Song of the Heart

Song of the Heart
Walking the Path of Light

Francine Vale

NEW YORK

World of Love Press LLC

Copyright © 2013 by Francine Vale

www.francinevale.com

Without limiting the rights under copyright reserved above, no part of this publication may be reproduced, stored in or introduced into a retrieval system, or transmitted, in any form, or by any means (electronic, mechanical, photocopying, recording or otherwise), without the prior written permission of both the copyright owner and the publisher of this book.

The scanning, uploading, and distribution of this book via the Internet or via any other means without the permission of the publisher is illegal and punishable by law. Please purchase only authorized electronic editions, and do not participate in or encourage electronic piracy of copyrighted materials.
Your support of the author's rights is appreciated.

To reach the author, email: songoftheheart111@gmail.com

Print ISBN: 978-0-692-21396-4

Digital editions available.

DESIGN: BLUE MOUNTAIN MARKETING

Published and manufactured in the United States of America
by World of Love Press LLC

My Child,

Time does not exist
And age is an elusive mist
Love transcends all space and motion
For Love is All There Is

Love, the only true connection
Binds us, one to another
The Light of Love and Sharing
Our only true protection

Mother

Song of the Heart is dedicated to the loving memory of my parents Mary and Matthew and my beloved Grandma Ida.

With love everlasting *Song of the Heart* is my legacy to my children Marcie and Ira and my grandchildren Steven and Brett.

I offer heartfelt gratitude to all my spiritual companions, beings of radiant light who stay beside me, guiding and inspiring me along the way yet never infringing upon my free will, providing beautiful poetic encouragement, having infinite patience with me, bringing healing through all the hard times and giving me the strength I prayed for to move forward and complete my destiny work.

CONTENTS

Foreword — xi

Introduction — xv

PART ONE

Angel of Death — 3

Matty's Life Review ~ The Early Years — 5

Guardian Angel Love — 24

White Dove on the Windowsill — 51

Prince on a White Horse — 77

Of Lost Wedding Rings and a Beautiful Baby Boy — 119

The Void — 149

A Beautiful Baby Girl	184
Golden Dreams	195
Conscious Intentions & Manifestation	242
Museums, Art & Culture	304
Afterward	326
My Son, My Guide	341

PART TWO

The Structure of All That Is	357
Purification	368
Crystal Library in the Higher Realms	417
Angels & Us	425
A New Millennium, the Year 2000	484
Angelic Healing & Light Beings	506
Temple of Light	550
Messages from the Angels	563

FOREWORD

The topics Francine Vale writes about in her book, "Song of the Heart: Walking the Path of Light" have validity and importance from my perspective and life experience. I welcome the opportunity to share with you some of my own mystical and healing experiences which over the years have given me invaluable insights.

When I was four years old I was home in bed with one of my frequent ear infections. I took a toy telephone I was playing with and unscrewed the dial and put all the pieces in my mouth as I had seen carpenters do with nails which they then pulled out to use. The problem was that I aspirated the pieces and went into laryngospasm. I can still feel my intercostal muscles and diaphragm contracting forcefully, trying to get some air into my lungs, but nothing worked and I was unable to make any sounds to attract help. I had no sense of the time but suddenly realized I was not struggling anymore. I was now at the head of the bed watching myself dying.

I found it fascinating to be free of my body and a blessing. I never stopped to think about how I could still see and think while out of my body. I was feeling sorry my mother, who was in the kitchen, would find me dead but I thought it over and found my new state preferable and intellectually chose death over life.

Then the boy on the bed had an agonal seizure, vomited and all the toy pieces came flying out. He began to breathe again and I was very angry as I returned to my body against my will. I can still remember yelling, "Who did that?" My thought as a four year old was that there was a God who had a schedule and I wasn't supposed to die now. So an angel apparently did a Heimlich maneuver on me is the way I would explain it today.

I really do believe there is a schedule we create unconsciously because of later life experiences. Twice I have had my car totaled by people driving through red lights and once I fell off our roof when the top rung on my wooden ladder snapped off. In none of these incidents did any significant injury occur to my body. Someone told me it was because I had an angel. I will add he always shows up when I call him in an impassioned way.

My next experience was with the healer Olga Worrall. I had injured my leg training for a marathon. It was very painful and not responding to rest or therapy. At an American Holistic Medical Association conference Olga was a guest speaker. My wife told me to ask her to heal me. I was embarrassed to ask and very frankly a non-believer. Never the less my wife pushed me forward and Olga sat me down in a chair and placed her two hands on my leg. The heat from her hands was incredible. I remember putting my hands on the opposite leg to compare the heat sensation. There was no sense of warmth from my hands coming through the dungarees. When Olga was done I stood up and was completely healed. The pain was gone and I could walk normally.

Another time Olga and I spoke at the funeral of a mutual friend. After the ceremony we were standing in a deserted hallway when she asked, "Are you Jewish?"

"Why are you asking?"

"Because there are two rabbis standing next to you." She went on to tell me their names and describe their garments, which included their prayer shawls and caps. Her description of them was exactly what I saw in my meditation and imagery sessions when I had met these figures while walking on my path.

Another evening after I gave a lecture, which felt like someone else was giving it and I was simply verbalizing it for them, a woman came up to me and said, "Standing in front of you for the entire lecture was a man and I drew his picture for you." Again, exactly the face and features of my inner guide. I still have the picture hanging in our home.

My next experience came when I was telling a friend about how busy I was and she said, "Why are you living this life?" Her intension was to get me to slow down and travel less but her question sent me into a trance and I immediately saw myself with a sword in my hand killing people. My first thought was that I had become a surgeon in this life to use a knife to heal and not kill.

I spontaneously went into a trance again a few days later and saw myself living the life of a knight who killed because he feared his lord and what he would do to him if he didn't carry out his commands. I killed my wife, in this life, and her dog and was devastated by the experience. But at the same time it revealed to me why my wife's face has always had a hypnotic effect upon me and why I am so involved in rescuing animals.

Ultimately it taught me about having faith in the true Lord and like Abraham, Jesus, Moses, Noah and others to understand that what our Lord asks of us is for the greater good and that if I had said yes I would have not been asked to kill anyone.

I learned from this that if I had faith in my lord I would have been asked to bring the families in conflict together and the solution would be for the young woman and myself to marry and be given the land that was being fought over to us as a wedding gift. Then we became one family with nothing to fight over.

Most recently one of our cats disappeared when a door was left open. After several weeks with no sign of her I was sure she was killed by a predator. A friend I had made, Amelia Kinkade, is an animal intuitive who lives in Los Angeles. We live in Connecticut and Amelia has never been to our home or near it. I pestered her to tell me where the cat was. She told me in an email, without my even sending Amelia a picture of the cat, "The cat is alive because I can see through its eyes." It detailed the house, yard, other animals and people who were involved in the cat's life. The next day I went out and found the cat exactly where Amelia said it was hiding.

If that doesn't make me a believer about the collective consciousness, nothing will. I totally believe that consciousness is non-local and not limited to the body. I also have experienced this through the drawings and dreams of patients I have cared for which allows them to know their diagnosis and what the future holds for them. As Jung said, "The future is unconsciously prepared long in advance and therefore can be guessed by clairvoyants."

I believe it is this unconscious awareness which we each are impregnated with when we are born. So I do not believe we literally live many lives but that we bring with us the experience of previous lives. Thus the wiser we get the better the future will be for those who follow us.

Dr. Bernie Siegel
Author of the new book, *The Art of Healing: Uncovering Your Inner Wisdom and Potential for Self Healing* (New World Library)

INTRODUCTION

Awake early on a summer morning in 1989, I watched the sun rise above the East River, above the tall city spires, filling a new day with its life-giving radiance. Simultaneously, a newly born thought arose in my mind and like the sun, the newborn thought blazed within me as if a shooting star had come to reside within my heart.

Suddenly, an open golden doorway appeared in my mind beckoning: come, step forward, move into the true light of your soul and find there your destiny. A moment later I had passed through the open doorway in my mind into a vast field of golden light where I saw a book infused with light blending its radiance with the golden light of the field. A title shone on its cover, *Song of the Heart*, and the entire book, every page sparkling and alive, was placed inside my mind, and all at once I knew every word, every phrase, every sentence inscribed on the pages of the golden book. "This is your destiny," the newly born thought expanded within me. "You shall bring this book into the world. Begin your task. You are not alone."

And so I retrieved from my desk a legal-sized note pad of light blue paper and a roller ball pen filled with black ink, and I wrote at the top of the first page: *Song of the Heart*. Words, phrases, fully formed sentences, freely flowed from the golden book inside my head onto the pretty light blue paper and the roller ball moved smoothly and with magical speed across the page, page after page, day after day, until October 1990 when the last word was transcribed from golden light into black ink. *Song of the Heart* came alive with a heartbeat all its own. The book's life became my life, and I became the book. It wasn't being created; it already existed. It needed to be brought into manifestation, and when the task was complete, the golden light remained with me, within my mind. A gift, I was told, for remaining loyal to the task, for bringing forth discipline of the mind to transfer all that I saw in the light onto pages for the purpose of helping others to see the same golden light and bring the light through, into their hearts and into their minds.

On March 1, 2012, a square of golden light suddenly appeared in the very center of my head, and as I observed this amazing phenomenon I saw four golden triangles overlay the golden square to meet at the precise central point, a view from above the Great Pyramid of Giza! As I continued to focus my mind on the light, I watched the four triangles open from the central point. Radiant golden light completely filled my head. Fully formed thought "packets" begging to be released into manifestation filled my head and began to flow into my consciousness. I went directly to my Apple laptop and out poured "The Structure of All That Is," the first chapter of Part Two of *Song of the Heart*.

Apparently, I needed to live another 21 years and experience all that I have experienced in order to complete my destiny work, *Song of the Heart*. Responsibilities of the past now fulfilled, "The Structure of All That Is" flowed through me in ten days. In six months Part Two was complete. Traversing space from distant stars, the golden light of the Great Pyramid of Giza, shone its wisdom through my consciousness, its sacred knowledge released in the year 2012 in accordance with the ancient timeline for the people of Earth.

It could be said that golden light is embedded on every page. The language and arrangement of words on the pages of *Song of the Heart* was designed to bring greater awareness of the absolute necessity for love and the power of love to shift the energy at every turn in our lives. It was designed to transform and uplift the consciousness of its readers into a higher frequency never before available, yet available now for all who so desire and open to receive it.

Part Two is presented in the form of a journal to maintain grounding in third dimension of its esoteric content. Also, there is soul travel and movement of consciousness within timeframes and dimensions. The journal form creates consistency in the comforting return to present time and space. It feels as if the sacred truth being revealed in Part Two, by the very purity of its frequency, uplifts and transforms everything it touches until nothing can be hidden in any way. The golden healing light of love shall overtake Earth and all humanity and raise us up to higher consciousness in all things until we see with clarity and speak with clarity of all the elements in our lives.

October 18, 2013, Scarsdale, N.Y.

Part One

Angel of Death

October 8, 1989.

The vaporous light that was his soul stirred within his worn out body and began its ascent. By some primeval sacred knowledge Matty recognized the moment, and he prayed. He prayed for another breath, one more breath...

Suddenly the Angel of Death appeared in the room and drew near the bed. "Why, Matthew Vale, do you require another breath? Why, after all these years, all the opportunities come and gone, millions of words you have spoken? All this you find insufficient? You will come with me now, Matthew Vale."

"No!" Matty protested, "... Francine!"

And the Angel understood. The Angel of Death, accustomed as he was to these last minute pleas nodded imperceptibly and responded, "Matthew Vale, by holding the bond of fatherhood close to your heart you have uplifted your immortal soul. Your request is hereby granted. You shall be permitted one final visit with Francine. But not now. Later. Now, you will come with me."

Abruptly, Matty's consciousness changed and memories,

beginning with his first, were revealed to him in the form of moving pictures right before his eyes.

Not even one complete second had elapsed since the Angel had first encountered Matty lying in the well-kept bed, engulfed in pain.

"Now, Matthew Vale, you will come with me." The Angel's intentions were clear and his luminous presence obscured for Matty everything in the room, even the walls seems to fall away. "You will see the rest," the Angel of Death assured Matty, "but you will see it from a different perspective."

"No! Please! Please, let me see her one more time!"

Matty was enveloped in unbearable sorrow, suffocating sorrow. He longed for the power of his youth. He struggled to summon another breath. A blood vessel in Matty's brain exploded. His body shuddered. His spirit soared free. And pain, in all its guises, ceased at last for Matty Vale.

Matty's Life Review ~ The Early Years

MATTY VALE'S earliest memory was of his mother's funeral. He was three years old, it was April 1918, and he was in a field picking yellow daisies. His father went away and Matty was taken in, along with his sister, to live in a big white house on Herzyl Street in Brownsville, Brooklyn, which was owned by his maternal grandfather, Wolff Friedman. Matty's aunts and uncles also lived in grandfather's house but they were young adults who went about their own lives.

While under his mother's protection Matty's complexion had been ruddy; now his skin had grown pale, now loneliness registered silently in his hazel eyes and mingled there with the gentleness of his formerly secure self. If anyone had cared to linger a moment and look into his eyes they would have noticed, also, Matty's eyes were deep and full; you could gaze into them forever, trying to discover their actual depth, and you might wonder if those were tears you saw glistening in the lamplight. Soon fear, too, came to reside in Matty's eyes; fear inevitably entombed by rage barely controlled by the force of his will, caused a small muscle in the hollow of Matty's right cheek to quiver.

Matty's loneliness found expression in his wanderings and in his fascination with trains. He would sneak onto the Saratoga Avenue station and ride to Forty-Second Street, or to the lower east side. He found his way to the freight trains, climbed aboard a boxcar where he remained hidden until the train arrived in Philadelphia. Like a perfectly formed tiger cub Matty leapt from the boxcar.

"Hey, hey! And what have we here?" A man's voice pierced the clamor of the Philadelphia railroad yard. The man wore rough grey overalls, and kneeling to appraise Matty correctly surmised his age to be five, although Matty's demeanor suggested the self-reliance of an older boy accustomed to being on his own. Matty, though startled, noticed the official railroad insignia on the man's cap.

Enveloped in the dusty haze of the railroad yard his thoughts fled back to the house on Herzyl Street where, for Matty, material comfort was overshadowed by loneliness. In Wolff Friedman's drawing room the light streaming in through leaded glass windows illuminated a collection of silver-framed photographs. One photograph stirred Matty's heart and pulled him like a magnet into the room.

Uncle Martin, a scholarly fellow of 29, had accompanied Matty one morning to investigate the source of his nephew's interest in the mostly unused room. Trying not to reveal his secret longing Matty listened patiently to his uncle's explanations of the photographs.

"And that's your Aunt Adeline on the occasion of her graduation from college. All the Friedmans are college graduates, Matty."

"And who are they, Uncle Martin?"

"Why that's grandmother Minnie and Grandfather Wolff . . . quite young . . . just purchased this big house. Yes, and then went on to fill it up with nine children, your aunts and uncles, Matty. Most unfortunate nephew that my dear mother passed on before you were born. It certainly would have been to your advantage to have your grandmother around now. Yes, as things have transpired, very much to your advantage."

Martin glanced at Matty. Reassured of his nephew's attention he continued. "Your grandmother was born right here, in Brooklyn, Matty, as were her parents, her grandparents, and even her great-grandparents. Now grandfather, he was born in Germany . . . hmm . . . family emigrated to England where he was educated, and soon after he made that marvelous decision to come to America, right here to Brooklyn. And right away he went into the business of manufacturing men's clothing, and as everyone knows, became quite successful!"

At last Matty pointed to the special photograph. "And who is that lady, Uncle Martin, and who is the man standing next to her?"

Martin placed his gentle scholar's hands on Matty's shoulders. "Well, now, aren't you an inquisitive fellow! Why, your mind is just insatiable, isn't it nephew, for knowledge of the world around you! And I see evidence that you can hardly bear the wait to experience your life, isn't that so? It's quite unfortunate, yes, hmm, most unfortunate, that already your path has been strewn with many sharp stones." Martin cleared his throat. They were facing the photograph, its sterling silver frame aglow. "The lady, Matty, is my sister, Francine, your mother."

Oval face, light-filled eyes gazing seriously into Matty's eyes, brown hair braided and pinned up like a crown, wayward strands lifted here and there by a long-ago breeze — his mother.

The man, appearing strong in a slim, angular way, stood smiling by Francine's side, one arm flung casually around her slender waist. "And the man, Matty, is Joseph Vale. Joe Vale, your father." A sob escaped Matty's throat.

"Yes, my boy, you may cry if you wish. Mmm . . . Certainly,

yes, go ahead and cry. Your poor mother passed away, yes my dear sister died. Mmm . . . Influenza, that terrible epidemic, surely will assume its place in the annals of medical history. And then your father, run off to who knows where, perhaps he, too, is dead and buried. Certainly, no Friedman has heard from the man these two long years."

When Matty's tears subsided Martin resumed the story. "Now, your paternal grandfather, John Vale, married a woman also named Francine, and they live in Boston. You see, the Vales came to America from Germany, back in 1785 I believe, and they chose to settle in Boston. Now we, the Friedman family, are Jewish, Matty, this you know. Your father, well, when you're older you'll be better equipped to comprehend this sort of thing but you may as well hear it from me now. You see, Matty, the Vales are Episcopalian, another religion, in the Christian faith. Well, my dear nephew, people can be pretty closed-minded about things like religion. Now your father has a sister and brother, both married, and you have five cousins up there in Boston. I have heard, by the way, your cousin Christian married himself a famous society gal. That's something to know. But if I were you Matty I wouldn't expect any communication to transpire between yourself and the Vales. Remember nephew, stay away from them, they'll never lift a finger on your behalf. You may as well know it now."

Observing Matty's sad expression, Martin suddenly worried his nephew might never smile again so he sought to soften the information which had already begun to circulate in Matty's blood, and lean its weighty message on his young shoulders.

Lightening the somber mood, Martin said, "See that swell cap your father's wearing?" Together they peered again at the photograph, Matty wishing it were clearer or larger. "Your father's a railroad man, Matty, with the Pennsylvania Railroad, and he's mighty proud to wear that engineer's cap!"

Matty's attention returned to the husky railroad man who

grasped his hand and led him directly to the nearby police station where a little kid alone and all the way from Brooklyn aroused the compassion of policemen.

"Well, now, laddie, what d'ye say ye name is?"

"Matty, sir. I used to be Matty Vale but my grandfather adopted me so now I'm Matty Friedman."

"Well then, Matty Friedman," the officer said with a big smile that his own seven kids were accustomed to "how'd ye like some ice-cream?"

"Thank you, sir." And Matty enjoyed the flavor of strawberry ice-cream. Awaiting the arrival of Martin Friedman from Brooklyn the police captain poured for Matty plenty of sarsaparilla too.

In the comfort of a plush Pullman car Matty dozed against the woolen folds of Martin's sweater. But as soon as Matty stirred and rubbed his eyes, Martin spoke sternly. "Matty, you may as well hear this from me. The family is very angry with this latest escapade of yours, very angry. I spoke up in your defense but unfortunately my sisters have determined that you are quite the renegade, in need of discipline. They're meeting tonight, nephew, to decide your fate."

THE FAMILY DECIDED to place Matty in an institution. Within a few weeks Aunt Goldie, teacher, resourceful woman, family representative, made arrangements for Matty's admittance to the Brooklyn Hebrew Orphan Asylum, and Aunt Anabel brought him there. However, one afternoon after the passage of several months, a diligent clerk in the office of the orphan asylum, while reviewing Matty's file, discovered that Wolff Friedman, a prosperous businessman who maintained a substantial household, had adopted his grandson. Matty belonged at home with his family.

Uncle Martin arrived to bring Matty home. "Well, dear nephew, I certainly hope you'll be a good boy now. Grandfather has taken a new bride, quite a fashionable lady, and I can tell you she may not be much inclined toward children about the house. No sir not the sort to tolerate children." Martin glanced at Matty. "Well, nephew, and how have you fared these past months?"

"They beat me! Every day, Uncle Martin! They're mean! They don't let you talk! They don't let you play! Locked inside scrubbing floors! Please don't send me back! Please! Oh, please!"

They were seated on a varnished wicker bench traveling to Herzyl Street by streetcar. Martin, proper gentleman in suit, bowtie and bowler hat, conscious of strangers all around, nevertheless gathered Matty into his arms and held him, all the way back to Herzyl Street.

In 1921 when he was almost six years old Matty was enrolled in first grade. One Friday afternoon as he came out of school a man and woman approached him.

"Hey, kid!" The man was tall and slim, neatly dressed, and his light brown hair was neatly combed. "You Matty?" the man asked and winked an ice-blue eye at the boy.

Matty nodded silently.

"I just knew it! See Mary what a fine lookin' boy I got? Yeah, you're lookin' at your Pop, kid!"

Suddenly, tears cascaded from the depths of Matty's eyes. Suddenly, the reason for holding back was gone! For here was Father come to take him home, protect him, keep him safe from those who sent him away to strange, scary places...

"No, no, kid, you got me all wrong, I just come to see ya, that's all."

"Oh, Joe," the woman exclaimed, "I'll take care of the boy he don't look so bad to me, let's take him home with us, please, Joe!"

Joe fixed his frozen pale gaze on Mary. "Look, this don't concern you, it's my kid, not yours, so just stay out, okay?" And he handed his son a package, a pair of roller skates.

The gift brought catastrophe upon Matty. The following day he went roller skating and to avoid collision with a horse-drawn pie wagon Matty skated under the wagon. At that moment his teacher passed by. The teacher shrieked, the driver pulled in his reigns, the horse reared and the wagon toppled over. Matty grabbed a pie and ran to a nearby park where he sat on a bench under a tree and ate the pie, a lemon meringue.

The teacher marched to the Friedman home where she embellished and exaggerated the pie-wagon episode to Aunt Celia. Inflated instantly with furious indignation Celia found relief in repetition. She discharged most of her wrath when Adeline arrived home, but managed to revive it in successive waves for Tillie, Jacob, Martin, her father and the new bride. That very evening the family met in the drawing room and concluded that the pie-wagon episode proved Matty's inherent evil.

So, on a day when the air was fragrant with Spring a stern man in a black suit arrived, frowned at Matty and escorted him from the house on Herzyl Street to the Manhattan Truant School. Here Matty passed the summer, the only outdoors a paved concrete yard surrounded by a high red-brick wall.

AT SUMMER'S END a school official summoned Matty to his office. "It has come to our attention that you are a resident of Brooklyn and the jurisdiction of our school is limited to residents of Manhattan." He handed Matty a nickel. "Do you know how to get back to Brooklyn, boy?" Matty nodded, dropped the nickel into his pocket and sneaked onto the subway.

FOR SEVEN DOLLARS a week paid by Wolff Friedman, Aunt Tillie who was already caring for Matty's sister, took Matty in. She handed him a pillow and a blanket and explained that the bathroom floor would be his bed. Miserable and alone Matty lay down at night and clutched his knees to his chest. The cold, hard tiles imprinted their pattern on his flesh, and he tried to remember his mother's face. Soon, Matty began to float far away from Aunt Tillie's bathroom floor. He wandered through space among the scattered stars, desolate and abandoned, searching for his mother.

SEVERAL WEEKS ELAPSED before Wolff Friedman learned of Tillie's cruel arrangement, whereupon he took his grandson back and enrolled him in school. Matty was seven.

SCARCELY ONE MONTH had elapsed when Aunt Goldie had Matty committed to the New York Parental School in Flushing, Queens; several buildings connected by underground tunnels. Now Matty rarely went outdoors. He wore a gray uniform and lived under a strict regimen of unbending rules. Any small infraction meant confinement to the coop, a small dark crawl space near the ceiling. Sunday, visiting day, the boys received packages of candy and cookies which they called boodles. No one came to visit Matty and Matty never got a boodle. One Sunday an older boy named Sparky stole a boodle and Matty saw him do it. "Keep ya trap shut, kid," Sparky warned.

LATER, WHEN the theft was reported the boys were lined up and questioned individually. It was decided that Matty must be the thief since aside from being the only boy who never received a boodle the expression in his eyes belied a secret withheld. First, Matty was thrashed until he bled. Then he was confined to the coop for two days; two slices of bread and a cup of water for each meal.

ONE SUNDAY Joe Vale showed up with Mary. "Take me outta here, Joe! please, oh please!" Matty begged. "They beat me! I don't get enough to eat! Please take me with you!"

Mary glanced around the place, looked at the child before them; paler, thinner, the shadows in his eyes even darker than she remembered and this time she saw clearly, his eyes were filled with terror.

"C'mon now, Joe, I'll take care of the kid, he won't be no bother to you."

Joe ignored her. "Hey, kid, there somethin I can get ya?"

If his father didn't want him Matty didn't want anything from his father. So he stared hard at a tarnished brass button on his father's jacket and remained silent.

That night at dinner there was a boodle on Matty's chair, a carton filled with treats. Matty cried brief, bitter tears and divided the entire contents among the other boys.

The veil over Matty's eyes which had lifted momentarily during his encounter with Joe, lowered once again, the hollow of his right cheek quivered with controlled rage, and his tears were sealed inside.

IN JUNE OF 1924, soon after his ninth birthday, Matty's case came up for review and it was decided that he had been a good boy. A few weeks later his Uncle Leo arrived to escort him back to the house on Herzyl Street. Once again the family gathered in the drawing room and right before the silver-framed photograph of Matty's mother they agreed to find an institution that would keep Matty until his eighteenth birthday when legal responsibility for his care would expire.

Wolff Friedman called on his lawyer to handle the matter and the lawyer chose the Gerry Society, a self-appointed group who looked after the welfare of unwanted children, to arrange Matty's future. Matty was removed from his grandfather's house to the society's building on Schermerhorn Street in Brooklyn where he was to await disposition in Children's Court. On the third day Matty got into a fight with another boy and his punishment was confinement in a discarded walk-in freezer of the sort used in butcher shops. There Matty remained in cold, silent total darkness until someone unlocked the door, placed a large hand on his shoulder and brought him before Judge Wingate.

The judge listened to a long list of complaints against the unwashed, untidy, gloomy boy who stood before him. The ruling he was about to issue constituted in the judge's mind one less file on his overcrowded desk, no more than a minute out of a day's routine, whereas for Matty the judge's dispassionate voice as he pronounced the fateful words was to be a haunting that lasted all the days of his life. Matthew Friedman, the judge ruled, was to spend the remainder of his childhood at the Jewish Protectory located in Hawthorne, New York, renamed the Hawthorne School in 1926.

A FEW DAYS LATER, on October 14, 1924, as Matty turned the corner from Blake Avenue onto Herzyl Street on his way home from school, he saw halfway down the block in front of the Friedman residence, Aunt Adeline in conversation with a large man and Matty knew that the man had come to take him away. He turned to run but Uncle Martin had been following him and now caught him and holding firmly Matty's arm, escorted him directly to the large man.

Matty was transported to the Jewish Protectory. The boys here were Jewish, the staff was not, and they showed no compassion toward their charges who were mostly truants and petty thieves whose sentences ranged from several weeks to a few months. Judge Wingate had sentenced Matty to nine years in Hawthorne.

Upon arrival he was issued four suits of clothing: two of khaki twill for warm weather, two of corduroy for the cold, two pairs of sneakers. No outer clothing. Everything at the Protectory was done military style. The boys lined up in formation and marched, whatever the destination. They were drilled in the manual of arms and Sundays were parade days. They assembled nightly back to back in the shower, but before they were permitted to shower the lieutenant called out the names of each boy who had committed an infraction that day. Moving one's head while in formation was considered an infraction. The captain, who most of the time was drunk, and who was fond of using a horse strap, administered an indiscriminate number of lashes on the backsides of the unfortunate boys. During one of these episodes Matty's thigh was slashed open.

Another time a lieutenant slapped Matty and threatened more lashes. Suddenly, an older boy, about fifteen, stepped forward and warned the lieutenant, "Hey, you lay a hand on this kid again you got me to deal with, hear? And I'll beat the hell outta you!" This older boy was Sparky, the boy who'd stolen a boodle at the New York Parental School, the boy Matty had not betrayed. Matty was protected for a few months at Hawthorne until Sparky was released.

The boys were served enough food to keep them going but never enough to satisfy their hunger. Matty wondered mightily about this for the Protectory was surrounded by lush farmland. Every boy shared in the labor of working the fields; they tended the fruit trees and vegetable gardens, watched the fruits and vegetables ripen and they harvested the crops. At dinner they might find at their places one small, half-rotted apple.

The Protectory was located on a scenic hill and Matty observed the natural beauty of the landscape, the lushness of the campus with its wide central lawn bordered by perfectly spaced towering oak trees, the sixteen Tudor buildings, eight on either side of the lawn, but he was unable to feel the calm usually inspired by nature or architectural beauty. The Tudor buildings were referred to as barracks and each housed thirty boys. Matty was assigned to barracks #4. The top half of the floor to ceiling windows remained open even in stormy rain or snowy weather.

Attendance at synagogue services were required every morning prior to breakfast, Friday evenings and Saturday mornings. The boys were made to stand at attention throughout the services and they were subject to the usual punishment for infractions. In Bible class each Thursday afternoon Matty's imagination soared. He found inspiration in the contemplation of God, and he recognized in the rabbi a source of fascinating knowledge. As his thirteenth birthday approached Matty studied for his Bar Mitzvah with great anticipation. He imagined that this important milestone in his life would bring about a reunion with his grandfather.

Grandfather will come to Hawthorne, Matty daydreamed every day, and in honor of my Bar Mitzvah he'll sit up front in one of the special chairs on the Bima. I'll introduce him to the rabbi and the rabbi will say, Mazel Tov, Mr. Friedman, you must be very proud of your grandson today. You know, Matty is a very good student, very good, and he has a real love for God. Grandfather will smile and pat my back affectionately. He'll look right into my eyes and say, "You recited your Haftorah like a man, Matty, yes you're growing into a fine young man. Would you like to come home with me now to Herzyl Street?"

The family was notified of Matty's Bar Mitzvah date, but no one came. And Matty endured the disappointment as he'd learned to endure all his miserable pain and loneliness – in bitter silence. In Bible class, not long after his Bar Mitzvah, the rabbi told the story of Joshua and how he had caused the earth to stand still. Matty questioned the rabbi who replied that one should never question anything in the Bible. But Matty persisted. He had to have an explanation of this astounding event. After class the rabbi summoned Matty to his study. Matty watched the rabbi unbuckle his belt and guide it slowly through the loops of his trousers. He listened to the sound of leather sliding against wool, the quiet clink of the buckle and he felt sweat breaking out uncontrollably all over his body. "Take down your pants, son ... I'm going to teach you a lesson you'll never forget." With each swipe of his belt the rabbi repeated, "Never question anything in the Bible!"

After the belt beating, the rabbi slapped Matty's face a few times. "Hereafter, young man, you will remain silent in my class! Silent! Do you hear me?"

THE RABBI, apparently concerned that Matty might forget his stern lesson, issued Matty a ticket. Each night the discipline officer called out the names of those boys who had received tickets. They were made to line up, fold their arms behind their backs and stand at rigid attention for an hour and a half. If a boy happened to move even slightly he was made to squat with his arms straight out and a broomstick was placed across his arms; a pail of water was hung on each end of the broomstick. As a result of the rabbi's ticket Matty suffered this punishment. The excruciating pain bolted through his body, crashed through bones, ripped through soft tissue, and settled in his spine, causing Matty to conclude that for him there was no God.

BOYS WERE always running away. Those who were captured were locked in a brick cell with a concrete floor for three days. The window and door were barred. It was an unheated cell, totally bare of furniture. One winter a boy managed to hang himself in that cell. Thereafter a punishment was devised which extended also to boys who refused to carry out orders: buckets were issued for the purpose of emptying the septic tanks and in this way they spent the entire day. At night the colonel and three of his henchmen led the boys one at a time into a small chamber in barracks #13. Here, with the aid of rubber hoses they executed cruel and memorable beatings.

THE FIRST TIME that one of Matty's teachers brought him to the library he stood in the arched doorway and stared with eyes of wonder, unable to move for several moments. He'd never imagined such a place, so many shelves filled with so many books. Immediately, Matty felt a yearning to read every book in the library and he wished he could remain there undisturbed until his goal was reached. His teacher instructed him not to remove a single book from the library; he'd be permitted to return once a week for an hour of reading. The librarian handed Matty *Tarzan of the Apes* by Edgar Rice Burroughs and when his allotted hour of reading expired Matty was already so engrossed in the story he decided to ignore his teacher's warning

Later, in the evening, the barracks lieutenant spied Matty reading in bed, grabbed the book and issued Matty a ticket. The next night he was beaten mercilessly with rubber hoses by four men in Barracks #13 until he almost lost consciousness.

A FEW DAYS LATER, John Klein the superintendent, happened to summon Matty to his office. John Klein sat behind his desk, his thick white hair and his white beard illuminated by the light shining through the window panes behind him. "Sit down, young man," he motioned to the chair beside his desk. "Tell me, Matty, how is it that you never have any visitors? You've been here now, what, five years? Five years with no visitors. And no packages either. How is that? Speak up, son."

Matty interpreted the superintendent's interest as kindness and the way the man's white hair looked all lit up, strengthened his confidence. So Matty felt certain Mr. Klein was a kind man. He was unable to answer the superintendent's question but felt he could unburden some portion of his misery so he proceeded to describe to Mr. Klein the terrible rubber hose beating.

John Klein glared at Matty with blue eyes grown suddenly menacing. He rose from his chair without uttering a word while simultaneously opening a desk drawer, removing a bamboo switch. "Let me see your right hand, son, palm up if you please!"

He raised the bamboo switch high above his head and three times brought it down hard: *whack, whack, whack* on Matty's outstretched hand. The third strike opened a gash and Matty's hand bled profusely. He endured this injury in his customary way, in bitter silence.

When he turned fourteen, Matty was appointed lieutenant of his cottage. His personal code of honor already firmly established within his heart and mind, Matty never, for the entirety of his term as lieutenant, put any boy on report.

That year he was awarded a gold medal for excellence in math. I guess that means I can put two and two together, he thought.

When he was sixteen Matty was appointed major which meant he was to march at the head of the regimen, carry a sword and shout commands given by the colonel. Matty found these privileges distasteful and told the colonel he wanted to be relieved of them. The colonel refused. At the next parade Matty failed to show up. The colonel went looking for Matty and found him. "Look here, boy, you can't ignore my command, don't you know I can have you beaten to a bloody pulp?" In all his years at Hawthorne the colonel's authority had gone unquestioned and unthreatened.

Matty stood before him fully grown. Lean, six feet tall, straight dark-brown hair combed back above a high forehead; a good-looking young man. The relentless lack of care and love, the absolute deprivation which for thirteen years had formed the dreary landscape of his life had been etched into the hard planes of his face, etched into the set of his mouth which had grown utterly unaccustomed to forming a smile. The quiet of enormously repressed rage burned in Matty's hazel eyes, darkened behind their veil of sorrow. Matty's voice reflected all that was in his face; his voice was quiet, hard, controlled and full of anger.

"I ain't marchin' in your parade, Colonel! I ain't takin orders from you or anyone else around here! An' if anyone ever tries to lay a finger on me again, anyone! I swear I'll kill 'em!" Involuntarily, in one smooth arc, Matty's right arm swung up into a threatening position, his calloused hand closed into a tight hard fist . . . "I swear! I'll stab anyone who tries to hit me again!" and his fist smashed down onto the colonel's desk.

Unruffled, the colonel turned and walked away. Matty strode directly to the superintendent's office where he demanded his release and received it. He knew nothing of the outside world, but Matty longed to go out into that world and make his own way. He boarded a train for the city. In Manhattan he ran into Nick, a kid from Hawthorne, who said, "Hey, no sweat, there's jobs like I got sellin' papers on the street . . . an' you got nowhere to go, no sweat, they let you stay free at the Newsboys Home." This is what Matty did.

THEN, ON NEW YEAR'S DAY, 1932, he ran into Tommy, another kid from Hawthorne. "Hey, Matty, you're lookin' swell! Sellin' papers, huh? Hey, I just quit this crummy job workin' at a print shop in the Bronx. Maybe it's good for you." Matty hopped a train for the Bronx and got the job. Seven dollars a week.

1941. MATTY SLAMMED down his fist and struck the kitchen table top. "I said, no abortion! Jesus! You out of your mind?" His booming voice filled the apartment; the raw vibrations issuing from his throat caused new cracks to appear on the walls. The torrent of rage thundered, and the walls strained to keep from exploding.

"I'm the goddam boss around here! And you're not gettin no abortion!" He pounded the table again with his powerful fist.

Mary sobbed, and prayed to leave this miserable world. Already the burdens of her life had been too much. "What do you care?" she screamed. "You don't have to figure out how to make a meal from nothing!" She flung out her skinny arms, encompassing their barren surroundings to support her argument, and despair filled her heart. "How can we feed another mouth on what you make in that damn print shop? We'll starve! Oh, my God, we'll starve!"

Mikey sat perfectly still in the next room. Starve? No! He would not starve! Mikey was four, a big four. Those who didn't know his age assumed he was seven at least, and Mikey loved to eat. The explosion of his parents' argument whooshed through the cracks in the thick plaster walls and holding his breath, Mikey listened, and suddenly understood. A baby was coming.

He imagined a tremendous mouth, gobbling, gobbling, feeding on all his favorite foods. And Mikey wished there was more to eat, not less! This was a bad thing to happen, a baby ... it made his parents mean, it spoiled the walls with dark, scraggly shadows.

Mary took no notice of Spring that year although Summer with its oppressive city heat could not be avoided. Soon enough the clothes were drying stiff on the line outside the kitchen window and as Mary reached over the snow-padded sill to pluck frozen towels and shirts from the grip of hard wooden clothespins she felt the first pangs of labor. A clothespin slipped from her grasp, somersaulted four stories to the alleyway below where it smacked the pavement and split in two. Just like me, Mary thought: falling, falling and breaking apart! I wish I were dead! Oh, God, let me die!

THE BABY WAS BORN. A girl. Lavendar eyes, black hair; a beautiful baby girl. And Friday evening Matty came home with a raise.

Mary decided the girl had brought them luck. "My lucky charm," Mary repeated to her infant daughter, "you are my lucky charm."

So this is the baby, Mikey thought, leaning against the crib slats and peering at his sister. He was prepared to hate this creature. It was she who had been responsible for those loud arguments which had caused their walls to crack. For all those long months he'd imagined this creature's gobbling, ceaseless gobbling, of piles of cherry pies, hundreds of charlotte-rooses. He'd imagined its mouth steadily growing just as his Mama's belly had grown. He looked at Francine's peaceful face. Her eyes were open and he saw they were the color of his favorite crayon in the box of twenty-four colors. He could read it, too: hyacinth. Her eyelashes, long slow curves of the most delicate black hairs, blinked gracefully, and he noticed that she kicked her tiny feet in a fascinating horizontal ballet. Mikey extended his hand through the crib slats and placed his sweaty palm gently on Francine's stomach. He pressed his face even harder against the wooden slats, trying to get closer, closer, wishing to devour his baby sister in all her sweetness. He was so big, the biggest boy in kindergarten, and here was his tiny, defenseless sister. In her presence he felt even bigger than he was. Gazing into her hyacinth eyes which captured his attention in the most pleasing, hypnotic way, Mikey realized he didn't hate her at all. It was impossible to hate her when it felt good just to look at her. Mikey loved her.

BUT LATER, lying in bed, he imagined again the gobbling mouth which he'd grown accustomed to hating and fearing. And that's how Mikey felt about his sister. Away from her presence he feared and mistrusted her. But when they were together he fell repeatedly under the spell of her sapphire eyes, and his love rekindled instantly. The problem was that Mikey had an incredible imagination which reworked reality and imposed fantasy in its place. Sometimes he dreamed his sister was a princess from one of his fairy tale books. Sometimes he stared at her, avoided the sapphire eyes and conjured up that old threatening, insatiable mouth which he hated and feared more than anything. Sometimes Mikey imagined he was St. George and sometimes he was the dragon.

MATTY STOOD BESIDE the crib and stared in startled wonder at Francine, his daughter. How amazing, he thought, admiring her loveliness. I protected her, I saved her and now I've been rewarded. At last I've done something right. Matty smiled, straining the tight muscles of his face.

As he stood beside the crib reveling in his own perfect instinct he felt the tension begin to withdraw in painfully slow increments from his body. From his powerful shoulders he felt a seemingly endless stream of sorrow flow like fiery lava down his arms all the way to his calloused fingers. The accumulated misery of his fractured, ruined childhood inched down his embattled spine, down his strong legs, until at last, in the timeless presence of his own newborn daughter lying in the crib right there before him, he realized the sorrow and pain had vanished!

And then the most amazing thing happened. Francine opened her beautiful almond shaped eyes, slowly blinked her long, black lashes and gazed directly into her father's eyes. Suddenly Matty felt overcome by a soft, floating sensation. Gentleness, until this moment an unknown foreign thing, consumed him and rushed into all the places in his body which for so many long years had been claimed by rage, and Matty acknowledged the existence of God.

Guardian Angel Love

THE BRONX, 1949. We lived on the fourth floor. I climbed the white stone steps to our apartment and noticed again how worn the center of each stone slab was. The sound of my footsteps echoed throughout the cold, bare hallways. I thought of my mother carrying heavy loads of clean, damp laundry up from the washing machine in the dark recesses of the cellar, I thought of my father trudging up all these flights of stairs after a twelve-hour day on his feet at the print shop, and I knew that if I stayed in this building, in this neighborhood, I would become worn like these steps, like my parents.

I turned the doorknob; the door opened onto immaculate pale-green linoleum, and the aroma of furniture polish welcomed me. To the right, beyond our sparkling clean windows, I could see the grimy brick building across the alley; clotheslines were strung between the buildings.

Our windows sparkled because every Friday morning my mother washed them with old newspaper and vinegar, even sitting on the stone window ledge to wash the outside of the windowpanes. When I was very little and followed her around the house I worried every time that she might fall so keeping my eyes focused on her, concentrating on my mother's safety, I prayed for her protection. Soon I imagined a shimmering light surrounded my mother; the light streamed like a golden cord across the room directly to me. And in this way I imagined I was keeping my mother safe.

I walked through the living room. Directly ahead, beyond the bedroom windows, were the elevated trains. The bathroom smelled of Lysol, and newspapers protected the clean floor. While washing my hands, disturbing the pristine cleanliness of our chipped white porcelain sink, I envisioned my mother, down on her hands and knees scrubbing the floor tiles, her left hand leaning on the gray metal pail of scrub water. Carefully, I smoothed the towel, then joined my mother and my brother Mikey for lunch at the small rectangular table in the corner of the narrow kitchen my mother called "two-by-nothing." The table had to be pressed against the wall to allow space for the chairs. My place was at the corner, to the right of my father's chair. I enjoyed the calm, quiet meal of a bowl of borscht with a slice of fresh, buttered rye bread. I loved to stir the pure white sour cream into the ruby-colored borscht and watch it grow pale pink.

My mother was dressed in a starched white blouse and plaid wool skirt protected by an apron. She looked trim and slender. "What happened in school this morning?" she asked Mikey and me, taking two clear glass dessert bowls of cold chocolate pudding from the Frigidaire.

I answered in a rush, "You know the assignment to draw a picture while listening to music and I chose one of Daddy's opera records? Well, my teacher loved it and she showed it to the principal this morning and they asked if I could draw another one just like it so Miss Lasker could have one for her office and I said I will try my best."

While listening to my father's recording of *Tales of Hoffman* I imagined the dark, murky waters of Venice glistening in the moonlight, and so I had used my best lavender and green crayons. A gondola was so romantic and I daydreamed and pressed hard with my crayons, covering every spot on the paper.

Mikey was discussing his morning classes and my mother was immediately drawn into his interesting stories. Mikey was a genius. He had been accepted to the Bronx High School of Science and I was proud to be his little sister. I loved my brother so much. None of the other kids in the neighborhood had a brother smart enough to answer any question or kind enough to take them to the American Museum of Natural History. Mikey knew how to get there by the subway train and we never got lost. He showed me the beautiful and rare gems like rubies and emeralds and the dinosaurs and models of cave men. But the most fun was when he took me to the Saturday movies. First we had a long walk, then my brother would stop at a candy store to stock up on rock candy and licorice. I liked the Jordan Almonds best because they were pretty pastel colors. One box lasted through the cartoons, the shorts, newsreels, serials and even through part of the first movie.

My brother was big for his age, almost six feet tall, and he had a bad case of acne. Sometimes on the way home from school I heard kids tease him and call him pimple face. I felt very bad and tried not to listen. But at night, lying in bed, I remembered and cried. I wished those stupid kids would stop it and sometimes I caught myself saying so out loud, in the dark.

After lunch Mikey walked me back to school and as we passed under the elevated trains he said that one day he would have a lot of money and then he'd cover our mother with furs, and take care of us all. I had nothing ever to worry about, Mikey assured me, as long as I had him. In the schoolyard we parted as we came to the third grade line. In the morning I always felt fresh and neat, my braids tight and precise, but by afternoon my scalp itched and I longed to shake my hair loose.

My mother declared that I was delicate, that I looked tired after a whole day of school, so at three o'clock we sometimes walked up our long, dreary block distinguished by an empty lot across the street which provided an open vista to the elevated trains and the dark, sooty neighborhood beyond where, for all the years we lived on Vyse Avenue, I never ventured. We walked directly to the luncheonette on 174th Street where they made delicious thick chocolate malteds with two scoops of ice-cream. We sat together at a small round marble table and my mother watched while I sipped slowly through a paper straw until I finished a whole glass of chocolate malted; she poured only a small portion for herself. Then my mother, feeling relaxed and I, feeling refreshed, walked home together.

Mikey was packing his knapsack for a scouting overnight. My mother slipped on her clean, pressed apron, tying it in the back, and got right to work at the stove burning pinfeathers off the chicken for our Friday night supper. A bowl of knaidlach prepared in the morning for the chicken soup sat on the ledge of the wide kitchen sink and a five pound bag of potatoes leaned against the sink leg waiting to be peeled.

My mother called out, "Mikey, here's your mess kit!" She interrupted her work to bring the mess kit into Mikey's room where all his Boy Scout things lay scattered across the big double bed. He was leaving right after supper.

My parents had given their room to Mikey and bought a Castro Convertible which they placed in the living room for themselves. It was very important, they said, for Mikey to have his own room, his own desk and privacy for studying because Mikey was going to be a doctor.

Grandma and I slept in twin maple beds in the smaller bedroom. My mother made the beds each day with clean linen and white bedspreads. On the wall above the headboards were two beautifully glazed French limoge plates decorated with paintings of birds, all in lovely shades of indigo blues and ocean greens, each plate arranged between two antique maple-framed watercolors of flower bouquets. A maple dresser was placed against the wall opposite the beds. It was so pretty the way she did things like that. The closet in our room was shared by my mother and Grandma. My father bought a fold-up clothing rod which he installed on the inside of the closet door and that's where I kept my clothes. Also, the bottom drawer of the dresser my mother gave to me and I kept it very, very neat.

Deep in our closet on the highest shelf was the ancient accordion which had belonged to my mother's father, Jacob Jacobson. Some dreary Saturdays Mikey would climb the stepladder, move a lot of boxes and things around on the dark shelves and after a while come back down into the room tenderly holding the revered treasure with which our grandfather had so delighted our mother when she was a little girl.

I was completely fascinated by the accordion which became for me, on those wintry Saturday mornings, a sparkling shower of musical joy. The size and weight of the instrument didn't discourage me from slipping my hands under the frayed leather straps, safely resting the accordion on my knees while seated on the edge of a small wooden chair by the doorway of my room. The delicately carved fretwork had cracked and in some places seemed about to splinter so it was with utmost care that I practiced for hours, teaching myself to play simple melodies like God Bless America.

In addition to the accordion, Grandfather Jacob could play the balalaika and the violin, our mother always told us, a faraway look coming over her deep-set Asian eyes. It was a wonderful blessing to be so musical and I wished I could be musical. To hold the accordion which our grandfather had loved felt good because it connected us to him, but it felt sad too. I longed to know him, certain that if he hadn't died I would have very much enjoyed having him for my Grandpa. But we had only a single photograph of a handsome, princely man with what our mother called, 'finely chiseled features,' we had our mother's stories and we had this accordion.

When my mother was twelve her father died of tuberculosis, leaving Grandma to raise her three daughters alone. Grandma went out early every morning to sell fabrics from a pushcart, and my mother, Mary, cared for her two younger sisters ages ten and nine. She cleaned, did the marketing, prepared dinner, saw that her sisters behaved and did their homework, and at night she had a warm bath waiting for her Mama's tired, swollen feet.

As they grew up, Mary remained caretaker of the family. She kept the image of her Papa before her. She used to sit by him listening to his dreams for her future. He had had great hopes for his bright, competent Mary to become an educated woman, a doctor perhaps. She recalled his aristocratic bearing and looked for his face in crowds. Whatever my mother did she wondered, "What would Papa think of this?" She often wondered how many things in her life would be different if her Papa had not died so young . . .

The winter afternoon faded quickly into evening. I brought my homework to the kitchen table. It was warm and steamy in the kitchen from the simmering chicken soup. My mother called out, "Mikey, please run down to the bakery and bring home a challah!" She handed him some coins, and admonished him not to eat the sweet-tasting freshly-baked challah on the way home, to wait for supper with the family.

My thoughts wandered to Lana, my lost friend. She was so pretty with her tan skin and long, black, curly hair . . . I loved my friend, the way she looked, the nice way she played, even her name. Then one day she didn't come to school. I worried that something bad had happened but my teacher said it was only that Lana had moved away. I wished and wished that one day I would see her again, so for years I kept a sharp lookout wherever I went, for my beautiful friend Lana. But I never found her.

Sometimes my mother put her arm around me and called me Sugarplum. It made me feel warm inside because it meant she was feeling good. But she didn't hold me too often. Her days were filled with work, beginning with her morning chores, during which she'd repeat again and again, "I wish I were dead! I wish I were dead!" Her voice was filled with anguish; her voice made her sound like she really meant it. She'd also say, "I look like a ghoul!" and I'd be too frightened to look. She'd yell about things without caring if anyone was listening.

Early Sunday mornings when there were hardly any people out on the streets my father took Mikey and me to the Bronx Zoo and before he moved away from our building to Long Island, my cousin Mitch who I loved so very much, came along with us. We loved feeding the goats and elephants old rye bread while the pathways and cages were still damp from hosing. When we returned home the apartment was immaculate but my mother was still yelling...

My mother called out that supper was ready just as I finished copying a list of spelling words five times. The doorknob rustled, Grandma was home. She came in slowly, tired, smiling. "My shayna maidela, my cameo face, come give your Grandma a hug!" I ran the few steps to her open arms and then let her get comfortable.

On this bitter winter evening Grandma had stopped on her way home to buy a gift. She handed the package to my mother. "Here, Mary, use this for supper tonight."

"What's this, Mama, fancy pickles?" My mother's voice came out high. "With all that we could use, Mama brings home fancy pickles."

"It's nice to have something special once in a while, Mary," Grandma said decisively, withdrawing her hatpin, removing her hat.

In another minute my father was home and I went to greet him with a kiss. My father was tall and strong, the texture of his skin was smooth, completely unblemished, and he was considered charming and handsome by the neighborhood women. He had already lost most of his hair and he was teased about it by Uncle Sammy, my cousin Mitch's father.

"Hey Baldy," Uncle Sammy laughed, thinking it was funny to greet my father this way. I was polite to Uncle Sammy but because he teased my father who was kind to my cousins, aunt and everyone and because my uncle, who had parents and a sister who loved him, failed to acknowledge the lingering sorrow of my father's heart, I never grew to love my uncle.

My father was the one who told me bedtime stories he made up just for me, like: "The Good Alice and the Bad Alice" and "The Munchkin Stove." He was the one who brought me a tall glass of cool water after I was in bed, sometimes even a second glass.

MY MOTHER was still complaining, "Mama, how could you spend money on fancy pickles?"

In the center of our small table the Sabbath candles were lit, the brass candlesticks framed the large round challah softly wrapped in an embroidered Sabbath cloth.

There was always enough challah left over for my mother to make us sweet challah French toast on Saturday mornings. We all took our places; my mother busily serving my father and Mikey first helpings. By the time she sat down everyone was almost finished eating, except for me.

My father smiled his soft-hearted smile, and chided me about my already famous-in-the-family slow eating habits, "How come, Francine, it looks like more food's on your plate now than when you started?"

Taking his gentle humor too seriously my mother said, "Well, she's not leaving this table until she finishes every scrap of food on her plate. Don't you know? They're starving in Europe!"

Every night while we ate our supper my parents told us their stories of years gone by. I wanted to scream, "No! No! No! -- it didn't happen!" Many of their stories were about their hard life during the Great Depression. Our mother was pregnant with Mikey and our father had no job and they were starving! They said the only way they could earn a few dollars was to sell eggs on the subway.

Our father often recounted his days as an orphan child and his life in Hawthorne. He was beaten with a rubber hose. He was alone. He felt he was smart, but who cared? The stories of his suffering and loneliness overwhelmed me. Inwardly, I begged, "Say it isn't true! This didn't happen to my Daddy!" And I knew I had to give my father a lot of love and be the best daughter to soothe the pain inside him, to make up for all the love he'd missed.

My mother often reminisced at suppertime about the way she and my father had met in 1932. She'd been walking in her neighborhood, 125th Street in Harlem which was quite fashionable in those days, when she met a girl she used to know, Essie, who said, "Mary, what are you doing tonight? Nothing? Then come to my house, I live in the Bronx now and I'm having a Washington's Birthday party." Noting Mary's reluctance, Essie urged, "You must come, Mary, everyone will be there." My mother's life was changed forever. There was irony in her voice each time she said, "I don't know why I went, I never liked that Essie. I was planning to become a nurse, I'd already been accepted to nurse's training school but they said I was too young, I had to wait a year, and along comes your father and convinces me to marry him instead. What dopes we were! Me only seventeen and him eighteen."

We were up to the Jell-O dessert. My father was giving us the latest installment about Eddie and Max, brothers who had also been in Hawthorne and now were his partners. There had been another argument over buying new machinery; my father was against it, but his share of the partnership was only fifteen percent so he lost the argument as he always did.

Then my father turned to me. "Now Francine, I'm very sorry to have to tell you this but you won't be able to continue ballet lessons. Your mother worries because on the way home you have to pass the Bar & Grill on the corner and some drunk might grab you and hurt you."

I swallowed and froze. I was best in the class! My place was first in the first row and the teacher never had to adjust my feet. It made me feel so grown up to turn left at the corner and walk to the ballet school above the RKO Chester. Even while recognizing the reasoning behind my parents' decision I believed there was a way for me to continue ballet lessons, but at that moment I couldn't think of what it might be. A lump had swiftly arisen in my throat, it prevented me from speaking so I left the table.

I sat in darkness on the edge of my bed and in the shadows of the room there suddenly appeared the ghostlike figure of Rose Poretzky, the girl with a hare-lip. Poor Rose. Her mother had asked my mother to ask me to be a friend to Rose, maybe walk with her to school. So beginning with the very next day when Rose came down the steps of her courtyard she sat on the bottom step waiting for me. I tried to avert my eyes from her disfigurement while we walked to school together as if we were real friends. The kids never tired of tormenting Rose. They called out in sing-song, "Rose has cooties!" and they danced around her laughing and pointing. One day Rose couldn't take it anymore; she struck back wildly and as I was walking right beside her I became the object of her misery and rage. A trembling sound issued from her wet mouth. Her long, bony fingers darted quickly, reaching for my face. She pinched and twisted a bit of delicate skin above my eye. A red mark remained. And now a question was forming in my mind, "Why was there such a word as fair when nothing ever was?"

The apparition faded. My father was standing in the doorway. "Here's my Pocahontas!" He switched on the light and in a moment leaned over to kiss my cheek with unsurpassed tenderness which was how my father always behaved toward me. "I have to go to the shop tomorrow. Would you like to keep me company, Francine?"

THE KITCHEN was quiet and spotless again and by the soft light of the Sabbath candles my mother and Grandma lingered over tea. Then Grandma came to me. She cupped my face in her tired hands. "My Shayna Maidela, let me look at my cameo face, my little Fagala. Tomorrow morning I make for you a beautiful dress. Shulman, he gives me a scrap of velvet, and I say, "This is perfect for my Fagala."

Grandma showed me a length of dark emerald green velvet, it shone in the lamplight, and a smaller piece of lovely white cotton lace which I guessed my Grandma would fashion into a round collar and turned back cuffs. I'd try to stand very still, but would probably giggle from the unintentional tickling while Grandma measured and pinned. "Thank you, Grandma."

Then Grandma took from her drawer a sepia photograph she had carried in her bundle all the way from Russia to New York City. This photograph was different from the ones my father took at his camera club. His were shiny black and white, modern looking, and you could bend them. Grandma's photograph resembled old-fashioned cardboard, crumbling and peeling around the edges, and the people looked serious and from another place and time. I peered closely at the images of family I would never know: my Grandma's Mama, her Papa and her three sisters. One little sister's face captivated me; she and I looked exactly alike! She was delicate-looking, pale and thin, and she gazed out of the photograph with fine, almond shaped eyes.

IN 1915 WHEN SHE was fifteen years old my Grandma came to New York all alone. She traveled steerage, her belongings wrapped up in a flowered shawl. As the ship sailed into New York Harbor my Grandma was one of those who leaned against the ship's railing and wept at the sight of the Statue of Liberty. And right away my Grandma went to school and learned the language of her new country, her new home. She became an American citizen. She marched with the suffragettes and never failed to vote in elections. Grandma represented her shop in the Ladies' Garment Workers' Union and she knew how to argue politics with my father. But my Grandma's gentle gray eyes were filled with sorrow. Her family waited too long to join her in America. Eventually, the Nazis invaded their town, rounded up all the Jews, marched them to a ravine near the edge of the forest, aimed their guns and murdered every one. Including Grandma's little sister who looked just like me.

I changed into flannel pajamas and climbed under the covers. My long hair, wavy from being braided all day, fanned out over the pillow; I felt the coolness of the fresh pillowcase under my neck and closed my eyes. But I couldn't sleep. The sounds of my parents talking, of the radio, of the trains rumbling over the tracks out in the darkness, the light from the living-room, and my thoughts, all kept me awake.

I was positive that my parents had adopted me. They didn't ask me what I thought or how I felt. Mikey had my father with whom he could discuss things I didn't understand, and they never explained their topics to me. My mother and Grandma confided in each other in Yiddish or else my mother was busy. Whenever I was sick and hoped she would stay with me, she never did. Instead, after finishing her chores and dressing, she'd say, "Now you stay right here in bed while I go out on errands. I'll be right back in a jiffy." I'd wait patiently, thinking that on her return she was going to stay with me but then she just gave me some Aspergum and got busy with other matters.

My hair was long, down to my waist, and the task of shampooing it fell to my mother. The water was always lukewarm so I felt cold in the tub, and the shampoo always got into my eyes. I cried, and my mother screamed, "Bastard!" and yanked my hair. My father came running. "What are you doing to my Pocahontas?" My mother yanked my hair again and screamed as if to herself, "She just wants his attention!" It wasn't true; my eyes were stinging from soap, I was freezing cold, but all I could do was cry even more. Later, when my father went to get me a glass of water I heard from my bedroom, "What does she want now?"

But no one ever yelled at Mikey. And my mother had a baby book for Mikey. Mine, she said, got lost. Whenever I was out walking with my mother and she met a lady she knew, she would discuss Mikey's latest accomplishments in school, the scouting merit badge he was earning, the overnights he went on. I stood quietly beside her, waiting for her to mention my name.

I was born with a cyst in my throat which protruded from my neck like a finger and it made me sick. One night when I was four years old the cyst ruptured. I was gasping for breath! My parents rushed me to the hospital where, following emergency surgery to save my life I remained for three weeks to recuperate, but my parents came to visit only on Sundays. I was lonely, everything frightened me and when they stood beside my hospital bed in their dress-up clothes my parents seemed like strangers. Later on they said they had no money for a doctor and that's why I almost died. But I never really believed them. I believed, instead, that I was adopted and that's why all the good things went to Mikey.

However, I found consolation in thoughts of Grandma's sister, the little girl in the photograph. How sad we'd never know each other. But the fact that I looked exactly like her dispelled the notion that I was adopted. Maybe I'm really her, I thought, she lives inside of me, looking out through my eyes, and everything I do is for her. The cracked and littered sidewalks in my neighborhood weren't so bad when compared to the muddy pathways that Grandma's little sister trod. Our apartment wasn't as bad as my mother made it out to be when I thought of the poor little broken-down one room cottage my Grandma had left behind in Russia. And my clothes! How Grandma's little sister would have rejoiced to wear the beautiful velvet and fine woolen dresses that Grandma made for me instead of the coarse old-fashioned dress she wore in the photograph. And we're safe here in America! No one's coming to round up the Jews on Vyse Avenue. But I better be careful, anyhow, and there's so many things to learn and accomplish, because I'm not living for myself alone.

At last I drifted off to sleep but then the nightmare returned. Two tombstones in the alley behind our building where I sometimes played. A dreary place, even for tombstones, and suddenly I could see clearly, horror of horrors, my mother's and father's names engraved on the stone. I bolted awake, too frightened to cry out, too frightened even to tell anyone.

After a while stillness came; and out of the stillness, my Guardian Angel, seeming as always to alight from somewhere above and although I couldn't see her I felt her luminous presence. I never knew when my Angel would arrive. I didn't even exactly think about her, yet she always found me when my need for her was greatest. Surrounded by peaceful silence my mind grew even more still and then somehow came the understanding that my troubling thoughts arose from unwarranted fear.

When I was three years old, rocking my dolls in their cradle was my favorite pastime; I played at adjusting their soft pink blankets, worrying my dolls were cold in the winter or not comfortable enough, crushed as they were in the small cradle. Enfolded in the peacefulness of my own little world of play, suddenly my attention was drawn to an extraordinarily loving presence right beside me . . . so I looked up. Right here in our foyer on the fourth floor in this old building in the Bronx, my Angel had found me!

"Francine . . ." she said without a sound, "why do you love your dolls so much . . . they are inanimate objects . . . it is your parents who need your love, Francine . . . your parents need the kind of love only you can give them . . . so love your parents Francine . . . it is your love that will heal them . . ."

QUIETLY, GRANDMA entered our room; on the far side of her bed she undressed in the dark so as not to disturb me. I listened to the rustlings of Grandma unhooking her corset, I listened to Grandma's soft sighing, and in this way I finally fell asleep.

On Saturday morning I dressed in my dungarees and plaid flannel shirt, grabbed the key to my bicycle lock and ran out.

My father's voice, calling my name, mingled with the sound of my desperate footsteps and echoed up and down the dank stairways. "Francine! Where are you going?"

"I'm running away! Leave me alone!"

I imagined that my father and brother laughed. They didn't think I could go anywhere by myself. But I knew the way to Aunt Margie's!

I ran across the rock and glass strewn vacant lot to reach the garage where my bike was stored. Entering the garage I was immediately engulfed by the stench of old jalopies with running boards, mountains of discarded rubber tires, exhaust fumes. I ran across the oil-soaked cement floor; I ran fast, unbolted my bike chain and pedaled out from the gloomy corner toward the bright morning light. My bike was new, a brand-new two wheeler, a gift from my grandfather, Joe Vale.

One evening a few weeks ago my mother had greeted my father at the door with a letter in her hand. Reading the letter which came from Joe Vale, the small muscle in the hollow of my father's right cheek began to tremble. "I want nothin' to do with him, Mary! Where was he when I needed him?"

"Just talk to him, Matty," my mother counseled. "Maybe he wants to apologize. He's an old man now, maybe he realizes..."

"Him? Apologize? What're you, crazy? Joe Vale don't care about nothin' but himself, mark my words. Sure, he's an old man now, an guaranteed he wants somethin' from me! An I ain't givin' him nothin'!" He slammed his powerful fist against the kitchen wall and everything in the whole building shook.

MY FATHER'S OUTBURSTS saddened me but never frightened me. His outbursts were a lamentable expression of a pain so deep that no matter how often he told us the stories of his ruined childhood, no matter how much love he received from us and my cousins and aunts, and even though he now had his own home to which he returned directly from work every evening, all the abuse that he had endured, the deprivations, the relentless lack of love for all the years of his childhood, had produced a kind of torment of the soul none of us could ever truly comprehend. I tried to comprehend it, I tried to imagine myself living his childhood. I soon became an observer in the past, able to see my father suffering through all his lonely tribulations, watching over him, sending out streams of love and comfort to him. When I saw his child self unbearably oppressed I knelt beside him and touched his shoulder and whispered gently of a better life waiting for him.

Eventually my mother convinced my father to allow Joe Vale one visit. So the old man came all the way from Brooklyn to Vyse Avenue where he then discovered he had to walk up dozens of stone courtyard steps and then the four long flights. When finally he entered our foyer I saw a spare man in a neat but threadbare dark suit. My grandfather spoke earnestly, with Brooklyn on his tongue and he was polite. But an invisible wall separated him from us. We gathered in the living room. I lingered in the doorway observing the scene, noticing again the quivering muscle in my father's right cheek. For a long moment it was the only movement in the apartment. And then my grandfather stated the purpose of his visit.

"It's not right, Matty, for you to carry the Friedman name. They had no right, changin' your name. You're a Vale and that's the name you should be carryin.' They had no right, changin' your name the way they did. After all, I'm your Pop, it's my name you should be carryin.'" My Grandfather was focused and intense. "An you got awfully nice kids here. They should have their rightful name. What do you say, Matty? Look at me, I'm an old man, an I made my mistakes, no worse than anybody else, but I got to die knowin' my name won't die with me."

My father's hazel eyes, always so kind, had hardened into dark gray steel. I noticed he had clenched his fists, and my mother reached out to cover one white-knuckled fist with her soft hand. The emotional tension between my father and grandfather was a powerful force that sent me from the living room into my bedroom, over to the window where the noise from the trains, the sounds that rose up from the street and the jarring landscape of elevated tracks, all kinds of buildings high and low seeming from my view out the window to intersect randomly, challenged my brain to create order from the chaos of it all, and the whole of it became a distraction.

Afterward my parents reviewed Joe Vale's request. "He said he wants to come and visit all the time, Matty," my mother reminded. "It's not just the name."

"You believe that crap? Well, I gotta a bridge I wanna sell ya."

"Maybe he does mean it, Matty. People can change, after all. Besides, what have the Friedmans done for you? Were they any better?"

My mother always turned to us and her voice rising, added, "What did they care about him? They threw him out like garbage! For reading a book he was beaten! Every day, they beat him for something else! Imagine! They locked him in a freezer! A boy like that! With his mind, and his sensitivities! He could have been anything, a professor!"

My grandfather returned for another visit. He gave my father money to buy me a shiny red two-wheeler. And in the middle of third grade my teacher had to call me by my new name, Francine Vale. After our name was changed we never heard from Joe Vale again.

Reviewing in my mind the route to Aunt Margie's I pedaled my shiny red bike out from the cavernous garage into the bright winter sunshine. My father was there! And he blocked the way!

My father grabbed the handlebars in his large powerful hands. He spoke to me in soft, loving tones and walked me back into the garage where he kneeled and locked up my bike.

"I have to go to the shop, Francine, would you like to go for a drive with me?" My father walked beside me, and his expression was serious. We walked home the long way around the block that I never used by myself. The elevated trains were passing overhead, the sun was blocked by a building and the wind was blowing cinders and litter all over the place. My father was holding my hand as we walked and now, during this unpleasant stretch of sidewalk, he put our interlocked hands into his flannel-lined jacket pocket as he always did when we walked together in the cold, to keep my hand warm. I glanced up at his face, he was grimacing from the grimy particles swirling around us, but when our eyes met my father smiled and inside his cozy pocket he gave my hand a loving squeeze.

My mother was frying challah French toast and already there was a golden stack in the center of the table. Mikey and my father had a contest to see who could eat the most. I ate one slice sprinkled with brown sugar, and then my father and I were on our way again, riding in the Buick to the shop.

"So, Fran," my father said, "are you asking at least one good question every day?"

I wondered every time he reminded me about this how my father knew I was shy in class and hardly ever spoke. Questions arose in my mind all day long but other kids raised their hands more aggressively than I. I turned in my seat and observed again my father's handsome profile: his complexion was wintry pale, smooth and unblemished as always. His nose, he'd explained, used to be straight until it was broken a long time ago while playing football. Still, it was a narrow nose and well-suited to his face. My father had good strong teeth and a beautiful smile. When he laughed he threw his head back in a very appealing manner and I always felt wonderful when my father laughed.

"Would you like to hear what happened at gym class the other day?"

"What happened, Fran?"

"Well, we had rope-climbing but everyone was just standing around doing nothing. So you want to know what I did?"

"What did you do, Fran?" My father was really interested so I felt good about telling him.

"I looked around at the ropes hanging down from the ceiling, I never saw such thick white ropes before, so I just grabbed one, and climbed up and up until all of a sudden I was at the very top! I even touched the ceiling with my hand! and it was so much fun to be up there, I could've stayed all day! but I wondered why no one thought about looking up, not even the teacher and I wished someone could've seen me!"

My father cleared his throat. "Well, daughter," he said, taking his eyes off the road to glance at me for a second, "I hope you will always remember what your dear old Dad has to say on the occasion of your climbing the rope to the top! You are a very capable girl. But you are never to concern yourself with people taking note of your accomplishments. Remember, daughter, it's what we do when no one is watching that really counts."

We had stopped at a red light. My father leaned across the seat and kissed my cheek gently. We rode on in silence for a while and then he spoke again. "I hope you will remember this, daughter, if ever you should become discouraged: always remember how happy you felt when you touched the highest ceiling. Never forget, my Pocahontas, how you grabbed that rope when all around you they were doing nothing, and you climbed and climbed without looking back until you reached the very top!" He paused another moment, thinking, and slowly added, "Just imagine ... there was no ceiling ..." My father threw back his head and laughed his wonderful life-affirming laugh and the car was filled with joy.

The print shop was located all the way out in a desolate

windswept section of the Bronx known as Classon Point. The shop was silent, the partners never came on Saturdays.

My father walked me around the shop explaining the function of each printing press. On this day he went to the trouble of starting up one of the enormous presses just for my observation. It was fascinating to watch the mammoth iron press repeating its deafening rotations, pushing out from deep inside itself, fragile fluttering papers which a second ago were blank and now had words printed on them and the papers settled into a stack. From time to time, my father would reach into the machine to adjust and maintain an orderly stack.

My father set type by hand. I enjoyed standing beside him on the cement floor. The floor, imbedded with thousands of metal slivers, shimmered with silver light. To my father it was a cold, hard floor that precipitated backaches and frozen feet in winter. To me, although I felt sad about my father's backaches, the floor was magical to behold, saturated with starlight. I watched the blur of my father's lightning-swift hands as he set up the type for some new job.

He worried I might not find it interesting so he gathered up a pile of pastel-colored papers of varying sizes and weights, all of which I loved, he cleared a place at one of the massive oak desks in the office, and said, "Now, Francine, you can sit here if you like and you can use any pen or pencil from any desk, to write or draw with. See here? There's pens that write with red ink, blue ink and green ink. Here's red pencils, and so on."

He positioned the swivel chair for me, made sure I was comfortable and then he leaned over and as lightly as a feather brushing my cheek my father kissed me. He never warned me not to touch important business things, he trusted me to be smart enough not to disturb anyone's work. But I preferred to be with him and watch his powerful, calloused hands which were also imbued with grace, arc back and forth across the type box, choosing from hundreds of metal pieces: upper case letters, lower case letters, numbers, punctuation marks, blanks for spaces. How did he do that? The dignity and concentration my father brought to his task recalled the image of a conductor standing before a symphony orchestra. When my father finished and the type was set the job was flawless.

So I came to know about the huge frosted glass windows that allowed a gray light into the shop, the white-washed walls that rose maybe forty feet high and the pressed tin ceiling. I learned about enormous iron-jawed printing presses clamping and unclamping in deafening repetition. When it was time to leave my father's custom was to recount the story, while he retrieved his key and unlocked the stark metal door to let us out and then relock it, of how some years earlier, before I was born, a press had tried to gobble his hand but, due to the quick response of Jack, a fellow worker who threw the switch, the press had only damaged a single finger on my father's right hand. He held out his hand to show me the scar. Then he warmed up the car and we drove home.

EVERY SUNDAY my mother and Grandma packed provisions unavailable to my aunts who had moved away from our building and now lived in Levittown: meat from the kosher butcher, fresh vegetables, fabric for dresses Grandma sewed for them.

Once we were out past the city limits, my father relaxed driving his sky-blue Buick along the open highway and he'd start singing in a clear voice, "Oh dear what can the matter be, Johnny's so long at the fair ..." and after a pause he'd launch right into my favorite, "The girl that I marry will have to be as soft and as pink as a nursery, the girl I call my own ..." I loved listening to my father sing, for his voice then did not contain a trace of his tough Brooklyn accent, and I could imagine that my father was a refined gentleman. But, if another driver cut us off my father rolled down his window and shouted a curse at the offender. I cringed with embarrassment. Then, as if nothing happened my father rolled the window up and resumed singing. A day away from the weary, worn streets of Vyse Avenue, away from the glittering shards of broken glass strewn in the path of skates or under the feet of girls who played jump-rope.

At last my father announced, "Here's Jerusalem Avenue, we're almost there, you can wake up now, Fran." In another minute we had turned onto Saddler Lane which looked identical to every other lane and street in the vast, sprawling town conceived and developed by Mr. Levitt for the returning veterans of World War II. We drove up to the white house with number eight on the door. Everyone awaited us! They had laid down boards from curb to doorstep to cover the mud and by the time we were in Aunt Margie's tiny, cozy kitchen, all of us were laughing.

My cousin Mitch and I played cards. Whenever he felt he was losing Mitch upset the cards. I knew he cheated but gave him endless other chances, hoping each time that Mitch would play straight, but he never did. We decided to go outside. It was cold; the mud was frozen and cracked. The landscape which surrounded us as soon as we left Saddler Lane consisted of endless rows of mud piles interspersed with wooden frames of new homes in various stages of construction.

"Want to go over there?" Mitch pointed to two large piles of dry, cracked mud; a board led from the peak of one pile to the peak of the other. "Want to walk across?"

"Okay, let's go!"

We climbed and climbed, and when we reached the top we looked down at the gully between the two mud mountains, stepped onto the board, Mitch first. Jackets flying, we ran across to the other side and skidded down.

"Want to go into that house over there?" Mitch called to me. We ran, we raced. We were going to explore a house with no walls.

After a while I said, "Let's go home, Mitch, we've been gone a long time." I began to worry that we were lost in the surreal landscape that surrounded us, devoid of any other human being, but Mitch knew the way after all.

As soon as we entered the house my mother grabbed my arm. "Where have you been? I've been worried sick!" Her voice was shrill and piercing. "Oh, my God, look at your shoes! You've ruined your new shoes! Look at them, covered with mud!" I looked down at my shoes while my mother carried on with her screaming. In our fun I hadn't given a thought to my shoes, and now I started to cry. "Take off your shoes! Oh, what am I going to do with her?"

Mitch took my hand and led me to the refuge of his room. As we passed the living room I glanced up for a moment and there was Mikey, reclining in an easy chair, reading science fiction. On the cover of his book was an illustration of a woman sprawled on a sofa. Instead of human skin, and except for her head which was the head of a normal woman, her skin was a coat of fur. Mikey's shoes were clean.

As they prepared the evening meal and set the table my mother and her sisters never lost the flow of their conversation. Their most often repeated discussion was, Do you think Papa knew he was dying? Then came the matter of settling accounts from the grocery store which was calculated to the exact penny. They discussed their husbands, and this is when they spoke Yiddish. The 'kinder,' they whispered, glancing at us. Then came conspiratorial tones followed by shrieks of laughter. Seeing my mother and aunts together like that I thought, They're so lucky to have each other.

Mitch and I usually got ourselves into trouble at the table because a single exchange of glances was enough to start us giggling. The harder we tried to control ourselves the more we giggled. If Uncle Sammy was not in a mood for a houseful of relatives he expressed it when Mitch and I giggled. First he turned a stern face toward us, then came warnings and finally he ordered us to leave the table.

When Uncle Sammy's parents came to visit they brought special treats. They announced, "This seven layer cake is from the best bakery in the Bronx and we brought it especially for Mitch. The brownies are for Jenny because Jenny loves them so much, and no one else is allowed to touch them!"

That's when Aunt Margie caught my eye and winked, her signal that when Uncle Sammy's parents weren't looking she'd come into Mitch's room with a serving for me. I loved Aunt Margie. She said I looked like Margaret O'Brien and that she wished I were her daughter. Her voice, when she called my name or spoke to me, carried the sound of love.

A half hour flew by from the time my father rose from his comfortable place on the sofa proclaiming it was time to leave until we were in the car. He and Uncle Sammy liked to joke about how long it took the sisters to say goodbye. They couldn't understand why there was always another kiss or another almost forgotten last word. I knew why. It was because they loved each other so much.

MY PARENTS RENTED a summer cottage in the Catskill Mountains; my father came up on weekends and Mikey went to Boy Scout Camp. A girl named Claire came to stay with her aunt in the bungalow across from ours. Poor Claire, my mother lamented, this aunt is her only family, Claire is a lonely girl. So every morning my mother hurried over to braid Claire's blond hair, and they lounged on the grass together.

I thought of my mother's fingers working in Claire's wispy hair; she was making braids for someone else! "No!" I said, when my mother summoned me, holding comb, rubber bands and ribbons, "I don't want braids anymore!" My mother turned me around, held my shoulders in her firm hands until I stood obediently still, and she braided my hair. As soon as she left the bungalow I pulled out the ribbon bows, tore the rubber bands free and tossed my long hair loose against my back, choosing to ignore the mounting humidity of a blazing summer day.

"Like a wild Indian!" my mother called from her lawn chair as the screen door banged and I ran across the field looking for Butch. Occasionally the boys invited me to join a game of baseball or tag but they didn't want a girl along for the best fun, the tree house in the woods. So, most of my time was spent exploring with Butch who was part German Shepard and part fox Terrier. Butch let me hug him and in response he licked my face.

The boys were going off to a baseball game. The sky was blue-white and I could see the heat shimmering everywhere. Butch and I watched the cars pull away leaving behind a dry, dusty cloud which floated around us. A dragonfly zipped by. I glanced at Butch and he looked up. "C'mon, Butch," I said, suddenly excited by my own idea, "take me to the tree house in the woods!"

Butch caught my excitement and off we ran. Now we were in the shaded woods, the sky barely visible. After a while I felt as if Butch was trying to tell me something, he started acting funny, he was running in circles around me, faster and faster. Then I heard the rumble and crack of thunder and as I looked up at the tallest trees I had ever seen, it began to pour. And now Butch was running away! I ran after him, trying to keep sight of his big fluffy tail, but he ran too fast and the pouring rain obscured my vision. I climbed under brambles which tore at my skin, exposed as I was in shorts and a midriff top. I tripped over fallen logs. I didn't feel any pain. All I felt was fear. The rain was teeming, thunder boomed and crashed all around.

Then I saw Butch again. Butch! Butch! You came back for me! He circled me furiously and then darted off.

Hours passed. I was lost amid the enormous power of Nature. I loved the forest and all that it held. I loved the blue sky and the sun and clouds and the sweet aroma of rain, too. I loved Nature! All the beautiful animals and birds ... I loved them all! I loved Earth! And in calm moments dreamed of exploring the highest mountains, the jungles, the wide flowing rivers I read about in school. I ran on through the forest, propelled by fear, not of Nature, but of being so lost in the vastness of a forest that spread over the mountains for hundreds of miles, that I might never find my way out! Fear prevented me from stopping even for a second. And even as I ran, the majesty and beauty of the forest remained in my consciousness. The mossy glens, the dried leaves and branches covering the forest floor, on a calmer day would have beckoned me to find a suitable sitting place from where I could observe all the miracles around me. The trees! So tall, reaching up higher and higher, home to birds and how I loved all the pretty birds! The fallen logs soaked with rain had their own kind of softness as I climbed over. How I loved it all! But I had to find my way out, find my way home and live my life!

Suddenly, a fence appeared! A fence indicated people, civilization! I followed the fence, by now completely unaware of the passage of time, and after a while an opening in the fence appeared. I climbed through the opening. Just then the storm abated and, except for the ethereal sound of raindrops dripping from leaves and branches, the forest became, after all the commotion of the storm, almost silent.

I felt different from before the storm, as though during the storm I had somehow blended with the forest; I was the glistening raindrop, the leaf, I was bark, moss! I was even the sky above peeking through the uppermost branches of the tallest trees! And now I imagined that woodland fairies were guiding me to safety, guiding me back to my life! Suddenly I saw a cabin! A cabin meant people! My heart was pounding, pounding as I ran to the cabin only to find it empty. A pathway led from the cabin door and I followed it. The path led to the edge of the forest and I looked up at the sky; it was a clear, fresh, deepening blue.

Across the field which lay before me I saw a bungalow colony. People were starting to leave their bungalows now that the thunderstorms were over and the sun was low and cool. I walked toward the people. I'll never forget the kind lady who hurried to take my hands in hers. She held me close. Then she looked into my eyes. She was asking me to tell her something. "What is your name?" I thought she said, and "Where did you come from?" She spoke very kindly but it sounded as if we were under water. Carefully, the woman began to pluck twigs and leaves from my wild, tangled hair. She touched my face lightly in places. Somehow, I answered her questions. Then I was sitting on the plastic car seat between the woman and her husband as they drove me home, and felt sorry when I noticed that rivulets of rainwater were running off me and making their clothes wet.

It was night, a full moon was shining, I'd been lost in the woods an entire day. Everyone from my bungalow colony was crowded at the entrance gate, waiting for my arrival. Butch was running in crazy circles. My mother ran over, grabbed my arm, twisted me around and there, in front of all the people, spanked me and screamed at me. Later, she hugged me and gave me hot soup.

White Dove on the Windowsill

MOVING DAY, 1953. We arrive in our new apartment. I come back into the living room to help empty another barrel. I face the window, struck by the loveliness of these new rooms bathed in crisp October sunlight and as I gaze outside through the open window at a wholly different landscape from the one we all were so relieved to finally leave behind, a lone snow white dove alights on the window ledge.

"Mom! Dad! look!"

My parents look up toward the window. "A white dove on the windowsill," my father explains, smiling, "especially on moving day, that means 'good luck'!"

The white dove is poised and still, her opalescent feathers shining, even glowing, in the sunlight, and I feel she is carrying a message. This beautiful lone white dove is telling me that although we've moved away from Vyse Avenue, my Guardian Angel knows how to find me! My beautiful Guardian Angel. I ask, "Dear Angel, how shall I call you?" The answer arises instantaneously in my mind, *Love, my name is Love*. Oh, how absolutely wondrous, my Angel's name is Love! With unsurpassed joy I dance and twirl like a ballerina through the rooms of our brand-new apartment.

Two-fifteen East 199th Street was a new brick building on the corner of Bainbridge Avenue, opposite the serene park-like setting of St. Ursula Academy in the Mosholu section of the Bronx. No gossiping yentas sat on folding chairs arranged on the sidewalk here, as in the old neighborhood. No Bryant Avenue gang here either, to threaten the Vyse Avenue kids as we turned the corner. Our neighbors in the buildings across the street were mostly Irish people and my father forbade me to have anything to do with them. The girls eyed me silently, but the boys were friendly and called out, "Hiya Green Eyes, what's your name?" At first I ignored them as my parents had instructed me to do but when they laughed and called out, "Whatsamatter sweetheart, cat's got your tongue?" I couldn't repress a friendly smile. I began to sort them out, especially Joey Boyle who had curly blond hair and was, to me, the cutest.

My mother recounted the story of when Mikey was a little boy the Irish kids in the neighborhood had threatened to throw him in the trash barrel and she had to go to the church to speak to the priest. But that was a long time ago, and times changed. Wouldn't it be a better world if kids didn't follow their parents' prejudices? We could decide who we like according to the individual. The world could start being better now, and I could make friends with Joey Boyle and his pals. I explained my philosophy to my parents, explaining how friendly the boys were and after all we're neighbors, and convinced them, sort of, to let me talk with them. The next thing I knew, I somehow became recognized on 199th Street as Joey's girl.

Every time he saw me out in the neighborhood Joey left his pals on the corner to walk me to the grocery store on an errand for my mother or to walk me home to my building. Evidently, even here on 199th Street there existed a territorial decree that I didn't understand at all; Joey and his friends hung out on their side of the block, never venturing across the street to our new building so it was a big deal when he crossed over for me. But I walked on both sides of the street according to where the sunlight shone.

My childhood was in the past, left forever on Vyse Avenue. Sometimes I awoke in the night, terrified, bathed in perspiration, having returned in a nightmare to our old fourth floor apartment, or the dingy sunless alleyways and glass-strewn sidewalks that used to be my playground, a playground still for other kids.

Here in my new neighborhood I was being given a chance to create a finer life. No plan was yet formulated in my mind of how to go about creating a finer life. I just knew that I loved the world and everyone in it, I loved the blue skies, the nearby Botanical Gardens filled with the beauty of Nature. I loved my life and all the possibilities that lay before me. I had no idea of how anything would come to be. I just knew that every day was filled with kids I could get to know, songs on the radio that I enjoyed listening to, books and classes I could learn from and from all this and all the other stuff that made up every day living I would somehow create a worthwhile life. My life was going to mean something, and I was going to fill my life with love. Whatever else I did with my life, love would be the most important part of it.

Our new apartment was very modern with its smooth, white walls and neat window sills. A half-wall dividing the kitchen provided a square dining area which allowed for a table in the center and a real brass chandelier above. It was wonderful to sit around the table with space enough for each of us.

Once again I shared a room with Grandma. It was carpeted wall to wall in dark forest green and gave a new look to the maple furniture. My mother added new white George Washington bedspreads, white ruffled muslin curtains, and then she went to Macy's and bought a drop-leaf maple desk just for me. The desk was fitted with cubbyholes and adorable little drawers and I so enjoyed arranging colored pencils, interesting papers of varied textures and hues which my father brought home from the print shop and all the little supplies that go in a desk. How I loved my desk. Then my mother found a flaw in the desk, had it shipped back to Macy's and chose a replacement which was similar but lacked the particular charm of the first one.

My parents argued over how to decorate the living room. My father got his way so it was bold primary colors and geometric shapes; this was the new modern Fifties look. We still shared one bathroom and still, there weren't enough closets for me to have my own.

The kitchen window opened directly onto a fire escape and trees. My favorite thing for all the years we lived there was to open the kitchen window wide, sit on the ledge with a book and a box of Cinnamon Crisps or Oreo cookies and enjoy frequent visits by neighborhood birds. The telephone had been installed on the wall right next to the window so altogether I passed more hours than can be counted sitting on that window ledge.

The laundry room in the basement was immaculate and bright with fluorescent lighting, so after school I helped with the laundry. No more trudging up endless flights of stairs, this new building was equipped with an elevator. And there were two young families on our floor for whom I babysat. I opened a savings account in the Dollar Savings Bank on Fordham Road and deposited every cent.

ELIZABETH BARRETT Browning Junior High School on the Grand Concourse. The faculty liked to call it a girl's finishing school. The girls called it, E.B.B., Everything But Boys. There were lots of rules forbidding things I never even thought of trying, like smoking and wearing lipstick to school.

Phyllis, who called herself Chico, sat in the last seat in the last row. She wore sheer stockings and capezio shoes, tight skirts and sweaters, and she liked to chew gum, making it crack during class even while Miss Saperstein was giving a lesson. Marilyn, who was called Babe, sat in the last seat in the first row. On Sunday nights Marilyn bleached her roots and re-dyed Chico's hair black. Marilyn wore black stockings every day, a black rayon skirt and most often, a white blouse. The underarms of her blouses were stained yellow. Chico and Babe delighted in calling across the room to each other as if they were alone. "Hey, Chico, what'd you do last night?" "Went out with Johnny! Want a smoke?"

Suzie Zimmerman was brilliant and nonchalant, creating on the morning they were due exquisite book report covers and 'A' book reports. She worked at her desk, seemingly oblivious of the lesson in progress. But if Miss Saperstein happened to call on her, Suzie had the perfect answer. I handed in pretty decent reports but needed to rewrite them neatly at home, undisturbed, while seated at my maple desk. Suzie was the type of girl who could travel the world with no more than a toothbrush yet remain confident and in control. Her clothes looked expensive but she didn't pay too much attention to them, and once Suzie brushed her hair in the morning she couldn't be bothered again unless she had a date. I wished I could be like her. Instead, I got to be her best friend. True to her style she chose the name Francesca for me, not caring that she was the only one who called me that.

Sherry Plotkin dated older boys she called 'men' and stayed out until 3:00 A.M. Sophisticated and smart, Sherry had aspirations to marry a wealthy man and she seemed to know how to go about it. She knew about makeup and how to cross her legs in a sexy way while casually holding a cigarette, and she had a beautiful smile.

Together with Roz and Sandy we bought navy blue and white college sweaters and had TEENETTES emblazoned across the back. We divided a silver dollar into five pieces and wore them on thin silver chains. We had Friday evening gatherings in each others' homes or, on irresistible Spring nights, at Jahns Ice-Cream Parlor on Fordham Road. Our distinct differences often became the focus of discussion, as did our hopes and dreams. We were determined to eliminate our Bronx accents and we chided each other when we slipped up. Everyone wanted to walk like me, kind of sexy, they said. And one day we'd live in a lovely Connecticut town and create our own Utopia.

In eighth grade Carol Cohen moved into the building on the first floor. Mrs. Cohen kept her hair shoulder length, dyed it black and wore a lot of makeup. She would tell us, "Remember, girls, it's just as easy to love a rich man as it is a poor man." And, "If you go to sleep with a pig you wake up with a pig." Mr. Cohen drove a taxi. He was a little man, slightly hunched from years of hugging the steering wheel. The skin beneath his day-old stubble was pallid. He couldn't sit and relax in his home. Maybe all he could think of was that he might as well be sitting behind the wheel of his taxi, earning a few extra bucks.

One Saturday night we were lounging around Carol's room with a couple of her friends from Music and Art when Mr. Cohen knocked on Carol's door and asked if we'd care to go for a drive. Would we! I ran upstairs to get my shoes and jacket.

"Mom! Carol's father is taking us for a ride, okay?"

"Where? Where is he taking you?"

"I don't know, just a drive."

"Matty," my mother called to my father who was relaxing in front of the television set in the living room. "Ed wants to take the girls for a drive. Is it alright if she goes?"

"Who's going?" my father asked as he left his comfortable chair and came right into the kitchen. "And where are you going?

"Just me and Carol and a couple other girls. I don't know where, just a drive, it sounds like fun, please, Daddy," I begged.

"You mean he's taking you for a ride at night and you don't know where? What kind of thing is that?"

I felt like screaming. Instead, I pleaded, "Daddy, please, they're waiting for me," and tied the laces of my white bucks. At last my father relented. "Thank you, Daddy! I love you!" I kissed him goodbye and ran down the stairs.

Mr. Cohen drove all the way out to Coney Island and treated us to Nathan's famous hot dogs. It was the kind of wonderfully spontaneous fun thing my parents did not do. The taxi radio blared Georgia Gibbs singing "Tweedly Dee." My hair swirled around my face in the breeze from the open car windows and I sang along with Carol and her friends, ". . . I got something that money can't buy . . ."

Suddenly, gazing out the open window, squinting my eyes against the hot blowing wind, I was alone with my thoughts, listening to my inner mind, or maybe it was my Angel Love seizing the moment to bring me an important message: Francine, you must cultivate all your personal qualities, improve yourself, develop yourself as much as possible; rely only on yourself.

Money was always a big issue in our house. My father earned a decent salary but Mikey was attending Columbia University where the tuition was expensive. My mother deposited half my father's salary into the bank for Mikey's tuition and managed the household on the rest. She complained a lot to herself when I was the only one home. Many quiet evenings while supper was cooking on the stove, waiting for the rest of the family to arrive home, my mother lay on the double bed, on permanent loan to Mikey all these years, curled up, holding her stomach, sobbing. My mother desperately needed relief from all the pressures and frustrations of her life but she never got any relief. My mother was prettier than any of my friends' mothers and prettier than any of our neighbors on 199th Street. Her youthful face, her mysterious deep set Asian eyes, her well-proportioned slim and neat figure, even the way she wore her tailored clothes set my mother apart from other women. And whatever she was doing my mother moved with grace. My mother was always reading books about history and world leaders; she loved the classics and read just about all of them including most of Shakespeare. She read biographies of all the royal families of Europe and Russia.

My father read ancient history. He knew about the ancient peoples of Greece and Rome and Egypt as if he had lived among them. Now that Mikey was attending Columbia my father set about reading all Mikey's college texts. So my parents were always content with one another's company, having so many interesting subjects to discuss.

But my mother's life was still consumed with too much housework, stress from worrying about where the money for everything would come from, and ongoing travails with her two sisters. I sat at my desk, homework laid out before me, listening to the soft sounds coming from the kitchen of soup bubbling on the stove, the sorrowful sounds coming from the other bedroom of my poor mother's sobbing. I wished I could make it all better for her. She ought to be dressed in the most elegant garments, I thought, knowing how she ruined her hands scrubbing the oven or the floor. She ought to go to glamorous night spots where she would converse with intellectual friends, and laugh her beguiling laugh, unconcerned about the cost of Mikey's education.

The important thing, my father warned, was that Mikey never know about the hardship involved in paying for his education. It might detract from his concentration and that must never happen. Nothing must interfere with Mikey becoming a doctor. We all were being called upon to sacrifice to help him reach his noble goal.

So for years my beautiful mother wore the same two skirts and rarely went anywhere, a few dresses sewn by Grandma remained on hangers in the closet, unworn. My father's dream was to have a drawer filled with neat piles of folded white shirts, but instead he alternated two plaid shirts my mother washed on the scrubbing board, and his trousers were threadbare. I got by with very little, took care of what I had and didn't ask for anything, determined not to add to my mother's nervous tension. I convinced myself I didn't need anything anyway.

IN THE CAFETERIA at E.B.B. I met Elaine and JoAnn. Elaine looked at the day's offerings, shook her head, and said to JoAnn, "This stuff stinks! Let's go up the block and get some fries at the deli." Struck by their conspiratorial attitude and humor, I laughed. They looked over at me and said, "Wanna come?" And that's how our friendship started.

Elaine was short; her skin was so dark she joked and said she was Negro. She lived on 200th Street and the Grand Concourse in a luxurious apartment, and her mother had a live-in maid. An elegant, black baby grand piano in their step-down living room held no interest for Elaine.

I decided not to tell her about my dream to play the piano as it would only give her another reason to act superior to me. From the time my ballet lessons had been discontinued I began to hope for piano lessons. I wouldn't have to go anywhere; piano teachers came to your house. My father finally explained that he might be able to buy a used piano if he saved very carefully but he did not have enough money for weekly lessons. From time to time, hoping that our financial situation might have improved, I asked again. But there never was enough money. Now that Mikey was in Columbia and I was old enough to understand, it was clear that there was no hope for piano lessons. I longed to feel the ivory keys beneath my fingers. I wrote poems and tried to turn my poetry into songs using symbols I devised to represent music notes. I placed my hands in position, imitating actors I observed in the movies, and even felt the rapture of music only I could hear.

Elaine explained to me and JoAnn that her Concourse address was high class and that Bainbridge Avenue where I lived wasn't. She said things like, "My mother is so exhausted from helping the maid clean all day." She had grandparents who showered her with gifts, and she told me the large amounts that all her gift checks added up to. One of the Four Lads who sang *Moments to Remember*, was Elaine's cousin and she thought that made her something special. And she was never ready when I arrived to call for her. Her older sister greeted me at the door, "Oh, make yourself comfortable, Elaine's in the shower." I waited in her stepdown living room seated on the edge of a puffed up white silk sofa.

JoAnn was tall and thin and kept her hair in a D.A. In most conversations JoAnn deferred to Elaine. They said I was good at attracting boys so I went along with them to a lot of neighborhood dances, in the winter mostly boring church basement parties, but exciting in warm weather at Poe Park where we met up with almost everyone we knew and looked around for cute boys we didn't know yet.

Sometimes after school JoAnn and Elaine came over to my house. We sat on the floor in front of my parents' up-to-date RCA cabinet radio with its woofers and tweeters and sang along with the music we loved. After my birthday we listened to the new 78s my father bought me. He had saved twelve dollars, he said, enough money to buy twelve records, so he asked me to give him a list of my favorite songs and that's exactly what he went out and bought for my fourteenth birthday.

Rock 'n' roll, the music of the '50s. When starting a conversation with someone new one of the first questions we asked each other was, Do you like rock 'n' roll? On Friday nights when we were out walking together we blasted the neighborhood with our transistor radios, singing along passionately: "Oh, yes! I'm the Great Pretender . . ." and ". . . down at the end of lonely street at Heartbreak Hotel . . ." and Alan Freed kept it going for hours on 1010 WINS. The music marked a passage from all that went before – the Great Depression, World War II, our parents' music. Rock 'n' roll belonged to our more hopeful generation, it provided a transformational experience that ushered in a new era, the idea that a world of infinite possibility lay before us.

I often tried to understand how it was that world events and social movements seemed to coincide in such a way that they all fit together as if according to plan, but what mind could devise a plan so vast that it included everything in the whole world? Mikey argued that everything was random, there was no God, but that made no sense to me. In some noble, majestic way that I could not grasp our lives were intertwined. We were all connected and it was inescapable; I held my own with my brother in an ongoing argument we never resolved between us. And even though he attended Columbia University, had been blessed with a genius mind, and I was still in junior high school I felt deep inside myself there was higher truth to my unexplainable knowing. Just when people were settling in to create a new life after the war, and new things unfolded every day, everyone hungering for the new, along comes rock 'n' roll, a new music perfectly suited for a new time.

A FEW NIGHTS AGO we were walking in a drizzly rain from my block to visit Mike, a pale lonely boy from the neighborhood who went to Clinton and owned a great record collection. *Come Go With Me* by the Del Vikings was blaring on our transistor radios.

I turned to look at my friends, feeling suddenly a great burst of affection for each one. The beautiful misty atmosphere brought into sharp focus these dismal streets we all longed to someday escape and the whole thought of it caused me to feel melancholy. But then, the aroma of rain always made me feel melancholy. If only we could be in a pretty meadow somewhere, wherever wildflowers blossomed, while it rained instead of on these old pavements.

To bring myself back to a lighter mood I said, "Isn't it exciting to be part of this amazing time? Here right at the beginning of rock 'n' roll? Just think . . . we'll always have these memories!"

"What is she talking about?" Elaine asked JoAnn and Roz and Sandy. To me she said, "Why must you always make everything so deep Francine? Just enjoy it!" Everyone laughed.

Elaine and JoAnn discussed their plans to join Shorehaven, a beach club in the Bronx, and invited me to join with them. It cost twenty-five dollars for a whole summer. I'd heard about

Shorehaven from a lot of kids and thought, At last I can have a real summer with my friends instead of staying at my aunt's house in Levittown where I slept in the attic and rode bicycles with Mitch and his friends.

But my parents said, Absolutely not! It was too expensive and besides, they didn't want me running around wild all summer.

ROOSEVELT HIGH SCHOOL. Overcrowded, kids from the East Bronx I didn't know and who didn't seem to care too much about learning, the Fordham Baldies taking your lunch money on line in the cafeteria, tough girls harassing me in the locker room. You had to be disciplined to receive an education in Roosevelt. I liked my teachers, felt they sincerely cared about their students, and a few took the time to encourage me personally, after class. My friends from E.B.B. were scattered to other high schools.

One evening in early October, as Grandma walked from the shop toward the subway, she stepped onto a cellar door set into the pavement, the type shopkeepers have outside their stores. At that very moment a man came up from the cellar and without warning pushed open the door. Grandma fell onto the concrete pavement. She lay in bed for days, ill and fevered, until the doctor diagnosed the cause of her illness: a diseased gall bladder which had to be removed immediately. My parents brought Grandma to the hospital.

On October 15, standing with my father in the darkened gray foyer, his expression solemn, my father said, "Francine, I have really bad news. The doctor says that Grandma has cancer and she might live six more weeks at the most."

No! Grandma can't die! Not yet! She's only fifty-seven! And she has to live! To see my wedding! And the children I will have! She always said it! And in six weeks it will be my birthday, December first I'll be fifteen! And Grandma can't die on my birthday! The next day after school, the bus ride to Royal Hospital on the Concourse was frustratingly slow and by the time I arrived visiting hours were over. I begged the nurse to let me see my Grandma.

I entered her room ... and there was Grandma, lying motionless in the white hospital bed, tubes in her nose and arms. My eyes followed the tubes to overhead bottles of liquid medication. I couldn't bear to stay there witnessing all this, I wanted to run away from the indescribable pain of being faced with Grandma's undeniable illness.

"Hi Grandma," I kissed her cheek, summoning all my willpower to hold back tears which threatened to overwhelm the visit altogether and then it would be just me crying by her side and Grandma lying helplessly sad.

My *shayna maidela*, my cameo face, her expressive eyes whispered to me.

"I came straight from school, Grandma, as fast as I could," and then my throat closed up tight. No more speaking, just sit and hold her limp, weary hand, don't even allow yourself to think.

It began to grow late, the nurse had peeked in several times motioning for me to leave, so I kissed my Grandma's hand and whispered goodbye. Outside her room I leaned against the wall, covered my face with both hands and cried and cried.

DURING THE WEEKS that followed I ran down the school steps every day in an effort to catch an earlier bus so I could sit one more time with my Grandma. Gently holding her hand, watching her gentle stillness, I remembered the happy songs she sang to me. When I was very little and she was my BeBa she bounced me on her knee, singing, "Hoo ta ta, hoo ta ta ..." She sang, "You are my sunshine, my only sunshine, you make me happy when skies are gray, you'll never know dear, how much I love you, please don't take my sunshine away ..." She had sat by my bed at night and taught me how to recite the Shema: "Hear, oh Israel, the Lord our God, the Lord is One . . ." At the Passover Seders Grandma's voice was stronger than anyone's. She sang Russian songs, *Toom Ba La, Toom Ba La, Toom Balaleika* . . . was my favorite. I wanted to remember my Grandma singing.

Grandma died on December First, after all. My fifteenth birthday. She always said everything was even-steven so her one-thousand dollars was divided evenly among her daughters, as were her few pieces of jewelry. That Spring Mikey needed an emergency appendix operation and my mother used her $330 to pay the doctor.

Steve Friedman, a friend of Mikey's from scouting, came around to visit. He said to Mikey, "I like your sister, is it okay with you if I ask her out?"

Naturally, the whole family got involved. Well what do you know, my parents beamed, Francine has a date! My father and Mikey joked how they'll beat him to a bloody pulp if he lays a hand on me, my mother chose my outfit and offered endless advice about how to answer if he says this or that. If only they would leave me alone and let me be myself! If only there was a place in our apartment where I could be alone with my thoughts!

My parents now slept in the room I had shared with Grandma and I slept on the convertible sofa bed in the living room. I liked reviewing my day in my mind lying in bed before drifting off to sleep. What could I have said more thoughtfully? How might I present myself in a more mature manner should the same circumstance arise in future? What can I do tomorrow to make up for the errors of today? But I had to wait for my parents to finish watching television, turn out the lights and, their voices fading, go into their room, and by then I was faced with the task of clearing my mind of all the chatter before I could begin to delve into my own thoughts. The Botanical Gardens, a short walk from our building, beckoned on sunny Saturdays and that's where I went for refuge and peace. Lying on the lush green grass in a little glen hidden away from the narrow pedestrian path I found the freedom to explore my thoughts fully, uninterrupted, and discover deep within my heart the truth of my life. I longed desperately for independence and spun visions of all I would accomplish and how I would fashion a sophisticated life for myself in Manhattan when at last my independence was achieved. Then later, at home, I found myself once again enveloped in the tragedies and sorrows of my parents' lives.

Steve was really cute. He was almost as tall as Mikey, he combed his dark wavy hair back on both sides and let the front section fall onto his forehead in the popular style, which on Steve looked natural and engaging. He lived with his widowed mother near Columbus High School and he was a senior. I felt so shy around him that I couldn't think of anything to say, so Steve talked about his life and his dreams. And walking along with him I felt so self-conscious I could hardly walk straight. I was sure he saw me as an ignorant little schoolgirl, someone he was wasting time with, but Steve asked me for another date, and then another and then I was seeing him every weekend.

One Saturday night, over burgers and fries, Steve asked me to go steady. I'd grown more comfortable with him but still felt somewhat awkward and felt that going steady was something other girls did, not me. Not yet. He tried to persuade me by offering me his senior class pin, but I refused.

I still hadn't begun to experience my life and besides, I wanted to feel at ease with someone. I dreamed of meeting a boy with whom I wouldn't have to say anything special, or do anything special. We'd feel at home with each other and be able to say anything at all. We'd gaze into each other's eyes and nothing else in the world would matter. And when he held my hand it wouldn't feel sweaty or strange, it would feel wonderful, and I would feel so alive and joyous I'd be smiling all the time.

The next day, Sunday, was a rainy day and Steve and I went to a movie, returning home to deserted, darkening streets. Suddenly, shivers of fear ran through my body for blocking the way to my building was a gang of neighborhood boys led by Joey Boyle with whom I hadn't spoken for a long while. The gang shouted, "Get him! Get him! Let's get him now!"

Joey pointed at Steve, "That's my girl you're with!"

We turned to run and the gang started after us. A speedy review of possible avenues of escape frightened me even more. Mt. Ursula Academy on the Bainbridge side of my building was blocked by the gang. We could run to the Firehouse but it was a full three blocks away and the gang would surely overtake us before we reached it. Steve froze! I felt responsible, I had to protect him! I grabbed his hand and we ran into a new building around the corner. We fell against apartment doors, pounding, ringing bells. No one answered. From the stairwell we heard wild shouts and thumping growing louder as the gang followed us! We screamed, tears streaming down our faces, the gang was upon us! They grabbed Steve, completely unaccustomed to fighting, fell on him kicking and pummeling. My screams echoed unanswered in the hallway. Why didn't anybody come to our rescue? At last a man, a large tough looking man, opened his door, yelled that he was calling the cops, stepped over his threshold into the hallway and raised his hand in a threatening gesture. The gang bolted down the stairs.

When he saw Steve my father clasped his hands to his head in outrage. Then, recovering his composure, he drove the car around to the front of the building and we drove Steve home. Later, on the phone with Steve, his voice raw and sad, he said he couldn't see me anymore, his mother forbid him to return to my block. For a long time afterward I walked the long way around the block to avoid Joey and his gang and I never did see them again.

AT THE 167TH STREET "Y" where I went a few evenings a week to socialize I met David Golden. One evening after watching me win a dance contest to *Rock Around the Clock*, he walked up to me while everyone was still applauding. He smiled right into my eyes and I liked him immediately. David's curly hair was the color of sand and his skin was golden, just like his name, and his eyes were lit with a soft golden light. He was a junior at Stuyvesant High School and he was proud of his school. Like all the boys I was meeting at the "Y" David had high aspirations; he planned on City College, the college of choice for most kids I knew, simply because it was affordable and provided a good education. David's goal was to become an engineer. He was very smart and savvy and I knew he would fulfill his aspirations.

"You're a beautiful girl," he told me often and sweetly, inclining his head toward me, "and besides that you're the most wonderful girl I've ever known!" He also sent me love letters and sang love songs to me. Dancing at house parties he sang along with his favorites, or while we waited on the subway platform for the next train to roar in he might start singing, "When I fall in love it will be forever . . ." Strolling in the Botanical Gardens where I showed him my favorite places, all of it more enjoyable sharing with David he sang, "I'll love you till the flowers forget to bloom . . ." Wherever we were David was singing to me. But David was also possessive. And no one was going to own me. In my struggle to hold onto my independence we began to argue but David always managed to win me back. After an argument he'd take me out special, usually to a restaurant in Manhattan. Once, he acted out the lyrics of a popular song, "A Rose and a Baby Ruth" and sent me a Baby Ruth candy bar stuffed into an envelope along with a note promising a rose if I forgave his foolish behavior. I laughed and agreed to see him again.

As the summer of 1957 drew near I begged my parents to let me accept David's invitation to visit his family's cottage in Rockaway. Everyone, it seemed, had somewhere to go for the summer, and surely David would find another girl to take my place in Rockaway. I didn't feel very independent then. I felt sad and worried. David had become my best friend. We talked on the phone after school and in the evening and saw each other at the "Y" and every weekend. I knew his parents, his little sister and his friends and I liked them all. I loved his seriousness, his intelligence, and besides, it felt good to hold his hand. Also important to me, we laughed a lot together. But my parents refused to let me go, even though David's mother called my mother to assure her that she would be around all the time and I would be safe.

Instead, my mother took me to Aunt Margie's for another summer of sleeping in my aunt's hot unfinished attic on a pull-out bed my mother and I shared. Every night my mother turned off the light, lay down and fell asleep while I lay awake and cried silent tears. David wrote long letters describing his days on the boardwalk, picnics at the beach, the books he was reading and wanted to discuss, the latest music he was into. In every letter he asked if my parents had changed their minds and would allow me to visit. I was still the one for him, he wrote, and on the envelope he added, Sealed With a Kiss! Mitch and I rode our bikes all around Levittown. We met his friends at the enormous community pool which they all found exciting. But, thinking about my good and kind boyfriend, and wishing I could be with him in Rockaway enjoying a carefree summer at the beach, I felt lonely and sad and went off by myself for long walks after dinner. When I returned to the house, everyone was relaxing on the patio. My uncle greeted me with sarcasm and thought it was funny to mess my hair.

One morning I overheard a conversation between my mother and Aunt Margie. "So, Mary, you like this boy, David?"

"He wants to be an engineer."

"And Francine, she likes him?"

"Well, she stopped seeing all the other boys that were after her … she must like him. And this David talks already about getting married!"

"You think she should marry him?"

"Why not? A fifteen year old girl knows when she's in love."

I almost collapsed right there on the attic steps. Married? My mother and Aunt Margie thought I was ready to marry David? I was happy to be his girlfriend but marriage, in my mind, was for a future time. There were so many things I wanted to do! And so far I hadn't done anything! I didn't even know how to play piano or dance ballet like so many of my friends were learning to do. Carol talked all the time about Music and Art but I went to Roosevelt where no one did anything. Even skating at the roller rink on Saturday afternoons ... my father didn't always have the money so I missed out while all my friends went.

Why did my mother want me to marry so young? And why didn't anyone ask me how I felt about marriage? Everyone assumed I would graduate high school and get married. I was impatient for the time when I would be old enough to move out, live like one of those smart young women in the movies; independent, earning their own salaries, enjoying the men they dated without being owned by them. I couldn't say this to my parents, though, and even thinking about it I felt a lot of anxiety knowing my parents would definitely and strongly oppose me. They didn't even imagine that I had ideas about my life that differed from theirs.

IN SEPTEMBER David and I happily resumed our relationship. I returned to Roosevelt where my art teachers complimented my drawings for their color and freedom of form and my English teachers gave me 'A's. My teachers spoke to me privately and told me I had great potential, that I was making a mistake by not applying to college. They didn't know that the circumstances of my life prevented me from considering college. Mike was about to graduate from Columbia and he had been accepted by New York University Medical School. The financial burden for my parents dragged on into eternity.

I decided the best course was, become an excellent

stenographer and earn enough money to ease their burden. I'd land a good secretarial job in a publishing company where one day my writing would be 'discovered' and my real career would be launched!

My grades in steno were consistent 99s and 100s which was not as simple as one might think. Mrs. Greenberg deducted points for the omission of commas, misspelled words as well as incorrect translation, and every kind of typographical error. While listening to my red and black transistor radio I practiced dictation from songs and newscasts. Radio news reporters, with their fast and clear diction, were an excellent challenge. I was hardly ever seen without my steno pad, practicing new words and short forms. Every girl in the class wanted to be as good as I was. Including Myrna Sprumm, who for the whole three years of high school trailed me by several points.

JUST AS SPRING was beginning my friend Sherry underwent spinal surgery and needed to recuperate at home for the rest of the semester. I brought the daily lessons to her and returned her completed assignments to our teachers. Sherry's mother kissed me and thanked me every day but I didn't think it was such a big deal. Now that the weather was growing warmer I enjoyed the long walks home which provided time for contemplation.

As I walked up Fordham Road I thought about Sherry and her plans for a summer tour of Europe. I imagined myself accompanying her, carrying chic luggage plastered with stickers from London, Paris and Rome. We'd meet exciting continental men and wear stylish outfits bought on our travels. Approaching Alexander's and turning north onto the Grand Concourse I thought, Even if every cent saved in my Dollar Savings account hadn't been spent on my winter coat or on gifts to my family, there still wouldn't be anywhere near enough money to join Sherry. Sherry could afford the trip and the luxury of taking off for the summer. I couldn't.

THINGS WERE DIFFERENT at home since Grandma had died. My mother interviewed at a nearby Yeshiva to teach fourth grade and to her surprise she was hired. Many mornings she left in such a hurry that the living room drapery remained closed so I returned home from Sherry's where the sun poured in while her mom bustled cheerfully around the kitchen, to a dark, lonely apartment. My mother's daily dustings and scrubbings, telephone calls to her sisters and her few friends, her constant surveillance of my activities were all held in abeyance by her mourning for Grandma as well as her new teaching responsibilities. Alone in the apartment in the afternoon when my mother had always been home I felt very sad. Remembering the days when my mother had cared about every little thing I opened the draperies and the windows. Then I vacuumed the carpet and made everything neat.

In the evenings my mother reviewed her lesson plans and corrected papers. My heart was filled with great admiration for her; my mother hadn't taught before. She enjoyed teaching but the boys in her class were difficult to discipline. My mother was accustomed to obedience and respect from Mike and me. I wanted to go to that Yeshiva and tell those rowdy boys, "Be nice to my mother!"

The days passed and June arrived. One lovely evening David suggested we go for a stroll in the park. As we walked along Southern Boulevard, which bordered the park, he said, "Fran, I have something to tell you."

An odd sound in David's voice, something I sensed before he continued, made me suddenly sick in my stomach.

"My mother wants me to spend more time studying and she says that you take me away from my studies. I'm sorry, Fran, but I won't be able to see you for a while."

What he was saying made no sense to me and sadly, I heard my own quivering voice defending myself. "But David, I want you to study. I understand how important it is, believe me. When have I encouraged you to go out instead of studying? Aren't you the one who decides when to go out and when to study?"

"I know, Fran, but the point is, just knowing you're there, waiting for me, entices me to go out."

I pressed my hands to my chest, trying not to cry, wanting to run, and at the same time wanting to hold his hands and beg him not to do this to me. He had pursued me!

I studied the bumps and cracks in the sidewalk. I looked toward the beautiful lush trees in the park on the other side of the chain link fence suddenly thinking, those trees I love must have been planted over a hundred years ago. Southern Boulevard was a busy thoroughfare and standing at the intersection all I could see was a discordant world. Telephone wires, traffic signals everywhere, noisy buses and trucks blowing exhaust fumes into the air, people crossing against the light, kids acting stupid. I looked up again at the beautiful trees, those old trees watched us all go by yet they remained steadfast and strong. The trees were my friends, and looking up at them for relief the leaves rustled a bit and seemed to be counseling me ... Hold onto your dignity, be strong like us, he's only a boy and now he's showing you he's not even the special one for you ...

"I'm really sorry, Fran, I don't want to hurt you. I'll never meet another girl like you, never, and I'm the first one to admit it. How can I forget our first date? Remember, it was raining and you met me at the bus stop with an umbrella. When I saw that I knew you were special."

What did it matter? David wanted his freedom. He was, after all, only eighteen. There was nothing to argue about. But a new kind of pain I'd never experienced before, an ache, actually, had already begun to change me. My girlhood had just ended.

I found a summer job with Office Temporaries in Manhattan and qualified for secretarial placement which paid $1.90 an hour, but Judy, the young woman who distributed assignments evidently saw me as just a high school kid and offered me mostly clerical jobs which paid only $.90 an hour. After a week or so I explained to Judy, "I want only secretarial assignments, that's my training and I'm better qualified than anyone else you have in your files." I didn't know who was in her files but here I was out in the real world and it was time to draw on the sense of self-confidence earned from endless hours of practice. It was time to speak on my own behalf. "I take dictation at 120 words per minute and I type at 80 words per minute. I am qualified for secretarial work and that's what I want." For the rest of the summer Judy gave me as many secretarial assignments as possible and she was friendly whenever I came to the office.

Subway tokens were fifteen cents and I could get by on a roll from the coffee wagon for twenty cents or a grilled cheese and a coke for sixty-five cents in a nearby coffee shop. My wardrobe consisted of three slim skirts and three blouses and from these separate pieces I created my own look.

Judy sent me all over Manhattan. Several offices were in peeling, mildewed buildings with unreliable elevators and depressing, narrow, high-ceilinged hallways. In these offices I worked at old-fashioned typewriters from the 1940s on large wooden desks, a fan rotating overhead, filthy gray windows open a few inches to reveal grimy brick walls opposite.

I observed other office workers, noticed how they distinguished themselves, and I learned from them. Quickly I learned how easy it is within the office setting to earn a label. So gossip, I decided, was not for me. Lunchtime was best spent in my own company, removed from office politics. People who maintained balanced, friendly relationships with their fellow employees were the wisest. I determined to follow that course.

A young man who had just gone into business requested Judy's speediest typist. The day I arrived the office suite still smelled of paint. I worked at a brand new IBM electric typewriter. I liked it there, it felt fresh and clean and new, filled with the promise of success. My boss was pleasant, bringing me coffee and a bagel whenever he had them himself. My assignment was to transcribe thousands of names and addresses onto sheets of labels. I was not expected to complete the job in five days, my boss politely explained as I quickly settled myself at the new white desk, but I challenged myself to do so.

On the third day a very attractive, well-dressed woman swept into the office, glanced at me without offering a greeting. I guessed she was the boss's wife. Above the hum and click of the typewriter I could hear her questioning her husband and from the inflection of certain words she used I surmised she didn't want me working in her husband's office. She was a sophisticated woman with style. I was a sixteen year old girl from the Bronx wearing three dollar shoes from Kitty Kelly and one of my put-together outfits. That day it was a black skirt and a white sleeveless blouse, the nicest I could find in Alexander's.

No more fine garments of elegant Italian fabrics, silk linings, French seams, hand sewn buttonholes sewn by Grandma on Saturday mornings. But I had learned from Grandma how clothing should feel and look on the body and preferred to have only a few pieces that were well-made than many shoddy items. Typing without the need to think too much about my task, I remembered my teachers in the lower grades asking me all the time, "Francine, where did you get that beautiful dress?" Maybe I was wearing the brown and green plaid taffeta dress that made crinkly sounds as I moved; how I loved wearing that dress. "My Grandma made this dress for me," I always answered and my nice teachers smiled.

So here I was, happy to be working out in the real world, making my way at lunchtime through the crowds, feeling peaceful inside myself and this week I'd gotten an especially good assignment. Later in the afternoon my boss came out of his office and said very simply, "Don't come in tomorrow, Miss Vale."

One man I worked for as a secretary offered me a permanent position for the remainder of the summer, but I told him it was against the rules of Office Temporaries to accept his offer. His office was in one of those old, broken-down buildings and he was sleazy; his rumpled shirt barely covered his protruding belly, a cigar stub always in his mouth. He had a way of leering at me over the rim of his wire-framed glasses that made me feel uncomfortable.

I often lost my way in the New York City subway system and watched, horrified and helpless as the Brooklyn Bridge materialized outside the train window signaling that I had once again taken the wrong train. I grew accustomed to wearing stockings in the summer. And the final week of the summer I worked for the owner of Office Temps. On the last day at four o'clock he summoned me into his office for one more letter. Then he suddenly reached out and touched my body, then with both hands he grabbed me. I twisted free, concentrated fiercely on the few steps toward the door, opened the door and heard him sneer at my back, "You can forget about your pay this week, Miss Vale!"

I stood on the subway platform, heard the sound of the oncoming train, the roar grew louder. No one would hear me if I screamed. But I disciplined myself to keep silent, be dignified and strong, and prayed that today no horrible man would try to feel me up in the crowded subway car, something that happened almost every day.

Senior year at Roosevelt. I found an after-school job as a part-time salesgirl in a children's clothing store on Fordham Road. The three brothers who owned the store were strict and nasty, but the saleswomen treated me kindly, explaining how to get along. I disliked the constant bending and fetching in that over-stuffed, foul-smelling store, selling poorly designed, scratchy little dresses and unevenly sewn boys shirts.

After work I walked home. One evening toward the end of September, when the scent of autumn found its way even to Bainbridge Avenue, I noticed a woman walking near me. She was burdened by two heavy shopping bags; she wore a flowered housedress, a black babushka and stockings rolled to her knees. Her face was kind. I approached her, reached for her shopping bags and told her she reminded me of my Grandma. Although

Grandma had not worn a babushka. Grandma had gone to the shop each morning attired in a pressed black suit, white silk blouse, black suede pumps on her tiny feet, her thick silver hair combed into neat, cropped waves beneath her stylish hat. And yet ... this woman reminded me of her. We walked together for several blocks and she told me she came from the town of Minsk in Russia and her name was Ida. "That's my Grandma's name!" I told her, "and my Grandma's town, too!" Then she said her husband had died many years ago and his name had been Jacob, the same as my grandfather! She spoke about her life and her children in a manner that communicated a particular acceptance of life with all its hardships and tribulations; the sorrow was gentle in her eyes and her eyes reflected also, an appreciation for all the simple joys of life. This reminded me exactly of Grandma.

We arrived at her building and I handed her the shopping bags. "You're a good girl, a *shayna maidela*," her smile held me and all the noises of the street seemed to fade. "May God bless you and may you have a good life."

For the remainder of my walk home and forever after, I felt Grandma's spirit beside me. Her spirit had found a way to reach me! It was really Grandma speaking through the woman, giving me her blessing just as she had always done! My Grandma's spirit was beside me, reminding me of her forever love.

Prince on a White Horse

SATURDAY, OCTOBER 4, 1958.

I called Suzie, "What are you doing? Finished your applications yet?"

"You don't sound so good, Francesca..."

"I guess I'm kind of down, you know..."

"Know what? Let's go out tonight. There's a dance at the Concourse Center of Israel. Take money, it's a dollar to get in, okay?"

All my friends were applying to college. Restlessness had seeded the landscape of my life, longing made each day feel more unfulfilled than the day before, and I was consumed with anxiety that life might pass me by and leave me stranded here on 199th Street where Joey Boyle and his pals still hung out on the corner. I finished reading *Candide* for Mr. Sage's honors English class, bathed and dressed in my light blue straight skirt and matching light blue cardigan buttoned down the back. It felt soft against my skin, like cashmere. Not that I ever really felt cashmere, but I could imagine.

The dance at the CCI was held in a dimly lit room which seemed larger than the gym at school. Rock 'n' roll music was blaring and hundreds of kids were dancing. I scanned the crowd and saw, way across the room, a handsome young man. He was also looking around. So many people moved between us I could only glimpse his face, his shoulder, depending on the movements of the crowd. I strained to see more of him.

"Suzie," I said, "See that boy over there, the quiet one looking at every girl? Well, I'm going home with him tonight."

"How do you know?" Suzie quipped, "Maybe I'll go home with him."

"Sorry, Suzie, you stay away from this one!"

I asked a few boys I knew if they knew my mystery man but they didn't. Then I spied Ted Zeiss with his buddies. Ted was a sweet boy, big and warm.

"Hi, Ted, I'm trying to meet that boy over there and I'm looking for someone to introduce us. Do you know him?"

"That guy? Sure, I know him, he lives on my block. C'mon, I'll introduce you."

Ted walked me over and as we approached the young man turned so that suddenly we were facing each other. Ted, Suzie, the boisterous crowd, all faded away as his eyes met mine, and my heart exploded. He took my hand and we started to dance, the room became the sky, and moonbeams showered us with brilliant light. The nearness of his face defined the meaning of delight. And the Platters were singing, "Only you and you alone can thrill me like you do . . ."

"What did you say your name was?" he asked, moving his head back a little and looking into my eyes. "Green Eyes?"

A laugh caught in my throat. "Francine Vale. And yours?"

"Danny Sachleben."

Just then the song ended. We walked a few paces together. "How old are you?" I asked.

"Nineteen," he paused, "but no one ever believes me."

"I believe you." I liked his straightforward manner. But just to prove it Danny took out his wallet and withdrew his driver's license. We talked about where we lived and our schools.

"I was supposed to be back at the University of Miami two weeks ago but my father wanted me home." A dark cloud passed briefly across his face, and his voice was earnest and trusting. "I was all packed and even had a deposit on an apartment with my roommate Seymour and at the last minute my father said I wasn't going."

"Doesn't your father want you to have a college education?"

"Well, he had a heart attack a couple months ago and couldn't run the lot by himself anymore. My father never liked my roommate anyway, he thinks he's too spoiled and wild and he wanted to keep me away from him. Besides, he thinks college is a waste of time and money."

"Is Seymour really wild?"

"He likes the horses and he likes to play cards, but he's alright. I wish my father had told me ahead of time. The way he did it was awful . . . my bags were all packed, standing by the door, and I even had my airline ticket . . ."

If your father hadn't kept you in town, I thought, you wouldn't be here with me, now.

"Come over here," he said in his quiet voice. "I want you to meet my friend Stan." Danny took my hand and led me over to Stan, a dark-haired, thin boy who had just met Linda who had a friend with her. Linda wanted her friend to meet Danny.

I held onto Danny's hand. I was not going to leave him for a second. A ChaCha was playing and Danny suggested we try it. I tripped and thinking I didn't know the steps he offered to teach me. I decided not to mention the many dance contests I won at the "Y" and he spent a lot of time showing me how to ChaCha. *Cherry Pink and Apple Blossom White* was playing. His left hand rested on my shoulder, we held hands and counted together, bumped into each other, and laughed, and every cell in my body felt alive.

After a while Danny took me aside. "Stan asked me to take Linda and her friend home. Do you mind?"

"Of course not." I smiled, elated that he felt my approval was necessary.

Danny drove Linda and her friend right up to their buildings. Then Stan leaned forward from the back seat and said, "Hey Dan, how about driving up to Adventurers for some hot dogs?" Stan was feeling restless. All of us shared one dream – to get out of the Bronx, even if only for a few hours.

Danny turned to me, "Can you go?"

"Sure, I'd love to go." I phoned my mother from Yonkers. "Mommy, I met the sweetest boy you ever saw!"

"Where are you? It's twelve-thirty already!" The usual panic was in my mother's voice.

"We're at Adventurers. He drove us. Me and his friend."

"What? You went in a car with two boys?"

"Mom, when you see Danny's face you'll see how fine he is."

"Danny?"

"Danny Sachleben. He's so sweet, Mom, please don't worry. I'll be home later. Remember, I'm almost seventeen!"

Later, after Adventurers and back in Danny's Buick my heart raced as he drove past the 200th Street exit and down to the West Bronx. Soon we'd be alone. Finally, Stan got out at his building.

"Stan's really something, isn't he? He has a whole fan club... lots of girls are crazy about him."

"He's nice," I answered, "but he doesn't compare to you."

"Well, he's a good-looking guy and knows how to be a lady's man."

"Danny, don't you know you're so much better looking than Stan... and anyway, I never cared for that type."

"Well, all the girls like him," Danny insisted.

"Danny? I'm not interested in Stan." I inched a little closer on the car seat.

When Danny drove the car didn't do anything he didn't want it to, and I felt completely safe. He glanced at me and smiled. We arrived at my street, he pulled over to the curb and I still didn't want to part from him. He put his arm around my shoulder and leaned over ... the ecstasy of Danny so close to me was overpowering my emotions, and then he kissed me!

My mother was waiting at the kitchen table. Hugging myself I told her, "Mom, I just met a wonderful boy."

"What school does he go to?"

"He doesn't go to school. He works in his family's business, they have a used car lot."

"So where does he live?"

"In the Bronx. I'm tired, Mom, see you in the morning." Drawing the blanket up to my chin, alone in the dark, I was overwhelmed with thoughts of Danny, his sweet, exciting, magical kiss, and I knew that my real life had just begun. I knew that Danny was the one. I knew he was the one I'd marry.

The next morning the telephone rang and my mother called out, "Fran! It's that boy, Danny!"

I threw off the covers and ran to the phone. "Hi, Danny."

"Hiya Green Eyes, how are you this morning?"

I loved the sound of his voice on the telephone. And he couldn't wait to call, I thought, checking the clock; it was only nine.

"Would you like to see me today?"

"I'd love to. What time?"

"I'll be over at twelve, okay?"

Unable to contain my joy I ran through the rooms and sang, "He called! He called! He called!"

DANNY ARRIVED neatly dressed in light tan chinos and a beige cashmere crew neck sweater; I admired the way he wore his clothes. Proudly, I introduced him to my parents, carefully observing their faces. My mother's eyes brightened and her smile was genuine. Then I noticed a strong resemblance between my mother and Danny. Danny's jaw line was very attractively defined while my mother's was softer; otherwise they had similar doll-like faces, straight dark brows and deep brown eyes that could turn liquid at any moment but most of the time were veiled behind private thoughts. And like my mother Danny's build was slender and wiry and his movements were quick and graceful. Danny was tall, but not as tall as my father who greeted him with a warm handshake. My father actually refrained from his usual inquisition concerning destination, curfew and unforeseen hazards.

Danny held my hand as we walked up the block to where he'd parked his car. "How come you're all dressed up?"

"You think I'm all dressed up? It's only a skirt and sweater, I always dress like this."

"You manage to look a certain way, I guess." He formed a frame with his hands and held them up to my face.

I smiled. The magic was still there. We were comfortable together. I felt as if we'd known each other for a thousand years, in other lifetimes, yet the feeling was also fresh and exciting. Danny's car radio was tuned to some great rock 'n' roll. "How about going up to Connecticut?" he asked. "We can get a bite to eat up there and see a movie."

"That sounds wonderful, Danny," I smiled. "So, what do you think of my parents? You know, my father never let me go in a car with a boy before. Once, someone came to take me out in his father's brand new Cadillac and my father still wouldn't let me go."

"Your father looks like a nice guy, and your mother is very attractive and youthful looking. Does your house always look this neat and clean?"

"Yes, my mother always keeps everything very nice like that."

"One thing I want you to do," Danny said, that liquid look

coming into his eyes, "you must take down all those Elvis Presley pictures around your mirror."

"What do you mean? It took a long time to collect all those pictures! Besides, the mirror is inside my closet and it's so exciting to me to have my own closet just the way I like it."

"They have to go," he looked at me and smiled, "put my picture up there instead." We laughed together and I knew I would do whatever he asked.

We shared a silence then, a comfortable one, filled with passing scenery and private thoughts. When we arrived in Stamford, Danny suggested a seafood restaurant up ahead.

"I never ate seafood before," I told him, "I won't know what to order."

"You mean you never ate clams or lobster?"

"No."

"Well, it's time you did. Don't worry, I'll order for you." Once again I was struck by Danny's kindness. His kindness illuminated every word he spoke and it uplifted his every act.

Danny ordered shore dinners, which began with clam chowder. The October sun streamed through the charming windowpanes and Danny's straight black hair shone in the sunlight. I stared at the cherrystone clams.

"You have to acquire a taste for them," he said.

If Danny liked cherrystone clams then I would too, and one by one I ate them. We finished the soft rolls in the oval wicker basket and then I was staring at a huge Maine lobster the waiter had placed in front of me. I felt as if I had entered a whole new world, a world where having a car wasn't such a big deal, a world where you could drive for an hour if you felt like it just to have a 'bite to eat' which turned out to be a feast. Out on dates or with friends it was always burgers and fries at a coffee shop, neighborhood pizzas or Jahn's. And every boy I knew was saving up to buy a car someday. In Danny's world beautiful restaurants were easily accessible, he knew where they were, how to get there. In Danny's world you didn't stand on drafty subway platforms or wait for buses in the rain. In Danny's world, it seemed to me on that Sunday, everything came easily.

Danny showed me how to maneuver the lobster fork. He ate with enthusiasm and didn't worry about a mess. I tried to emulate his style but I did not like the sloppiness of food on my hands.

"Danny, this is the most wonderful meal I've ever had! I never knew how delicious lobster is!"

"Didn't your parents ever take you out to eat?"

"Yes, but not too often. Actually, it's been a long time since we went out for dinner."

"How come?"

"Well, my brother is in medical school, so we can't spend money on anything that isn't a necessity."

"But you look so well-dressed. How come you have such nice clothes?"

"Thank you," I laughed. "My grandmother worked in the garment center and she made all my clothes so I learned all about fabric and things like linings and buttonholes and seams . . . you know, how a well-made garment should look. But since she died it hasn't been easy to find quality clothes I can afford, so I don't buy too much, but once in a while Alexander's has something nicer than usual."

"Well, I have cousins who have money and they spend a lot on their clothes but they don't look as good as you."

No one ever treated me like this, no one ever cared like this. Does he feel the same way I'm feeling now? Does he want to put his arm around me? Kiss me?

After our lobster feast we went to a movie. Danny held my hand, put his arm around me and I leaned my head on his shoulder. When I turned my head slightly his smooth cheek, which felt as if he hadn't yet begun to shave, touched my cheek. I was with a friend, the most wonderful, delightful friend I ever had.

I hated to see the exit sign on the Thruway leading us closer to the Bronx and the moment when I'd have to part from the warmth of Danny's hand. But he drove right past my neighborhood! "I know a place where they make the best sodas. Would you like a soda?" he asked.

Coming out of the soda shop he said, "How about another movie?"

Afterwards, Danny drove to a quiet place and put his arm around me. I let my head rest against his arm and he leaned over me. His kiss was as soft and warm and exciting as it had been the night before.

"See you tomorrow, Green Eyes."

"I can hardly wait, Danny." It was seven o'clock when we drove up to my building. All I wanted was to be with him, hold him, kiss him. And when he held my hand it felt to me like all the world was blessed. He called me Green Eyes and Sexy and Elizabeth Taylor, declaring that I looked like my favorite actress. When Danny said, "I'll see you tomorrow," I knew I could count on it.

THE PREVIOUS JUNE, working in the Program Office at Roosevelt, I had arranged my own senior year program so with study hall and lunch eliminated I was out by 1:05. I walked up Fordham Road to the children's clothing store where my responsibilities were now routine and greeted the saleswomen.

"What's that big smile about?" Maria poked my arm.

"Oh, Maria, I went to a dance Saturday night and I met a wonderful boy! The one I'm going to marry!"

"Really? That's nice sweetheart. But how do you know?"

"I don't know how I know. But as soon as I saw him I knew right then that he was going to take me home, and he did! And then later, I just knew he was the one. I can't tell you how I know ... it's a feeling I have, a very big feeling."

Then, glancing at one of the brothers she whispered, "He's in a really foul mood today, be careful." The hours passed and at last

I was walking home. As 199th Street came into view I heard my mother's voice calling, "Fran! Fran!" I looked up to see her waving and smiling from our window. "Danny is on the phone! Hurry up!" I ran the remaining distance to our building and took the stairs two at a time.

I ran to the window ledge and grabbed the phone from my mother, "Hi, Danny."

"You're five minutes late," he said, laughing.

I laughed too. It was a beautiful day. I pushed up the window wide, kicked off my shoes, positioned myself on the ledge and leaned back. "How's your day going? Sell any cars?" I closed my eyes, and the only thing that existed in the whole world was Danny's voice. I concentrated on his voice and listened to every nuance, every hesitation and I heard between the words. So I knew there was no need for wondering, does Danny really like me, I knew he was drawn to me in a powerful way.

"I wrote a few deals. Did you read about the hockey game? Do you know the score?" he kidded me. I never paid attention to sports news. "Well, you'll have to start reading the sports pages so you can give me a report."

"And will you take my American History test for me?"

He laughed, a wonderful laugh whose tones resonated deep inside me, and I heard the melody of our destiny together. "I'll call you later after I close up and you'll keep me company while I get a bite to eat, okay?"

"What time?"

"Until there are no more customers, nine-thirty or ten. It seemed awfully late to be eating and besides, I never went out at that hour. "I'll be waiting for you, Danny," I promised.

I was eager to be with him again, to sit beside him in his car and hold his hand. I brought my history notes to the window ledge but found it impossible to concentrate. After dinner I combed my hair and sat neatly in the green chair near my desk listening to Alan Freed on the radio. The Skyliners were singing, "To know,

know, know him is to love, love, love him, and I do . . ." so how could past events interest me? At last the phone rang and I ran to get it.

"I'm leaving now, Green Eyes," Danny said, "so I'll be there in about fifteen minutes."

Danny's car braked to a stop below the open bedroom window and he signaled with two soft taps on the horn. Tonight he drove a white Oldsmobile. I had to get used to this business of different cars. I slid into the Olds and greeted him with a kiss. The radio was on and Lloyd Price was singing *Personality*. "That's you, Honey," Danny smiled, and slipped his arm around me. I leaned against him.

He drove down the Concourse to Fordham. At every red light he leaned over to kiss me. He chose the corner deli, and I watched him eat a steak sandwich and fries. Danny was tired. His black chinos were dusty from a long day on the unpaved used car lot, and his hair was mussed. He ordered apple pie and encouraged me to have some too. "I love to watch you eat, Honey, how you hold your fork and put it in your mouth and never get messy, I've never seen anyone eat the way you do." A great tenderness for this gentle boy welled up inside me.

Back in the white Olds Danny drove to University Avenue and parked under the tall trees by the fence. Alan Freed was on the radio, reading kid's names and dedications. "What's the matter, Danny?"

He turned toward me and leaned back against the car door. "I had another fight with my father today. He screams at me. My brother just agrees with everything he says so he gets along fine. But I just can't keep it to myself when I think he's wrong. He treats me so awful. He always wanted me to be like Edmond, but I can't be like Edmond. He really let me have it right in front of the salesmen."

I put my hand on his arm. I understood. In his family, too, the firstborn son was forever superior and therefore entitled to a greater share of everything. No matter what Danny accomplished in his life, to his parents his brother would always occupy first place.

"I've never known anyone like you, Honey," his voice was soft and low. The headlights from a passing car illuminated the emotion on his face. "I've never been much of a lady's man. In fact, no one would go out with me."

"Who would be so crazy to turn you down?"

"I'm very fussy ... I only like a good-looking girl, and real sharp girls always turned me down. You're the only one who ever made me feel like this." He reached for me.

"All I think about is you, Danny."

We kissed then and Danny asked that big question all the boys wondered about. "You're a virgin, aren't you, Honey?"

I nodded. "And you?"

"Me too."

I moved back into his arms. "Then I'll be your first."

I reached up to touch his face and discovered his tears. "My only, Danny, my first and only."

The next afternoon I paused at the top of the school steps to adjust my jacket and heard Danny's voice calling, "Hey, Green Eyes!"

I ran down the steps, aware of heads turning and Danny kissed me right there, everyone looking on. My classmates were watching me open the car door and slide into Danny's car of the day, an open red Chevy convertible.

"You left work early just to see me?"

"I thought we'd have a quick bite together. I have to eat, don't I?" He grinned.

After lunch with Danny I hurried into the children's clothing store. Two of the brothers had been watching me through the window as I said goodbye to Danny and greeted me with scowls. I stowed my books and purse in a cardboard box beneath the front counter and began refolding a pile of little polo shirts. The store was busy and I waited on customer after customer without a moment's pause. Finally, after returning a plastic box filled with pajamas to its proper placement on the shelf I noticed the clock over the cashier's counter read seven-fifteen. At that moment a customer approached me, "Do you have this dress in pre-teen?"

I didn't know if we did or not, I would have to hunt through stock, and it was already late. So I said to the customer, "I'm sorry, I was supposed to leave fifteen minutes ago, you'll have to ask someone else."

Suddenly I noticed one of the brothers standing to my left. "Miss Vale!" He barked, "You are fired! Pick up your pay at the cashier and leave this store at once!"

The saleswomen gave me sympathetic glances, too intimidated to speak. I hurried next door into Woolworth's and dialed Danny's number at the used car lot.

"Don't cry, Honey, I'll be there in five minutes."

As soon as I saw Danny's face that stupid job and those horrible brothers no longer mattered. "Come with me to my night class, Honey. You can take notes for me with your shorthand, and afterward we'll have something to eat."

"How can I just walk into a college marketing class and sit there taking notes?"

"C'mon, Honey, I really need you. I'm very bad at taking notes. It's not easy running downtown after a long day on the lot. And it's hard to concentrate on the classwork. My mind is on the deals I'm involved with. You'll see, the professor won't mind having you in class."

I wanted to be with him, it didn't matter where, so when he leaned over and kissed me, it was decided. After that, on Tuesday and Thursday evenings I went with Danny to N.Y.U. night school and learned about product marketing. I kept good notes for him and after class we had Chinese food in a little place near the school.

On school mornings Danny picked me up and drove me. He

said it was getting colder now and he didn't like to think about me walking halfway across the Bronx to Roosevelt.

Classmates started asking questions and soon everyone knew about my Danny and how it was that he drove so many different cars. Kids let me know how impressed they were. The funny thing was, cars had never impressed me. I didn't measure people by the cars they drove. Under the terms of my father's partnership agreement my father was entitled to a new car every year. My mother always complained that she'd rather have the money, she felt uncomfortable when neighbors decided she was rich because my father drove a shiny new car. That's the way things were. People decided things about you based on appearances and then you were stuck with a label. I hoped my appearance reflected the real me but didn't know if it did or not, or even how to make it happen.

EVERY DAY after school Danny waited for me in his car in front of Roosevelt, always with a reason. Either he needed a sweater or a suit or socks and wanted my opinion. Or he had to buy a gift. "Rainy weather," he told me smiling, "isn't good for business, people just don't come to the lot in the rain . . . so we can take our time with lunch." I grew to love the rain.

He enjoyed taking me out to eat and encouraged me to order something more expensive instead of choosing the least expensive item on the menu. I grew accustomed to leaving my house at nine-thirty at night to keep him company while he ate his dinner. Then we'd go and park by the fence on University Avenue where we talked until it grew late.

Sometimes we talked about Danny's friends who were going with girls far less interesting than my friends. We talked about our day. Danny taught me about used cars. Getting credit and the best financing for each customer, as Danny explained it, was an art form. Danny worked hard at it and he was good at it. I had never thought about these things. I was learning the intricate details of the business and what it took to make a deal.

"You and me, Honey," Danny grew fond of saying, "we're going places."

I loved the shape of Danny's fingers, his palms, his wrists. I loved the way he looked in his chinos and imagined his legs were beautiful. Danny was my prince. In another lifetime he surely must have appeared at my doorstep mounted royally on a splendid white steed. But now, in 1958, my prince arrived in a used car.

I SAW LESS and less of my friends. I heard a rumor that Suzie required hospitalization for an undisclosed disorder, and had been sent by her parents to an institution out west.

The last time I saw Elaine she asked, why did I like Danny so much, was he a good dancer? I recalled our first ChaCha and laughed and told her he had many appealing attributes but I didn't love him solely for his dancing. "He's my best friend," I told her.

"Well, he looks too wealthy for you," she said.

I turned the corner without saying goodbye, her fancy building passed from sight, no longer considered her my friend. Other than Sherry, the Teenettes drifted out of my life. Fanny Cohen from Vyse Avenue came to visit my mother and told her, "Oh, Mary, you'll be so lucky if Francine makes a catch like Danny Sachleben. Remember Zelda from the building? The blond one, all the time screaming from the window ... now she's Doris, well! She married the older brother and what I hear, the family is wonderful to her. Oh, it should only happen to your Francine, she should live and be well!"

Danny invited me to his family Thanksgiving dinner. The Sachlebens greeted me politely although somewhat coolly. Mrs. Sachleben said, "I'm worried about my brother Dave who's in the hospital, so we're going to visit him as soon as we finish eating."

Edmond's wife Doris was busy on the phone making arrangements for show tickets and her anniversary dinner reservation, and Edmond barely spoke at all. When I looked at Mr. Sachleben, who sat directly across from me, I discerned an exceedingly private cautious man; he spoke judiciously, peering directly into your eyes.

I had anticipated sitting in the family living room, listening to family anecdotes, having the family albums out, being shown Danny's baby pictures. Instead, his parents hurried off to the hospital leaving Doris and I to clear the table.

My seventeenth birthday. We parked in our usual spot by the fence on University Avenue. The car windows clouded over as soon as Danny turned off the defroster, the bare branches swayed above us and reinforced our feeling of being enclosed in our own private world. Danny had driven here directly from the theater on Broadway where we had seen West Side Story. The play had been wonderfully entertaining, but sad, too. Maria had lost Tony. But Danny was here! warm and exciting! He leaned over and kissed me with his sweet kiss.

"I love you, Danny." I couldn't hold back the words even though I had longed to hear him say it first. But 'love,' the most important word in all the world, was a word Danny was reluctant to use. Suddenly, I felt confused. Maybe he was frightened of its implications, maybe all this closeness was really an illusion and I was making a big mistake, imagining that all I felt was inside him, too.

"How can I be sure?" Danny asked. "I've never been in love. I don't know if love is what I feel for you."

My heart was already pounding. What was he doing, then, driving across the Bronx every morning to drive me to Roosevelt, leaning over to kiss me at every red light? meeting me every afternoon and hurrying over after he closed up the lot every night? Was he just playing with my heart? No . . . not my sweet Danny.

Was it possible that he really didn't know what it felt like to love someone? I will help him.

"Believe me, Danny," I said, "how we are together, what we are feeling, is what love is."

When he was alone in his car, driving home, Danny thought, "What's love anyway? I've never thought about it. I love kissing Francine and I love the feel of her body and I'm dying to make love to her. Is that love? I want to take care of her and I like to please her. Is that love? I know I don't want to lose her. She's come into my life and opened it up. I know I don't want to hurt her. I just don't know if I love her."

Parked in Danny's red Chevy convertible, his favorite, we listened to Alan Freed playing songs which perfectly suited our moods. The Big Bopper, "Oh, Baby, you know what I like . . ." Danny talked about his day on the lot, his frustrations with his father and brother, his deals, and somehow I understood his struggles.

For my birthday I had expected Danny to give me an ankle bracelet; instead he gave me lipstick. I thanked him for it, the lipstick was in a pretty gold metal case. But a little while later when he leaned over to kiss me I didn't feel like kissing him and carefully expressed my honest disappointment. "Why did you give me a lipstick, Danny? My friends are all wearing ankle bracelets from their boyfriends, remember I told you? I really thought you were going to give me an ankle bracelet."

"Well, Honey, if I give you an ankle bracelet it will mean we're going steady and I don't want to give the wrong impression."

"What are you talking about, Danny? What are we doing, seeing each other every day, sharing our lives with each other . . . you don't think this is going steady? Whatever you want to call it, Danny, to me I'm going steady with you. I don't see anyone else, you're the only one."

"Well, Fran, I guess I'm just not ready to make a commitment."

Our conversation went round in circles. Danny held to his

original statement with unmovable determination and after a while, with great exasperation, disappointment, confusion and anxiety all swirling around in my mind and in my heart, I let it go. Surely he loves me, I reasoned, reviewing in my mind his way of looking at me, the trusting way he confided in me, the way he reached for my hand whatever we were doing. More than anything I wanted to be with Danny. I decided that patience was a worthy attribute and I was being called upon to practice it.

Danny came to our family Passover Seder in Levittown. All the relatives treated him as a special guest and I was proud of him. We rode home with my parents and Mike. Suddenly, Mike turned around from the front passenger seat and addressed Danny. "You know, Danny, you're a pretty nice guy, you've been dating my sister for quite a while now. You've taken up her time to the exclusion of all other boys, you see her every day, and I would like to know exactly what your intentions are."

Why was Mike interfering with my personal life? I was polite to his friends and his girlfriends and even though he still called me his baby sister I never embarrassed him. I was sensitive to his vulnerabilities and I respected him. If I wanted to see Danny forever without a commitment, I would!

"I like you sister very much," Danny responded clearly and quietly.

I was dying! "like!" he used the word "like!"

"I enjoy seeing her very much," Danny squeezed my hand, "and I would like to continue seeing her for as long as she wants to see me. I'm just not ready to get married."

Silence reined in the car. There it was, out in the open. Francine had fallen for a guy who merely "liked" her, who was not prepared to marry her. Danny grasped both my hands in his. Our eyes met. I respected him for remaining forthright and honest. I loved Danny even more.

Mrs. Greenberg nominated me for a special award for maintaining a ninety-nine average for three years. And then, two weeks prior to graduation my award was suddenly rescinded. Apparently, I had been falsely charged with accosting the Dean with four letter words.

"That's not true, Mrs. Greenberg! I've never used that word in my life! I haven't even seen the Dean! Mrs. Greenberg, you know me! Please, tell them it's a terrible mistake!" But Mrs. Greenberg failed to support me.

Through the years I'd watched my brother bring home awards. Dozens of patches and merit badges from scouting, intellectual achievements, school acceptances. This was my only award, an honor I could bring home to my parents; I had earned it by personal diligence, a great desire to succeed in the way that was open to me. And it was withheld from me by a woman who never knew me.

When I walked into class Myrna Sprumm gave me a triumphant look; she was next in line for that award. My eyes were stinging. It hurt to look at Myrna but I looked at her anyway and suddenly her face reminded me of a horse – the length of it, her protruding teeth, the way her bangs fell over eyes ... I loved horses but I wouldn't want to look like one and I turned away from Myrna.

I no longer cared about my grades. The three-thousand students at Roosevelt who crowded the halls, or hung out on the front steps, the Fordham Baldies who still collected lunch money in the cafeteria, the tough girls who smoked in the bathroom instead of attending class or threatened to beat me up in the locker room, all became a blur and whatever the teachers were saying became inconsequential. The night before English regents I stayed out late with Danny and the day before American History regents we went to a double-header at Yankee Stadium.

Mrs. Greenberg summoned me to her room. She had just completed the job of gathering papers and packing personal supplies;

I guessed that speaking to me was her final task of the semester. I glanced at the vacant seats and desks, at the blackboards she had already washed, at the large windows already shut despite the heat spell. This is the way I'll remember Roosevelt, I thought, devoid of life and suffocatingly silent. Danny had often asked me, "Honey, why didn't you go to Music and Art, with your talent, that's where you really belong." I didn't know where I belonged. I only knew it was always somewhere else.

"How are you, Francine? Do you have a job yet? I know it's not easy with this recession." Mrs. Greenberg addressed me in her kind and gracious manner.

"I have an offer from the City Water Company, a couple of insurance companies and an import company. I don't know where to go, I think the Water Company is probably best but my father says an insurance company is better for advancement."

"You know, Francine, in every teacher's career there's one student who comes along and makes it all worthwhile. And for me . . ." Mrs. Greenberg smiled warmly and then continued in her perfect diction, "That special student is you, you Francine. Remember that. I hope you understand about that messy affair with the Dean, there was nothing I could do." She appraised my face and waved her hand back, as if to wave away the memory. "Well, let's get down to business. My brother-in-law is an executive at Bache & Co., down on Wall Street. I've told him all about you and I've arranged an interview for you tomorrow." My beautiful, lovely teacher handed me her brother-in-law's card, 'Gerald Green, Personnel Manager.' "You can do very well at Bache, my dear."

The following morning at nine o'clock I walked into Mr. Green's office for my interview and he hired me as his private secretary at a salary of $65 a week. Mr. Green politely escorted me to my desk right outside his office and I began immediately to get acquainted with my duties. At lunch hour, already feeling the sophistication of my new position as well as completely elated and amazed, I called my mother and gave her the good news. Dressed in a new narrow-belted light blue dress in a pretty cord fabric with matching light blue pumps, I leaned back in Bache & Company's desk chair, crossed my legs and smiling, dialed Danny's number at the used car lot.

JULY 4, Danny's twentieth birthday, we went to the Riviera Club in New Rochelle with his family. A beautiful scene of pools, beach umbrellas, cabanas, all immaculate and elegant, built on the shore of Long Island Sound in a protected inlet; a heavenly retreat. Everyone here looked so content, gathered with friends, relaxing on lounge chairs, enjoying tall summer beverages. All those wealthy suntanned girls with nothing more to do than take care of their appearance, enjoy themselves and look glamorous. How easy it would be for Danny to go with one of them instead of me, and in that moment I knew it was inevitable.

About a week later, on a lovely summer evening, Danny drove to our usual spot by the fence on University Avenue. The Skyliners happened to be singing that melancholy song, *Since I Don't Have You*. Danny's voice was soft as usual but also held an unusual note. "Honey, I think it's time for us to have an intermission."

A searing pain flashed in my heart, radiating through my body, and my whole body instantly became damp with perspiration. I heard a voice, too tiny to be my own, the voice sounded shattered, it was my voice, for all of my dreams of a future with Danny were crashing and shattering from the blows of his words. If only the love I felt for him would shatter, too, or fly away toward some distant star. Who wanted a used car dealer anyway? I could marry a doctor instead, one of Mike's friends. How did I ever allow myself to get drawn in by Danny's delicious kisses, warm hands, soft voice? Why did I allow myself to feel the excitement of his nearness. I should have been more cautious.

"What do you mean, intermission?"

"I haven't gone out with anyone but you, Honey, in such a long time, I want to find out if I can like someone else."

"But why? Why do you want to like someone else when you have me? You know you love me, Danny." I sounded so desperate. Why didn't I just slam out of his car and get myself home? I was used to walking everywhere, for miles.

"That's just it, Honey, I really don't know if I love you. I have to find out. So I'm going up to Grossinger's for a week, I need a vacation, anyway."

A vacation? Away from me? Why? Why do I love this foolish boy? This cruel boy? "Please don't go, Danny! Please don't!" Why was I begging him? I ought to turn away from him immediately and tell him, Fine! Go! You don't deserve my love and I'll find someone who will! But how could I? My heart had grown so entwined with Danny's.

He put his arm around me and kissed me so gently it felt unbearable. "I'm really sorry, Honey, I don't want to hurt you, you're such a wonderful, sweet girl." I cried, and he held me for a long time. Suddenly, I became aware of Danny's tears, hotter than my own, on my face. And for one fleeting moment my pain diminished.

Danny drove me home. Exhausted, I gathered my self-control, my parents were sure to interrupt their TV program, peer at me expectantly, Maybe this was the night that Danny proposed. I turned the doorknob and tried to imagine a whole week without seeing Danny's face, without hearing his voice or touching his hands. I lay on the sofa bed, blanket drawn over my head, immersed in the blackness of despair, and whispered again and again, Come back to me, Danny, please, please come back to me.

A few days later Danny called from Grossinger's. "How are you doing, Honey?"

"Fine, I'm fine. Have you met anyone interesting?"

"There's one nice girl," he said, "she has dark hair, she's up here with her parents."

The lucky girls, whose parents take them to places like Grossinger's.

There was a young man at Bache who was working as a messenger for the summer. He was tall and blond and tan and he had sublime pale-green eyes. "Girl of my dreams..." he sang, clasping his hands in a dramatic pleading gesture. Then he smiled and leaned across my desk. "You have to go out with me! I want to marry you! Let me have a better look at those eyes of yours! Oh, my God, they're so beautiful! light green with these yellow flecks, and you have these turquoise rings around them! Think of the gorgeous green-eyed kids we'd have!" I laughed. He was an Adonis, he was charming, and he liked me. I told him I had a boyfriend.

Danny returned home. He'd enjoyed his vacation but he still didn't know if he loved me.

My brother became engaged to Sarah Slater and I loved Sarah's mother, Belle, a truly gracious woman. The Slaters lived in a home which looked like a mansion to me, and they invited our family out to Long Beach for Sunday visits which always included a sumptuous luncheon in their elegant formal dining room, their maid serving us from heaping platters. The enormous proportions of Sarah's private suite startled me. While showing us her white marble dressing room Sarah casually noted, "Oh, I see the maid forgot to clean my hairbrush."

"That's easy to do," I answered.

"Oh, no," Sarah laughed, "it'll just wait until next time."

One Sunday at Long Beach, while Danny and I were out on the beach, a strong wind arose which blew sand into Danny's pomaded hair. We went back to the house to wash the sand out of his hair. The airy marble bathroom, which seemed larger than our living room on 199th Street, felt cool and refreshing after the hot beach. Danny and I laughed. We splashed water as it cascaded from elegant faucets. This water felt more wonderful than water had ever felt before. How I loved the feel of Danny's wet hair tangled in my fingers.

Suddenly, Danny pulled me close and kissed me. His mouth tasted of the ocean, the taste of everlasting life was on his tongue. Before I met Danny other boys had tried to kiss me like this and I had pushed them away. But with Danny I loved it. We were wearing only bathing suits, and his chest pressed against my body; his bare arms around me, my whole body tingled with the realization that Danny had the smoothest, silkiest skin imaginable. "C'mon, Honey," he breathed against my neck. "Not here, Danny! Not now!" I laughed and made him chase me back to the beach.

In August, Danny took off for Grossinger's again.

Mr. Green was preparing for his two-week vacation. While he was gone, he said, I was to consider Miss Shannon, the personnel office manager, my boss. Each morning I now discovered stacks of folders on my desk, piled so high as to make one marvel at this remarkable talent Miss Shannon had for balancing folders. A hand-written note leaned against the phone: 'Miss Vale, These are for filing.'

When only a few folders remained and my hands felt grimy from the handling of so many dusty folders, Miss Shannon squawked, "Miss Vale, can't you see that everyone has gone to lunch?" When I returned an hour later my desktop was again obliterated by new mountains of folders. One of the women told me that those folders had been lying around in boxes for as long as she could remember. Whenever I re-entered the office after a ladies' room break Miss Shannon glared at me and tapped her watch. The other women left and returned unnoticed by Miss Shannon. Day after day she tirelessly piled hundreds and thousands of folders on my desk and I filed every single one of them, until finally, every folder in the personnel office of Bache & Co. was filed.

Having failed to break my dignity, unmoved by the silent yet obvious sympathies offered me by the other women in the office who brought me paper cups of water, patted me on the back and even hugged me, Miss Shannon decided one afternoon to follow me into the ladies room. From within the privacy of a bathroom stall I suddenly saw Miss Shannon's angry face! She was kneeling on the floor to observe me from under the door! "Miss Vale!" she shouted, "you've been in here long enough! Return to your desk immediately!"

At last Mr. Green was back and I waited at my desk for him to buzz me for dictation. In an unemotional and resolute tone I described how Miss Shannon had treated me in his absence. Then I said, "Mr. Green, I enjoy working for you and I thought you were my only boss. But I cannot and will not take any further abuse from Miss Shannon."

"I know Miss Shannon's ways," he answered, "and it's obvious, Miss Vale, that she's developed a dislike for you. Look ... she's been with the company forever, she was running this office when I arrived ... so unfortunately, my hands are tied. I'm very pleased with your work and I'd like for you to stay. It's always possible that things will work out with Miss Shannon."

"I'm sorry, Mr. Green, but I think the reason Miss Shannon doesn't like me is because I'm Jewish, and that's not going to change."

"I understand, Miss Vale."

Maybe Mr. Green really did understand, maybe his name used to be Greenberg.

OUTSIDE, the narrow streets baked in the oppressive August heat. People were off to Labor Day Weekend destinations. Relief blazed inside my heart and I felt like flying, up to the tops of the Wall Street buildings which appeared to lean toward each other, sharing endless secrets, secrets I'd never know, but it didn't matter

... I had my own secret ... I had been confronted with rudeness, harassed for no reason, but I had responded with poise and grace. I had retained my dignity. I was only seventeen but felt I had earned my place in the adult world.

The day after Labor Day I went to an employment agency and within the hour I was at the offices of Lionel D. Edie & Co., an investment counseling firm on Fifth Avenue and 47th Street. Mr. Hammond, who interviewed me, was a tall, trim, refined gentleman, silver hair perfectly styled, dressed in a dark gray pin-striped suit. "We're a conservative company," he explained, "and our girls are expected to dress appropriately and that includes makeup, we don't like made-up secretaries here." Mr. Hammond paused and smiled in a fatherly way, "I can see you won't have any problem with that. Also, you ought to know you are the only private secretary in this company without a business school degree, and the youngest." Mr. Hammond rose and came around the desk to stand near my chair, so I rose, too. "I'll have to ask you to obtain working papers as soon as possible. Now, if you will, please come with me." And he extended his arm in a courtly gesture to show the way. I followed, light as air. This means I'm hired! I got the job! Seventy-five dollars a week and only a half-hour subway ride!

MR. WAGGONER, an account executive, was a handsome fellow in his late twenties. Although not very tall he carried himself well. He had a freckled complexion and wavy auburn hair and he wore the look of one who had grown up amid the security and comfort of proper schooling and social ties. In his small, glass-walled cubicle he politely indicated for me to be seated in the chair across from his and he proceeded to explain my duties. His swivel chair could not contain Mr. Waggoner's energy. He was in constant motion, even as he spoke, so that the chair turned first this way, then that way, it rolled a little closer to his desk, then away from the desk until it bumped into his console which stood against the wall, and as he crossed and uncrossed his legs the chair squeaked and tilted. And all of this motion was not disconcerting, it suited this beautiful man-boy, my new boss.

"So, Miss Vale, if you don't mind, I like coffee first thing in the morning, and I like this pitcher here kept filled with ice-water. You'll have to open the mail of course, and arrange it like so," he arranged several envelopes and letters, clipped them together in the precise way he preferred. "Oh, you'll have to keep my files organized," he flashed me a dazzling smile to soften all the instructions, "and answer the phone, are you good at messages? Yes, of course you are, and also, most important, my letters must go out as quickly as possible." Mr. Waggoner leaned back in his chair until I feared he might topple over, and he smiled. When he smiled it felt as if a window had just been carved into the windowless office wall permitting the sun to fill every crevice and cause the fluorescent lighting to dim in comparison.

Mr. Waggoner dictated long and difficult letters filled with unfamiliar, complicated phrasing and terminology. From his letters I learned of the existence of a world which had previously been unknown to me: trust funds, bonds, the madness of tax season, IBM stock splits. I became acquainted with myriad facets of the investment world, the worries that accompanied wealth and the manner in which wealthy people preferred to be addressed. Occasionally, I'd glance up from my typewriter which faced Mr. Waggoner's glass wall to find him staring at me, then I'd become flustered and lose my place. While transcribing I sometimes got stuck on a word and had to approach him for help. This lovely man followed me with his eyes as I entered, he'd fidget in his chair, and then very kindly instruct me.

Mr. Waggoner often initiated conversation, seemingly unaware of my ignorance regarding worldly matters. He talked about his summer home in a town with an upper-class sounding name that I had never heard of, his two show dogs and the shows he entered them in. He told me about some women clients who flirted with him, they kept their fingernails long and red and he disliked that. My fingernails, short and bare, suddenly looked good to me. He discussed his various clients' idiosyncrasies, and he showed me it was alright to laugh about them. Mr. Waggoner entered my dreams where he usually took me in his arms and kissed me, thrillingly, of course. He entered my thoughts as I rode the subway, and during lunch at the Automat where I ate macaroni and cheese for fifteen cents, thoughts of him looking at me, silently and openly through the glass wall, made me wonder what he really thought about me. He certainly didn't dream about me, I concluded. Educated, refined men like Mr. Waggoner were bred to stay away from Jewish girls who lived in the Bronx.

FRIDAY EVENINGS after work I walked up Fifth Avenue to Temple Emanuel where I sought sanctuary from turmoil, where my thoughts might assemble into orderliness, where meaning and solution might emerge and bring me peace. Why did I always have to analyze everything? Did other people do that? Was it a good thing to contemplate and reflect upon every circumstance and conversation as I did? If I disagreed with many things my parents said and did, could I still be a good daughter? I hated prejudice but was not about to get on a soap box. Would it be enough to live my own life free of prejudice? And what of my dreams? My plan to work for a publishing company where I'd be surrounded by those to whom the written expression of thought was all, exposed to writers, have the opportunity to learn from them and maybe even advance. Somehow, I'd find my way, become a journalist, call attention to the plight of the downtrodden. But here I was involved instead in the world of high finance, money people, those who dealt with the accumulation of wealth, all of which was foreign to me. What happens to dreams when they're packed away? Can dreams be safely kept, retrieved intact?

And what about that strange light? A beam of blue-white light ... streaming down from heaven as I walked along the crowded city street ... people hurrying by ... I saw the light not with ordinary vision but inside my mind ... flashing right into my head. And suddenly I had knowledge of my own death ... I was going to die young. But I had already evaded death; my hand reached up and touched the ugly scar on my neck which I kept covered as often as possible with high neck sweaters and scarves ... and even before I was born my life had been saved when my father convinced my mother not to have an abortion. My life, I felt, was a gift from God and there was something to be given in return but I wasn't sure what it might be, so I lived in anticipation of finding out ... one day an opportunity would present itself ... I'd seize the moment and then my true destiny would begin to unfold. But I worried I might not recognize this most significant moment ... so I decided to seize every opportunity until the right one, the real one, the one for which I came, the reason my father convinced my mother to have me even though they had nothing and she was already overwhelmed by everything. I longed to know when this big opportunity to meet my true destiny would present itself ... having no answer I decided to keep myself ready ... every day ... to meet my destiny ... to give something back to God in return for my life, for however long my life would last.

Oh, how I wished I were wise and understood all the mysteries of the universe!

IT WAS INDIAN SUMMER, the most beautiful time of year in New York, so on Saturday morning I went to Orchard Beach. That evening I wore my pale yellow dress, actually a sleeveless blouse and slim skirt in a crisp cotton fabric, yellow pumps kept meticulously clean. The color looked pretty against my tan. I carried the white silk purse Belle Slater bought for me in Bonwits, the gold hoop earrings Grandma had given me 'to remember her by' and my parents' graduation gift, a gold-filled Bulova watch with an expandable bracelet.

Danny had the top down on his red Chevy convertible. The radio was blasting, *Personality,* one of *our* songs. Danny maneuvered the Chevy out from the parking spot with only two fingers on the steering wheel, his right arm around me. "You look gorgeous tonight, Honey. I love the way you fit into that dress!" He kissed my cheek in his gentle way. "Edmond and Doris are having the Sachlebens over to see their new apartment in New Rochelle. Is it okay if we go?" That's how he was, casual about things which to me were a big deal. I wished I, too, could be less serious but for me it was a task that required concentration.

"My aunts are bleached blonds, you know, the glamour type with the clothes and the jewelry. They're very different from my mother. My mother is more practical, so she has trouble with them sometimes. My cousin Larry will probably be there, too, and his wife Mona is also a bleached blond." Danny glanced at me for a reaction.

My sunburn suddenly felt very hot. "I'm looking forward to meeting them, Danny . . . I'll be fine."

He went on with a quick rundown of the relatives. His father's brothers and Larry were butchers, his father's sister was married to a man who provided her with a lovely home in New Jersey but his money was 'tied up' so she never gave gifts to anyone. Aunt Maizy was in the fashion business, which made her the family maven on style and taste. Aunt Fay, Uncle Louie's wife, was the one with big mouth, the one his father couldn't stand, because she spent Louie's money faster than he could earn it. Danny's parents bought all their steaks from Uncle Louie. Fay and Louie lived in an expensive home in Scarsdale, and although Louie was the sweetest guy, Fay tended to look down upon anyone who still lived in the Bronx.

Doris had hired a decorator with a fondness for large wall

hangings of framed dried flowers. The relatives sat, perfumed and perfectly groomed, on the long beige sofa and dark green chair, forming an oval. Danny introduced me all around, then placed two bridge chairs for us at the far end of the oval. I sat neatly, placed my purse under the chair and facing Danny's attractive family. I looked at each aunt and uncle but no one looked at me.

Several conversations were under way. Fay, who was an animated speaker and fun to watch, was telling Mona about her princess Lisa's many suitors. Lisa went out with this gorgeous Italian boy whose father was a doctor and the whole family wanted her to marry him, Lisa could have anyone she wanted just by nodding her head. Larry sat on a folding chair next to me. I looked at his profile, hoping he would turn his head, and speak to me. I reached for a piece of cheese and handed it to Danny. Maybe someone will see me move and remember I'm here. Fay's bragging continued and I hoped my mother didn't do that when she visited in Levittown. Danny's parents, Rose and Leo, sat at the other end of the oval. An hour passed and still, no one spoke to me or even seemed to notice me.

When the maid began to serve coffee Danny suggested we leave. He deftly maneuvered the Chevy out from the tight parking space, reached across the seat and opened the door for me.

"Well, what do you think of the Sachlebens?"

"They're a handsome family, very nice people."

Danny was angry. "Honey, never lie to me! The truth is they were awful to you! No one spoke to you!"

"Danny, I thought I was invisible. Why were they like that?"

"That's just the way they are, Honey, very self-centered and very cold. Let's get something to eat." He put his arm around me and, as usual, managed the steering wheel with two fingers of his left hand. "Next week," Danny said, "Doris is having my mother's family over. The Steinbergs are much warmer people, you'll see. Especially Aunt Millie, my mother's sister."

The following Saturday when Danny called for me he gave me

a long look. "I have to have you, Honey, you can't keep saying no all the time. I want you so badly."

"I want you, too, Danny."

"You're almost eighteen, you're working, you're old enough. And you know how much I care for you, I'm crazy about you, Honey." He enfolded me in his arms and caressed my back with his strong, gentle hands.

"I know, Danny, I know..."

"So, what is it, then? Why do you keep saying no?"

"It's just not right." It must have been the hundredth time I'd said those words to him, and they were beginning to lose meaning. My mother's admonishment rang in my ears, That's all a man wants from a girl... and once they get it, it's all over, and besides, good girls don't do it.

"Honey, you're supporting yourself, you're a grown woman, you can do anything you want. This is your personal life, our personal life. It'll be alright, you'll see." He pressed his cheek against mine. I loved the smell of Danny's skin, the whisper of his breath against my hair. "Come live with me, Fran," he pleaded, "and then we'll be together every night."

My eyes brimmed with tears of longing and I felt weak against his body. "How can I just go and live with you, Danny? I'm just a plain girl! My parents would be heartbroken!" If only I were carefree, able to cast aside my fears, cease agonizing and just do it.

The Steinberg aunts gathered around me for a moment as everyone arrived together and crowded near the door, but soon the evening descended into a family quarrel. Aunt Rae did not want to host a twenty-fifth anniversary party, and the nerve! After Gladys and Herman, and Millie and Max had already made theirs, and even invited Rae's brother-in-law!

Georgie, Doris' brother, remembered me from years back on Vyse Avenue. "I remember your long braids," he smiled, "and your wild cousin Mitch... my mother didn't let me play with him, remember?"

I laughed and Georgie confided, "You know, Fran, from the first minute I saw you and Danny together, I could tell you're in love. You'll get married someday, I predict it. And I already told Danny."

I felt like throwing my arms around Georgie. Instead, I laughed, "Thanks, Georgie, you're really sweet."

ON MY EIGHTEENTH BIRTHDAY, in the back seat of Danny's white Olds, I finally gave in to him. Despite Danny's reluctance to admit his love I felt sure he loved me, or maybe it was only hope, and I was the one who couldn't admit even to myself that he wouldn't say he loved me because he didn't love me. In my dreams Danny was romantic and whispered low in my ear, "Honey you're so wonderful, I love you more than anything in my life."

The next day, Sunday, Danny arrived early. As soon as we got into his car I touched his arm and he turned to look at me. "Now you're really mine, my sweet Francine."

I was with my Danny, so everything was right and good. Lucky for me, I'd found him. At last all uncertainty melted away.

Several weeks went by, we were up in Stamford having dinner at our favorite Chinese restaurant, seated in a red brocade booth. Danny poured tea into white china cups decorated with blue dragons. I played with my cup and turned it until the dragon's head, breathing fire, faced me.

Danny began to speak and immediately the day shattered; his words broke the lovely evening into slivers of glass which swirled before my eyes, slicing the air and creating a turmoil of dragons and fire and broken glass. "You're not the kind of girl who should be strung along like this, Honey ... you're the kind of girl guys want to marry, and it's not right for me to do this to you."

Danny had recently moved with his parents to New Rochelle, and now he wanted another intermission, this time he wasn't going away, he was just going home to New Rochelle.

He called the next day, his voice soft, and I felt myself sinking. "How're you doing, Fran? I worry about you."

I MUST remain composed, Mr. Waggoner is watching me through the glass wall of his cubicle. "I'm going to miss you, Danny."

"Don't worry, Fran," he tried to comfort me, "I'll call every day. I have to do this, I have to somehow find out if I really love you."

It was then I should've walked away from this boy who failed to blend with me in the depths of my heart. Instead I held fast to a dream which wasn't even my dream. It was, after all, my parents' dream to see me safely married.

Life was waiting for me and it looked on the surface like Danny was my life but how could he be with all his uncertainties, not even knowing what love is, when I had always known about love and still remembered the angel who came to remind me when I was only three.

"Take care of yourself, Honey."

A FEW NIGHTS LATER I went out and called Danny in New Rochelle. "Honey, I'm coming down right away."

Making the call I felt completely unlike my true self, I felt as if I were losing myself in some crazy drama. This tearful, emotional person wasn't me! I was strong! I had climbed the rope all the way to the top! Now I paced back and forth beneath the street lamp, wiping my tears with cold, frozen hands, counting the seconds, shivering. At last he arrived! Holding me in his arms Danny soothed me, "No more intermissions, Honey, no more. Look what I'm doing to my Green Eyes." I felt the stream of Danny's tears mingling with my own.

A few weeks later Danny came up with the idea of going out with other girls on Friday nights. The first Friday night I stayed home, bathed, shampooed my hair, and suffered. Now Danny is calling for his date. I shaved my legs and saw him opening the car door for her. Reaching for the towel and crying I pictured them sitting in a restaurant – was he ordering for her as he did for me? Was he holding her hand, looking into her eyes, making her happy while I was so sad? Sleep was impossible. My legs shivered, and I clasped my hands to a broken heart.

A COLD, WINDY Saturday night in March and we were driving to a party at Aunt Margie's in Levittown. Danny paid the toll at the Whitestone Bridge.

"Well, how was your blind date last night?"

"Nice girl," he answered. Then, keeping his eyes fixed on the road, he added, "Honey, last night I realized something. All these intermissions, all these dates, what I'm really looking for is to see if there's another Francine. I compare every girl to you, Honey... and last night I was out with an intelligent, pretty girl... but, she wasn't you. There's only one Francine. I guess I'm saying I love you... I want to marry you, Honey." Danny glanced at me, the highway lights illuminated his eyes which glowed with an unbelievable brightness and the look in his eyes made time stand still.

From somewhere inside me I heard myself speak, "Will you ask me, Danny?"

"Honey, will you marry me?"

"Yes! I will marry you! I will be delighted to marry you!"

Danny's arm around me, I leaned my head on his shoulder, and he whispered, "You and me, Honey, we're going places."

My parents were ecstatic. It wasn't education or sophistication they dreamed of for me, it wasn't to see me dance ballet or create artistic masterpieces or write to my heart's content. Pursuit of those goals would lead me out into the big wide world and God only knew what could happen to me, the many strange and dangerous people who lurked, waiting for an opportunity to take advantage of their tender daughter. A married daughter would give them grandchildren, and there would be happy, warm family gatherings. Oh, what a life awaited us all, now that Francine was getting married! And what a catch! A fine, handsome Jewish boy from the Bronx who would never take their daughter far away from home. A boy from good hard-working people, business people, no less, with financial security. And oh! how he adores her! Every night – he wouldn't miss a night – he comes to see her and never lets go of her hand, you should see them together! Yes, my parents had their sunny time in life when I became engaged to Danny.

Danny's parents did not object. After all, Edmond married young, why not Daniel? And a Jewish girl, that's the important thing. Look, she doesn't come from money, but money isn't everything. You go to their house, it's clean, but you can see they're not up to us. And she's not the best-looking girl we ever saw. Not glamorous like Doris, with the beauty parlor hair. Francine's plain, so, she'll learn how to be glamorous. And her clothes, eh, nothing special, that she'll learn too.

While Danny was growing up his mother always knew when she needed him to run an errand she could find him at the neighborhood pool hall. Her time was spent at the business, even cooking their meals in a makeshift office kitchen. She never worried, as she managed the books, about her Daniel. He was a good boy, what's to worry? Now her son was going to marry a girl who was too quiet and knew nothing from nothing. She, Rose, had better look out that their money shouldn't be squandered.

On Sunday Danny drove me up to New Rochelle and I sat on the living room sofa with his mother. "Do you have any money saved up?" she inquired.

In my usual straightforward way I answered, "I have about two-thousand dollars," proud of my savings and the discipline it represented.

"That's all? How come that's all you have?" she probed. Rose

Sachleben was a woman of generous proportion, only a half inch taller than I, but beside her I felt microscopic.

"I'd have saved more but I've had electrolysis on my legs and it's expensive." I wanted to tell her about the special price I'd negotiated with the owner, about the cheap hot dogs eaten while pausing at a Cuban lunch counter on treatment days, how it was always a mad rush because the reduced price was based on lunch hour treatments. But I decided from observing Rose's imperious expression that it would be useless to explain.

"What's that, electrolysis?"

"It's a way to remove hair permanently."

"What do you need that for? Can't you just shave your legs like other girls?" She inhaled deeply, drew herself up and looked down at me as if I were the most wasteful of creatures.

Rose's face, in repose, might be described as pleasant but when she looked at me the tilt of her chin and the way she barely parted her thin, straight lips, sucking in little gasps of air, the way she kept her eyes slightly diverted from my face as if refusing to completely acknowledge my existence, made her appear ugly to me.

"I had a baby boy before Daniel but he died an infant."

"I'm sorry to hear that, Mom." An uncomfortable silence hung over us which I tried to overcome. "Well, you have two wonderful sons, I'm sure they give you lots of happiness."

"He would be twenty-two now," Rose prevailed, solemnly.

"How is your leg?" I asked. She'd broken her leg several months ago and I'd visited her in the hospital.

"Okay, my leg's okay." Silence again. "So, you have no money and you hardly earn anything. Do you know how to cook?"

Why was Rose being so unfriendly? Did she consider one's bank balance the sole measure of one's worth? Would her view of me improve if I told her about my grandfather Jacob who had come from a wealthy family back in Russia where they had owned forestland until it was seized by the Czar? What was it?

We'd already seen each other several times but we sat on the sofa like strangers. I wanted to be friends with her, feel comfortable addressing her as 'Mom,' but how could this cold, distant woman be 'Mom'? And yet, she was Danny's mother, so I respectfully called her Mom and referred to her son as Daniel in her presence because she required it.

Rose defined our relationship with her endless comments and demands. "Why do you wear such red lipstick, it's not so nice a bride should wear such dark lipstick, maybe you could do something with your hair, it's too long ... Doris was shopping and she found this pearl necklace she likes and we were wondering if you could buy it for her matron of honor gift. And listen, you can't send out thank you notes from the wedding that don't have your picture on them ... everyone uses that kind and you have to also, why do you always have to be different? Can't you just do like everyone else? I'll order the thank you cards and make sure you have them, and use the photographers Doris used, they were good enough, listen, why should you knock yourself out on looking for a photographer, he already knows the family. And by the way, Aunt Maizy called up and she says those silver shoes you wore to Norman's Bar Mitzvah were the worst! Who ever heard of silver shoes! Yeah, and Fay said, if you don't buy bridesmaids gifts with diamonds her girls don't want them ... Doris and I found a perfect place for your parents to make the engagement dinner so tomorrow you should go take a look ... here's the address, we spoke to a Mr. Amiel. So, who are you asking to be flower girl, and what about a ring bearer? Too bad Eliot isn't a little older, Doris said. Oh, and you don't buy furniture with too many legs showing in wood ... it's not the way decorators do it ... and listen to me, your headboard has to be ordered in gold leaf, it's the only way ... I know, you already said you're not fancy, but believe me, you'll grow into it. I told Daniel, Don't let her buy it any other way. I'll make the engagement party for your friends in the apartment, you don't need to invite your friends to an expensive dinner in a restaurant. And by the way, you'll have to change the wedding date, Doris and Edmond already have a wedding over Thanksgiving weekend and another one will just be too much ... I know you don't like me, that's why you gave me that horrible Mother's Day gift. Alright, the terry robe I can use at the club, but the matching beach bag! I'll never use it, it's the worst! I even told Daniel, She hates me and that's why she doesn't care about anything I say!"

I felt lost in the eye of a raging storm. No more time for quiet contemplation. The Bible, which I'd been studying daily since graduation, lay unopened on my desk. I gave up browsing in bookstores, and my newest purchase, a two-volume set of the Complete Works of O'Henry, remained half-read in my closet. I even lay aside my compelling interest in the Holocaust which had been aroused by Leon Uris' book, *Exodus*, which I had read last summer on the long subway rides down to Wall Street. At night I dreamed I was lost in the woods again, only this time the lightning never ceased, the storm never abated and I failed to find the hole in the fence.

Rosy brick houses were under construction in the neighborhood near Terrace on the Sound, the apartment complex where Danny's parents and Doris and Edmond lived, and the sign advertised ONLY $18,000.

"Danny, we could use the money we're spending on furniture as a down payment," I suggested. "I'd much rather buy one of those houses and we'll buy furniture later."

We drove by the construction site but Danny argued against it. He said his parents wanted us to live in Terrace on the Sound.

"When we moved to New Rochelle," Rose explained, "I asked Daniel if he planned on getting married and he said no, so because of him we took a two-bedroom. Now we're stuck with an extra room and it's Daniel's responsibility so you have to take our apartment, anyway it's perfect for you ... and don't worry about us living next door, I mind my own business. Look, it's important for us to live close by ... this way when it snows we can all go to work together."

When Danny and I were alone I protested.

"I can't fight my mother, Honey, she's too tough."

As December 11 drew near and the matter of where we were going to live remained unresolved, Rose exhibited her true power in the family. She issued her final decree, "Daniel, you go and tell Francine that if she doesn't want to live where she's told there'll be no wedding!"

My parents, in anticipation of my marriage, had rented a lovely new apartment in Terrace on the Sound, peaceful landscaping right outside their windows. They pleaded with me to surrender. What was I arguing about, my mother wanted to know, moving into a beautiful apartment?

A beautiful apartment. Next door to Rose. Married to Rose's son who stood firmly with his mother in opposition to my desires. No one heard me, no one was listening. Everyone responded to my anxious worries with dismissal. With every passing day I was filled with increasing nervous tension. Most of the time I was hearing a roar inside my head, making errors at work.

"Mom! Please! I'm not feeling right about all this, everything that's going on! All these arguments! Now she's telling Danny she doesn't like my dishes, I have to return them! She doesn't like anything I choose! She wants to be the one to choose my stuff! She doesn't stop complaining about me!"

"Francine, all the arrangements! Invitations! We have a pile of response cards! The gifts! You know Danny loves you ... and you love him! Everything will work out, you'll see! After you're married it will all settle down. Don't be foolish, Francine."

Sunday, December 11, 1960, dawned cold and overcast. This was IT, my wedding day! But everything seemed strange and unreal. And even my face felt odd, too frozen, too tense to smile.

In the Bridal Suite at the newly-completed Fountainhead I applied lipstick, brushed a little Maybelline onto my lashes and combed out my hair. My hair had set too tightly; I felt disappointed. Tomorrow, I thought, my hair will fall in loose waves the way I like it best. My mother assisted me into my bridal gown and guided the zipper quickly up its long path. I stepped into pure white satin pumps and together my mother and I adjusted the pretty pearl crown and net veil purchased in the wholesale district on 32nd Street. We gazed at our reflections in the bridal suite mirrors. My mother looked dazzlingly beautiful and happy in her silvery-blue lace dress. Arms around each other we smiled into the mirrors, and my mother laughed, her eyes closing as they always did when she laughed, "Come, Sugar Plum, it's time for your wedding!"

Suddenly I recalled a long-ago birthday when my father had asked me what I wanted. Oh, how my six-year-old self had longed to have a bride doll. And my father had somehow managed to find a bride doll, a doll with green eyes dressed in a satin bridal gown. "This will be you someday, my Pocahontas." As soft as a feather's touch, my father kissed my cheek. "One day some boy will come along and take my daughter away from her dear old dad." My father's eyes had grown misty at the very thought. He'd leaned over and kissed me again. My new doll was accompanied by a beautiful birthday card, its cover embossed with a perfumed and padded bouquet of red roses, painted on a circle of shining silk. It opened to my father's lyrical handwriting which resembled music notes: "Adversity's sting has become a gentle kiss and my heart is ever light because of you."

The next day my father had taken me for a walk up Tremont Avenue to the store where he'd purchased my birthday gift. "Look up there, Francine ... see all those pretty dolls sitting on that shelf? Do you see a doll you like better than the one I chose for you?"

Kneeling beside me his face was very close to mine. A fleeting moment embedded in my soul, remembered for all time. Suddenly, I felt my father's sensitivities, the longings buried deep within his heart for everything to be better than it was. All I could do was feel the biggest, saddest love for him and assure him that he had chosen the most beautiful doll any little girl could ever have imagined.

Now I'm a bride! And Danny's waiting for me under the chuppa! The night we met the room became the sky. In another moment we will be standing side by side under the chuppa, my groom looking like Clark Gable, attired in high hat and black formal tuxedo, his black hair slicked back, a mischievous twinkle in his eyes. For a brief moment I'm transformed into pure spirit, soaring with joyous anticipation! My angel must be here ... she must have touched me ever-so-lightly with her gossamer wings.

The first chord of the wedding march is struck. Now I'm clutching my bouquet of white gardenias in fiercely trembling hands, my heart is pounding beneath the satin and lace bodice of my gown. My parents are leading me down the aisle. My heart is jumping out of my body! Danny is striding toward me, standing right in front of me, turning, taking my arm. My parents are walking to their places under the chuppa which is beautifully decorated with garlands of white roses and gardenias. The wedding march is playing just for us. Danny is guiding me through space, gardenias and roses perfuming the way. We're standing under the chuppa and Danny's face is shining just for me.

We hold hands as the Rabbi intones the ancient Hebrew prayers and blessings, then pronounces us man and wife. Danny crushes the traditional wine cup under his heel, so that even in our supreme moment of happiness we might recall the sorrows of the Jewish people which began with the destruction of the First Temple. Mazel Tov!

I'm in Danny's arms, he's kissing me, long and steady. Long enough to convince me this is real. And steady enough to make me feel secure. And now, I'm smiling!

Of Lost Wedding Rings and a Beautiful Baby Boy

OUR WEDDING CELEBRATION was drawing to a close when suddenly everyone's attention was drawn to the windows. Outside, the evening winter landscape was becoming rapidly obscured by heavily falling snow; the historic blizzard of December 11, 1960 had begun during our wedding dessert. As the storm grew more intense with every passing moment our guests hurriedly gathered up their coats and rushed out to their cars.

Miraculously, Danny and I finally arrived at Idlewild Airport in a battered old taxicab that surely must have been watched over by God throughout the treacherous drive, first to get to the Whitestone Bridge and then to cross over in blinding wind-driven snow into Long Island where the blizzard was even more fierce. With all flights canceled the airport closed, and we were stranded at the airport motel for three days.

When the airport at last re-opened we departed on the first flight out and arrived in Jamaica, at the Montego Bay Hotel, our honeymoon destination ... and almost immediately, Danny lost his wedding ring. After a brief search I retrieved it from behind the bed. The following day he lost his ring in the waste basket and once again I found it. Then Danny lost his ring in the sand of Montego Bay Beach, or maybe he tossed it into the beautiful aquamarine sea.

"So you lost your wedding ring on purpose, didn't you, Danny?" My loving message had been engraved by hand inside the ring. "Why did you ... oh Danny ... why did you throw away your wedding ring?"

Unable to suppress a smile Danny bit his lower lip, sneezed and pulled his nose. "Oh, Honey, you know how I hate wearing jewelry ... just kiss me with those luscious lips."

Returning from the hot beach to our room one day I went directly to the sink and splashed handfuls of cool refreshing water onto my face and hair and paused a moment before the mirror, looking deeply into my eyes, searching for the truth of everything which I knew was somewhere inside each of us if only we could access it.

I felt that my real self was an immense fullness of spirit, barely able to be contained by human form. My real self was loving kindness, an awareness of being one with the eternal universe which had been conceived in love, created out of God's desire to share love. When I opened my mouth I felt an enormous energy connected to my tongue, as if every word spoken was spoken for the entire universe. What would God say? I gazed more deeply into my eyes, beyond color, beyond form, and felt my heartbeat. The tongue was meant to express whatever the heart felt. Only kind words, words designed to help and heal, ought to be spoken. A shimmering light was shining through my eyes, obscuring my reflection in the mirror. The heart, the voice, the soul, the universe, God ... whoever or whatever God was! Everything is connected. But how? how is it all connected?

Danny isn't searching for the truth. Danny makes his own truth. When Danny looks at me does he see the fullness of my love for him? Does Danny think about his love for me? He must love me ... after all, he decided to marry me and he says he loves me.

Danny needed a way out when Uncle Sam came calling; the war in Viet Nam was on everyone's mind and all the young men we knew were searching for deferments.

"Let's have a baby, honey," Danny said, coming up behind me, startling me out of my reverie. I smiled at his reflection in the mirror. "Let's start our family right away, why wait? A baby will keep me out of Viet Nam!" I turned around; we kissed and hugged and laughed. And so it was settled. "We'll call him G.I. Joe!" Danny said. We hugged and kissed and our hearts were filled with happiness.

So on the fifth day of our honeymoon, gazing ever more deeply into my own heart, I understood a most significant truth: I'm Danny's wife now ... we're going to begin our family together ... I will be dependent on him ... my whole life will be from this moment devoted to his well-being. I will bring to my marriage all the fullness of myself and express it with love and harmony, the sacred language of the universe! Someday Danny will grow to truly love me, he will come to know the fullness of my heart, all that I wished to share with him, and Danny will grow to cherish me.

As soon as we returned home my mother-in-law established herself as the arbiter of all our comings and goings, our plans and purchases; even our discussions grew out of her demands, complaints and critical observations.

"Here, take my orange-juice squeezer," she said as she barged in and set it on the kitchen counter. "Be sure you make Daniel fresh-squeezed orange juice every morning."

It was time consuming to squeeze out a second glass of juice for myself, so I placed the tall glass of fresh orange juice in the refrigerator for my sleeping prince and hurried down the steep, icy windswept hill to catch the commuter bus to the eight-o-five train to the city.

"Daniel," Rose said, sometimes in my presence other times Danny just reported back to me, "don't let her get rid of that dark green carpet in the other bedroom, it cost me a fortune, dark green is fine for a nursery."

"Danny, I don't want that old carpet for our baby's room."

"Honey, I can't fight my mother, she's too tough."

"How about that old sofa your mother left here, why must I keep it? She never asked me if I want it and I don't."

"Leave it stay awhile, Honey, just till she calms down."

"It's not nice a married woman should have such long hair, and it's so thick, go to Doris' place and just tell him to make it short, that's all."

I obeyed her. On the long walk home I chastised myself: Francine where is that independent girl you used to be? You're in danger Francine! Look at you! Becoming subservient to an aggressive domineering mother-in-law! Serving a husband who cares more about pleasing his mother than he does about pleasing you! You're in danger Francine! Don't lose yourself!

"I don't care what you saw in the city, painted flowers on baby furniture, who cares for that? There's a store here in town, Doris and I were in there already and he has a very nice crib set, walnut, and we'll pay for the dresser."

"Honey, my mother wants to know why you didn't call Doris today, she's sick with a cold and so is Edmond. She says you don't care about the family."

"Danny. I can't believe you're serious! I'm at work all day . . . exhausted when I finally get home, and besides, who called me when I had a cold? And what about Edmond? Before we were married your mother said he'd drive me to the station but he hasn't taken me even once! What does everyone want from me, Danny? I don't understand!"

"Don't find fault with my family, Francine!"

"They're the ones finding fault, Danny! They're causing us

to have all these stupid arguments! What have I done so wrong? Why does everybody hate me so much?"

"Because you deserve to be hated!"

Danny's love had flown to the furthest star in the universe! His eyes grew distant. His heart closed.

Sobbing, I ran into the bathroom; Danny didn't follow. I leaned both arms on the sink, my forehead leaning on my arms, sobbing into the cold, hard sink wishing to remain like that forever! Oh! what have I done to myself!

Despair held me in its arms. Sadness enveloped me like a shroud. And, as new life bloomed inside me, a part of me was laid to rest.

Not long after that night I became very ill, worse each day, each week, until I awoke one morning uncontrollably vomiting on the bed, unable to move. A kidney infection was the diagnosis. Dr. Kappler ordered total bed rest, it was absolutely imperative until the infection healed.

At the office Mr. Wagonner conferred with his superior and it was decided that the company would pay me a full month's severance pay. I was entering my third trimester and it was the belief of Lionel D. Edie & Co. that a very pregnant woman might embarrass visiting clients, so I wouldn't be returning to work.

Eventually, Dr. Kappler declared the infection healed but my feet had swelled to such enormous proportion walking had become a painful ordeal. Apparently, there was nothing to do but wait it out until the baby was born.

Then, as we entered the hottest August anyone could recall Danny began having dizzy spells. The doctors decided to do some tests, and Danny was hospitalized for ten days.

Every morning I went down to the city to stay with Danny in his room at Mt. Sinai Hospital. I brought meals from home and games for us to play. Alone at night I wrote prayers for Danny's good health. Danny told Rose she needn't visit, he was happy having me with him and was enjoying our private time together. After all the tests, the final one a spinal tap which left Danny feeling worse than when he entered the hospital, the doctors decided it must be some kind of inner ear imbalance, not to worry. He returned home, went back to work on the used car lot, and we resumed our life together.

On October 21, 1961, I gave birth to Neale.
"Honey, you should see him! He's so big! Eight pounds, fourteen ounces, wow! He's so strong looking! You should see those little fists! They put a torn undershirt on him and he looks like a tough little guy, he's really something . . . he's gorgeous, Honey!"
"Oh, Danny, I'm so happy."
"How do you feel, Honey? Kappler says you had a rough time." Danny leaned over and kissed me.
"I feel kinda weak, Danny . . . guess it's natural, I'll be alright."
"I don't know, Honey, Kappler says the baby was much bigger than he expected and you had some pretty big lacerations. He says you have to take it easy for a while."
At last the nurses brought the babies out and I held my beautiful son. Before he was born the soul of my son had come to visit me so now I looked into the precious face of my child who I already knew from so many dreams.
Welcome to the world Neale, darling! you're so beautiful, the most beautiful baby I've ever seen! almond shaped eyes, long curly lashes, long tapered eyebrows, rose bud mouth and your ears, my son, so tiny and close to the head, and look at that . . . no earlobes! soft, downy hair, blond for your entrance into the world . . . and all in perfect proportion.
My son looked directly into my eyes . . . a bond of trust was born.
Whatever you choose to do with your life, my darling, whatever you choose, you're going to be dynamite!

His intelligent, steady gaze told me that Neale understood and waited patiently to hear more.

Yes, you're going to be something special, my son, and ... you'll always love your Mama.

After a while I decided to get off the hospital bed and go for a little walk down the hall to the nursery and peek in at Neale, but discovered that I lacked the strength to stand. The next morning I tried again, this time with a nurse's assistance. As soon as I stood upright and stopped leaning on the bed I almost collapsed and the nurse quickly helped me back onto the bed. I forced myself to try again and again until I made it to the door. Every step was agony. I looked down at myself; my stomach was flatter than ever. On the third day I made it to the scale outside in the hall and was shocked to see that it registered twelve pounds below my normal weight. But I couldn't pay too much attention to my weight. My thoughts were centered on caring for my baby at home when we were alone together, no one around to help. Waves of anxiety and nervousness washed over me throughout the day. Now the nurses are changing my baby's diaper and preparing his bottles but once we go home the responsibility is mine and I don't know anything about caring for a baby! And now ... oh, Francine, what has happened to you ... so thin and weak just when you must be strong ... you must find the strength to be a good mommy!

As it turned out, caring for Neale was the most rewarding and pleasurable task imaginable, for he responded to every touch and smile and sound as if we'd known and loved one another forever and this was a time of re-discovery. By the evening of our first day home I had it all figured out and knew how to do everything! I rejoiced over the bottles and the sterilizer that I'd worried about. As it turned out nothing was difficult as I'd imagined and worried over. Gently and lovingly, I massaged my precious baby's tender body with baby oil. I made diaper changing into a fun time by smiling with him and speaking cheerfully to him through the whole procedure and he, enthralled with the sound of my voice, gazed into my face and lay still in quiet contentment. When I laughed, Neale laughed. I exercised his plump arms and legs and sang to him, "You are my sunshine, my only sunshine ..." I described to him in a soothing voice all that was happening in our day.

"Daddy is working now, my darling, but he can hardly wait to come home to you ... Daddy loves you so much."

Danny came home late every night, going after work to the racetrack or basketball games or poker with his buddies from the old neighborhood and I worried about Danny's absence from Neale's life so I created with little stories an image for Neale to hold in his mind. In this way, with love, I sought to soften the absences that caused me so much distress.

"Mommy is going to bundle you up nice and warm and take you outside in your beautiful silvery coach! and Grandma will come to visit! And Mommy will play with you!" I kept it up for as long as he looked interested, then I left him safe in his crib to kick his strong baby legs and to think and grow. Seated on a chair in his room, while listening to the melody of my son's musical baby talk, I managed small and quiet household tasks and wrote letters to my friends.

I carried Neale on 'tours' of our apartment, explained to him what each object was and its purpose. I lifted the delicate English porcelain birds from their places on our shelves and right away he reached out to pet them. I showed him my books on the breakfront shelves, and let him feel the pages; and then, holding his little hand, we petted the leaves of all our plants. Neale looked directly at me while I explained things, and he touched each object carefully, the way I had demonstrated. The lovely antique clock I'd purchased in the city one day after work in that now past time, I held up to my son's ears; "tick-tock ... tick-tock" I whispered. Neale held his breath for a moment, listened to the rhythmic sound and laughed. Every day I poured the fullness of my nourishing love into my infant son and watched him blossom from moment to moment. One day he'd become a man, he'd leave our home and go on to create his own life and home, but always he and I would share a bond of trust and love that neither distance nor the stresses of life could sever.

My parents were ecstatic. They felt as if their lives had begun anew. My mother arrived in the morning and followed me around, going on and on about her problems, while I completed my household chores, cared for Neale and prepared lunch. I was happy for my mother; her life had at last become easier. But most of her pleasure hinged on her time with me and Neale. My mother enjoyed an everlasting youthful glow which lit her dark, deep-set eyes, lent a light spring to her quick steps and made her look like the mother of my plump baby who lay content in his elegant, polished coach. My mother proudly steered the carriage along the narrow suburban path as I, like some visiting aunt, followed. My mother still possessed a nervous energy which drove her to pursue her errands with an edgy determination and wherever she wanted to go I drove her; frustrating hours of the day with Neale in his car seat while I so longed to be sharing our precious fleeting time alone together. I tried to tell my mother how I felt but her hurt feelings prompted my father to call and ask me if I knew how deeply I had hurt my mother. My father spoke sternly to me and the depth of his emotions reminded me of my duties as a daughter. So my mother continued coming over early in the morning, usually before Danny left for work.

ONE MORNING Rose arrived at my door from her apartment down the hall even earlier than my mother's usual arrival, her hair a maze of wild steel wool, her nightgown unkempt beneath her sloppy robe, and she screamed, "Doris is outside with the kids already, they're up since six o'clock, children need fresh air, and you! a young woman should be so weak like you! I never heard such a thing, it's natural to give birth!"

Completely taken by surprise I faced her, somehow summoning from somewhere a calm composure. "Well, Mom, Neale sleeps late so I'm on a different schedule than Doris … and you know, I had a big baby and lacerations that are still healing … you know I'm still underweight … remember the kidney infection, it kept me in bed for over a month … the pregnancy took a lot out of me …"

"I don't believe you! There's just no reason to be so weak! You had a baby! Everyone has babies!"

Rose kept me standing by the open door, refusing to come in and refusing to calm down and return to her apartment. "I'm reporting you to the Child Welfare Bureau!" her screams echoed in the hall, up and down the stairwell, and throughout my entire life. "And always your mother is here! Why don't you make friends with the other women your own age!"

The day after Rose accused me of being a bad mother my hair started falling out.

My father looked forward to Saturday morning visits and when Leo heard my father's footsteps in the hall, he'd come in to visit too, followed in a moment by Rose.

"So, what's doing? Your father's here already? How's Neale? How come you aren't outside yet? Here's your mixer, I borrowed it yesterday when you were out, how come you don't get a better mixer, they make such good ones these days, this one's impossible."

Why should I even bother to explain that this mixer had belonged to my Grandma and I had no trouble using it.

Grandma would have set matters straight on the double. I could picture Grandma baking one of her huge, delicious sponge cakes, filling the kitchen, the apartment and the hallways beyond with an aroma capable of activating salivary glands all over the neighborhood. Then, with flour still dusting and mingling with the silver white of her hair, she would carry her loaf of ecstasy down the hall to Rose. Settling into a kitchen chair, Grandma would sip her tea and wait for Rose to finish at least one slab of sponge cake.

Then my Grandma would speak. "So, what's the matter Rose, you're not happy with my Fagala? Such a sweet maidela, always good to her mother and father and everybody. You should know, you're a mother, what it's like to watch the little ones grow up, and such a beauty my Fagala, inside, Rose, you know what I mean? Let's not meddle with the children, they have enough, so young and a baby to care for. Such long hours your Daniel works, such a wonderful boy, Daniel. And how my Fagala loves him. What for we should make them unhappy, Rose? So, they make mistakes. Remember when we were young, everything wasn't so perfect. But somehow we managed, fachtait, Rose, understand? Give the girl half a chance, you'll see, believe me, no one knows her better than me, she wants only for you to love her, that's all Rose, only love is in her heart. I should know, my Fagala and me, we slept in the same room for years, don't ask how long, it wasn't easy. Okay, Rose, you should remember what I'm telling you, you shouldn't forget. Here, keep my sponge cake, there's plenty more. Next time I bring a honey cake."

But Grandma wasn't there.

ONE EVENING as I rested on the sofa with a book and a chocolate bar, and Neale slept in his crib, dreaming his sweet baby dreams, the shrill ring of the doorbell suddenly pierced the silence and Leo entered.

My father-in-law's pride in his fine physique and youthful appearance was apparent in his confident, purposeful stride. In his native town in Austria he had been a runner and had tended his body well, lifting weights to expand his naturally muscular chest and eating good, thick steaks from his father's butcher shop. All the young girls in town knew him, he bragged to me, and I even met a woman, a perfect stranger, who upon hearing my last name inquired about the family's origins and then declared she'd known Leo and his brothers. They were all good-looking, the woman had confirmed, but Leo was the handsomest. Leo loved the outdoors and Sachleben skin took a beautiful tan. Even now, with only a few silver-gray strands combed back over his tanned scalp, Leo was a fine-looking man. He always spoke in soft, low tones and required total silence when he was speaking. If he was interrupted, he stopped in mid-sentence, waited for the intruder to pause and then asked, "Are you finished now, may I continue?" He often came to apologize for Rose's bad behavior. He was kind to my mother and on pleasant evenings joined my father for long walks and conversation.

Now he made himself comfortable beside me on the dark-green sofa which Rose had selected for my home, and reached for a Nestles chocolate bar from the platter on the cocktail table. He unwrapped the thin chocolate, careful not to let tiny slivers escape the shiny white paper wrapping, and spoke.

"Mom tells me you're giving her a hard time with this dinner party you're making for the family. What's the matter?"

I knew that Leo would listen attentively to my reply, but I knew, also, that when he walked back down the hall he'd be able to report to Rose that Francine would now do things Rose's way. I realized that if I didn't comply after this quiet, earnest appeal from Leo, he'd return tomorrow night, Rose would join him, and the next time Danny would be brought into it and I would give up the fight eventually, for the sake of peace.

"Mom wants me to let her prepare all the food and tell everyone I did it and I don't want to do that . . . it's not honest. I don't think the family expects me to be the best cook in the world, but I am capable of preparing a meal for my guests."

"Look, if she wants to do it, let her do it, what do you care?"

"I care because I don't want to lie."

"Don't you see, Francine, the family likes her cooking, she wants them to be happy and maybe you won't make everything just the way they like it."

"Dad, they're coming to my house, they expect to eat my food. When they go to your house they eat Mom's food."

"Why cause trouble, Francine, do it for me, I can't take the yelling, she doesn't let up, you don't know what I live with."

We went back and forth in this vein for a little while longer and then my father-in-law and I sat in silence for a moment. I looked into his fine, serious eyes and I didn't see the tough businessman I knew he was, I didn't see the father who favored my husband's brother, I saw a beleaguered husband, a sweet man, and I did not wish to prolong his unhappiness.

"Okay, Dad, tell her I'll do it her way, but please remember that I'm not happy about it."

OVER MY OBJECTIONS Rose bought a playpen for Neale – Doris kept Elliot and Laura in playpens. I dragged it out to the terrace, thinking, well, maybe out here it can serve a purpose. One Sunday, alone for a brief minute with Neale, Danny decided to play one of his humorous games, humorous to him only. He placed Neale in the very center of the playpen and as I was returning to the terrace, opening the door, I see Danny attempting to close the playpen with my baby sitting there, innocent and smiling. I screamed, "NO!" and ran the few steps but Danny had already stepped on the lever to bring the center up into its fold. Neale's sturdy weight, however, kept the center anchored, causing the playpen to crack and break. Naturally, Rose accused me of lying, Danny would never do anything like that she asserted, and she called everyone in the family to report that Francine had broken her beautiful gift, what nerve! The most expensive playpen on the market.

Danny resolved the issue of telling his mother the truth by insisting, "Oh, Honey, what does it matter? She won't listen anyway."

At mealtimes Neale flipped his light blue rubber spoon over his shoulder, sending his baby food splattering against the wall, and he laughed. He piled applesauce into his hair, rubbed it in and laughed at his own antics. I laughed with him, he was so funny and joyful in his play. Entering the kitchen Rose uttered sounds of disgust. "Don't worry," I assured her, "he's having fun . . . after lunch I wash his hair and explain that he shouldn't put food into his hair or throw it around. Leave him alone."

I didn't want Neale to see disapproving looks directed at him. In any case, by the time he was ten months old, shampooing his hair with applesauce ceased to amuse him and thereafter Neale became exceedingly well-mannered at the table.

In Rose's eyes nothing Neale did could match what Elliot, her first grandchild, did. When I described to her how Neale could sit quietly absorbed in a book, turning pages as if he were actually reading, she immediately commented, "Oh, Elliot is so adorable, you should see what he did today." This became her lifelong habit.

EACH MONTH Dr. Zimmerman weighed and measured Neale and compared his findings with a national growth chart, and each time his comment was the same, "You have quite a big fellow here, Francine, he's in the ninety-ninth percentile!"

Dr. Zimmerman's nurse, Diane, was a lovely, softly-rounded young woman whose deep voice sounded as if she had a sore throat. "I see plenty of mothers in here, believe me, but you are something. Tell me, did you have any special training? And this little Neale is so beautiful I just love whenever you come in!"

And that's how our friendship began. Diane came to visit and soon we discovered that Barbara Goldberg was a mutual friend.

I recalled Barbara talking about her friend Diane, the nurse, and Diane had heard about Barbara's lucky friend who married this great-looking, wealthy guy and then had a gorgeous baby.

My brother's engagement to Sarah ended. Sarah's father, Dr. Slater, expected Mike to join his dermatology practice but Mike was planning to become a surgeon. There was no middle ground. When Dr. Slater finally understood that Mike had no interest in dermatology and was completely committed to surgery he ordered Sarah to return the ring, called off the wedding and didn't even consider relenting when for a whole year his daughter sat in her closet, crying and clutching her expensive hand-sewn wedding gown. I suggested to Mike that he meet my friend Barbara Goldberg, who'd waited a long time for this opportunity, and Mike agreed.

"Remember," my father warned Mike, unknown to me at the time, "Barbara is a friend of your sister's and I hope you will refrain from making any improper advances."

After their second date Barbara came to visit. "Oh, I'm so jealous every time I come here," she greeted me with her big wide smile. "Just look at this apartment, this baby! You're so lucky, Fran!"

"Yeah, I'm so lucky ... look at me, I'm so skinny is what you mean, and my hair ..."

"You do look thin. You know, Franny, women sometimes lose a little hair after childbirth, but it'll grow back, you'll see. Here, let's have the brownies my mother baked for you, and fatten you up a little."

"Thanks, Barbara, it's so good to see you, come, sit down, I'll make cocoa, one of the few things Danny says I do well in the kitchen."

"Franny, since you're my only married friend, I have to ask you something."

"What?"

"Well, I'm trying to understand how a woman stays faithful to one man . . . isn't it difficult? I mean, don't you want someone else occasionally?"

"You know, I've never thought about it . . . I don't want anyone else but Danny. Actually, I don't think I'm a good person to ask . . . I think maybe someone who's been around more can answer better. I mean, Danny's the only man I ever . . . you know."

Barbara paused for a moment and then she laughed in her hearty way. "It's true, isn't it? You're not kidding!"

I was surprised at Barbara's response. "No, I'm not kidding."

"Well, I wish I could say that after I'm married but I go to bed with all my boyfriends. My father even walked in on me once when I had a guy in my bed . . . ha! I told him he ought to knock before entering." Barbara laughed.

"I would have died of embarrassment."

"You ought to learn to let yourself go, Franny."

"So, tell me, how was your date with Mike?"

"You know, Fran, I'm really confused," Barbara turned serious. "Is something wrong with your brother?"

"What do you mean?"

"Well, we've gone out twice and he hasn't made a single move. Nothing, nada, zilch, not even a kiss, I don't get it."

"Maybe he's just being polite."

"Well, I don't know, Fran, he's very nice and everything but I don't think he's for me . . . I was thinking, though, remember I mentioned my friend Gloria? Maybe we could fix Mike up with her."

"Alright, I'll ask him."

IN MAY 1962 Mike graduated from medical school and he met Gloria the very next day. Two weeks later in my mother's kitchen, Gloria by his side, my brother announced, "This is Gloria, the girl I'm going to marry. You're looking at the future Mrs. Vale."

My mother almost dropped the platter of roast beef she was carrying to the table. My father's mouth opened but he made no sound.

"I love Mike," Gloria proclaimed, and repeated often. Gloria's fair complexion made me think of cold porcelain, and her hair was colored light auburn, cropped and neat. Her eyes reminded me of translucent waves in an arctic spring thaw. Gloria was tall, she didn't need a stepladder to reach the top shelf of the kitchen cabinets, and she seemed robust and healthy. She said her collection of cashmere sweaters was legendary. She had decided to marry a doctor and now her dream was coming true. Gloria was very happy and satisfied and she knew this was only the beginning. She was marrying Mike, who belonged to a family who loved him dearly, but Gloria wanted him all to herself.

TUESDAY AND THURSDAY nights Danny went to the racetrack. Friday nights he went over to Fred's in the old neighborhood for poker. Alone, I wandered through immaculate rooms. I stood by Neale's crib; it was so quiet, his sweet little baby breaths were audible. I watched for the gentle flutter of his beautiful lashes, patted his back and adjusted the blanket. I tried to read for a while or watch television. I polished all our shoes, watered and trimmed the plants, sewed buttons onto Danny's shirts, rearranged drawers. I wrote long letters to Sherry who lived with her husband in Poughkeepsie now. I wrote stories for Neale which I illustrated and bound in leatherette folders. Every few minutes I checked the clock. Finally, I sat on the clean, fresh bed, made up so pretty with a quilted white silk spread since morning, and cried from loneliness.

On Sunday morning Danny awoke early and began immediately to dress in his basketball clothes.

"Danny, please don't go, stay home with me." I went to him and put my arms around him. "Kiss me, Danny."

He pulled my arms away. "I'm going to play basketball ... leave me alone."

"I don't want to leave you alone! You leave me alone too much! You're never here!"

Danny continued dressing and then moved to the sink to wash his face. I followed him, fear and distress mingling in my stomach. "I need you, Danny, I'm lonely for you! Please stay home with me!"

Danny combed his hair. Then he brushed his teeth and turned to leave the bathroom.

"Didn't you hear me? I can't bear it when you ignore me, Danny! Can't you just stop and listen to me?"

"Get out of my way, Fran, I'm going to play ball."

"That's all you care about is playing ball! What about me? Don't you care about our marriage?"

Danny opened his top drawer and took out a pair of white sweat socks.

"Answer me, Danny!"

"I'm playing ball. Leave me alone."

Danny pulled on his socks and laced his sneakers. He reached for his Jacket.

Panic filled my heart. What is he doing? Rejecting me? Walking out on me? My throat hurt, my stomach ached. "Danny, please, please ... don't do this, stay home with me ... I love you ... I want us to be together ... we'll do something together ... it's Sunday ... let's have a picnic ... please, Danny, just this once!"

I reached out to him. With all his strength Danny leaned across our king-sized bed with the gold-leaf headboard that Rose had insisted upon, and pushed me. I lost my balance and fell backward off the bed. My head struck the cherrywood bedside table. He was walking toward the front door. I stumbled back up and ran to the door, turned to face him, my back against the door. "Don't walk out on me, Danny! Don't treat me like this!" Danny reached behind me and tried to pry my hands from their grip on the doorknob behind me. My face felt distorted with misery, drenched with tears. My head throbbed. Why would anyone want to stay home with a wreck like me? I was locked into a frenzy of emotion, unable to extricate myself from it, and clung to the doorknob with all my strength. Danny reached behind me and pulled at my fingers until I thought my fingers would break, until I let go. Danny opened the door and went out.

Splashing cold water on my face I felt a swelling on my forehead and looked up into the mirror. A huge purple lump had arisen on my forehead! right on my left eyebrow! so now I knew which part of my head had struck the bedside table.

Not the time to think about myself, I went to check on Neale. He was standing in his crib, lifting his arms to me. He had heard our terrible quarrel. "I love you, sweetheart . . . Mommy loves you so much." I held my baby close, pressed my face against his and kissed him. All I wanted to do was get into bed and cry but Neale needed to be changed and fed, so I attended to his needs.

From that Sunday on married life was for me a form of imprisonment. Locked up in a world where everyone seemed to be blind. No one noticed the horrible bruise on my forehead. I showed my bruise to Danny when he returned later from basketball, he gave it a glance, never referred to it again, behaving as if it hadn't happened. He never asked me if it hurt. He never referred to its healing when it finally healed. It's true, I did my best to camouflage the nasty purple lump with my hair and keep my left side turned away as much as possible from my mother and others. Yet, how could people not notice? Couldn't anyone tell that I was not myself? My real, true self was now imprisoned deep inside my heart, leaving my body to somehow perform all the necessary tasks our life demanded. I became a shadow of myself. My former enthusiasm for all of life became narrowly focused on my child. Nothing else mattered. Danny made no time for me, his mother never ceased her criticism of me, my mother's daily complaints about everything in her life obscured her awareness of everything else. Her daughter was living in a beautiful apartment she herself would have loved to live in, and she now had a beautiful grandson to play with and brag about. And based on reports of my mother's bragging to the family not only about Neale but also about my marriage to Danny she never developed a deeper understanding of my life.

Also, disturbing memories were already piling up and becoming imprisoned inside my mind. A cool, sunny day at the Beach Club should have been a wonderful, happy day. But returning quickly from a visit to the ladies room I looked across the lawn to where the family was gathered. Danny and Rose were playing catch with my baby! Shocked, I saw Danny toss Neale to Rose and she tossed Neale back to him! as if my precious baby were a football! I reached them in a second, took my son from Rose's loose and sloppy hands and held him close.

"Are you both crazy! What are you doing with my child!"

"We're just playing! calm down!"

"You call this play? Endangering my child's life is playing to you? What kind of father are you, Danny!"

I walked away from them and sat under a tree alone with Neale until it was time to leave. The incident so distressed me it became a haunting I wished I could wipe from memory; I became overly fearful of leaving Neale with anyone, whether family members or babysitters.

Later in the morning my parents arrived, smiling. "Where's the handsomest and smartest little boy in the whole world?" my father beamed, heading straight for Neale's room.

I had already showered, brushed my hair best I could to cover the bruise, and had somehow managed to regain my composure. This is how it's going to be, I thought. No one will know. Let them think everything is fine. My parents have suffered enough. Just now when they are in the happiest years of their lives, their burdens at last lighter, their lives easier, how can I destroy their rosy illusion and give them something new to agonize over? It was actually easy, as my mother went right into her usual dialogue about my aunts which lasted until we were interrupted by Leo coming in, followed by Rose.

"We heard you in the hall so we figured we'd come in and say hello."

They focused on their own conversations awhile until I carried Neale out from his crib and then our home was filled with happiness and laughter.

At twelve-thirty Danny came home. My parents left for their usual Sunday visit in Levittown. Rose and Leo remained; Leo had business to discuss with Danny. Rose said, "Let's go into my place, I made stuffed cabbage." Danny left with Rose and Leo and I followed with Neale.

Late at night Danny asked, "Why are you crying, Honey?"

TONI, one of the neighbors, invited me up to her place for an afternoon visit. She showed me her collection of wigs, and drawers over-stuffed with make-up.

"I'm gonna make you glamorous, babe, you're wasting your natural good looks. Believe me, if you don't fix yourself up your husband will notice every chick who does."

Toni took a long drag on her filter tip, leaned her tall, slender body against the wall, ran a manicured hand through her long blond hair. She was wearing a black leather pants outfit and high-heeled boots.

"You think Carmine would look twice at me if I didn't doll up with all this crap every day?" She directed a long, red fingernail at her false eyelashes.

"Show me how to line my eyes, Toni, but I'm not ready for false lashes."

"Okay, Babe."

It was a snowy day, there was nothing else to do. Neale was cozily napping in his stroller, his afternoon bottle having fallen to the side. Toni and I stood before her large bedroom mirror.

"Let's see how you look as a blond. With your eyes you'd be a knockout." She pulled a blond wig in a flip hair-do from one of her high round boxes and fitted it onto my head. We looked at my reflection and frowned. "Uh,uh," Toni said, "no good . . . let's see you as a redhead, redheads are hot. Carmine loves it when I wear this one."

"He wouldn't if you looked like this," I said, pointing to myself, and we laughed.

"Listen, Babe, maybe you oughta stick to your own hair."

"You look great in the wigs, Toni, it's just not my style, I guess."

Toni showed me how to line my eyes with dark green pencil and how to apply eye shadow. She instructed me to throw out my old-fashioned cake mascara, to use instead a new mascara wand. She said, "This is my blusher, Babe, you got to use it, it goes on like so . . . Carmine gives me plenty of bucks but he has no idea how much I really spend . . . I tell him a bunch of crap about the supermarket and John's stuff . . . you gotta do it, Babe, otherwise they screw you every time . . . keep your face tilted this way . . . yeah . . . soon he'll finish this new deal he's working on and he'll be making real money and it won't matter anyway what I'm spending . . . he's my second marriage, believe me, I know . . . me and my first husband, we had this really cute place . . . I kept it like a dollhouse . . . I know you wouldn't guess it by this mess . . . you never care about anything like you do the first time . . . so, where did it get me, huh? Nowheresville, that's where . . . now I'm in it for whatever I can get . . . he wanted a kid, I gave him a kid . . . now he's gotta give me . . . there! wow! look at you, a regular movie star!"

I hugged her, "You're great, Toni! Thanks a million! I can't believe it's me! Think I can do this myself?"

"Here, Babe, take these to practice on till you get your own, I keep buying new stuff anyway." Toni filled the stroller pouch with a heap of compacts, little tubes, pencils and brushes.

"Oh, Toni, you must tell me, what can I do for you?"

"You know, if you don't mind, you can watch the brat for me, I'll bring him down to you in his carriage. I gotta get outa here for a while before I go nuts." Toni extinguished her cigarette in the large crystal ashtray overflowing with stubs, and exhaled a long curl of smoke.

The following morning I viewed my freshly showered face as an empty canvas for a new art form. My understanding of color and my steady, precise hand created anew each day a face which came alive with just the right shades of pale pink and lavender. Compliments from saleswomen at the makeup counter in Bloomingdales, where I went to purchase new makeup, gave me confidence.

When Barbara came to visit she said, "You're amazing, Fran, how long do I know you? Since Joanie's sweet sixteen? I've never seen you in anything but lipstick, and now you're always made up, even when it's just me coming over."

My mother commented, "What do you need all that make-up for? You always look very nice without it." My mother-in-law scrutinized my face in silence.

Danny said, "You look really terrific, Honey. You're doing a good job, not too much, just right."

On ordinary days and on days when I thought my life was falling apart, I applied makeup which disguised private emotions and I felt better prepared to meet the world.

Neighbors and friends noticed the change. I began to hear the comment, "You look like you really have your life together, you're so lucky!" I loved hearing it and began to grow attached to my self-created illusion of perfect marriage, perfect life.

THE FOLDING TABLE was set up in Neale's room with brightly colored party decorations. October sunlight filtered softly through corn-yellow curtains, alighting gently on his big fire engine and yellow derrick. Horsey, Neale's most beloved possession, lay safe in his crib.

Last winter we were in the children's clothing department of a local branch of Arnold Constable, shopping for warm pajamas, when Neale became excited by a large colorful display of stuffed animals, pointing to a friendly-looking black horse with a white face, loving blue marble eyes, a golden mane the color of buttercups bathed in sunshine and a silky golden tail. I placed the horse in Neale's arms while I paid for the pajamas and Neale laughed with joy, his eyes shining. The horse was expensive, twenty-five dollars, so when it was time to leave I returned it to the display. We went home to our quiet evening routine. "Up into the cherry tree, who should climb but little me . . ." and Neale was fast asleep. Outside, thick, heavy snow flakes were blowing all over. I stood by the terrace door mesmerized as always by the ethereal whiteness of it all, remembering the intense look on Neale's face as he sat in his stroller squeezing the plush horse tightly to his chest; the horse stood upright on strong legs yet was also very cuddly to hold and hug. The French cloisonné clock on the breakfront shelf chimed seven times. It was Monday night, the store was open another hour, but my car was parked in the garage we all shared, blocked by Edmond's car.

I closed the door to Neale's room so as not to disturb his sleep when the key turned in the front door lock, I lifted the telephone off the hook, grabbed my envelope of savings, threw on my coat and boots and ran all the way to the store. I raced up the stairs to the children's department and there, exactly where I had replaced it a few hours earlier, sat Neale's horse, waiting to be reunited with the sweetest little boy who had in a fleeting moment instilled so much love in him, the horse now felt ready to love him in return! Outside a strong wind swirled the snow, obscuring all the hard edges of the world. The universe consisted of a golden maned horse held close to my pounding heart, and my son. I fought my way through the storm, through snow which fell now in blinding fury. At last I was home! As soon as I entered the apartment I heard Neale stirring in his crib. He lifted his head and quickly stood up. I enfolded my precious son in my arms and extended the wondrous plushy horse. "Look, sweetheart, who has come to be your friend." In his dreamy sleepiness Neale clasped the horse tightly to his chest, and lay down contentedly. Every night, for years to come, Neale slept embracing Horsey.

The birthday table glowed in stripes of sunlight. A fairy had come by and sprinkled the party hats and candy baskets with stardust. Neale was dressed in navy slacks, a light blue sweater and navy and white saddle shoes. I held him so that he could have a good view of his birthday party table.

"This is your party, sweetheart ... you're a big boy now, two years old! And Susan and Elliot and Laura are coming to help you celebrate. See all the pretty hats and funny horns? That's to make it special for you, Neale, darling. Everybody loves you! Mommy will take care of everything and Neale will have so much fun!"

Neale looked at the table, he looked around the room and then at me. He pointed to himself and said, "Me a big boy now!"

I kissed his darling, rosy cheeks and Neale hugged me and pressed his mouth hard against my face in his version of a kiss. His beautiful hazel eyes shimmered with delight. He blew out the candles, everyone clapped and sang Happy Birthday.

Happy second birthday, my angel boy.

SARAH ADAMS, who lived downstairs on the ground floor, reminded me of Suzie, my pal from junior high. Sarah's gorgeous chestnut hair cascaded in shining waves onto her shoulders. She was forever trying to lose the ten pounds she'd gained from the birth of her two young boys. Mark had left law school to get a job and marry Sarah; now he worked for the Westchester County Administration.

To prepare for one of their frequent evening engagements Sarah began searching her closets at three in the afternoon. "Everything looks like rags to me," she complained, then gathered the boys, along with supplies of milk and cookies, and dashed off to Lord & Taylor where her favorite saleswoman settled Sarah and her boys in a spacious dressing room and brought her dozens of outfits to try on. Sarah selected a short, tight black dress, the saleswoman fetched accessories, including stockings and shoes. Then Sarah was ushered into the beauty salon where Fred put up her hair and Donna applied her makeup. Sarah rushed home, threw a couple of hot dogs into a pot, placed an open can of beans to heat in a pan of water and called around for a sitter.

When Mark opened the front door he was greeted by the vision of his elegant, sophisticated wife serving hot dogs to Steven and Josh, a babysitter waiting in the living room. Mark needed a shave before going out again but first he scooped armloads of toys from the floor, and soon you heard a great clanging and crashing from the boys' room. "Sarah!" he shouted, "how many times must I ask you to please teach the boys to put their things away!"

"Mark, you don't know how busy I am all day . . . I didn't have time!"

Mark began gathering up a second load of toys. He was tall and pale and his face was sweaty, a lock of dark hair fell across his damp forehead.

"Don't worry about it, Mark! They're only going to mess it up again tomorrow!" And Sarah rolled her eyes heavenward, long wavy strands of hair escaping the pins.

In a few strides Mark was at her side, kissing Sarah and the boys. "Want to dance before we leave?"

Sarah was always ready to dance with Mark. "Cathy! You take over here please, and would you bring them into their room as soon as they're finished eating?"

Then Sarah went around the place turning off all the lamps. She got out matches to light dozens of candles, turned on their favorite music and rushed to push the club chair back to its place against the wall. Cathy led the boys into their room, Mark held Sarah in his arms. In the candlelight you couldn't see the many deep scratches on the bare wooden floors, or the stains on the peach velvet sofa. The smudgy hand prints on the walls faded into the flickering shadows as did several toys that still remained scattered in corners and under tables. Sarah and Mark were lost in each other and as a result arrived at the dinner party an hour and a half late. "It's not easy, when you have two small boys, to get out on time," Mark apologized to their hostess.

Sarah got pregnant again.

Neale stared at Sarah's belly, turned to me and very seriously said, "Me want baby, too."

"Yes, sweetheart, I know ... Mommy will have a baby, too, someday ... but it takes a long time and meanwhile ... Mommy has lots of fun with you!"

I BOUGHT NEALE a G.I. Joe doll with outfits. Before he went to sleep Neale put G.I. Joe into a miniature sleeping bag. In the morning he dressed Joe in one of the khaki jackets. I was always helping him search for a misplaced G.I. Joe boot or vest or knapsack. Once, while walking on Main Street, Neale discovered that Joe's new leather pouch was lost. We retraced our steps, carefully searching the sidewalk, and miraculously Neale spotted the precious pouch, clean and undisturbed. We laughed as if we had discovered gold!

Neale climbed into his car seat with the toy steering wheel and round red horn. "Dis Mommy's little blue Falcon." He called his daddy a "car man," and loved to watch him in his fast-paced stride, moving between the colorful, neat rows of a hundred gleaming cars.

Danny still dressed for work in black chinos, a hip jacket and thick-soled black shoes. There was a trailer-office for shelter but

Danny was out on the lot in every type of weather, showing cars to customers, looking over trade-ins, appraising cars. He'd call after the porter or a salesman who needed assistance. When his son arrived, however, Danny hurried over, greeted him with a swoop into the air and a hug. He showed Neale things as he went on with his work. There was hardly a moment in Danny's day to pause and rest. Constant telephone communication in the trailer regarding credit applications to banks and finance companies. Incoming cars were designated "creme puffs" or "hairy." Customers, body shops, tire shops, transmission shops. Danny was often on two phones at the same time with a third lying on the desk or in a drawer if the caller was screaming.

Soon after Neale and I arrived Danny gave detailed instructions to the salesman, "Lopez'll be in to pick up that blue '61 Chevy over there, have Pedro put gas in the tank. If Banco calls back on the Colon deal take the numbers for me, I'm going out for a bite."

Finally, we were together in the Falcon. Danny drove the few blocks to Howard Johnson's. Over fried clams on a roll and chocolate marshmallow sundaes Danny kissed me and I reached over to smooth back his hair. Neale held onto Danny's hand. The maroon plastic-covered booth became an oasis. Neale learned what it meant when I told him his Daddy was at work, working hard for Neale to have a good life. I yearned so much for love to paint my days; I felt that love colored my thoughts, and I allowed love in every way possible to fill my life with beauty.

DRESSED IN his nightshirt, robe and slippers Leo spent hours on the phone, picking the brains of men who had information he needed. From conversations with two men who once worked for him and who now owned Volvo and Saab dealerships Leo realized it was a good idea to move into the new car business. As a businessman he appreciated the credibility and recognition a new car agency would earn from banks and finance companies, plus the used car business would become more secure. Leo applied for Volvo and Saab dealerships.

Danny worked the main used car lot and a smaller lot about a mile up Bruckner Boulevard. The two lots had a combined inventory of about a hundred and fifty cars. Danny managed three salesmen at the big lot and two salesmen at the smaller one, and many months they delivered more than a hundred cars.

No one understood credit as well as Danny. Most of the time the success of the deal depended on getting credit approved for the customer. Many of Danny's customers held short-term jobs, lived with relatives and had little or no credit standing, but Danny knew which car to put the customer into by the monthly payment the customer could afford. He called this method, "working the deal backwards."

Danny knew the people who worked in the credit departments of C.I.T., Chase Manhattan Bank, Manufacturers Hanover, Banco dePonce and small loan companies such as Guardian Loan, H.F.C., Neighborhood Loan, Rapid, and Family Finance. When a loan for a down payment was required, as well as for the regular car payment, Danny took the deal to two finance companies. This kind of deal was called a "Mickey Mouse" and the small loan companies "blood banks" where the customers were taken for a "transfusion."

The most crucial aspect of the deal was in qualifying customers well enough so that their credit would be approved. Danny got hold of rent receipts, pay stubs, telephone bills, W2 Forms, anything he could, to verify employment and home address. If a customer needed a co-signer Danny took a credit statement from the prospective co-signer over the phone. He took complete financial statements from his customers. Since he knew the varying requirements of each bank and finance company, he knew where to go with each deal. When it came to financing customers no one could make a better judgment than Danny.

Because of the intense competition from Jolly Charlie, Five County Motors, and Don Q Motors, all nearby dealers in the Bronx, Danny often had to move fast for an on-the-spot delivery. In order to accomplish an on-the-spot delivery he needed to get the down payment immediately. Danny kept a handy supply of withdrawal slips from all the banks, ready for customers to sign in case as often happened, he was working on the deal after bank hours. Then Danny drove the customers to their homes to get their bankbooks. The customers signed blank contracts, which wasn't exactly in accordance with the law, but Danny always filled in the exact amount he quoted. If they didn't have license plates Danny immediately got the insurance broker to issue insurance I.D. cards and then dealer plates were issued temporarily to the customer. If the customer had a trade-in, the trade-in became the down payment. Danny delivered the car on-the-spot.

A garage was needed to service the huge volume of used cars being sold. Leo bought a garage at 766 Southern Boulevard. When the Volvo and Saab franchises were approved the garage was divided in two, a plate glass window installed in front and this became the new car showroom. The back portion was set up for service for both new cars and used cars.

A deal was struck with King Ford on Bruckner Boulevard which allowed Edmond and Leo to appraise and select a tremendous amount of first-choice trade-ins. They worked with Angelo, the manager, and bought the used cars at good prices. Edmond accompanied Leo to all the real estate meetings and new car factory meetings. A buyer was hired to relieve Edmond, whom Leo was grooming for the new car business.

Danny continued to run the used car operation which was indispensable. It was needed to finance the whole new car enterprise. It provided income for three families. Danny was twenty-four years old.

The Void

It was May when I became pregnant with our second child. I felt at last that life with Danny was unfolding as I'd dreamed it would, like the tender green curls of leaves on the maple trees outside our building, like the pink azalea buds alongside the clean, swept pathways, like the forest green bushes fuller and stronger than ever behind the low black iron fences.

I explained to Neale that a baby was growing inside my tummy. Each morning he reached up for a hug and kissed my belly. "The kisses are for my baby, Mommy, I want the baby to love me."

"Sweetheart, the baby is going to love you more than anyone."

Mike and Gloria, married about a year now, were making preparations to move to White Sands Missile Base in New Mexico. Doctors were required to serve two years in the Armed Forces and were permitted to choose the time of their inductance. Mike had completed his internship and half his residency and felt this was a good time. He and Gloria came to visit. They sat side by side on the sofa and we paused in our conversation to look at Neale as he climbed up onto Danny's lap.

"I hope I can have a little boy just like Neale," Gloria remarked, "he's so perfect."

"You and Mike will have a beautiful family, Gloria, I know you will, you'll see . . . you know, we have some news."

"Oh, really? Tell us," Mike said.

I looked at Neale and Danny, my heart was full, bursting with happiness. "We're expecting a baby in January!"

Gloria and Mike exchanged serious glances. Gloria began counting on her fingers. "That means you'll have two children before we even have one . . . you have this beautiful apartment, we'll never catch up."

"You want another baby so soon?" Mike exclaimed in a high note of surprise.

"Yes, of course, Neale is almost three, why not?"

Were they jealous? Innocently, I had assumed our joy would be theirs.

"I'm just living my life, Gloria, and I don't think of my life as a contest. While I was home with a baby you were in college having a whole different experience, an experience I'll never have."

Their blank expressions, the lack of smiles and laughter at my very happy news, were making me feel awfully uncomfortable. What was going on? I tried again to smooth over the discordant energy sweeping through my living room by shifting the focus onto their life.

"You know, I wish that Danny and I had the opportunity to be far away from home when we first married. It will be so romantic living in a little house on the base, making friends with the other officers and their wives. You'll see, it'll be good for your marriage to be on your own."

But my brother and sister-in-law had already given me the evil eye.

ON FRIDAY of Labor Day weekend, Danny took off from work and we set out with Neale for the 1964 World's Fair in Flushing Meadow. It was a sweltering day, long lines at every exhibit, but we were enjoying an amazing adventure! We began with an imaginary journey to the moon. We took a ride through a futuristic home fitted with fantastic robotics. Another exhibit depicted the harnessing of nature's energy sources from the discovery of fire all the way through human history to atomic energy. We watched the story of human communications from smoke signals to the Telestar satellite. We felt so happy! We were enjoying a real family day.

At home Neale went directly to his bed and a moment later was fast asleep. Danny and I lay down to rest awhile. Suddenly, we were covered with blood! Blood was spreading over the sheets!

"What's happening, Honey?" Danny cried out in alarm.

"I don't know ... I don't feel so good ..." Blood was running down my legs! I tried to calm myself but blood was gushing and pouring from my body. "Danny, quick! call Dr. Kappler!"

He was already dialing. He explained the situation to the doctor, then called Rose, who in a minute was in our room, taking in the scene. Danny assisted me into some clothes, trying to wipe blood from my legs with one towel after another.

"See what happens when you don't care about your baby?" Rose screamed. "You went and walked all around the World's Fair and now you have this! You don't go to the Fair when you're pregnant! Just like Rae, hanging drapes when she was pregnant, she brought on the miscarriage herself and then they had to adopt! This is all your fault!"

Inside my head an explosion, enormous clanging and ringing vibrations. The doctor never said to stay away from the Fair! He hadn't issued any warnings at all; I was a healthy young woman of twenty-two. Sobbing, I wished that Rose would stop hurling hateful remarks at me. And then, suddenly, like a ray of healing sunshine into the darkness of this terrible moment, an old movie began to play in my head: my father, young and handsome at the steering wheel of his Buick, singing that wonderful song we all so enjoyed, "Oh, dear, what can the matter be, Johnny's so long at the Fair . . ."

Neale was asleep. When he awoke Rose would tell him, in a most unkind way, that his mommy was in the hospital. While I lay helpless in a hospital bed, completely unable to comfort my child, Rose would frighten him and with her unharnessed biased attitude begin to turn my child against me as she had already been doing with Danny at every opportunity.

Danny carried me to the car and we sped off to New Rochelle Hospital. From deep within my heart I cried, Neale! Neale! my darling son! I'm so sorry all this is happening! I don't even know what's happening!

Dr. Kappler had joined Dr. Forman's practice as an associate and that year Dr. Forman retired. I lay on the hospital bed, calm in an otherworldly way, the hemorrhage had slowed to an even flow. I sensed the presence of both doctors. From somewhere above the bed I heard Dr. Forman's professional soothing voice, "You're young, you have plenty of time for more pregnancies."

But I want this pregnancy! This is a baby of mine! I want this baby! From within this otherworldly space came a solemn knowing: my baby is not going to make it into this life. Yet, my will was strong and I was determined to fight to keep my baby. I pushed the solemn knowing aside.

"We're doing all we can to save it, but you must realize, we never can be sure."

I'll do anything! Tell me what to do! Tell me! I want to save my baby!

"All we can do now is wait and see. And try to understand, Fran, every year a certain number of pregnancies end in miscarriage and we don't know why. Think of it as nature's way of eliminating unhealthy babies."

My baby unhealthy? No! My baby is fine! He looks just like Neale and he's fine! He's fine!

"We're going to keep you here a few days, so just relax now. Try to get some sleep, you need it."

I spoke to Neale on the phone. "Hi, sweetheart, Mommy had to go to the hospital because I wasn't feeling well."

"You get better, Mommy?"

"The doctor wants me to rest here a few days, sweetheart, and then I'll be home with you again."

"I love you Mommy and I miss you."

"I love you, too, darling and I miss you too. Grandma will take good care of you. She'll read you lots of stories and make you good things to eat."

I knew what my mother was like when she was nervous. I pictured her in her robe, cleaning as if the apartment needed cleaning, repeating over and over, "Oh God! What's going to happen to my Francine? Oh God!" When my father comes home from work she will cry to him, her voice will rise and my father will shout, "Calm down already!" Neale is accustomed to the peaceful environment of our home. My parents will discuss loudly and repeatedly every detail of the tragic circumstances. My mother will have the longest phone conversations with Aunt Margie and Aunt Natalie, all of this without considering that my child is right beside her, seemingly deep into his drawings at the kitchen table, yet listening intently.

How helpless I felt lying in the hospital bed, unable to comfort my child, unable even to fully understand how this pregnancy would affect the rest of my life, that the repercussions of this pregnancy would echo through all the years of my life, eventually opening my mind in the most transcendent way. How could I understand anything? I was in a state of shock, Dr. Forman had said. But the vision of my son linked me to life.

THE NEXT DAY my mother reported that Neale was sick with the flu. He missed the Labor Day festivities at day camp. I lay in my sterile private hospital room overwhelmed with sadness while my son's sweet voice rehearsing his group song arose inside my heart. His adorable lisp which would soon be gone, his wavering two-year old singing, made it all more poignant. "It's a jolly holiday with Mary..." and I cried.

On Tuesday the bleeding stopped. Wednesday I returned home, still pregnant. The following week I began to cough. It was an unusual cough in that it wrenched my stomach and shook my whole body. I had to hold my stomach and lean over. How long could a cough last? In a few days or a week it will be gone, I was sure.

We renewed the lease on our apartment and the landlord sent the painters over. What colors did I want? Keep everything white. You want your closets done, lady? No, don't bother. The odor of paint was nauseating and though it was cold outside I agreed with the painters when they opened the windows all the way. The cold in addition to the stench of the paint made me feel even more ill. With each cough I ran to the toilet expecting to vomit. The cough had an ominous sound, like a wolf devouring me.

"Honey, this is terrible, you must see a doctor, I'm taking you right now. I don't care if you never go to the doctor for a cough, you're going now." Danny wrapped a coat around my shoulders, he put his arms around me and kissed me. "Come, Honey, I'll stay with you."

WE WENT to Dr. Weissman whose office was on the ground floor. Dr. Weissman diagnosed whooping cough. A few cases were cropping up that year, he added, although not around here, he had heard New Jersey. But due to the pregnancy he couldn't prescribe the appropriate medication. Dr. Weissman gave me instead, a mild syrup which did nothing to alleviate my symptoms and I was afraid to take it anyway, it might harm the baby. Expect the cough to last another eight weeks or so, the doctor predicted, and don't be surprised if it gets worse before it gets better.

It did get worse. Each morning, doubled over at the sink, clutching my belly, I coughed uncontrollably. The coughing fits lasted for hours. At night I whooped again, that's all I did was whoop, run to the bathroom, spit and hold my belly, trying with my touch to protect my baby inside. Autumn passed. Slowly, the coughing fits lessened; I was getting better.

FIRST WEEK of November I went for a check-up with Dr. Kappler. I wasn't gaining too much weight, which pleased him, and my belly was nice, not too big. Less than three months to go. The home-stretch. Neale hugged my belly first thing every morning and throughout the day. "I'm sending kisses to my baby, Mommy." Danny and I chose the name Adam. I just knew this baby was a boy and was already looking a lot like Neale. My mind raced ahead reaching into the future with unwavering enthusiasm. With two sons I will definitely be pregnant again, to bring my daughter into the world. Somewhere the soul of my daughter waited patiently to join our family. My visions of the future comforted me and made me smile.

THE DAY AFTER the check-up my head started to ache. Unaccustomed to headaches I shrugged it off. The headaches grew in intensity and duration, forcing me to lie down, but cushioning my head on pillows did nothing to alleviate the pain. Don't be nervous, I counseled myself. You got through the bleeding, you got through whooping cough, and now you'll get through these headaches. I prayed to see my baby's face in my dreams as happened when I was pregnant with Neale, but my dreams were barren.

By the end of November the headaches had become unbearable. I awoke with a pounding headache, it stayed with me all day and into the evening and at night the pain persisted into the dark hours. On the Sunday of Thanksgiving weekend we drove out to

Long Island for a reunion with friends we'd met last summer. The intensity of the headaches heightened daily to such an acute stage it was difficult for me to do anything. And it wasn't only the headaches. I was feeling very, very ill.

"Why don't you call your doctor tomorrow," my friend Rena suggested, and the other women in our group gathered around looking at me with grave concern. "Believe me, it's not normal to have such a headache," and everyone agreed. They insisted I lie down on Rena's bed awhile but nothing helped me feel any better. We left early, right after dinner.

The next day was December first, my twenty-third birthday. My head was pounding. Pounding worse than any headache could. Unimaginable pain.

"Dr. Kappler, I've been having awful headaches."

"How long have you been having these headaches, Fran?"

"Almost a month, they started right after I saw you last."

"Look, Fran, I want you in my office as quickly as possible, can you come right over?"

THE NURSE USHERED me into an examining room and Dr. Kappler was there in a minute. He studied my face and said, "Do you know how many calls I get each day from women with headaches? But something in your voice got to me, I know you're not a complainer. Can you leave a urine specimen?"

"Dana," he turned briefly to his nurse, "work up Fran's urine immediately."

"Okay, Fran, lie down and we'll have a look." He wrapped the blood pressure cuff around my arm and pumped it up. The color drained from Dr. Kappler's face. "Let me do that again, Fran, maybe there's a mistake." He pumped the cuff again and winced. With his medical flashlight he examined my eyes. Dana came back in and whispered to him. Dr. Kappler started sweating.

"Fran, your blood pressure is dangerously high, your eye ground has changed, you have severe edema, protein in your urine, all the symptoms of acute toxemia. I want you to take Neale home, get a few things together and come right back to the hospital. I'll meet you in the emergency room in one hour, okay? Can you do it?"

I nodded, too frightened to think or ask questions. When we arrived home I took Neale in my arms and sat him on my lap. I explained that I had to go to the hospital again and he would be with Grandma and Grandpa. I hugged him and kissed him, and felt a surge of love passing from my open mother-heart directly into the heart of my child. In that moment it felt like we were one heart. "I love you, my sweet, sweet boy." My poor nervous mother, unusually silent, or maybe I just didn't hear her, was gathering up some of Neale's clothes to bring over to her place.

I called Danny. "I'm very sick, Danny, I have to go to the hospital."

"I'm leaving right now, Honey, wait for me."

My mother took Neale's hand. She was crying. Thanks, Mom, I love you so much, what would I do without you?

I stood by the door and watched my boy walk down the hall. My heart was breaking. He held onto my mother's hand. With her other hand my mother carried Neale's clothes in a large Macy's shopping bag. Neale was carrying G.I.Joe.

Danny came home. "What is it, Honey? What's the matter?"

"I have acute toxemia, Danny, my blood pressure is 210 over 130. That's why I've been having headaches." Danny's eyes filled with tears and he kissed my cheek. "We have to leave right now, Danny."

As Danny drove to the hospital I explained the little I knew about toxemia. I didn't know how close I was to convulsions or coma. I didn't know that my life was in danger. I didn't know toxemia could bring on labor and that the life of my baby was in danger. I thought I was going to the hospital so that Dr. Kappler could cure my illness. I didn't know that in a few hours my life would be changed forever.

My roommate in the hospital was a woman fifteen or twenty years older than me, a mother of five who had just had a miscarriage. She told her relatives and friends about it over the phone. Her last line was always the same and so I heard her repeat it over and over again; and each time, even though her life circumstance was very different from mine, it hurt my heart to hear it. "I'm so relieved," my roommate said, "the last thing I needed was another kid."

I stared straight ahead at the square of gray winter light framed by the window directly opposite my bed. Neale must be sitting at my mother's kitchen table now, playing, while my mother prepares dinner, talking to herself, crying over me.

I'm sorry, Neale darling, for disrupting your life. I'm sorry, Mom, to put you through all this. And Danny . . . I'm so sorry, Danny. I wish this wasn't happening. I wish I was home, getting Neale ready for his bath, preparing the ground beef for hamburgers, deciding how much onion to chop and trying to slice the tomato into perfectly even slices.

Suddenly, a great pain sweeps through my body! I cry out! Instantly, Dr. Kappler and a team of doctors and nurses surround my bed. "This is what we were waiting for, Fran," Dr. Kappler says. "I was hoping nature would take its course and save me the job of making a decision." He issues directives. Fire courses through my veins. My whole body is enveloped in flames! I'm on fire, I'm burning! I hear myself crying out, Oh! it's hot! it's so hot!

"You're a lucky girl, Fran," Dr. Kappler speaks again, measuring his words as he goes about the task of saving my life. "If you had been anywhere else, say, walking down the street, right now, when labor started, you'd be a dead girl. You'd never have made it to the hospital in time. The poisons would have shot right through your bloodstream and killed you."

Somewhere in my mind I understand, it's the poisons shooting through my bloodstream that feel like flames inside my body! I'm losing myself in a fog of fear, struggling to remain alert, determined to hear every word the doctor says and to remember every word.

"Yes, lucky for you, Fran, I told you to come in this afternoon. There was something in your voice . . . now we can save you."

What's happening to me? Did he say labor? But it's too early, seven weeks too early . . . I don't feel labor, I just feel sick . . . very, very sick . . . am I dying? he said, 'dead girl' . . . dead girl . . . dead girl . . . it's echoing in my mind . . . suddenly that beam of blue light is also in my mind . . . I was seventeen . . . I remember . . . walking up Fifth Avenue to Temple Emanuel on a Friday evening in the summer . . . a blue light had come down from heaven . . . and then I knew I was going to die young . . . but I'm not ready to die! I don't want to die! Neale needs me . . . who will love him, care for him, watch over him, like I do! Danny! Our life together . . . I don't want to lose it! Everyone's voices are fading away, I'm leaving them behind . . . moving so fast . . . toward the light . . . enveloped in light . . . so soothing, calming . . . I surrender and the light embraces me . . . fully and completely . . . the light is love! the light is God! Everything is God . . . God and love!

SUDDENLY, everything is fraught with difficulty and fear again.

"The baby is coming!" a nurse calls out.

A flurry of activity, they're moving me . . .

Oh! there's Danny! and Mom! they're standing by the wall, looking at me and crying! wait! stop! I want to touch them . . . feel Danny's hand . . . my mother, her face is so sad I must comfort her . . . oh, the look in her eyes . . . if I can touch Danny and Mom, hold their hands, I'll know I'm still alive! Suddenly, I know! I'm back from the Light . . . about to give birth . . . and my baby isn't going to live . . . I hear myself screaming, No! No! I promised Neale!

What did she promise Neale? everyone hearing my screams is surely wondering.

I promised Neale a baby! And now my baby is being born seven weeks early! While immersed in the Light I was told, my baby won't be able to breathe on his own!

It feels late, usually I can gauge quite accurately the passage of time, but now I'm drifting outside of time . . .

"FRAN? FRAN? Can you hear me? Open your eyes, Fran . . . listen, Dr. Forman's here . . . I called him in . . . we're concerned about you, Fran . . . hold on, Fran . . . stay with us . . . open your eyes, Fran . . . listen, we think the baby has a better chance if we don't use anesthetic . . . so far we haven't given you any anesthetic . . . Fran, do you hear me? We can't give you anything if we want this baby to make it . . . we need your approval . . . is it okay with you, Fran? Once we get this baby out you'll be fine! Will you fight with us? Fran! We need you awake! Open your eyes!"

Oh! My baby has a chance, he says. My baby has a chance! I nod, with all my strength I nod, yes . . . anything! I'll do anything to save my baby! I can do it! I can . . . I will!

I'M BEING MOVED AGAIN. This must be the delivery room. I'm on the table, they're spreading my legs, telling me to push . . . I'm trying . . . I haven't any strength! Push! Push! Someone keeps insisting. Oh, God! I'm pushing as hard as I can . . . I can't anymore . . . I'm dying . . . there's no strength left in me . . . the poison has taken hold . . . I'm dying! Oh, dear God! this is what it feels like . . . no strength to even breathe . . . I'm fading . . .

"C'mon, Fran! One more push! Let's have another good push! Stay with us, Fran! Stay with us!"

I'm done . . . no more . . .

Oh! I hear a sound . . . a baby is crying! My baby! A pathetic cry . . . a kitten mewing.

"Here he is, Fran, here's your son." Someone lifts my head. It's the anesthesiologist. "I haven't anything else to do, I may as well help you see your baby."

I see him! He's very small . . . but he does look like Neale . . . and he's alive! Oh, thank you God! My baby is alive!"

Want to hold him, mother? someone asks.

Too tired, I gasp, later, I'll hold my son later . . .

THE ROOM IS DARK, silent, a blank wall immediately to my left. I turn my head. Danny is lying on a cot a little to the front and right of me. What are we doing here? How long have we been here?

A young doctor is leaning over me. "Fran? I'm sorry to tell you," the doctor pauses a moment, "your baby has just died. Hyaline Membrane Disease, insufficient lung capacity."

I turn my face back toward the blank wall. The Light already told me.

Several days later I overhear Dr. Kappler explaining to someone, "She's had a very rare type of acute toxemia. It occurs in only one-half of one percent of all toxemia patients. When she goes home I don't want anyone to bother her. Someone is calling my office, keeps asking about the baby, someone named Rose? Please keep that woman away from Francine. She's still in shock and she needs peace and quiet."

I SIT in the club chair. It's a cloudy day but who wants to bother with lights? I like it dreary and dismal like this. Perfect. Neale is downstairs at Sarah's. Thank God for a good friend like Sarah, she invites Neale to play just about every day now. I want only rest. And to gaze across the living-room at the living-room drapes. The way they hang in dark folds even though they are light beige is very interesting. The apartment is cleaner now than ever. I vacuum the carpet every day in order to eliminate all those footprints everybody makes. I never noticed all those footprints. But now I do. And I don't know how I ever got away with dusting only once a week, anyone who looks hard enough can see the accumulated dust on the furniture. Who cares if it takes me longer to apply makeup and fix my hair, I'm just more diligent than I used to be, I am requiring perfection of myself. And throwing away everything in my closet felt liberating. Everything is different than it was before. Nothing will ever be the same again.

I stare across the room at the drapery. I've let everyone down. I was responsible for having the baby and I failed. I must find a way to make it up to Danny and Neale. I must be a perfect wife, a perfect mother, a perfect housekeeper. But however hard I try I cannot undo the tragedy. During the day I'm composed. No one will ever see me cry.

But late at night I cry . . . endless tears.

"It's so cold outside, Danny, my baby is under the ground, so cold, do you think they wrapped him in a warm blanket? I hope he's in a warm blanket . . . I wish I'd seen him before he was buried . . . I never even got to hold him . . . I should have held him when I had the chance . . . but I was so tired . . . take me, Danny, I want to see his grave."

"Shh, don't cry anymore, Honey, I love you, please stop crying. You have me and you have Neale."

"I want to go to his grave, Danny."

"No, Honey, it'll be too much for you, I can't."

"But I want to go, Danny. A baby should be warm, in his mother's arms, not cold, under the ground."

"Honey, please, you scare me when you talk like that. C'mon, Honey, I love you, please don't talk like that, don't do this to yourself."

During the first week when Neale came to hug me in the morning, he'd wrap his arms around my waist and, looking up at me, ask in a voice too somber for a little boy, "What happened to my baby, Mommy?"

Immediately, my eyes filled with tears, but I knew it was

important for Neale to understand as much as he could. "Our baby wasn't strong enough, sweetheart, to live in this world."

Neale searched my face with his beautiful serious eyes. "Am I strong Mommy?"

"Oh, yes, my darling, you are very strong. Come, let's look at your baby pictures, let's see those little fists you had and the strong body you were born with!"

"But why, Mommy, why wasn't my baby strong like me?"

"Well, sweetheart, Mommy got sick. Remember when I was coughing a lot? A mommy has to be healthy to have a strong and well baby." In my mind, while I struggled, unprepared to answer my son's questions in such a way as to comfort him in just the right way, I hoped my responses were the best responses, but I worried that they weren't. "Neale, darling, I also wish our baby could be here now just like you do."

"Do you think he knew when I sent him kisses?"

"Neale, my sweet boy, while our baby was growing inside Mommy's tummy, he was very, very happy whenever you sent him kisses and whenever he heard you saying sweet things to him. And Neale ... it matters very much that you loved him when he was inside my tummy because that's the kind of boy you are and the kind of man you'll grow up to be ... loving and caring."

Neale hugged me. "You are a wonderful son, my darling, and I love you with all my heart."

MY FRIEND BARBARA CALLED. "When you were in the hospital," she said, "I called to find out how you were feeling and your mother-in-law answered and all she could do was cry over the baby. I kept saying, "But how's Francine?" but she wouldn't say anything except, 'the baby is dead.'"

In the kind voice he reserved for me my father said, "You know, Fran, my mother died when I was only two and losing her destroyed my life. You wouldn't want that for Neale, would you?

Believe me, sweetheart, it's better this way ... better for you to live, Fran ... if we had lost you ..."

My father's eyes filled with tears. I kissed his cheek and nodded.

My mother just looked at me and cried.

Aunt Margie called and Aunt Natalie, too. They told me they loved me and cried over the phone. My young cousins, except for Mitch who was still in Viet Nam, eventually summoned the courage to call.

My brother could have flown home from New Mexico as a guest of the United States Army and I hoped he would. Instead, he also made a phone call. He was sorry about the baby but the important thing was, he said, that I had come through it okay.

If you were here, if you could look into my eyes, you'd see that I'm not okay. Apparently, it was easier for him to believe I was okay, that it was unnecessary for him to comfort me when every day I was struggling not to fall apart.

My friend Diane had fallen in love with an Israeli, Chaggai was his name, and she was preparing to leave for Israel. "Oh, Francine, I'll never forget those afternoons we've shared, playing with Neale in his sunny room, solving all our problems over cocoa in your pretty white and aqua kitchen."

"And sitting in your mother's herb-scented garden. Oh, Diane, I'm going to miss you so much! You've been a wonderful friend!"

Ordinary memories suddenly bittersweet. We embraced and promised to write. Like every close friendship since my beautiful friend Lana moved away from Vyse Avenue so long ago, Diane was now moving far away.

EVERY DAY I heard Doris out in the hall, going into Rose's apartment for lunch, but she didn't walk the few additional steps to come and sit with me awhile. She had visited me in the hospital, all done up, unable to say anything warm or comforting, and even when the nurse who was in the room with us intervened and said, "You can't imagine what this girl has just gone through," Doris only said, "Mmm."

The Sachlebens and the Steinbergs were silent. Since Labor Day, Rose had spread the word that by going to the World's Fair I had brought disaster upon myself. Everyone believed whatever they heard and no one from Danny's family offered sympathy.

My father-in-law had a cousin who owned a funeral parlor so the arrangements were made with a phone call. No one from the family witnessed the lowering of the tiny casket. No one saw the tombstone. Everyone was ready to forget. Everyone except me.

And when at last my crying stopped it stopped for everything. Grandma had died on my birthday and now Adam, my infant son. I had come so close to dying on my birthday. I'll watch others enjoy birthday celebrations, I decided, but mine will be a day of mourning.

On a snowy day in January I dialed Sherry's number in Poughkeepsie. "I'm very insulted that you didn't call me right away," she responded when she heard my voice. "I had to find out from Elaine."

"Sherry, please try to understand, I didn't call anyone. Danny made the phone calls and he must have asked Elaine to call you."

"Well, I can't help feeling insulted. You were my best friend, not Elaine, and you should have called me."

"Sherry, please, my judgment would definitely have been to call you before Elaine, but Danny doesn't know this stuff, please, you must understand how difficult all this has been for me."

"I'm sorry, Fran, that's no way to treat a friend."

"Sherry, I can't believe you're saying this to me ... not you! I need a good friend now, someone who really knows me. Remember when you needed a friend, when you had your back surgery? I was there for you."

"This is different! You didn't call and I'm not forgetting it!"

"Sherry! Remember when we signed each other's yearbooks and then we saw we had written the identical message? Remember what it was, Sherry? It was about our friendship lasting forever."

I couldn't take any more. I poured a cup of coffee and sat at the kitchen table flipping through a copy of Good Housekeeping trying to focus on one article. All I could see was myself at sixteen, carrying the daily assignments to Sherry's house after school, sitting on her sunny rumpled bed, dictating Mrs. Greenberg's business letters of the day so Sherry could maintain her shorthand speed, keeping her up to date with school gossip.

IN FEBRUARY I started coughing again. My head ached and I felt feverish. My lips could barely form a whisper. Danny called Dr. Weissman who came up, sat on the edge of my bed and spoke very gently to me. "You're very sick, Fran. I'm taking a culture to be certain but it looks like a serious case of strepp throat. You belong in the hospital."

Slowly I moved to protest but all I could do was whisper, 'no.'

"I know what you've been through. You're a very brave girl, my dear, all of New Rochelle is saying it. I understand that you'd prefer not to go back to the hospital . . . if you can arrange to have your mother take care of Neale I'll allow you to stay home . . . but you must promise to take your medication and stay in bed."

Very slowly, I recovered. The winter of 1964 was over.

IN EARLY May I became pregnant again. Dr. Kappler assured me that all was proceeding well and I felt healthy, until September when I began to feel something was wrong. And then one morning I awoke to find the sheets stained with blood. Dr. Kappler was not alarmed and advised a few days of bed rest. But the next afternoon I felt a sudden onset of extreme weakness followed by an ominous stirring in my womb. Immediately, I feared more blood.

I didn't want to stain the bed or the carpet so I hurried to the bathroom a few steps away. I looked down and saw a flat, round blood clot the size of my hand.

Suddenly I felt enclosed once more in tight world of fear. I needed to reach the white princess phone on the bedside table but another clot, as large as the one before, came sliding silently, cruelly, out of my body. Then another clot and another and another. Never had I known such fear as engulfed me then. Fear with an aching heart of sorrow, fear which bore knowledge of imminent tragedy. The clots let up momentarily, and I rushed, shaking, to the phone. Dr. Kappler's service answered.

"It's an emergency!" I cried, "please get him for me!" I lay down, trying to calm myself. Oh! Another clot sliding out of me! I rushed back to the bathroom. A terrifying mass of clots came tumbling out of my body! I couldn't count them, and each one was large and round and flat. My belly didn't seem big enough to have contained so many clots. And then I felt a sharper pain accompanied by an even larger clot. Chills spread from my scalp all the way to my feet... oh, my God, what is happening to me?

At last Dr. Kappler returned my call. "You sound hysterical, Fran. Now first, calm down!" he shouted, and continued in a loud, stern voice, "You're pulling me out of the operating room! Just lie down and try to calm down! You've had some spotting, just relax and stay calm. I lay back against the pillows. Calm, stay calm. Then the blood started flowing. The pads soaked in a minute. I went through a box of pads. I grabbed the phone. "Please get Dr. Kappler for me! Please! Tell him I'm hemorrhaging!" I dialed my mother, then remembered my parents were away for the weekend. I dialed Rose, "Mom, I need you! Please hurry! I'm hemorrhaging!" Rose came running in. "Mom, please take Neale down to Sarah's for me!"

Dr. Kappler finally returned my call and told me to meet him at the hospital. Rose hurried back from Sarah's to help me. She called for a taxi. She helped me into a loose dress and half carried me down the hall, into the elevator and through the lobby doorway into the sun-soaked peak of a September day, past startled neighbors, into the waiting taxi.

"Why did your mother have to go away when she knew you weren't feeling good?" Rose repeated all the way to the hospital. I had left a trail of blood behind me, and a pool of blood was forming in the taxi. The driver turned around in his seat, took in the scene with eyes that already saw what he thought was everything, "Jesus, Mary and Joseph . . . why in my cab?"

Blood continued running down my legs until at last I was lying in a hospital bed. A nurse provided giant-sized pads.

"Tell Dr. Kappler I'm in terrible pain," I pleaded.

"He knows, dear, he knows."

"Where is he then? Why doesn't he do something to help me?"

"Just rest, dear, Dr. Kappler wants you to rest."

The night shift came on. The pain grew even more intense. The bleeding stopped. Then I felt a sudden wetness. I pulled back the covers and saw that my water had broken. Frantic, I called for the nurse. "Look! I think my water broke! I'm four-and-a half-months pregnant! Why can't Dr. Kappler help me?"

"There's nothing he can do, dear, he'll be here in the morning."

In a few hours everything came out. Dr. Kappler arrived in the morning and performed a dilation and curettage.

Once again I began to have headaches. Terrible ceaseless headaches. I made an appointment with Dr. Fisher at N.Y.U. He took my medical history.

"You know you're a very courageous young woman. You've been through a lot but no one would know it to look at you. I'm going to help you as best I can."

Here was another doctor talking about my courage. I didn't understand what it was that was so courageous about me. I was just trying to have a family so Neale wouldn't be an only child.

I was holding onto my dream and trying to make it come true: a happy house filled with love and the laughter and joyfulness of children.

After taking my blood pressure he said, "Let me do this once more, just to be sure." My pressure registered 200 over 105. "The first thing we have to do is get your pressure down, and that means a few days in the hospital. Also, while you're there I'd like to check out your kidneys and so on, you know toxemia sometimes creates various problems."

I stayed at N.Y.U. Medical Center for five days. Dr. Fisher stopped by on his rounds but instead of hurrying off he sat with me and we talked.

"What is it that bothers you so, Fran?"

I explained my desire for another baby, the sadness and guilt I felt for the constant disruption in my son's life caused by my illness.

"Okay, I understand that, but I'm detecting something deeper that seems to be disturbing you. And knowing what that is may assist me in treating you successfully."

I was in the care of a true disciple of Hippocrates so I began to speak of things which I had never shared with anyone. "Well, I believe more than anything in love and harmony ... I try so hard ... but Danny ... well, he makes everything so difficult ..."

In a gesture of kindness and seeking to offer comfort as my voice was breaking, Dr. Fisher took my hand in his. "Like what, my dear?"

"Oh, Dr. Fisher, I'm worried that my husband doesn't really love me ... and that he's deceiving me ... it's so hard to say all this ..."

"Well, now you're with your private physician and you can trust me to keep your confidence ... I will help you, my dear."

"Well, for example, I'm in the supermarket with Danny's mother and she's asking me why I'm buying so few groceries, why don't I stock up, so I told her all I have is $25. She was so surprised so I explained that he makes $50 a week and gives me half. What half? Danny makes $100 a week. She knows because it's a family business and she's the bookkeeper. So as soon as he came home that night I confronted him. He looks at me like nothing's wrong and says, "Yeah, sorry Honey, I lied ... you have everything you need ... and you have more with me than you had with your parents ... and I need the money for the racetrack."

I needed to pause to keep myself calm, otherwise I was going to descend into tears just remembering the overwhelming frustration of explaining ethical behavior to Danny.

Dr. Fisher touched my arm lightly, "Go on Francine, how did you handle this?"

"Well, I tried to explain to Danny about trust in a marriage. I asked him if he was worried that he couldn't trust me with money and pointed out that I am completely trustworthy, I'm very careful with money. So, it turned into me becoming defensive and then he became defensive and shouted that I didn't know anything about money, he did, so he has to be in charge. I went to take his hand and get both of us calm but he pushed me ... I fell against the doorknob, right here, and hurt my back. It was just terrible ... terrible."

Suddenly, all this was pouring out of me, the gateway to the sorrows of my heart had opened wide. "And his mother right next door, monitoring every minute of my life, yelling at me all the time, criticizing me for everything right in front of my son. Oh, Dr. Fisher, I used to be a very independent girl! And healthy!"

Dr. Fisher took out his notepad. "I'm giving you the name of an excellent marriage counselor. Call him, my dear, he may be able to help you."

I took the slip of paper into my hand but even as I thanked the doctor I knew Danny would never go and never pay for me to go. The kind physician went on to complete his morning rounds.

Alone, praying for my blood pressure to recede to normal, I gathered up all the sadness I had just strewn about, like petals torn from a blood-red rose, and buried each one in that dark corner of the heart reserved for betrayals and loss and the tears you don't want others to see. I locked the fragile petals in, even deeper than before. Go on with your pretense, I counseled myself. Allow everyone to go on believing that everything was wonderful, Francine just had pregnancy problems. Concentrate on all the good things, the blessings in your life . . . smile, laugh, remain optimistic. Danny needs so much love, see only the best in him. There really was nothing else to do . . . my parents, Danny's parents . . . they maintained a major presence in our lives. Divorce was perceived as a shameful blot, a curse even, on all the family.

And Neale so needed a father. I knew my husband would never be the father my son needed if we lived apart. And if Danny agreed to any sort of generous financial support, which was unlikely, Rose and Leo would swiftly dissuade him. Arguments would consume my life and already my health was compromised. Better for us all, I decided, if I went on loving Danny, overlooking his flaws, after all no one was perfect. I would use all the power of my soul to overcome negativity, to create harmony and a loving home. I knew how to do it. I could do it! And I would!

After five days of monitored bed rest my pressure had come down to near-enough normal to go home. Dr. Fisher gave me a prescription and instructed me to rest whenever possible.

DR. NOLAND, my new obstetrician, referred by Dr. Fisher, was young and I liked his kind face. After the physical exam I sat with Danny in the doctor's office to receive prognosis.

"Anatomically," Dr. Noland said, "there's no reason why you can't have another baby. What happened to you is unfortunate and tragic but they were accidents of nature, not because there's anything wrong with you. My advice is to wait a few months, rest, get stronger and by May you can try again."

And sure enough, in May I became pregnant again. At the end

of June, two days after Dr. Noland confirmed the pregnancy, I started getting cramps. The following day I started to bleed.

"Stay in bed, Fran," Dr. Noland advised.

I stayed in bed. The bleeding increased. "I'm losing it, Dr. Noland!" I cried into the phone.

"Alright, Fran, listen, have Danny drive you down, take some things, you may have to stay."

By the time we reached Dr. Noland's office I was hemorrhaging. I stayed in the hospital for another D&C.

IN JULY we returned for a checkup.

"Okay," Dr. Noland said, "you had another miscarriage. But I think I understand what's going on here now. I shouldn't have given you an internal exam." He looked earnestly into my eyes and I admired him for his honesty. "I stand by everything I've already told you," he continued. "You can have another baby, this I promise you, but," and now he enunciated each word slowly and emphatically, "are you willing to do everything I say?"

"Anything . . . just help me have another baby."

"And you, Danny? How about you? Are you prepared to make sacrifices to have another baby?"

"My wife has been through a lot and she's the one who has to go through another pregnancy. I'll do anything to help her, anything you say." Danny squeezed my hand.

"Okay, then," Dr. Noland's smile was sincere. "We're a team! This is it. Relax over the summer, go away, take a vacation. In the Fall you can try again. When you get pregnant you will stay in bed. Total bed rest. You will go nowhere and do nothing. The only time you will leave your house is to come here for checkups and hormone shots. In the beginning every two weeks and later, once a month. You will have no intercourse, none, for the duration of the pregnancy." He looked at Danny. Danny nodded and squeezed my hand again. "Are you both in agreement? This won't be easy, you're both very young. How old are you again?" he asked, reaching for my folder.

"Danny just turned twenty-seven and I'm twenty-four."

"Well, you're a beautiful couple and I guarantee you'll have the family you want." Dr. Noland smiled, rose from his chair, and we shook hands across his desk.

I felt completely joyful and filled with renewed hope. My baby is waiting! The soul of my daughter is calling, Mother! Mother! I'm here beside you, waiting! Now my baby's spirit is soaring and waltzing with mine! I am finding a way to bring her into the world!

Outside by the elevators Danny said, "Let's have lunch in the city, Honey, before we go home."

THE ATMOSPHERE around us was charged, I could feel the current running through me, we now shared a sacred goal, and Danny was being called on to step into a higher way of being in his role as husband. Away from the daily influence of Rose and Leo, the anxiety of used car deals on the lot, his mind was free to focus on my well-being, on us as a couple. I felt sure on that day that Danny truly loved me.

With all the exuberance of the moment I answered him, "I love you, Danny!"

"I love you, too, Honey and I'm happy I married you." He held me in his arms and kissed me so sweetly I was reminded of other kisses in a different life when I'd imagined, you just got married and then had children, like everyone did.

"I'm sorry, Danny, to put you through all this."

"No, Honey, don't talk that way. We're in this together, I'll take care of you, I promise."

In October I was pregnant again. My mother left her job. "I'll go back to work after you have your baby," she decided. "Meanwhile, you'll need me. I'll go shopping for you and help with Neale."

Rose said, "We'll order a hospital bed for you, it can go right here, next to your bed."

"I don't need a hospital bed! And I'm not getting one!" She argued and tried to convince Danny.

"Mom, Francine doesn't need a hospital bed. She doesn't have a contagious disease, she's just pregnant."

The longest nine months of my life had begun.

I SET UP the living room sofa with pillows and a blanket and moved the cocktail table close to the sofa. A half-hour in the morning to shower and straighten up the apartment, a few minutes every few hours to move about. All the rest of the day on the sofa.

What can you do to fill the hours of the day when you're not supposed to move? How can you keep your life in balance when the living room sofa becomes your cage, when a walk to the kitchen to prepare a quick meal turns your heart cold with fear that a spot of blood will appear, that the slightest activity might trigger the end of another tiny life.

I focused on my love for Neale and Danny, for my parents, the family, everyone I knew, the Earth, the universe, my love for life, for God.

Lying on the sofa, contemplating the life I had so far created for myself, I determined to put all the sadness behind me, to let go of a family legacy of all kinds of suffering. I decided to let go of it all, to create at last the life I always dreamed of, a cheerful house filled with love and kindness. I believed it was possible to create a beautiful life. I focused on the present. I sent my thoughts up to Heaven and prayed that God, or the Angels, would hear me. "Help me!" I prayed every day, "I cannot do it alone! I need your help!"

Lying on the sofa my concept of time changed. Mornings drifted into afternoons which drifted into evenings. Days drifted into other days, all the same. Years were passing. The six years between Neale and this baby will be greater than I could have imagined when Danny and I set out on our honeymoon to begin our family. A house filled with children, that's what we talked about. Now, please, God, let me have just two.

When Neale played alone in his room, or when he came home from afternoon kindergarten and saw that I was always on the sofa, he patted my belly and kissed me. He went by himself down to Sarah's and on nice days, outside to play. In the mornings my mother took him for walks to the supermarket or to Main Street. On Sunday mornings Danny took Neale along to play basketball. One time Rose and Doris took him to a movie with Elliot and Laura. Mike and Gloria came home from New Mexico with Andrew, their one-year-old son, and moved into an apartment identical to ours in Terrace on the Sound. Twice, they took Neale to the zoo with Andrew.

Every time I watched my adorable son leave while I remained on the sofa I felt searing emotional pain for I'd never have this time with him again. I was missing out on irreplaceable moments with my child and my heart cried.

My hours of solitude collected and gathered, and built a mountain of empathy for any type of life which unfolded inside a cage. Empathy especially for the physically impaired.

I gazed out the window. People walked to their cars, or down the hill. Children played. The world went on turning and I wasn't part of it.

As I entered the second trimester of pregnancy Dr. Noland prescribed Phenobarbital three times a day for the prevention of toxemia. Not many worries invaded my mind during the months I took Phenobarbital, but on days when Neale was outside playing, I walked slowly, carefully, down the hall to the single narrow window that overlooked the playground. I hoped that Neale was playing within the boundaries of the view from the window. Sometimes he was, and from the dark shadows of the hallway, I blew him a kiss.

Once, while I was watching from the hallway window, I saw

Neale sitting on a bench with four or five other boys. He sat on one end and the boy next to him pushed him off. C'mon, Neale, I whispered, get back up there! Neale got up from the concrete and sat back on the bench. The boy was older and bigger than Neale, and he pushed him off again. C'mon, sweetheart, don't let him bully you! Neale wiped his hands on his jeans and got back on the bench. The older boy insisted on pushing him off again, the other boys looking on, and Neale kept regaining his piece of territory on the bench. When finally the older boy grew weary of pushing and the other boys included Neale in their conversation I whispered my cheer, Hooray for you, my son! Slowly, mustering all my inner strength, I walked back to my sofa-cage.

SEVERAL TIMES during the course of the long day I lay down my book, clasped my hands over my belly, closed my eyes and prayed. Please keep growing, my baby, please keep growing, please wait for June to be born ... I petted my belly, caressed it ... I love you, baby, I love you ... This was definitely a daughter growing inside me, a gentle, darling daughter. Her movements were never abrupt. I felt her slowly stretch and yawn ... stretch and grow, my baby, rest with me and grow!

The hours and days and months drifted on. My right foot and calf swelled. I felt the pain even lying on the sofa. At the fifth month checkup I called Dr. Noland's attention to my foot and calf. There were bulging blue lines and red splotches on my swollen foot.

"After you leave here go down the hall to see Dr. Imperato. He's a vascular specialist and he'll know better how to advise you regarding your leg."

DR. IMPERATO'S large corner office had two long walls of wide, sunny windows. In the glare of blinding sunlight and a high beam above the examining table my foot appeared hideous. The doctor's expert fingers touched my calf, followed the lines of pain to my foot. "Considering your condition there's really nothing I can do for you, aside from giving you advice and checking on your leg whenever you visit Dr. Noland." He paused, "How many pregnancies have you had?"

"This is my fifth."

"What are you trying to do, start your own baseball team?" My eyes filled with tears. The only thing that could make me cry was trying to explain my medical history to doctors. They never got it straight the first time.

"Well, let me tell you, this will be your last pregnancy. Unless you wish to spend the next one in a hospital."

I tried to avoid the sight of my blue-lined pink foot. I wanted to say, So, Doctor, tell me what to do and let me remove my foot from the glare of this harsh light. Let me run from this office where I'm hearing things I don't want to hear. But my voice was lost in swallowed tears. Why does he have to be so harsh? But Dr. Imperato was an expert, highly respected in his field of vascular surgery, and I needed an expert.

"You must keep your legs elevated higher than your heart . . . can you do that?"

I visualized the sofa. I could pile the thick sofa pillows under my legs. What a position to lie in! What a sight for Neale and Danny!

". . . and stay that way!" Dr. Imperato emphasized in his direct manner to which I was quickly growing accustomed.

During the course of this initial visit with Dr. Imperato I began to realize that my doctor had witnessed and had been deeply affected by much suffering among his patients. It seemed entirely possible that much pain and suffering could be prevented by following common sense guidelines. This idea appealed to me. It opened my awareness, it redirected my thinking, and I never forgot this most wise lesson from my brilliant doctor. I applied the idea instantly to my own life. Of course, it required thinking ahead, an extra task many people didn't bother with. But thinking ahead suited me just fine. My mind was always racing ahead, providing visions of the future. From now on I would discipline my mind to take advantage of its future-oriented focus. I would make precautionary and preventive measures part of my everyday life. As much as possible.

"I've been taking an hour a day to care for my son, divided into brief periods . . . following Dr. Noland's instructions."

"Not anymore! From now on you can shower and so on, maybe fifteen minutes of walking around the house in the evening, and that's that! You must take care of your leg."

ROSE WILL HAVE TO cook for Danny, was my first thought. He complained about my cooking anyway, whether it was steak for dinner or eggs for breakfast, I could never get it right for him. Before this pregnancy I prepared a nice breakfast for Danny, but he'd leave as soon as he finished and go next door into Rose's apartment. Then later while wiping my hands from washing the dishes I'd hear him out in the hall saying goodbye to Rose and Leo. I always wished he'd walk back to see me again even for just a few seconds. It would be romantic. We might smile, feel warm inside and speak lovingly to each other. Those few moments would help create a happy day. Okay, Francine, that's enough daydreaming. Focus on the present. Neale and I will be eating very plain meals. My mother, in addition to the marketing will put the groceries away as well. And Neale will take his own bath. We can keep the bathroom door open a little and I'll be able to hear him from my sofa-cage.

I HAD DEVELOPED thrombophlebitis in my right leg, which meant that a superficial vein had first become inflamed, then a blood clot, or thrombus, had formed within the inflamed vein, interfering with the flow of blood to my heart. My case was unusual because I had not had varicose veins, a common prelude to thrombophlebitis.

What happened next made my case even more unusual. The deep veins of my leg became involved in the inflammatory process and clots formed within them. Deep vein involvement is the most serious of the inflammatory venous conditions of the leg veins.

Even the few moments of moving around the apartment was a painful ordeal. I limped badly. My leg swelled horribly, stretching the skin thinner and thinner until my leg no longer looked like a leg. The blood vessels and capillaries in my foot began to break down. My foot turned purple. Even so, every day that passed was a blessed day, my baby continued to grow safe within my womb.

The fear of toxemia was soon replaced by the fear of a pulmonary embolus, or blood clot to the lung. I lay on the sofa, legs elevated on three sofa pillows. Carefully, I wrapped my leg in an ace bandage as Dr. Imperato had taught me. Touching my leg, even gently, was extremely painful. Relentlessly, my leg throbbed and throbbed. My leg will return to normal, it must, after the baby is born my leg will return to normal.

My belly grew rounder and I embraced it tenderly. Keep growing, baby, it's all right, you just keep growing, you need to be strong to survive in this world. Now and then a tear escaped. My baby mustn't feel me cry! I brushed the tear away and bit my wrist to shift the focus of my thoughts.

In the morning, on her way to errands on Main Street my mother stopped by to visit. In the afternoon she stopped by again and brought me whatever I needed. My mother walked Neale to school and met him there at three o'clock. My father came over every Saturday morning. On Wednesday evenings I heard Doris walk down the hall to my neighbor Marsha or to Rose, for their weekly game of mahjong. Sometimes she arrived with the other women and I heard their voices echoing loudly in the hall, laughing and chattering.

THE SEASON OF SPRING arrived. I kept the windows and terrace door open wide, listened to children's voices and the click of their mothers' shoes on the pavement as they walked to their cars. Car doors slammed shut, motors turned over, and off they drove. Planes flew overhead, dogs barked, a mother called her child. And then as evening approached I heard the cars returning to the parking lot. Soon, the women would be in their kitchens, mixing and chopping, preheating their ovens, phoning each other with plans for tomorrow.

Dinner for Neale and me was pan-fried hamburgers and Birds Eye quick-frozen vegetables. Friday nights I roasted a chicken.

I recalled the elegant dinner parties I used to have and my careful attention to setting a beautiful table with an embroidered linen tablecloth, fine china, Orrefors crystal goblets and sterling silver flatware. Will I do those things again?

In early May Dr. Noland said, "At this point, Fran, if it weren't for your leg I'd say you could go outside and walk a bit." He paused and took my hand in his. "Look, why not pick a night, one night a week, and go out with Danny to a nice restaurant. I don't see why you shouldn't be able to do that. Just go where you can keep your leg elevated."

Danny suggested we go to the Washington Arms in Larchmont. When we first met Danny had sent me a postcard from the Washington Arms where he went one Sunday with his parents. I could still recall the thrill of receiving the card and reading Danny's message. "This is a nice place, Honey. I'll have to take you here sometime."

And then, during the summer of 1960 my parents made our engagement party at the Washington Arms. We had a beautiful private room, an enclosed terrace actually, with a long curved wall of a hundred white-framed windowpanes, and outside, towering oak and pine trees. I wore an aqua and white checked cotton halter dress and a silver bracelet with three round turquoise stones.

Danny was tan and gorgeous, his dark eyes sparkled, and his black hair glistened in the candlelight. My skin tingled with excitement. Danny was my prince. We'd always be in love.

Now, on Friday evenings we went out to dinner with Neale to the Washington Arms. Danny carried me down the hall to the elevator. From there I limped to the lobby doors, then Danny carried me up the few steps to his Chevy, which he'd driven around to the curb. At the restaurant I limped to our table where the waitress set up a chair and pillow and helped me elevate my leg. They still kept the place painted a glossy white and lit with tall white tapers. We were always home in time for Neale's favorite new TV program, Star Trek, which the three of us watched together.

Once in a while I sat out on the terrace. Not too often, for it required carrying out and arranging the pillows and besides, I couldn't hear Neale from the terrace. One Saturday morning, however, my father got me settled on the terrace; he was taking Neale out for one of their Saturday adventures around town. Just then Doris arrived, her only visit during that long and difficult time. My father escorted her from the door to the terrace.

"Oh, this isn't so bad for you. It's nice out here. I wish I had the time to lie around like this, ha, ha!" Once in a while Gloria and Mike stopped by for a visit.

My cousin Alice was marrying Norman and she asked me to be her matron of honor.

"Thank you, Alice, for asking me but I'll ruin your ceremony, I can't even stand. I think you should ask someone else."

"I want you, Francine. You've done so much for me. I'll never forget all those times you made Norman feel so welcome, the fun we had playing monopoly, all your advice, and this is my way of thanking you. And I don't care about how it will look to have a pregnant woman in the ceremony, not if it's you ... they'll look at your face and you'll make my wedding more beautiful. Please say yes?"

Dr. Noland said yes, why not, but have a chair provided for me.

My mother shopped in Bloomingdales and brought home a simple short-sleeved aqua-blue maternity dress with a high scooped neckline. I limped down the aisle, sat under the flower-strewn chuppa, and held my cousin's bouquet.

Danny quit the racetrack. They cut out the twin double anyway, he said. He brought home extra heavy chocolate frosteds from a soda shop in the old neighborhood. I relished every spoonful of thick, icy-cold, almost liquid chocolate ice-cream.

Day after day Sarah could be counted on to invite Neale over to play with her boys after school.

As JUNE APPROACHED the color of the skin of my leg whitened. Phlegmasia alba dolens, or 'milk leg.' The deep vein in my thigh had become involved. My foot and calf ballooned. Dr. Imperato examined my leg, shook his head and announced, "I've never seen a case as acute as yours. Unbelievable. Very rare. I'd like to have this leg photographed by a medical photographer here in Manhattan. He's not too far from here. Can you go?" His look was serious and penetrating. "You see, I'm writing a paper on your leg and can use the photographs." I accepted the card he handed me but when I got home I threw it away.

My leg throbbed with unremitting pain, from foot to groin. The last days of June were especially unbearable. The prescription ended for phenobarbitol, for the threat of toxemia had passed, but the phenobarbitol had relaxed me.

I lay on the sofa, elevated thighs pressed against my belly. Grotesque! I couldn't lay there another day, another minute. My mother brought me an embroidery sampler, Home Sweet Home, to help pass these restless days.

She said, "Here, sweetie pie, this will keep you busy for the next couple of weeks." I finished it in two days.

The baby was developing well, Dr. Noland assured me. He had amended the due date to July 6, but as the end of June approached and my leg continued to swell, he consulted with Dr. Imperato and it was decided that labor should be induced. The doctors feared the skin of my leg would burst.

On June 26 Dr. Noland called. "Look, Fran, you're coming in tomorrow for a checkup? Bring your suitcase, I may keep you here overnight."

On June 27 after Dr. Noland examined me he said, "I'd like to induce labor, Fran. We're very concerned about your leg. I'm afraid it's become too dangerous for you to remain pregnant any longer. I would have preferred taking this baby along for another week, but really, we have no choice."

Right away my hands felt cold and sweaty.

The following morning, June 28, 1967, as I lay on a bed in the labor room, Danny was beside me, dressed in hospital whites. I tried to keep my mind blank. If I focused on my leg, which Dr. Noland had wrapped in layers of soft white protective toweling, I would cry. If I thought of our baby, the answer to all my fervent prayers, about to be born at last, I'd surely cry. I looked into Danny's face, the tranquilizers worked and I slipped into dreamless sleep.

I'm weightless, floating in a cloud, looking into Danny's face... he's floating too... he's very happy... he's ecstatic... he's telling me something. What?

"Honey! Honey! You did it! You did it! You had a girl!"

Me? I had a girl? The cloud is changing, quickly now, into a hospital room, a happy hospital room. I'm lying in bed. And I feel healthy! A girl? A daughter? I'm laughing! Laughing!

"Yes, Honey! A beauty! A little black-haired beauty! You did it, my Fran baby, you did it!" Danny's laughing. A wonderful sound, our laughter. Danny leans down and kisses me.

"Is she alright, Danny? Healthy?"

"Yes, darling, she's perfect! A perfect baby girl!"

A Beautiful Baby Girl

ANNIE. The chorus of infant cries grows louder and nearer. The nurses bring the babies out. A nurse is entering my room. She is walking past the other beds. She is coming to me. All I can see of the infant she is holding is the top of her head, whispery black hair. The nurse is leaning over. She is placing the baby in my arms.

I reach out for you. I have you. Ah, Annie, my precious, precious daughter. You are awake for our first moments together. I hold you close, you are secure. I look into your beautiful dark brown eyes, fringed with the longest lashes I have ever seen. Your lashes sweep into a delightful slow curl. Your eyebrows are long, too, and tapered, black, like mine. You are looking into my eyes. We gaze into each other's eyes, seeking recognition, which we find. You look at me with intelligence and warmth. You remember me, don't you, my sweet angel? And I remember you!

I offer you my index finger to hold and soon you reach out with your other hand and tightly grasp my thumb. I can't get enough of looking at you. And you keep looking at me. You even recognize my voice, don't you Annie, my dearest daughter. Hear me now, my precious.

Your mommy adores you. You have a family who wants you so very much. Welcome to our family! We are going to give you a wonderful, good life, Annie. Mommy will teach you and guide you. You are smart, my precious, you will be an educated woman, an independent woman.

You look into my eyes with extraordinary perception. Oh, my darling Annie, I love you, love you, love you! Doesn't this feel wonderful, nestling your delicate face so sweetly against my cheek? I will comb your dark hair long and loose, my darling, the way I liked it best when I was little. And I'll dress you in the softest little cotton dresses with smocking in front and white eyelet collars. I'll buy dolls for you; dark-haired, dark-eyed baby dolls for you to cuddle and play with. You will be respected my darling, and appreciated for your intellect and independence. You will be loved for your beauty and sensitivities. You will be loved for your great capacity to love. For you, Annie, I will educate myself and accomplish things. For you, Annie, I will mold myself into a woman you can learn from. You have made my life complete and in return I can never do enough for you. So, welcome to life, my little Annie! My own sweet daughter!

My mother called and put Neale on. "Neale, darling, how's my boy?"

"I miss you, Mommy. Is my baby okay? Does she have a cute little baby face?"

"Oh, Neale, you have a beautiful little sister! Her name is Annie! I told her all about you and now she can hardly wait to go home and play with you!"

"Kiss her for me, Mommy, okay?"

"I will, darling. I love you, Neale. And in a few days I'll be home with Annie and we'll all be together!"

"Mommy, can I hold Annie?"

"Of course, Neale darling, you can hold her and kiss her and rock her, too!"

Neale laughed and we laughed together.

THE FOLLOWING DAY Dr. Imperato, accompanied by a team of medical students, crowded around my bed. They all stared at my leg which had returned to its normal size. "Amazing," Dr. Imperato addressed his student doctors. "You should've seen this girl's leg only two days ago. This is a miracle."

He proceeded to describe in medical terminology what had happened to my leg, stroking his chin while he spoke, his eyes fixed on my leg. When he finished, he turned and left. One student smiled at me, waved and wished me luck. I smiled back. I sure was lucky. The nightmare of suffering with my leg was over. Dr. Imperato did not consider that I was still lying in bed and hadn't yet resumed a normal life. Neither did I.

The following day Dr. Noland came in to report that my Annie had become jaundiced. I couldn't take her home until her liver was working properly. "I'm not going home without my baby," I told him.

So on Saturday, the fourth day, I remained in the hospital. Danny called. "I'm going to the track tonight, Honey."

"Oh, Danny, can't you come here? The nurses are making a party tonight, the husbands will be allowed to stay past visiting hours."

"Sorry, Honey, I feel like going to the track."

"Please, Danny, don't do this. I want you to be with me. Don't you want to be with me?"

"I want to go to the track tonight, Honey. I haven't gone in a long time."

Suddenly, a great gray mist of sadness enclosed my heart. Before Danny called I was praying for my Annie to be well. Now that old sadness that only Danny could evoke enveloped my body. The sadness pushed me back against the thin hospital pillows and made my limbs weak. My eyes closed.

"Don't do this to me, Danny, please don't do this."

"I'm going. I made up my mind and you can't talk me out of it."

"Danny, if you don't want to come here, then stay home with Neale tonight."

"I'm going to the track, Honey."

The wedding! He's actually going to the wedding! He's lying again! Danny's cousin Fay of his mother's age had called last week to ask if we'd be able to attend her son's wedding together or if Danny would go without me. I'd told her it was impossible for me to go and I didn't think Danny would go without me.

That night I'd pleaded with him, "Don't go and leave me alone on a Saturday night, Danny ... I'm so miserable lying here ... I look forward to the time you are home, keeping me company."

"The family expects me, Honey."

"Doesn't the family expect you to be a good husband? Doesn't anyone care about me, this ordeal I'm going through? Twenty-four years old lying here alone day after day."

"You're being unreasonable, Fran. Why should I miss a wedding?"

"Look at me! Look what I'm going through? I can barely take another minute of this. What do you think it's like to lay on this sofa with this leg, trying not to become bitter or crazy?" My throat was already feeling raw from the stress of the argument.

"Look, Honey," Danny relented, "if you feel so strongly about it, I won't go to the wedding. But I think you're wrong."

I, too, thought it was wrong of me, to expect Danny not to attend his cousin's wedding, yet my emotions were overwhelming all common sense. What difference did it make if I lay here another night consumed by loneliness, no one to have a conversation with, to share an adult meal with? Danny was out all the time and even on ordinary nights, since Rose was serving him dinner he was next door in her house, not here. If he had been in the habit of hurrying home to me at night my whole thought pattern would be flowing with ease. But the stress of Danny's constant activities away from home had created a thought pattern of heartache. A pattern of neglect. There was always some activity luring Danny away from home. And now, even though it wasn't on his customary list of activities, this wedding which he himself would scorn if we were attending together; a wedding all the way out in Jersey with cousins he never saw or cared about, suddenly held supremacy over being with me.

"Promise me, Danny, promise you'll stay with me, you won't make me lie here all alone all those hours."

"Okay, Honey, I won't go, I promise."

Now, lying in the hospital bed I wanted to scream at Danny, scream into the telephone, that he better come and stay with me. "Danny, you're breaking your promise, aren't you? You're going to the wedding, aren't you, Danny?"

"No, I'm not, Honey, I'm going to the track." He could repeat it a zillion times and yet I knew he was lying.

My white hospital bed was really an island which had just broken away from the continent of Happily Ever After and it carried me off to the dismal plight of a broken heart.

Later in the evening when the husbands arrived, the nurses brought the babies out for a special unexpected visit with their Dads. I held my Annie. "I love you, my precious. Whatever else may happen in my life I'll always be your devoted Mommy. You and Neale will always come first in my life."

By Sunday morning Annie's jaundice was clearing. Danny arrived and Annie was placed in my arms. "Annie, my doll, we're going home!" I love you, Mommy, Annie said with her beautiful alert, almond-shaped eyes.

July 4, Danny's birthday. Rose invited her family to the club. I sat in my shady kitchen, feeding Annie, my right leg elevated on the other kitchen chair. Dr. Imperato had advised me, "Keep your leg elevated whenever possible."

The first day home my leg had started to throb again and by evening it was swollen. My leg was supposed to be normal now. How was I going to be a good mother with a throbbing, swollen, painful leg? How was I going to do everything? The clock on the wall ticked the seconds away while my infant daughter sucked slowly on her bottle.

Rose had, in the past, held family parties in her apartment next door. Just now, when Danny and I should have been together with Neale and our new baby, she held Danny's party away from home separating not only me and Danny but my children as well. In keeping with her usual habit she disrespected me while Danny's allegiance to her remained as firm as ever. I had longed to have a good friendship with Rose, I felt no need to compete with her. But our lives had settled into a pattern of her design which I felt helpless to adjust. How might I shift the dynamics of our relationship, I often wondered. Whatever offering I made proved inadequate. She disrespected me, judged me without compassion and showed no interest in talking to me about anything meaningful. I couldn't find my way in the family. And after she chose to make this party away from home, a day after I came home from the hospital with my new baby, making it impossible for me to participate in my husband's birthday celebration, separating my little family, much of my enthusiasm for a good relationship with Rose simply evaporated.

Later, while Annie napped in her crib, I went to put away some of Danny's clothes, and there in the drawer lay his rumpled tuxedo shirt. Danny came home from the club with Neale, suntanned and gorgeous.

"Danny, I found this in your drawer."

Danny stared at the shirt in my hand and with no show of emotion looked straight into my eyes. "I'm sorry, Honey, I wanted to go to the wedding."

"What about your promise, Danny? Doesn't your word mean anything? Do you know that I was the only mother without a husband at the nurses' party?" I started to cry.

Danny put his arms around me.

"Why did you do it, Danny? Why? You betrayed my trust, when I was helpless. You chose to be with your mother's family instead of your own. I'll never forgive you for that!"

Danny stroked my hair. "I don't know, Honey, I felt like going, my mother really wanted me to go, I didn't think you'd get so upset."

"Well, you are responsible for your own actions, Danny."

"It's not like I was unfaithful, I'm not a bad person, Honey, I just went to my cousin's wedding, that's all."

There are all kinds of faithfulness but Danny was incapable of understanding.

Danny enrolled Neale in day camp for the summer but Neale didn't want to go to day camp.

"Let him stay home, Danny. He can go to Hudson Park with me and Annie. It's so beautiful there. I miss going places with him and I would love being in the park with Neale and Annie together."

"Are you kidding? My son is not spending the summer with his mommy and baby sister, he's going to camp!"

"Danny, Neale is my son, too, and I love having him around."

"Absolutely not! Neale is going to camp and that's that!" Danny turned to Neale, "You're going to camp tomorrow, Neale! No more nonsense!"

Rose yelled, "We paid for the club, a beautiful club, and you come only on weekends with Daniel. And you know, you're not as slim as you used to be!"

Each morning after Neale left on the camp bus I packed up the silvery coach and wheeled Annie to Hudson Park. There, we staked out the tallest oak tree on a bluff overlooking Long Island Sound, the narrow beach thirty feet below, and stayed the whole day.

One afternoon Neale came home with a cold. The next day I took him to the park and he lay on the blanket watching the swaying branches of the majestic oak, mesmerized by the lacy pattern of leaves through which he could see the clear blue summer sky. Neale's cold was whisked away on the summer breeze.

I gave him two dollars to buy hot dogs and soda from the park vendor across the path. The mid-summer sun waltzed on the waves just beyond our wide grassy veranda, and Annie napped in her royal coach.

"Can I come here with you and Annie tomorrow, too, Mommy?"

"Of course, Sweetheart."

"I like to be here better than camp."

"It is beautiful here, isn't it, Neale? And peaceful, too." I hugged my son. That day, that very special day, before summer ended and he entered first grade, lives in my heart; it lives in vibrant colors of summer-sky blue and oak-leaf green, butterfly colors, and silvery-tan in dappled light.

The butterflies of Hudson Park discovered Neale and engaged him in games of follow-the-leader. Whenever he captured one in his net, Neale examined its colorful wings close up.

"It's mean to keep the butterflies, Mommy, and stick pins into them, like it says in the book." And then he set the butterfly free.

Annie wanted to play with her brother so I placed her on the blanket beside him. Neale held her hands gently in his, moved her arms up and down like I showed him and crooned, "Exercise Annie, exercise . . ." He petted her tenderly and kissed her. Annie looked directly into Neale's eyes, smiled and kicked her little baby feet.

"See how Annie knows you love her?" I said.

"Does Annie know where we are, Mommy?"

"Well, sweetheart, Annie probably figures we're somewhere in a sweet land of love."

Later, he rocked her gently in the silvery coach that had been his. "I think she's sleeping now, Mommy," he whispered.

My cousin Mitch was preparing for his discharge from the Marines and needed a job. He had a wife now, and an infant son. It was my hope that Mitch would have the security of a job with

Danny. I showed Danny the recommendation, sent to me by Aunt Margie, which described Mitch's performance in the Marines as "exemplary." Danny called Leo in.

"You could use someone like Mitch in the company," I urged Leo. "He's smart and he's trustworthy."

They decided to offer Mitch a job in the Volvo parts department on Southern Boulevard and asked me to compose the offer. If Mitch proved himself in the parts department he'd become a trusted employee, he'd be promoted; in sum, this was Mitch's "golden opportunity." Danny and Leo approved my letter and Danny signed it.

"There's no reason, Francine," Leo said, "to tell your cousin that you wrote this letter, just let him think Danny wrote it."

I promised not to tell, and I kept my promise.

VIET NAM had taken its toll on my cousin; now that he was home he had to find security and since his return Mitch could not find security. When he received the letter which would be remembered in the family as the "golden opportunity" letter, Mitch was overjoyed. He accepted the offer and the whole family was pleased. But in the Volvo parts department Mitch worked for Edmond, not Danny.

"Why can't he work for you, Danny? You're the one he has the relationship with. And Mitch could make life easier for you."

"Edmond needs him in the parts department, Honey, what difference does it make, anyway? The important thing is, he's with the company."

I was concerned, too, about my parents' financial security. Eddie and Max, my father's partners, decided to accept an offer from the mayor of Burlington, Vermont and relocate their printing company. But despite the allure of major contracts, the seductive appeal of wealth at last within their reach, my parents were not persuaded to leave their lovely life in New Rochelle among the children and grandchildren. And my father was worn out from all the arguments with Eddie and Max. But now, at the age of fifty-two, he had to find a new way to earn a living. Finally, he found a job helping a businessman establish a branch office. A better arrangement, I thought, would be for my father to sell cars, so I proposed the idea to Danny. It wouldn't take very long, I knew, for disillusionment to overwhelm my father and then he'd be looking to Danny for an offer.

Danny was making his own changes. Tired of working until 9:30 every night he promoted a salesman to manage the lot and he came home for dinner. "I want more time with Neale and Annie," he said, and his late hours at the lot were over. Now we ate dinner together as a family at the dining-room table. Neale told Danny about his day at school and I turned to Annie in her recliner, "And what did Annie do today? Annie had fun today? You will be talking soon, my love, and your opinion is going to count." Annie smiled, and the world was a pleasant place.

"If you become pregnant again, Fran," Dr. Noland warned at my next checkup, "You'll be forced to make a choice between staying in the hospital for the entire nine months or an abortion. In my opinion we just can't risk another pregnancy. I suggest you think about a tubal ligation. I'll tie your tubes and you won't have this constant fear of pregnancy hanging over you."

After the operation which required another hospital stay we went up to Kutshers' Resort for three weeks where we rented a room by the lake and I recuperated. There were moments when I rested alone on the patio by the peaceful lake, watching Annie nap in her summer carriage. I was twenty-six and my reproductive life was over. Because of my age I had been required by hospital protocol to appear before a board of physicians. However, my considerate and kind doctor arranged for one female doctor to represent the board while he asked the questions.

"Do you understand," Dr. Noland began, "that after this procedure you will no longer be able to conceive a child?"

I sat on the edge of an office chair and watched my knees betray the anxiety of my heart. "Yes, I understand."

"Suppose one of your children were to die. Wouldn't you want to be able to replace that child with another baby?"

I closed my eyes and saw Neale and Annie playing horsey. She begged him not to stop so he took her for another ride across the living room. She rubbed her hands in his soft light-brown hair and they giggled. "Neither of my children could ever be replaced."

"How about contraceptives? Why don't you just rely on them?"

"We do, but I get pregnant so easily and every time my period is late I worry . . . I'm so frightened of another pregnancy."

"You know," Dr. Noland continued, looking significantly at the other doctor, but addressing me, "that you can have a legal abortion whenever you need one?"

Suddenly, anxiety threatened to obliterate my thoughts and my whole body was trembling from the formality of the setting, the finality of my decision, a decision I had never even considered having to contemplate. Suddenly, it was impossible to speak without falling into an abyss of emotion.

And then I felt it, the presence, right beside me, and recognized the familiar energy of my Guardian Angel Love. I felt her touch on my right shoulder and on my arm like the softest cloud of comforting love, infusing me with her love. She had come with a message. It wasn't in words, it was more like a transfer from her mind to mine, a message contained within an imprint, a symbol made entirely of light. "The light of truth reigns within your heart, truth is your enduring power. Dearest Francine, claim your power!"

Then I heard myself speak and my voice was strong. "I believe in the absolute right of every woman to have dominion over her own body, even to end an unwanted pregnancy. But for myself, after losing babies I wanted and having babies like Neale and Annie, I don't know how I could ever have an abortion. It would be an impossible dilemma."

Golden Dreams

MOVING DAY, JUNE 29, 1969. I stand among the barrels and cartons. Nine-and-a-half years. Many dreams have broken here, and some dreams have come true. Friends and relatives have envied us for living here, in this apartment I never wanted to live in.

Now I want to leave all the bad memories behind but some memories hurt forever and they remain deep inside my heart. Rose, in one of her abusive tirades shouted, "You only married my Daniel for his money! You wanted to live in this beautiful apartment!" She had chosen her moment carefully. My family was expected to arrive any minute for a dinner party in celebration of my parents' wedding anniversary.

Rose wore her dove-gray satin dress, her pearls and diamond earrings. Her hair, usually in disarray, was coiffed and she looked quite prosperous. She had opened the door and walked in without knocking as usual, to see "what's doing." Neale was playing around the house, Annie slept in her crib. I was wearing an apple green silk Chinese style pants outfit for the occasion. The table was set and everything was on schedule. Apparently, Rose had felt obliged to damage, once again, the serenity of my home. She may even have considered it her obligation, considering how consistent and effective she was. She ignored every good thing about me, and she ignored my recent plea. "Mom," I had said, "I really want to have a better relationship with you. I admire you for so many things, and now I have Annie, let's be real good friends from now on."

Now, on moving day, Rose came in, picking her way among the barrels. "What a mess!" She opened a kitchen drawer, "Aren't you taking these?" She pointed to two battered knives.

"No, I bought new knives."

"What about this? You're leaving the hot plate?"

I definitely was leaving the hot plate. Leo had bought it, Danny had insisted I use it to broil steaks, and because it had no handle, I was always burning my fingers on it no matter how carefully I tried not to. "You can have it if you like, Mom, I don't want it anymore."

The movers arrived. I lifted Annie into her stroller, looked around for the last time. I'd grown up a lot here. I felt like crying but didn't. There was a chasm inside me that I was growing accustomed to, between the feeling of wanting to cry and being unable to.

"Let's go, my Annie doll! Our new house is waiting!"

A lucky star shone above Two Flower Place in the north end of New Rochelle. The rising sun lit up our house with soft golden rays. The noontime sun supplied clear, white light. And the western sky filtered all the varied hues of gorgeous sunsets through our sixteen west-facing windows. When a sudden January ice storm blasted the neighborhood encasing the branches of young pine trees and newly planted white birches and lovely apple blossom trees in sheer ice, the storm winds shearing branches off the trees which slammed against houses and cars, we discovered when the storm abated not a bit of damage on our property. During Spring thaw when heavy rains and melting snow flooded basements, our lower level remained dry. Houses up and down the street were burglarized. Our house never was. I often found myself wondering, as years passed, if the magical light shining through the many windows of our house and which so delighted me also surrounded us, even above the rooftop, and in some mystical way was protecting our house. I had stood on the land when it was just a meadow, it had felt good to me, and then I learned it had formerly been farmland and so I had chosen this piece of land for our house.

Danny said, "I'm busy at the lot all day, Honey, and then I have my activities, and anyway I'm not good at that stuff. You do it, Honey."

I had accepted the responsibility of monitoring the construction and had watched over the construction daily, setting out with Annie right after her early afternoon meal, conferring with the builder, checking on progress, and arriving home in time for Neale.

Now it was our beautiful new home. I was filled with happy enthusiasm. Danny surveyed our half-acre and envisioned football games and softball games. Neale and Annie saw freedom to run and run and still be on their own lawn. Rose looked at the fourth bedroom and saw a room waiting for her and Leo when they needed relief from the hot southern summers of Florida. My parents were overjoyed to think of their daughter as the mistress of such a house and they saw Paradise awaiting their Sunday visits. We all saw a good life awaiting us on the corner of Flower Place and Wilmot Road.

ANNIE WAS DRESSED in her pale-yellow and white plaid dress with the long yellow satin sash tied into a bow at her waist, her full chestnut hair brushed past her shoulders.

It was the day of her nursery school graduation. She posed in the fragrant June morning light outside our front door. The pink azaleas still glistened with dew, the flowering apple blossom tree,

Annie's favorite, was heavy with scented pink and white blossoms. The morning enhanced in an enchanted way Annie's ever-present glow. Too bad the whole town didn't show up to see her, five years old, a thoroughly beautiful and lovely child. I snapped her photograph, then off we drove in the dark-green Volvo. No more used cars. Now that we lived on Flower Place, Danny and I both drove new Volvos.

ANOTHER IMPORTANT EVENT in the neighborhood! Incoming kindergarten students and their mothers meet the kindergarten teachers. Annie held my arm. "Mommy, there's Mrs. Drier, my Spanish teacher from nursery school, remember? I want you to meet her." Annie introduced me to her former teacher, "Mommy, this is Mrs. Drier, Mrs. Drier, this is my Mom."

About my age, Mrs. Drier had light-brown swingy hair which every now and then she tossed back from her round, freckled face. She pronounced her syllables with precision, "Oh, I am delighted to meet you, please call me Sue ... this is my daughter Jodi. I want you to know I just adore your Annie ... she is so enthusiastic and bright, just wonderful to have in class!" Sue tossed her swingy hair. "Why don't you and I have lunch sometime, perhaps next week after the girls start day camp?"

During the brief drive home Annie bubbled, "I knew you'd like Mrs. Drier, Mommy, you need a good friend." She squeezed my arm affectionately.

I pulled into the garage and we entered the house. "I love you, Annie doll."

Annie threw her arms around my neck and kissed my cheek. "And I love you, too, Mommy. Would you like to rest now? Does your leg hurt?"

"Yes, sweetheart, I would like to rest a bit before Neale comes home from school. What are you going to do? Would you like to play in the family room and we can keep each other company?"

Annie went to get her Barbie dolls. The afternoon sun streamed in through the picture windows. I closed my eyes and felt comforted listening to Annie unfold the story of her dolls' afternoon adventure.

Annie was right. I did need a good friend. Danny and I were on friendly terms with our neighbors, and we socialized with many couples on a regular basis. I visited occasionally with several women, mostly mothers of Annie's or Neale's friends, but I didn't feel especially close to anyone.

Ellen, den mother of Neale's Cub Scout troop, had asked me to be her assistant. I'd agreed, and we'd become good friends. Ellen was an artist, a sensitive woman with whom I'd shared many pleasant hours visiting, in her airy living room surrounded by her paintings which were reminiscent of Georgia O'Keefe, sipping chamomile tea. Then Ellen moved two-thousand miles away; another good friend gone.

The front door slammed. "Hi Neale darling, how was your afternoon?"

"Hi Mom ... we played kill-the-carrier and Bernie tore his pants."

"I wish you wouldn't play that wild game, Neale."

"Everybody plays, Mom."

"Get washed, Neale, okay? and I'll make ice-cream clowns."

I treasured this after-school hour when it felt to me as if the house vibrated with love. Gathering with my children, serving them ice-cream clowns, listening to their sweet voices recounting their day's experiences or planning the next few minutes, the whole room flooded with warm sunlight. My heart swelled with golden light. My heart was full, and yet there was room for so much more. I felt then and held the feeling throughout all the years that came after, if only exquisite moments such as these could last forever.

IN THE WINTER of that year I'd spent a week in the hospital undergoing tests on my leg. A venogram and an arteriogram had determined that the extensive damage to the deep veins and arteries of my leg was beyond surgical repair. Nothing could be done about the broken capillaries and blood vessels. Stripping the superficial veins was considered a cosmetic procedure, of little help in alleviating my pain. My leg would never heal. My condition was progressive. All I could do was try to keep the swelling to a minimum.

We are so intimate with hope that only in its absence are we reminded of the comfort that hope affords us. Despondency and pain, experienced in silence, twisted their dark way around my heart. I had lost weight in the hospital and had become anemic as well. Beside my flourishing family I felt inadequacy rise inside me. Inadequacy filled me, and took the place of hope.

Fired by some unidentified power my will engaged itself in daily battle with my physical weakness. Each morning I wrapped my leg in elastic bandage, went through routine chores, was showered and dressed by ten. My leg hurt so much by then that I was forced to rest. It didn't matter how long I rested for as soon as I resumed activity the pain in my leg returned. I felt it was important to maintain calm composure even while experiencing the pain of lifting my leg to a chair. I needed to be strong, stronger than anyone imagined I could be, and believed I was.

Then, something went wrong with my stomach; sharp, nasty pains. I went to the bathroom ten, twenty times a day. One small meal sent me running to the bathroom five, six, even seven times. After each episode my face looked pale and drawn.

After undergoing every imaginable intestinal probe it was discovered that I had ulcerative colitis. Mike prescribed medication. We kept increasing the dosage until it achieved its desired purpose of relaxing and coating my colon; twelve azulfadines and three lomotils daily. Even with medication any disruption – irritant food substance, or unexpected aggravation, and the symptoms erupted.

Danny came home from work and everyone came to the dinner table. I set out the salad, we began our meal, and the phone rang.

"I bet it's Grandma," Neale said.

"Want me to take it, Fran? You sit down, I'll get it."

"No, thank you Danny, I'll get it." My mother called every evening at the same time and the conversation never varied.

"Hi, Fran, how's my girl?"

"Fine, Mom, everything's fine. Can I call you back? We just sat down to dinner." I sponged the counter as we spoke and started on the stovetop.

"C'mon, Mommy, come eat," Neale called out.

"Just tell me," my mother continued, "how's my adorable Annie?"

"Fine, Mom, Annie is fine."

"And how's my Neale? Everything okay with that precious family of yours?"

"Yes, Mom, nothing to worry about. I promise to call back as soon as we finish dinner."

"I just got home, you don't know the day I had in that store. People treat you like garbage when you stand behind that counter." My mother had switched from Sportswear to Fine Jewelry at Bloomingdale's.

"I know, Mom, please, let me eat, I'll call you later."

"Honey, get off the phone already!"

"Why does Grandma call every time we sit down to dinner?" Annie asked.

"Well, sweetheart, she thinks about us all day and she can't wait to get home to call."

"I'll tell your mother not to call," Danny said.

"No, Danny, you'll hurt her feelings."

"So why don't you tell Grandma not to call?" Neale asked.

"Because, sweetheart, you have a responsibility to treat people with kindness, even if it's not always convenient."

I served the steaks. Danny poked at one steak with his fork,

"You did it again, Honey, the steaks are too well done! You ruined the steaks!"

Annie reached for mashed potatoes and asparagus. Like me, she didn't like to eat meat.

"I'm sorry, Danny, I really tried." I looked at the steak where he cut into it, it looked good to me. Annoyed, Danny shook his head and sliced Neale's steak.

Neale refused vegetables. "Yuck!" he said, and made a face.

"I like it, Mommy," Annie consoled me.

I looked at her little face, how her chin was just beginning to reach the tabletop. My daughter looked at me and I saw compassion in her eyes. Looking at her I thought, I will remember for all eternity, my Annie, how your soul had called out to me, 'Mother! I am waiting for you to bring me into the world!,' and now she was here, beautiful child; insightful, compassionate, intrinsically good. We all were blessed to have her. "Thank you, Annie."

"What a difference at work," Danny said, "Now that the lot is paved, so much cleaner and it's definitely better for my hayfever."

"Too bad it wasn't paved years ago. All these years you've been breathing that grimy air, surrounded by weeds!"

"That's my father, he could never take spending money on improvements." Danny turned to Neale, "Did you play basketball today?" And they launched into conversation about basketball maneuvers.

Annie and I discussed her ongoing game of school with Jodi and Lisa. I served fruit for dessert, Danny went outside to have a catch with Neale, Annie followed them. I returned my mother's call and while she described her difficult day behind the counter in Fine Jewelry I cleaned up the kitchen.

This, I thought, this life I'm living is the stuff of golden dreams. Children, home, husband, all here in the great land of America. I ought to feel jubilant. So where is this melancholy feeling coming from? What am I missing? I plugged in the vacuum cleaner, gave the carpet a quick going over, and drowned out the roaring commotion of my thoughts.

As I'd foreseen, my father left his pleasant position in Manhattan. Danny agreed to offer him a job selling used cars and my father gratefully accepted.

GLORIA AND MIKE moved into our neighborhood. Sometimes on his way to the hospital Mike stopped by to visit. "I've been asking around," he said one morning over coffee and donuts at my kitchen table, "trying to find something that might provide relief for your leg, and I discovered there's a machine called a Jobst Intermittent Compression Unit... I think it can help you, Fran. It's meant to be used in addition to elastic stockings and you still need to elevate your legs several times a day."

The Jobst Unit consisted of a black vinyl boot into which I inserted my right leg. This vinyl boot was attached by rubber tubing to a black box about the size of a professional makeup case, which housed a pump that forced air through the tube into the boot. As the boot inflated my leg was compressed by the air pressure in the boot which held steady for several seconds before deflating. For the first few minutes the pressure on my leg was extremely painful; as the cycle continued my body relaxed as relief washed through my leg, the pain eased and the swelling was reduced. The process was so exhausting and the relief so dramatic that it put me to sleep every single time. The kids and Danny grew accustomed to hearing the drone of 'Mommy's machine' and they never disturbed me during its use.

IN 1972 EDMOND was completely involved in the new car business. Danny's continued success with used cars had financed all new car expansion although he remained in the background, unknown by factory people and banks, while Edmond enjoyed the limelight, fancy lunches and dinners, as well as business trips extended into vacations. New car dealers were respected in a way that used car dealers would never be.

Danny deserved recognition and respect, and I wanted him to have both. "Why don't you get into the new car business, Danny? Do you want to spend your whole life on the used car lot?"

"I like used cars, Fran, I'm good at it and we still need it to finance the new showrooms."

"You'd be good at new cars too, Danny, and you'd make just as much money with new cars. Haven't you had enough years of being outdoors in every kind of weather?"

"Honey, this is what I know . . . used cars . . . I don't know anything about new cars."

"So, you could learn, Danny, you could learn." Edmond Motors had expanded to Manhattan and another showroom on Jerome Avenue. Leo and Edmond had established each franchise agreement – Volvo, Saab, BMW, Fiat and in 1973, Honda – with Edmond as the dealer principal.

A new Japanese car, Mazda, was gaining a good reputation in California since its introduction in 1971, and now Mazda was moving east. The factory was coming out with a new '73 model which had a rotary engine and the company was canvassing existing dealerships for qualified dealers.

Danny began to think about acquiring a Mazda dealership. It would provide him entry into the new car business. And as he lived with the idea a while he realized that Mazda was going to be 'his baby.'

Leo had just purchased a two-story building on Jerome Avenue, expecting to use it as a service department for Volvo and Fiat. When the Mazda people came to the Bronx, Danny and Edmond proposed this building as a Mazda facility; they would build a showroom in front, service and parts departments in back.

Early in 1973 the doors at 2100 Jerome Avenue opened for

business and Danny became a new car dealer. We emptied his drawers and closet of faded old banlon shirts and worn black chinos. We went shopping and bought suits, white shirts and ties, and winged-tip shoes. Now when Danny left for work in the morning he looked like a businessman and as I watched him drive away I saw in my mind, me and Danny working at the dealership together. I didn't know how it would come to be but the images flashed clear in my mind. Danny continued to run the used car lot on Bruckner Boulevard. He had not been groomed for the new car business as Edmond had been; Danny had to learn as each situation presented itself.

The service manager and the bookkeeper were accustomed to Edmond and they took their orders from him. Edmond spent most of his time at the Manhattan location but he stayed in touch with his people in the Bronx, too. When Danny attempted to implement his own ideas, Edmond stepped in and changed it back to his way.

During the summer we learned that several dealers were going for their insurance broker's license, it meant an opportunity for additional income on mandatory automobile insurance.

"I can't do it, Honey, I hate sitting in a classroom, but you like to study, you're always taking classes, how about if you go? Think of it as just another class. I'll get all the information."

"I don't know, Danny, insurance is not the sort of thing I enjoy. I choose my classes based on my interests and insurance is not one of my interests. Besides, who knows if I can do it."

"Believe me, Honey, if these dealers can do it you can, too."

The course consisted of two evening classes a week from seven to ten, September to May, preparation for a six hour exam in the city.

"I really don't want to do this, Danny. I find insurance so dry."

"It'll be good for business, Honey, and you'll get your commissions, it will be your money."

What lured me more than anything Danny said was the

amazing opportunity he was unwittingly presenting to me. An insurance broker's license would provide a legitimate opening for me into our business which I envisioned as experiencing phenomenal growth in the years ahead. As I saw it in my mind there were no limitations, nothing to hold us back, success was waiting, we just had to make it happen, and we would.

A buzz of invigorating hope entered my life. I would show Danny what I could accomplish outside the home. I would prove my worth to him in his business. And Danny would come to respect me. I would be a role model for my daughter. The world was changing and women were assuming a greater presence in the business world and I didn't like the housewife identity which was viewed in general as demeaning, even though in truth what could hold greater importance than maintaining a nurturing, stable and secure environment for growing children. The feminist movement was a big topic among my friends and I realized that enormous change was upon us. I was going to be riding that wave of change. So many women had passed this way before, struggling for respect and equality in a patriarchal society. Even my own Grandma had marched with the suffragettes so long ago, fighting for equality. All the discussions at Hadassah meetings and with friends at parties and over coffee were having an effective influence not only on me but on an entire generation. It was bristling in the air around us. Now here was my husband, himself being influenced, not even realizing how deeply his offer was resonating within me.

Tuesday and Thursday evenings Danny made sure he was home early, we had dinner a little earlier than usual, the kitchen clean by 6:30 and I was ready to go. Annie practiced writing at her white desk on which I had painted narrow candy-pink borders. On her chair I'd painted her name and a bouquet of flowers. All her friends brought their mothers in to see Annie's room; white, ruffled eyelet curtains dressed her windows, a graceful bell-shaped canopy of white ruffled eyelet above her white four-poster bed. Annie's dolls sat in friendly groups beside her books on polished white shelves and on the dresser-top. As I entered her room I was struck once again by the glorious sight of the sunset as it transformed the west-facing window into a rectangle of golden light, in turn flooding the windows of her doll house with a golden glow.

"Bye, sweetheart, I have to go to school now."

"I know, Mommy, I'll be fine, don't worry."

"I'm not worried, Annie, it's just I'd rather stay here, in this lovely room, with you."

Yes, my visions of the future were exciting and filled with joyous hope, yet the heart-centered pull of my child's company which so delighted me, was also strong.

"Bye, Neale darling, remember guitar practice, you have a lesson tomorrow."

I kissed him and tousled his hair, and rushed down the stairs to my Volvo in the garage and drove twenty minutes to White Plains High School.

THE OTHER STUDENTS in the class were already in the insurance field. Some were agents, others had Life Insurance licenses and wanted their General Insurance licenses. Some were clerks in insurance offices and wished to get ahead. I was the only student in the class who knew nothing about insurance. Ironically, Danny didn't believe in insurance so I didn't even have a life insurance policy. The course was organized into various categories of insurance and each week we studied a different category; Glass Insurance, Boiler, Machinery, Fire, and so on.

"I hate it, Danny ... it's so boring, and I'm so ignorant I didn't even imagine all the types of insurance there are. I wish you'd go."

Danny put his arms around me. "It can't be that bad, Honey."

"It is, and I'm not going back. You go, see how much you like it."

"Oh, Honey, you can do it, I'm so proud of you!"

"How are the kids? Is Neale in bed?"

I went to Neale's room. He was watching TV. "Hi, Neale darling, did you finish your homework?"

"Yeah, shh, I'm watching!"

I went into Annie's room. It was dark and quiet. As my eyes grew accustomed to the darkness I saw that Annie's eyes were wide open. "Annie, my doll, why are you still awake?"

"I was waiting for you, Mommy." She hugged my arm the way she liked to do and rubbed her face against me.

"Oh, Annie, my dear, sweet daughter."

"You're my queen, Mommy. You're so beautiful and perfect, I wish I could be like you."

"No, no, Annie, I'm just an ordinary woman."

"But you can do anything, Mommy. I hope that I can do things as good as you when I grow up. But I don't know how."

"Oh, darling, I can't do everything. And someday when you are older you will discover that I'm far from perfect. I hope you won't be disappointed."

"No, Mommy, you will never disappoint me. You're my beautiful queen!"

I held her close. "Annie, do you remember, almost three years ago, the first week we lived here, we all went out for a walk after dinner..."

Annie lay back against her pillow, "I remember ... that time we got locked out!"

"That's right, my love, and all the windows were shut tight except one ... and that one only opened a little, and Daddy said we'd have to break a window..."

"But we didn't want to break a window in our new house!"

"So what happened then, my love?"

"Everybody looked at me 'cause I was little enough to go through..."

"And you and Neale were frightened of the downstairs, it was so big and dark and Rudy hadn't finished making it a real room yet, and all his building supplies were scattered around..."

"Yes, Mommy, and me and Neale thought you were so brave to go down all alone for the laundry!"

"But you were very brave, Annie, and you were only two years old, your birthday was just the week before, remember? and Daddy lifted you up and helped you climb into that big, dark room, and then you ran all the way across to the garage, and you had to open the door and stand on tiptoe and reach up very high to push the button for the garage door to open..."

"I remember being so scared, Mommy, it was so dark I could hardly see, but you kept calling to me and telling me what to do next, and finally the garage door opened and then you and Daddy and Neale were already standing there, you must have run very fast!"

I cupped Annie's beautiful face in my hands, and her luminous eyes, so trusting and loving, reinforced once again my overwhelming desire to protect her from every potential harm, however slight, and melancholy swept over me for I knew it would not be possible.

"We were so proud of you, Annie, you were our heroine! I knew right then that you possessed great determination and courage ... I love you so much, my sweet, and you'll be able to do everything you want to do, even things that I could never do ... you'll see ... pleasant dreams, my Annie doll."

Annie sighed. By the time I reached the door of her room she was sleeping.

ON THE APPOINTED DAY in June I drove down to Manhattan for the insurance exam. Miraculously I'd managed to hold my own in class, and discovered an ability in Fire Insurance in which I'd earned a perfect score. The first half of the exam consisted predominately of questions on Fire Insurance. During lunch break there was a great deal of speculation among the group as to whether or not we'd have to deal with No-Fault in the second half of the exam. No-Fault was an innovation in New York insurance law, it hadn't been included in our curriculum and we'd been told not to expect it on the exam. A rumor which proved correct, flew through the crowd, the second half included No-Fault. Three weeks later a notice arrived in the mail. I'd failed by two points.

A woman from Danny's broker's office supplied me with pamphlets and mimeographed papers explaining No-Fault. I took another exam in July, and this time I made it! With Danny's guidance and help I started Francine's Brokerage Company, Inc. And within a few years' time the convenience of purchasing auto insurance at the dealership became an accepted practice.

One day, Danny hoped, he'd be able to say to Leo, "See Dad, I did it! Me, Danny! I'm successful in the new car business even though you didn't choose me to be the one!" But he had many obstacles to overcome. The gas shortage of 1974 signaled the downfall of Mazda's rotary engine which got only thirteen miles to the gallon. The used car lot on Bruckner was well-stocked, as always, with big American cars. People stopped buying big American cars. Our bank accounts were needed to save the business. So on his birthday I surprised Danny with a check for $10,000, everything I'd saved from my insurance commission checks.

Danny had hired the new Mazda sales force, but the parts and service people and office people had already been hired by Edmond or Leo and these employees still regarded Edmond as their boss, not Danny. Danny had immediately recognized inconsistencies within the service department, and he struggled to institute corrections. However, over lunch with Edmond the service manager complained about every change that Danny tried to make. Edmond encouraged the manager to continue as usual and disregard Danny's instructions.

Edmond had not instituted, nor did he explain to Danny, the need for a checks and balance system. It came as a shocking revelation to Danny when he learned that in addition to incompetence, his service manager was guilty of being a thief. The same situation prevailed in the parts department with the parts manager. The accountant, also loyal to Edmond, did not report the bookkeeper's incompetence to Danny. Danny uncovered it through his own investigation and then he dismissed the accountant from the Bronx corporation. The bookkeeper was under Leo's protection.

Edmond reported to Leo every error Danny made and exaggerated in a way that threatened great catastrophe. Edmond ruthlessly belittled Danny, and Leo revered Edmond's every word.

Each evening Danny came home steaming with angry frustration and aggravation. After dinner he tried to rest in the leather club chair by the window and read the newspaper as usual, but found himself too upset to concentrate on anything.

"I can't believe it! All these years my father had me believing Edmond was some kind of genius! And he does know a lot... the trouble is he doesn't do anything! He doesn't check anything! All he does is bullshit with his buddies, his spies! I like to get things done! Make things happen! He just sits and bullshits! I can't believe it, Fran, and then he undermines everything I try to do! Without telling me! I walk into the service department... I ask Charlie why he's not carrying out my system and he says, 'While you were in Florida over Christmas your brother came in and he agreed with me that your system stinks.' I felt like grabbing that no good son-of-a-bitch and ripping his head off! The place is so disorganized, we're losing so much money... I'm killing myself on the used car lot all these years, thinking Edmond had everything under control... nothing's under control! Everything's a mess! One big fucking mess!"

"Danny, listen Danny, this isn't good, this aggravation. You can't go on like this, there's got to be a solution."

And we talked for hours. The natural solution was for Danny and Edmond to separate their areas of responsibility. This level of aggravation was a new element in Danny's life. He was accustomed to being in control of his life and suddenly everything seemed beyond his control, outside his grasp, overwhelming his nervous system. His doctor prescribed tranquilizers. We decided the best resolution would be achieved by offering choice of location to Edmond. We knew that given the opportunity to own the prestigious Manhattan location Edmond would more readily agree to separation. Danny asked for a meeting with his parents and Edmond. He explained why the business was losing money in the Bronx and in Manhattan and why separation of responsibility was necessary if the business was to survive the major challenges which lay before them.

Mazda's rotary engine was a disaster. Volvo had just moved into a higher price range and wasn't selling. Saab's new '99' model wasn't selling. Our only success was Honda. Interest rates were high. New York City was experiencing major financial problems, and many of our customers, firemen, policemen and other municipal employees, were being laid off.

"Daniel, you will not get your way!" Rose screamed.

"I'm shocked at the amount of anger in you, Daniel," Edmond remarked.

Rose and Leo refused to hear of such a thing as separation. Why, the two boys should always get along! Danny was all wrong! Crazy! Mixed up! The business stood a better chance of pulling out of hard times if both brothers worked together just like Rose and Leo had planned. And besides, how could Danny run the new car business without Edmond's expertise?

I wanted to accompany Danny to their meetings to lend him my support but he remained adamant, the ignoble family scenes that arose during these meetings were off limits to me. Asserting himself with his parents and brother required an enormous emotional effort and as the arguments dragged on Danny's blood pressure became elevated; the doctor adjusted his medication. Edmond told everyone he met that Danny was having a nervous breakdown. They had one meeting at our house, downstairs. I sat unseen on the top step and listened to Rose and Leo berating and ridiculing Danny without mercy. Danny, with complete loss of composure, argued vigorously and screamed at them relentlessly.

The summer passed and one fine September day, without warning or explanation, Edmond suddenly approached Danny with a change of mind; Okay, Daniel, you win, I'll keep Manhattan and you take the Bronx.

NEALE HAD ONCE AGAIN left his clothes lying on the bathroom floor. "Please put your laundry in the hamper, Neale."

Ignoring me, my son searched his room for a favorite sweatshirt. "Neale, did you hear me?"

"I don't have the time! Can't you see I'm getting ready for school!"

"You still have to pick up after yourself."

"Why? You're home all day with nothing to do! You do it!"

"Neale, you know I do lots of things for you but some things you have to do for yourself!"

"What do you do for me, huh? Did you pick up my blue pants at the cleaners yesterday?"

I would've gone to the cleaners, Neale, but my leg hurt so much after marketing ... the long check-out line ... I had to come home and rest ... and your anger is a wound to the center of my heart! I was unable to say it, unable to defend myself. I so wanted to be a perfect mother but I felt, with unconquerable sadness, the physical limitations forced upon me by my swollen painful leg. And faced with the anger fueling my son's dialogue I felt helpless, wishing I had pushed myself a bit more and stopped at the cleaners for his favorite pants.

"Neale!" I called after him, "Why are you talking like this? I'm your mother! I love you! Please don't walk away while we are talking!"

When he was two and we came home from marketing he used to run to bring his little red wagon right to the door. With sweet toddler's hands he'd unpacked the groceries from the brown paper bags, piled them into his wagon, and taking care not to topple anything, pulled his wagon into the kitchen. "Here, Mommy, take this," he used to say, so quickly handing the groceries to me I laughed and we laughed together, "here, Mommy, take this." How proudly he'd proclaimed, "Me help Mommy!"

Now he was fifteen, growing tall, perfect posture, handsome every day. But every day he was angry with me for something, or, for nothing at all. Just yesterday I'd said to him, "Neale, I don't want to argue with you . . . you're my son, I love you, darling. I'll try my best not to bother you about little things . . . will you try to be nicer to me?"

"Nice? What's nice, Mommy? You want everything to be so nice!"

"Neale, let's talk like we used to. Come, sit with me, we'll talk a while."

"I'm busy, see you later, Mommy. Try not to burn the steaks tonight, okay? and could you pick up my contact lens stuff?"

I read psychology books, including Robert Coles' entire set of child interviews, and I sat through several semesters of parenting classes. Finally, I went to see a psychologist.

"You know, Francine, you have this wonderful calm aura about you, I don't see that too often in here, believe me, and those beautiful cat-eyes, how does your husband resist you?"

A visual of Danny flashed across my inner mind; sitting in front of the TV watching whatever game was in season until he fell asleep in his chair.

"Tell me what to do to help my son, Dr. Rabinowitz."

He paused, lit his pipe, and peered deeply into my eyes. "Well, you see, even though you and Neale argue, you are communicating, that's his way of communicating."

"Wonderful . . ."

"Your son needs more time with his father, Francine, and you need to do a better job of asserting yourself. It sounds to me like Neale is emulating his father's attitudes. It's coming from your husband. What's wrong with the man, anyway? Your son will get over this stage in time. But I'm sorry to say, the problem lies with your husband, and my guess is, you're blocking a lot."

CONVERSATIONS which centered on issues other than business concerns and which did not serve Danny's own immediate interests or which may have called for a bit of personal sacrifice always resulted in overwhelming frustration for me. Danny locked into his own position, refusing to acknowledge there was anything worthwhile to discuss, and usually moved toward exiting the room while I was speaking. My efforts to resolve a problem, whatever research I had done, whatever wise counsel I had sought to validate the knowing of my heart, went unacknowledged. Usually, Danny just walked calmly out of the room, waving his hand dismissively in my direction, the original significance of the conversation lost in the insensitivity of his response.

"I'm a good father, Honey. Neale knows I care about him."

"Don't you understand, Danny, Neale is at an age when he needs more time with you. He hangs around his room with his friends on Saturday mornings just waiting for you to come home from your game. I hear them. It's sad, Danny, he's waiting for you and then they go out. Don't you see? What does it take for you to understand?"

"There's nothing wrong with him spending Saturdays with his friends, I was always with my friends when I was a kid. My father was never around on Saturdays."

"Oh, Danny, just because your father didn't pay attention to you doesn't mean it wouldn't have been good for you. Can we just focus on the present needs of our son? Neale needs you, Danny, he needs his father! Your presence in his life when he needs you, and be assured this time will pass quickly enough, is far more important than any tennis game or whatever it is you're doing!"

"You're trying to coddle him again, Fran... didn't I coach Little League and go to his games? And don't I play basketball with him?"

"Sure! Sports, sports, sports! There's more to life than sports! And Neale hated Little League, you insisted he play when he would rather have been at home doing other things. Neale is not you, Danny, he doesn't want to be playing games all the time! Why don't you just sit down and talk with him? He's trying to figure things out, how life works and stuff like that! I talk to him all the time but I'm his mother, he's a growing boy and needs to relate to his father! Why is it so hard for you to get that?" Danny was already near the door.

"Danny, please don't walk away, we haven't resolved anything! We're talking about Neale's well-being! I know you're worried about all the problems at work, I understand that tennis relaxes you. But you really must find a way to spend more time with Neale."

Surprisingly, Danny paused, his hand on the doorknob, and turned to look at me. "I'm a self-centered guy, Honey, you married a selfish guy and I'm not going to change. Get used to it."

I said to him, "How about, instead of reading the paper in the family room after dinner you visit Neale in his room? Just go in there and keep him company. You'll see, Neale will start a conversation, he loves a good conversation. Oh, God! Just do it, Danny! What does it take!"

"Okay, I'll think about it."

Victorious me! Danny will think about giving his son a few minutes of his time! Danny Sachleben! I'll never get used to being married to a selfish guy! You think you own me! You think you'll have me forever! I give my love to you, my loyalty and devotion, and you disrespect me right before the eyes of my children! Criticizing every night my bountiful meals served with love! Ignoring me except when you need me! Withholding money from me except for household expenses, but there's always money for gambling and season tickets to sporting events! I will keep my family together until they are on their own and can take care of themselves! Then, Danny Sachleben, you, who believe that gifts for me are no concern of yours! You, who refuse to provide insurance for me, joking that you don't want to be worth more dead than alive! You, who find humor in discussions with our son of how to get rid of your wife and get away with it. I will be patient. I will continue to be a good and loving wife to you to ensure a stable home for our children. But the day will come ... I will leave you, Danny, even though in leaving my dreams will crash! And then I'll live my life away from you!

I held these thoughts to myself, confided in no one, turned the force of my will toward maintaining well-being within the family. How proficient I'd become at blocking, as the doctor had expressed it, all my disappointments and sadness; shoving them all away, into that dark corner of the heart, keeping them hidden from the light of truth! even forgetting for a while ... you must forget ... while you are busy fulfilling responsibilities!

I felt despair with nowhere to turn and suddenly the calming presence of my guardian angel was beside me! "Life is calling you, Francine! Transcend! For the health of your children, all the challenges thrown in your path. You are being called on to find the highest, most loving and patient and kind expression of your soul ... you are being called on to apply the highest way of being now ... to transform the madness of daily life with Danny into golden halcyon days! Be the alchemist that you are! This is, truly, no small task Francine. Yet, with the power of love informing every thought, you can do it. You can and you will!" All that my angel imparted to me became woven as one with my thoughts.

A FINE, SILENT DRIZZLE glistened on the pastel stone pathway and from my view through the kitchen window the grounds looked exquisite. I was tempted to leave the Passover dinner I'd spent the last two days preparing, there on the counter ... grab Annie's hand, and go outside to run and play with her in the rain ... allow ourselves to be embraced by the sweet aroma of damp grass and earth!

ON VYSE AVENUE the streets had been strewn with broken glass and everything was stark, even on sunshiny days. See what you have created, Francine, for your children! Come outside, Nature beckoned as I gazed, mesmerized, through the window ... become one with Me and with all My beauty! How I longed to dance on the beautiful green grass, barefoot in the misty drizzle ... how I longed to fling my arms up to the sky and sing!

Annie was in her room dressing for our Passover Seder. My parents will arrive soon, carrying a huge pot of matzo ball soup and boxes of Passover nut cake, honey cake and sponge cake. Any minute Danny will be home. Where was Neale?

A sudden deafening roar out on the driveway sent me running downstairs, and there I saw my son maneuvering a monstrous black motorcycle into the garage. "Neale! Where did this thing come from?"

"I just bought it! Isn't it a beauty?"

"What do you mean, you just bought it? Where did you get the money?"

"I went to the bank and took out the money."

"But Daddy's name is on your account, it's a trust account!"

"I signed Daddy's name to the withdrawal slip. It was easy, just told the manager my father was outside in the car. It's my money, Mom, I can do whatever I want with it."

My thoughts were tumbling, searching for comprehension. The beauty of Nature was no longer beckoning; the Passover dinner I'd worked so hard preparing, making everything perfect for my family, suddenly of little importance; sweet Annie upstairs and innocent in her lovely room; Danny, who will leave Neale's latest rebellion for me to resolve while he retreats into his mind, a mind that somehow turns foggy whenever faced with a request of mine, almost home; my parents who worship their first grandchild almost here; this monster sitting in our garage. Somewhere, somehow, I must have lost my way as a mother to Neale. But how could I have? Affectionate and warm, home and available whenever my son needed to talk, teaching ethical behavior naturally, by example, sincerely interested in his activities, creating a welcome space for his many friends. My mind was buzzing, my whole body was buzzing. The moment felt like time was standing still.

Then I heard my son speaking again. "I got this ad from the newspaper. Some guy was selling his motorcycle."

"Didn't he realize that you don't have a driver's license, that you're only fifteen?"

"He didn't care, he just wanted the money. Here's the receipt." Neale handed me a scrap of yellow paper with a name, address and telephone number on it and $700 scrawled across the bottom.

Cymbals crashed in my head, drums banged in my chest. I ran up the stairs to the serenity of my room and dialed the bank. "Mr. Hanson? My name is Mrs. Sachleben. You just handed over $700 from a trust account to my son, a minor. We've been banking with you since we live here, seven years, but I'll be there first thing in the morning to close every account we have with you!"

Then I called the man who sold Neale the motorcycle. A scene completely foreign in my life was unfolding, I was creating the script and acting without time to think. My head was exploding. "Mr. Blackstone? You just sold a motorcycle to a young boy! My son! Do you have any idea how old he is?"

"Sixteen?"

"He happens to be fifteen! Didn't you think it prudent to ask to see his driver's license? I expect you to take it back tonight and return our money!"

"Are you kidding, lady? A sale's a sale."

"Listen here, sir! You had no right to sell that motorcycle to a kid! You acted irresponsibly, don't you understand?"

"Sorry, lady, too late!"

"It's not too late! I'm taking you to court, Mr. Blackstone, and you'll be forced to take that monstrosity back, you might as well do it now and save us all a lot of trouble. No judge will uphold the sale of a motor vehicle to a minor!"

"Yeah? Go ahead! Take me to court!"

I slammed the phone down and, catching a glimpse of myself in the mirror above the dresser, was startled by my own image; my eyes were the eyes of a wild woman! I wanted to run! run far away! to peace! I needed peace!

Annie came in. She hugged me. "Calm down, Mommy." She patted my back caressingly, as if I were her child. "Everything will be alright, you'll see, shhh. I love you, Mommy."

"Oh, Annie, I love you too, sweetheart. Thank you, my love, for helping me. I'm sorry for getting so upset, sweetheart. I'll be okay."

"Neale doesn't mean to upset you so much, Mommy. He really loves you. He's just going through a difficult period in his life."

I looked into her serious eyes. Nine years old. God had truly blessed me.

"Don't get married too young, my Annie doll," I stroked her lustrous hair. "You must go to college and finish growing up first." I drew my precious daughter close and enfolded her in my arms. "Listen, Annie, we mustn't tell Grandma and Grandpa about the motorcycle, they'll get upset and it will ruin the Seder."

"Don't worry, Mommy, I understand . . . then the whole Seder that's all they'll talk about and the dining room looks so beautiful we should talk about only good things, right? . . . don't worry, Mommy, I won't tell."

Neale was still in the garage admiring his treasure. "Neale, you have to get cleaned up for the Seder. I spoke to Mr. Blackstone, we'll have to take him to court." I put my hand on his shoulder.

"How could you do this, Neale, especially on the first night of Passover? Grandma and Grandpa will be here any minute. It's best if we don't discuss this motorcycle thing tonight, okay? I'd like us to have a nice Seder."

Love and compassion for my son swept over me and filled my heart. He could hardly wait to be a grown man and do exactly as he pleased.

"I hate holidays and big dinners!" he said as we climbed the stairs.

"I know how you feel. Let's try to make the best of it, okay?"

My leg was throbbing, I couldn't bear it anymore! sharp pain shot through my stomach, I desperately needed to lie down and rest! The drizzle had become a downpour.

My parents arrived and waited in their car for me to open the garage door like I always did when they visited on rainy days. But they'd see the motorcycle! Because I never told my parents about my troubles, presenting always for them a lovely picture of complete harmony and grace, the expression of Neale's rebellious behavior - that monster in the garage - would come to them as out of the blue and as shocking as anything could be. The illusions I created were to my parents, the reality of my life. My lifelong determination to protect my mother and father had led me to the very edge of holding it all together. How far-reaching was my responsibility for their happiness? Now was not the time for introspection. My parents walked around to the front door laden with shopping bags and pots.

"What's the matter with you, Fran? Why didn't you open the garage door instead of letting your mother and I get all wet like this?"

"Don't complain, Dad, just come in and relax."

"So," my father asked, "is your brother coming over?"

"I invited him, Dad, he said they might be here for dessert."

"Such a disgrace! The family can't even have a Seder together!"

"Mom, please don't start, you know how it is, we all know."

"My sisters have their families together, but I have this! My son, my wonderful son, is married to a woman who keeps him all to herself. I denied myself everything, a lifetime of denial, so he could be a doctor, and now, he lives in a mansion, a beautiful mansion, and we're not even welcome there! Disgrace!"

"C'mon, Mom, let's enjoy our Seder, this is nothing new, it's years since they came to a Seder, and they won't be here later ... he says the same thing every year and they only came once. You have to accept it, this is the way it is, and it's not changing."

"I can't accept it! I'll never accept it!"

"I know how you feel, Mom. But when I look into the future I don't see anything different. Remember that aggravating conversation I had with him, when he said not to expect them anymore, too much trouble for Gloria when it was her turn? And even when I said, just come so we'll be together, Gloria doesn't have to reciprocate, he still refused. Over an hour on the phone. So I'm telling you, Mom, accept it, this is the way it is. I know how you feel, Mom, believe me, but there's nothing we can do."

"Everything came to nothing! That's my lousy life!"

"I don't understand, Mom, isn't it good enough to be here? You're in my house, I'm happy to have you here together with my children, everyone loves you, and look around, how it's all so beautiful. I've been working so hard to make everything nice."

"Fran is right, Mary. Just take a look here, what our daughter does for us." My father turned to Annie. "And look at this sweet angel doll. How's my favorite granddaughter?"

"Go call him, Matty," my mother wouldn't let go, "maybe if you ask, he'll come."

SUE DRIER, Annie's former nursery school teacher, had become my close friend. She liked to call in the morning, as soon as she finished blow-drying her hair. "I'm so bored, Fran, how about breakfast at the diner? I'll pick you up in five minutes."

I threw the wash into the dryer, left the dusting for another time, and ran out to the sound of Sue's horn. Both of us were restless and longed to be engaged in interesting activity. Sue did occasional substitute teaching but she felt dissatisfied. I did posting for Danny. He brought home the computer print-outs from the parts department and paid me five dollars an hour.

"Do you know what my mind is filled with, Sue?" We buttered our toast. "Numbers. And I mean numbers. Each part has an eight or ten or twelve digit number and I've memorized every one of them."

"You're so lucky, Fran, your husband has a business."

"Do you really think I want to use my mind for posting parts inventory? I'm only doing it temporarily, until Danny gets the parts department organized. If I didn't do it, he'd have to, and he's so tired at night. And someday I'll be working with Danny . . . this vision keeps showing up at different times, of being his partner in business. I don't know how it will come about, I just see us working together."

"I admire you, Fran, you know what you want and you go after it. You knew you wanted a wealthy boy and you went after one."

"What are you talking about? I didn't marry Danny for money! Why do you say that, Sue, it really annoys me. I don't understand why, but his friends used to say things like that to me, and it's plain offensive."

"Well, you had to want things or else you wouldn't have them. I know, I studied psychology."

"What things, Sue? You mean my house? You think I married Danny so I'd get to live in a big house?"

I still remembered the cozy little houses for sale near the Sound when Danny and I were first married. To have bought one of those houses and furnished it simply, inexpensively, would have delighted me. Instead, my mother-in-law had dragged me to fancy furniture stores and my mother had urged me to go along; it gave my mother so much happiness to see my home furnished with expensive furniture she herself could not afford. I was eighteen years old, so I had gone along and pleased the mothers. Rose believed I should be grateful and my mother believed the expensive furniture made me happy.

"Well," Sue was saying, "when I married Robert I expected him to provide me with certain things. Only in my case it hasn't happened yet, I'm still waiting."

"There's more to life than material things, Sue. Believe me, all I ever wanted from Danny was his love."

"Come on, Fran, admit it, aren't we friends?"

"You're so wrong, Sue, and you're upsetting me. My mother-in-law always says those things to me. What you're doing is invalidating my love for Danny, and it's my love for him that's directed my life since the day we met. Sure, there are times I wish I didn't love him, he knows how to hurt me ... it's a major issue with me, Sue, so please get off the material track ... please!"

"So, what are you saying, is Danny into the control thing?" I was startled by my friend's question and became immersed momentarily in my own deep thoughts. Sue looked into my eyes for an answer while we sat across from each other in silence. "So, why do you put up with it? Look, whatever else he's doing, trying to control you, or whatever, Danny loves you. How could he not? You're beautiful." She scooped her home fries onto my plate, "Here, you take them, somehow they don't show on you." Barely pausing for a breath my friend's mind was already spinning with another issue of mutual concern.

"By the way," Sue said, "what do you think of Ellen Larkin and the book she goes around with on open marriage? Do you think Larry goes along with the idea?"

"She really got me annoyed at the party Saturday night. Did you hear her, going on and on about it with Danny. I was upset with him when we came home."

"Why?"

"Why? He was flirting with her! Didn't you see it? I just don't know how to handle it when he does that? You think I should just go over and interrupt? That seems so . . ."

"Oh, come on, Fran! Whatever's going on in your head? You two have a great marriage! Gorgeous kids, smart and good, every night your husband comes home to you. I wish Robert loved me like Danny loves you!"

People's perceptions, as I'd learned long ago when my mother complained that the neighbors would think we were rich because my father drove a new car every year, were based entirely on appearances. No one could know what another person's truth was. Especially when most people didn't even know their own truth. It seemed that everyone was living with their own illusions; even within one greater illusion that encompassed all our lesser ones. How could you ever break out from under the weight of it all and just be free?

"Well, be careful with your judgments, Sue, you may not be seeing the whole picture. So happens, Danny ignored me the whole party and he didn't stop joking around with Ellen."

"Don't be so sensitive! He was just having fun."

"But that's just it, Sue, I'd like my husband to flirt with me sometimes . . . I need some fun, too!"

"But why do you worry about Ellen Larkin? And why would Danny be interested in her when he has you? Besides, you flirt with other men!"

"I do not! How can you say such a thing? Who do I flirt with? Tell me!"

"Every man you talk to, Fran, don't make believe you don't."

"Sue, you must be crazy! I just talk, that's all! Friendly talk!"

"Well, when you talk you look right into a person's eyes and then you smile and you look like you're flirting!"

"I've always looked into a person's eyes when I'm talking to them, and I smile when I feel friendly."

"Maybe you ought to think about how you look when you're talking to a man."

"Oh, Sue, to me, flirting is saying coquettish things like Ellen says to Danny, like, 'How do you like my new sweater, Danny? Larry says I have great tits.' That's flirting! Or else she says, 'Do I hold my tennis racquet like this, Danny? Show me.' And then she stands in front of him and leans against him. That's flirting! Not the kinds of conversations I have!"

"Well, in a way you're right, Fran, I can see your point. But you have this certain way about you, so you don't have to do what Ellen does. And truthfully, Fran, some women resent it."

"You know, Sue, I really don't understand ... but because you're so sure of what you say I'll give it some thought. But honestly, I have no intention of flirting ... maybe I have to adjust my style a bit, hold back ... I don't know, I'll think about it. I just want people to like me, that's all. And I guess smiling comes easily to me. But, thank you, I'll think about it."

Sue leaned back in the booth, patted my hand and swung her shiny hair the way she always did, probably unconsciously. Her hair was lovely. And she was a very pretty woman. A good friend.

"You know, Sue, even though what you've just told me is hurtful to me I do appreciate it. We just don't see ourselves as others do. We see ourselves from the inside, it's a feeling thing we have about ourselves, and others see the outward appearance, and usually without compassion. I've noticed people tend to judge each other quite carelessly."

"Yes, you have a point there, Fran."

"I do believe that if we expect this women's lib sisterhood thing to be successful it ought to begin with women being kind to other women. And that includes not trying to steal other women's husbands."

"Well, one of the guys, I can't say who, told Robert you licked your lips while looking straight at him. He took it that you were after him."

"What! That is the most ridiculous thing I ever heard! Who are you talking about?"

"I can't say, I promised Robert."

I watched her sip her hot cappuccino. "This is really nice, Sue, some idiot says some stupid thing and right away my friends are ready to believe it!" With this new accusation my mood shifted considerably and now I suspected that Sue's real motive on this otherwise pleasant morning, was to disrupt my peace and maybe even to aggravate me. "It would be nice to know you had some sense of loyalty, Sue. After all, we talk about everything, don't you know me? I thought you were an intelligent woman! Really! Oh! I can't take this, why am I even having this conversation with you?"

I pushed my full plate away, appetite completely gone, even though I loved bacon and eggs and home fries at the diner. "Whoever this person is, he's crazy! I wish you'd tell me who, so I could at least confront him and straighten this out! Besides, why are you saying all these things to upset me?"

"I'm really sorry, Fran, I like you a lot and you're a great friend, but you're so beautiful, and you have this perfect life, I just get jealous sometimes, I can't help it."

"I have plenty of my own struggles, Sue, and jealousy is a destructive force, it blinds you to our true purpose, the task we all share ... creating a life of harmony ... jealousy, or envy, interferes with that. So maybe we should just see less of each other for a while."

A few days later Sue began acting strangely. She called on me for help so I drove her to the doctor and then to the lab for blood tests. When the doctor called to report that the test results were negative Sue asked me to drive her to other doctors and other labs. She decided she was allergic to everything in her house. Her nervous anxiety began to overtake her life. She called a dozen times a day for moral support. Her daughter, Jodi, began spending more time at our house. Sue began complaining about tiny red bugs crawling around inside her mattress. She insisted that Robert discard their mattress. When she complained that her attic was also infested with tiny red bugs I became alarmed. Houses can become infested, doctors and labs can make mistakes and people can go through difficult phases but it wasn't only my friend's complaints that alarmed me. Her whole demeanor had changed.

After deliberating for hours, not wishing to interfere, yet seriously concerned, I called Robert at his office. His silence had also been disturbing me and I felt a talk with him was necessary. "What's happening, Robert?"

"I'm trying to convince her to see a psychiatrist but she gets angry. She needs you more than ever, Fran. Will you stick by her? You're the one person she really trusts."

The following morning I went over to Sue's house. The door was open so I went in to find Sue sitting immobile on her sofa in her otherwise nearly bare living room which had been fully furnished the last time I was there, and she was staring at the floor. I sat beside her, held her hands in mine, and searched her vacant eyes for signs of my vibrant friend. "Look at me, Sue, look into my eyes!"

Slowly Sue lifted her head, looked at me, finally acknowledged my presence and then she began her lament.

"Robert's having an affair with his secretary! We go away for the weekend and he takes his secretary along! My kids are getting used to having her around and they're turning away from me . . . I'm so strange these days . . . and they're turning to her for consolation!"

My friend was losing her mind over her husband's infidelity. I stroked her hands. The ramifications of his behavior within their family stood starkly before us and as we sat together on her sofa, I realized she was a shadow of herself yet still aware enough to understand that her life was falling slow-motion into a swamp, and I shared her grief.

"He was my high school sweetheart, Fran," she sobbed. "My first boyfriend. He used to say I was the prettiest girl in the class, that's why he married me." She twisted and knotted long sandy strands of hair until her hair was completely tangled and disheveled.

Later in the week Sue had a handyman come to the house and remove all the insulation from the attic. Then she said there were tiny red bugs in the bedroom carpet, and in the living room carpet. Four rooms of carpet were ripped out and discarded. Sue's parents came to stay and added to her grief by screaming at Robert.

The neighborhood women began avoiding her and whispering about her unusual behavior. Everyone started asking me questions. Is it true Sue's crazy? We hear her house is bare inside, is it true?

"Sue's not feeling well," I told them, "and she needs understanding. She'd really appreciate a visit from you."

But this was suburbia, land of perfection. Perfect untrodden front lawns, pedigree pets, ideal kids, sublime marriages.

"Poor Robert," everyone said.

The tragic turn of events in Sue's life caused me to examine my own life under a more urgent lens. Maybe I didn't see little red bugs in my home, but I cleaned every day as if I were warding off an infestation. I worried, also, that Danny might fall for another woman and turn my world upside down while my kids still needed a stable home. I, too, needed the comfort of friends. Instead, I felt alone and isolated. There was a core of strength inside me, though, and if I stayed connected to it nothing would unravel me as Robert was unraveling Sue. I peered into the hallway mirror. The sunlight was shining so pleasantly, softly through the white silk drapery in the dining room. Peering into the mirror I saw the light reflected in my eyes, in fact my eyes were glowing. 'Know yourself,' a silent message arose in my mind, 'your strength is in your soul and in your loving heart.'

Hours later, deep in the night, I awoke to find that Grandma's spirit was standing at the foot of my bed.

"Why do you not come to see me Fagala? You know I long for you."

"Grandma, how can I come? I have my children to care for, and you are in another world."

"Never mind," her spirit continued, "You must find a way to make your Grandma not feel so lonely."

"I understand . . . you want the family to be together, to honor your memory by remaining united. I'm trying. I remind them, whenever they're arguing and angry with each other, and I can't convince them to make peace, to remember you. But Grandma! Everything's changed! Do you still love me, Grandma?"

"Who else but you, my Fagala . . . you are the one who listens . . ."

"Grandma, tell me, will my children be alright? Will they have good lives?"

"Everything will be good for your children," Grandma's spirit consoled me, and it felt like she was smiling and her smile was a blessing, "Don't worry, my Fagala . . . your Grandma's always with you . . ."

In the morning Annie came into my room, put her arms around me in her gentle way, looked up into my face and on this ordinary school day said, "I love you, Mommy."

DANNY LIKED to scan Westchester used car listings. Generally garaged and cleaner than city cars, they were a good source and Danny didn't mind paying above wholesale for a creme-puff.

One Sunday afternoon, while relaxing in his leather chair in the family room, the Sunday papers scattered on the floor, Danny looked up from the automobile section and said, "You know something, Honey? I bet you could do this. All you have to do is learn how to qualify over the phone. You have a good eye. When you go there, if you like the car, make an offer, and then I'll come back with the check at night."

Danny circled with red marker the cars he liked and I made a list. He explained how to qualify the seller over the phone in order to avoid making unnecessary trips.

In a few minutes I was ready to make my first call. "Hello, Mr. Simpson?"

"Yeah, that's me."

"I'm calling about your ad in the 'Times' for a '75 Olds Cutlass Coupe."

"Yeah, that's my car."

"Can you tell me about your car? Is it in good condition?"

"Oh, yeah, excellent condition."

"Any scratches?"

"Nah, I got a perfect car here, no scratches, no nothin.'"

"You mean you're driving the car for two years and you never got a scratch?"

"Well, maybe some very small stuff, like on the fender, but no big deal."

"What about dents?"

"Well, we got a dent in the back, where the trunk handle is, some joker in a pickup got me at a red light, but you can hardly see it."

"I see, thank you for telling me about that. Mr. Simpson, has your car ever been in an accident?"

"Nah, never, no accident."

"And you use it mostly for local driving or for long trips?"

"This car? I take it up to my house in Vermont, maybe once a month."

If the car had mileage, that is, more than fifteen thousand miles a year, and had been used primarily for local driving, the general rule was that it suffered more abuse than a car with high mileage driven primarily on highways. Mr. Simpson's Cutlass had 25,000 miles on it. For a two-year-old car the mileage was good.

"How about the interior, Mr. Simpson? Is it clean?"

"Oh, yeah, the inside's beautiful!"

"Mr. Simpson, are you willing to consider less than your asking price of $4,600?"

"Well, I dunno, I got another party interested besides you."

"If your car looks as good as you say it does, I'm prepared to bring you a check tomorrow, no hassle, no delay."

"Well, then, how about you come an' have yourself a look?"

"Thank you, Mr. Simpson, I'd like to. Is tomorrow morning at ten okay for you?"

The car had to be seen in daylight, Danny said. When I drove up to Simpson's house I recognized the white Cutlass in the driveway. I walked around my first prospective buy, carefully examining the car, and realized how much I'd learned from Danny. The car had to have a sharpness to it, eye appeal. This white Cutlass Coupe had it. I spotted the scratches Simpson had described plus a dent he hadn't mentioned, in addition to the one by the trunk, near the bottom of the passenger door. The tip of the front left bumper was bent out. Even if the car looked really good you had to find flaws to use in bargaining. The finish looked smooth and original. I opened the door on the passenger side, the interior looked clean and crisp, the corners of the upholstery weren't even frayed.

Mr. Simpson stood by, watching me. Danny had cautioned me not to go for test drives; he'd do that before he paid.

"You do have a decent car, Mr. Simpson, but it's far from perfect. We're going to have some expenses with those scratches and the dents over there, all additional costs. I think you may have to come down a bit on your asking price."

The car, after these minor inexpensive repairs, would be a creme puff.

"Well, how much you want to pay?"

"How about $4,100? You'll have your check in a few hours."

"Nah, forty-one is too low, I can't sell my Cutlass that low."

"There's not much demand right now, Mr. Simpson, for this model." Maybe there was and maybe there wasn't, actually, I had no idea. Danny would know. "And a lot of people bother you afterward with all kinds of problems. With us you'll have no problems, we'll give you a check and take care of the rest."

"I don't know... maybe forty-three."

"Forty-two-fifty, Mr. Simpson, a check in your hands tonight."

The man hesitated another minute and then agreed.

At home, while setting the table for lunch with Annie and one of her friends, I called Danny at the Mazda showroom. "It's a great-looking car, Danny! A few scratches, two tiny dents, immaculate interior."

"How much did he come down?"

"I got him down to forty-two-fifty."

"Honey, you're terrific! See you tonight!"

After dinner Danny and I rushed out and drove to Bronxville. He gave the Cutlass his expert appraisal, checked the trunk, the engine, and drove around the block. He took out a check, looked at Mr. Simpson and said, "You know, you did okay for yourself."

"Oh yeah? Your wife here is some tough cookie, pal. What's she like to live with?"

Danny smiled, enjoying the whole scenario. "My wife? A tough cookie? Nah, my wife's a pushover!"

I drove the Volvo home and Danny followed in the Cutlass. Back on our driveway it was twilight and every leaf was still. The air was fragrant with another Spring.

"Danny, did you hear what he said? He said I was tough! Tough, Danny! Better watch out!" I laughed.

Danny laughed and grabbed my legs in a mock tackle. "You're terrific, Franny baby, terrific!"

For every car bought on my recommendation Danny paid me fifty dollars. It wasn't always as easy as Mr. Simpson's Cutlass, but it was always fun.

My friend Sue lamented that Robert was destroying her. "He's the reason I am the way I am, Francine. He did this to me! With his woman!" Sue had summoned me, in desperation, as she had nearly every morning, "I really need you, Fran, I'm so lonely."

It was a calm, sunny morning in April, the aroma and the breath of cool, damp air giving way to a fresh Spring day, inspiring memories of other days, when I'd walked the Concourse and Fordham and Valentine, visiting Elaine and JoAnn or bringing the homework to Sherry, keenly aware of the lovely weather and aware, also, there were places where a lovely Spring day could be far more beautiful and certainly healthier than on broken, littered, sooty pavements. What a lovely life, surrounded now by manicured lawns and fragrant landscaped gardens. And instead of walking everywhere, I drove, even if my destination was around the corner. So, on this beautiful day I drove the few blocks, one more time to comfort my friend.

We sat on her navy-blue sofa, our conversation echoing in the bare, chilly house and Sue's eyes beseeched me to save her. I put my arm around her too-thin shoulders. "Sue, you're an intelligent woman, you have to be strong now, use your intelligence. Don't let him do this to you, show him your strength!"

"That's the problem, Fran, I don't have that kind of strength! I'm not like you, and I know it."

"Come on, Sue, of course you have strength! I'll help you. First thing, you must groom yourself. Go take a shower and put on one of your pretty outfits."

"I don't want to, Fran, I take these pills now and I just want to sit here."

"What pills are you talking about?"

"Robert found this doctor for me. Robert controls everything. He tells the doctor all about me, what a bad mother I am, how I don't want sex anymore."

"Do you tell the doctor about Robert and his secretary?"

"Yes, I do, but he doesn't believe me. He listens only to Robert, and Robert tells him I'm crazy!"

"Sue, listen to me, are you listening?" Her eyes were vague and staring. "You're allowing yourself to be manipulated. Sue! it's your heart and your soul, no one owns you! You must take back control of your life. Do you hear me? Look at me, Sue!"

Her gaze traveled slowly upwards from the bare wood floor. "How? Tell me what to do, Fran."

"Do you want to go on like this? Do you want Robert back? Or something entirely different?"

"I want Robert back, Fran. Before, I wanted too many things from him … I got nothing anyway. I want my children to love me and respect me like they used to, only I don't know how to go about it."

"Think of how you used to be and what it was they loved about you."

"I used to teach. I never stayed home like this, day after day, doing nothing."

"Do you want to go back to teaching?"

"To tell you the truth, I don't think I could handle it now."

"How about a different kind of job, something you can handle?"

"I used to be a secretary …"

"Would you like to try that again?"

"I don't know, maybe … but who would hire me? Look at the mess I am."

"Sue, listen, Robert just opened his new office, right? He's on his own now, right? How about if you worked as Robert's secretary? You'd get dressed in the morning and go to work with him. You'd be helping him and the two of you might regain your closeness, mend your marriage."

"You think so, Fran?" A wan smile fluttered across her face.

"It's worth a try, I think, and it beats moping around the house all day!"

The next morning Sue called. "Robert says he could use my help. You were right, Fran, he's been paying these girls from Office Temps and he says he'd rather have me."

"Sue, that's great!"

"Yes, the only thing is, he says I shouldn't go in with him in the morning. He wants me to come down to Manhattan at one o'clock. I'm scared, Fran, will you drive me tomorrow? Annie can have lunch with Jodi at school and they can come over here at three-fifteen. Josh will be home, so they won't be alone."

Robert's office was small and sparsely furnished. I rested on the brand-new Danish leather love seat. Robert gave Sue his address book. Her assignment was to transfer all the information to Rolodex cards. Sue immediately set about her task. Her progress was impeded by her need to check and double-check the spelling of every name. She tossed dozens of Rolodex cards into the basket, some easily correctible, others hopeless messes.

Robert sat silent at his desk. Was he hoping, as I was, that Sue would rise to the occasion and perform her task professionally? Or was he using this opportunity to prove his own case more thoroughly? I watched Robert clip his nails, arrange paper fasteners and rubber bands in his center desk drawer and sharpen his pencils. I thought of Danny, managing three phones at once, driving across the Bronx from the used car lot on Bruckner to the Mazda showroom on Jerome, back and forth all day, running with me at night to look at used cars all over the neighborhood. Where were Robert's clients? Didn't accountants have tons of paper work, file drawers filled with forms, and busy phones? At four o'clock he told Sue he had a dinner engagement so it was time for her to go home. She left her desk littered with Rolodex cards, a few neatly typed and correct.

The next morning Robert called. "There's nothing more you can do for her, Fran. She's a very sick woman, she needs her medication, that's what she needs. And I'd like you to stop seeing her, from now on just leave her alone."

A few weeks later, while working on the daily entries in the parts ledger, I received a frantic call from Sue.

"He's taking me to an asylum, Fran! This weekend! And we have that wedding! I was looking forward to it, and he says I can't go, I'm too sick!"

I dropped my pencil. "Oh, my God, Sue!"

"What should I do?" she cried.

"We'll come over, Danny will be home soon, and we'll talk to Robert, we'll protect you, Sue, I promise!"

We sat on the navy-blue sofa in Sue's living room. Robert stood, facing us, pacing back and forth.

"Please, Robert, don't do this! Sue does not belong in that place! She can stay in her own home and still have good therapy!"

Robert shouted, "Don't tell me what to do with my wife!" Danny sat in shocked silence.

"I know what's good for Sue and you don't . . . she's crazy, don't you understand, out of her fucking mind!"

Jodi had come down from her room. She sat on the bottom step and stared at us, motionless and silent.

"See what he does to me?" Sue said, too calmly. "I told you, he tells everybody I'm crazy."

"Robert," I pleaded, "please, let's talk it over. There may be other options less extreme. Maybe this doctor you have now isn't good for Sue. Maybe we ought to find someone else. Anything, only please, don't put her in an institution!"

"Fran, this guy she sees now is good, he knows."

"He's your friend, Robert," Sue snapped, pointing her chin at him, a faint reminder of her old assertive self.

"Robert, please, let's talk."

"You've been causing trouble here long enough, Fran! Why don't you just go home!"

"I'm taking Sue with me! She'll stay in my house! I'll take care of her! C'mon, Sue!"

Robert shouted at Sue, "Don't you dare go with her!" In the

shadows of my mind there lingered still, and forever, painful memories of my father's institutional years. So long ago my father had been a helpless child in desperate need of an advocate, and no one, not one person, had stepped forward to protect him. Now my friend was like a helpless child and it felt absolutely natural for me to be her advocate.

I took my friend's hand, "Come home with me, Sue, I'll take care of you, and I'll find you a good doctor."

Sue looked at Robert. His eyes were burning into her. "Sue, you stay right here where you are! I'm your husband! You listen to me!"

Sue remained seated on her sofa. "I'm sorry, Fran," she said, in an expressionless voice, never looking up at me, "thank you but I can't go with you, I have to listen to my husband."

Danny and I walked toward the door, near the steps where Jodi was sitting. "I'm really sorry, Jodi, I love your Mom and I wanted to help her. Call any time you like, okay? And remember, you're always welcome to come over." Jodi nodded solemnly and continued to stare straight ahead.

The next day I waited in front of the school for Annie.

She was walking too slowly, and her chin almost touched her chest. What could've happened to dim the scintillating glow that my angel daughter wore like a crown and which distinguished her in any group. She opened the car door and climbed in.

"Sweetheart, what's the matter?"

"They won't talk to me! And they won't tell me why! Not even Jodi, or Tracey. At recess I asked Jodi what's wrong but she wouldn't tell me. Then I asked Tracey and Carol and Lisa but no one would tell me anything!"

"They've done this so often, Annie, to other girls, and now they're doing it to you! But they can't stay mad at you, sweetheart, after all, you're the one who helps the others when it happens to them. They'll remember, you'll see, Annie."

"No, they won't, Mommy, they really mean it."

At three-fifteen I met with Annie's teacher. Tall and blond and kind, Mrs. Young wore a tailored white blouse, tweed skirt, sturdy brown oxfords, and traces remained of bright red lipstick which had worn off during lunch and which she'd been too preoccupied to retouch. At our conference in November Mrs. Young had shown me papers indicating Annie's citywide and national test scores. Annie had scored in the ninety-ninth percentile in every area. She'd said to me that day, "Once in every teacher's career a very special student comes along, someone who makes it all worthwhile. For me, that student is Annie." Regarding the ostracism occurring now Mrs. Young assured me, "Mrs. Sachleben, nothing like this will be permitted in my class, you have my word. I'll speak to the girls tomorrow. And I'll keep my eyes open." She smiled warmly and took my hands in hers. "Don't worry, I'll look after Annie."

For three weeks Mrs. Young kept her promised vigil and a strained peace prevailed. Then she took a leave of absence to nurse her mother who was suffering the final stages of breast cancer, and the girls stopped talking to Annie.

The substitute said, "I know all about it, Mrs. Young told me, and I'm doing my best. These girls aren't easy, you know, they smile and say, 'Yes, Mrs. Marcus' and I can't tell if they're sincere. And your daughter doesn't complain. She sits at her desk and does her work and participates in class, so everything looks good to me."

MANY YEARS LATER, after her discharge from another sanitarium where she'd been recuperating from another suicide attempt, Sue found me in my new home, and in a flat, dispassionate voice apologized. "There's something that's always bothered me, Fran, and I must tell you. I'm so sorry for what happened back then with Annie and the girls. It was all because of me. Jodi was angry and she took it out on Annie. I saw it, and that was one thing I could've done something about. I think about it all the time, and it's one of the things I'll never forgive myself for."

THE SUNSET. I lie down on the light-blue damask sofa in the family room. My leg is hooked up to the machine. The shutters are open, revealing the three large picture windows which face west. It is the peak of the hottest hour on a summer's day. Above the roof the sun advances, and the heat from the sun can be felt, magnified, through the window glass.

The sunlight is going to fade the upholstery. But I need the comfort and the warmth of the sun, and I like how the wood paneling looks in sunlight. The wine-red and light- blue of the Persian carpet are prettier in the wash of light. All of this will outlive me. The floors I vacuum and scrub, the furniture I polish, will remain long after me. Who will care about my immaculate floors and gleaming woods? Why do I care?

At night I dream I'm in my house, walking through each room and looking beyond for the end, for the last room. I wander. Each succeeding room grows smaller and smaller, the work I must do is endless. Less time for achievement.

Too much time wasted waiting for maintenance men. They come to turn the lawn sprinkler on and off with the season, they come to spray the trees, fix the washer, repair the refrigerator, replace faulty shower lead pans, mend the gutters, install attic fans, repair the air-conditioner, repair loose stair tiles, put up and take down the patio awning, fix the telephone and TV cable. They track through my clean house in their work boots, appraise my home with raised eyebrows, ask for drinks, to use the phone, do not apologize for arriving late or tracking mud. I count the hours and minutes until they finish and leave.

Strangers somehow choose my bell to ring when their cars break down or if they're lost, or caught in a thunderstorm while biking. Always, I open the door and welcome them. Once, in the middle of the night, a young woman knocked on our door. She had been thrown from a car by three men, she sobbed. I took her in.

My eyes close and I feel the sun still warm on my face. The Soviet Union and the United States' build-up of enough nuclear arms to destroy the world no longer exists. The persistence of anti-semitism in the world, even here in our town, does not exist, nor the prospect of war in some far-off land drafting my boy into danger. Danny going off to work each morning, dynamic and handsome, a challenge to his bookkeeper, does not exist. How am I going to make it through the rest of my life with this leg? The sun is lower in the sky. The machine is pumping and droning. With all my heart I call out to my body, to my colon! be calm! please! I want to live a normal life! "Hear me now," quickly comes the reply, "hear me! for my dysfunction is the manifestation of all your fears! Take control of your days. When your leg throbs and you can no longer bear the pain and you are frustrated with yourself, I churn and twist and create more pain. Be kinder, therefore, to your leg. Love your leg! Love me, your body! And love yourself, the heart and soul of you! Then, Francine, your life shall become transformed!" I understand, my mind responds, I understand. My face feels cool. My eyes open. The sun lies low in a blazing sky of fiery red and yellow streaks. The thing I love most about this house is the sunset, painted and framed anew each evening in the picture windows of the family room. There is a sunset inside me, too! A new day will dawn tomorrow! A day without azulfadines, a day without lomotils! And soon a day without the machine! I make a silent heartfelt pact with myself, and vow to keep it.

Conscious Intentions & Manifestation

EAST TREMONT AVENUE, 1978. After school Neale goes directly to his job at the warehouse. Annie is in sixth grade, in the Gifted Program. Soon I'll be thirty-six and I realize that for the first time since Neale was born, when I was nineteen, there's no reason to be home for lunch. So I drive to the showroom on Jerome Avenue.

A little over a year ago at 9:34 PM on the night of July 13, 1977 the lights went out in New York City. Throughout the night and into the next day lawlessness prevailed, looters rampaged the neighborhoods, stealing, smashing, burning everything they could. One of the hardest hit neighborhoods in the city was Jerome Avenue; it would never be the same for fear now discouraged customers as well as employees. We had to relocate, but every minute of Danny's day was crammed with running the business and there was never enough time.

Danny's reputation as a knowledgeable, reliable automobile dealer had earned him a substantial customer following. He spent evening hours advising customers as to which particular car would best suit their needs. He invited his customers into our home to sign contracts, review their owners' manuals and satisfy all their questions. Out on the driveway he attached their license plates and delivered their cars.

When a car required service or repair, Danny arranged for the customer to exchange his car for Danny's dark green Volvo. Every night another of Danny's customers would arrive on our driveway to return Danny's Volvo and pick up their own car which was always waiting for them, service or repair completed. Then another customer would arrive for his exchange, pick up Danny's Volvo and leave his own car for Danny to drive in for service in the morning. Occasionally, a customer failed to return Danny's Volvo on time. On those evenings Danny drove to the customer's house to make the exchange and hurried back to our driveway for the next pick up.

It was not unusual for Danny to drive a customer who lacked funds to buy a new car from the showroom to the used car lot. One afternoon two male customers said they couldn't afford a new Honda after all, they'd like to see a used one, so Danny drove them over to the lot on Bruckner Boulevard. After showing them several used Hondas he got back into the Volvo with the men and when they were just a few blocks from the showroom one of the men reached into his jacket, pulled out a revolver and held it to Danny's head.

"Turn off here, man, right here at the corner."

Fear drained all color from Danny's face, he felt himself grow cold, and he did as ordered.

"Get out!" the other one shouted, "an gimme everthin you got!"

Danny handed over his cash, his wallet and his Seiko watch and got out of the car. The hold-up men drove off in the Volvo leaving Danny sweating and shaking on a street of abandoned, burned-out buildings. At the police station a few days later we learned that the day after they robbed Danny these same two men had held the same pistol to the head of a young supermarket check-out girl and the faulty gun had accidentally discharged, killing the girl instantly.

"This is it, Danny, we've got to get out of Jerome Avenue, find a safe location, and soon."

We were lying in bed, talking in the dark; Danny leaned on one elbow and a narrow beam of light from the street lamp outside gleamed through a space in the shutters and captured the sparkle in his eyes. "How about if you help me, Honey? We'll look together! You have good judgment, I can use your help."

Yes! Yes! Of course I'll help you! I will, of course, defer again my dream to become a writer. Here, in the present moment, practical needs are pressing and immediate. In fact, while fully immersed in family concerns I had devoted very little time to honing my writing skills. And while I wasn't paying attention my dreams had shifted.

Striving for harmony within the family and within our marriage had led to personal evolution, Danny and I working together to ensure financial security for our children, this was harmony! As well as an opportunity for us to grow closer, for me to earn Danny's real respect out in the world away from home. So it was with joyful enthusiasm that I flung myself into a new expanded life, my own golden opportunity.

When I arrive at the showroom, Danny's working several transactions simultaneously. In the parts department disorganization and inertia envelope me like a thick fog. Here emerges a row of dark narrow shelves crammed with boxes of parts, large and small jumbled together; there, a gruff hand reaches, shuffles some stuff around, clanking noises, hairy voices, curses. In the bookkeeper's office Maria sashays over to Danny, cracks her chewing gum and smiles, "I'm getting the statement out on time this month, Danny, will you take me out to dinner?"

At last we were in the car together. "How's my gorgeous baby, huh?" Danny leaned over and kissed me. "You're looking too thin,

Honey, I want you to eat something before we go looking at real estate."

I'd been infected with a strange virus during the summer and had lost weight.

"Danny, why can't you find another bookkeeper? Maria's behavior is very unprofessional … in her approach to her work and in the way she behaves with you."

"I know, Honey, but it's difficult to get a bookkeeper and she knows the routine."

"I don't like the way she flirts with you, Danny, it's inappropriate and you shouldn't be encouraging it."

"Don't pay attention to that stuff, Honey, it's nothing."

"Nothing? What's this dinner thing?"

"I told her if she finished the statement on time I'd take them to dinner, all of them." Maria had hired her friends.

"I've never encountered a situation such as you're setting up here, Danny, and I've worked in lots of offices. Isn't it her job to get the statement out on time?"

"It is, I know, but let her just do it. I didn't think of going without you, Honey."

Oh, sure, Danny, that's why you never mentioned it to me. I decided to let it go for the present, and turned my attention back to more important and pressing issues.

It would have been ideal to relocate in Westchester. But an automobile franchise agreement is valid only in the area of responsibility, known as a 'Point,' for which it was originally issued by the manufacturer. Our 'Point' was, of course, the Bronx. We were free to relocate within the Bronx provided the factory saw it as an upgrade and granted approval. Coming out of Jerome Avenue any neighborhood at all had to be an improvement.

Danny and I parked outside automobile showrooms and watched the traffic flow. We examined the side streets, observed other small businesses in the dealership neighborhood. We went inside the showrooms to examine their design, what the personnel were like and if the place was busy. We were searching for a location with good public access, growth potential, active neighborhood businesses and stability.

At night we reviewed the pros and cons of each location until we narrowed the choice to two neighborhoods: Fordham Road near Southern Boulevard or East Tremont Avenue near Westchester Square. Fordham and Southern Boulevard was known as automobile row, plus it was a high traffic area; it was also somewhat seedy and rundown. Westchester Square was bustling with successful small businesses. The neighborhood side streets were lined with neat, well-tended homes. Major highways connecting the Bronx to Long Island, Westchester, Manhattan and New Jersey crisscrossed the outskirts of the neighborhood. Several well-known, long-established auto dealerships were located there.

The showroom available on East Tremont Avenue, old Grand Ford, was large enough to accommodate our three franchises and it had wonderful growth potential. The owner of the property, petite and lovely Carlotta, was a pleasure to do business with and Danny signed a ten-year lease.

Our task was to give the place a new look on a shoestring budget. One of our office employees, through a family connection, negotiated a wholesale price on terra-cotta tile and recommended three buddies who, for an after-hours low price, handled the installation with professional expertise. In a neighborhood supply store we selected coordinated wall paneling. We painted and carpeted the back offices, scrubbed the outside aluminum siding.

Danny ordered signs: HONDA. MAZDA. VOLVO. We moved in January 1979. Out from under the dismal Jerome Avenue 'El' and into the sunlight of broad and clean East Tremont Avenue, number 2455.

At dinner one night, having had the inspiration only a few minutes earlier while setting our places at the table, I suggested we try a specific kind of family discussion; we'd take turns describing a pleasing, helpful thing each of us had done over the past week and also, something bothersome. To my delight everyone agreed.

"Alright, Neale, would you like to go first?"

"Okay." He looked across the table at his sister. "You ate my yogurt, Annie. I bought it with my own money and you ate it!"

"Did you Annie?" I asked.

A worried look came over her face. "Yes, but I didn't know it belonged to Neale and I like yogurt."

"Okay," I said, more aware than even a few minutes ago of the minor family annoyances that could so easily be rectified, not only with polite manners but also with a little humor. We were enjoying our dinner, we were smiling and even laughing. "Okay, I'll buy enough yogurt for both of you. Tomorrow, I promise, we'll have plenty of yogurt."

Neale sat back in his chair, satisfied. "Now," I prodded, "what has Annie done to please you?"

"She rubbed lotion on my shoulders and on my back." He smiled at his sister, she smiled at him.

How joyful I felt! It was really working! I thought of the spacious, cobalt-blue and white bathroom Neale and Annie shared; two sinks opposite a mirrored wall. I called it their conference room because they were always in there, grooming and talking.

"Okay, Neale, now do Daddy."

He turned to me. "No, I'll do you now. Why can't you stop arranging my papers and books into piles? I like my stuff left alone."

"I do that when I'm dusting, but thank you for telling me, Neale, from now on I'll dust around your papers."

"Yeah, sure you will."

"I will, Neale. Now tell me something I did that you like."

He thought for a moment. "Oh, yeah, you made my deposit for me. Thanks."

"You're welcome, sweetheart. Now do Daddy."

He looked at his father and back at me. "I can't think of

anything bad for Daddy. Daddy doesn't do anything wrong. Daddy gave me my car, he took me for my college interview, Daddy does everything right." Neale rose from his chair and leaned over to kiss Danny on the cheek. "I love Daddy, Daddy's Mr. Wonderful."

Annie's eyes met mine and we exchanged a smile. "Okay, Danny, you're next."

Danny looked across the table at me in that mischievous way of his that said, You asked for it so don't complain.

"I don't like the fish tonight, it's awful, what did you do to it? Can't you learn to broil fish right?"

"I like it, Mommy," Annie interjected.

"It's disgusting!" Neale said.

"I'm sorry you don't like the filet of sole, Danny, maybe I ought to just make scallops next time. What did I do this week that you liked?"

Danny winked at me. "C'mon, Danny!"

"You're a good wife, Honey, a good wife."

"That's it? Oh, Danny!"

He looked at his son. "Be nice to Mommy."

"I don't bother Mommy, she bothers me!"

"For something I like about you," Danny continued, "you're a good son."

He looked at his daughter, at me, then back at Annie. I read his mind. It was difficult to come up with a complaint for Annie. "I can't think of anything Annie did to annoy me. Annie is a very good daughter." Danny was the only one who could get away with these answers and he knew it.

"Thank you, Daddy," she answered. "Now it's my turn."

Annie looked at her father. "It would be nice, Dad, if you learned my parakeets' names and which was which." Neale laughed and then we all laughed. We never knew if Danny was teasing or if he really couldn't keep track. He smiled at Annie.

"I'll try, I promise. Show me again, later, okay?"

"Okay. Thank you, Daddy, for playing pool with me and ping pong, too." Annie gave him a big smile.

"You're welcome, Annie, I like to play pool with you, and you're getting really good at it."

Annie looked at Neale. "You used my towel the other day. Can't you use your own towels?"

"Big deal, so I used your towel, what difference does it make?"

"I don't use your towels . . ."

"So what? So who cares?"

"C'mon, Neale," I said. "You know your towels are next to your sink and Annie's are on her side. And this isn't even about towels, it's about respect."

"Use your own towels, okay, Neale?" Danny said.

"Thanks, Neale, for giving me advice."

Neale's face softened. He loved his position of older brother. He nodded and smiled at his sister.

Annie turned and looked at me with her deep, liquid eyes. "You don't do anything to bother me, Mommy. You take care of me and teach me stuff, I don't know what I'd do without you." She patted my hand.

"That's sickening!" Neale said. "It's your turn now, Mommy."

"Let's hear it, Fran!" Danny called out.

I looked at him. "You made such a fuss over Arlyne's meatloaf last Saturday night but you complain whenever I tell you we're having meatloaf even before you taste it!"

"That's because he already knows how bad your meatloaf is!" Neale laughed.

"I'm telling you, Danny, the day will come when I'll never cook for you at all, just you wait and see!"

"I'm sorry, Honey, I guess I'm fussy, I can't help it."

"Okay, for something good. You remembered to take off your sneakers when you came home from tennis so I didn't have that gray sand tracked through the house. I appreciate that." Neale often left his key on the outside ledge above the garage door and, ignoring my warranted concern about security, reached up in plain view of the whole street to retrieve it. "Neale, please, I've asked you so many times, don't leave your key outside. What good is the alarm and the wrought iron on the downstairs windows if there's a key outside?"

"No one knows it's there."

"But anyone can see you reach for it, Neale."

"Who's looking? No one's out there. Don't be so neurotic, Mommy."

"You went to the deli for me yesterday and I really appreciate it. Thank you, Neale."

"It's okay."

Annie waited. Finally, I said, "You left your light on late last night, Annie, after I asked you to turn it off."

"I thought you said I could read in bed if I couldn't sleep. I was reading."

"But not so late, Annie. And for something good, thank you for keeping your room neat and clean."

"My room is too beautiful to let it get messy."

This is what we did on Monday nights until Neale's enthusiasm faded and our engaging family conversations dwindled away.

AT THE DEALERSHIP Danny rarely paused to rest. Sitting behind a desk was too confining for him; Danny was a whirlwind of nonstop action. Every interaction with employees took place at their station, and Danny had so many deals on his mind and felt so overwhelmed by the new car business, his nervous energy kept him always on his feet. He needed a quiet break in the day which on his own he didn't take, but when I showed up he looked at me and said, "You have to eat, Honey, let's go have a bite." Just the way he used to say it when he picked me up at Roosevelt. Then he talked about the day's aggravation and accomplishments and calmed down.

Driving under the noisy elevated trains one day we noticed a restaurant with brick-framed arched windows; we'd found Joe's. Even though the 'El' ran by outside the place was crowded with business people and Bronx politicians, limos waiting up and down the block.

During the five minute drive from Joe's back to our showroom we passed Sander's Buick, Pape Chevrolet and the newly constructed Grand Ford showroom.

Suddenly struck with a vision I said, "Someday, Danny, we're going to own all of this!" I was so filled with a grand burst of energy I flung out my arms to encompass three long blocks on East Tremont Avenue.

Danny smiled.

"You'll see . . . all this will be ours . . . for the kids . . . for their future."

"These guys have been here for years, Honey, and they're not going anywhere. And the Ford store is owned by the factory."

"Doesn't matter, Danny, it's all going to be ours. I'm seeing the future!"

Danny leaned over and kissed me.

One Spring evening after dinner, instead of leaving the kitchen as he usually did, to go outside and relax, Danny remained at the table and waited for me to finish cleaning up.

"Come, sit down a minute, Honey." He took my hand. "You know the dealer who has his wife on TV doing commercials? Well, I was thinking, if she can do it, so can you!"

"You want me to make a commercial?"

"Yeah! You'd be good, Honey! They'll see your face and hear your voice and they'll come running to buy cars from us!"

"Danny, are you crazy? I can't just go and make a commercial. I don't know anything about how to do it and I'm not making a fool of myself."

"You can do it, Honey. And you'll be good, I know you will! Write up a few lines and tomorrow I'll get in touch with my advertising agency."

"Danny! Just like that?"

"Yeah. You can do anything you set your mind to, Fran. And we'll work together. We'll have fun! I'm going to make you famous, Francine baby, famous!"

"Well, I'll try . . . but I don't know . . ." I rose from the kitchen chair to find some paper.

Danny grabbed my hand and kissed it. What wouldn't I do to make my marriage strong? To show Danny there was a lot more inside me than he imagined when he drove to 199th Street, dusty from a long day on the lot, just because he had to see me and didn't even know why.

I worked on and off, between phone calls and pressing interruptions from the kids. "How does this sound, Danny? And time me with your second hand, okay?"

It ran to thirty-one seconds. I scratched out a couple of phrases and he timed me again. "Twenty-eight seconds, perfect! Say it again, Honey, I love it!"

Now Danny was my audience, but how would I manage when this thing was for real, in front of a camera, a host of people looking on? Suddenly I remembered my third grade class play, *Sleeping Beauty*; someone had submitted my name for the lead role, my classmates had voted and given it to me. Under the white dotted Swiss cotton dress Grandma had sewn, its hem touching the floor, my knees had trembled violently. But when the curtain rose I simply forgot my shyness, I forgot to be frightened, and had concentrated on the performance.

The idea of making a commercial was only a few hours old but already it had crystalized into the next stage of my legitimate place in Danny's business life. I determined to be strong, to be smart, to do whatever it took to help Danny build our business, to be successful, to ensure financial security for Neale and Annie. My kids will never live on Vyse Avenue. In my mind I saw the future – my kids will live in lovely homes. I held the vision. I was going to breathe life into my vision. I couldn't do it alone. So I called on God, and then I remembered my Grandma promising to always be with me, and my guardian angel, Love, also beside me. And suddenly, a big truth was revealed to me. We may feel alone yet we are not alone.

"Here goes, Danny . . . wait, let me step back, you're going to make me laugh with that expression on your face."

Our Bronx dealerships still went by the name, Edmond Motors, the original name decided upon by Leo years ago, and which hadn't been amended to include Danny's name. I'd been urging Danny to change the name of our dealerships to DAN MOTORS, but he wasn't quite ready for another round of arguments with his parents and brother. And now it fell to me to deliver that name, Edmond's, as if I loved it with all my heart.

I cleared my throat and began. "Hi, welcome to Edmond's newest showroom at 2455 East Tremont Avenue. Sure, you can buy a new Honda Accord, Volvo, Mazda GLC or RX7 somewhere else, but here at Edmond's we want to make you happy! At Edmond's you'll be greeted by one of our friendly, helpful salesmen who will cater to your needs. When you drive out of Edmond's in your new Honda Accord, you'll feel comfortable and relaxed knowing you got the deal you wanted!"

The president of the advertising agency sent his son, Alan, to handle our TV account. Danny and I decided to film the commercial on location, freeing us from the burden of transporting cars to Manhattan plus we'd get outdoor and indoor shots of the showroom, and it was cheaper than renting a studio. Alan needed a few weeks to get a camera crew together. Meanwhile, I practiced my lines every day in front of the large mirror in the blue bathroom, scrutinizing every detail of my thirty-second performance. As I noticed personal flaws I corrected myself, subsequently becoming more professional. I practiced and practiced until the mirror showed me I had conquered each flaw.

In mid-May the day of the filming dawned sunny and cool. Immediately upon awakening I felt with dread the familiar monthly pain. Intense rhythmic pain traveled down my legs and the veins in my legs hurt more than on ordinary days. On the days of my monthly cycle it was difficult to leave the house. My uterus swelled and the discharge of endless blood clots caused a terrible personal problem. Today I'd have a lot more to transcend than shaky knees at school plays.

Call Danny, tell him to reschedule the filming, I thought, then decided against it. The arrangements had been complex, involving a lot of people. The head cameraman had even called last night for confirmation. If I wanted to be respected and taken seriously in business, canceling for female problems was out of the question. Imagining the usual comments and jokes by the men who would be sorely inconvenienced was enough to thrust me forward into the day.

The automobile business was traditionally dominated by men. Wives who worked in the dealership were bookkeepers who ran the office. I surely was not the only one, but I certainly was one of the first, to break into this male-dominated world. I couldn't have done it alone. Danny was my support. His mantra became, 'You can handle anything, Honey,' and he delegated to me many responsibilities.

Maybe he was not inclined to deal with those responsibilities, he'd rather go off to the tennis court, but still, he entrusted me to always do the right thing. And he really did enjoy having me by his side at the many functions that crop up in the course of doing business. The men were growing accustomed to my presence and I felt respected by them. So it was imperative to maintain my fledgling reputation, and not only for myself. At those meetings where I was the only woman I felt my presence spoke for the emergence of the feminine, a strong, capable feminine energy, an unstoppable movement, for the planet had begun to cry out for major re-balancing of everything.

I dressed in my dark-brown velvet jeans, sand-colored hand-knit sweater and dark-brown suede platform sandals. I would have preferred to wear a more sophisticated outfit but there rarely was time for shopping and suddenly the day was here, so I told myself this was better, I'd have the next-door-neighbor look instead of trying to impersonate a model. For good luck I wore my gold seaplane charm suspended on a gold necklace; it was set with two large oval cabochon emeralds and a large round cabochon ruby. Danny had bought it for me on our honeymoon in Montego Bay, for twenty-five dollars, and the salesman had told us the stones were glass!

The first problem we encountered at the showroom was power; the ancient wiring in our showroom couldn't accommodate the crew's lighting requirements. Cables covered the floor tiles in organized chaos. Lights and tripods teetered beside gleaming Mazdas, Volvos and Hondas. Camera equipment lay scattered on salesmen's desktops and on the low ledge which spanned the length of the plate-glass windows. The crew shouted orders at each other trying to resolve the power problem.

I tried to rest in Danny's office. "Want some lunch, Honey?"

"Not today, Danny, thanks."

A timid knock on the door and Alan entered. "It's nice in here," he said, looking around. "They want to check you out under the lights."

It was one o'clock. Feeling ill I left the comfort of Danny's leather recliner and immediately, those horrible clots again! sending me into our private bathroom, peaceful and charming, the sun casting a dim light through the cloudy leaded glass of an old-fashioned skylight.

Out on the showroom floor John, the head cameraman, held light meters to my hair and face; adjustments of tripods and angles of light. Glare that bounced off polished fenders and hoods was eliminated but they didn't want to lose the shine on my hair.

"Got the lines down?" John asked. "So let's run through for timing, okay?" The timing was perfect. "Put more excitement into your voice, Fran," he coached. I tried.

They took shots of the salesmen, and Maria and Carol posed as customers. They needed shots of cars, of course, plenty of car shots. The commercial would open, John said, with one RX7 headlight cover blinking open. Nice touch, wish I'd thought of it.

Three o'clock came and went and still they weren't ready for me. I was exhausted. Rotating blades in my uterus, heavy, weighted pain in my leg. I daydreamed longingly for my bed at home.

"Okay!" John shouted out so that everyone in the whole showroom heard him, "Let's go! Francine! Take One!"

Curious neighborhood people crowded outside the showroom window, peering in. The salesmen, Maria and Carol stood to one side, the whole crew, Danny, oh, my God! They're all looking at me!

I felt the heat of the lights, saw the mic extension, the red eye of the camera, looked into the camera's eye and did my bit. Just the way I practiced at home in front of the mirrored wall in the kid's bathroom. Finished, whew! Then I heard John shout, "Francine! Take Two!" Over and over he called out takes, I didn't understand why. I hadn't flubbed or paused or looked to the side.

"Technical problems!" John boomed. And then I began having trouble finishing within twenty-eight seconds. I was slowing down with fatigue. How could I pick up speed? "Faster, Fran!" John roared, "More excitement!"

This is it, the rest of my life I'll be standing here, repeating my twenty-eight second spiel into infinity. And then I heard John's booming voice, "Cut! That's it, Fran! We'll stay and finish up whatever shots we need, you can go."

Outside it was growing dark. Danny came over and wrapped me up in his arms. "Francine baby! My star! I love you, baby!" He kissed my face, my hair, my lips, a tangle of cable wires at our feet, cameramen rushing about, employees and neighbors looking on. "You and me, Honey," Danny whispered sweetly in my ear, erasing all the hard times, leaving them in the past, "we're going places!"

Only two miles south and east of here was 1816 Vyse Avenue where I'd climbed endless flights of white stone steps, and dreamed of a finer life. I had dreamed in those days, while my child-self slept, of standing fearless, full of joyful wonder, an adventuress, in a sparkling crystal elevator rising, rising, gaining speed, and when the elevator reached the ceiling which I saw was an enormous crystal dome, the ceiling gave way to a gorgeous open blue sky and my crystal elevator rocketed up into the sky, the sun shining gold, and rainbow beams, like guides, alongside the elevator.

NEALE'S HIGH SCHOOL GRADUATION. My father scanned the program and I read his mind. "Hey," he leaned over, "where's my grandson's name on this list of awards?"

"Stop looking, Dad, Neale isn't getting an award."

"What? What kind of school is this that doesn't give my wonderful grandson an award?"

Awards meant nothing to Neale. I looked over at Annie, so pretty, only she didn't know it.

"We know how smart Neale is," she said.

"I know, sweetheart, I know," and I patted her hand. When he was three my precious son had stood in the living room, strong and sturdy little boy, and with both hands he'd pointed and looked up at the breakfront shelves filled with books. "Someday," he'd declared firmly, "I'm going to read all the books in Mommy's shelves!"

Neale was almost six feet tall. He carried himself with perfect posture, and he'd developed a strong physique. His face resembled mine, the timber of his voice was pleasant to the ear. One morning he'd looked in the mirror and exclaimed, "See! Look at my eyes! I prayed so hard for my eyes to change to green like Mommy's, and look! they did!" Completely surprised, Annie and I had peered into Neale's eyes, and sure enough, the color had shifted from dark amber to radiant bronze green. My son had to finish the job of growing up. Independence of mind, clarity of thought, an unfailing ability to view life objectively without succumbing to the whims of others. These were his natural gifts. He was seventeen, he'd soon be entering the University of Miami; I didn't think Neale would find his path to fulfillment there and I'd argued about it with Danny, who'd encouraged him to attend his alma mater ever since Neale could talk.

"Look, Mommy, there's Neale! He's the easiest person to find in a crowd!"

I see him, Annie, I see him ... Neale, my darling boy, I love you so!

And while the day's ceremonies unfolded before us a kaleidoscope of memories began spinning in my mind. Here we were, together at Neale's graduation, a family, and the kaleidoscope turned; out of the fractured beauty one solid thought emerged – if only we could do it over again! Next time around, when Danny, in a rage, beat my son with a strap, I'd take my kids, run out the door, and drive far away! And even though I hadn't enough money I'd call a taxi to bring them home from summer camps they both detested, where Danny had insisted they go for eight weeks, and leave Danny, car keys, his ultimate power, in his pockets, leave him insisting to the wind that Neale and Annie stick it out. Instead, I'd argued all through the years, always trying to help him understand. In anger he'd overpowered me, I'd fallen against doorknobs and furniture. Terrified, I confided in no one. Years later, after a bone scan to rule out suspected myeloma, bone cancer, the radiologist had taken me aside and asked if my husband was hurting me. Immediately frightened, I asked why. "Because," the doctor replied, "your bones, according to this MRI, indicate long-term repeated trauma. How long are you married? Wouldn't you like to tell me about it?" I remained composed but was unable to speak. "Here, take my card, Mrs. Sachleben, if you feel like talking please call me. But you should know, your bones have multiple tiny fractures many going back at least twenty-five years. It's what we see when women have been pushed into walls and that sort of thing." I still couldn't speak but I smiled and took his card. The kaleidoscope turned and beautiful flower-like patterns exploded right before my eyes. I believed that somehow the power of love would heal everyone's wounds and my task was to hold the vision. The power of love. I still believed. If only we could do it over ... I would be so much wiser!

Neale and his friends tossed their graduation caps high in the air. He saw us approaching, came over to greet us. "See, Mommy! told you I'd graduate!"

MY FIRST MEETING with Alan regarding the purchase of commercial TV time was a disappointment. Alan hadn't come up with a sensible plan and his ideas ran counter to mine. The key to TV advertising on our scale was to keep expenses low. Alan showed me reams of surveys and polls and percentages of male and female viewers. Traditionally, automobile ads were directed at the male audience.

I suggested to Alan that we run the commercial on the new morning talk show, "Phil Donahue," viewed primarily by women. Alan hadn't heard of the show.

"Well, price it for me, I want to run on 'Donahue.'" Later, over lunch at Joe's, I told Danny, "I can't deal with this Alan guy. He wants to spend our money on game shows and expensive sporting events."

"I'm not impressed with him either." Danny ordered Joe's famous lentil soup for the two of us. "We'll go down and meet the reps at Channel 9 and 11," Danny said. "We'll introduce ourselves and I'll set you up as my advertising rep."

"What about Alan?"

"We'll let him set up the meeting and we'll give him the commissions, he won't care about you taking over as long as he gets the money."

"I guess he deserves the commissions, he arranged the filming for us."

"But the next commercial will be all yours, Fran."

"What do you mean?"

"Well, we can set up an advertising agency for you and then you can make more commercials and earn commissions, too."

Vinny approached, served salads and smiling, extended an extra-tall peppermill above my plate. "Thanks, Vinny."

He poised the mill over Danny's plate. "Pepper, Boss?" Danny nodded and smiled at me.

"I like having you at work with me, Honey. You can help with other things, too."

"You mean, like be your partner, Danny?"

"Yeah! Franny, baby, you'll be my partner!"

Danny leaned over the arugula and endives and the purple onions which gave me heartburn, and kissed me.

Alan discovered who Phil Donahue was and bought a spot for $250. At 9:42 on a July Tuesday my commercial aired for the first time. I was alone in the house.

It's you, Francine, it's you! I called to the image of myself on the screen. My eyes blurred with incredulity. You did it! You did it! I repeated, trying to ground myself in reality. There was no one to hear me but my feelings needed expression. So I hugged myself and sang to the shiffalera plant next to the bird cage, I sang to Elvis, Priscilla and Angel, Annie's parakeets, to the squares of sunlight on the taupe Berber carpet. I danced through the house and sang to the white opaline lamps in the living room, to the walls and the windows, to the immaculate home which was mine, "If they could see me now, that old gang of mine . . ."

The phone rang. "Were you on?" Danny asked.
"Nine-forty-two. We got the last spot in the second break."
"How'd you look?"
"Danny, no one will ever guess how sick I felt that day of the filming."

ALAN BOUGHT TIME for our commercial with Channels 9 and 11, and we learned what it meant to get 'bumped.' If another client made a last minute offer of more money for our spot, if a baseball game ran into extra innings, or if there were last minute programming changes, we didn't get on. The billing department was not always notified of cancellations so I learned to monitor the schedule and keep careful records.

"Well, that's it," Danny said, maneuvering the Volvo up the garage ramp and onto the melting asphalt of midtown. He turned the air-conditioner up to High. "You're in charge now, Honey."

"This is my wife, Francine," Danny had introduced me to the executives at Channel 9, "she's president of Francine's Fine Tuning, Inc., our in-house agency, and she'll be making the buys from now on."

We headed north on the FDR Drive; thirty-five minutes to home.

"I don't have a lot of confidence in 9 or 11, Danny, they seem so unprofessional."

"You know, Honey, why don't we meet with the other networks . . . let's see what they're like."

"You think so? It's not like we're a real agency, it's only me and our one commercial."

"Why not try? We'll call the sales departments and make appointments. It's like anything else, Fran, they have something to sell, in this case it's air time, and we want to buy . . . why shouldn't they talk to us?"

Neale was packed and ready. We gathered by the Japanese maple tree, snapped a roll of farewell photos, and suddenly, it was time for my son to leave. And then ... Neale was gone.

Two Flower Place was silent in a new and lonely way. I opened the door to the pantry, empty now where he'd stored his supply of protein powder and vitamins. He wouldn't be here tomorrow but I longed to have him back! I longed to spend more time with him! I walked down the long hallway to his room and sat on the edge of his bed. The walls were paneled with white wood and white shutters filtered the August light at the wide double window. Neale had loved his room. Sitting alone in my son's room felt strange, memories began to flow and swirl around me, beginning with the first September that we lived here.

While preparing lunch one warm, sunny day, and expecting Neale at the door any minute, the bell rang but it wasn't my child. A woman stood there and in a flat voice announced, "I don't want to alarm you but your son was just hit by a car."

I bolted across our lawn, the small crowd which had already gathered, parted. Neale was lying, pale and still, eyes closed, on the sidewalk. Someone approached with a blanket, someone else had brought out a pillow and placed it under his head.

"Neale! Open your eyes! Neale, please, open your eyes! I love you, wake up! Neale, darling!"

I turned to the people standing by, "Anyone call an ambulance?" I asked them. No one had. I flew back to the house, through the open door, up the seven steps to the kitchen, and dialed the Scarsdale Ambulance Corp, a short distance down the road. They served Scarsdale residents only. I dialed New Rochelle Hospital, twenty minutes across town, then called Danny. I ran into Annie's room, picked her up, grabbed the keys and raced across to my neighbor's aunt who was always home. "Annie, sweetheart," I said in some other woman's foreign voice, "you have to visit Aunt Rae a while, Mommy has to go with Neale to the doctor."

I hurried back to Neale and knelt beside him, very close. "Wake up, Neale, open your eyes and look at Mommy!" Neale remained ghostly pale and motionless. "I love you, my darling, you must wake up, please! Neale!" Seconds and minutes hung suspended, time did not exist.

A police officer arrived, "Excuse me, Mam, have you locked up your house?"

"What? Oh, yes, yes."

At last the comforting wail of a siren. The attendants lifted the still body of my beautiful boy onto the stretcher and carried him into the ambulance. This couldn't be happening! Not to my Neale! In desperation, I called on Grandma's spirit, Grandma! Save him! Save my precious child! He carries your name!

Neale's eyes fluttered open! Then I knew that relief had a taste, it had an aroma, and relief had a sound which was ringing in my ears. I very gently kissed his cheek. I love you, darling, Mommy is with you.

The day after a snowstorm when Neale went out sledding, another boy had slammed his sled into Neale's sled and he had come home with his left eye swollen like a purple golf ball. "I left my sled on the hill, Mommy ... that was a good sled, the best ... and my name was on the bottom, do you think someone will return it?"

"Material things come and go, Neale, and can usually be replaced. But remember, my love, you only have one body, and it has to last you a long time, your whole life, that's why it's important to watch out for yourself."

The golf ball had looked like it was there to stay, until one night Neale called me and Annie into his room. His eye, he showed us, had opened a bit. "Cover your right eye with your hand ... do you see us, Neale?"

"Yeah, I can see you, Mommy, and I see you, too, Annie."

"Just a minute ..." I grabbed a school book and held it up. "Keep your right eye covered and read a little." He read a few words. When he was three and I thought he was reading, my friend Diane had laughed, "He's not reading, Francine, you've read those stories to him so often, he's memorized them!" Now, to more accurately test his vision, I opened another book. "How about this, sweetheart?" Neale read a paragraph. I dropped the book, and the three of us hugged and danced around Neale's room.

When he was twelve Neale fractured his shoulder playing touch football. When he was fifteen he broke his right foot playing basketball on our driveway with Danny, and I'd been furious with Danny for playing so competitively with his own son. When his foot was almost healed Neale broke his left foot.

My gaze traveled around my son's room and I remembered how each thing had come to be here: his perfectly placed wheel of banners mounted on the wall, his telescope, the charms he'd collected as a small boy. How he'd loved his fish and cared for them, and had tended his two fish tanks diligently. He had trusted only me to empty the tank and clean it when his broken foot was healing. "Not like that, Mommy! What's the matter with you, you'll kill my fish!" Unable to do it himself, watching me do it without the expertise he brought to the task, made him anxious, but he knew I cared about his fish and he had, as he told me from time to time, a lot of trust in me. I sat on the edge of Neale's bed, and let the memories sweep over me.

The following week Danny and I introduced ourselves at Channel 5. We were assigned an account manager, a pleasant man, fiftyish, easy going Dave Bloom. We agreed that David Susskind's Sunday night talk show and the Sunday afternoon movie were good buys for us so I signed a contract for eight spots per month at $100 each and called Dave every Thursday to find out how the weekend schedule was going and to remind him to give us good time slots.

At Channel 4 our account manager was Sally Weber, a tall, slender black woman, married to a Jewish man; she wore a gold Star of David around her neck. Sally wrote up several possible combination packages and we set up a luncheon meeting.

"I'm impressed with everything you're doing, Francine," she said, "and I'm going to try and help you however I can."

Sally was the most sophisticated, attractive woman I'd ever met; I admired her cosmopolitan style and we soon developed a warm friendship. Channel 4 sponsored parties for their advertisers and even though our account was a relatively small one Sally invited me, and in this way I got to meet a few celebrities.

At the showroom I worked at Danny's desk. A lot of the time he was out, still making rounds between the used car lot on Bruckner and the service and parts departments on Jerome, but we always had our lunch together at Joe's.

I recorded every TV buy according to date and promised air time. I also recorded the actual time the commercial aired and used this information when bargaining with my reps. For instance, if the commercial ran during the last break of Susskind for two weeks in a row I worked Dave Bloom for a cheaper price the following month. If we got a good early spot I called the following day and thanked him. If we ran sandwiched in during the hourly break I worked him for a better spot.

After a while, as soon as he heard my voice Dave immediately said, "I know, I know, I'm trying to get you into a good position. How would you like next to last break, first spot?"

"Next to last break? You gave me that last week. C'mon Dave, get us on during the first half-hour, you can do it. I mean, I love watching Susskind but when it gets late I fall asleep and then I wake up when I hear my own voice. Don't you want me to get a good night's sleep?"

He laughed, "You know, Fran, you aren't exactly paying top dollar for these spots."

"Just think, Dave, someday we'll have a lot more money to spend and we'll be a bigger client and give you all our business. You'll be able to say you knew me when!"

Dave laughed again. "I'll see what I can do for you, my dear, I promise."

"Thanks a million, Dave, I really appreciate it."

At Channel 4 I tried a month with Sunday afternoon golf, the Saturday afternoon movie and Phil Donahue. Sally gave me prices well within our budget and even managed to work in an occasional five o'clock news spot for only $350.

Tony, at Channel 2, gave me the Sunday morning news for $200 and late shows for $50, $75 or $100. He drew up flexible monthly contracts enabling us to add spots if prices went down. He taught me about quarterly price fluctuations, daily and weekly price fluctuations. The contract was written for four spots per week on the Late Show at $100 each. I'd call Tony at four-thirty, he'd punch into the computer and say, "It looks light right now, Fran. If it stays this way by the time I go home I'll put you in for a second spot and keep the price at $100 for both. If it fills up I'll try to lock it in before 3:00 A.M. for $75 but I can't promise."

I lunched with Tony, too. He showed me surveys, graphs and ratings sheets, he explained statistics. None of those things meant anything to me; everyone watched the news and besides, the Bronx was a difficult market for automobiles which tended not to follow network surveys.

Sometimes Tony would call with questions like, "You're scheduled late tonight, Fran, around 4:00 A.M., want to let it run or should we move it up to tomorrow and hope for better luck?"

I learned that in addition to shift workers lots of people suffered from insomnia, they turned on their TV's all hours of the night, so I usually let it run. Wherever I went someone said, "Hey, didn't I see you on TV last night?" People were impressed. In some restaurants Danny and I were given priority seating just because the maître d' recognized me. So we learned firsthand the awesome power of television; ideas and images, however self-serving, delivered with authority directly into the viewer's mind.

THE DINING ROOM looked warm and inviting, the dore' bronze chandelier gleamed golden yellow in the cool October sunlight. The table was set. Platters of smoked fish, bowls of salads and assorted herrings all arranged, bagels hot and sliced. At last I rested on the azure-blue sofa, my legs already swollen and aching. From the driveway came the familiar sounds of car doors slamming followed by my aunt's excited exclamations, and my mother ran to the window.

"Margie and Sam are here! Where's Mike? He should be here already! Matty!" she called in a loud, nervous voice, "you call and see what he's doing ... go find out when he'll be here!" My mother hurried ahead of me, opened the front door and embraced her sister.

"Hi, Sweetheart!" Aunt Margie sang out across the center hall. "It's so good to see you! Where's that doll of yours? Oh, here you are, Annie, you're just like your mother! Come, give Aunt Margie a kiss! Your place is so elegant, Francine, warm and beautiful, just like you! Sam, tell her, hasn't everyone in Levittown heard about my lovely niece?"

"Aunt Margie, it's so good to see you, come, sit down," and we kissed on both cheeks and hugged, she held me at arm's length for a moment as she always did, and exclaimed again, "I'll never forget, when you were a little girl how you looked just like Margaret O'Brien!" My aunt had a way of making me feel so very loved. And she never wavered, from the day I was born until a time still some years off in the future, which I never saw coming, when my mother passed and with her passing everything in the family I loved so dearly, changed. Even Grandma's spirit couldn't help.

"Hey! I want to eat!" Uncle Sam shouted good naturedly.

"Not yet," my mother spoke with authority, "We have to wait for Mike!"

"You always have to wait for Mike! We're here, isn't that enough?"

"No! Go sit with Matty, Sam, and behave!"

"Your sister is very bossy, Marge, look how she bosses me around."

"Sam, be quiet!" Aunt Margie made the command sound like an off-beat melody; although she was funny no one laughed, but Annie and I exchanged smiles.

Sam maneuvered his large, heavy body into an armchair in the family room and the chair creaked.

"Matty," my mother nagged, "Go call Mike and find out what's happening!"

"What's the matter with you, Mary? He's probably waiting for Gloria to get dressed."

Then I recognized the distinctive sound of Mike's Mercedes on the driveway. My mother and aunt rushed to greet them.

"Look at them run!" Uncle Sam laughed. He lifted his heavy bulk from my lovely french side-chair. "Now, maybe Mary will let us eat."

"What are you doing, Mike," Uncle Sam bellowed, "hogging the chopped liver all to yourself?"

My father crooned, "Fran, dear, would you kindly pass some more of that delectable whitefish?"

"Fran," Danny complained, "why can't you remember to set the table with two butters, one at each end?"

Gloria sat beside Mike engaged in her customary practice of whispering in his ear.

While buttering his second garlic bagel my father looked up

and spoke in a clear, smooth voice; I suddenly realized that my father now spoke with barely a discernible trace of his former Brooklyn accent and that he'd accomplished this by his own determination. It had happened somewhere along the way, and I supposed that by reading and studying ancient civilizations, the great philosophers, Mike's college texts, listening to his beloved recordings of classical music, an integral part of his life all these years, he'd transformed his tough-guy younger self into his now more refined self. The way he was with me since the day I was born had become a template for all his relationships! My father, I realized while observing in his eyes the mist of joy arising from being with his family, especially his grandchildren, had arrived at that exalted place for all human beings, living with a loving heart.

"Isn't your commercial coming on soon, Fran?" My father bragged to everyone he met about his daughter, the TV star. He announced to anyone who'd listen, "See this beautiful young woman here? Well, she's my daughter and you can see her on TV! Also, she's given me two outstanding grandchildren!" He memorized the schedule and told people exactly what program to watch to catch my commercial.

Now everyone at the table focused their attention on the commercial. Aunt Margie and Uncle Sam wanted to hear all about it, how it was made, how did I know how to buy time on TV, all the details. Gloria and Mike were silent and after she whispered to my nephews David and Andrew, they remained silent.

At 2:15 when the commercial was scheduled to appear on Channel 4's Wide World of Sports, the family hurried from the dining room and gathered around the television console in the family room. We saw the red Mazda headlight cover blink open, and there I was, looking like your friend, telling you about a great place to buy a car.

"What do you think of that?" my father addressed the family. "Isn't she terrific? No training! Isn't my daughter something?"

"Francine, baby, you're so cute on TV!" Danny hugged me.

My mother smiled, "Who wouldn't want to go straight to Edmond's," she said, "after seeing my sweetie pie on TV?"

"You were great, Mommy!" Annie put her arms around me. Everyone returned to their places at the table.

"Well, Margie," my mother prodded, "wasn't she terrific?"

Aunt Margie replied with pursed lips, "Why did you do that thing with your hands?" She pushed back her chair, stood up and gestured with her own hands. "As you're talking," she continued, "you move your hands up and down, like this!"

"What are you talking about Margie?" my mother shouted defensively.

"Mary, please, I recognized that from when she was a little girl and she used to do that with her hands, it's like a little flutter, like a little bird."

"Well, when you do it Margie," my father said, "it looks funny, but on Francine it's graceful and charming."

An argument then ensued, Did this hand movement add or detract from the overall quality of the commercial? I did not participate in the argument.

I cleared the table and brought out the coffee service, platters of chocolate danishes, apple strudel, fancy cookies, Margie's pink and white cake from Levittown, and a generous slab of seven-layer cake, the kind that Sam's parents used to buy exclusively for Mitch and Jenny and which I still found delicious.

Gloria, Sam and Margie soon realized there were other aspects of the commercial worth debating. I poured the coffee. My leg was hurting so much it was unbearable. I wanted peace! Quiet! Danny tried to explain that the important thing was, people took notice of the commercial, came to the showroom and purchased cars.

A well-known columnist wrote an article about local homemade commercials and he mentioned "that raw talent who is asking us to pick up a Honda at Edmond's." Aunt Margie disputed with my mother, "Was the line in the newspaper meant as a compliment?" They argued as if all America awaited a resolution.

"You know, Honey," Danny suggested, "you're so good at buying time I bet you could do newspaper ads, too, place them through Francine's Fine Tuning and earn the commissions."

Buying time on television had opened new doors for me; I met interesting people, stretched my mind in new directions. Newspaper ads were an anxiety producing drudgery. You worked solitary, created a perfect ad, and then sweated production, deliveries and final outcome. The ad in the paper never looked as good as the ad on your drawing board. But for the challenge of it, to help Danny, for another meaningful way to earn my place in the life of the business, I would do it.

We went to the N.Y. Times building on Forty-third Street and introduced ourselves to John Tolesor, manager of the Automotive Advertising Department. "My wife will be doing our ads," Danny explained, "So I want her to meet everyone she needs to know. And someone has to go over the routine with her."

Bob Roselett, V.P. of General Advertising at the 'Times,' explained the procedures. He gave me a sheet listing every type size available and how many letters to a column. He explained deadlines and prices. Then he handed me an application for credit. "We'll accept your ads temporarily on Danny's credit after we receive Danny's guarantee in writing, but you'll need credit in your company name."

Danny invited John and Bob to join us for lunch and they suggested Sardi's, their favorite place. So there I was on an ordinary day, lunching in Sardi's with Danny and two executives, when for most of my life a day like this was spent running errands, doing endless household chores and arranging my life according to the kids' activities. Would I ever really get an ad together? It seemed so complicated now that I was faced with the actual procedures. But I knew that somehow I would learn and do it.

First thing next morning I filled out the N.Y. Times application for Advertising Agency Recognition. November 19, 1979, total assets $3,200. I typed up a letter in which Danny guaranteed all expenses incurred by Francine's Fine Tuning and sent it on to John Tolesor who then approved me for temporary credit. February 1980, the Times sent me a letter of recognition granting Francine's Fine Tuning, Inc. fifteen percent agency commission, a credit amount of five-thousand dollars and an account number.

Over lunch in Joe's, Danny gave me the facts for the ads. Back at his desk, working on graph paper, I worked out the ads figuring point size and number of letters to a line. I had to learn when to use upper and lower case and when and how to combine them for the most effective results and costs. Instructions to the printer had to be clear and perfect to avoid errors. In the beginning we ran three prominent ads three times a week, one each for Honda, Mazda and Volvo as well as a half dozen or more used car ads.

All ads were clipped for proof of insertion. I checked every charge on the invoice, filled out forms for credit on errors and sent payment immediately. Eventually, I worked out display ads as well.

I was Danny's secretary, taking phone calls, writing letters. And somehow I became a purchasing agent for everything from carpet in the bookkeeper's office to all necessary office furnishings. My opinion was sought regarding car arrangement on the showroom floor, placement of factory posters and window shades for the floor to ceiling showroom windows.

Danny and I entertained factory reps, bankers and insurance people at Joe's. I was accepted as a businesswoman. I was asked innumerable questions regarding the commercial which seemed to interest everyone, and I was treated with respect by everyone. Employees came to me with problems. They rushed to open doors for me and hold my coat; they laughed at my humor! For several consecutive years I was invited by "Who's Who in American Women" to add my name to their roster. Danny said it was nothing more than a money-making scheme, not to bother. Nevertheless, many years later when those golden days were no more, I regretted having been influenced by his opinion. I would have had something in my hand that spoke for my achievements.

I made a second commercial. This time we filmed it in a studio at Channel 5 and displayed one special car, my silver Volvo Bertone. The Bertone was a limited edition, two-door model with a low-slung black vinyl roof and Italian hand-stitched black leather interior. It was just me and my Volvo and I knew my lines.

"How do you like my gorgeous new Volvo from Edmond's in the Bronx? I love my Volvo and I love Edmond's. My Volvo gives me luxury, safety and that all-important gas economy. Edmond's gives me low price, quick delivery and efficient service. At today's prices Volvo is worth a long, hard look and so is Edmond's. So look for me in my Volvo with the blue and white Edmond's sticker on the back and I'll be looking for you at Edmond's in the Bronx!"

The engineers found technical errors in every replay so again there were endless takes until finally they ran off on a monitor what they considered the three best versions and asked me to choose one.

I was in solid with Tony at Channel 2, with Sally at 4 and continued buying economically sound spots. Phil Donahue's morning talk show had become a huge success by this time and prices for a spot on his show were escalating. We were the only automobile advertiser on the program and I wanted to stay with it. Sally made a terrific offer. For the same $250 I could have the last spot on Donahue; the hitch was, it might get cut off, there was no guarantee. Every morning for a week I watched Donahue to the very end before driving to the showroom. Only once were a few seconds clipped. So I decided to go with Sally's offer twice a week. That and the CBS Sunday morning news were our most substantial spots. The rest were Late Shows on Channel 2. All around, prices were doubling and tripling.

In a few months the Donahue show became too costly even for the last spot and our limited budget forced me to withdraw our commercial. My spot had made an impact. Some automobile advertising executives had begun to acknowledge what I'd been speaking about to them at every opportunity: that in addition to purchasing cars on their own, women also influenced men regarding the purchase of cars, and that the time had come to recognize the presence and importance of women in the automobile marketplace. With the passage of time this became accepted wisdom, yet in 1979 this was a breakthrough, part of a new era in marketing. Manufacturers' advertising budgets were considerably larger than the budgets of individual dealers. And whereas our commercial ran only on local networks, a factory ad ran nationally reaching a broader audience. Now targeting the women's market Volvo took my place on Donahue with a short factory ad and ran it for years in the spot I had pioneered.

DANNY WAS on friendly terms with the inspector from the Occupational Safety and Health Administration, the agency which, in accordance with the OSHA Act of 1970, checks on job safety and health protection. On a blustery November day in 1979 he stopped by the used car lot and mentioned to Danny that the Chevrolet store on East Tremont Avenue, two blocks down from our showroom, was about to close. The owner, Mr. Dade, had sold the franchise back to Chevrolet and was looking to sell the property.

This was the break we were waiting for! That property would provide us with 50,000 square feet of space, half indoors and half outside, which we'd use for service, parts, an exclusive Honda showroom which the Honda factory was clamoring for, plus a used car lot; the whole business in one location!

Mr. Dade, an elderly gentleman, lived in Scarsdale, a few minutes from our house. Danny lacked experience negotiating the purchase of major property, so he asked an old family friend, who had sold us the Jerome Avenue building, to accompany him to Mr. Dade's house. A supermarket chain was competing with us and we entered a stalemate, but the supermarket deal eventually fell through and we moved up to first position. Our lawyer closed the deal for $390,000. An investment which has, as they say in the business, paid for itself a hundred times over.

MY FATHER AWOKE one Sunday morning suffering excruciating pain in his left leg. He was unable to leave his bed. Danny and Mike carried him down to the car and we drove him to the hospital. Based on his symptoms the medical staff at Montefiore couldn't come up with a diagnosis so they began a series of tests.

ANNIE'S BAT MITZVAH was coming up in June and to mark the occasion we'd been planning a trip to Israel. Days and weeks passed, my father remained ill with an undiagnosed disease without a course of treatment. The day of departure for Israel was drawing near and I knew by their expressions and silences that my parents were hoping we'd cancel our trip, although they never actually asked me to cancel. I felt torn between the pressing needs of my parents and my promise to Annie. Finally I reasoned that Mike was at the hospital every day, he'd look after my father and drive my mother home at night. The doctors and Mike assured me that my father's life was not in danger. So we went.

Our two weeks in Israel were soul-stirringly beautiful and memorable. I cherished every moment of every day with my beautiful daughter; planting a tree, dining on Mediterranean fish high above the blue sea, floating in the waters of the salty Dead Sea, white stone of Jerusalem, the digs, the hills, the land that everyone is fighting for. My Annie, dignified and filled with grace, receiving a certificate from the Rabbi at the Mount of Olives.

The day of our return we drove from the airport directly to Montefiore. My father, strong and youthful all his life, looked aged and frightened in his hospital bed. With thin, quivering hands he gripped the edge of his blanket and tears welled in his sunken eyes. "Fran, my Fran," he wailed in a frail voice. "I thought I'd never see you again!"

This aged man couldn't be my father! But here was my mother, forlorn, her face streaked with tears. I kissed my father's cheek and held his hand. Come back, Daddy, I want you back, the way you were! Annie stepped forward and gently leaned over to kiss him. A band of steel tightened around my chest.

"You don't know," my father moaned, beseeching me with hollow eyes, "they want to give me a terrible test, it might kill me, and I said I have to wait for my Francine, she'll help me decide . . ."

"Oh, Dad . . ." The band of steel squeezed my heart. "What about Mike? What's his advice?"

"Ach!" my father tried to wave his hand, his large, warm hand, which once upon a time had held mine cozily in his coat pocket as we walked in the early morning chill with Mikey to feed the goats in the Bronx Zoo. "You know, Fran, your brother didn't even drive your mother home once. She had to take the bus and then walk that long distance from the bus stop, in the dark and cold." My father was crying again.

"Danny, would you call Neale?" We carried our luggage into the house, "and let him know we're back?"

At that moment the phone rang and Danny got it. "Honey," he called out, "pick up in there, okay? It's Neale, he wants to talk to both of us."

"Hi Mom . . . listen . . . I have to tell you and Daddy . . ."

"What is it sweetheart?"

"I decided to leave Miami . . . it's not the right school for me."

We talked for a little while and then I said to my son, whose inner conflict was already burning within my own heart, "Your room is still here, Neale, just the way you left it."

Danny had blatantly disregarded my presentiment that Miami was not the right school for Neale and had encouraged him, since early childhood, before my son even had a chance to form his own opinion, to go there anyway. I felt a surge of annoyance and maddening frustration rise up also within my heart.

IN FORTY YEARS Mr. Dade hadn't made a single improvement on his property. We were faced with a project of total renovation; major electrical work, new plumbing, roof repairs. The ceiling in the service department was black with the grime of four decades, the cement floors were thick with dirt and grease and surely the walls had never received a coat of paint. The whole place had to be steam-cleaned before repairs could even be attempted. Then the ceiling, twenty-five feet high, was power-sprayed twice with white paint, as were the walls; the cement floor was repaired and painted grey. New fences and lighting were installed on the outdoor lot which was repaved. The large expanse of old paneling in the showroom was steam-cleaned revealing attractive lighter walls. We covered the shabby old tile floor in the showroom with industrial carpeting.

THE EXTERIOR BRICK we painted a shade of terra-cotta, and signs in aqua blue were painted directly onto the brick wall: Service – HONDA MAZDA VOLVO. Danny felt ready, at last, to assert his autonomy and he gave the business his own name. Above the showroom window we installed blue and white lighted box signs: DAN MOTORS – HONDA.

In order to obtain official recognition from American Honda for an exclusive Honda showroom and our new service location we were required to submit plot plans, floor plans and an artist's rendering of the facility. "You can do it, Honey," Danny urged.

I visited an art supply shop down the block, wandered among the varieties of papers, pens, brushes and paints; all things I used to love, and selected the largest, weightiest drawing paper with a smooth surface and clean-cut edges, three widths of black marking pens. The widest point I'd use to define the exterior walls and the finest point to designate measurements and names of areas. I bought a ruler mounted on a cork base to prevent smudges, and rolls of brown paper on which to mount the finished drawings, figuring that rolling them would make them look professional. Later I learned that was exactly how professionals do it.

The plot and floor plans had to be drawn to scale and the property was angled on the side and curved in front, following the line of the sidewalk. Crumpled papers piled in the wastebasket.

To accomplish the artist's rendering I sat in my car across the street and sketched the property. At the desk I painstakingly added details and color. I couldn't draw cars well enough for this project so I leafed through dozens of automobile brochures and magazines and clipped appropriately scaled renderings of cars, pasted them into the drawing of the showroom and created a showroom window of clear paper-thin plastic. Meticulously, I lettered the signs. In my drawing I transformed the lone half-dead plane tree and weeds along the border of the used car lot into lush, wooded glens and flower beds. Smartly dressed customers peopled my drawing. My paints assimilated nature's loveliest hues, and altogether our property appeared to be an automobile paradise. I rolled and tied my three masterpieces and Danny hand-delivered them to American Honda. We received official recognition, of course, and I imagined that my drawings received a cursory glance before someone filed them away in some cabinet drawer.

The contractor we'd hired at the outset grew weary of the

job so Danny replaced him with Rocco, a master carpenter from the neighborhood. Rocco became our most loyal employee and friend. He took over all construction and maintenance of the company. Every time the heat or air-conditioning or plumbing went out of order, the call went out, Where's Rocco? And there he was in a minute - resourceful, dependable, even driving in on a bitterly cold Sunday to turn on the heat for Monday morning, and to check things out.

My cousin Mitch left Edmond and came to work as service manager for us. Mitch asked if he could maintain a small body shop business on the side, Danny consented and introduced him to the best body shop man in the business who'd been doing our work for years. Mitch organized our new service department and kept it running efficiently.

Even though our neighborhood was clean and safe, like others in the Bronx, we had to contend with its unfavorable reputation. People who'd never been to the Bronx decided that the whole of it lay in ruins, discounting the broad geographical scope of the borough, its numerous diverse neighborhoods. Our task lay before us: Establish a reputation for standards higher than those of our competitors, get the word out that our neighborhood was not only safe but attractive as well. Danny's personal reputation was an advantage and our image together was an advantage.

When we first arrived on East Tremont Avenue I had prophesied that one day Danny would own every automobile property on our street. The vision of it had arisen spontaneously in my mind and I knew it would be so. The acquisition of the Dade property signaled the beginning of that prophecy's fulfillment. Danny and I had to build an organization of good people, a stable customer base, and in 1980 there was still a lot to learn.

APRIL 15, my father's sixty-fifth birthday, was drawing near. "I want to go home," he pleaded with anyone who'd listen, "my

Mary will cook for me and I'll get better." When he'd entered the hospital my father had weighed two-hundred-twenty-five pounds. The day he went home he weighed one-hundred-seventy-five pounds, he leaned on a cane; a diagnosis had not yet been made.

My father suffered his illness in silence. Shadows veiled his eyes ... this must be how he endured the suffering of a deprived childhood. The silent shadows of pain in my father's kind eyes haunted me, and led me to volunteer at Children's Village in Dobbs Ferry, a charming river town alongside the Hudson.

Richard, the director, said the best contribution would be to take a boy out for an hour or two, or even a whole afternoon. We walked from his office along the single lane roadway. Richard was about my age, medium height, slender and he needed a shave. The rolling expanse of meadow, tall oak trees, leaves swaying softly in the summer breeze, butterflies and dragonflies, all provided a visitor with a sense of peace. The worn clapboard houses we passed might have belonged to any ordinary family trying to get by. I viewed this bucolic scene through the suffering eyes of my father's childhood, and knew it was a facade.

Richard led me up a steep flight of hewn gray stone steps set into the grassy hillside. At the top a gentle breeze entered the house through a dilapidated screen door. Here I met my boy, nine-year-old Christopher; grimy hands and elbows, neglected teeth. Chris stared at the worn linoleum floor.

"Hi, Chris, would you like to go for an ice-cream soda or something?" I extended my hand, "Come." Chris glanced at me, put his hand in mine and stared at the floor again. "Come on, Chris, I'll show you my car. Do you like cars?"

I led him down the stone steps and back up the road to my Volvo. "This is the radio, Chris, would you like to choose a station?" Chris accepted each offer in silence. I reacted to him as if he had spoken. Chris' mother, Richard told me, had kept him locked in a closet for days at a time. She had tied him up and blindfolded him and locked him in a small room. While Chris stayed at Children's Village, his mother received psychological counseling.

I drove to a diner in town as Richard had suggested. A glass dish of chocolate pudding in the refrigerated case behind the counter captured Chris' attention so I ordered it for him. I watched him slowly eat the pudding, relishing every mouthful, remaining silent. "Do you know, Chris, when I was your age chocolate pudding was my absolute favorite food in the whole world!"

"It's mine, too," he answered seriously. He looked up and our eyes met. That's how Chris and I connected, and a great warmth for the child surged inside my heart.

A few days later I took him to our local beach club. He stayed close by my side and I kept a protective arm around his scrawny shoulders. I thought my father would show interest in Chris but to my surprise he didn't. Later, my father explained to me that he saw too much of himself in Chris, and it hurt.

When school resumed I stopped at Children's Village on the way home from work and took Chris home with me. The first time he entered my house he ran to the bathroom to vomit. Annie showed him her parakeets, we played together, ate dinner together and then I drove him back to Dobbs Ferry.

One winter afternoon I went to see Richard in his tiny office; books, pamphlets and papers piled everywhere, and explained that the routine was becoming difficult. I didn't want to complain about my health to Richard, but I had become anemic. My blood count had dropped to the middle twenties, even with iron pills. Richard assumed it was the usual burn-out syndrome; it wasn't easy to hold onto volunteers. "How about if you just stay here in town with Chris," his eyes squinted with anxiety, "just take him for an hour or so?"

I empathized with his plight, "Okay, I'll try it that way."

"You know, Fran, the other boys envy Chris every time he goes with you ... think you can handle a couple more?"

Those yearning unwashed faces; those abused, discarded

children, paraded across my mind. "Sure, Richard, I'll take a few more boys. Who do you have in mind?"

So after that I took Chris and three more boys. Enraptured, they listened to everything I said. They stayed close beside me and looked up at me with love-starved eyes. They competed for my attention with an endless stream of jokes and questions. I drove to a nearby park, not much of a place but to them it was 'outside' which made it wonderful, and then off to the diner for burgers and ice-cream sodas. People in the small town diner stared at us; Rigo was Puerto Rican, Edmond was black, and Juno was blond like Chris. Enthusiastic to hear about my life I told them about the commercial and my stories excited their imaginations. Juno decided he'd become a cameraman. Edmond declared that because he was so handsome and looked like a movie star he'd make commercials, too! Mostly, they were interested in how to get into the car business. When we parted back at the cottage each boy had to have his hug.

"Go there," I urged my friends and acquaintances, "these boys are desperate for a little love, a little attention."

People feared that a kid might steal from them, or worse, harm them. "No, no, no! Believe me, they're just as lovable and bright as any kid anywhere!"

Richard fell into an evening routine of calling me. We discussed the boys and he talked about himself. He was well-educated and could have entered a more lucrative field, but he felt committed to social work. He asked me to go out with him.

"You know I'm married, Richard."

"I just thought we could talk over dinner for a change, that's all."

I sighed.

"I'm sorry, Fran, I don't want to cause you any problems, it's just that you seem to understand me so well, it's hard not to ask."

I did understand him. I understood the challenges of his work and I admired his commitment. Richard was devoting his life to work I could easily see for myself. It called out to my heart and stirred dreams of a never-forgotten time when I wanted to go out into the world and do good things for people. Our first year on Flower Place I had ambitions to open a home for children, had even gathered a group of qualified professionals who agreed to help. But illness had interfered with my ambition. Now, once again, my health was threatening to restrict my activities. My blood count dropped even lower, to twenty-one. For some reason I didn't understand my body had shifted to a twenty-one day monthly cycle, and my periods were lasting as long as ten days. Three D&Cs had failed to correct the problem and at the last few annual checkups Dr. Nolan had advised a hysterectomy. He'd scheduled surgery against my wishes but I canceled the arrangements.

"You're making a big mistake, Fran, I have the operating room reserved, I'm strongly in favor of doing it now. I'm concerned that one of these days you're going to hemorrhage and then you'll be brought in here bleeding to death."

"But I'm not ready emotionally, Dr. Nolan."

My body would tell me when a hysterectomy was unavoidable and then I'd have no reason to be plagued afterward by doubt. Dr. Nolan was annoyed by my opposition, and I was disappointed by his lack of respect for my very personal decision regarding my own body.

Chris finally returned home to his mother and I prayed she was healed of her compulsion to abuse her child. I met Richard for lunch and confided in him about my health, how difficult it was to continue my visits with Rigo, Juno and Edmond and he was sympathetic as well as forward-looking, assuming the attitude that my problem wasn't permanent. Richard had a way of inspiring me to see myself as an independent woman who could find success away from the world that belonged to my husband. He re-connected me to exactly how I felt about myself before I married Danny.

"Someday I'm going to open my own facility," Richard brought up his favorite topic, "and I want you to work with me. You don't belong with cars, Francine, or even hidden away in the Bronx. It's so clear, for goodness sakes, can't you see it? You belong with kids – it's your God-given talent, and you know it. There's no limit to what you can accomplish in this field, in every way!"

I looked across the table at him. He needed a shave as usual. Richard took my hand in his "Maybe you haven't noticed, Fran, but I'm in love with you, and I know you care for me."

"If my Grandma were here she would say that you and I are like ships in the night. How could I not care about you, Richard? You're the most interesting person I know, devoted to work I so admire and understand. I do have a real affinity for your work, and besides, you're really very attractive, in case you haven't looked in the mirror lately," which I guessed he hadn't. "But what you want is impossible, Richard. I could never leave my children as you're asking me to do."

"Why couldn't I have found you earlier, before he got to you?"

I remembered my green-eyed Adonis long ago in Bache & Co. I had fallen for Danny. We had created a life together, a beautiful family. Danny certainly had a way of taking advantage of my love. He'd broken my heart repeatedly, and there were plenty of times I wished I were free of him. My love for him kept me in a prison of my own making. Now we were working together, Danny was learning to respect me, and that was something I'd longed for. Here was Richard: refined, intelligent, declaring his love for me, a serious man. Sitting in that quaint little restaurant with its lace curtains and tablecloths, mostly empty of other diners at this hour, it was very clear to me: I could've had all that was important to me without the endless anxiety that was part of my life with Danny. If I'd waited for Richard to come along I'd be respected and easily loved, just for being me. Richard would never criticize my cooking every night. He'd be loving just because he was a loving man. Richard would surprise me with thoughtful gifts on my birthday, he wasn't the kind of man to ignore me and then claim he couldn't help it, his parents hadn't been the giving type. Richard wouldn't come home empty-handed on our anniversary, asserting the wastefulness of buying flowers. And Richard was not the kind of man who'd run out to play every kind of sport while I was home, begging him to stay with me. Richard would sit with me and we'd talk together, about books, or important issues. Richard would have been a tender father for my daughter, a strong father for my son. He never, ever would have raised a strap to our son or ignored our beautiful little daughter just because she was a girl. He'd know how to relate. He was in fact, a perfect man for me, and if I'd been with Richard loving kindness would have filled my life instead of the stress and anxiety and constant emotional turmoil which had compromised my immune system and caused my own body to rebel against itself. And even though we'd never kissed or even embraced I was certain that if I'd married Richard instead of Danny I'd know what it felt like to be cherished.

Several weeks after our lunch Richard called to say goodbye. He was heading out to California, accepting a top position in a well-known boys' institution.

AUGUST 1980. The new, exclusive Honda showroom opened for business. I put together a one-page flier and Danny drove to neighborhood hospital parking lots, placing the fliers in windshields of foreign cars, and wherever else he spotted a parked Honda, Mazda or Volvo. He decided it was time to make a third commercial.

"Meet me at DAN MOTORS! We're offering for sale or lease most models and colors at fantastic savings. You can lease this new Accord 4-Door from DAN MOTORS with no down payment at the low price of $188 per month for thirty-six months. So come to our beautiful new showroom and visit our outstanding new service department and find out why DAN MOTORS is the fastest growing dealer in the East!"

I used the tag line, 'fastest growing dealer in the East' in our display ads as well. "That's a good line, Francine, keep it going!" factory representatives called with praise and encouragement.

Prices for air time had skyrocketed and Channel 2 Late Shows were the only spots we could afford. At the end of September I took this commercial off the air and advised Danny that our fling with TV had expired.

MY FATHER'S health declined still further and in October his gall bladder was removed. The day after surgery my mother stood beside him as he lay asleep in the hospital bed, drugged up with pain medication, and horrified, my mother noticed a fast-growing pool of blood staining the sheets. My father was rushed back into surgery. The surgeon had accidentally left a small surgical tool inside my father's body!

After his recovery, sitting in my kitchen, my father related how he had felt himself rise above his body and feeling himself suddenly weightless, ascend to a place near the ceiling from where he witnessed his own blood flowing onto the sheets. He'd felt enormous relief, for his pain had ceased. He saw the pool of blood, his own blood, to which he felt no emotional attachment. He watched my mother sobbing. "This is not the time to leave my Mary," he decided, "she still needs me." Instantly, he assumed the weight of his body, and the pain. After this my father recovered. "You know, daughter," my father said, "I'm beginning to understand all those things about the soul that you talk about."

AT AN ANNUAL business affair Danny and I learned about Northwood Institute, a college in Midland, Michigan, supported in part by General Motors. At Northwood automobile dealers' sons learn to become successful dealers. Northwood operated on a tri-semester schedule; a new semester would begin the day after Thanksgiving.

Neale was reluctant to go, but a few days later he got another speeding ticket, the third in a twelve month period, and his license was revoked. Neale applied to Northwood, Danny accompanied him there for an interview and Neale was accepted.

Danny brought home a Ford Bronco; a rented U-Haul was on the driveway, tightly packed and hooked up to the Bronco. The shingles on this side of the house, which faced north, had weathered and grayed. The steel gray basketball pole, its net rigid with cold, blended into a bleak November sky. The silver birch trees, the azalea bushes, slumbered in the gray winter morning. Even the stone retaining wall, usually reflective of soft, pastel light, was gray today.

MY BOY was going off to the gray wasteland of Midland where the Dow Chemical Company poured pollutants into the air and water. Danny and Neale travelled north to Niagara Falls, stayed the night, then west and south, down into Michigan. Danny helped Neale set up the apartment, and flew home.

When he wasn't attending classes Neale spent the dreary, frozen hours of a Midland Winter in his apartment working on assignments and staying ahead of his classes. He prepared healthy dinners of broiled fish, steamed broccoli and brown rice. And he made the Dean's List.

Sunday nights he called home. "What am I going to do in the business, Dad?" he asked every week. "I don't want you creating a job for me or making up some dumb thing for me to do."

Every Sunday I reminded Danny to reassure Neale that his help was definitely needed. The business was expanding faster than either Danny or I could imagine. We really did need him.

Located one block north of our Mazda-Volvo showroom there

was a Ford factory showroom. We were surprised to notice, one Monday morning, that over the weekend the windows had been boarded up. A sign posted a phone number; Danny called immediately and opened negotiations for purchasing the property.

A week later the Buick dealer on the corner passed away. Buick closed the point; there were two remaining Buick dealers in the Bronx and that, they felt, was sufficient representation. Danny applied for a Buick franchise anyway, figuring it couldn't hurt for them to have his application on file. Then ... one of the remaining Buick dealers went bankrupt, Buick took another look at Danny's application and chose him as their prime candidate for the open point. The Buick execs drove down from their offices in White Plains. Danny showed them our facilities, gave them a tour of the neighborhood and we went to lunch at Joe's. They liked us.

At one of our many subsequent luncheons with Rick Thurber and other executives involved in the process of dealer selection, I mentioned that our lawyer was working on the Ford property deal but it was dragging. I looked up from the broiled red snapper on my plate and noticed, at the mention of the Ford property, a certain light in Rick's eyes. Up until that moment I thought as Danny did, that we'd renovate the old Sander's Buick showroom and service department on the corner. But that light in Rick's eyes ... I suddenly understood. Buick had had it with that old place. They wanted the quarter million dollar facility which Ford had built plus the acre and a quarter lot adjacent to it. A commitment from Rick had not been forthcoming and we had wondered why. It was obvious he preferred Danny to the other applicants.

"You know, Rick," I ventured, "that Ford property might be perfect for Buick."

"Now you're talking!" He laid down his fork, real excitement rose in his voice and his eyes shone with the promise of promotion back at corporate headquarters.

I glanced at Danny and back at Rick. "Well, we'll have to make that our priority then."

"I think you have got a very good idea there, Francine!" Rick nodded emphatically.

At home that night Danny and I relaxed in the living-room on the white leather chesterfield sofa and love seat we bought in Bloomingdales for our twentieth anniversary. We'd finally discarded the old sofa which Rose had insisted upon so many years ago. The new sofa was placed against the west, or main wall, and the love seat opposite, in the wide bay window. I had removed the heavy dark green draperies and shag carpet of the seventies and replaced them with white shutters and bare, white oak floors. The room looked fresh and elegantly youthful.

"What do you think, Honey?" Danny worried, "do you think we'll get the Ford place? can't get the lawyers to make anything happen."

"Danny, you'll get it. But you have to fight for it! Do it yourself! After all, the lawyers don't share our urgency for the deal. And that place is the key to a Buick franchise. Did you see Rick's face at lunch today when we talked about it? They want that Ford place, Danny, and they're just waiting to see if you'll give it to them. I'm positive that's what they want."

The next morning Danny contacted the Ford lawyers in Detroit and made his offer. He stayed on top of it. He negotiated the deal on his own. He promised Rick Thurber the best looking Buick dealership the Bronx ever had. On the strength of Danny's word Rick sent us a Letter of Intent and began processing the paper work.

Rocco set to work repairing the Ford showroom. The back wall was sun-faded ochre brick and the floor was a coordinated shade in ceramic tile; three walls were tinted windows. I designated the large, airy corner office for Neale. It looked out onto the adjacent lot and down East Tremont Avenue toward the Honda showroom. When Rocco completed the office we locked the door, it would wait clean and new for our son.

Danny hired Vinny, sales manager from Sander's, to be our

Buick manager and get the place set up. There were many luncheon meetings and dinner meetings and Vinny became a good friend.

June 1981. The sign went up over our new showroom: DAN MOTORS – BUICK, and we opened our doors for business.

December 1, 1981, my fortieth birthday. We bought a treadmill and set it up, along with a small TV, in Neale's workshop, which we renamed the exercise room, so that I could keep my legs strong and healthy. I walked thirty minutes every night. Attending to my legs had become automatic, almost like breathing. Lying down, legs in the air, a hundred bicycle rotations every morning; legs raised on two pillows at night prior to going to sleep, until the pain drifted away. Morning and night I massaged my legs and feet with body lotion to heal the continually drying and flaking skin which had taken on the appearance of transparency, like an onion skin with myriad tiny cracks. I pulled on heavy elastic stockings. Mornings my legs looked trim and slender but I knew that as the day progressed they'd swell as they did every day. I prayed for a small miracle anyway, maybe today the swelling wouldn't be too bad. At home the only way I sat was with my legs elevated.

As I dress for work on this, my fortieth birthday, a scene unfolds within my mind. Seated at a round birthday table are all my friends, all my dear lost friends who I loved so much. Here's pretty Lana, eight years old forever! Oh, Lana, I've stopped looking for you lately. And Sherry! Too sophisticated for Poughkeepsie where Jerry took you to live. Suzie! Wherever you are, you're also here with me now. And Diane! In Israel, dark circles too soon beneath your eyes, smiling, sweet, here with me, too! Barbara! Sarah! Sue, well and whole once more; light brown hair swinging at your chin. We hold hands, my dear, lost friends and I, and they wish me a happy fortieth.

NEALE EXCELLED in Accounting, he maintained his place on the Dean's List, graduated and returned home. We rented an apartment for him, small and new, seven minutes from the house. "Now I really appreciate all the things you did for me, Mom," he greets me with a kiss, always a sweet kiss. My son has become a man, and yet, the little boy I adored and cherished has survived. It's wonderful to have him back.

The first business day after Memorial Day Weekend, Neale came to work. He loved his office. "Find your own way," Danny advised him, "stay here in Buick for as long as you want and when you feel ready, go around the dealership and see what interests you."

MITCH HAD BEEN our service manager for three years but he'd left because of a falling out between him and Danny regarding body shop work. Mitch defended himself, "I don't owe you anything anymore!" He opened a body shop two blocks away, hoped to get work from DAN MOTORS, but avoided us.

A whole year passed when Mitch stopped by the Honda showroom looking for me. "I resent having to be grateful to Danny forever," he said, "just because he helped me out? Didn't I work hard for you? I did my part... we're even!"

"Who expects eternal gratitude?" We were standing in the doorway of my office. Once upon a time my cousin had hung on my braids. He'd cried whenever I played with someone else. We'd climbed trees together, raced our bikes through the winding lanes of Levittown, we'd giggled and shared secrets and gotten into mischief together... and we'd felt each other's pain. "Danny treated you like a brother, Mitch, and you let him down with your stupid cheating."

"There are times I want to apologize, Fran, but I can't. What if Danny won't accept it?"

"Remember when we were kids, and you were always cheating at cards? But I played with you anyway, we loved each other. Danny will accept your apology, I know it, he wants to hear it, believe me."

Mitch promised to apologize. It took him a long time to actually do it, about five years; and then he sent his son to hand-deliver a letter. Danny read it and showed it to me. There were tears in his eyes. Mitch had described in the letter his appreciation for many things, among them, having Danny for a 'brother.'

EVERY MONTH Maria, the bookkeeper, and her assistant, Judy, messed up the DAN MOTORS payments to Francine's Fine Tuning. I couldn't decide if these errors were due to incompetence or mutiny. She still behaved unprofessionally flirtatious with Danny and we still took her and her office friends to dinner on the occasions when she got the statement out on time. The whole situation was an irritant to me, yet nothing I said to Danny could convince him to find a more competent bookkeeper. Then one day Judy argued with Danny, demanded a fifty dollar raise, and this became an ongoing issue between them. She and Maria complained all the time that the salesmen, who they called jerks, earned more money than they did. "Let us sell Volvos, Daniel, we'll show them what we can do!" And Maria still wanted Danny.

"What is she thinking, Danny? She sees us together every day, why doesn't she get the message that you're unavailable?"

"You can't blame her for trying," Danny said, claiming to understand her.

"Well, what are you doing to encourage her when you ought to be discouraging her? You're playing a role in this, too, with your constant kidding around with her. Why don't you just be serious in the office?"

Then one morning I entered the Volvo showroom where Maria's office was located to review an ad with the manager. A loud argument under way in the office drew me to investigate. On Judy's behalf Maria had incited the other women in the office to cease work and hold a sit-in until Danny capitulated to Judy's demand.

I hurried back to the Honda showroom. "Fire them now, Danny! This is your opportunity!"

"I can't do it your way," Danny explained, visibly upset. "I'll be stuck with no one to run the office. I'll do it my way, Fran, don't worry, I know how to handle it."

Effectively disguising his disappointment required major discipline, for the one thing which hurt Danny more than anything was employee disloyalty. He walked into the office and announced in his usual easy-going way, "You win, Judy, you got the raise. Now you can all go back to work."

Danny stopped being friendly toward Maria and a few months later she told him the job was too much, she had migraine headaches all the time and wanted to leave. A week later Judy gave notice and the week after, Carol. Danny hired Martin to replace Maria and under Martin's competent watch the office finally ran without delays or errors.

My father had become diabetic and my mother was his nurse. She supervised the morning urine test and injection of insulin. She massaged his legs and carefully powdered his toes. She prepared three meals a day and under her watchful eyes every morsel of food my father consumed was in accordance with the diabetes diet. But now, in December, my mother was ill. She was unable to eat.

Her plate before her, she lifted the fork hesitantly, slowly, slowly raised a tidbit of food to her lips, and dropped the fork back onto her plate, food uneaten. Every evening Annie and I brought my mother all her favorite foods and laid out her dinner. When my father saw she wasn't eating he grabbed the food from her plate.

"Grandpa!" Annie protested, "don't do that!"

"It's alright, Annie my sweet, I can't eat it anyway."

"She's going to leave it over ... she always does," my father rationalized, "so I may as well enjoy it while it's hot."

Although my mother monitored all my father's medical appointments she refused to make one for herself. Finally I told her, "Mom, I made an appointment with Dr. Conti. I'm taking you and you have nothing to say about it."

"Involuntary Anorexia," was the diagnosis; my mother had to be hospitalized. I left work early and spent every afternoon in my mother's hospital room. My father sat there utterly lost. My mother's voice grew weak, her eyes became hollow. Annie and I brought family albums to her bedside and we made a happy fuss over old memories, although my mother couldn't take too much excitement and looked at the pages for only a few minutes. At work or when I went on errands I saw my mother's face in front of me; I felt nauseous and faint.

On a Friday in March I sat on the edge of her bed and held my mother's hand. My mother was a dignified woman. The nervous yelling when she was well was not the real Mary. That was Mary helplessly drowning in a life over which she'd never mastered control. This woman, calm and serene, was the real Mary.

My mother mustered the strength to speak. "Dr. Conti asked me this morning, have you had a happy life?"

"Oh yes," I told him. "We never had too much money but we always had plenty of love. And we brought up two wonderful children. No one has a daughter like my Francine."

My mother was telling me goodbye. I leaned closer and looked more deeply into her sunken eyes. What I saw frightened me, and all I could do was hold her hands and pray for her recovery.

AT HOME I nervously cleaned until exhaustion forced me to stop. I called on God, on the spirit of my grandma, my guardian angel Love: "Please restore good health to my mother!" I prayed. "She is needed to care for my father!" I implored. The next day when I arrived at the hospital the door to my mother's room stood ajar and I recognized the distinct outline of her feet beneath the blanket, her big toe was half an inch longer than the second toe. Her hands lay motionless by her side. My mother's face, no longer round, was beautiful still. And her eyes! The haunted look of yesterday was gone!

"Fran," she smiled at me.

"Mom! You look so good today!" I leaned over, kissed her soft cheek, and then I finally lost control and cried.

"What's the matter, dolly?"

"Nothing's the matter, Mom, everything's wonderful!"

"I made up my mind last night," she told me then, "right after you were praying for me, Fran . . . I decided no matter how difficult it is I'm going to eat, I'll force myself!"

"MOM, YOU'RE a wonderful mother," Neale said. I was loaning him $40,000 savings from Francine's Fine Tuning, to enable him to buy an apartment in Bayside. "I really appreciate what you're doing for me, Mom, and I promise to pay you back."

"You don't have to, Neale, I'm just happy to give it to you."

"No, I want to pay you back," he hugged me affectionately.

"I'm really sorry, sweetheart, for all the times I failed to understand you. If I had another chance I'd understand you better."

"No, no, Mom . . . I really gave you a hard time for a while and I'm really sorry about that. I love you very much, Mommy."

HONDA WAS the first Japanese automobile manufacturer to build a plant in the United States; Marysville, Ohio, was the chosen site.

In preparation for the extra availability of cars and also, in expectation of increased competition from other manufacturers Honda initiated a program to upgrade their dealerships.

ONE HOT, HUMID August morning, the kind of morning that inspired Danny to toss his tennis gear into the backseat of his car in anticipation of leaving work early, he said as we drove south on the Hutchinson River Parkway toward East Tremont Avenue, "You know, Honey, everything in the business is under control, we have Ronnie in the service department, the operation is making money . . . I feel terrific! And I have Neale, he's really a help. I'd like to start taking it easy, play some more tennis, get to work a little later. Why not, right?"

I agreed with him. Maybe there'd be some time left over in his day for me. Not the kind of time we spent together at Joe's talking business, going over ads, entertaining bankers and factory reps and insurance people. Not the kind of time we spent together in the office we shared, me doing ads, keeping my books straight, writing letters for Danny, both of us interviewing job applicants, talking business, business, business, a million interruptions. He looked at me but didn't really see me. If my conversation wasn't centered on the business, well, he just didn't listen. I had to remind him to look at me.

Then he'd say, as he had last night, while relaxing in his leather chair in the family room, "Sorry, Honey, my mind wandered for a minute."

"But your mind doesn't wander when you're talking business." I was standing, having just finished cleaning up after dinner.

"I guess I take you for granted, you know, you're my old lady," Danny smiled his mischievous, teasing smile, a smile that signified his habitual and determined refusal to take me seriously away from business, especially when I was sharing with him the feelings of my heart.

"I don't want to be taken for granted! I'm still a young woman, Danny, and I want to be treated like one! You never walk into a place with me anymore! I always have to look for you. And when we're at a party I always have to look for you! If I'm not discussing business you don't hear a thing I say!"

"Oh, come on, Honey! You know I love you, and I think you're beautiful!"

"Words, Danny! When did you kiss me last, and I mean, just a nice kiss? When's the last time you put your arms around me, Danny? It's not enough to say, Oh, Honey, I love you. Act like you love me, Danny! Act like you love me!"

"You're not wrong, Fran, I forget … I get tired … I don't know. Come over here and kiss me. I'm going to try." He reached out for me to take his hand but remained seated, comfortable in his chair.

I was standing where the kitchen flowed into the family room, a blue sponge still in my hand from a final swipe of the counter. My leg was hurting beyond recovery for the day. "You have the energy for everything else, Danny, running around the tennis court, whatever it is you want to do. And when it's my turn you won't even walk across a room for me! I give up!"

"No, don't give up on me, Honey, I'm going to be more attentive, I promise."

"Oh, Danny, I'm so weary of begging for your attention! I'm in love with you my whole life! And I've watched you charm every woman who comes along. You listen to them, talk to them, they all love you! And you have me, praying for you to pay attention to me that way, but you don't! Ach! We've been through this so many times."

"Look, Fran, you have your leg, you're anemic, you're always sick with your period. I think I'm a pretty understanding guy. And, I'm good to your parents."

To excuse his own failings as a husband Danny always cited my personal tribulations as if they detracted from my appeal as his wife. It was a triumph of my spirit that no one guessed from looking at me the adversity I conquered each and every day.

"You're not being fair, Danny, and you know it. I'm a woman and I want to be treated like a woman!"

"I'll try, Honey, I promise."

He always promised. Then in a few hours he forgot.

LAST MAY while rushing to throw a late wash into the dryer during a commercial break in the Monday Night Movie I'd slipped at the top of the stairs hitting my head on every stair all the way down to the last, and I'd suffered a concussion. The headaches and stiff neck lingered still. I had too much on my mind, always too many responsibilities and too much work. I longed to have someone take my hand and say, Let's just relax together, don't think about anything except how we love each other. There's nothing to jump up for, just lay here in my arms and let me love you.

Neale lived in Bayside now, Annie was out, driving around the neighborhood in the navy-blue Honda Prelude Danny gave her. My parents still waited on the driveway or on the patio for me to arrive home from work and I served them refreshments when I just wanted to lie down and rest.

Every responsibility in the house was mine. Danny wouldn't even change a light bulb. "Later, later," he put it off, leaving for me whatever was required, even when it was a "man's job." We needed a new roof and now I was choosing roof tiles and rushing home to wait for roofers who came to give estimates.

I wandered through the rooms of my house. Annie had wheeled her doll carriage back and forth in this hallway. Neale hadn't been able to pass through without jumping up to tap the beam. On dark winter evenings, sitting on the family room floor, Neale and Annie had watched "Batman" and "I Dream of Jeannie," and I was right here in the kitchen, enjoying the sound of their laughter, slicing tomatoes and rinsing steaks.

The house was silent now. In two short years Annie would be off to college. And then what? I'd be home, waiting for repairmen, dusting, waiting for Danny to come home from tennis. On weekends, as soon as he peeled off his sweaty tennis clothes, I ran down with them to the laundry room. Immediately after he showered I cleaned the bathroom and waited for him to wake from his nap so we could have lunch at the corner deli.

Danny was strong. He'd go on playing tennis, carefree, business under control, while my responsibilities were endless. It was time to liberate myself. It was time to move.

At the office Danny was going through his messages when a call came in from our Honda zone manager, John Conners. He and our rep, Tom DelFranco, would be stopping by. Twenty minutes later John and Tom sat opposite Danny in the brown tweed guest armchairs, and made the following proposal: they were after exclusivity; they'd like the old Sander's Buick place on the corner renovated and transformed into an exclusive Honda facility for sales, service and parts.

Danny hesitated. He didn't need additional expenses when everything was going so well. Tom smiled his friendly smile, he leaned forward laying an arm across his knees, and enunciated each word with intense concentration. "Daniel, listen to me. We're making you an offer you can't refuse."

Reflexively, Danny glanced at me. I responded silently with a half-nod.

"You do this for us," Tom prompted, "and we'll see to it that you grow. We'll feed you cars." They talked for a long time and I continued to work on the billing at my desk.

Danny agreed to the renovation. "How about some lunch, John? Tom?"

Over Joe's veal topped with ripe tomato wedges and sliced onion, Tom explained how important it was to him, personally, for the dealers in his area of responsibility to upgrade their facilities. I surmised that Tom's success in this endeavor determined his future with Honda. John told us their plan was to approach every Honda dealer with a similar proposal.

"You're the first," he said. "And we'll remember anyone who doesn't go along."

DANNY REFUSED a hundred times to consider moving. He was content to remain in his comfortable house, his house with the low mortgage, located only fifteen minutes from his business. And then one day, to my amazement, he agreed.

"I'll design a house, my dream house, Danny, with no steps, so I can't fall again, and we'll buy some land and have it built."

Night after night I worked at the kitchen table trying to transfer the vision of my imagination onto graph paper. This new house would be the jewel of my imagination: spa room, central Japanese style garden room, an enclosed courtyard for almost every room and for the entryway. I planned every detail, from the white stucco walls and pecan paneled ceiling in the den to the wide, built-in shower seat in the master bath.

I visited a real estate agent in Larchmont; an architect friend of his happened to be there when I arrived and he asked to have a look at my plans. He found them interesting and asked permission to make a copy.

The agent drove to a quiet street near the Sound where he showed me half an acre of meadowland. Wildflowers peeked from behind small boulders, butterflies rode the hot summer breeze. We were standing in the shade of an old, gnarled apple tree and I visualized my dream house centered in this sunny meadow. The agent explained that this piece of land was owned by the previous residents of the house on the adjoining lot. Then, despite the bucolic field and the heat, a prickly chill crept up my arms.

"Tell me about that house," I said.

A fine family had lived there. One day the wife fell down the stairs, became a quadriplegic and after several years of enduring her tragedy, had enlisted the aid of her physician husband to end her life. The sorrowful energy of her tragic demise hovered in the meadow, and I felt it. I thanked the agent for his time and went home.

An agent in Rye brought us to land near the water where marsh grasses grew and hundreds of wild birds nested. Too remote. A lovely wooded plot in Harrison but we could hear the constant noise of trucks on Route 687.

While driving around the neighborhood on a Saturday afternoon in late September we spotted a corner lot on a slight rise, bordered with lush foliage, opposite a golf course whose great expanse of green sloped down toward Mamaroneck Sound, and the blue shimmer of the Sound was visible. We had finally located the perfect land on which to build my dream home. A builder owned the property, we quickly learned. His plans for a colonial style house had been approved the previous night following a wait of several years and he refused to even discuss my plans.

I reconsidered my plans. Why was I looking at land all over Westchester? I recalled the ordeal of building Two Flower Place. Did I really want to go through all the phases of construction again? My dream house was laid out on graph paper, Neale and Annie were excited about it, and in my imagination I'd already walked through the rooms and basked in the courtyard sun protected from the wind. Specimen trees had already flowered on either side of the winding path. These were daydreams of the mind. The next morning my private, secret dream, held so long within my heart, suddenly shone as clear and bright as the sunrise pushing through the spaces between the shutters and the windowsill.

When, at seventeen, I'd traveled the subway to my job from the Bronx to Manhattan I'd imagined living in the city. Evenings at the Ballet, the Philharmonic, dinners in fine restaurants, and elegant friends who'd gather in my chic apartment for luminous conversations and intelligent laughter. Whenever Danny ignored me or used me for his own needs, ignoring mine, this fantasy rose from within my heart and my anguish fed it life. My own comforting reverie. And now fantasy suddenly emerged into the realm of possibility! Everything suddenly appeared in sharp focus. All those occasions I was angry at Danny and accused him of keeping me last on his list, I was really angry at myself because I was last on my own list.

Neale was acquiring power in the business and Danny often discussed with Neale, things he had once discussed with me. At Joe's lately, I was left out of the conversation. Neale understood business finance, he was becoming the financial controller. He had taken over Danny's role in laying out the advertising budget and the ads now required Neale's stamp of approval. I was witnessing my son's growing sophistication and his willingness to accept responsibility, an enormously gratifying life passage. But I recognized also that my son's growth signaled a new era in DAN MOTORS, an era that would make my contributions obsolete.

Danny hadn't issued stock in my name as he'd promised, nor had he given me a title. But he'd given Neale stock and made him Vice President. The dealership and property ownership had bolstered Danny's ego like nothing he'd ever experienced in his life. He'd maintained full control and when we began to achieve real success he chose to share it not with his wife, but with his son. I would always be 'Mommy.' I had no desire to control anyone's life, my desire was to gain control of my own life!

"I HAVE SOMETHING to discuss with you, Danny, and I'd like to discuss it over brunch."

Danny shot me a look. The resolve in my voice sounded an alarm which motivated Danny to be alert. He looked worried while driving twenty minutes in silence to a new restaurant in White Plains; pure white walls, bare, bleached floors, pink-clothed tables set with bouquets of fresh flowers. We sat by an open window. I ordered eggs Benedict and a Bloody Mary. Danny remained quiet, not his usual inattentive quiet, frightened quiet. He knew I rarely ordered alcoholic beverages. "Same," he nodded at the waiter.

We sipped the Bloody Marys. "So . . . Fran, what is it you want to talk about?"

"I've made a decision, Danny, and nothing . . . nothing will change my mind." It hurt to see dark clouds in his eyes, but I continued. "I hope you'll go along with me, but even if you don't, my mind is made up."

Danny covered my right hand with his, his palm felt cold and sweaty. "What is it, Honey?"

"I don't really want all the headaches of building a house, I went through all of that when we built Two Flower Place. I don't want a monument to material possessions, it never was my style. What I really want is an easier life . . . I want an apartment in New York."

Instantly, Danny exuded relief, his expression brightened and he smiled, which made me wonder for a long time afterward, what secret worry had he been harboring? Had he committed a deception that he worried I'd discovered? Or was it just the stuff I already knew held within a guilty mind? To ask was to invite further deception.

"Honey!" the words burst out of him with gusto, "wherever you're going, I'm going with you!"

Museums, Art & Culture

NEW YORK CITY. 1983. Tara Sunshine wore a wide-brimmed black straw hat, a snug beige suit, and she walked comfortably in four-inch heels. "First place I'm taking you I think you're going to like," she said. "Museum Tower on 53rd Street, above the Museum of Modern Art."

A doorman attired in a smart, dark-gray uniform pushed the heavy glass and brass-trimmed revolving doors for us and we entered an elegant lobby, bronze sculpture on the left, walls lined with paintings by famous artists. A concierge greeted us, entered our names in the Day Book and handed Tara an elevator pass. Three elevators, and three operators, each attired in smart, dark-gray twill uniforms and white gloves. On the thirteenth floor Tara led us to the 'B' apartment; the door, eight feet high, was constructed of sleek teakwood and it swung open with reassuring solidity.

Danny and I stepped into the entrance foyer. Before us lay a room of magnificent proportions: a ceiling nine feet high, the southeast corner on the left, thirty feet from where we stood, was solid glass set six feet wide on two walls. Windows were set two feet above the floor and reached to the ceiling. The room seemed to be about twenty feet wide. The floor, of finest teakwood, was laid in tongue and groove herringbone pattern with straight borders. It was a cloudy day, yet the room was suffused with a beautiful light!

I flung my arms wide and danced in a circle. "I love it, I love it, I love it! We'll never find another place like this, Danny!" I grasped his hand and together we explored the entire apartment. There were three bathrooms of marble the color of sand, a marble shower stall in the master bath as well as an oversized tub fitted with a French shower and a bidet.

We discovered a huge walk-in closet. The master bedroom was larger than our bedroom at home, and a second bedroom suite with dressing area and its own full bathroom, perfect for Annie and in years to come, a study. The bedrooms and the kitchen had the same tall windows as in the living room. The apartment measured almost two-thousand square feet.

Museum Tower was considered the finest new building in the city. The Rockefeller family, the original owner, had donated the land to the City of New York as the site of the Museum of Modern Art. The building rose fifty-two stories high, the apartments began on the ninth floor, above the museum, and each succeeding floor cost an additional $16,000. The next available 'B' apartment was on the twentieth floor, so it was imperative that we arrive at a timely decision. But how could we buy an apartment, even this perfect one, without comparing it with other available apartments? Tara showed us apartments in all the new luxury buildings but nothing felt as right as Museum Tower.

On October 7, 1983, we went to contract. Closing date was set for June 6, 1984. Scheduled moving day, June 7. It was happening for me! I was making it happen!

Annie brought home a private school directory, sought advice from her teachers, made a list and began the application process. Neale understood and agreed with our decision, and after some inquiries he learned that despite the high cost of the apartment, according to the New York market it was good value.

"We're not going to build a house," I explained to my parents, "we bought an apartment in New York." Shock registered on my mother's face. "It's what I've always wanted, Mom."

"Why, Fran, I think that's wonderful!" my father exclaimed. "That's what I wanted to do a long time ago, when you and Danny first got married, but your mother refused..."

"Wait a minute!" my mother interrupted in a shrill voice, "What do you mean?"

"She's moving to Manhattan, Mary! Our daughter is going to have a wonderful life with her husband!"

"What about Annie? She has to finish school!"

"Annie is applying to schools in the city, Mom, and she's excited about it."

"What? How can you let her go to school in the city? Anything could happen to her there!"

"Mary, keep quiet a minute! Let's hear about their apartment! Tell us, Fran! I want to hear everything my daughter has to say!"

I described Museum Tower. "Mom, I never have to carry clothes to the cleaners again, there's a valet service! And security you wouldn't believe! A package room, no more waiting for deliveries! Maintenance men, right there, to fix anything! Don't you understand, Mom, my life is going to be easier! I'll feel better, I'll have more time to pursue my interests! It'll be so much easier to take my classes!"

My mother repeated herself over and over. "Why do you have to go and move so far away? I love your house! Your house is your Camelot!"

"It's not so far, Mom it's only Manhattan, it's not California!"

"But your trees! All your things! How can you leave that beautiful house?"

"Mom, a house is only walls! It's not material things that make a home! It's the people who live within those walls! It's love that makes a home! Wherever I live will be my home! I'll fill this new place with love! And Museum Tower will be my home!"

Rocco started renovating the old Sander's place. I began the drawings and plot plans. We selected taupe ceramic tile for the showroom floor and suede-like wallpaper in a lighter shade; we met the designer-owner of an office furniture store in the city and we collaborated together, deciding on a smart, practical desk design for the sales force which we ordered in a complementary shade of taupe. Tom DelFranco sent us to another Honda showroom to look at their new lighting system and we had Rocco order it. Rocco and I reviewed the dimensions for new bookkeeping offices. We installed new enlarged windows and wide double doors, tan pebble siding and dark brown mansard, which altogether brought the building into the modern age.

Neale patched things up with Mitch and they struck a new deal. From a box in his closet at home Mitch retrieved a photograph of Neale, two years old, sitting on his shoulders, and pinned it on his office wall where, with an affectionate smile he pointed it out to everyone who entered his office.

THIRTY-EIGHT DAYS of menstrual bleeding. A hysterectomy can no longer be avoided. A solitary tear escapes my left eye and rolls into my hair. This is it. I'm icy cold and shivering on the gurney. A nurse approaches offering three pills in a tiny white cup.

"Are you sure these are for me?" I ask, my practical, cautious self proving more powerful than fear. Or maybe fear made me practical.

"Francine Sachleben?" the nurse responds, "Dr. Nolan's patient? Hysterectomy?"

I nod.

"It's for you, dear."

I swallow.

"Francine Sachleben?" Another nurse enters to administer an injection.

I nod and turn a little, feel the sting of the needle. It doesn't bother me. What's one needle when I'm about to be sliced open.

No more anemia with blood counts of 21 or 22. This is emergency surgery, as Dr. Nolan had warned. I'm consumed with fear. Dreadful fear that my eyes will never open again! Don't close your eyes! Keep watch over yourself! When they were ill I'd watched over Neale and Annie. Last night they called, "Good luck tomorrow, Mommy. Hope everything goes okay. Love you very much."

Now I'm about to lose that part of myself which brought my children into the world, mysterious cradle of creation. Sadness descends not only for me, but for all the women of the world who endure 'women's problems,' and I'm blanketed in sorrow. My eyes close.

They're wheeling me down the corridor. Did I expect to lie there for a thousand years? I feel the lights above as we pass under them ... bright ... dull. We've come to a halt, must be waiting for an elevator. Trembling of my body is fierce but they can't see the trembling, for I'm wrapped up tight, like the mummies Mike used to take me to see in the museum. Ancient bodies wrapped in yards of fine white linen cloth, detailed likeness of the deceased beautifully rendered on the sarcophagus in gold and turquoise, black and coral, lapis lazuli ... how I've always been mesmerized by ancient Egyptian artifacts and timeless treasures. The ancient Egyptians glorified their dead with material wealth. But now I know that when we pass into the next world we take with us only love.

SURGERY. My gurney has halted again. Above the door to the operating room a light is blinking. Controlled discipline all around. My eyes are closed but I realize my feelings tell me everything as if my eyes are open. Dr. Nolan issuing orders. "Fran," he is saying, standing by the gurney now, his face floating above me, "Fran, there's another emergency, a woman is bleeding to death, I've got to take her in before you. I'm sorry, Fran, are you alright?" Don't use up your day's supply of miracles before you get to me, Bob! Save a little miracle for me! I don't want to die! Can you tell someone to cover me with another blanket? Bob goes to his emergency.

I'm freezing, shivering. I keep vacillating between semi-consciousness and total blackness. If you die they just pull that extra flap of white cloth over your face. But shivering is painful. The gurney is moving again. Any moment now Bob's hand will guide his scalpel across the smooth, flat skin of my belly.

My spirit rises to preside over my funeral, a room in shadows, crowded and hushed. My spirit hovers protectively close to Annie and Neale. My children, I whisper, you will miss the sound of my voice, my gentle touch, my tender loving kiss. When you are going about your days you'll think of me, unexpectedly. A woman with hair like mine will momentarily capture your attention, or someone will call out, Francine! and you'll think of me. You don't need things to remember me by, I learned that when my Grandma died. Neale will say, No one will ever love us like Mommy loved us. And Annie will agree.

My spirit moves on to Danny. He's sitting beside our children, yet my spirit sees him as solitary. You'll remember our first kiss, Danny, parked in your Buick on 199th Street, our week of heaven at the Laurels. You'll remember me begging you, when we were young, stay home with me! Be romantic! And someday your soul will join mine and we'll frolic hand in hand in the flowers of eternity, as we did in a vision I had long ago . . .

MY EYES OPEN and focus on the window, beyond which all the world proceeds as usual, but here in this room, in this hospital bed, all the world is pain. My uterus is gone, my ovaries are gone, but I am here! I made it! I love you, Bob Nolan! God channeled His will through your hands, and I love you!

During the course of surgery Dr. Nolan discovered cysts on both sides of my fallopian tubes, an infected gland within the left ovary, an enlarged uterus, and a pelvic cavity filled with blood clots.

"You know, Honey, President's Weekend is coming up. Maybe you should place an ad for the house, we might get lucky."

I began packing, starting with the storage room and closets to preserve the serenity of my home for as long as possible. Packed cartons were stacked in the exercise room.

Sunday morning the phone rang. "I'm calling on your ad," the man said. "I know your neighborhood because we've been looking around there for over a year already."

"Oh, so, you're interested in this neighborhood?"

"Yes, we have relatives in the new development near you and as a matter of fact we almost put a deposit down on the Schiller house around the corner from you."

"Oh, yes, I know the house. If you thought you liked that house, wait till you see ours! You'll love it!"

"Fine, when should we come over?"

"Well, we're just finishing our bagels."

He laughed. "That's what we're doing."

"So come over later then."

About an hour later the doorbell rang. The sun was unusually bright and warm for February and it had melted all the snow. The sunlight worked its magic and Two Flower Place was glowing.

I opened the front door and there stood the young man and his family. Why, this was us sixteen years ago! A little boy peeked out from behind his father's legs and the young woman was holding her infant daughter in her arms.

"Welcome! Come in! Your husband says you've been looking for a long time. Well, I think you can stop looking . . . this is the perfect house for you. Come, I'll show you around."

They followed me through the hallway to the bedrooms, Rose oohing and aahing, David nodding and smiling.

"I like it here," the child said as he entered Neale's room.

"Of course you like it! I have a boy, he's grown now, but once upon a time he was a little boy just like you, and he loved this room!"

Annie's room always looked like a page from a picture book, white ruffled curtains pressed just so with spray starch, the prettiest room in the house. Rose and David were impressed, they obviously loved my home. I led them downstairs and that's when they were absolutely sold.

"Oh, Davy, look! She has an organ!" They were ecstatic. David turned to me and said, "It's been a standing joke with us that when we have our house Rose was going to buy me an organ, I've always wanted one, and here you have this beauty!" He turned back to his wife, "It's a good omen, Rose."

Their little son found the cozy room under the stairs where Annie had played years ago, and he happily refused to leave.

"Come, sit down," I indicated the white director's chairs at the round white table in front of the wide double windows which looked out on our back lawn and garden.

"This is a good luck house," I told them. "We've never had a flood or a leak or hurricane damage. We've never been burglarized, and I've never even needed an exterminator. You can see that everything is well-cared for. A house like this is hard to find, believe me."

"Oh, we can tell," David agreed, "This is definitely the cleanest house we've ever been in!"

They left, promising to call soon and a few hours later they returned with David's parents. Immediately, his mother and I hit it off.

"Oh, she exclaimed, "this house is gorgeous! And so immaculate! How do you do it?"

"Well, to tell you the truth, I haven't been keeping up as much as usual, I just had a hysterectomy a few weeks ago."

"Oh, darling, please sit down. Rose, let's not keep her standing like this."

"No, it's okay ... come, I'll show you the rest of the house, then we'll sit."

By the time they left David's mother had her arm around my

waist, proclaiming what a doll I was. "The kids will never find another house like this one, I don't care how long they look! And just to own your house, that's something!"

"You know, Estelle, it's really important to me that a lovely family like your son's should live here. I'll really feel good to know that the next owners will love the house and take care of it. And really, it's the perfect house for them!"

Estelle nodded and smiled, and at the door we hugged and kissed.

I gave away a lot of stuff. To synagogues, churches, Salvation Army, employees, friends and relatives, until everyone we knew and almost every local organization had some memento from Two Flower Place. I sold all my jewelry. From now on there'd be no room in my life for the accumulation of unnecessary or unimportant belongings. No more saving interesting newspaper and magazine articles to which no one referred anyway, or Playbills. Our new closets and drawers were going to contain only those things which are useful in the present.

Possessions stored on closet shelves become so familiar they cease to be noticed. But now we're moving. I reach up to clear a shelf, hold the object, examine it and ponder: should this article be kept? If not, what should be done with it? I can't throw away a perfectly good thing, someone else might enjoy it. But who? About halfway through the task of clearing and packing I am seized by an urge to gather all these possessions into one huge bonfire and be done. But I am a reasonable person, so I bend and reach and clear and pack, drawer by drawer, room by room, and swear I will never own so many things again.

On June 6, our closing date, Rose and David arrived on time. I gave them the booklet I'd prepared listing all the people who serviced the house. I withdrew from my purse the key ring I'd carried for fifteen years. Seven keys: front door – upper and lower locks, back door, outside garage door key for times the automatic opener didn't work, inside garage key, two alarm keys.

"Here are the keys, Rose. I hope you and your family will enjoy many, many years of good health and happiness in Two Flower Place."

I felt as light as the angel food cake Annie and I used to bake on winter afternoons. Now I'd carry a sterling silver Tiffany key tag inscribed with 'Museum Tower'; on the ring were two keys for the sleek teakwood door of apartment 13B.

The skies on June 7 were clear and blue. Annie left in the morning for her last final exam at Rye Country Day. The movers arrived and swung open wide the extra high double doors. A bee hovered near the azalea bushes, but for once I didn't worry that it would find its way inside.

The movers carried out Danny's beautiful Directiore chest of drawers, the one Mike had hoped we wouldn't take to New York, and give to him instead. Our furniture, carried down the pastel stone walk, the walk we'd paid for with proceeds from a Cadillac Danny won with a raffle he'd bought from an old-timer on Jerome Avenue, could be seen by the whole street. But no one was there.

Our neighbors directly across the way had already left for work. Our next-door neighbor, well, she used to yell at Neale when he was a little boy and his ball rolled onto her grass. Five of our neighbors, all women, had died; five out of thirty-two. One of the women, named Fran, had been my dear friend. She died in the Spring, the week our apple blossom tree flowered into a gorgeous cloud of pink and white blossoms.

My parents arrived. My father had recently given up the cane he'd used since the by-pass operation on his leg that winter. Tears brimmed in my mother's eyes. "We'll never again drive past this corner."

Annie came home exactly on time to climb into the back seat of the Buick. I helped her position the round white domed birdcage on her lap. Prissy, Sweetie (who replaced Elvis) and Angel seemed to be chirping a farewell chorus. I kissed my parents and got in beside Danny. The movers pulled out in front. At the stop sign I turned and looked back at my house. My flowers had come up full this Spring.

By noon the movers arrived at Museum Tower and by four our furniture was in place. I transferred from the closet where I'd stored them when we'd brought them down earlier in the week, my antique vases and lamps, and arranged them in their new places throughout the apartment. I made up the beds with new linen. Violet and white towels were already laid out in the bathrooms and my dishes were on the kitchen shelves, all arranged the previous night.

I was consumed with relief, knowing no household chores awaited my attention, knowing there was no need to run downstairs one more time to make sure Danny hadn't forgotten to close the garage door.

I was filled with the joy of freedom; freedom from carrying groceries up steps, from setting automatic light timers to fool potential burglars, and all the other chores that Danny wanted no part of.

Annie went up to Harvard for a summer program and Danny and I were alone. Liberating myself from his command ... I was going to accomplish that, too. Would Danny love me if he couldn't own me? He enjoyed saying he owned me and that he was my boss.

He'd moved out of his comfortable home and brought me to Museum Tower. Francine Vale from Vyse Avenue, living in a luxury New York condo. To Danny it meant I was expected to socialize with people of his choosing, eat whatever food he approved of, continually take on business projects under his direction, continue in the role of 'good sport,' leave him alone when he didn't want to be touched and be ready whenever he was ready. But now I craved my freedom.

I longed to be free from the kind of love that kept me in bondage. I didn't even know what it felt like to love in the absence of anxiety. Awareness of these feelings provokes a great tension within my heart. Suppose it turns out that Danny is immovable, he can only love me if he controls me? Then what? I pictured myself getting into our bed without him there, waking up alone in the morning. Could I do it?

THE FIRST STEP toward personal autonomy would be not to share every single thought with him. He didn't listen anyway. And sharing yourself so openly only to be ignored or waved away with a callous hand leads to a profound sense of feeling unloved. So stop reaching for his hand, I counseled myself. Stop hoping to catch his eye as if you only exist when Danny notices you. If I could contain the urge to touch him, I'd also learn to be more in control of my life. Make appointments for myself, take more classes and study whatever I like. Come home after him. Let him discover what it feels like to wait. Don't melt when he flashes that gorgeous smile of his. Flash your own smile and become again the strong woman you were before you were interrupted.

IN LATE AUGUST our exclusive Honda facility was complete and Danny and I moved into our new office. The cars looked outstanding in the elegant taupe setting and under the new lights. As a temporary measure, until Danny acquired a franchise for the showroom just vacated, he designated it for 'creme-puffs.'

Plans were being formulated by Hyundai, the Korean automobile manufacturer, to introduce their car into the American market and Danny applied for the franchise. The car was already well-received in Canada where it was known as the Pony. Hyundai was part of a huge conglomerate of heavy industries, including one of the world's largest ship-building companies. The reputation of the

Pony, plus the enormous production power of the Hyundai factory, put them in a position to create an elite dealer body.

Qualification required a combination of several factors: financial substance, proven success with several franchises, a good C.S.I. record (customer satisfaction index), a willingness to provide top-flight facilities, and of course, location in an open point.

On June 27, 1985, the day before Annie's eighteenth birthday, and a year after we moved to the city, notification arrived that we were granted a Hyundai franchise.

ANNIE NOTICED an ad in the Times for a summer study program sponsored by Tulane University. Eight weeks in Paris studying Art History and Sociology. Annie was an excellent French student; she was going to have a wonderful summer.

Neale bought an apartment in a new luxury building on the upper east side; twenty-ninth floor, wide open views in all directions. From Neale's apartment you could see the bridges in Queens, the Bronx and New Jersey.

After dinner Danny and I strolled up Fifth Avenue. Passing the Plaza and alongside the park, Danny said, "You know, Honey, you hardly ever touch me anymore. You used to be all over me."

"Oh, you noticed."

"Yeah. Actually, you've been a little cold to me."

"Well, why do you suppose that is, Danny?"

"Are you angry with me? Did I do something wrong?"

"That's just it, Danny. You don't do anything. All you do is get into bed at ten o'clock and go to sleep. The only way I can stop feeling hurt is if I don't care, so I've been teaching myself not to care."

"But it turns me off when you aren't nice to me."

We were up to 69th Street and continued walking north.

"Oh, Danny! What about all the years I fell all over you! You can be distant, forever if you want, but I have to remain warm and loving? Why is our relationship my sole responsibility? I don't know what it feels like to be hugged anymore!"

The thing was, I didn't even feel like crying. I should have felt the ocean welling up behind my eyes; I'd waited a long time for Danny to realize there was something to discuss. At 74th Street he put his arm around me.

"Let's turn back, Honey, it's starting to get dark. Look, we've been married a long time, we're going to have our ups and downs . . . you know I love you, Honey."

He kissed my cheek and drew me closer to his side. It didn't move me. I felt like a piece of stone. "You've hurt me too much over the years, Danny. I always imagined if we ever reached this point, just the two of us, the business doing well, you not running out to play every sport there is, I imagined I'd be so happy. But now I see it wasn't activities that kept you from me, Danny, it's just you . . . you keep yourself away from me. And I don't want to live that way anymore."

"I know I've been difficult, Fran, but I'm really trying. I do my work-outs at the health club early in the morning so they won't interfere with our day. That's an improvement, would you prefer I didn't work out?"

"Of course not! It's good for you and I'm glad you're working out . . . but you leave the bed without a kiss, without a touch, as if you lived alone. That's what you ought to do, Danny, live alone! Call me when you want to see me!"

"Never say that, Honey, please don't say that. I love you so much, I'm a certain way, my father was never affectionate with my mother and I guess I can't help it."

"I'm not your mother, and it's more than affection, Danny. You don't talk to me, unless it's business. What's that? Oh! I can't stand it anymore!"

"Give me another chance, Fran, please don't be disgusted with me. I have no life without you! You and the kids are my whole life! I'm not an intellectual or a brilliant speaker, I'm a plain guy.

You've got so much class, I can never be like you, you could be married to the wealthiest, classiest guy and you'd fit in. But I love you, Honey, and I want to spend the rest of my life with you."

"Oh, Danny, what am I going to do? I can't keep going through all this emotional stuff!"

"Why don't we go on a trip? Somewhere romantic. Let's go to Paris! We'll visit Annie. We'll fly the Concord! From now on only the best for my baby! First class all the way! I want you to love me like you used to, Honey, and forgive me. I'm sorry for hurting you."

My feet ached. I was glad to reach 53rd Street.

The Concord, Row 3, Seats A and B.

"See?" Danny smiled. "I take you first class now! Only the best for you, Honey." He held my hand and leaned over to kiss me.

"You know how long we'll be married soon, Danny?"

"Twenty-five years! December 11th it'll be twenty-five years! And I'm the luckiest guy in the world . . . I have you! You're more beautiful than ever! If I met you today I'd ask you to marry me on the spot!" He kissed me again.

"Would you, Danny? You wouldn't want to change me?"

"No. You're perfect just the way you are." He squeezed my hand. "I want to start over with you, Fran." He looked into my eyes. "My Green Eyes. Remember I used to call you that?"

Danny's hair had grown silver at the temples, and it was thinning. But I saw instead, the darkest hair, slicked back in the pomaded style of the fifties. I closed my eyes and saw his face, young and sweet, totally irresistible to me.

"Yes, Danny, I remember . . . I went to a dance with my friend Suzie, and there you were, looking every girl up and down. I asked that boy, what was his name again?"

"Ted Zinn."

"Yes, Ted Zinn. He walked me over to you. You were so gorgeous Danny, and so sweet. Right away you called me Green Eyes. And all I ever wanted since that moment was to be with you, to feel your arms holding me close, to hear you say, 'I love you.'" A great emotional tidal wave swept over me, I was drowning.

"Don't cry, Honey, I love you so much! You're my whole life! I'm nothing without you!" Danny leaned closer. "Let's get married again, Honey."

The notion uplifted us, like a rainbow our love blessed the world. And there, in Danny's eyes, or maybe it was in my heart, I felt our unshakable bond.

"We'll do it for our twenty-fifth!" Danny raised my hand to his lips and kissed my palm. He buried his face in my hand. "Will you marry me, gorgeous? Huh?"

I nodded. "I still love you, Danny Sachleben." I leaned over and kissed him.

MID-AUGUST and Annie was due to arrive home from Paris. She had met great kids, and one young man in particular who was about to enter Law School had made her summer perfect.

The call came from Edmond; Rose had passed away in her sleep. She had made it to seventy-nine.

We met Annie at the airport and drove straight to Edmond's house because Leo was already there and the Rabbi was there. Neale drove up on his own. We gathered in the living room to talk about Rose with the Rabbi.

Elliot said, "Nanny brought us up, she was more like a mother to us." Laura nodded in agreement.

"She did things with them," Doris laughed, "I couldn't be bothered with!"

I studied my children as they sat composed on Doris' sectional sofa. Just turned eighteen and almost twenty-four. My children carried themselves with grace. I felt more proud of them than ever.

Elliot and Laura told the Rabbi all the reasons they had loved their grandmother. Neale and Annie listened respectfully. Now they knew for sure how partial Rose had been. My children hadn't needed anyone else to be their mother, they had me. But it would've been wonderful if Rose had shown more interest in them.

After a while the Rabbi turned to Annie and Neale. "What about you two? You're both so quiet, were you close to Rose, too?"

Neale nodded, Annie nodded. "Oh, yes," they answered politely.

Danny and I made the funeral arrangements but he left to me the selection of the coffin. So, in the end, I was the one who chose the box in which Rose's bones will lie until they turn to dust. The funeral director led me down the stairs to the windowless room where the caskets were displayed.

"Whatever you think is best, Honey," Danny said.

I could get even with her and put her in the cheapest, plainest box. That's probably what she'd do for me. I examined every casket and listened while the funeral director explained the differences. I'd be good, of course, very good. "I like this one," I told him. Elegant mahogany, lined in quilted white satin.

In the twenty years which had passed since the death of my infant son I'd never been to his gravesite. I nudged Danny, "Ask the director to look in his records, I want to know where my baby is buried, please, Danny."

After a surprisingly brief investigation the director handed me a slip of paper: Baby Adam Sachleben, Block 14B, Line 1, Grave 40.

BABY ADAM ... the memory of him had remained with me, like a task you can never complete, or a wound which never will heal, or a teardrop poised on your eyelash forever. My lost baby was not discussed in the family. I wished we could have talked about him, perhaps on those snowy nights when we felt the particular closeness and comfort of togetherness, but even then I couldn't bring the words out, as if a connection between my heart and my tongue had ruptured. I cried on my birthdays, however, usually in the shower where the rushing water obscured the sound of my private sorrow. But the passage of time had not diminished my need for something outside myself to substantiate my lost baby's brief existence. Surprisingly, the funeral director's slip of paper provided this. A strange foreign feeling washed over me. Peace.

THE SACHLEBEN AND STEINBERG families gathered around Rose's open grave. Once, long ago, I'd longed for them to love me, accept me. Every one of them had been to my home for dinners and parties. Some of the relatives probably liked me, but I no longer cared like I did in the beginning.

I stared at the polished mahogany coffin, poised at the side of the open grave. The Rabbi opened his ancient prayer book and began to pray in Hebrew...

Can you hear me, Rose? Danny told me about your conversation, the one he had with you the last time he flew down to get you and Leo into a hotel for the hot summer months. He asked you, finally, Why did you treat Francine so badly all these years, when she was always so good? You told him you were sorry, that you'd made a mistake by favoring Doris. Why didn't you tell me, Rose? I needed to hear it from you! Anyway, in your will you left all the good stuff to Doris and to me you left your 'trinkets.' That wasn't a nice thing to do, Rose...

Six weeks later, peacefully asleep, Leo passed away. He'd lived to see Danny's success. And while Danny and I were cleaning out his parents' apartment, sorting through thousands of papers stuffed in manila envelopes or bound with rubber bands, we discovered that Leo had left a letter for Danny, an attempt to explain his life. He explained how and why the business came to bear the name Edmond's; apparently it was a simple matter of convenience.

When he read the letter, Danny cried. The last line read, "When I married Rose I had the best bookkeeper."

DANNY BROUGHT HOME a station wagon, we were driving Annie up to college! Cornell, Arts and Sciences! Ivy League!

All my life I'd tried to educate myself and still, I felt uneducated. But Annie, her opinion will be respected and she'll hold her own in any discussion or group. My daughter was fulfilling my dream for her, she was becoming an educated woman! We attended the Dean's reception in the crowded gym and the pride of so many parents in one place was palpable. The Dean spoke of dreams and accomplishments. I glanced at Danny, his eyes were glistening. I hugged his arm. "Just think, Danny, our daughter is part of this! Our Annie has made it to Cornell!"

We returned to the city and faced a whole new life. I was no longer anemic! I could go through a day without the naps my body once required. Together Danny and I left for work in the morning, at the end of the day returned home together, freshened up and went out. Every night. Opera, theater, ballet, movies, dinners, interesting new friends. Was this really me?

THE HYUNDAI SHOWROOM was completed in February 1986. We utilized the same design scheme as in the Honda showroom and it came out sharp and sleek. On Zerega Avenue, an industrial park a few minutes' drive from the showroom, we purchased a large, square brick building for Hyundai service and parts and it became the model for all our other service departments.

On a cool, sunny day the sign went up over the new showroom: DAN MOTORS HYUNDAI, and on our opening day customers jammed the showroom. It buzzed with excitement! Never before had we opened to such a crush of customers. Danny had picked a winner!

I initiated a personnel department, interviewed almost everyone in the company, over one-hundred-forty employees, expanded from thirty back when Danny had first asked me to be his partner, and set up a folder for each. In addition, Danny gave me the task of interviewing new applicants. Combined with the insurance and advertising and showroom design projects, it was a tremendous amount of work. When I completed the plot plan for the Hyundai showroom I told Danny, In the future we will pay someone to do this.

The advertising budget, after we acquired Hyundai, increased even more, and often, at six o'clock I was still immersed in meeting deadlines. So, in January 1987 I hired a man to help out and by April I'd allowed him to take over most of the ad work.

Hyundai invited us to spend a week in Korea. When we returned home Danny called Neale, who was in Florida, and after a few seconds Danny exclaimed, "You bought a house? I'll put Mommy on, describe it to her, I don't understand these things."

"Mom! You won't believe the house! I just left a deposit on it today! Remember we passed a house on the intra-coastal side, in Highland Beach, facing the ocean, the one with the blue porcelain tile roof? Well, that's the house! It has a suite for you and Daddy in your favorite colors!"

"You mean aqua?"

"Aqua and violet! And my suite is black and gray, with a huge black marble bathroom! Our suites are upstairs with a bridge that goes over the living room, and there's a room downstairs for Annie, very pretty, like a lavender color.

A pool, with decking all around, and the intra-coastal is in our backyard! Mom! Remember the house you designed before you moved to Museum Tower? The whole idea you had of private courtyards? Well, this house has it! Every room has a courtyard or a private terrace!"

"Oh, Neale! It sounds spectacular! I'm really happy for you, sweetheart!"

"I got a good deal on it, Mom. It's completely furnished, the same design team that did the architecture. We don't have to buy a thing! Just bring down some clothes!"

"What a wonderful greeting to come home to, Neale! You are really seeing your dream come true!"

"I did it, Mom! I bought us a beautiful house! You and Daddy come down on Mother's Day, the closing is the day after!"

THE PLANE LANDED at Palm Beach International Airport. Who could've guessed, when I was eight, playing in the back alley on Vyse Avenue bouncing my pink Spalding and turning my leg over the ball a hundred times without losing my balance, wishing with every turn of my leg for a finer life, that someday I'd have a son like Neale? A son who brings me to the paradise of Highland Beach and says, "This house is for you, Mom . . . Happy Mother's Day!" A son who pauses in the midst of a busy work-day to say, "I love you, Mom, and you're looking very beautiful today."

And who could've guessed I'd have a daughter like Annie? A daughter whose path is a path of compassion, helping others, doing good in the world, also one of sharing, from the first tiny steps of her life, never wavering. A daughter who says, "I love you very much, Mommy. Everything I am, I owe to you."

NEALE'S AND ANNIE'S children will never know about climbing to the fourth floor or longing for a better life. Will my grandchildren think life is all sparkling waterways and enough money for everything? I had better write it all down, I thought, leaving the airport with Danny, before I forget.

DURING THE SUMMER Danny received a Letter of Intent from Acura. We built twin showrooms on the lot next door to Hyundai, the lot we once designated a permanent space for used cars. In recent years we stored new cars there. We'll store the cars somewhere else, and utilize the valuable frontage for an Acura showroom and an exclusive Mazda showroom. Neale is supervising the entire project from ground-breaking to wallpaper.

The signs have already been ordered: DAN MOTORS ACURA.

NEALE IS LOOKING to buy his own dealership in Florida. And Annie worries about getting into Law School. My children will succeed in accomplishing their goals and each goal reached will lead to greater wisdom and lift their souls higher, for they've learned success is possible while remaining forthright and kind to those they meet along the way. This, above all, is the legacy I've prayed they'd inherit from me. For as I learned a long time ago from my beloved father, what matters most is what we do when no one's watching. And from my Guardian Angel Love I learned it is by loving kindness infused into each moment that merit is accumulated.

SOMEDAY I hope my children will hold in their hands a book called, "Song of the Heart," open the book and read it, and say to themselves "This is the book our mother wrote. She decided to write her story for us. And then she went and did it."

Afterward

The morning sun rose pale and distant, hidden from our street view by the Citicorp Building. At the entrance to Museum Tower a few leaves, their edges crisp, fluttered to the pavement. The pink granite stone sidewalk was fragrant from its early hosing; no breeze stirred as Danny and I walked a half block west to the garage. I carried a briefcase, Danny still got by with a slim black calendar book (he now preferred the Manhattan Diary) and a few papers folded into his jacket pocket. We held hands and walked together.

"Hiya, gorgeous . . . hungry? How about a bite to eat?"

"Oh, I'd love to, I'd love to not go to work at all, it's such a beautiful day. But Nancy is bringing her Volvo in for service and we planned on lunch."

Danny drove leisurely as we entered the drive through Central Park. We enjoyed this route to the Bronx although the harsh reality of Lenox Avenue as we emerged from the park on 110th Street filled me with distress; why, I wondered, appalled at the sight of fellow citizens living wounded and scarred among ruins, why can't we as a nation re-assert our heritage of compassion and hope, why can't our government rediscover its soul and rescue our people from despair?

My mind wandered. October again. The month of my parents' wedding anniversary. October was the month Danny and I had met. Neale was born in October. Leo had died. And last October my father died.

SUNDAY, OCTOBER 8, 1989. Upon awakening I'd worried it might happen that day and urged Danny to hurry, we must get up to White Plains quickly. Erev Yom Kippur, eve of the Day of Atonement, holiest day in the Jewish year, and it's written that whosoever shall die on this day shall be considered among the righteous.

Three blocks from my parents' home Danny stopped at a gas station. My sense of urgency overarched all else. "What are you doing, Danny, I'm counting every second and you're stopping?"

"We need gas, Honey, we're on empty."

Regarding things like turning off the stove or locking the door my mother had all her life been vigilant, but strangely, this morning the door swung open almost by itself and for the first time since I left my parents' home to marry Danny, I entered it without my parents greeting me. With great foreboding and heaviness of heart I headed directly for the bedroom and called tentatively into the silence, "Mom?"

"Oh, Fran," my mother answered nervously from the bathroom, "I'm combing my hair, your father's waiting for you, every minute he keeps asking, 'Where's Francine, doesn't she know I'm waiting for her?' See, Matty," my mother sprayed her hair, "here she is."

My father is lying in bed, his eyes are closed as if he's napping, but my father's skin is gray! I lean forward to examine his face, no breath issues from his open mouth. Panic and dread overwhelm my heart.

Following me into the bedroom my mother leans over and touches his face. "Matty! Matty! Wake up! Fran is here! Wake up!" she screams, "Matty, wake up!" Wailing now, falling to the carpet, "No, no, no! Oh, God, no!" I turn away and cover my face. The sound of my mother's wailing is a terrible thing to hear. Matty, wake up, wake up, Matty! I turn and Danny is there, lifting my frail mother, carrying her out of the bedroom into the living room, holding her in his arms; the only time I've seen Danny expressing tenderness or compassion toward my mother.

Gently, I touch my father's cheek. Poor Daddy, no more pain, no more suffering for you, Daddy . . . I love you, Daddy. I look up. Your spirit is here, right here, watching us.

My gaze returns to my father's face. Still, so still. No raising or lowering of the chest, no flicker of the lash, no movement of any kind. Skin is gray. Stone. Sleeping gray stone. But my father's spirit rocks me in its arms - transcendence - the spirit is comforting me, calming me, loving me. The fear is leaving me. My body stops trembling. And I walk out to the kitchen where my parents keep the phone.

So my father died before I could reach him, and although we'd sat together often and had shared thousands of conversations, I knew there was something, the kind of thing reserved for the last moment, that he'd wanted to tell me. Often, while watching my father suffer the ravages of diabetes, I'd prayed for God to grant him mercy, but now, faced with this, the absolute finality of death, I prayed to have him back.

BARELY ONE MONTH after his passing I began to feel my father's presence around me; he had a message for me. So I dialed Frank, a psychic friend, but Frank was out of town on an extended journey. As I turned away from the phone I felt my father's presence beside me. "What do you need a psychic for, Fran? You can hear me on your own!" A few days later I awoke just before dawn, and my father was there! His upper body, composed of glistening pure white light tinged with violet light hovered above the foot of my bed. And without a sound my beloved father spoke to me:

> Francine, my dearest daughter, please remember me, do not forget me ... I wish to live on in your memory. Even though I am no longer with you in human form my love is with you and all the gentleness of my spirit. Fran, dear, you have been an exemplary daughter, one whom any father would be proud to call his own. The message I care about most right now is this: keep me alive in your memories, think of me and speak of me and light a candle for my memory on the day of my birthday. Do not commemorate the date of my death as that is a date of sorrow in your memories and in mine, the date on which I left you. However, the date of my birthday is a date on which we all celebrated together, so that is the important date on which to remember me. I do not wish to make your mother cry, but you might say this to her: Mary, as we were one on Earth so we shall be one again. The time of reunification must not be hastened even one minute sooner than ordained by our Holy Source of all life. Fran, my best daughter, all is well. Your father is in a good, calm place at the present time which, in all the wisdom of the Highest One, is perfect for me. You must not be sad when you think of me for this is the way of God our Creator. Your light is one of perfect kindness and gentleness and your love heals all who open to you. So think of your father from time to time and allow me to live on in your memory. That is all I ask. I know you will think kindly of me for I always managed, however clumsily, to get the message to you that I loved you with all my heart. You know, daughter, that I always tried to say to you words of

comfort when you were faced with difficulty. And, my daughter dear, you always listened, not only with your ears, but with your heart. This is part of what makes you the blessed one you are. Farewell for now, daughter, may all who come your way recognize your goodness and treat you accordingly.

DANNY BACKED INTO the parking space reserved for us, adjacent to the side door of the Honda showroom. As usual I quickly arranged, according to importance, my paper work for the day, organized in piles, and noted once again with great relief, the absence of advertising tasks. After my father died I made a deal with an agency eager for our account, and then Neale assumed responsibility for the ads as well as all the invoices which for him was a far less laborious task than it ever was for me. Lately there was less and less for me to do here, my focus had changed, for my mother needed me. I'd moved her into a charming L shaped studio apartment in an attended building on the Upper East Side, I accompanied her to doctor's appointments, kept watch over her grocery supply as my mother tended lately to claim she was full after two or three swallows, refusing salad and dessert, and in general I worried over her. The stress had culminated for me late last Spring in the form of stomach ulcers, finally healing, and I prayed every day for my mother to find her independence.

PAPER WORK COMPLETED, I glanced at my watch – 12:00 NOON, exactly – and there was Nancy, driving right past the Honda showroom where I was, and stopping outside the Acura showroom. I took the indoor back way to the Acura showroom as was my custom for I enjoyed the greetings and friendliness of my relationships with our 200 employees, most of whom had visited at one time or another in my office. I walked toward the extra-wide glass doors to greet my friend. What a lovely day it was. What a nice life. See? We'd overcome all the challenges and it had all turned out so well, just as I had always believed-behaving ethically, conducting your affairs morally, treating people kindly-evolved naturally to a finer life. I smiled to myself, walked toward the sunlight, and breathed the last breath of a thoroughly innocent life.

Two-dozen government agents, wearing dark navy-blue hip jackets, initials DEA, FBI, IRS emblazoned in white, or was it yellow, across their backs, charged into the Acura showroom, guns drawn; their chief demanded to see the owner.

Neale was there in a minute.

"You are hereby charged with failing to file Reporting Form 8300 involving all sales in excess of $10,000 in cash as required by law. Punishment for failure to file is as follows: 1. Fines of $10,000 for each occurrence. 2. Imprisonment in a Federal Penitentiary for a period of up to five years for each failure. We're here to seize and impound any and all records pertaining to transactions over and above $10,000 between DAN MOTORS – ACURA and its customers."

"You can have anything you need," I heard my son reply, "the office is back here."

Nancy came to the door. "Are you alright?" she asked immediately, "You look like you're going to faint."

"I can't talk, Nancy, please, I can't have lunch with you after all, I'm so sorry, please forgive me, I can't ..."

"What happened? What are all these cop cars doing here?"

"I don't know what's happening, I don't know, but whatever it is, it's terrible, please Nancy, I'm sorry ..." Nancy left.

Neale came back and instinctively I reached for his hands. "They're seizing files ... I told the office to cooperate and give them everything they need ... they think we're laundering drug money ... they want to close the place down ..."

Overwhelmed by fear, suddenly I felt bereft of whatever illusion of security I'd imagined we'd achieved. I pledge allegiance to the flag of the United States of America ... and Danny was a Yankee Doodle Dandy, born on the fourth of July!

"You have your apartment, Mom, that's safe." Neale's voice was quiet and steady, but I saw fear in the fullness and softness of his lips, in his eyes I saw an intense prayer that all this trouble would somehow go away, disappear.

"And you have your house," I answered.

We offered comfort to each other. It is strange how our minds protect us; questions regarding the whole episode were momentarily held at bay, the need to reassert our sense of security was powerful and foremost. They could have our files, they could have our business, we could always work somewhere for sustenance, but our home symbolized security and safety and we couldn't bear to imagine losing it. Nevertheless, we stood there, in the center of the Acura showroom, stunned, shocked, profoundly aware that our lives were no longer under our control, profoundly wishing that our lives once again be governed by daily mundane problems which challenged us but never threatened us and which now were utterly inconsequential.

SOME MOMENTS LATER my mind began to seethe with questions. A few answers were immediately available, others required patience; each answer inspired more questions which meant renewed suspense, renewed shock. Facing each new day was unbearable ... Please, God, don't make me live through this.

The Drug Enforcement Agency had planned a 'sting' operation. The object of the sting was to uncover automobile dealerships which were not yet in compliance with new regulations regarding the transfer of cash in excess of $10,000. In an effort to thwart drug dealers from unloading large amounts of cash by purchasing high-priced items, retailers were now required to file an 8300 Form for every such transaction.

The DEA might have informed automobile dealers of the new law in a straightforward manner. They might have sent, directly to each dealer's attention, a booklet setting forth a detailed description of the law's many intricacies. In fact, many months later our lawyers provided us with a copy of the law, several pages of fine print, and it fell to me to disseminate the information throughout the company. There was so much confusion among bookkeepers and salesmen and sales managers as to the law's true meaning, I sat with each employee and reviewed individually, the highly detailed information.

The truth of the matter was that the DEA saw its opportunity to acquire cars, lots and lots of cars, by running a sting operation involving four dealerships in the area. The operation would provide media coverage of the law in a way sure to capture the attention of every automobile dealer in the nation and the DEA would emerge looking like heroes, thereby ensuring their continued employment despite the fact that in reality the so-called War on Drugs, if waged wholeheartedly and honestly, would have by now been won. In our case the agents ordered, in anticipation of seizure on the day of the sting, seven expensive Acuras, loaded with fancy radios and CD players, just the way they wanted them. Another benefit for the government was the huge amount of proceeds from the imposed fines garnered by the sting.

But when the government becomes your adversary, fear muddles all your thoughts. You're thrown into a world of lawyers who never reveal everything they know, although if they did your fear might be lessened, but this way they retain the power to charge, and in fact, you're happy to pay whatever they charge because after all the hope is that they will find a way to minimize your ultimate loss.

Tapping into your phones is a strategy employed by the government to keep you nervous and frightened. It certainly isn't a cost-effective way to gather information. However, every time you use your phone and hear those clicks, or get another strange call from a man with a nondescript voice, your thoughts rearrange themselves and wear you out.

But this is America! Sweet land of liberty! I pledge allegiance to the flag... and my hand is on my heart.

I grew angry. At my country. At my husband. He was the boss, after all. Why hadn't he read every piece of mail and paid closer attention to business? He might have caught the article in the industry newsletter about the 8300 Forms.

In consideration of Neale's polite and immediate cooperation, the agents who stormed our premises did not close us down as they did some other automobile dealers included in the sting. But nothing in our company would ever return to the way it was prior to the sting.

A group of agents, posing as customers, had negotiated a deal to purchase seven Acuras, proposing to pay cash for one of them. They made it clear to the salesman that they were unwilling to sign any forms. The salesman and the manager, hungry as always to make another sale, accepted their proposal. In addition, one of the agents transacted a small drug deal with one of the salesman. These transactions meant our case came under the Federal Sentencing Guidelines statute which left no room for negotiation.

Our attention was drawn away from business and focused instead on important conferences with lawyers who described the possible danger all three of us faced. All three of us, they said, could go to prison! While in the process of acquiring Acura, Danny had suggested it was time for me to become an officer, so I'd filled out an application, had been accepted and was Vice President of the Acura Corporation.

After several weeks passed it became evident that the government had set its sights on Danny and Neale. Some weeks later we learned they wanted only one.

Danny and I argued. Oh, God! Is this what everything comes to? Please let me die!

IN THE OFFICE and in public I kept my fear and misery hidden. But one morning I lay on the bed, unable to move, agonizing cries tearing at my throat. The decibel of my cries filled the apartment, the hallway outside, the whole of 53rd Street; my vocal chords felt ravaged and still, I cried out to my guardian angel Love. And, seeking to restore me to my essential self my angel responded! A light cloud of warmth descended and covered me. In the presence of my angel my sobbing ceased, replaced by a lovely memory, a day from my girlhood, a summer afternoon. While exploring the countryside near our summer bungalow, and pausing beside a lake, a beautiful wild bird, black iridescent feathers tinged with turquoise, alighted on my shoulder. I turned my head to look at the bird, we became instant friends, and the beautiful bird had remained on my shoulder the entire morning and afternoon. My father took a photograph. It was in an old family album. I remembered walking around the entire bungalow colony, introducing my shining bird-friend to all the people who were sitting out in their deck chairs. Then, still immersed in my angel's comforting cloud which was all the while restoring my energy, I remembered every detail of my entire life. I then arose from my bed with its tear soaked sheet, newly inspired, feeling guided and determined, to get us through this crisis.

Quickly, I learned that determination alone wasn't sufficient, so every night I drank two Bloody Marys and some mornings I poured vodka into my juice just to still the constant shaking. Danny took tranquilizers and got some for Neale. Mom, Neale had held up a box of jello in the kitchen on Flower Place, don't you ever read ingredients, this stuff is all chemicals, how can you buy it? I was hurtling, wandering lost in phantoms of thought.

LIKE THE DISMAL rainy March evening when Danny stopped to buy some fruit on Lexington Avenue, and while I waited in the car a man and a woman happened to pass by and the woman was laughing! Laughing! An anonymous woman was laughing ... and suddenly I wished I were her. While Danny and I dined on healthy meals arranged on the plate like works of art, other people right here in our city, suffered from hunger. While we drew a cashmere blanket up to our chins in a heated apartment where the temperature exactly suited our comfort, others lay on frozen sidewalks in cardboard boxes. Cognizance of these others had always diminished my comfort, so I sent checks to all kinds of charities. On our planet misery was plentiful, abundant and everywhere. Millions of people never laughed; now the surging tide of misery had risen to my doorstep, its stench had penetrated the life I'd believed secure, it had penetrated 'The Wall,' a very high and wide wall, constructed and reinforced daily by years of living on Flower Place and then in Museum Tower, the wall had kept me insulated against the dreary sunless alleyways and worn stone steps of Vyse Avenue. I knew the wall was an illusion, but apparently my security was an illusion as well. Was all life an illusion? Even laughter? Never in my life had I wanted to be someone other than myself and now I wanted to be this anonymous woman, just because she could laugh ... the lowest moment of my entire life.

SEVEN MONTHS into the case, during a visit with Neale at the house in Highland Beach, I lay awake listening to the night wind in the palm trees outside. Suddenly I felt myself falling apart again, flying in a million directions. Can't lay here another second, must go out, walk, must move to stay whole ... pull on jeans, lace up sneakers, hurry, got to get out!

The sky was a midnight dome of stars, it was so quiet I was sure the stars could hear my thoughts, and mesmerized by the starlit sky, walking slowly, I allowed myself to cry out, "Grandma! Where are you, I taught my children to revere your name, to love your memory! I don't want to live if they send my son or my husband to prison! Grandma! Save us!"

All the stars blurred into streams of lights and Grandma answered me. *Fagala, Fagala, I am with you. Think, Fagala, the most important thing you should learn in this life . . .*

Continuing to walk along the path, my gaze fixed on arcs of starlight which held the Earth in a loving embrace, I knew the answer, had always known: I must learn to live my own life!

And this you will do, Fagala. Everything will be alright, sorrow will be as a faded memory, and joy will be restored to your heart. The business trouble was a lesson for others, not your lesson, Fagala . . . and many other troubles that you take on belong to others. Learn to see this. Be free, my shayna maidel mine, walk your own path. So no more crying, Fagala, all will be good for you and your family.

Slowly, I turned and walked back toward the house, the sapphire house set like a jewel between the ocean and the intracoastal, feeling weightless and flushed with the loving kindness of Grandma's spirit, keenly aware of my own spiritual capacity to transcend the physical world and open to the endless world where the Light of God illuminates and lightens all burdens.

"Where were you?" Danny tried not to let on that he was worried.

"Danny? I just had the most incredible experience, everything will be alright, I'm sure of it now, oh, what a relief to feel calm again!"

He reached out to hold me.

"Danny, are you listening? You've got to hear what just happened while I was walking outside . . ."

At the next lawyers' conference we learned the case was almost settled, they were in the process of negotiating fines - feed the beast and he'll go away. Another six weeks and it was all wrapped up; the manager who handled the sale of Acuras to the undercover agents was sentenced to six months in a residential work-release facility, our fines were substantial and additionally, the seven seized Acuras were never returned.

The business had sustained irreparable damage and the anxiety we'd suffered left its legacy. Neale lost the last of his enthusiasm for doing business in the Bronx, and now, except for a few days each month when he came up to check on things, he focused his full attention on his dealerships in Florida where he could run a business unencumbered by the negative associations we battled constantly in the Bronx. Danny lost his life-long love for the automobile business. He no longer cared about this deal or that deal, this or that used car. "The American Dream is dead," he asserted.

Furthermore, the word 'recession' had begun to surface in private conversations and in the media; on the basis of business conditions in the Bronx Danny had been foretelling a recession for over a year. Downsizing, consolidation – we grew familiar with the painful language and requirements of survival which accompany recessionary times.

THE KEY TURNED in the lock, I went to greet Danny and Neale, and we walked into the living room together. Danny and Neale chose the white leather sofa so I took the loveseat and looked with love at the two men in my life. I cannot bring to mind how this conversation began but I know very well how my life, how the meaning of my life, how my emotional self, was changed when the conversation ended. My presence in the business they were saying was no longer needed. I should come in to wrap up loose ends.

My body froze. My thoughts blurred. I could not summon one word. Neither could I stand up to the two men in my life, who I suddenly realized, had never really come to know me. They had chosen to define me narrowly as 'Mommy,' and this view of me apparently, despite all my striving, had not evolved past a mother who knew little more than how to nurture small children. My husband did not, I was suddenly and painfully forced to acknowledge, have respect for me. And he had been, of course, the significant, defining role model for our son. Had Danny ever respected me? Had he ever loved me? Neale hugged me affectionately at the door, and then he turned around, before he left, for another hug. And yet I felt unloved.

"Danny, did you know about this yesterday? You were sitting here in silence letting Neale do all the talking."

Danny stammers and stumbles, unable to answer.

"You knew, didn't you? Didn't you? Danny! You betrayed me! You arranged this whole scene with Neale behind my back! You've been teaching my son to disrespect me! You want me to fight my own son? I won't Danny! I'll never fight with Neale! What are you doing to our family? You asked me to be your partner! It was between us! I'm your wife, Danny! You sat in silence and gave our son permission to push me out of the business! What kind of husband are you? What kind of father? Don't you know anything? All these years! I thought we were growing closer! I thought our relationship was growing stronger!"

It must have been a dream... a dream, what else could it have been?

I WAS TOTALLY and completely unable to ponder anything. I went into a state of emotional shock. I walked through my daily life smiling, explaining briefly to my friends that I decided to retire. A lifetime of protecting Danny's reputation was locked firmly into place and so I kept to myself the raggedness of my heart, the shredded pieces of my deepest 'knowings,' the angelic wisdom placed by Love into my open heart. And where was my guardian angel Love anyway? Maybe Danny and Neale were only playing their roles on Earth and maybe it was time for me to really be on my own, pursue my own desires, truly become my own woman, rather than a woman who basked in the light of her man, who supported his image to bolster her own. Isn't that what women did, when it came down to it?

And so, in my struggle to re-define myself, as Grandma's spirit had counseled, to plunge finally full time into my own life, I decided to respond to a full page ad in the Times for Columbia's School of General Studies and attend daytime college. Re-centering myself, I got busy filling out an extensive application and studying for the entrance exam scheduled for August. Why, I worried, would Columbia accept me, an almost-fifty woman with nothing but an old Commercial diploma and a string of adult education classes? I studied hard anyway, for the sample SAT tests were a challenge I enjoyed, and besides, with every hour of study I could feel the wounds of the past nine months fading.

The case had happened and now, curiously, the memory of it was growing less and less painful. The betrayal, which is how I came to view 'the late-afternoon conversation in the living room,' would be one of those forever wounds. Nevertheless, I felt myself healing.

ANNIE LIVED in a studio apartment on the Upper West Side, near the law school she attended, and as her busy schedule permitted we grabbed snatches of time together. She would call and say, 'Come meet me for coffee, Mommy, I have a free hour.' And out I would fly to be with my loving daughter.

My Son, My Guide

I LOOKED FORWARD to quiet, recuperative weekends at the beach in Cape May, at the southernmost tip of New Jersey, where the Atlantic coincides with the Delaware Bay in a great folding-in of water. Each summer for a few years we'd been reserving a suite in an historic Victorian Bed and Breakfast right on the beach. The ocean spray sailed on the breeze right up to and even through open windows and porch doors. But July 4th weekend, 1991, our suite was inadvertently rented to another couple and we stayed in a small room, west-facing, hot and dry, on the uppermost floor, somewhat removed from the rest of the house.

Since my last birthday, my forty-ninth, I was filled with a 'knowing' that something momentous was going to enter my life but I had no idea what form it would take. I knew that whatever it was would happen before my next birthday, my fiftieth. So I carried a little notebook and a pen with me wherever I went, prepared to write about it, whatever it turned out to be, as soon as it appeared.

JULY 4, 1991. At dawn he comes, a light-being, moving toward me from a great distance. I think as he advances and becomes more solid, that he is Neale for he so closely resembles Neale, but this young man is slender, as Neale was before he developed his body with weights. My etheric body rises up to greet him and he comes right up to me and embraces me with incomparable gentleness. He kisses my face tenderly, all-encompassing love flowing from him to me.

"I love you, Mother," is his greeting. And I'm overwhelmed by the purity of his vibration, feeling so loved and joyous, beyond this material universe!

"My son! Unable to breathe on your own, you went home. And now you are here, embracing me with so much love! How shall I call you, my son?"

"Mother, you may call me, 'your son, your guide.' You may call me that, only you, my Mother. To all others I shall be known as 'Adam.'"

"Oh, my son! I'm aware of your intimate knowledge, not only of my life, but my soul's entire journey. You see all my flaws, my weaknesses, and yet, you love me anyway!"

"I see your golden light, Mother! I see the beautiful light of your soul! From distant stars, dearest Mother, your light is seen and recognized. Mother, We Are All One!"

I lie down and immediately feel a powerful energy vibration, simultaneously warm and cool, it sweeps upward from my toes, blending and rising up from the base of my spine, upward to the top of my head, where I feel an opening as the powerful energy bursts through, sweeping around again, rising up my spine again. I am enveloped in ecstasy! Every cell in my body is stimulated and tingling beyond any feeling previously known. This must be kundalini rising, as mystics describe it. Again, the powerful vibrations surge upward through my spinal column and I am absolutely ecstatic! Yes! Kundalini Rising! Gratitude, my son, my guide, from my deepest heart, for this gift of ultimate cleansing and purification and spiritual opening that you have bestowed upon me!

Now whatever else I'm doing is of no account. All I'm waiting for is another chance to lie down and feel again the spiritual ecstasy of kundalini rising. Several times a day, every day. I'm walking around emerged in this transcendent sensation of joyous ecstasy, so I'm smiling all the time!

Back in the city I lie down on the daybed in the study to elevate my legs while the rays of the sun rising over the East River transform the windows into panes of liquid gold. I close my eyes and he is with me. Vibrations enter my body through the heart chakra now and quickly flow up and down my spine, spreading down into my toes, reaching into my fingertips and upward into my scalp. This is the signal that my son, my guide is with me.

His name lives within my heart, but its sound has never crossed my lips, and now, the profound beauty of his spirit revealed to me, I am too humbled to utter his name.

He understands. "I am your son, Mother," he repeats, never tiring of bringing me comfort.

"My son! You are so gentle, no one could imagine such gentleness my son. You are the essence of love, so intrinsically good, so comforting."

"We are all one, Mother. I am one with your son, my brother, Neale. I am one with your daughter, my sister Annie. We are all one!"

"And what of your father, why do you not mention him?"

"You are my mother, he is not my father."

"I don't understand."

"You are the one who has held me in your memory, in your deepest loving heart. He never has. You are my mother, he is not my father ..."

AND IN THIS WAY began a most unusual, yet completely authentic, personal journey of remembrance, a re-learning of metaphysical wisdom we are born into forgetting. A time of preparation. Learning from pure Spirit whose only purpose is to bring enlightenment to humanity. Teaching me how to view life on Earth from the perspective of the Endless World where all is Truth, not according to the restrictive laws of man but according to the eternal Laws of Creation. But, it is here on Earth that humanity must learn to incorporate into our lives these life-enhancing, soul-enriching, ways of expressing our unique gifts for the purpose of helping one another!

BUT FIRST, MY SON, my guide had some deep healing work to accomplish in order to strengthen our bond and bring our bond into a place of pure being with no lingering pain between our souls. "Mother, where is my birth certificate?"

Immediately, I go to the drawer where such things are kept, take up the envelope labeled Birth Certificates, and unfold each square of paper only to find that his is not among them. I feel the vibrations of his urgency. I recall holding the death certificate in my hand, taking it out and touching it year after year, until one day I tore it into a thousand pieces. Proof? The hollow place in a mother's heart is proof enough. I open another drawer, searching organized papers in chronological order, lift the entire neat pile and lay it down in a golden shaft of light. Neale's birth announcement, Annie's, dozens of certificates - trees planted in Israel honoring their births, cards and letters, no birth certificate for him! Go through it again! Again! Think! Then my hand rests on a lavender-bordered envelope, Annie's Bat Mitzvah invitation, and inside, a folded paper. There it is! How did it get in there? Never mind! Quickly, I transfer it to the envelope marked, Birth Certificates and tuck it in between Neale's and Annie's.

"Now you are pleased, my son, for tangible evidence of your

existence as part of our family has been restored to its rightful place. I feel your relief and your joy!"

And a moment later, unable to conceal the truth of my heart from my son, my guide, I'm asking him and re-discovering, in the higher realms there is no such thing as secrets or guilt or embarrassment or any of the ego-driven false emotions we feel as humans. Questions are responded to with love and respect. The veils between our third dimension and the higher dimensions are seen and understood completely by Spirit.

"Perhaps, my son, all of this is my imagination and you don't exist at all! Give me a sign, my son, a sign!"

And then, demonstrating to me how in the higher realms all is known, and coming from the highest wisdom a wondrous sign had already been prepared for me. My son, my guide responded, "The simultaneous phone calls from Annie and Neale, which have confounded you and made you smile happily these past two years . . . it is I who influence them, Mother. This has been my way of preparing you for our meeting. Simultaneous phone calls from your son and daughter are proof of my existence."

TWO, OFTEN THREE, times a day, my children called, and always within a few minutes of each other or on call-waiting. If Annie happened to call at eleven-thirty at night then Neale called at twelve. If Neale called in the morning at nine, the very next call was Annie. And sometimes one might call right back with an almost-forgotten message and sure enough, the other called back, too. Three days might elapse when neither Annie nor Neale called and then Neale would call, followed in a moment by Annie.

And, from that day forward the simultaneous phone calls, having served their worthy purpose, ceased.

So I know my son, my guide is with me.

LATER, as Danny and I were driving up to visit friends in Westchester, I gazed absentmindedly at the passing scenery and realized, had my son lived he'd be twenty-six now, and indeed, he appears to me as a young man of twenty-six.

"Danny? When our baby died did you mourn him? Have you ever mourned him? Do you think about him from time to time?"

"Did I mourn the baby? No, I didn't... at the time I was concerned only about you, your health, and then I guess I put it out of my mind."

"Didn't you cry even once?"

"No... why do you ask?"

I told him. But there was no response.

As soon as Danny leaves in the morning I lie down on the daybed and call on my son. When he comes to me the vibrations are more subtle, as if his vibrational level has been fine-tuned to align more harmoniously with mine. Or maybe my vibrational level has risen to align more harmoniously with his!

"Are you really my son? Can you explain what is happening?"

"My dearest Mother, I am your son, your guide! I come to you in love, according to our pact, for we have been together for all eternity!"

"Can you speak aloud, through my voice, my son, to make our communication more real for me?"

"Yes, my mother, I will speak through you if this is your desire. You and I come from a light-being realm far removed from this planet Earth. Where we come from our light is of the most glorious nature. Gentleness is the most superior attribute. For from gentleness springs all the good and all the kind and all the love which is needed. And you, my mother, are there the most gentle of all! The gentleness and grace of your human body cannot compare with the gentleness and grace of which you are capable in your light-being form."

"Tell me, my son, why have I been denied your presence in this life? You would have brought great happiness to all of us. After all, you were the link between Annie and Neale."

"Ah, dear Mother, you are so wise! You use the exact word! Yes, I am the link! You and I have predetermined that this is how it would be. I am the link! This is my role! And how much better I am able to fulfill this role in the form which now I inhabit. I am the link! We are all one! I will watch over you and you will be protected as if by a shield of the strongest matter. For we have much work to do. You will choose and whomsoever you shall choose that is whom we shall help. Together, we will work to help others, for this is our plan. I have been with you forever. I come to you now, your fiftieth year, when your children have become independent of you in their human lives, when your responsibilities in this life have been fulfilled. Do you not begin to see the wisdom of our plan, my mother? Now we have become reunited, you are aware of my presence, and in time you will appreciate all that I am imparting to you. This I promise you, my dearest Mother!"

"My son, only one week has passed and I can't imagine not having you with me. I thank you with all my heart for the joy you have brought into my life. Can you advise me, my son, with regard to my health?"

"You have already begun a new and healthier path for yourself, my mother. You have applied to Columbia, this will be for the health of your mind. You have joined the new Spa, this will be for the health of your body. And you have opened yourself to discover Your Son who is here for the health of your spirit. Mind, Body, Spirit. You are doing very well, my mother. Study for the purpose of knowledge and understanding so that we may advance our work with greater ease. Keep your body healthy in order to maintain our tie. You may choose to eat more fruit and vegetables, otherwise you eat healthily enough. You will live a long and healthy life, my mother, for you and I have much to accomplish. And I will guide you. Mind. Body. Spirit. You are well-balanced, my mother."

ANOTHER DAY. "My son, what can you say to reassure me that our conversations are not conjured up by my imagination?"

"It is with great difficulty that the human mind can accept such telepathic communication, my mother. Do not worry, all is well. The future will show."

A WEEKEND AT THE BEACH. My dear mother, people enter your life for reasons, and you must learn to understand the underlying reason for each encounter. The woman you just met who lives with the aftermath of a diseased leg, serves as an example to you of one who allowed bitterness and pain of affliction to alter her demeanor. Take notice of this and learn to appreciate the strength and power of your own spirit. For although you have suffered great pain, your face reflects serenity and you are filled with harmony and grace. You are to understand, dearest mother, how much you have overcome, the extent to which you have conquered your body with the power of your mind and spirit. And you are to go forth from this moment with greater awareness of your personal power.

I thank you, my son, for all that you share with me. In so short a time you have transformed my life and shown me a higher way of looking at things. For this I am ever grateful.

No, no, my mother, it is I who lay bare at your feet. I worship you, for in our realm you are the most gentle of all. The sacrifice of your health for the purpose of bringing the soul of your daughter Annie to life as a human being will be recalled for all eternity. It is recorded. The selflessness, the dignity, with which you endured those days and months of your young life, the peacefulness and harmony which you achieved and maintained as a result of this birth is a measure and indication of the beauty of your light-being form when you are in our realm of gentleness. All is well, my mother.

Another day. My son, I have been advised to communicate with you through the action of pen to paper.

My dearest mother, there is no need to worry. All is well and all is as you so choose. We may proceed in this manner if this is your choice. I am your son, your guide, we are all one, through all time, through all eternity. One in gentleness, one in love, one in kindness. You must learn to let go of all controlling with regard to others. This is for your well-being as well as for the well-being of those you love. You are on an accelerated path of spiritual awareness and you must rise above human weaknesses if you are to achieve our goal of enlightenment and wisdom. You must not expend precious energy worrying, for you need all your energy for the achievements which will enlighten your life as a human being and in turn enable you to enlighten the lives of others.

My son, what have you to say about religion, about the man, Jesus, believed to be the Son of God by all Christians?

My dear mother, the question of religion is many faceted and complicated, a cause for war, destruction and great sorrow upon the Earth. We are all one. Religion is no more than a path to the Oneness of our universal life force. To each human being his religion is the true religion. In truth it matters not which manner or form the individual chooses to recall his origins, but the qualities of good which are discussed in each religion are significant, providing each human being with a framework within which he may pursue his role. The choice is always a free one. The paths to holiness are innumerable, as there are human beings in high numbers. Each is provided a framework, each may choose and each choice is valid for that human being who makes it. Good will - this is the thing - intent. Kindness above all. Freedom, too. No human is to be captive, whether in mind, body or spirit. The man Jesus was a son of God as we are all of the all-knowing Oneness. It was not his intent to leave in his name war or hatred. Jesus followed his path as a human being and he died as all humans must, each in his own manner, according to plan. We Are All One. We are all possessed of holiness and for our deeds we are remembered. Who among us desires ill fate upon another in our memory? This is a sorrowful outcome.

You do well in your studies, mother, for you are capable of great understanding and compassion. Your studies will provide the language and language is your path. You understand the importance of clarity for the purpose of avoiding discord. You learn from all you encounter.

Last day of July. Seek intelligence, my dear mother, but notice where it departs from the harmonious nature of the soul. Seek balance. Seek for your friendships those who dwell within an alignment of intuition, openness of mind and gentleness toward others. Such are the characteristics you must seek. An unbalanced intelligence may impart as much injury as ignorance.

In August. We work in quiet ways, dearest Mother. We do not seek glory, nor success as soothsayers or fortune tellers. We are 'helpers.' Let us practice helping, then, and be satisfied with such a skill for helping is quite important. Remember, gentleness does not mean weak, no dear mother, gentleness means of nobility, the fairest and the kindest, the wisest and the quiet. We work in gentle ways. You shall see. All is well.

October. With regard to your question, "Why are we so intense and filled with longing?" Deep in our sub-conscious mind is a memory of the time of glory when our souls were joined in golden light, when sorrow and physical struggle were not part of our existence. The soul's awareness of a state of perfect harmony and grace, what you may describe as Utopia, creates a longing for that which is unattainable here on Earth.

DECEMBER 1, 1991. Fiftieth birthday. You are doing well, my dear mother, absorbing so many new ideas and concepts in so short a time at Columbia. It is remarkable. And learning is not only derived from books but from observation and contemplation as well. Learning continues even without the classroom. Therefore, go forth and meet your days in joy, seeking new wisdom in each day's experience. Your light is filled with an effervescence of love for humanity and with great determination to grow in wisdom. Be a source of love for all who need love. Do not withhold love from any. Give to all. You will discover that your capacity for love is vaster than the oceans, and holds great power!

ANOTHER DAY. All goodness and all love is derived from Source, our Holy of Holies. There is no good which exists independently of our Holy Source. Therefore, all love and goodness are part of our Holy Source and those who agree to do His good work are blessed throughout all eternal time and space. Such are you, my dearest mother. Therefore, the guidance and protection bestowed upon you are blessed as well, and I am in my turn, blessed through the good which you do! You see, dearest, we are all one! You are brave, for you have accepted the task with full knowledge of the obstacles, with full knowledge of the ignorance you will encounter. All will be revealed to you in time. For now, continue to listen, continue to observe and continue to learn. For these are the days of preparation.

ANOTHER MONTH. My dear mother. Have no fear. You ask for further assurance of the reality of our encounters. You ask why anyone would listen to you, citing inadequacy and other fears. I am your son, your guide, your protector. The forces which inspire all human activity are more awesome than the human mind can accept. Even those minds of great intellect are reluctant and for the most part closed to receiving information of such powerful import.

THIS, HOWEVER, in no way diminishes the validity of how the human experience is realized. You, in your light-being form are a being of enormous capacity. This, you feel, even now, sometimes, although your fears prevent you from free expression of these feelings. However, you know of what I speak. Inadequacy is no more than a human fear, superimposed upon the glorious spirit of eternity. Whenever the beauty and love of eternal life manage to penetrate the many barriers to the soul's encasement, fear prevents full acceptance. This communication of ours is even more valid than the usual communication now in vogue between human beings. Very minute numbers of spoken words or written words, or telecast words have value in the course of human time. Our communication is part of our pre-determined plan in which we were aided and guided by other loving and gentle guides for the sole purpose of bringing peace to mankind. How, you ask, are you, unknown, not of greatness in your media, not of political influence, to fulfill such a role? Ah, my dearest, it is precisely the working out of such seeming problems, the way in which all that is promised shall come to pass ... it is in the result, the outcome, that you shall know the truth. I am with you, I shall always be with you. I shall guide you and protect you for all the holy days of your blessed life. Go in peace, go in joy.

ANOTHER DAY. My dearest mother. Too many human beings view the concept of non-human entities with a too-narrow mind. They ought to open their minds as a camera lens widens, allowing more of the scene to be captured on film. If the aperture remains narrow does that mean the landscape outside the perimeters of the photograph does not exist? You see, my dearest, your mind is open, you understand. There are others whose minds are open, and here we encounter degrees. There are degrees in everything. Thousands may compose music, however, how many Mozarts have there been? Continue to learn, remember to be wise.

Another month. My dear mother, You are on a path of righteousness, a path of kindness, a path of Oneness with all. Do not permit yourself to stray from your path, not even when it seems to be otherwise. I am your son, your guide, and I shall lead you to all fulfillment. Therefore, dearest, stay on the path of kindness which is your sign and your light for all eternity. Stray not, even for a single moment and all the good shall be revealed in your behalf. I am your son, your guide who has come to you in love according to our pact and I am with you always.

Another day. All pain of the body shall be removed, all shall be healed, all bodily ailments shall be healed and pain will cease.

My presence shall be reflected in your eyes, your eyes shall reveal my light.

Remind people as you walk along the way, as you gather in your homes:

> Do kindness unto your neighbor
> And enjoin love one to another.

Part Two

The Structure of All That Is

MARCH 2012.

Imagine a long, long sheet of paper, rectangular in shape, so long you cannot hope to see its end. Now imagine vertical lines printed on this very long paper. The lines are very close together but do not touch. These lines cover the entire length of paper all the way into infinity. Now see this paper rectangle upheld to form a spiral. This image represents our world. We will bring refinement to this image and understanding to this concept.

Each line on this paper spiral model represents a moment, a single moment in time, which progresses to the next line/moment in time. We are, each of us, always in a moment. For as long as we are living here, in third dimension on Earth, life leads us into each succeeding moment yet the moment we have just left is still in existence. It always will exist. Just as the moment we move into exists, waiting for us, existing forever. We are all progressing from moment to moment and every moment exists forever, whether we are in it or not.

Now understand that the paper model described above is, in reality, pure living crystal. Each line/moment is embedded in the magnificence of soaring, spiraling crystal walls alive with harmonious vibrations of light and sound, sending forth a symphony of unsurpassed musical majesty and beauty. The symphonic vibrations thus created are intended to resonate within the central point of every atom and molecule for the purpose of maintaining a brilliant harmony among all of life; joyful well-being.

Vibrations of purest light radiate out from deep within the One Infinite Living Crystal Spiral; the heartbeat of the vast immeasurable spiral which encompasses All That Is. We may refer to this cosmic heartbeat as the Heart of God. In cosmic language God is love. This great pulse, this heartbeat, is the source of all life. This is the heartbeat that breathes light eternally into the great Oneness. It is that which maintains and assures the continuity of life with all its ebbs and flows throughout the entire living, breathing spiral, renewing and regenerating itself by means of its own all-powerful pulse pushing forth emanations of purest light to emerge into the All That Is, enhancing the overall inestimable power of love in the cosmos.

Pure light vibrations radiating out from the Heart of God surge forth and flow through the walls of Living Crystal, thus calling forth into the Structure of All That Is, vibrations of sound. This Divine light is encoded with infinite love and infinite intelligence. The interaction of Divine light with Divine harmonics produces Divine life. This grand cosmic interplay between vibrations of light and vibrations of sound creates atomic particles, celestial seeds of life.

Differing from the hard formations of crystal we on Earth are familiar with, the living crystal walls have a plasma-like fluid quality and an elegant transparency. The power and strength of the fluid crystal walls have never, since the beginning of creation, been harmed or weakened in any way. What occupies the channels between these fluid crystal plasma-like walls, which appear to human beings as vast empty space? Billions of spirals. Between each liquid crystal wall of the One Infinite Living Crystal Spiral there exist billions of other spirals.

Each channel represents what we would refer to as a dimension. There are twelve major dimensions within the One Infinite Living Crystal Spiral. In addition, there exists a vast unknown number of minor dimensions within the twelve major dimensions. Each exists to fulfill its own purpose and each supports its own life forms which are birthed by the unique harmonics of its own galaxy. Each and every particle of creation serves its own unique purpose and each is equally important to the overall well-being of the One Infinite Living Crystal Spiral. All the dimensions, the twelve major dimensions as well as the vast unknown number of minor dimensions, contribute to the balance and harmony of the One Infinite Living Crystal Spiral.

The Living Crystal walls are conductors of all light and sound vibrations as well as amplifiers of all light and sound vibrations. Sound vibrations travel in massive waves throughout the entire Structure of All That Is. As waves of light and sound vibrations surge through billions of Living Crystal Spirals, touching every particle of living crystal, innumerable light and sound patterns arise. A symphonic majesty of music comes into being and flows throughout All That Is, giving rise through endless vibratory patterns, to infinite combinations of light and sound, in this way creating life in every form imaginable. Creation abounds in the All That Is.

THE CENTRAL POINT of the physical human body, that which takes form before all else, is the human heart, repository for our DNA, that which holds the key to physical form. The design of our DNA, a spiral, adds clarity to the understanding that we have been designed to resonate with the majestic symphony of light and sound emanating from the central point of the One Infinite Living Crystal Spiral. When people live in true freedom, uninterrupted from the natural flow of life, in harmony with the Heart of God, people prosper in a state of well-being for this arrangement evokes an environment that encourages growth and evolvement within a vibration of peace.

The collective tones of all humanity blend and also surge forth in powerful waves of sound. The sound waves created by humanity affects the symphony of unsurpassed majesty and beauty sent forth by the central pulse of the One Infinite Living Crystal Spiral which amplifies humanity's sound as effectively as it amplifies the pure light and sound waves emanating from the central point of the spiral. If humanity's vibration of sound is discordant the cosmic symphony of Oneness becomes impacted negatively. Negative vibrations create discord, disharmonious sound patterns which disrupt the flow of love causing instead, fear and confusion to flow. All life forms feel the discordant sound vibrations which interfere with instinctual behavior patterns and fall gradually out of harmony with the cosmic symphony of love. Striving for survival within the flow of nature's harmony is disrupted, causing havoc in the natural world. And indeed, this is true for all living species on Earth.

For humankind in particular the advent of negative interference, whether by means of human dominance over others or by means of electronic intervention, has caused the frequency of light and sound which produces life-sustaining harmonics to be interrupted, thereby producing ominous imbalances within Earth's spiral. Such imbalances inevitably lead to disharmony and weakened connection to the central point of the One Infinite Living Crystal Spiral. From this weakened connection flows all fear, all conflict, all illness, all pain and sorrow.

Long sequences of time encrusted with dark destructive energy forms have created an environment of disease for mankind. The entire spiral feels this vibration of disharmony, and disharmony within a spiral threatens the well-being of the entire spiral. Therefore, Infinite Intelligence has sent forth its urgent directive:

Humanity, Hear the Call! The Time is Now! Return to Harmony with Divine Love!

WITH DIVINE URGENCY humanity is being called on to remember: more than any other vibration coming to us from other diverse lesser sources, however tempting or alluring, it is the frequency of love and truth radiating out from the deep inner pulse of the One Infinite Living Crystal Spiral, the Heart of God, that will bring to us the peace and love we seek and long for. It is this true eternal pulse that most naturally resonates within our hearts and minds for our souls sprang forth from this true eternal pulse. And yet, mankind behaves in opposition to the heartbeat and vibration of the Heart of God and chooses instead, the pain and sorrow that derives from association with destructive vibrations.

Although humanity has passed through centuries of war and destruction, and light and love in the form of peace on Earth has passed into ancient myth, Divine harmony embedded within each moment remains true and constant. Although generations have been taught that war and destruction are human destiny, and they pass through the moments of their lives distracted by chaos, thereby permitting chaos to expand and gain dominion over the moments of time, Divine love clothed in grace awaits the transformation of humankind. How shall we, as individual human beings taught to believe in the doctrine of individual powerlessness, respond to this directive?

We may be assisted in this task by remembering that our true authentic self is in truth an unlimited spiritual being of beautiful light and that we assume our physical body with its limited capacities for the purpose of learning that which is incomprehensible to a light being whose awareness includes knowledge of the One Infinite Living Crystal Spiral. Once we begin the process of remembering who we truly are the burdensome cloak of powerlessness begins to fall from our shoulders.

Gradually at first, our minds soon quicken to the memory of our light being form. Our minds are challenged to seek and discover ultimate truth. All that went before is questioned and largely discarded, until our physical self enters the alchemical fulfillment of dark into light, and fear into love. Our energy, uplifted by the joy of remembering, moves by means of resonance, into the eternal flow of life-sustaining vibrations of love emanating from the central point of the One Infinite Living Crystal Spiral. The all-powerful creative frequency of light and sound welcomes us, embraces us, and our individual loving soul power is enhanced beyond human imagination.

Within the flow of the Essence of Divine Love, our physical vibration enhanced, our capacity for love is also enhanced and with every thought, emotion and action transformed by the frequency of Divine Love, we become enabled to uplift the energies of every moment we pass through. Uplifting of the frequencies of thousands of people gathers momentum. The Law of Love gathers momentum. A new wave of higher awareness, a more evolved frequency, sweeps over encrusted deposits of destructive energy in the moments of time. The all-powerful emanations flowing from the Heart of God, now focused through the emerging power of millions of human beings experiencing higher frequency, explodes with unbounded joy as the healing of time, that which once seemed impossible to the limited physical brain, is accomplished by minds awakening to the Law of Love!

The mind of mankind, when open and bound to an evolved soul, is capable of accessing various moments on living crystal spirals which lie beyond the reach of five-sense third dimension reality. The mind of mankind is capable of traveling beyond known reality to arrive at any moment on a spiral. The mind, however, is limited by limiting thought.

It is now essential that we understand, mankind's brain is terrestrial. It is of the Earth, of third dimension. It is structured in physical form which gives it limitations and exists within third dimensional time. Mind of mankind has no limitations of form or structure. It is not of Earth. It is of the great Oneness, unity consciousness. It is through the discipline of the mind, the open evolved mind bound to the evolved soul, that humanity has capabilities which soar beyond time as it is known on Earth. The closed mind remains bound to the physical brain and its reach is limited to the brain's physical capacity.

All is accessible through the mind of mankind. The mind of mankind exists outside of time. It is through the timelessness of mind, which is bound to soul, that mankind seeks the wisdom of the stars, stars being symbolic of that which lies beyond our reach, unendingly stirs our imagination, inspires us to seek beyond that which is already known. It is through the timelessness of mind which is bound to soul, that mankind longs for the peace and love that is our heritage yet seems to lie beyond the stars. Yet the vibrations of peace and love radiating toward us are more powerful than the accumulation of millions of impressions of negative human actions imbedded in the moments of time, patiently awaiting transformation into loving peace.

As conceived and designed by Intelligent Infinity, We Are All One. All that ever was, or is, or will be, is connected. This idea is expressed with clarity by pure Logic. All that is, throughout all the vast cosmos, is contained within the One Infinite Living Crystal Spiral, the vastness of which cannot be conceived by the human brain. All That Is owes its primal beginnings to the Heart of God which in one sacred burst of all-knowing infinite intelligence birthed the One Infinite Living Crystal Spiral with its unsurpassed elegant design for ongoing renewal and regeneration.

WE ARE NOT the creators of time. "Infinite Intelligence," not humanity in its present limited form, created time with an intention of loving unfoldment. Due to profound forgetfulness of the Law of Love which is the Law of Harmony, each moment of time has been and continues to be, altered negatively. The pure and perfect moments of time intended to unfold with loving kindness have been altered by certain portions of the world's people who have lost awareness of the Essence of Divine Love which glows like a flame within each human being. Those portions of the world's people who still remember identify this flame as our soul.

We pass through the moments of time which have been created for us, known to us as linear time and exists only in third dimension. Higher dimensional life exists outside of time as we know it. We are on a journey. With this awareness we can understand that here on Earth we are actually travelers through time! And every human being has an opportunity to experience everything, absolutely everything that can ever be experienced. The thoughts, emotions and actions we leave on each line/moment as we pass through them depends upon our individual consciousness, our own unique soul consciousness, and the way in which our unique soul consciousness responds to the millions of thoughts, emotions and actions impressed into each moment.

Understand that each line/moment contains the accumulated imprints of the thoughts, emotions and actions of millions of people who have, in the course of their lives, progressed through each moment. As we approach each moment we may or may not resonate with particular impressions imbedded within that moment. As we advance through each succeeding moment we may expand or modify our thoughts according to the imbedded energetic influences we encounter in that moment.

Generations of people progress together through time, each generation being offered the opportunity to remember their souls, their divine connection to All That Is, and devote their time in this world to accomplishing the uplifting of the energies encountered in each moment. The generation immediately following ours, for example, passing through the same moments we have passed through, is called upon by the Law of Love, just as our generation and every generation previous to ours has been called upon, to respond with enlightened hearts and minds to the thoughts, emotions and actions embedded in eternal time. The generation immediately following ours may choose to answer the call to expand on the imprints of goodness and loving kindness imbedded in the moments of time or they may choose to build instead on the energies of fear, war and destruction in the moments of time. In this way humanity creates, from moment to moment, with its gift of free will, the world it chooses to live in.

How MANY cycles of time must humankind experience before it chooses to turn its back on a world dominated by destruction and suffering and create in its place a world shaped by a new paradigm built on the Divine qualities of love and integrity?

For the purpose of understanding the concept of a far more expansive reality than life as we know it in linear time third dimension reality the human brain with its limitations of physical form impel us to move into our mind which is capable of journeying beyond third dimensional understanding. In the greater reality, which may also be referred to as the true reality, beyond the limitations of linear time as known on Earth, everything is happening simultaneously. We human beings, as we have noted, are composed of light and sound vibrations. In third dimension we are vibrating at our lowest point of light and sound. In third dimension our light, for the majority of humanity, is no brighter than a spark and our sound is expressed, in spiritual terms, as a single tone. The heaviness of our physical body weighs upon us, limiting freedom of movement. Simultaneous to this life in third dimension we are also experiencing other lives in other dimensions where we are not constrained by the limitations of third dimension, the lowest dimension capable of supporting sentient life.

In other lives in higher dimensions our light shines forth freely unencumbered by dense physicality. Our single tone of third dimension expresses itself as melodious song. We resonate without complications with other beings of light and song whose frequency matches our own and this brings unbounded joy to our soul. In each distinct life we progress upward within the spiral, moment by moment. In higher, finer dimensions we move with ease for purposes of service and to increase experiential knowing, into lower dimensions. However, in accordance with unwavering universal law our journey upward is limited by our own unique frequency of light and sound. Here in third dimension as we spiral upward, by slow rudimentary steps through a process thousands of years in duration, we learn and relearn, we experience spiritual growth while within a human body, a most daunting, though certainly not impossible, task. The culmination of humanity's journey upward is occurring now. To assist humanity at this momentous time this course in higher understanding is being offered.

ALL PEOPLE now living on Earth are being called upon to remember: Unending emanations of purest love are sent forth with every pulse, every heartbeat, from deep within the Heart of God, reaching out to every molecule and atom that has emerged and begun its own journey. These emanations are sent forth as light. From the action of light passing through crystal, arises sound. We are composed of light and sound. It is the same harmonious vibrations which support and nurture billions of spirals held within the One, which maintains the spiral within which Earth is held. And as it is for the billions of spirals held within the One, Earth's spiral is itself held within its designated position relative to all other spirals through a system of magnetic resonance.

All people now living on Earth are being called upon to remember: Love may be accessed at any moment through the awareness of an open mind. Immersing the mind in loving thoughts joined by the sincerest emotion of a loving heart is all that is necessary to attract our portion of love from the great ineffable Heart of God whose love flows in an eternal stream throughout the entire spiral system. Indeed, it is the enduring power of everlasting love that provides and promotes balance among all life within each spiral, from the smallest to the most vast all-encompassing spiral.

Every planetary body, every cosmic seed, every star and every moon, every worm hole and every galaxy, is held within its own spiral. Minor spirals are held within major spirals. And every spiral is structured as an exact replica of the One Infinite Living Crystal Spiral. Fractals. Every spiral holds within its center, a pulse, or heartbeat. Every spiral is composed of Infinite Living Crystal walls. Every spiral sends forth from its heart center vibrations of light which birth vibrations of sound. Every spiral sends forth its own harmonious, melodious symphony whose sound vibrations contribute to the over-all well-being of the One Infinite Living Crystal Spiral. Without these melodious vibrations of light and sound which radiate the purest creative power of love and light from each and every spiral the entire structure of crystal spirals would become unstable and disintegration would follow.

Now we may begin to understand interconnectedness on a cosmic level. We begin to understand Unity Consciousness of the One. The Structure of All That Is may now be understood as elegance, dignity, purity and goodness kept in balance by the flow of light and sound emanating from the source of all, the Heart of God, the eternal heartbeat of Love Everlasting. The Heart of God never rests, never pauses. Its pulse is eternal, its love is eternal, its creative force is eternal, its infinite intelligence is eternal, its life span is eternal.

Purification

JANUARY 1, 1996 – Soul Travel Experience.

I am in a foreign land preparing for a journey, among a group of people whose identities are unknown to me. We know that in the past many others have journeyed this way and many will come after us. Thousands of people, too numerous to count, are walking steadily single file.

A circular gazebo, constructed of pure white light, its roof supported by arches of white light, appears on a gentle slope to our right. In the center of the gazebo stand two translucent beings suffused with white light who telepathically transmit directives; all-knowing, exalted beings who record all events. To reach the gazebo, they have told us, we must pass fully clothed through a shallow murky pond.

Concerned about ruining my fine garment of pure white linen, I lift the long flowing skirt above my ankles so as not to sweep the dusty path. My feet are dressed in white feminine slippers. I proceed only because I must, having observed those who precede me emerge from the murky pond mud-splattered and disheveled. I reach the waters of the pond and step into the pond. A moment later I emerge from the unwholesome waters, and see that my gown is miraculously clean. My slippers are a bit damp, otherwise undamaged, and the hem of my gown, as I observe it, is clean and soft, strewn with sparkling lights.

In a steady procession we ascend the few steps toward the holy beings who stand behind a low podium formed wholly of light in the center of the gazebo and to whom we must relinquish all that we carry. I suddenly notice that I am holding in my hands two bottles of water prominently labeled, "PURIFIED." The water is accepted into the outstretched hands of the holiest being and my trust in the safekeeping of these two vessels is absolute. The second glowing being, the helper, who stands beside the holiest being, inscribes carefully and studiously alongside my name in the largest book I have ever seen, "Two vessels of water - Purified." Much attention is given to the accuracy of record-keeping.

If my spirit guides are intending a purification process for me I will need to be my own careful record-keeper so the very next day I buy a new journal. In this way the new year, 1996, begins.

FEBRUARY 21. Driving along an upstate parkway, the winter sun glaring on the windshield, a sudden flash of white light blocks the passing scenery. I see the name, YEHUDA, spread across the windshield. The letters appear in black typeface resembling Hebrew letters.

Instantaneously, the memory arises of the day we were driving home from Cornell University after Annie's graduation. Suddenly against the windshield appeared my grandma's face. "Fagala," my grandma's spirit urgently imparted, "you must get off the road, now!" I suggest to my family that we pull into the rest stop coming up on the left. After some light refreshment, resuming our trip home, the sharply curved route led us into a hugely tangled traffic snarl caused by a horrific accident involving many vehicles. If we hadn't gotten off the road we would've been involved in that accident. My grandma's protective presence, proven.

The name YEHUDA as I saw it spread across the windshield is guiding me to discover profound meaning in my life. At home, in the Encyclopedia Judaica, I research the name Yehuda, and learn that in the year 757 there lived a blind scholar, head of the academy of Sura. His life's goal was to bring worldwide unity to the Jewish people through the authority of the Babylonian Talmud. Yehuda was revered for his piety, purity and humility.

Just as I lay aside the large heavy book and momentarily close my eyes to dwell a moment on the struggles of Yehuda's life, another name in black Hebraic style letters, AHIKAR, flashes in my mind. Surprisingly, this unfamiliar name is also listed in the Encyclopedia Judaica. Ahikar was a scholar as well, a wise man who lived in 5th century Egypt, author of the Book of Ahikar, in which he recorded the accrued wisdom of his life. Ahikar the Wise is mentioned in the Book of Tobit as one of the exiles of the Ten Tribes of Israel. Ahikar, having no children of his own, adopted his nephew. With devotion he taught his wisdom to his nephew but his nephew betrayed him and planned to murder Ahikar. Ahikar, calm and loving, reminded his nephew that he, Ahikar, had been foremost in helping him when he'd been a vulnerable child. The wise persuasion of Ahikar turned the nephew away from murder, thus averting tragedy for both.

The next morning, a moment before awakening, my son my guide who I was accustomed to calling on for clarity before drifting off to sleep, appeared in my inner mind. You are them, he said, and they are in you. You lived as Yehuda and you lived as Ahikar.

MARCH 18. I am very sick, suffering a lot of abdominal pain, able to eat only liquids, mostly soup and ice-cream. This is the eve of surgery. I close my eyes, feel the presence, and a vision arises within my inner mind. Native Americans gather as I lay on a woven blanket. I recognize my chief from long ago, leaning over me, speaking about protection. Strong young men of our tribe have formed a circle around me, dancing to the rhythm of the drums, a dance of healing, a circle of protection. The women of our tribe form an outer circle, arms entwined, close together, humming a repetitive melody that harmonizes with the drumming. Beyond the women an assembly of young children and elders, gathered in silent prayer. Now, my father's face appears, and now Grandma's face. And my children are here with me. Overwhelmed and with silent tears I thank everyone for being with me, praying for my good health and providing protection.

During surgery the doctor discovered my inflamed fallopian tube, two inches in diameter and six inches long. This monster was jammed into my intestines, creating an intestinal blockage. Painstakingly, my doctor peeled the fallopian tube from the intestinal wall and re-positioned my intestines. An ovary, which I had mistakenly believed removed along with my other ovary at the time of my hysterectomy, the doctor found buried in a large mass which overgrew part of the tube.

Surgery successfully completed, I return home to recuperate. Offering heartfelt gratitude to all my loved ones every day, is an important part of my healing.

APRIL 1. Dream. Mom is in my apartment in the clear glass stall shower. Too weak to wash herself or even stand on her own she falls to the shower floor. I rush to lift her. "Bring me a Francine robe," my mother can barely speak; I hear her thoughts telepathically and awaken filled with dread. For it was only a few weeks ago that Grandma had appeared in the night at the foot of my bed. "Fagala, you must take care of your Mama." "Grandma," I'd replied, "Don't you know I always take care of Mom?" "This is different," Grandma had answered, "You must take care of your Mama." "I will, Grandma, I promise."

APRIL 8. Mom is in Montefiore Hospital. She's been coping with an incessant cough. The pulmonary specialist has removed a quart of fluid from her lungs.

I call Aunt Margie at my cousin Mitch's house. The family is gathering at my cousin's house in Virginia in anticipation of a family reunion this upcoming weekend. I explain to my beloved aunt, with whom I've shared a special bond since my birth, that my mother is sick and I cannot leave my mother home alone to attend the family gathering.

I call my brother. . He informs me that our mother may have lung cancer, but I don't believe him. Not my beautiful mother, who still adheres to the healthy diet she began with my father's diagnosis of diabetes. Not my mother, who walks for miles to her daily destinations in the city and is still slim and fit. Not my mother, who at 79 years of age maintains lifelong habits of cleanliness as well as careful attention to a neat, attractive appearance. No! My brother is being mean!

Neale, arrives for his monthly visit. He calls me every day from Miami where he now makes his home. When we embrace, my world is complete. My son takes a moment to look into my eyes as he always does as if searching for reassurance that his Mom is the same as always, the Mom he knows, unchanged from childhood memories; and he says, "I love you, Mommy, you're still beautiful, Mom." Satisfied, he turns his attention to ongoing business dialogue with Danny.

APRIL 10. Annie calls from her office at the prestigious law firm where she labors long hours in her chosen field of employment law. "How is Grandma?" Annie is worried.

"I've been resting, sweetheart, I'll find out and get right back to you."

Very much in the midst of a six-week recuperation period, I rouse myself and call Dr. Conti. I learn that Mom has widespread cancer. Lungs, liver, pancreas. His diction is precise but I'm unable to grasp the meaning of his words. Once again the dialogue of disbelief fills my head: my mother is youthful and energetic, my mother doesn't drink or smoke; she's intelligent, still reading books of world interest, walking ten blocks to her favorite trimming store just to buy a button.

I dial Mom's room at the hospital and my brother picks up her phone. At this very moment, he tells me, he himself is giving Mom her diagnosis.

I toss back the blanket and find myself confusedly rushing from room to room, now in the living room in my nightgown, turning in circles, seeing nothing.

I call Danny at the lawyer's office. He's involved in a big lawsuit, we're being threatened with loss of one of our franchises and Danny's adrenaline is pumping. Their meeting just ended. He and Neale are returning home.

Annie calls. Oh, I forgot in my confusion to call her back. "Can you come over, sweetheart? Daddy and Neale are on their way."

"Is it Grandma? I'll be there, Mom."

I call Aunt Margie and Aunt Natalie, to give them the tragic news.

Annie arrives. In another moment, Neale and Danny are here. How odd: all of us together in the living room at noontime on a Wednesday. I call my mother.

"Francine, darling, my precious girl. They say I have cancer and there's nothing to be done."

I grab a lavender Bergdorf Goodman shopping bag, quickly fold the gown and robe, washed and pressed, bought scarcely a month earlier for my own hospitalization. Knowing Mom's desire to remain well-groomed I pull a few things from my shelves and drawers and throw in a book I'm reading, a light anthology of women authors.

We're in the car together, a family, driving up to Montefiore, Annie holding my hand all the way. After our greetings Mom's first words, "I have cancer."

We crowd around her, hug and kiss her and she describes in detail, events of the past 24 hours. Danny and Neale depart for the dealerships. Annie and I help Mom into the gown and robe, Mom protesting that I shouldn't have brought such a beautiful gown, she doesn't need it. But when she leans back against the pillows, smoothing the soft fabric of the robe with her worn hands my mother whispers, "A Francine robe." She gazes up from her hospital pillow, her sad weary eyes connecting with my sad eyes, "Thank you, Dolly, very nice."

Annie and I climb onto Mom's hospital bed. "When I retired from Bloomingdale's your Mommy promised me she'd see to it that I'd always have pretty clothes, and I want you to know, Annie," Mom pauses and reaches for a tissue, wiping her eyes, "your Mommy has kept her promise. I sometimes think she buys things she doesn't need just to give them to me." Now Mom's tears are a waterfall. "I always liked to wear nice things, you know, especially when it comes from your Mommy." Annie is trying not to cry. She's holding her Grandma's hand and she reaches for my hand. My other hand Mom is grasping tightly. The mingled sound of our quiet sobbing overflows the hospital bed.

At home all I feel is misery. Annie tells me, "I know how you feel, Mom, because that's how I felt when you were in the hospital. I just sat at my desk and stared out the window, not knowing what to do."

And in the middle of all this the business troubles grind on. Danny's nerves are somewhat calmed by my assurance that I'll help him, but the subject makes me sick.

I learn from my cousin Mitch that my brother has instructed Mom's doctors, his colleagues, to provide health bulletins to no one but him. This explains why I haven't been able to gain access to Mom's internist, or the pulmonary specialist or any of the doctors on her case.

APRIL 11. I cab it up to Montefiore and against the nurse's protest that more tests are needed, I get my mother signed out and take her home. The doctors remain aloof but I can see for myself my mother's condition. In a voice devoid of emotion my brother describes in excruciating detail the cancer in Mom's left lung, her liver and spleen.

APRIL 16. My four-week check up with Dr. Orlando. The doctor is angry because I've suffered a setback in my healing process and he orders me to rest. He doesn't want to hear about family responsibilities. Rest, rest, rest, he commands.

Danny needs me in the deposition room, it's only a few hours so I go, but all I can think of is my mother.

The very day that I take Mom home from Montefiore Hospital Mike and Gloria drive to the family reunion in Virginia, passing right by the city. Leaning back on pillows arranged on her sofa, still dressed in the neat gray slacks and white blouse she wore home from the hospital, Mom wonders hopefully if they will stop by, but as the sun sets and night comes on, Mom's hope fades.

"They've left for the weekend," she cries, "to see my sisters. I'm dying and they didn't even stop to see me! My son has abandoned me!"

My mother cries deep heart rending sobs and searing pain stabs my own heart. Mom waits for a call from my brother. Late on the night of his return from Virginia he calls to say he's home, he can only talk for a minute because tomorrow he has to be at the hospital early.

These days all illusions are crumbling, a most unpleasant process. Yet, I embrace it. The light of truth helps us gather wisdom. But for now, being with Mom consumes all my energy.

MAY 8. Mom confides, "When your grandma lay dying I remember feeling that my world had turned upside down." The mail brings my favorite astrologist Maya del Mar's monthly Daykeeper Journal. The Journal falls open and I read on the open page for Sagittarius, "Your world has turned upside down."

Falling asleep an image of Grandma suddenly appears beside my bed, soft waves of thick silver hair framing her face, wearing her precious gold locket; silver and gold light shining all around her. She is cradling in her arms a little girl and Grandma's smiling at me.

MAY 9. Mom is sleeping on her sofa, her daytime bed. Beethoven's Ninth is playing. My eyes are closed and the room is peaceful, sunlight peeking in from behind the shades. Grandma's image comes before me, smiling, transmitting love, and she speaks so softly, "Fagala . . ." Then she moves spirit-like and is standing behind Mom, leaning over her protectively. Grandma's spirit is radiating pure white light which spreads like the wings of an angel to surround Mom. As I'm watching I notice suddenly Dad's image kneeling on one knee beside Mom. Deep in afternoon slumber Mom becomes aware of his presence and with sudden silent tears flowing Mom is whispering, "Matty . . . Matty . . . oh my Matty."

MAY 10. Mom is suffering this morning, loss of breath from the effort of holding onto her independence by dressing herself. I lead her to the sofa, sit on the edge and hold her weak hands. Mom reaches up, and with surprising strength pulls me down to her, kisses my face and cries, "Francine! my Francine! I'm so frightened! I'm not getting any better! You've always been so good to me! Always understood me! Oh, my darling Francine! I'm never going to see you again!"

The air grows heavy with my mother's anguish. Her hair has turned to pure silver. Her eyes are swollen, overflowing with pain.

Friends ask, How do you spend so many hours with your mother? I meditate, pray for strength, hold her hands, listen to her sorrowful stories, comfort her, care for her. I must be strong for the responsibility has fallen to me ... no, I have chosen it. It is my choice, my decision, to be the one, a decision I'll never regret.

I pray for Mom a lot and practice my spiritual healing. Currents of energy pass through my body. The currents feel like smoothly flowing streams of golden light vibrations. I lose track of time. I lose awareness of physicality as if I'm in another dimension. When I open my eyes Mom is sleeping peacefully. Hours pass.

Mike and Gloria arrive. I stroke Mom's cheek and call her name several times to waken her for their visit.

"I heard sounds and wanted to open my eyes," she says, "but couldn't, until now. I feel so calm and restful. Thank you, Dolly, I just love that thing you do."

"Your sister is a sorceress," Gloria remarks.

"All I do is pray for peace."

My brother nods, silent, thoughtful.

MAY 14. Mike calls. "Have you done 'that thing' again? I think you should try it more often." My brother sounded friendly.

I ask Mom's permission to do spiritual healing for her. "Yes," she answers, "I like the way it feels, it's very nice."

Mom goes right into a peaceful sleep. I watch her sleep, her breath coming slowly and evenly. After about forty minutes or so Mom begins to speak trancelike: "I'm in a very peaceful place ... my sweet, dear Annie ... Francine ... Francine ..."

When she awakens I ask her, "What were you experiencing, Mom?"

"I saw a golden glow," she answers, "right where the blinds are."

We look across the room at the blinds which are drawn closed the way Mom likes them now although all her life she loved the sunlight pouring in, and in the cloudy afternoon the blinds appear gray. I feel peaceful and Mom's voice is unusually calm. When I serve her dinner she declares she is hungry and she eats with appetite sitting upright.

MAY 19. No longer able to make her body respond to her will my mother now requires assistance for everything. "Fran! I can't get out of bed! Fran! Fran!" she cries. I help her. To propel herself forward one step at a time is now immensely difficult for Mom. She leans on both my arms, pauses to catch her breath. Also, I am feeding her now. A few spoonsful of Jello, tiny slivers of papaya, sips of water or prune juice. I bathe her while she lies in her bed and with utmost gentleness massage her limp hands and cold feet with Shalimar lotion. She is barely speaking. My mother's eyes stare past me, observing a world I cannot see. Suddenly, she returns to present time and her eyes tell me she is enjoying the massage, the scent of Shalimar.

"Keep my memory alive, Fran," Mom beseeches me.

When I speak to my mother of how she saved her Mama's life, when her Papa died, she seems comforted that I remember her stories, sharing the memories, however sad. "And you were only twelve, Mom. Grandma was so despondent and you convinced her to go on for you and your sisters. You were just a child but you kept your family together, running the household, taking care of Grandma, Margie and Natalie. Without you, who knows what would've happened!"

Lifeless tears trickle from Mom's eyes.

"And you saved Dad's life, too. You gave him a life, you gave him love, a loving family to belong. Who knows what direction his life would've taken when he got out of Hawthorne if he hadn't had the amazing good fortune to meet you."

As if in trance Mom whispers Dad's name. "Matty, I love you, I love you, Matty."

June 5. Past midnight. Dad's spirit appears in my room, hovering above my bed. "Dearest daughter, yes I am your dear old Dad. I am in your mother's room all the time and she feels my presence but she is confused. When she calls out my name this is the signal that she sees me. Please continue to be the good daughter that you are, Fran, for all you do adds to the love in our universe and there is no task more holy than manifesting love, especially under trying circumstances. I am here, I rejoice, for it will not be long now when your mother and I are reunited and all this pain will be healed and she will find comfort and soothing atmosphere all around her. And then, of course, all shall be well."

June 6. Mom is sleeping for most of the afternoon. I gaze at shadows, at sunlight streaking across the walls, sadly thinking that Mom and I will never again stroll together window shopping, talking, her arm linked in mine, stopping at one of our favorite little places for lunch or coffee.

I close my eyes and see Dad seated right here in Mom's studio apartment. He repeats some of last night's message and goes on to say, "You mustn't mourn afterward, Fran, for it is time; your vigil here shall suffice. Your mother and I shall be with you for all the blessings which are yet to come. Do not concern yourself with the ways of your brother. Just be yourself, kind as always. If I have one regret, Fran, it is that I should have hugged you more often when you were a small child. But, dear daughter, we are what we are and not always so wise."

JUNE 8. Looking over records of last year's ordeal with a malignant melanoma on my left eyebrow, I am seized by an urge to release traumatic memories, so I rip all my research notes into tiny pieces; self-determination, anti-oxidants, vitamins, the importance of breakfast, the importance of self-nurturance as well as self-esteem. All the teachings to heal cancer and stay healed imbedded in my mind.

Then, the hour growing late, I come upon a description I'd written of a day during my recuperation. Lying in bed, awakening from a peaceful afternoon nap, I'd switched on the TV just as the opening credits for "A Tree Grows in Brooklyn" flashed on the screen. Through the years Dad had often asked me to read the book. "I want you to know how I've always thought of you, Fran," he usually added. Yet I'd never followed Dad's suggestion.

Immediately immersed in the film's imagery, which evoked in me a strong emotional response, I'd felt my father's spirit beside me, bringing me this loving, healing message. The old neighborhood of stoops, streets teeming with people's lives, the way people used to know and care about their neighbors, fire escapes, cramped old-fashioned kitchens, mothers wearing aprons to protect their cotton dresses, hallway scenes; the humid air of trapped lives. In the midst of it all, a serious dark-haired girl whose dreamy eyes glowed with a special light, searching her imagination for something grander, something beyond run-down streets, wanting to write about it all someday, in the meantime worrying about everyone she loved. The girl's name was Francie.

So this is how my father had seen me! My father had, with eyes of love, seen inside my heart! And he'd tried in his gentle loving way to transmit his feelings through a book I'd resisted reading. Oh, Dad! I felt my father's spiritual presence in the sun-filled serenity of my bedroom, rejoicing that at last I was going to gain deeper understanding into our relationship. "A Tree Grows in Brooklyn" would be the vehicle and my father was with me. The memory of that day when my father's loving spirit had come to assist me in the reclamation of a lost part of myself, the memory of that day when my real recuperation had begun, remains vibrantly alive in my mind.

A few years afterward I happened to wander into a local book store. And was I happily surprised to discover there a prominent display of, "A Tree Grows in Brooklyn." I quickly bought a copy and a coffee and began reading.

Mom is quietly dozing again. A little while ago she awoke to a frightening crisis of choking. Shaking with anxiety I administered a double dose of morphine. I bathed her face with a cool, damp washcloth, sat close by her and held her hands. I listen to my mother's labored breathing: Mom inhales; waiting for her out-breath I hold my own breath. I must regain composure, focus my thoughts and return to my journal, the keeper of my heart life here on Earth.

FOLLOWING an intriguing conversation with my dear friend, Susan Wine, regarding past-life regression therapy, Susan had sent me a copy of Roger Woolger's "Other Lives, Other Selves" which I very much enjoyed reading.

Over lunch with Susan I had recounted my experience at a seminar with Dick Sutphen. Expecting only a lecture I was surprised when Dick began, with brief introduction, to regress the audience of several hundred people. Despite my reluctance to have this unexpected experience while seated on a plain chair among people I didn't know, to my astonishment I went immediately into an altered state while remaining aware of Dick's instructions. Guided by his voice I found myself focused only on the tunnel I was swiftly moving through with no time to wonder which important day of a past life that still bears influence on my current life I would emerge into. My tunnel has transformed into a vast forest and I emerge from the forest into a clearing. "Notice the year, look down at your feet and observe your clothing," comes the next instruction. The year is 1869, I'm a girl of fifteen, and this is my wedding day! I am wearing a sun-bleached deerskin dress adorned with carefully chosen turquoise beads sewn with my own hands and beaded deerskin moccasins.

The daughter of our Hopi medicine man, I am being wed to the chief of a neighboring tribe, this decision handed down by the wise elders of both tribes who seek to restore our tribal strength. The Hopi elders in particular seek through this marriage unity among the decimated tribes.

But I, Singing Bird, am in love with White Eagle to whom I have pledged my undying love since childhood. Off to the left, mounted on his spotted white pony, White Eagle watches, standing apart from the wedding assembly. The strong planes of White Eagle's young face are aflame with burning tears. My father has been steadily passing on to me, since early childhood, the Hopi knowledge of healing as taught him by his grandfather. I come from a respected line of Hopi medicine men and women. On this day, my wedding day, I can recall grandmother singing, "O, daughter of heaven, the day you arrived, star of the healer rose in the skies." The tribe of my husband has lost their medicine man as we have lost our Hopi chief so this marriage is deemed a most important occasion. It is my duty, my responsibility to my people, to subjugate my own personal desires for the welfare of the tribe. On this sad wedding day, I present myself with devotion to our tribe; yet my true heart love remains unwavering with White Eagle.

Dick Sutphen brought the audience back from wherever our minds had traveled and I was shocked to discover my face streaked with tears, my body bathed in perspiration. I felt overwhelmed by the sadness of the young Indian girl's heart.

After this past-life regression with which I resonated deeply, I began to dream almost nightly of the young Indian girl's life until one day I contacted Don Morris, Roger Woolger's assistant and good friend of my friend Susan. Don came to my home, his clipboard ready, and gathered information from me about my consciousness and spiritual awareness. The following Saturday Don arrived to facilitate a more in-depth investigation into the life of a Hopi Indian girl whose inner world, whose sorrows, whose very consciousness felt exactly like my own. I lay down on the carpet in my study, Don held my feet for grounding, and I was off on my journey to a time and place that exists within our individual soul consciousness although from our third dimension reality perspective seems no more than imagination. In a moment I was off on my own, as Don later emphasized, back in the life of the Hopi girl, barely aware of anything he said after his initial instruction to describe aloud all that I was experiencing. His only task, he later said, became to hold my feet and listen.

I AM SINGING BIRD, whose soul is my soul, and I'm revisiting through her eyes, my life as a Hopi medicine woman. I live in the American Southwest. I make poultices from herbs, grasses, leaves, flowers and tree bark gathered fresh from streams and fields and forest to use for the healing of wounds. I place my hands above the affliction, invoking the names of ancestors as well as celestial powers.

Inside my tepee the light is muted and it is peaceful. A thick woven blanket covers almost all of the earthen floor and I feel fortunate for this comfort. I sit cross-legged on a fringed blanket and notice to my right a careful arrangement of little woven baskets each one containing a particular ingredient for poultices. I have exchanged with traders, beadwork for glass jars, and in the glass jars I store especially revered scraps of tree bark, leaves and such. I am at this moment ministering to a Hopi brother who lies upon a mat set in the center of my tepee. I have prepared a special poultice for him and am placing it upon his upper chest where he has received a serious wound. He is young and he will be healed. Outside, a few mothers with children have gathered, waiting patiently.

My father has spoken firmly the decree of the elders. I must wed the chief of a neighboring tribe, for since the white man has come to our land, seizing our land, murdering us, our numbers have been decimated. My father has made the dreaded pronouncement and I must obey; I must turn my face from White Eagle who I dearly love and have, since our seventh Harvest Moon, been secretly pledged to wed.

We ride on White Eagle's pony to our favorite place beside the running waters in the cool of the forest; his arms hold me and we laugh easily together, finding much to admire in one another and in the glorious land around us. I do not want to marry the chief! He is old! I want to be with White Eagle whose smile makes my heart soar high above the treetops! Sometimes I know of events before they transpire and this decision of the elders I have foreseen. I look down at my dress sewn by candlelight. Deerskin, fringed, embroidered with tiny shells and turquoise beads. Pretty. My handiwork is admired by others. My hair is black, long, braided. I weave narrow strips of beaded deerskin into the lower plaits and fasten the braid ends with these beaded strips.

I BECOME AWARE of Don's voice guiding me to a future time. I have a son. Soon he will be permitted to hunt with the men. A new infant, another boy, designated by the stars, as I was, to learn the ways of healing. I feel burdened by the needs of my people. I've grown weary of responsibility and long to be just a girl today. So I take up my newborn son and go down to the shore of the pond. This is forbidden. Women must never venture alone from our tiny village. But I long to be free! I unfasten the baby from my back and lay him down beside me while I sit crosslegged on the shore. I lift my face and close my eyes to the sun. A lovely day in planting season, sunlight filtering through bowers above us. Suddenly appearing from among the wooded grove across the small pond, many warriors. My newborn son carries the blood of chiefs and medicine men and they are here to capture him, keep him for their own! The warriors steal my baby!

Oh! Foolish woman! What have you done? Foolish, foolish woman! You, who counsel others! You, who bring healing to others! What have you done? By disobeying the law of your people you have brought great tragedy upon them! You! who have known only service to your people now have fallen to disgrace!

Struggling not to collapse I return to the village. A sister at her loom aware of my approaching footsteps immediately notices the absence of my little one. A cry goes out, my people gather round me, reach out to embrace me. With feeble gestures I communicate. The chief is summoned.

I have no defense. I disobeyed the law. I am consumed with misery, heartbreak, despair. Oh, foolish woman! I crawl onto my sleeping mat, the drums are pounding, my heart is pounding. Kidnapping of the chief's son must be avenged!

DON'S VOICE instructs me to move ahead to another important day. All around they are dying in the bloody field. My son is lying in my arms. Scattered white clouds are reflected in his eyes. His eyes, like great black pools of shining light, beseech me, "Help me, Mother, help me!" My arms are soaked with the blood of my first born son. I cannot see his wound but I know where it is, for I feel a breathless pain in my back on the side of the heart.

I am rigid, like stone. Frozen, as in the season of white storms. Why do I alone survive? Why? Dearest child of my heart, I am unable to move ... I feel your pain and cannot help you. Only hold you and mourn. Blood has been shed everywhere and everything lies in ruins. The light of day is fading.

Mounted on a speckled horse a man approaches. I sense he is a man of honor so I am not in fear of him. Dismounting, he draws near, kneels beside me. He gathers my son in his arms. The man's skin is pale but he is familiar with our ways, wrapping my son's body in deerskin from his own bundle, building a twig pyre, igniting the fire. With large hands he raises me up from the blood-soaked ground and stands beside me respectfully until only ashes remain. The man is strong but he is also gentle. He lifts me onto his saddle and guides his horse toward his home.

The man, Henry, can read the stars as I do. Rarely does he live in his home, he tells me, but many relatives, all women, live there and Henry supports the household. He is a trapper, friend to Indian and white man alike, and makes many fortunes so his relatives live in comfort. All along the trail I feel safe with Henry and foresee that he will be kind and we will be together.

The women of Henry's household - mother, sisters, cousins, aunts - run to greet him but cast scornful eyes on me. Filthy savage! Henry leads me inside the house but I cannot tolerate being enclosed by walls. The walls contain darkness. The women gather beside the door, whisper and mock me: Savage! Wild animal! I rush outside and raise my arms to a starlit sky! Henry will not part from me. We lie together on the soft grass and he tells me stories of the star patterns, of his travels, and feeling safe, I sleep. When dawn arrives Henry secures a tent for me, right there on the great expanse of green meadow. The women hold a meeting among themselves and agree to scorn me away from Henry's eyes. They'd hoped that he would marry one of the cousins.

I have a daughter! Mine and Henry's. We married according to the white man's law. Henry and I never tire of lying together on the sweet fragrant grass, gazing up at the forms in the sky. Star maps, cloud shapes, moon phases, birds in flight. He calls me his beautiful Indian princess. I lean over the rippling stream trying to see what Henry sees, and suddenly I am crying for all I have lost. Henry takes me into his arms and I cry for all that I have found.

The women relatives want my daughter to be like them. They are teaching her their customs and have fashioned dresses for her in their style. I teach my daughter the ways of my people, to ensure our line does not die, to ensure the wisdom of our ancestors not be forgotten. But my child is fond of their ways. She sits with me in my tent and says, "Dear Mother, why sit upon the hard ground when you may rest upon a soft cushiony chair? Dear Mother," she says, "allow me to bring you some of their thick loaves or sweets, you will find them tasty."

A messenger on horseback gallops toward the house. What terrible news he brings! Henry! We haven't had enough time together! Our daughter has not yet reached womanhood! Henry! My dear Henry!

I am alone. My daughter sleeps within their house. Oh, sorrow! I was spared at the time of the massacre to bring forward the wisdom of our people. It appears the wisdom will be lost. I cannot walk in your shoes, my daughter says to me. The women rejoice with the laughter of triumph. Without Henry to protect me they are free to scorn me openly.

I'm walking along the road. One of Henry's cousins, seated high on the wagon bench, rides up from behind, reining the horses to the right and a wagon wheel bears down on me! My leg! My leg is crushed! The beginning of my end.

A narrow cot pressed up against the wall of a cabin. This is the day of my passing. My daughter is with me. We have been living in this little cabin, my daughter and I. Now she is sobbing and stroking my arm, "I love you, Mother!"

"Please, my daughter, remember all I have taught you. Be wise. Do not allow the line of our great Hopi people to wither!"

DON'S MELLOW VOICE is telling me to rise above the pain and go to the very moment after death. I am now in the next world. And here is Henry! We are holding hands! Floating and holding hands! Henry is smiling and I am smiling. Now we are laughing! And here is my son, smiling. Greetings, dear Mother! And he is holding the hand of his younger brother! Floating, we are holding hands in a circle. We arrive at the enormous base of glorious

Golden Mountain where Great Father resides and we come to the marvelous Tree of Golden Light beyond which we cannot go for the light above in the Tree's uppermost branches is blinding. Oh, I am so joyful to be reunited here in my true home, to be done with that heavy, sorrowful life on Earth.

Now I see gathered before me all those of my tribe and they are bowing low. Their hands touch the 'ground.'

"Arise dear ones, do not bow, I am unworthy."

"No, no, no," they respond in one voice. "Great Father is pleased to have you home. He has decreed that we shall bow until you are thoroughly healed of your wounded heart of sorrow."

"Oh, Great Father! Forgive me! Forgive the transgressions of my life!"

"Dearest daughter, you have accomplished much good in your life, soothing fear and pain of many people, bringing wisdom and love to Earth, healing all who asked. You have done very well, dearest, and now you must permit your own healing to transpire. Accept yourself, embrace yourself, the woman you were. It is in your embrace of self that you shall find healing."

"Oh, Great Father! I do not wish to embrace that foolish woman who disobeyed the law of her people and brought catastrophe upon them through her own irresponsible desires."

"You must embrace her, for she was only being human, and she suffered great distress, and as part of the long march of human history, bore a heavy burden. Now you must embrace her, forgive her, and in so doing, become healed."

Obeying Great Father I embrace the young mother I was and feel immeasurable relief. Singing Bird is transformed by joy and within the golden shimmer of my light being form my daughter and I are reunited. My daughter stands before me. Her spirit has come on the wings of a dream! We embrace and she is healed. We are all one!

I RETURN TO PRESENT TIME. "Wow! What happened? What was I doing? What time is it?" I feel as if I've just returned from the longest journey.

"You had quite an experience," Don tells me. "I've never witnessed anything like it."

"I was having this conversation with Great Father! He told me my life is very important to him because I am his helper. He made me feel I am his helper in all my lifetimes, whatever era or culture I'm born into on Earth, my connection to Him is never forgotten. He was welcoming me Home. His words were just and true and there was no such thing as disbelief."

IN THE LONG HOURS of my mother's afternoon naps, while keeping watch over her I also ruminate on the wisdom to be gleaned from revisiting my life as a Hopi medicine woman. The first awareness that comes to me is one of the biggest teachings in metaphysics. More than any other influence we are our souls, meaning our soul determines our character and whatever other influences come to bear on our life, whether through early childhood indoctrination or through the society we live in, it is ultimately our soul coming through as character that will determine how we respond to our experiences. Each response leads us to the next experience and in this way, from moment to moment, we create our lives. We are bound, along the way, to make what we, with imperfect judgment, call 'mistakes.' Yet each 'mistake' brings us further along in the lessons we are here to learn as individuals as well as in the overall plan for our generation's lessons. And let us be mindful as well that we progress as souls and contribute as human beings to the history of humanity on Earth, through all the good we do, the merit we earn, in our lifetime.

I see the character of the Hopi medicine woman in myself. I see how even character that is deemed *good* can become entangled with the sorrow of others and even with harm to others, however unwittingly. Great Father, in the higher realms where all is Truth reminded me, with utmost loving kindness, of the imperative to forgive ourselves. After all, each one of us is taking part in 'the long march of human history.' We often choose, as intrinsic to our personal forgiveness, to take up another life on Earth where we will be given opportunities to make restitution. In this way we raise the vibration of our soul and gain inner peace for our human self, enabling us to function more fully with optimum well-being.

We return through birth into another life on Earth, refreshed and renewed and determined to get it right this time. We are provided clues to help us remember. For me, in this lifetime as Francine, one of my clues was the word, 'responsible.' 'Responsible' has always been a big word for me. Now I understand its genesis. I understand now my strong drive to be, above even my own needs, responsible in all things. The Native American theme runs through my entire life. Not only did my father affectionately call me Pocahontas, but my mother used to call after me when I was a young girl feeling the freedom of country life in summer, Wild Indian. Were they with me in the Hopi lifetime? Was my father the medicine man father of the Hopi lifetime who in this lifetime devoted himself totally to supporting my brother on his path to becoming a doctor? And was my mother one of Henry's sisters who never understood me and had to make restitution in this lifetime by loving me as her daughter? If you seek carefully you may find the whisperings of the past. And what about Henry? Is he my husband in this lifetime, providing but always running away? My Hopi son who died in my arms, is he my son now? My daughter, the one who so loved and sought to protect her Indian mother she felt herself to be her mother's guardian; it feels in my heart that Annie was my beloved Hopi daughter.

It is intriguing. Yet, we are meant to live in the present. We come away understanding the imperative to forgive ourselves so that we may then go on to forgive everyone else now that we see so clearly how we are all together in this thing called 'Life.' We offer gratitude for the wisdom gained in the transcendence, the balancing of weaknesses and strengths, the understanding achieved from seeing those we love playing different roles designed to help each one of us evolve. With everlasting love we accept the retrieval of lost parts of ourselves and integrate all of it to create a more whole self, a more wholesome self.

JUNE 15. Mom had a crisis. The Hospice nurse advises hospitalization. Mom laments, "Oh, what's going to happen to me?" Every passing day feels like forever. I can barely maintain myself. In the morning without caring I throw on the same clothing I wore the day before. Annie interrupts her overwhelmingly busy day at the law firm to taxi over to Mom's apartment and voices concern when she sees me wearing the same clothing day after day. She is stressed and anxious over her Grandma and now I've added to her stress.

Mom cannot hold herself upright for meals on the sofa so I feed her propped up on pillows. She swallows each spoonful slowly, with enormous effort. As the day flows into evening and Mom is washed, lying exhausted in her bed I sit beside her. My mother tightly grips my hands, kisses my hands, her tears flowing while moaning and recounting sorrowfully, heart-wrenching memories.

JUNE 21. Mom awakens with a jolt from a long nap. "Fran darling, tell me, what happens to you in those first minutes after you die?"

Fighting back tears, holding her hands, I seek to comfort my mother. "You know when you come to my house, Mom, I open the door wide for you, greet you with a smile and a hug, take your hand and lead you to a nice chair where we rest, feeling warm and happy to be together? Well it will be like that, only so much more joyful. All your loved ones who are there will be waiting to greet you. They will call your name and embrace you and lead you to a wonderful safe place where everything is loving and harmonious."

Mom smiles her little girl smile and reminisces with struggling breath, "I always loved coming to your house, the way you greet me."

My brother is on a Sunday afternoon visiting schedule of precisely one hour. Following Annie's advice that Mike's visit is a good time for me to take a short break, after he and I exchange greetings I go out feeling grateful for some fresh air and a tall iced coffee across the street. A few weeks later my brother changes his schedule so now he arrives at nine o'clock on Sunday morning during Mom's hygiene and grooming time. Mom settles refreshed and clean into her bed against pillows adjusted just right, coverlet tented above her feet; Mike presides a few moments longer and then, his visiting hour expired, he leaves.

JUNE 28. Despite her fourteen hour days at Skadden Arps, Annie visits every day. May God bless my beautiful loving daughter every day of her blessed life, and today especially, on her birthday!

DREAM: I'm out in space. A meteor is hurtling at incredible speed toward Earth and I can see, as if I'm very close to it, the crevices and holes on the meteor's surface, yet I do not feel it's stormy passage.

JULY 9. My brother calls at 9:00 A.M. to describe in detail the lovely barbeque they all enjoyed yesterday with our cousins.

Found a few pages of dreams at home so I'm writing them into this journal. The task helps to temporarily shift my focus away from the misery that fills my mother's tiny studio apartment. For a little while by exploring my inner world I find some peace.

A dream about my son, 1992. I see my son, a strong, powerful king. A vine grows from his right arm. The vine is lush with large ripe green grapes. From the trunk of his body emerge strong healthy roots.

Another dream about my son, 1992. I'm facing a closed door, its upper half milky white glass, the edges and the front of it appear cloud-like. Merely by the projection of my thought the door opens and fades away. Standing before me is Neale, looking quite angelic and surrounded by pure glowing white light. Upon seeing me his face lights up, he smiles, opens his arms in greeting. "Mommy!" Delighted and joyful we embrace. "My darling Neale!" A few hours later Neale calls, "This is your lucky day, Mommy. You're having lunch with me."

A dream about Grandma, 1993. Grandma is my teacher, imparting specific information to me. It's an unemotional yet familiar setting, apparently we are accustomed to seeing each other this way. The information this time is about Mom's care.

A DREAM ABOUT STARLIGHT, 1992. I am moving along swiftly, gliding actually, as my feet do not touch the pavement on 53rd Street where I live. I pass many people, arrive at closed, almost sealed but not fully sealed, large metal doors. An elderly man in the corner, in response to my urgent request, grants me permission to pass. Now gliding through a long, curved tunnel I arrive at a waiting area where the remaining distance of the tunnel is hidden from view by the bend in the wall. A few people have gathered. I understand that we have passed over, the others seem very confused. A graceful beautiful woman attired in a long white flowing gown is guiding several people further along in the tunnel. Soon she comes to me, takes my hand and leads me to a stone bench carved into a niche in the tunnel wall. She appears to my eyes like an angel and it is with utmost gentleness and kindness that she instructs me: "Dear Francine, you may not pass beyond this place. You are to return, for much remains for you to accomplish." The angel has spoken and I obey. Hordes of distressed souls are rushing by me into the tunnel, so for safety I keep close to the wall unseen by the others. I hear a loud crashing noise and I'm outside again.

A magnificent being of radiant light, upholding like a lantern a majestic crystal sword, is waiting for me. Protectively, he takes my hand and leads me to an unadorned silent room which feels to be in a higher dimension as it seems to be made of pure white light. We are seated on two plain white chairs facing one another. Our knees are touching, indicating an intimate relationship. He is beautiful and god-like. His third eye glows in the center of his forehead; three glorious eyes shining and radiating streams of turquoise blue and white light, simply gorgeous. Elegant streams of violet light form the language of his thoughts, and pure violet light glows with refinement around his head and shoulders, all around him. Glorious streams of indigo blue light emanate from his being to create deep serenity within me. He is fair-skinned and blond, his physique is healthy and balanced in all ways, reminiscent of the olden gods of ancient Greece. This magnificent being takes my hands in his while his gaze, with glorious light continually streaming forth, is focused on my eyes. He communicates telepathically: I must not give into despair. I must remain courageous in all things. I must never forget who I am and remain always in my dignity. He has removed me from the path of obstacles and has guided me to an open clear path free of interference from negative forces. He will continue to be my guide, my protector, on this path toward enlightenment for all of my days on Earth.

I worry that, dazzled as I am by his presence, by his effervescent light, I will not remember the transcendent wisdom he is imparting to me. "You will remember, dearest, when the time comes you will remember everything."

May 2012. This magnificent being remains with me to this day. For several years after the meeting just described, whenever he arrived, crystal sword in hand, to transmit an important message, to heal a client or to guide me through a personal illness his noble presence struck me speechless. Then one sunny morning in April 2001 he unexpectedly appeared before me and finally I had the presence of mind to ask, "How shall I call you?"

"My name is Starlight." As he transmitted to me I saw continuous streams of beautiful violet-blue light radiating all around him, sparkling and glowing.

"Dear Starlight, can you speak to me of our connection?"

"We are spiritual soul mates." And then I heard within my soul, floating on the softest musical field, Starlight singing:

> *From beyond the whirling galaxies starlight shines*
> *As the light of distant stars shine forth, so do I*
> *From within the great Oneness I am by your side*
> *As the Heavens alight in the night streaming*
> *Memories of everlasting love glistening as morning dew*
> *So I shine forever for you ... I am Starlight.*

Enormous vibrations of purest love accompany the Song of Starlight, coursing through me like primordial waves at sea; I am transformed into a great light-infused water being, I become a being of liquid light!

Our thoughts are blended like waters of the deep. "Have we ever shared a life together on Earth?"

"No, dearest, we have not. Through all eternity we choose to keep our connection pure. We choose multi-dimensional lives of service and while one of us is in human form the other of us remains in our light body form to provide protection, guidance and loving support."

"And what of other guides, angelic beings and Masters who make themselves known to me?"

"Beloved, we are all of the Light. We all serve the Light. We Are All One."

A DREAM ABOUT TEACHING, 1994. Classroom setting, high school students. I've been summoned by the High Ones to teach the meaninglessness of prejudice. I hear a voice from above telepathically providing wise counsel. The voice belongs to a spiritual Master with whom I am well acquainted but cannot identify in this dream. I am here to translate this wisdom teaching into language that will resonate with the students. I have their attention and am simply saying, "Each human being has a soul which comes from God. Beneath the surface of our skin our souls are related through our connection to God. This is why it makes no sense to hate people based on appearance of skin, or religion, or nationality, or for any reason. Please, dear ones, remember, we are all one." Much more followed, all from presence above.

A DREAM ABOUT SATAN, 1994. Suddenly, an unknown man of towering presence entered our home at Two Flower Place. He produced from the side of his belt an enormous sword which he immediately began to swing menacingly. With deliberate intent the man proceeded to destroy each object on every shelf and then destroyed all the shelves. With an explosion he caused just by pointing his sword he destroyed our living room. He slashed at doors and cupboards. He tore open his shirt to reveal a broad strange-looking flat chest. It was at this moment that I understood this man to be the personification of Satan.

Strangers in my home were unconcerned with my welfare.

Some form of judgment was taking place. Widespread destruction of my home. I locked myself in the bathroom but Satan banged it open, grasping at me, threateningly.

"Let us negotiate!" I cried, "why do you want to destroy me?"

Satan replied, "There is nothing left to say, we have already negotiated."

"What do you mean? Why do you seek destruction? Why not pursue those who harm others?"

Satan laughed, "That would take a thousand years!"

"Fine," I answered, "all the good and helpful people would live in peace."

"No! You don't understand! We had this conversation ten thousand years ago! Now it is time!"

"But I don't remember!"

Satan said, "I will have all the world to myself and my rogues. We will own Earth! Earth will come under our reign of darkness!"

"No!" I answered, suddenly unafraid of Satan, suddenly connecting with my inner spiritual power. "You will never succeed! You cannot stop the sun from bringing light to Earth! Things will grow! Beauty will always exist!"

"No! It will end! I will destroy you and all the righteous ones, every last one! And God will no longer care about the world! He will abandon Earth and leave it to me and my rogues!" While shouting these threats Satan swirled his sword high as if he were challenging God Himself. "Now, I start with you!"

"No!" I was standing up strong to Satan, seeking compromise. "Let us retreat to an island!"

"Ha!" Satan laughed mockingly, "What kind of life will you have? You will live with endless fear of our arrival. No! Ten thousand years were you granted to uplift Earth from darkness; now over!"

I called on my Guardian Angel, Love. "Where are you, my Angel? Come and save me!"

Instantly, my Angel answered, "I am here! And I shall save you! I shall make you invisible!"

A great circular wind blew, forming a column around me, rendering me invisible.

But Satan was not to be outsmarted. "I know you are there!" he thundered with enormous rage. And Satan became a whirling dervish, swinging his enormous sword every which way, slashing the air with powerful strokes. Satan was outsmarting my Angel, when suddenly he roared, "Yes! You shall go to your island! Go, and live in fear of my arrival!"

Mom is still sleeping her morphine-induced sleep, afternoon naps are longer these days. Suddenly, she coughs a terrible cough in her sleep, frightening me; leaning closer I see perspiration glistening all over her skin, so I run to dampen a washcloth with cold water. Another mini crisis settles down. The hours wear on. I retrieve my folder of notes written on all different papers, searching for another dream worthy of this journal, sometimes wondering about the ones I didn't save and sometimes thinking I have saved too many, and I'm surprised to find a moment in time: a scrap of paper stuck in a book and transferred to this folder.

August 1994. In bed with a flu; call from my son. "Mom, I love you very much. And when I was growing up I always knew you loved me very much, I always felt very loved. And I know you did the best you could. So I wanted you to know I love you."

Unusual experience, March 1995. Hyatt Hotel in Scottsdale, Arizona. 3:00 a.m. I close the bathroom door behind me to emerge into the absolute blackness of our room, blackout drapery closed by Danny. Not wishing to disturb Danny's sleep and unable to see my way around the bed back to my side, I speak aloud, "I can't see in the dark." Suddenly, a glowing ball of white light appears right in front of me, transmitting telepathic thoughts, "I am your guiding light." Love radiated from this ball of light and I felt the love inside my heart. It illuminated only its own space, it did not light up the room. Around the king sized bed to the narrow passage alongside the wall the ball of light guided me directly to my pillow. While following this extraordinary globe of light, which hovered at my chest height, I'd paused a few times sort of playful and each time the light had paused with me, resuming its role of guide as I again walked forward.

Later on, at a seminar in New York City, I learned about the mysterious Arizona phenomena of 'orbs,' as they are called.

JULY 12. Annie just called to report a most strange occurrence. She awoke in the night to see me standing in the doorway of her bedroom. I was wearing a long white nightgown and was smiling peacefully. She felt my love for her as real as if my physical self were there. "It was quite a powerful experience, Mom, to see you standing there watching over me as if you were my guardian angel. Very powerful, Mommy, and I want you to know how much I love you."

JULY 25. Late at night reading in my study a few pages from "The Tibetan Book of Living and Dying" I notice a glimmering, shimmering shape of light. Amazed and delighted, I watch it streak across the floor displaying a robust life force. Within the dazzling light is silver light and there is such a profusion of silver light it reminds me of pure mirrored glass, and suddenly with great speed the shape expands to an almost unbearable brightness, yet I cannot turn my eyes away. This light shape remains with me for about an hour. The light transmits to me, happiness and abundant joy.

JULY 30. As soon as I'm awake in the morning Danny tells me that I had a busy night. Three times he woke up to go to the bathroom and each time he watched my hands moving rhythmically above my head, my crown chakra. He said at first he thought I was awake but then thought I was in a trance. Do I practice healing in my sleep? he asked. This morning I do feel cleared of depression.

AUGUST 5. At mealtimes today Mom is clamping her mouth closed. Her mouth is rigid. Walking her to the bathroom in our usual posture of Mom holding on to my arms while I step backward, the few steps taking forever, today my mother suddenly froze, unable to move forward, except that her whole body was shaking uncontrollably. I held her, kissed her forehead and reminded her once again of my eternal love for her. I promised to remember how much she loves me.

"I'm slipping, Fran darling ... I don't know what world I'm in ..." my mother whispers, "I love you, darling." We are crying together.

AUGUST 7. Oh, dear God, there are black spots on my mother's heels and bruises on her feet. While I very gently prepare to massage her back I stop abruptly, shocked by the sight of two large bleed-throughs where cancer is devouring the lining of my mother's lungs. "The house is flying in the sky," Mom hallucinates, "How did I get here?" I search deep inside my heart for more strength; strong, stronger, strongest.

AUGUST 9. At 4:30 I decide to awaken Mom from a coma-like sleep. "I feel a whoosh, Fran, going through the windowpane, somewhere dark and lonely, terrifying!" At bedtime Mom is afraid to lie down, worrying she might be better off in the hospital. She begs me to summon Dr. Kochen, a psychiatrist she visited a few times prior to her illness. Dr. Kochen arrives at midnight, suggests anti-psychotics, advises against hospitalization, strongly recommends 24 hour nursing care. Xanax eases Mom to sleep.

AUGUST 10. This morning Mom's legs are covered with swirls of purple and blue. Her hands are blue and her fingernails black. The customary queasiness arises in my stomach. I hold Mom in my arms, "I love you, Mommy." Within a couple hours her skin returns to normal color, the discoloration faded, completely gone.

Also, this morning, my father has returned in spirit, his powerful spiritual energy evident. My father speaks thusly to me: "Your mother requested a clean death with no form of intervention, no unnecessary effort to prolong her life. The oxygen arrived and in accordance with her wishes you returned it. Your brother re-ordered it. You returned it again and again he re-ordered it. Your mother's suffering is being prolonged. She clings to you, and you, who believe in freedom for all human beings, have shackled yourself to a dying woman whose death has been needlessly delayed."

In the book "The 36 Hour Day" on page 115 oxygen is listed among other life-support interventions. I read in "Dying At Home" about the issue of lack of family support for the caregiver. In most cases the caregiver does receive family support. Annie found her way to the same books and we discuss these serious issues. Addressed in the book is the open secret of administering a dosage of morphine. Years afterward I deeply regretted my inability to relieve my mother of her tragic suffering. If I had known the extreme suffering she was to endure before her final day, would I then have found the inner resources to administer the required morphine to end it? The end of life suffering from lung cancer is known very well, however, by the medical profession. In the beginning, the first week she was home from the hospital in fact, her reasoning ability as sound as always, Mom called

Dr. Conti and asked him in a steady voice to please end her misery. The good doctor laid down his phone and while I waited with Mom, phone resting in her hand, he never returned. Doctors, I have learned from a Hospice nurse, receive monthly payments from Hospice in return for supervision of their patients. Dr. Conti hasn't made one visit, violating the terms of the Hospice agreement to visit the patient once a month, minimum.

Mom is sleeping her long afternoon sleep. I am watching her while she sleeps. And then I glimpse in the room with us my Grandma! and Grandfather Jacob who I never knew yet in an instant I know it's him. And my father is here in the room with us again! Smiling gently they transmit love and reassurance. Suddenly, I am smiling and feeling good.

The room is suffused with peace and love. I am receiving a spiritual message: "You are a soul who has come to Earth from a highly evolved civilization to live as a human. Your purpose here is to help, teach, heal. Your karma differs from karma of human beings. Many lifetimes you have lived on Earth and in each you sought to manifest healing through the power of love, even loving those who do not love you. You are not here to suffer. You are here to love. Remember who you are."

Hospice has sent us Virginia for the twelve hour day shift and Sharon for the twelve hour night shift. I explain to Mom that every effort is being made to keep her home in her own bed. Mom smiles, relieved, and says, "I'm glad you're my daughter." Then she cries. Annie is here for her daily visit, "You could have been a psychiatrist, Mom."

AUGUST 11. The profound spiritual interaction of yesterday fulfilled a purpose which the events of this morning are bringing into focus. My father's loving spirit, Grandma's loving spirit and grandfather Jacob's loving spirit, with knowledge of what was unknown to my mother and I, came yesterday to prepare us for today. The reasons for the messages become clear today.

Early in the morning a call from Hospice. Mom's case has been reviewed by the Hospice medical team, influenced by an apparently forceful crusade by Dr. Kochen, Mom's psychiatrist. "Prepare to bring your mother into the hospital. She is suffering from psychosis and paranoia, she needs a thorough medical exam which she hasn't had for months; your mother requires intensive care."

AUGUST 15. Head nurse from Cabrini calls, summary of report from visiting nurse: Bleed-throughs on Mom's back require special treatment; the ulcerations on the heels of her feet require special treatment; her left arm is swollen. My mother's body is shutting down.

AUGUST 19. Annie is upset over everything and worries incessantly about my health. She speaks eloquently, imploring me to agree and allow Mom to go to Cabrini. Intellectually, I understand the wisdom of my daughter's plea, yet my heart refuses to abandon my mother to the system. Falling apart physically and emotionally, holding on for as long as possible to my promise to let my mother die at home, I sense the time is rapidly approaching when I will break my sacred promise.

Annie implores me, "How do you think I feel when I'm sitting in my office thinking of you at Grandma's day after day, all these hours alone and miserable. I'm losing time from work running over here in the middle of the day. I can't do it anymore, Mom!"

My physician, when he sent me home wearing a heart monitor, my aunts, my brother, have all been arguing since June to let my mother die in the hospital.

August 21. I consult with Kabbalist Rabbi Kessin who I regard as my spiritual mentor. "Rabbi, please advise me regarding one's responsibility in the care of a terminally ill parent."

Rabbi Kessin deliberates for a moment before speaking. He answers, "It is the highest mitzvah to care for one's parent. However, can you determine how much time you can be with your mother while maintaining your own health? Your health, your life, must not be compromised," he admonishes. Then the wise Rabbi elicits from me what I really didn't want to disclose, that my brother comes for an hour once a week. At this disclosure Rabbi becomes very upset. "Abandonment," he pronounces with sincere emotion, "is a terrible sin. You are the teacher, it is your job to make your brother understand. I know you well, I've been to your home, you are a pure and righteous woman. You are one of the 36 souls who uphold the world!" Rabbi is getting overly emotional.

But it is Annie, my beloved daughter, who speaks with the deepest heartfelt love for me and her Grandma, who in the end convinces me. I am, above all, a mother.

August 29. Mom is in and out of reality. I struggle to bathe my mother, brush her teeth and comb her hair. She wore her clothes until the end of June. Now I dress my mother in her favorite tee shirt. She wears a diaper. With monumental effort we complete her outfit with the pretty pink robe I brought to her that day in Montefiore, and tie the belt stylishly.

An ambulance arrives at the entrance to Mom's building; attendants are at the door. One attendant admires Mom's apartment and takes her blood pressure in a surprisingly kindly way. The second attendant comments that I look like Natalie Wood or Liz Taylor. On another day I would have smiled and told him that a long time ago when we first met, my husband used to say that; now all he talks about is his golf swing.

I stand by and witness the transfer of my mother from her

four-poster bed, made up with white eyelet sheets and embroidered quilt, to an ambulance gurney. She will never lie in her four-poster bed again but Mom is certain she is coming home soon.

Slowly, the attendants begin to wheel the gurney toward the door and my mother raises herself up on one elbow, suddenly imbued with newfound energy, an angelic glow on her face. A soft light is shining in her Asian eyes, even with her pain, and through all her terrible suffering my mother's sweet face remains unwrinkled, truly lovely, beautiful. Now we are walking out, a lost, helpless expression in my mother's eyes, and as our eyes meet I feel my mother's broken heart inside me, blending with my heart. How can I live through this moment? But blending with us also is the most tender love, a love that transcends time and space, a strong love imbued with renewed spiritual strength we both need to carry us through this time; the eternal love of my father's soul, grandma's soul, and the soul of my grandfather. Only a few days ago they had used their spiritual energies to make their presence visible, to transmit strength to help us through this passage.

LABOR DAY WEEKEND. Despite hallucinations Mom remains calm but when a nurse enters her room she becomes frantic "No! Leave me alone! I want my Mama! Matty! Matty! I want to go home!" She sits bolt upright, eyes flashing, arms flailing. "I will never forget this as long as I live!"

Saturday. My brother arrived for his visit. Mom becomes severely disturbed. I suggest to my brother that he give Mom some loving comfort and he replies by reading aloud a list of nursing homes.

Sunday. Mom is semi-comatose. I stroke her forehead, hold her in my arms. She focuses her eyes and whispers, "Fran, darling, you don't know until you're faced with it." I know, Mom, you're right. She rallied a bit, grew peaceful, and more present.

As I lay in bed at night, just as the warmth of sleep is washing over me, I see my lovely mother dressed in her favorite dark green suit from the years of my childhood, her crescent moon brooch positioned perfectly on her jacket. Close behind her stands my father, wearing his hat and two-tone forties style jacket. My parents smile and give me a blessing.

SEPTEMBER 3. Stroking Mom's forehead. Suddenly, she opens her eyes and speaks in the voice I remember from before her illness. "There's nothing you can do, darling." Except for tiny sips of water my mother is refusing nourishment.

Suddenly my brother calls. I hear a lot of noise in the background coming from his end and Mike remarks, "You don't know what torture it is to live in this house."

SEPTEMBER 10. While I'm massaging my mother's arms she has a lucid moment. "My life stinks, I want to die, this is no life."

"Mom, you always say it like it is and I agree with you."

"Fran, I kiss the ground you walk on."

SEPTEMBER 13. My mother's 80th birthday. She knows her age and she knows it is her birthday. I relay birthday messages from the family.

When visiting hours end a nurse rides the elevator down with me. "You're not just beautiful," she suddenly remarks, turning toward me with a smile, "You have style and grace, and you make a woman feel good just to be around you, and you have a special attitude, it adds to your beauty."

Imagine! Almost every day lovely people reaching out to me with kind messages. All these lovely people! I feel so very blessed!

Outside, crossing to walk up a pretty tree-lined street, I think about a little scene that happened to unfold earlier in the afternoon. While Mom slept, I'd walked into the visitors' lounge where a patient's wife in desperate need of comfort was looking for a counselor though none was available just then. So I spent some time with her. While I was helping her through her difficult hour the nurse I met in the elevator happened to step in for a coffee, and she'd come over to sit with us. The caring energy this nurse brought into our space was so very comforting I felt that she exemplified her profession.

In truth, we are not separate at all. The idea of separation is an illusion into which we are born. In truth, as Adam my beloved spirit guide, taught me, We Are All One, his first wisdom offering to me. And in those first months after revealing himself to me, whenever I asked for a sign he replied with another wisdom offering, The future will show. Loving kindness. Patience. Profound teachings offered with transcendent love and meant to be shared with everyone! Practicing lovingkindness and patience every day with everyone we meet brings the energy of lovingkindness and patience into ourselves. After practicing a while we begin to notice that the energy of these attributes blends comfortably with our energy and through a most gentle, natural transformation we become more kind and loving, patient human beings.

SEPTEMBER 15. I am awakened at 5:00 A.M. by sharp stabbing pain in my left eye. To accomplish self-healing I immediately cover my eye with my left hand, call on my son, my guide and with my inner vision I see five beings of white light standing in a row. With one synchronized action the light beings snap their fingers; I open my eyes and the pain is gone!

It is not the purpose of this book to recount the untidy details of family gossip and false accusations but there were at the time of my mother's illness disturbing and deceptive behind-the-scenes goings-on among my brother, sister-in-law, my aunts and some of my cousins. I avoided getting involved in family discussions regarding such things as my mother's jewelry or the clothing chosen for her burial, responding simply, "My mother has a legal will and we shall abide by my mother's wishes." These ongoing discussions caused me additional emotional stress, as well as causing me to doubt their love for my mother. Did they suppose that upsetting me with false accusations while my mother lay suffering in the last months of her life would soothe my mother's pain? If either of my mother's sisters were dying my mother would have been beside her sister with devoted loving care; this I knew with all my heart.

SEPTEMBER 16. Automatic writing. Dearest Mother, I am your son, your guide who has come to you in love according to our pact. The anxiety you are feeling comes from a negative energy force intruding on your peace. This force can reach you through telephone wires. Therefore, Dearest, keep not only personal meetings to an essential minimum but phone calls, too. Never be the one to initiate contact. Never be the one to open communication with negative forces. When it is thrust upon you, as will occur from time to time in the course of human relations, you may be comforted in the knowledge that I am ever by your side and you are surrounded by the light of our Creator. Be not fearful. Follow your path of enlightenment. We will maintain always a shield of light for your protection. Fear not, go forth in joy. Be not sad, rejoice, for your mother is in the hands of loved ones who watch over her. Her ordeal is drawing to a close. Adieu for now, dearest.

SEPTEMBER 18. Mom is transferred from Cabrini to Little Sisters of the Poor in the Bronx with whom my brother has a professional association. I remain beside my mother, walking alongside her gurney, holding her hand as she is wheeled into the ambulance and throughout the drive from downtown in the city up to the Bronx. I hold my mother's hand as the gurney is removed from the ambulance and wheeled through the corridors of the nursing home, to her room at the very end of the long corridor. Silent tears never cease flowing from her eyes but my mother, nevertheless, looks elegant in her embroidered white cotton gown. The Sisters are exceedingly gentle. As soon as Mom is settled in her new bed in this immaculate, spacious room, silent tears still flowing, she falls asleep.

Mike comes into Mom's room, adjusts his attitude so as to impress whoever of the staff might enter while he is present, a studied superiority I've grown so weary of these past months. How often I have held my sobbing mother in my arms, trying unsuccessfully to soothe her uncontainable heartbreak, "My Mikey doesn't love me anymore!" I say a silent prayer and summon my spirit guide for protection. Mike moves his chair around the bed to where I'm sitting in the corner close to Mom, stretches out his long legs, a life-long habit. In the presence of the Sisters he adopts a soft, sweet voice and pretends a caring attitude toward Mom which I perceive as stilted. Later, after the Sisters leave, my brother turns to me with an edge of familiar ridicule in his voice and sarcastically questions me regarding my children. His unloving energy is sickening me. A Sister enters. Mike rises, walks to the foot of Mom's bed and announces with a flourish of grandeur, "Gloria, my wife, is going to buy you some nightgowns, Mom," and then he walks out.

Dad's image flashes in my mind and Mom whispers, "Matty?"

SEPTEMBER 24. I arrive at Mom's bedside and feel the absence of her soul. Then I feel her soul's brief return.

SEPTEMBER 27. Mom stares unseeing. Tenderly, I caress my mother's face, "I love you, Mommy." In this moment my mother's soul is present, she knows I'm with her. "I love you, too," she responds, barely audible. Another coma-like sleep.

Lightly massaging Mom's arms and shoulders I begin to feel the presence of Dad and Grandma so I pray to their spirits, "Will you watch over Mom? Will you be there for her? Will you hold out your arms to her? And show her the way?"

Suddenly I am pulled toward the window which on this day frames a cloudy gray sky above Bronx tree-tops and architecturally familiar distant red brick buildings. Appearing in mid-air between myself and the window panes are hundreds of sparks of golden light, floating. Living, vibrant, graceful. Dipping and rising, with intelligence and coherence.

Among these floating golden sparks of light tiny rings are also floating, some singly, some in pairs and some in threes. Each appears to me as a delicate double ring consisting of one very tiny ring contained within a slightly larger protective ring. These rings move in a steady upward stream. At a certain point in their ascendance the rings vanish right before my eyes.

Has my vision grown faulty? Perhaps I should look away. Returning my gaze to the space between myself and the window panes I see that the sparks of golden light are indeed still floating, vibrant and alive, and the delicate rings are still streaming toward an unseen yet reachable Heaven. What is the significance of this I ask, and receive a profound reply.

A vision of Dad appears, and Grandma and grandfather Jacob. They transmit this message: "You are being granted opening into another dimension. We are with you. We shall surely remain with your mother, protecting her soul as it is released from its time-worn vessel. We shall surely welcome her and your mother shall find peace and love."

And then, wonder of wonders, I see Mom in spirit form! She appears beside the loving, comforting spirit forms of Dad and Grandma and grandfather Jacob. My mother's spirit is speaking to me! "I shall always be with you, Fran, my dearest, in love forever."

My mother appears restored to her energetic, youthful beauty, smiling unburdened by worry. Her smile transmits pure joy, her face is radiant! "The sparks of golden light are a gift, Fran," my mother's spirit, fully aware and awake, tells me. This golden spirit filled with strength and well-being is my mother! "A gift for you to more surely know of our higher world, the world of which you dream, the world of universal love and kindness. To inform you on your path of wisdom."

Each of us is a brilliantly designed physical vessel which draws its life force from the Heart of God, located at the central point of the One Infinite Living Crystal Spiral. An eternal pulse sends forth that which is known as the Essence of Divine Love, a spiritual force composed entirely of light which holds within itself ultimate universal creativity. This Light is the source of the souls of humanity. We Are All One.

Our souls spring forth from the Light, a unified consciousness of Love. The light of our soul is encoded with knowledge of the Oneness from whence we come. Our soul, as it emerges from out of the Oneness is guided by angelic beings who offer self-understanding. Our soul is sent forth into the cosmos, thus beginning its long journey during which our soul may lose its balance, lose its way, forget from whence it came, feel separated from and forget the Oneness, searching for Home.

A beautiful blue planet called Earth, positioned in the cosmos near the Heart of God, beckons to our soul who recognizes familiar flickering lights from the Oneness, and the lights call out to our soul who, in its confusion during descent through the dimensions of space and motion which surround Earth, arrives through birth into human life in third dimension, hoping it has at last found Home.

The greater portion of our soul remains safe in the higher realms. We may refer to the greater portion of our soul as our Higher Self. For the duration of our life on Earth a spark of light from our greater soul resides within the center of our chest, within our heart chakra, and may be referred to as our soul. Our souls come to Earth to inhabit a physical body, to blend as one unit with our physical body. The ultimate purpose of our soul's journey is to uplift the lower fear-centered survival energy of the physical vessel which sometimes struggles in opposition to its soul's mission through deliberate acts of harm and destruction. Our soul's mission, in service to the Heart of God, is to transform fear into enlightened heart love.

While we are living our stream of physical Earth lives in third dimension, the upper dimensions are veiled from us, allowing us to have an illusory experience of separation from All That Is. Feeling alone and separate the lower body consciousness falls into the lower energies of fear. The force which seeks to cause harm or gain control over others originates in fear. From the dark energies of fear flow all negative thoughts, words and actions.

The power of Love holds the power to transmute the dark energies of fear into higher awareness, into Peace and Love. Our higher selves, our spiritual guides and masters, transmitting inspiration to us through our dreams, through synchronicity, through every-day experience, patiently await our eventual upward seeking which places our feet firmly upon the path of light. By our deeds of kindness, by sharing love with all who come before us, we earn merit. By this process, readily available to everyone, higher truth is revealed to us.

This is the way of the Light. It is a way that inspires well-being and harmony within us. The way of the Light uplifts our thoughts and helps us remember All That Is. It is a way of life that causes harm to no one, seeks control over no one. We may take note of the supreme genius of this process: a Divinely inspired inner process simultaneously beneficial to all who associate with such an upward seeker.

When our life on Earth is complete the spark of light that is our soul returns to the higher realms where it blends with the greater portion of itself, bringing with it all it has learned from the trials and tribulations of life on Earth, adding to the overall vibrancy and wisdom of the greater portion of its soul, expanding the glow and radiance of its soul's light.

On Earth the Light of All That Is as expressed through the human vessel shall overspread the world's civilizations. Remembrance of the Light shall overtake the affairs of humanity. Planet Earth shall evolve as well to its new state of enlightened planet and the cycle of confusion and heartbreak, its genesis in ancient times, shall draw to its weary conclusion. The planet and all humanity shall move through an open golden portal, into a higher plane known as Fifth Dimension where loving kindness and service for the greater good prevail.

The above wisdom teaching was transmitted to me by the hundreds of floating sparks of light on that day of amazing grace! That day when my mother's spirit left her dying body to show herself to me in spirit form; that amazing day when I saw standing before me the spirit forms of my mother, my father, my grandma and grandfather all transmitting love and comfort to me. An amazing demonstration of the power of love!

And afterward I feel an incredible sense of freedom, of having been released from overwhelming burdens. My balance is restored, my peace of mind is restored. I am feeling blessed.

SEPTEMBER 29. My mother's suffering is over. Sister Theresa greets me at the front entrance and takes my hands in hers, "... slipped away peacefully in her sleep ..." is all I recall of her kind words.

Annie calls at the very same moment. Then she calls Neale and later tells me his first question, "How is Mommy?" Neale asked Annie, "What time did Grandma die?" He realized he was thinking about his Grandma just at that moment. How did Annie know the time of my mother's passing? While walking with her boyfriend she suddenly felt a lightening of the burden she'd been carrying all these months and she felt relief for me. She'd felt the presence of her Grandma around her and had glanced at her watch.

> Love, the only true connection
> Binds us, one to another...

I WALK INTO my mother's room. "I love you, Mommy," I whisper. "You are free now, Mom, free. Go in peace dearest Mom, go in love." I pass my hand over her body from her forehead to her feet. I feel the absence of my mother's soul. I look around the room; her presence is no longer here. The spirits of my father, grandma and grandfather have already been here and have led my mother's spirit to a better place.

In the corridor Sister Theresa has been waiting quietly. Now she steps forward to embrace me. She has changed from her spotless white habit and is all in black. I am moved by her show of respect. "Sister," I tell her, "You will always be in my memory for the tender loving care you gave my mother."

In the car my children seek to comfort me. Neale says, "You know, Mommy, I'm almost 35 and I've never seen a woman age as gracefully as you. Daddy's really a very lucky guy to have you for his wife, the best wife anyone could have. I just don't see anyone look like you. Mom, you're a beautiful, beautiful woman." I turn around and Neale notices my surprised expression, "C'mon, Mom, isn't it obvious? Really, it should be obvious to anyone."

Annie reaches forward and takes my hand. Silently, she nods and smiles, her eyes glistening with emotion. My daughter understands the preciousness of Neale's sentiments. An exceedingly loving daughter who understands. My children. How blessed I am.

NOVEMBER 2. Returning to normal. Seeing Annie and Neale regularly again.

Dream. Kaleidoscope in glorious color, swiftly moving presentation of humanity and the civilizations humanity brings into manifestation. Each picture intricately drawn, surrounded by borders of living light. Images grow larger, turning, spinning, glowing, signifying arrival into manifestation, passing into history, rotation left to right. Buddha images, cars, buildings, people, depiction of Depression Era, flowers, the natural world, humanity. The illuminated zigzag borders pulsate with life, the scenes within each border shifting. Wanting to carefully examine each scene I try by force of will to slow the scenes from rushing by in this swiftly rotating kaleidoscope, yet it continues on and on until I awaken.

NOVEMBER 5. Virginia Dutton, my healer friend, came over to give me a healing today. Warmth filled my body and color filled my inner vision. Time stood still. I felt my mother in the room. After our session we sat together sipping tea, quietly discussing what Virginia called our shared healing. Virginia said she'd never experienced so much love. She, too, felt my mother's presence in the room with us and while transmitting healing energy she received a repetitive message: "This kind of love is what life is about!" Virginia thanked me and through her tears said, "You are love personified, and you have just healed me!"

DECEMBER 1. I'm having a massage on my birthday. Suddenly, I see Mom as she looked on the day she was taken from her apartment to Hospice. She's leaning on one arm, her face glowing, our eyes meeting, as it happened on that day. My mother's spirit speaks to me, "It was time," she says, "I had to go." She shows me flashes of us in her apartment: I'm feeding her as she lay on her navy blue sofa, we're praying together, I'm sitting beside her praying for her while she sleeps. Mom shows me our painfully slow walks, she leans on my arms pausing to gain strength for the next step as I walk backwards with her to the bathroom; holding onto her dignity for as long as possible had been supremely important to my mother.

Next, I see my mother standing, youthful and pretty, smiling at me. "You loved me, Fran, and you did everything you could for me. Don't cry, live your years on Earth in joy." She leans toward me as if to embrace me. I see my father standing beside her. In unison they speak, "We love you, Fran, daughter dear. You always brought us so much happiness. Do not mourn us. See, we are happy and at peace here, and we are together." My parents kiss. They transmit waves of love to me and a few times throughout this incredibly marvelous visit my parents sing, Happy Birthday, just the one main line. I remain very still, sending thoughts to tell my parents I miss them and love them. My parents smile and bid me farewell. A minute later the massage is over.

DECEMBER 13. A Magical Experience. Noticing that I was still in need of solace and healing, my compassionate friend Sharon invites me to join Rebbetzin Jungreis' Torah study group on the Upper West Side. One afternoon our elegant Rebbetzin withdraws from her purse a hopelessly tangled ball of red thread and asks for a scissor. The red thread is worn as a bracelet on one's wrist to recall the rare spiritual merit of biblical matriarch Rachel and to provide protection to the wearer. Offering to untangle it, I reach out my hand and Rebbetzin tosses the ball of thread into my lap. I lift up the ball of thread, tug gently on a tangled loop and in seconds with everyone watching, the red thread untangles itself into a nice long length. "How did you do that?" everyone asks.

Crystal Library in the Higher Realms

SOUL TRAVEL to a higher realm away from Earth. I'm floating up a broad expanse of white steps. I have arrived at a building in the classic Greek style of architecture. This magnificent building is a library constructed of pure crystal which is known to me as, "The Crystal Library." Whenever I am brought here by my spirit guides I notice small groups of angelic beings in white robes gathered on the broad steps engaged in peaceful discussion, just as you might see college students gathered after class. As I float up the steps I look upward toward the two large crystal doors that stand wide open. Inside there is a vestibule where a luminous being, my teacher, awaits my arrival. He is holding an enormous crystal book. The book is suffused with light, illumination from within. With knowledge of my visit he welcomes me with friendly thoughts. Before we begin our work I always enjoy peeking inside the crystal library. With unbounded joy and reverence I observe a vast interior, its vastness beyond imagination, its walls lined with crystal bookshelves, all the way up to the high-domed ceiling.

Unusual light, soft and also illuminating, filters in through the crystal dome, infusing this holy place with the essence of truth, intelligence and ultimate peacefulness. Crystal shelves hold enormous crystal volumes like the one my teacher is holding. As I look down the length of this heavenly library the crystal shelves lined with crystal volumes seem to reach into the distant cosmos.

It is time to turn my attention to my teacher-guide, a youthful male unknown to me on Earth but familiar in this setting of soul travel experience, and I pay close attention to the lesson for which I have been brought here. The crystal book that my teacher is holding open could not exist on Earth and he places it before me. It is a book filled with important knowledge and sacred wisdom pertaining to life on Earth. As we look into the book together my teacher's luminosity increases in radiance, he is methodically and helpfully testing me one 'page' at a time. I am infinitely grateful for his help. Information as it appears in the crystal book is composed of hieroglyphs and symbolic shapes. Before my gaze the hieroglyphs and symbolic shapes fade from the center of the 'page' outward as questions and responses posed in the manner of a vibrantly colored hologram arise within a bubble right there in the enormous open crystal book. As the play-act ends the text is restored. My guide speaks informally as if we are close friends. He is skilled at incorporating himself into each scene and teaches me with great earnestness. In the pure crystalline atmosphere of the higher dimension, I understand all that I am taught and eventually realize that these sacred teaching sessions are the source of my 'knowings' here on Earth.

DECEMBER 25. Dinner with Neale and Danny. There is no acknowledgment by my husband of my presence at the table. When I begin to speak Danny speaks louder to override my voice. He directs his comments exclusively to Neale. He doesn't reach over to touch my hand. His dinner table posture blocks my presence; elbow on table, palm against his face, head turned away from me. I'm waiting for an opening to speak with my son and when I finally find an opening Danny adopts demeaning facial expression plus a dismissive hand wave toward me and he finds an excuse to leave the table.

In Danny's brief absence Neale turns to me, "Mom? You know this healing energy you talk about? Why don't you bring some of it to our employees in the Bronx? They could use it." Looking into my eyes as he always does Neale adds, "You should do it, Mom." My son's suggestion stimulates my thoughts and I begin to envision a lunch hour healing circle at the business.

JANUARY 3, 1997, Neale in New York. Sushi dinner, then he shows us his new apartment on the Upper East Side. Brunch with Annie, then up to see her new apartment on the West Side. We had fun, we hugged and kissed a lot. She told me that she thinks about her Grandma and Grandpa every day.

JANUARY 13. Lunch with publisher JoAnn Pello who has read the manuscript of "Song of the Heart" and tells me she would like to publish it. Her new start-up company is not ready yet so in the meantime we maintain our friendship.

JANUARY 17. We hold our first Healing Workshop in a sunny corner of the Honda showroom. We order pizza and set up a circle of chairs to accommodate our eleven women employees. We begin with a discussion about their most pressing needs which leads me to decide upon stress management as the focus of our first meeting together. The guided healing meditation provides healing for one woman's back pain, another's shoulder pain. Our first Healing Workshop is a success!

JANUARY 19. My daughter is loving and affectionate, consistently reminding me of her love. My parents come into my mind offering messages of protection. I heed their counsel which always proves well-placed and wise.

The most powerful force in the universe is Love. Love can pierce the veil between dimensions. Love heals, protects, comforts us and lives on forever. We need only trust enough to allow our hearts to open to the ever present stream of love flowing forth from the Heart of God and allow it to flow through us.

FEBRUARY 15. This morning I awaken to a miraculous gorgeous shimmering light which forms an arc that streams from my upper chest, from the shoulder area, and up over my head, vividly glowing in all colors at once, mostly violet white. To attempt a description of the colors is to diminish the effervescent glory of their presence. The band of light shimmers in a zigzag pattern which melts after about ten minutes into a wavy line, its points softening, while the band, or arc, continues shimmering in vibrant motion.

I leave my bed and stand before the mirror where the shimmering light is reflected all around me. I close my eyes. The light remains so brightly vibrant it's practically blinding even with my eyes closed. The light holds a frequency of loving intelligence and communication. The light speaks to me and raises my awareness of the unseen reality all around us.

FEBRUARY 16. During meditation this morning another communication from my parents. I ask for a physical sign to once again prove they are truly with me and they assure me a sign will be forthcoming.

Afternoon visit to the Metropolitan Museum of Art, a fine setting to receive a sign but although I am alert for it no sign comes.

Philharmonic in the evening, seated in the orchestra, enjoying

Rachmaninoff. I close my eyes and immediately see Mom and Dad. "We are honored, Fran, to have brought you to life on Earth. Many high souls have been assigned to protect you and these protective ones are honored to have this assignment." My eyes are brimming with tears, an abundance of love is filling my whole body and I can hardly contain myself. My parents speak telepathically and I can't tell which of them is speaking; it feels as if they are in a state of pure alignment, their minds having blended in unity, a completely transcendent moment of harmony, for I feel my mind is part of their unity. In this higher place of unity consciousness all is truth.

My parents go on to tell me that my brother was their karma, important for their evolution, not part of my karma. "You were born without negative karma yet you hold yourself to an impossibly high standard, remaining unaware of the truth of your own goodness. You must accept yourself, love yourself and stay away from people who cause you pain. Now that we are no longer in physical life you are free to disassociate from your brother to whatever extent necessary for your well-being. Your love for us brought you into our affairs with him and you took them on as your own. But, Fran, your well-being is of utmost concern to all of us here, watching over you."

Through the layers of my sweater and winter jacket I feel a touch on my upper right arm. A gentle ripple on my arm, like a musician playing flute! Three consecutive ripples on my arm. Instinctively I reach over with my left hand, hoping, almost expecting to feel the physical presence of my parents beside me, but of course all I feel is my jacket. The fabric of my clothing hadn't pressed against my skin, just a beautiful melodious touch. I ask for another touch, this time I will be more alert, and my parents comply. Once again, with no sense of fabric being pressed against my skin, there is definite pressure on my arm! The orchestra soars to Adagio, and Mom and Dad are dancing, smiling, graceful and so very happy that I brought them to the Philharmonic!

At home I take out an old photo album and a picture falls out, my favorite of Mom and Dad. Oh, my! I cover my face with my hands. What's becoming of you, Francine, sitting alone late at night looking at old photographs, crying, talking to spirits all the time! Yet, I know this part of me is just as vital as any other.

FEBRUARY 17. Reading Stanislav Grof's "The Adventure of Self-Discovery," pages 121 to 123. "... encounter with guides, protectors, from spiritual world. They appear spontaneously at a certain stage in an individual's spiritual growth, continue appearing on their own terms or at request of protégé. Messages conveyed by telepathic transfer of thoughts ... intervene in dangerous or difficult experiences on subjects' behalf, give intellectual, moral and spiritual support, help combat evil and destructive forces or create protective shields of positive energy. They introduce themselves by name."

FEBRUARY 18. Very much enjoyed Rabbi Kessin's Kabbalah class. "Our world, here on Earth," Rabbi Kessin teaches, "is governed by justice. The endless world is governed by love."

FEBRUARY 25. Bickering among our employees, particularly between office staff, and the sales department, is causing undo stress for everyone so my current plan for our healing workshop at the dealership is to focus on conflict resolution. In addition to conflict resolution the women enjoy discussing dreams and spiritual experiences. Time management is also an important issue. Altogether, our healing workshop is a rewarding experience and although it is tiring for me I do enjoy interacting with the people, our employees, who I feel a responsibility for as if they are my family.

MARCH 15. Danny attended an NBC business dinner declaring that wives were not invited which I declared preposterous. Many of the executives and celebrity reporters from the network are women. When he came home after the event which took place only a few blocks from our apartment he admitted that other dealers had brought their wives. "Oh, well, sorry Honey," he said, "you were right." Ignoring our theater tickets and dinner reservations for tomorrow night he accepted an invitation to a hockey game. He left at seven this morning for another golf outing without saying goodbye knowing he won't be home until very late tonight.

MARCH 21. This morning Sharon, Mom's home health aide, calls to check in with me. It's so kind of her to call but it brings me back to those terrible days. Instantly, I'm immersed in sadness, back in Mom's studio apartment watching my mother suffer, and a great melancholy sweeps over me. "I called just to say, Francine, you are the most angelic person I've ever known." Imagine.

APRIL 8. When Danny momentarily leaves the dinner table tonight Neale turns to Annie and observes, "Daddy is a superficial guy. If Mommy didn't look as good as she does, if Mommy wasn't one in a million, Daddy never would have stayed married." Imagine.

JULY 1. Visit to friends' summer home in the Hamptons. My friend invited her neighbor to join us for lunch, hoping that I might help him in his battle against cancer. The neighbor, a physician, is sitting across from me. My friend serves a lovely summer lunch and after a while I introduce the subject of spiritual healing to which the neighbor offers no response so I decide not to pursue it. In that single moment I see his left arm and hand as if my eyes have suddenly acquired x-ray vision. I'm looking at the man, at his physical self, and yet the flesh and soft tissue of his left arm and hand do not exist. I see instead a sickly green skeletal arm and hand. This highly unusual vision is accompanied by a knowing that this man's unfortunate fate is to lose his heroic battle and he will pass within two weeks.

July 13. My friend calls from her home in the Hamptons. Her neighbor passed away this morning.

Angels & Us

JULY 14. At six o'clock tonight Neale called. "Mom," he said, and was unable to finish his sentence.

"What is it, Neale darling? Are you alright?"

"Well, Mom, Tracey needs a doctor."

Tracey is Neale's current girlfriend and suddenly I knew the cause of my son's distress.

"I've been honest with her, Mom. I've told her I will assume all responsibility for her welfare and for the baby's welfare but I don't want to get married. Mom, Tracey is not someone I want to be married to."

"Well, a baby is always a blessing, Neale. I love you and I'll always be there for you."

I lie down flat and commune with my spiritual guides. This child's soul is from the soul group of my spirit guides. He is arriving in accordance with a prior agreement. I will transmit unconditional love to this baby's soul, the child of my son. To balance the disharmony surrounding the circumstances of his birth it is essential to impart to this baby a strong sense of family, of belonging, a strong sense of being loved.

The future is crashing all around me and flooding my mind, I can think of nothing else. I see heartbreak for Tracey. I will be supportive. Neale must investigate his legal rights. My guides have spoken. In accordance with our pre-arranged plan I am to be a guardian angel on Earth for my grandchild, the firstborn son of my firstborn son.

And in conjunction with all of this, my daughter is engaged to be married! Annie is entitled to her own share of happiness and I will help her through her passage and do all I can to sustain an aura of joy around all her wedding plans.

Into our lives our new baby is crash landing, like a startling shooting star. As both my children move through their individual life-changing events each has a need to reach out every day to their mother for comfort and practical advice.

This child, I assure Neale, will surely look like him and be a lovely, charming child. Neale says that his most vivid childhood memories are of being with me. As we talk I sense my son is growing calm, moving from initial shock to excited expectation.

This baby is barely formed and yet, his effect upon our lives is truly profound. The future is constantly on my mind. All will be blessed in Heaven and on Earth. When Neale holds his baby for the very first time and looks into his eyes for the very first time he will fall completely in love and he will be a wonderful loving father.

JULY 19. Dream. Seated ancient Asian woman, motherly demeanor, and on her lap she holds two delightful babies. One is a boy, one is a girl. The babies, very alert and very beautiful, are facing a visitor, me! The babies, the woman says, are soulmates. Which one will come to be our blessing? Suddenly, the baby on the left, the boy, becomes extraordinarily radiant, surrounded with glowing light and then he looks directly at me as if he has something to tell me. We have been together in many loving lifetimes, he tells me! He smiles a glorious sun-lit smile and his smile shows him to be a perfect replica of his father!

So, I have been introduced to my grandson! In the higher realms he and I are well-acquainted and we share an ancient bond of love! He is a soul to whom my son is profoundly connected. I offer heartfelt gratitude to my spiritual guides for arranging this transcendent meeting! Oh, how my heart is singing!

Annie tells me that Neale is very concerned about me. How does Mommy feel? he asked her. Is Mommy angry with him? Neale requires more reassurance, she tells me, he needs to know more clearly that I am happy about the baby.

At lunch with Tracey today I tell her we love her, the baby is already part of our family, and very loved. Tracey's eyes fill with tears. I tell her she is my daughter and I will do anything for her. She is worried about being accepted because she is not Jewish and she heard that Jewish families are not at all happy about interfaith relationships. I told her that for us religious differences are of no account and in no way shall dampen our love for her. "Neale is so very loved and so very precious to us in every way. You are having Neale's child and we accept this child fully as our own. We already love this baby! And we love you!"

The baby's soul has already entered its body. We all feel its presence. This must be an extraordinarily loving and evolved soul to be affecting each of us so positively at such an early stage.

JULY 29. Our marriage is eroding. My husband's lack of interest in me brings emptiness into every area of my life. He demonstrates no desire to become more accommodating or respectful toward me. I tell him we are separating. He doesn't argue.

JULY 30. The large mirror in the master bathroom is a portal, a window onto another dimension. Lights off, door open just enough to permit a stream of light from outside, I call on my spirit guides and ask, "Please, dear guides, show me who I am." Then, in place of the light being forms I usually see reflected in the mirror, in golden light, I see a violet light emanate from the top of my head. The light pulsates and is enhanced. I feel Kundalini force rise up my legs from the soles of my feet, through the base of my spine, right up to my crown chakra. Pulsating violet light all around me, Kundalini force soaring through my body, accompanied by a simple message: Gentleness. You are gentleness, Mother. Go forth in peace and in love.

Driving home after ordering flowers for Annie's wedding, big discussion in the car. In Annie's opinion we are all responding to the baby's arrival extremely well and for her part she looks forward to becoming Aunt Annie.

AUGUST 2. Dream. In Tanglewood for the weekend. Dreamed all night long of flying accompanied by strong feelings of foreboding. I was flying above Manhattan, looking down on the city at night but the city was dark, completely black and eerily disturbing.

Like a bird following its instinct I'm flying to a vantage point several blocks north of Battery Park high above the city streets. Focusing on my location I recognize across the Hudson River the familiar Jersey shoreline. The Statue of Liberty easily identified is exactly where it's supposed to be, on Liberty Island in the Harbor. Turning my gaze eastward expecting to see the Twin Towers to my surprise the Twin Towers, which ought to be looming above me, are not there. I look around and am shocked to see nothing but empty space where the Towers ought to be. Alarmed, I turn in all directions hoping the Twin Towers will reappear exactly where they're supposed to be.

Widening my investigation, I fly to an open window in a rather tall nearby building and settle myself just inside the room. Looking downward to the street I have a perfect view of the strangest sight: a lone remaining remnant of the Towers leaning, covered and surrounded by some kind of ominous white mass of dust on the ground. Growing frightened I see a large bombed out open space where the Towers had stood. Moving away from the window, looking around the room in which I have landed, everything in the room which seems to be a living room, is blanketed completely by the same white dust as outside. The white dust which I begin to realize is actually white ash, gives me an uncomfortable creepy feeling. The interior of this room appears altogether surreal. I find myself standing by the sofa, facing a cocktail table set with what I presume to be a china tea pot and tea service, all completely enveloped in the white ash. The window through which I entered is now directly opposite and I notice it's an unusually large square window, architecturally attractive. The scene is captured in my mind like a photograph, indelible in my memory for its utter strangeness. A shudder runs through me. What has happened here?

Next, I find myself in mid-town my vantage point now the rooftop of one of the office buildings. I view the surrounding buildings, the Hudson River beyond, the Jersey shoreline. Then I'm standing on the street and feel a strong desire to get away. I must escape! With that thought I lift up off the sidewalk, fly to the Upper East Side, and feeling increasingly disturbed, observe a massive blackout. Everything has changed in my city!

Awake, back in our hotel room in the Berkshires, I am thoroughly shaken, lacking comprehension of what I just experienced.

On September 11, 2001, I understood my prophetic dream. During that awful week the New York Times published a photo on Page 1 of Ground Zero as seen through the window of an apartment overlooking the site. Immediately, upon seeing the photo, I gasped and clasped my hands to my heart! The large square window was distinctively recognizable. The photographer's camera had captured the delicate china tea service set on the cocktail table covered with white ash from the catastrophe as was everything else in the room. The room appeared exactly as I'd witnessed it on the night of August 2, 1997.

AUGUST 11. Dinner with Annie, her fiancé, Neale and Tracey. Humorously, Neale says, "Mom, I want you to take care of the baby for his first five years and then I'll take over. So will you do that, Mom?"

I look over at Tracey and she is smiling. Everyone is smiling. "If that's the way things turn out then I will."

Annie says, "I would very much love to take care of my nephew." The whole family is in a wonderful mood. I assure Tracey and Neale that they will both be very good parents. Neale has chosen the name, "Steven," for his son and we all agree it is a very good name that will suit this child well.

AUGUST 17. Happy Dream. Steven is a little boy and he and I and Annie are walking in midtown in New York City. Steven is an adorable child, smart and witty. We enter an office building through revolving glass doors, Steven turns around to look at us through the glass panels of the doors, winking and blinking with great humor and electric energy; his mind alert and inquisitive. Shining dark brown eyes filled with a wonderful zest for life. A most appealing child walking with a straight and steady gait, quick and agile.

I also feel, while immersed in the dream, that my grandson will 'know' people, understand who people are. He will be wise for his age, insightful beyond his years. Steven will be known by many people, loved by all, held back by no one.

The imagery of revolving glass doors in the dream is telling me that we have been "around together" in other lifetimes and that although Steven is not yet born he can see us and he's happy. By winking and blinking he's saying, "Hi, Grandma! Hi, Aunt

Annie! It's me, Steven!" He's happy and excited about coming into his new life and can hardly wait to get here!

Speaking to Neale on the phone I ask him, "Remember my search for a healer and psychic person to help you and Annie? Well, guess what?"

Cheerfully, Neale replies, "Wait, don't tell me, you're it, Mommy!"

Then I pass on to him the following message. "This is a soul of great kinship with Neale, desiring to be reunited. Father and son will share a wonderful bond of love and closeness destined to enrich Neale's life beyond measure. Bring this message to your son."

"That's really wonderful, Mom. The only trouble is, the baby comes attached to a mother."

"Neale, it's natural when we face change to feel a little scared of it and this is certainly a major change you are facing in your life, but ultimately it will be wonderful for you, Neale, you'll see." He listened quietly.

OCTOBER 8. Eight year anniversary of my father's passing.

President Clinton dream. I am speaking on the phone with President Clinton, and yet, simultaneously, I see him seated at his presidential desk. He is intrigued with my message of using the power of language, in which he is so skilled, to lead people toward the highest vision of themselves. Specifically, not speaking down to people, or blaming others, or taking out one's personal feelings of anger and frustration on others, but moving beyond all that, completely rising above personal feelings into a place of altruistic service. Focus only a person's best qualities, help people envision their own higher selves and move into their own higher selves. The president smiled, acknowledged the wisdom of following this philosophy in his efforts to create a better world.

OCTOBER 10. Neale called, happy and excited, from the doctor's office. He and Tracey listened to the baby's heartbeat and ultrasound confirmed it's a boy! Expected birth date March 9. The doctor says the baby is big, with big hands and feet.

OCTOBER 11. I'm resting in bed with a flu when Neale calls and says he and Tracey will be here in a few minutes. I rush to make the bed, brush my teeth and splash cold water on my face. We have a lovely visit, filled with excitement over Steven. Tracey and Neale watched their baby move his arm to rest his hand on his cheek exactly like Neale! Tracey asked me to be her partner for pre-natal classes. I showed Neale a closet shelf where his horsey is resting, waiting, and he is very moved that I've saved it all these years. Suddenly, so many things are important to him, memories which for years have lain fallow in his mind.

OCTOBER 21. For Neale's 36th Birthday.

>
> The measure of a man is taken
> Not on a tranquil day
> When all the winds are still
> And flowers barely sway
>
> But when the tide comes crashing
> And storm clouds are gathering
> When a man's freedom is ebbing
> That's when Heaven's assessing

Francine Vale

The man's measure is taken
While his mind is on the struggle
While he's thinking and planning
The strategy of the battle

And while Heaven is watching
The man considers his options
Deciding hour by hour
Discovering new convictions

And as he draws ever nearer
A just and fair solution
Clouds grow lighter and disappear
The struggle that seemed oppressive

Fades in rays of sunshine
His path grows ever clearer
As new love removes the shadows
And the man is redefining

The meaning of the battle
The definition of his freedom
And that's when his measure is taken
And Heaven, well Heaven, is smiling

My spirit guides transmitted to me the following message: Steven will look like, walk like, talk like his father. He will be smart and humorous. He will love you all. The boy will be delightful. No hardship will cause him to err, being of strong mind, body and spirit. A most wonderful son. You will feel familiar with him as he is one of us. Your grandson Steven shall inherit all the finest characteristics of the family. You shall see.

October 23. At Annie's request I accompanied her and her fiancé to be their marriage license witness.

November 7. Every day, all day, Danny is studying the racing form in anticipation of the Breeder's Cup race. And every day he manages to bring me to tears.

Tracey and Neale have had a fight and Neale has flown off to Las Vegas with Jeff, his best buddy. He just called me with two requests: Tracey needs money to buy an outfit for Annie's wedding. Also, can I pick up a tuxedo shirt for him.

"Neale, this impromptu trip of yours a day before your sister's wedding, is causing a lot of aggravation."

"Mom, I don't want anyone forcing me to do anything!"

I'm feeling sick inside, and then Annie calls, "Mom? Where's Neale?"

Knowing how upset she will be I have to tell her, and I want to cry for my daughter's disappointment and her worry that her brother might miss her wedding, which is tomorrow.

At bedtime, replacing the long fluorescent bulb in our bedroom cabinet, the bulb slips from my hands and shatters into millions of slivers, catching in the threads of my brocade robe and across the length and width of our grooved wood floor. And as usual I'm barefoot. Danny remains in bed, watches while I clean up the dangerous glass and when the floor is finally clean my beautiful robe, which I bought on our trip to Japan, now hopelessly embedded with hundreds of slivers of glass, has to be disposed of.

Tomorrow is Annie's wedding day! Years later Annie tells me that the night before her wedding, at approximately the same hour that the fluorescent bulb slipped from my hands, shattering into millions of slivers, she and her husband-to-be were engaged in an argument and my daughter felt inner foreboding that her marriage would become a hurtful time for her. But she did what many of us do; she cast the foreboding aside and turned, with all her heart, toward the positive, hopeful path.

To calm myself from nervous tension I decide to listen to a Nigel Taylor guided meditation tape. The opening minutes of the meditation are soothing my nerves. Suddenly, I find myself inside an ancient Temple. Appearing spontaneously before me, is an altar on which is set the sarcophagus of a royal man. I know he is the King, his young and slender likeness painted on the sarcophagus which will soon be placed within a larger sarcophagus. The spirits of those who assisted me in the beginning of my life's lessons materialized in a semi-circle guarding the sarcophagus in the center of the Royal Ancient Egyptian Temple. All my loved ones in that lifetime, who are once again my loved ones in this life, form a semi-circle before the sarcophagus. We gather this way in love and support. Then the spirit of the man inside the sarcophagus appears, and it is the spirit of my husband. He does not take a place in the semi-circle with us. He hovers from one to the other. No one is solid, I can see through them! The spirit of my husband communicates love and gratitude for the companionship we provided one to the other, for the joys and sorrows we shared.

I request healing and restoration and then I sleep an otherworldly sleep. When I awaken the sparks of light are all around me and I feel restored to peace and strength.

November 9. Annie is a bride today! She is beautiful, refined and poised in the gorgeous lace gown we chose for her in a Madison Avenue bridal shop. The gown hugs her slender body and opens to a graceful flair. Exquisite. She is glowing and compliments abound. People are struck by her loving presence which enhances every encounter with her. At the wedding table a light shines above Annie, her illuminated veil casts a remarkable holy light around her face. It is an elegant wedding and now I have a married daughter. Later, Annie tells me that everything went by so fast it seemed that her wedding party was over in a flash. With all my heart and soul I pray for my daughter's happiness.

November 13. Concert at Philharmonic. I close my eyes and see beautiful indigo and golden light. Warmth engulfs my face and my sharp headache fades away.

Then I see Mom and Dad. They have chosen to appear in the downstairs sitting room of my house, a room they had so enjoyed, and Dad is seated in his favorite chair. The house is symbolic of one's self, one's heart. And so often my parents have chosen for their visitations, the setting of the house we lived in while my children were growing up, a place that symbolizes for them, true heart love. When he was alive with us, my father often thanked me for the loving acceptance and comfort they felt in my home. My home, he told me, was a special place for them where they felt even happier than when they were in their own home. Whenever he said this my father's eyes grew misty, I felt his tender emotions, and quickly became emotional myself. "Oh, Dad," I always answered inadequately, standing before the profundity of his gratitude. So it is in perfect keeping with the characters of both my parents, this strong soul desire to bring into open awareness all the deepest feelings of their hearts; even now, when they must reach me through dimensions of time and space, to satisfy this deep urge to make things right.

My parents have decided to reveal to me the following story and my father is the one to speak while my mother sits on the arm of his chair in agreeable support.

"As your life is moving forward, Fran dear, into a new cycle," my father says, "It is now time to complete an outworn cycle. In a previous lifetime your brother saved our lives." I am shown a scene of a near drowning in the rapids of a great river, maybe the Columbia River. A canoe has top-sided, and a man and woman are struggling in the white foaming water. A strong, young man who happens to be on the bank of the river jumps in and breathtakingly rescues them. "Time went by," my father continues, "and it came to pass that our rescuer needed help and he asked for help in his time of trouble. While it is true, as you are now thinking, that your mother and I are mostly kind toward people, at that time we made a regrettable choice, the reason is of no importance, we did not come to his aid. It was, therefore, decreed in the higher realms that restitution must be made and so we agreed to give the better part of our lives in service to our rescuer, who it was decided would be born into this life as our son. You, Fran, were not required to alleviate anyone's burdens, you were born to us for other reasons . . . to find your own inner strength, to discover your spiritual power despite the roadblocks on your path."

I am seated in the orchestra, the New York Philharmonic is extraordinary tonight, the music is building to a crescendo, tears are running down my cheeks. My father goes on to explain, "The abundance of loving support you gave your mother and me through all the years was never required of you, dearest daughter, nor was the infinite compassion you felt on our behalf, you 'owed' us nothing, but it was," he said, "a measure of who you are. We have looked into it, Fran," and I was shown an enormous crystal ball, representative of Earth, wherein holograms appear in response to understanding sought by inquiring souls, "and it has been given to us: you hold no anger toward your parents for whatever lack we imposed upon you, and we find a complete absence of bitterness within you. What we have been shown is a beauteous being of light, who while in a human body, remains aware of her soul consciousness and holds an intention to radiate love to all. These rare qualities, daughter dear, allows us and all who enter your life to proceed on our paths with purity and love abounding between us, with no negative karma accrued between us. We are free, dearest Fran, to move along without encumbrances between us. This is the highest gift any soul, living as a human being, can bestow on others as all of us proceed on our journeys."

The Law of Karma, judging none as good nor bad, seeing all as it is, calls for balance in all manifested energy. The soul's journey is a journey toward balance where it ultimately discovers to its unbounded joy and bliss, harmony and lovingkindness do prevail like a canopy of glorious golden light shining over and above and within all things.

Morning meditation brings yet another spiritual visitation; today my mother is by herself, reclining on the sofa in her studio apartment, appearing healthy and very pretty. Immediately, tears well in my eyes. My mother is telling me that she was wrong to have been so demanding of me and she is asking for my forgiveness. "I was stupid," she says, "but now I'm wiser."

"I forgive you, Mom," I answer through my tears, "and I love you both so very much."

Now Dad appears and they are speaking to me of Annie's wedding, how they'd been present and how when she was little, Annie Angel Face, the affectionate name that Dad gave her was really perfectly suited to Annie. "We just couldn't have lived long enough, Fran dear. We will always be near you, protecting you from harm. There's still a lot more for you to do with your life, daughter dear."

Although my mother and father lived humble lives their soul energy reveals Masters of caring love as well as an awesome power to manifest in visual form, to communicate with me creatively and in the language of the heart which is always telepathic! I somehow know that in the distant past they lived exalted lives. An orator in ancient Greece, my father was also a revered scribe in the ancient way of carving great wisdom into stone. He had been fascinated by his ability to become as one with the tools of his craft. This art remained as a soul quality and so he had chosen for this life, to create with his hands a harmony of lead, ink, paper and machinery, a printer who would always earn enough to maintain his family yet never enough for luxury. He had chosen a challenging life. A Master of loving kindness and time-honored skills had lived in the Bronx on Vyse Avenue!

And so, we know not who any of us is. Therefore, it becomes clear that the highest way to move through our days is to choose loving kindness in every encounter. And as we help one another progress, with love and kindness, throughout our time here, humanity becomes uplifted.

The souls of my mother and father are wise. Coming to me with transcendent love they display great skill in assisting me through this current life passage in which my life is bound up with the lives of my precious children. The wonder of it all is overwhelming so I lie down to take it all in and then arise to go for a long walk.

November 26. Today I spoke to my palm tree. "Thank you beautiful tree, for your many years of loyalty. Thank you for providing beauty in our home. Thank you for bringing me peace. Thank you!" Then, one palm frond bowed. Ever so gently, the palm frond bowed! So moved by my plant's response, I rose from the sofa, walked over to my palm tree in the neighboring window and here, too, a single frond bowed toward me. I then walked over to my palm tree in the expansive corner window, this tallest one reached up to the ceiling, and to my amazement it happened again, a palm frond bowed to me! Imagine!

NOVEMBER 28. Message from spirit guide:

> The boy, Steven, is to be yours to nurture. The boy will require maturity coupled with capacity for selfless love which you will provide. He is a gentle soul whose light is a brilliant one, a shining star destined to be seen by all the world! And you shall be as a guardian and in this role you shall enjoy a wonderful adventure. And we shall be with you, helping you to bring out the child's gifts and reveal them to the world!

DECEMBER 5. Tracey called from Los Angeles but I missed her call and when I returned the call she didn't pick up.

DECEMBER 8. Neale called early, he's flying up this evening for our monthly family dinner. He tells me that while exercising Tracey felt sharp pain in her back and a blood test indicated kidney infection. Neale told her, Forget Hawaii vacation, return promptly to New York. He said Tracey will meet us tonight at the restaurant.

We're seated at our favorite table at the Ocean Club, the round table in the corner, porcelain Picasso plates illuminated on the walls, worried about Tracey, when Neale receives a message from her. She has decided to continue on to Hawaii after all and will be back in ten days. Neale's thoughts are centered on the future. To us he proposes, sell the business, move to Florida, Dad will run a used car operation, Mommy will help care for Steven. He wants his son to live in his house with Tracey. Danny laughs and waves his hand in dismissal.

The urgency of my son's request, his deep heartfelt desire, reaches directly into my heart. His plan calls for upheaval in my life, yet I must go. Seated here in this lovely restaurant, feeling my son's anxiety, his trust in me, feeling the love of my children here at our special table, where they came to celebrate their parents' 37th wedding anniversary, I decide to fulfill my son's request.

December 16. 11:30 a.m. Danny calls. Enza, Tracey's friend, called from California with a message for Neale. Tracey's water broke and she's in an ambulance on her way to Freeman Hospital in Englewood.

11:45 a.m. Enza calls me. Tracey hasn't arrived at the hospital yet and Enza is crying.

11:55 a.m. I put in a call to our doctor here in New York. Baby is 28 weeks.

12:00 noon. I call Annie.

12:05 p.m. I call Frank Andrews, my psychic friend; instead of getting his usual answering machine Frank actually answers the phone. Says he will meditate on it and call me later.

12:15 p.m. I call Danny. Says he will fly out with me.

12:40 p.m. Neale calls. He's upset and angry with Tracey. Before she left he'd argued with her, adamantly opposed to her traveling.

1:10 p.m. Neale calls. Tracey called him, hysterical. She wants me to call her.

1:15 p.m. Tracey is crying uncontrollably and while we are on the phone the doctor enters her room to explain his plan. "Call me back," she cries.

1:55 p.m. "Have you spoken to Tracey?" Neale asks. We are waiting for ultrasound report. Heartbeat good. Maybe the baby's weight will be good, he's big for developmental stage. Neale's in a terrible state.

"Neale, darling, the baby's not going to die! He's going to pull through! I know he will!" Hasn't it all been arranged in Heaven?

"Mom, can you get better information from the doctor?" My plan to fly right out to L.A comforts him. God help me!

2:25 P.M. New York doctor returns my call. Tracey has ruptured membrane, danger of infection, doctor in Englewood giving baby medication for his lungs. Maturity of baby's lungs is crucial. Old sorrow of baby Adam, my own loss, my own broken heart, washes over me. Doctor says the mother's travel was detrimental to baby's well-being. Neale screaming on the phone to Tracey, worried about bringing a retarded baby into the world, did not endear him to the doctor.

2:40 P.M. Danny calls. If I wait for tomorrow to fly out he'll go with me.

3:00 P.M. Call Tracey. Usual hospital woes. They aren't telling her anything. She has IV with antibiotics, trying to eat.

3:20 P.M. Call Neale. Relay doctor's latest information. He reports that Tracey is feeling very guilty. Neale is distraught, says she should feel guilty. He told her to stay home, sit on the couch for the next three months and go nowhere. He asked me if he should call her. "It would be very comforting to her if you do and upsetting her any more is not going to help," I said. Maybe the baby is bigger than the doctors' estimate. Oh, God, please help us!

4:05 P.M. Annie calls from work for update.

4:15 P.M. I call Tracey to offer comfort. Neale's terribly frightened, I tell her, and his fear, his anxiety, is coming out as anger. Neale did call her, she tells me, and she is relieved to know that I'm flying out tomorrow.

4:30 P.M. Danny calls for update.

5:00 P.M. Frank Andrews returns my call. He doesn't feel a tragedy. Will be scary, he says, but will be okay. Tough situation, Frank adds.

5:10 P.M. Neale calls for Frank's insight. Neale very concerned about baby receiving steroids. Doesn't want his baby harmed by drugs. The thought makes him crazy. Also, waiting for latest blood test results. If baby has infection, nothing will save him. No infection, doctors will work to save him.

1:00 A.M. I, who rarely drink alcohol, am saved tonight by two strong Bloody Marys.

DECEMBER 17. 9:00 A.M. Plane lifting. I pass every moment of the entire flight immersed in prayer for Steven's well-being.

11:00 P.M. In our hotel room in Marina Del Rey, reviewing the day's events. At 1:30 this afternoon we arrived at the hospital. With mutual feelings of enormous relief that I am here with her, Tracey and I held onto one another's hands. I remained at her bedside for the rest of the day. The ob/gyn doctor as well as the neo-natal doctor explained the situation to us. Daniel Freeman Hospital has an unusually well-appointed neo-natal care unit. They dutifully explained all the terrible dangers our baby is facing. I won't allow my thoughts to dwell on even the possibility of one more thing going awry. I discipline my thoughts to focus on the remarkable strides in medicine. I focus my thoughts and visualize Steven in excellent health.

Tracey asks me for a healing. I feel strong energetic activity within her womb. I feel a beautiful stream of love emanating from within Tracey's womb. Steven wants to be born! He wants to be with us on Earth! But to satisfy some mysterious spiritual purpose, it's up to us, his family, to prove our love for him! My hands held above him, transmitting Divine healing light to him, purest love to him, sends the message to Steven's soul that he is greatly desired and will be loved beyond measure.

As a result of the healing Tracey says she feels lighter and less frightened. She asks me, "Francine, will you do healings for me every day?"

"Of course, I will, sweetheart." I lean over to press my cheek against hers. "For you and for Steven, every day. When I arrive in the morning we'll do a healing right away, then later in the afternoon and then at night before the nurses kick us out we'll do another one to get you through the night. And Danny found a golf course somewhere around here so he'll drop me off, then go play. He says he'll come back to the hospital when it starts getting dark and bring you whatever you want to eat. Sound good to you?"

"Oh, Francine, I will never forget what you and Danny are doing for me."

"I love you, Tracey."

"I love you, too!" And then we embrace.

On the phone with Neale and Annie I focus my conversations on the positive. Neale's personal challenge is to calm down and as much as possible, remain calm. I call on the angels: Please, dear angels, I call on you to stay beside my precious son and bring him assistance in meeting his challenge.

For now, the healing love and light pouring through me from the angels, spiritual beings advanced in healing who are here to help and guide us through our crises, is filling my heart with more than hope; I am filled with certitude that this baby's destiny is to be with us, beautiful and healthy. Our love for him, our dedication to his well-being, and most of all, the dedication of his mother and father to his well-being, is noted in the higher realms. Especially important is the willingness and readiness of the father to devote his best and most powerful energy to the highest good for his child, which demonstrates to the angels that the time is now, to move fully into healing mode for this baby.

While engaged in transmitting angelic healing, deep insight regarding the human drama unfolding before me is often imparted by means of the light. Within my mind arises an open portal of golden light and a process I have come to know as 'blending' occurs. We carry within us 'soul memory' of who we are, our destiny on Earth, memory of people, opportunities and events we have agreed before birth to experience in our lives. In spiritual terminology, these memories are enclosed within the spark of light that is our soul which resides in the center of our chest, within the heart chakra. These memories may also be envisioned as held within the cellular structure of our physical bodies. One single enlightened thought becomes a catalyst to prod open a single cell, like a tiny flower blossoming under a shining, golden sun. One cell vibrating at a higher frequency, as scientific studies have shown, raises the frequency of surrounding cells, a cascade of blossoming cells ensues, and a higher, finer vibration comes into being. This may be recognized as a human becoming enlightened.

Every time the angels blend their energies with mine for the purpose of helping others additional cells within my body begin to blossom. In this way, I become blessed with increased light, golden light, a glowing inner sun. The spark of light which is my soul expands within my heart chakra allowing me to become more of my true authentic self. An inner signal similar to a current of electricity transmits in a flash to my mind and the portal of light opens. This process holds true for every human being on Earth.

The angels have advised me to share their wise counsel, intended to help each one of us manifest all the goodness we hold within ourselves: "When we take steps in our own behalf, the angels smile upon us. When we take steps on behalf of others, the angels blend their energy with ours." We are designed to help one another. Whatever life work we may have chosen, opportunities to help others will arise, for helping others is meant to be foremost on our journey toward enlightenment. We may notice that every time we reach out in service to another our inner light expands and along with this, our personal growth accelerates. We feel good inside; on those days we have abundant smiles to share with others, we feel closer to our higher self. On those days the angels draw very near to us.

While engaged in transmitting healing to Tracey and Steven the angels are blending their energies with mine. Later, while alone and peaceful, awareness of new insight unfolds gently within my mind. The soul of this child, which is in truth an enlightened soul, has a great mission to fulfill in the life he is about to enter. As with many enlightened souls the mission is many-faceted, requiring multi-dimensional capabilities while in human form. First, the angels have told me, his very presence will be a catalyst for his mother, who is being guided to learn selfless love.

In a past life as native Americans, Steven was my infant son, son of a Navajo chief and Hopi medicine woman. He held within him a mighty acorn which in time would grow to confer wisdom as well as strength, upon his tribe. To gain possession of his unique power a warlike tribe, known by the sign of the Thunderbolt, traveled westward and stole him away. My baby's nurturing was entrusted to a female member of their tribe. She was a wild woman and it was thought by the elders of the tribe that caring for an infant would create healing for her. My infant son was handed over to this wild woman so that she might learn, through caring for a helpless baby, a sense of responsibility. However, the plan failed.

By the Law of Karma and the Law of Grace she is being given, in this current life, an opportunity to make restitution, and rise to responsible motherhood. Steven, in an offering of service, will help her accomplish this. He will engage her sensibilities in every way. By his physical beauty, his gift of insight, his intellect; by all this and more he will help her. But, it is known in the higher realms that despite her close proximity, once again, to a highly advanced soul, her ability to learn selfless love shall remain elusive within the span of this lifetime. The contract between Tracey and Steven is limited in time as we know it on Earth. This is also the Law of Karma.

The open portal within my mind revealed to me that my son, Neale, had been in our native American lifetime, my firstborn son then as now; Neale and Steven had been brothers in that lifetime. A prior soul connection exists between them, a connection of love and goodness, even mutual protection. In this way I am shown that wondrous blessings await them both, all within the fullness of time.

DECEMBER 18. Tracey is in better spirits today. She talks about her terror in the ambulance. I try my best to comfort her. "Well, you moved past it, Tracey, and now you know you possess resources of inner strength you didn't know you had." At 10:30 A.M. we begin the first healing of the day.

In the afternoon we do another healing. I tell Tracey to visualize golden light coming down from God and surrounding the baby. I feel a tremendous stream of heat flowing from my hands. Tracey says she feels the heat strongly and it relaxes her. I feel waves of energy coursing through me while simultaneously, Tracey's eyes are flowing with tears.

I explain to Neale all the developments since yesterday. I tell him only positive news. Replenishment of amniotic fluid, the focus of my healings, is occurring. Measured in half ounces, the baby is gaining weight and is healthy. Tracey is calmer today. Annie is in Arizona with her husband and she phones directly after Neale. I am exhausted.

DECEMBER 19. I call Tracey's grandmother today to assure her that Tracey is in good hands and she should try not to worry. I call our doctor in New York to keep him abreast of events. The doctors and nurses here offer compassionate and knowledgeable care. Steven is receiving excellent medical support. Tracey says Neale wants to bring her and Steven to live with him in Florida. In the meantime, Danny and I are renting an apartment here.

DECEMBER 21. We're up to 29 weeks and are praying to make it to 30.

DECEMBER 22. Neale is here; it is a comfort to be together. We finally get Tracey transferred to a private room. As if an invisible star fills the room I feel an enormous energy of love dashing about the room, from one to the other. Steven is surely absorbing this abundance of love. For hours on end Neale massages Tracey's feet. At first he is reluctant, but finally he agrees, to tour the neo-natal unit. He's wincing at the sight of all the medical technology, the painful thought of his son being hooked up to these machines. Neale reminisces with me about his childhood. We discuss his many boyhood accidents. "My son," he declares, "will never be permitted to ride a motorcycle!" He's telling Tracey that she needs me to help her take care of the baby. I feel as if Tracey is my daughter. May God protect all my children!

DECEMBER 23. When I awaken I feel as if I've been soul traveling, and although I have no memory of where I was I have returned knowing that Steven will be healthy and there is no longer any cause for fear.

While transmitting healing today my spirit guides tell me that healing is complete.

Doctor stops by on his rounds. To our delight he tells us Steven is a smart baby. Sonogram shows him moving all his fingers as if he were a pianist. The medical staff is pleased with his progress. It is noted that in the recent 36-hour time period no amniotic fluid has been lost!

Danny is off playing golf. Neale, Tracey and I talk about Neale's childhood. He's thinking a lot about his childhood these days which he recalls, was bound up with me.

"Your son will require a lot of love and nurturing," I say. "You'll have to tell him every day he's a good boy and you love him."

"How do you know?" Neale asks.

"He's making that aspect of himself known right now."

"Suppose he isn't a good boy?"

"He's a very good boy, you'll see."

DECEMBER 25. We're all in Tracey's room. Stress is showing in Neale's face; I offer a healing and it relaxes him. It's getting late, and as Danny and I are leaving I turn around and smile. Neale is sitting on Tracey's bed, his hand on her belly, sending healing love to his son.

DECEMBER 28. Tomorrow is 30 weeks. Doctor has just frightened Tracey. The latest sonogram is showing amniotic fluid loss again and she tells Tracey that the threat of cerebral palsy passes with week 32. A doctor told me on the first day about this threat but I have kept it to myself. Tracey is crying and asks for healing.

Loving healing vibrations are flowing through me into Steven. Oh, my dear spiritual companions, I pray with all my heart and soul, if ever a healing is accomplished let it be now, for our Steven!

DECEMBER 29. Early morning, terrace door open to a new dawn and crisp fresh air. I'm praying as usual. Suddenly, I feel lightheaded, removed from my physical environment.

Angels are here! In the room with me! I'm in the presence of a very large angel! An amazing cloud of glowing luminescence, white and violet light all around! I see the angel's large graceful wings! He is very tall, about nine feet tall, clothed in white silken robes, a small harp held in his left hand nestles against the folds of his shining robe. The harp is radiating supernal healing music of celestial origin. The angel is accompanied by a host of smaller angels, six on his left side and six on his right side, and their feet do not touch the floor. Altogether they form a semi-circle above me, an arc of angels, suspended in mid-air!

The large angel speaks to me, telepathically. To receive his message I have somehow been elevated to a higher frequency. The transmission feels more refined, more highly esoteric, than any previous spiritual communication.

"Don't cry Francine. Everything will be okay. The baby will be well."

I'm not actually crying tears but angels see right into our hearts. There is nothing to worry about! My heart and soul are comforted beyond measure!

After the angels depart I feel myself back in my chair, aware again of the open terrace door welcoming breezes sweeping refreshingly across the marina, streaming sunlight calm in the room. I am unable to reason or even think. I can only be and being is loving serenity.

Imagine! The messenger angel, Archangel Gabriel, chose to descend and lift me up, give me strength, enfold me in angelic light. A blessing of immeasurable love to last for all time. In gratitude, I am to speak of Gabriel, to let people know of his presence, to let people know of his most loving magnificence. Yes, dear friends, angels are real! Angels watch over us! Angels heal us!

Within minutes the phone is ringing. Tracey is bleeding. Sonogram indicates the baby has turned completely around. Now he's in breech position. Possible placenta damage. Awaiting results of blood tests.

6:45 A.M. Tracey calls again. The baby will be born Cesarian. We are rushing out to the hospital. Unable to reach Neale. I call Annie. We're at the hospital, Enza greets us. Tracey is in the delivery room and we are in the waiting room a few steps away. I'm praying, praying, praying; a beautiful vision of Archangel Gabriel fills my mind.

Suddenly, delivery room doors open! I rush forward! A fleeting moment to catch a first glimpse of Steven! He's being rushed to the N.I.C.U. but the nurses are wonderful and pause momentarily. I look down into Steven's gorgeous almond shaped eyes! His eyes are open and he's looking up directly into my eyes! Beside myself with excitement, I recognize this baby! Oh, God, I know him! Then the moment passes, he's screaming, kicking, moving his little hands up to his cheeks. Lively! Active! Wonderful signs of good infant health! Quite beautiful little round face, perfect pink fingernails. Doctors rushing by pause to tell me, "This little guy is bigger and in better shape than expected!"

I call Neale and relate everything. He is so very overjoyed and asks me to repeat every detail. And he's so relieved that we are here. He returned to Miami to attend to a major business deal he's putting together, describes it as a mess he can't leave. Will return in a few days. I call Annie, Aunt Annie now, and she is elated, also wants to know every detail. It's so good to hear her voice.

Donning gowns, we follow Tracey into I.C.U. Steven's skin is tan, his hair is wavy black. Remarkable for a three pound, three ounce premature baby Steven's Apgar score is 8.9! The doctor tells us he will probably be ready to go home in four to six weeks, a full month sooner than previously expected.

I call Neale with this wonderful news and then I call Annie.

I feel the presence of a host of angels! Smiling and rejoicing! They have ushered Steven into the world!

Precious Steven! Someday I will tell you about the angels! About their wings of glorious effervescence! Angels from the highest reaches of Heaven who came to announce your blessed birth!

Somehow, against hospital regulations, I am permitted alone time with Steven in the N.I.C.U. My heart is bursting with joyous love. Steven opens his astounding eyes to reveal an evolved, ancient soul. Cooing and singing low, I extend my ring finger and stroke his downy head. I pet his shoulders and tiny feet, so delicate now but destined to grow big and strong. Steven is enjoying our communication. With infinite gentleness I place my pinky against his tiny palm and he quickly and firmly grasps my pinky. While we are holding hands this way Steven yawns and bubbles, opens wider his rosebud mouth permitting a peek at his lovely pink tongue. He is basking in my love. We're going to be very good friends. Oh, thank you, angels! Thank you, God! And thank you, to all the stars in Heaven!

A nurse later commented that she'd been observing me with Steven and she noticed I was bonding well with him. Tracey came in and the nurse then informed us that Steven's physical signs indicate he was born at 32 weeks, not the estimated 30 weeks. A crucial difference lies in those two additional weeks of gestation.

DECEMBER 30. A spacious, furnished apartment, including food in pantry and refrigerator, now awaits Tracey's homecoming. Danny returning to New York; I am exhausted beyond anything. Tracey is forlorn and lost. I encourage her to visualize the future: Steven playing, all of us together. "You will always have me to help you, Tracey. I will always be there for you." I am haunted by the sound of Tracey's voice and pray for her well-being.

DECEMBER 31. Tracey tells me it was decided that the baby was too hyperactive so they've given him a sedative. Uncomfortable and angry with the intrusion of wires and tubes in his body, I feel Steven's cries, "Get all this stuff off me!" He kicks his feet in frustration. His hands, beautiful expressive hands 'playing piano' in utero, now stuck with needles and strapped to miniature boards.

JANUARY 1, 1998. With discipline of the mind I transform worry into prayer. I visualize Steven surrounded by protective angelic beings, golden light all around, immersed in heavenly glow. Yet, everyone with whom I speak inquires, "You sound so tense, what's the matter?" So begins 1998.

JANUARY 3. Ventilator tube removed today. Steven screamed for hours until he finally fell asleep. I was shopping for baby supplies. At the very moment that Steven's ventilator was being removed I was in the infant department feeling faint. Without understanding the reason why this was happening I began to cry right there in the store. A saleswoman came over, put her arm around me and helped me to a chair, but within a few minutes I left the store to go outside and breathe. Then I called Tracey and learned of Steven's ordeal.

Later on in the day Howard, a physician friend, called to check in. Feeling somewhat sensitive himself these days Howard's very kind words set me crying yet again. "Let me take this opportunity to tell you," Howard began, "the world needs more people like you, Francine. Your children are very lucky to have you." People are so very kind.

JANUARY 7. Today I hold Steven in my arms! He opens wide his beautiful eyes and makes a concerted effort to focus his eyes on my face. He closes his eyes and opens them again; his focus improved. He is struggling to greet me, to say, "Hi Grandma!" So I say it for him! No longer stressed, Steven is calm in my arms. He is still being fed through a feeding tube and I observe his growing contentment as his little belly fills with formula. Steven grasps my pinky and I massage his tender back, ever so gently.

I offer infinite gratitude to all my spiritual companions, to the angels, to God and to the grand universe. I'm sending out a thought to the angels, "Now you have one less among yourselves." The angels reply directly into my mind, "We Are All One!"

JANUARY 9. The developmental psychologist has declared Steven well and fine. Tracey is making herself unavailable to me. The daily stress of watching her learn basic mothering skills from the nurses is overwhelming to me. While I am holding Steven she watches the monitor closely as if my holding him might cause harm. She is growing unduly possessive. Danny is spaced out, leaving me to feel even more isolated. I have no friends here, no one to talk with. I do my best to assure Tracey that after Steven is home she will feel his rhythms and enjoy a comfortable routine. The technology in the N.I.C.U. interferes with the establishment of natural rhythms. Nothing of normalcy here. Very stressful.

JANUARY 10. Oxygen removed; Steven is breathing on his own!

In the apartment Tracey stays to herself, locked in her room, until the very moment we leave for the hospital. I stay in the open living room, restless and nervous, trying to concentrate on my book, waiting for her company but it just isn't happening. The rest of my life is fading away, as if belonging to a distant past.

After dinner I wander through a charming maze of narrow streets where I discover a spiritual bookstore. The resident psychic greets me warmly, invites me into her cozy little curtained space and says the following to me: "You and this grandson have a strong spiritual connection. You have shared many past lives together, probably mother/son, and will once again share a closeness. You are a very powerful spiritual influence over your family, more than most. You are talented, with many gifts, a very high soul. Wise, unusual reading in your palms. There is no challenge you cannot meet, nothing you cannot accomplish. In the past people tried to block you but all that is over and gone. Your son is angry that this happened to him but he cares very much about his child's upbringing and loves and cares very much for his child. You can provide comfort to your son and show your grandson the spiritual path. Your daughter is very talented in business. She's been hurt in the past, she still feels it emotionally and is disappointed with her marriage. You can provide comfort to your daughter and show your daughter the spiritual path as well. You have requested protection for your children and it has been granted. Your guides will guide you. All is well."

January 11. Neale is here. We had a good talk over lunch. Only two visitors permitted in the N.I.C.U. for each infant but no one is bothering us so I am sharing with Neale these precious first moments when he sees his son for the very first time. In full admiration mode, Neale is in love with every little feature of Steven's face, his sweet fragile body. With an incredulously happy expression transforming his usual serious demeanor, Neale admits to me, "Yes, Mom, you're right! He does have an intelligent look, especially around the eyes." Neale is completely charmed by his infant son and when Steven opens his eyes I notice that Neale is charged with immense protective, loving emotion. He holds Steven for a long time, showing no sign of wanting to give him up.

He admonishes Tracey for being too rough in her handling of the baby, especially at diaper changing when Neale becomes visibly upset. "Hey, that's enough! Leave him some skin! Can't you see how delicate he is?" Tracey does not appreciate his comments. But where Tracey requires instruction, Neale knows instinctively.

Neale tells us later that Tracey wants him to be here with her, not his mother and father, yet I am here at Neale's request. She is on Prozac, he says. Danny spoke harshly, telling Neale that Tracey is a liar who says whatever comes into her head, a thief and a slob. There was no stopping Danny.

In an effort to soften the harsh energy of Danny's comments I reminded them, "Tracey has stated more than once that she wants to be part of our family and I have welcomed her with warmth and love, sensitive to her position."

"She meant it when she said it," Neale replied, "but she changed her mind."

I'm in great emotional turmoil; away from home, away from my daughter, my work, my whole life in New York fading into oblivion; immersed in Tracey's needs and schedule with no personal connections or relief. I do it willingly, lovingly, ultimately for the sake of my grandchild's well-being, a cause I see as the highest.

JANUARY 12. We are shocked and saddened. Danny's brother, Edmond, 60 years old, has suffered a heart attack while playing tennis and has died suddenly where he fell, on the tennis court. We must now fly to Long Boat Key in Florida. God, give me strength. It was Edmond I called when our crisis with Steven began and Edmond, not my sister-in-law, who stayed in touch regularly. Edmond's death is truly a terrible loss to everyone.

With love and trust, my son has 'appointed' me his representative with Steven here in L.A. and this is not sitting well with Tracey. Eventually, when Steven grows past these first crucial months Neale will bring him and Tracey to Florida but for now, while Steven is still a fragile infant, he wants Steven to go home to New York where he can benefit from my care.

Prior to our flight to Edmond's funeral we stop at the hospital for a last look at Steven for the next few days. The IV is out and his little hands are at last free. He's gained two ounces, bringing his weight up to three pounds, five ounces. His cheeks are rosy and his hair has turned light brown. Most of all, it's Steven's eyes, this tiny infant's magical eyes that transmit love and wisdom.

Neale calls us to meet up for lunch. To facilitate our tight departure schedule he orders ahead for us. He speaks only of his son. He loves the way Steven raises his eyebrows, opens his enchanting eyes, makes expressions with his mouth, the way he moves his hands still playing an imaginary piano. All Steven's charms lure Neale, with every passing moment, more deeply into the world of fatherhood. We all concur that whenever we speak to him Steven opens his eyes, responding to our presence. And Neale is thrilled because while he was holding Steven, his eyes remained open the whole time.

JANUARY 16. My children have arrived in Long Boat Key and we drive together to Edmond's funeral. Neale's only thought is the well-being of his son and he returns immediately after the funeral to Steven and Tracey. Annie stays a few days longer.

My healing services are being sought by everyone here. A family member who suffers from M.S. related symptoms, after a healing, walked without need of her cane, no sign of a limp, diminished hip and back pain. Now she wants me to move here. My niece requests healing for her little son who they fear may be autistic; Edmond worried terribly about his grandson. As soon as healing energy begins to flow I feel a rush of powerful energy accompanied by Edmond's presence. The energy rushes come crashing like ocean waves through my body and I feel Edmond's love for this grandchild. "Do it, Francine, you can do it," his powerful hope arose in my heart. Afterward, my niece and her husband who watched the healing, were crying with deep emotion. They, too, had felt Edmond's presence.

Word has spread so in the evening while everyone gathers in the living room in observance of shiva I'm in another room accommodating requests for healings. My sister-in-law says she really loves me and needs me now. I give her what no one else can, she says; we embrace and cry together. As friends and family are parting there is an enormous outpouring of love for me, from everyone. Tears fill my eyes. That for which I have yearned is coming to pass and yet it's all eclipsed by pressing concerns over Steven.

JANUARY 30. "My dear guides, please tell me the truest and the highest meaning of Free Will."

"Dearest Francine, we come to you in peace and in love, in the golden healing light of our Creator. The truest and highest meaning of Free Will is this: to choose to align oneself with God our Creator, the Oneness of All Creation, which is an alignment with Love, or to choose to live in opposition to God and the Oneness, a choice to live in Fear. Let every choice go forth in Love and manifest with Love on Earth."

FEBRUARY 7. Steven now weighs four pounds, five ounces. The feeding tube is out and he is sucking slowly but well. And, he has been transferred from the N.I.C.U. to a nursery room!

Neale wants the baby to bond with me, he feels it is best for Tracey to stay in New York with Steven for a few months. He also wants Annie to have a chance to know Steven. He is talking to Tracey, trying to convince her.

FEBRUARY 12. Tracey left a message for Neale. She will not return to New York, neither will she go to Florida. She still insists on taking Steven to her grandmother's house in Los Angeles. Neale is terribly distressed about Tracey's inability to be a responsible mother and he wants Steven to stay with me in New York. Across the miles the anguish in my son's heart fills my heart as well. "Neale," I answer unhesitatingly, "of course Steven can stay with me."

Neale calls Annie and immediately she agrees to be there for him in any way he needs her. "I love you so much, Neale, I'll always be there for you," Annie told him. "And Mommy has always been there for you and me and she'll be the same way with Steven."

Annie explained to us that since no agreement has been signed neither parent is breaking a law by taking the baby, but whoever doesn't have him has the task of getting him back. So if Tracey is serious about keeping him in California it will be necessary for us to take Steven back to New York. She has no means of support or even a home of her own. She can, however, cause Neale plenty of grief. Annie told me she is very upset over the state of Neale's emotions.

I call on my guides who are always near and awaiting the call. We transmit loving healing light to Tracey. We surround her completely with golden light. I hold the image and grow peaceful. Then I call her on the phone.

"Tracey," I say, "I know you're upset and nervous about taking care of Steven all by yourself." She agrees. "That's why, Tracey, I want to help you. I'll be available for you every minute of every day when you are in New York." Tracey is silent. "I don't see how you can count on your grandmother for support, Tracey, she hasn't even come to visit you once. And you and Neale may have issues to work out but Neale's the one paying for everything, he's supporting you, your schooling, your psychiatrist. You need to be practical, Tracey. Consider where life will be easier for you. In New York, I'll take care of Steven whenever you want, whatever you want to do, see your friends, go on errands, go work out, I'll be there for you Tracey, I promise."

FEBRUARY 14. I'm awake very early. Neale lets me know he's going to call Steven's doctor. "Mom, we must stay focused on getting Steven to New York. He must be with you, it'll be equal to him being with me." My son's voice is filled with desperation. A little while later he calls back. Doctor reports that Steven is doing well with the bottles. Main concern, he still has apnea and if it continues he will require more tests which will delay his release. Steven will be discharged three or four days after he outgrows the apnea. The danger of apnea is, it can be a precursor to Sudden Infant Death Syndrome.

FEBRUARY 15. One stressful day follows another. How much can I take? Neale expects so much of me, he counts on me to do everything right for Steven and I will, but it's so difficult with Tracey's instability and now, here in this apartment we're sharing, she's hostile toward me. I feel it through the locked door of her bedroom, through the wall when I'm in the living room alone with a book, waiting for her to come out.

When I told Neale that Steven will need a lot of love he replied, "No one can do that for him as well as you, Mom."

FEBRUARY 16. Awake at 3:00 A.M. Not feeling well. In the bathroom mirror I see large red welts on my neck and arms. My breath is coming hard. A sharp pain in my left eye. Back in bed I'm shivering and suffering unbelievable itching. A warm compress on my eye seems to offer some relief there. Suddenly, Danny's sleep is disturbed by a nightmare so I set aside the compress and soothe him. It's 4:00 A.M. I get out of bed, stand before the bathroom mirror again and raise my nightgown. Horrified, I see huge red welts, the size of my palm and even bigger, covering every inch of my skin. Too painful to touch even gently. I'm feeling sick inside.

A shower will help, I decide, but the shower spray is terribly painful. Danny applies to my back an ointment he has for relief of eczema. My back is completely covered with enormous red itchy welts. I swallow two antibiotics we happen to have and soon the episode grows less dramatic.

At the hospital Steven is sleeping on his tummy. I sit beside him and watch him breathe. He's stirring and making little baby sounds, so I place my hand on his back and transmit love and light to him. Tracey is supposed to be here at 1:00 P.M. for his feeding but it's 2:30 and she's not here yet.

Danny and I drive to Brentwood, find a shop for infant supplies, and I buy a small white crib along with other necessary items for Steven and have the whole order shipped to our New York apartment. Praying for strength, I walk through this very attractive, well-stocked store, call Tracey, describe to her what I'm looking at and choose according to mutual agreement. We pack these infant furnishings into the rental car. I'm beyond exhaustion. For some undisclosed reason the night nurse is hostile, claiming there are no plans for Steven's release and that he needs another transfusion. I feel like I'm going to faint but instead I sit down and sip a cup of water.

FEBRUARY 17. Enormous overlapping red welts, difficult to measure for their varying shapes, some look almost ten inches wide, cover my entire body. My body is screaming for peace! Instead I'm here, in the midst of a brewing storm between Neale and Tracey, praying with all my heart and soul, for Steven's well-being.

Neale is flying out tomorrow. I overheard Tracey's mean hostility toward Neale, refusing to divulge information about Steven. She hasn't attended the class on infant CPR, a hospital requirement for Steven's release. She hasn't had the time, she has other things on her mind.

FEBRUARY 18. My New York dermatologist has referred me to Dr. Cheryl Rand. At 10:00 A.M. I am greeted by Dr. Rand, who I quickly learn, is highly regarded and known on both coasts. I am so grateful to my dermatologist and to Dr. Rand who has taken me in while her scheduled patients are kept waiting. She examines me, asks a few questions; the diagnosis is a mammoth case of hives. The astute and thoughtful doctor gives me two kinds of ointments in full-size tubes and a full supply of super-powerful antibiotics. Within the hour I begin to feel relief.

From the doctor's office we go directly to the "Firehouse" where we meet Neale, Tracey, and two of Tracey's friends for lunch.

And then, directly to the hospital, to bring our baby home! At last, after several hours of an official release process, we leave the hospital. Our precious, beautiful Steven, in our arms! No tubes, no needles, no restraints, no technology. Just Steven, wrapped in a blanket purchased in Brentwood. We each take turns holding him and then he lays on his Daddy's chest where he falls asleep, fully content for the very first time, and sleeps for most of the day.

Whenever Neale asks Tracey a question, such as the size and use of Enfamil bottles, she answers tersely with a flash of rage. It hurts me to witness such negativity against my son. Tomorrow they are going in the morning to work out and I will be alone with Steven.

Before retiring for the night Neale embraces me in the living room. "You didn't expect a grandson so soon, did you Mom? See? Sometimes you get the best when you least expect it."

Alone with Steven I watch him raise his arms and stretch as babies do. I hold his little hands and he responds by grasping my fingers. Then I very gently stretch his arms forward and in this way we discover, Steven loves this exercise! When he feels the stretch his eyes light up in joyful surprise. When I release his hands he reaches up for more! Steven and Grandma are playing!

FEBRUARY 19. Under Neale's tactful guidance, Steven and I are alone together again today. First, I enjoy the singular pleasure of feeding him. And then, as if he knows a fun playtime awaits, he naps a scant hour. I change his diaper and dress him and now he's ready to play.

Ever so gently I touch my nose to his, make a playful sound, and there arises in his face that wonderful expression of surprised delight that we can never get enough of. I repeat our nose-touching game and Steven becomes excited from the stimulation so I hold his hands and bring his arms in close to his body, my open hands embracing his tiny fragile body. I whisper, "shush, shush, shush," and in a moment Steven grows calm. He loves playing and he hungers for the stimulation but I'm careful not to over-stimulate him. He reaches to grasp my thumbs and tries to pull himself up! Once he discovers this remarkable new ability Steven shows an unquenchable desire for repetition. Ever watchful of his responses I lead him again through calming exercises and he enjoys the calming, too. I use the black and white giraffe toy as a focus to exercise his eyes from right to left and back again. I show him a little book of baby animals on glossy pages and this proves quite a hit with Steven.

Looking at each colorful picture is completely intriguing to him and he listens attentively and watches my face with pleasure when I imitate the various animal sounds. Steven already knows our play routine and to help him feel secure I maintain consistency from one playtime to the next. I tell him a little story pronouncing our names and how much each one of us loves him, and to accustom him to the sound of "Daddy" I repeat "Daddy" often. He slept in my arms today while I transmitted healing love to him.

Observing Tracey at Steven's bath I almost have a heart attack. She sets the plastic baby washtub into the bathtub which she has filled with water for her own bath and while holding Steven with one arm, steps over the side of the tub past the obstruction of sliding glass doors. "Why not let me hold him, Tracey, until you are safely in the tub?" As soon as I place Steven back into her arms she immediately plops him, without any warning, into the water. Clearly, Steven's expression indicates discomfort, yet Tracey seems not to notice. Later, I suggest that the baby tub be placed directly on the carpeted floor; after all, how much water is required to bathe this tiny baby?

Eager to hear every detail about Steven, Annie calls, "I hope you're telling him about his Aunt Annie," she reminds me every day.

FEBRUARY 20. Doctors here are recommending a certain eye exam and test which requires needles to penetrate the baby's eyes. As he has already undergone this test in the hospital I see no benefit from inflicting any further trauma upon Steven, especially when it's obvious to me that his eyes are perfectly fine. Neale passes this on to Tracey and she is angry, banging things around, storming through the apartment.

A dear friend in New York, a psychologist who works with mothers and children, has previously recommended a pediatric specialist, Dr. McCarten. "Call her, Francine, tell her you're my personal friend." Immediately, I had followed my friend's good advice, and now I put in a call to Dr. McCarten. Even though we have spoken briefly only once back in January, Dr. McCarten remembers me right away. "I do administer the eye test if needed," Dr. McCarten says in her clear, measured speech, "at three months, when the eye's development is complete. In your grandson's case I'd say there's no rush. Bring him in when he gets to New York, and we'll have a look."

Tracey will listen to no dissenting opinion, angry at Dr. McCarten for having one. I place one hand on Tracey's back, the other on her shoulder and look directly into her fiery eyes where I see the bottomless pain of her soul. "Don't be angry, Tracey. We all want the best for Steven." I embrace her, press my cheek against hers, and transmit love to her heart. Nevertheless, Tracey remains blind to Steven's discomfort and the dangers of premature testing. She refuses to reconsider.

"Dear Angels, you who have heralded Steven's birth, you who have watched over him, protected him, brought him to this moment. Please, come and look into it, cast your light upon us and protect Steven!"

I accompany Tracey to the doctors' office, taking my usual place in the back seat of the car next to Steven, filled with dreadful premonition that this is not a good idea. The energies in the offices repel me and the staff strikes me as technicians rather than compassionate physicians. I feel a lack of heart energy here. Drops are administered to Steven's eyes to dilate his pupils and we are shown into the waiting room.

I feel the familiar warmth around me signaling the presence of angels. Vibrations of light are filling my body. Tracey asks, "Would you like to hold Steven?" and I gather him into my arms. My precious Steven looks up at me, our eyes meet. After a while, someone comes to check Steven's eyes but his pupils are not yet sufficiently dilated. We are here almost two hours, an attendant comes out to check again. There is a consultation among the staff and finally we are informed that for some reason the baby's eyes have failed to dilate, therefore the test will have to be rescheduled!

We play together. He looks at me like he really knows me and is happy to be with me. He reaches up to grab my thumbs and pulls himself up! Over and over again. He loves to do this. When we look at the book of baby animal pictures Steven grows very calm. Incredibly, Steven can play, pleasantly interested, without interruption, for ninety minutes or so. He drinks his bottle and then he naps, contentedly.

Steven is a clean baby, quiet and expressive, alert and aware. When Danny joined us on the sofa Steven turned his head and looked at him in a most interested way. Earlier, he was fussing while Tracey was changing his diaper. I came over and with one little hand he reached up, grasped my finger, looked at me and grew calm. The hospital and all its attendant fears are over and in the past. Steven is healthy!

FEBRUARY 21. We are in the living room together. Tracey hands Steven over to me. Neale observes Steven's delight in the little book of animals so now he understands what I've been describing to him. He watches Steven grow very still as I hold the book in front of him, his eyes sparkling with enjoyment. An indescribable look comes over Steven's face, as if he's bringing something from Heaven down to Earth.

Neale holds him on his lap and Steven is content. They look

into one another's eyes. I've never seen Neale like this. He is absolutely crazy in love with his son! A special expression of pleasure comes over his face when I say to Steven, "You look just like your daddy!" So I say it again, and the expression returns. Each time I say, "Neale," Steven's eyes shine and sparkle with joy.

Tracey went to sleep early and left Steven awake with us and we had a wonderful time. Neale so enjoys the look of wonderment on Steven's face when he looks at the animal book, mesmerized by all the colorful pictures. So we turn the pages again and again. Steven looks at Neale sitting across from us. He definitely knows his Daddy. He responds to our words as if he understands. Neale calls it coincidence but I believe Steven truly does have remarkable comprehension. When he's looking at the book and I say, "You can touch the book, sweetheart," Steven reaches out and touches the book with both hands.

Hospital nurse arrives and Steven is weighed. He has gained six ounces since he's home with us. Six ounces in three-and-a-half days. The power of love!

FEBRUARY 22. Neale inquires, "Did I make all those faces when I was a baby?"

"Yes, darling, but you were calmer. Steven's expressions, though, are exactly like yours."

Neale and Tracey take Steven for an outing and Neale leans into the carriage and kisses his sleeping son. It's a painful separation when Neale returns to Florida. And it's difficult for Tracey, enduring her own problems of depression, insecurity, anger.

We shared a memorable week of being together, a moment in time I will remember for all time. Like a rainbow the power of love arcs over all. Scientific and technological advancement hold their rightful place of honor in our lives. But a moment comes when the institutional setting shifts. In that shifting moment we are challenged to grow beyond ourselves. We are presented with an opportunity to discover the true power of love, an opportunity to seize the helm when it's pure heart that is needed most and allow love to conquer all.

FEBRUARY 23. I visited Doris, a Jin Chin practitioner recommended by Annie. Doris balanced my energy meridians. Afterward, she shared with me her insight. "In your case it's all about heart. Your concern is love and you want everyone to 'get it.' Most people are concerned only with their personal life. In your case you want everyone to love this child and you want this child to receive all the love he needs."

Holding Steven this morning beautiful sparks of golden light floated all around us. Danny returned to New York, Tracey went out with friends and I am cozy home with Steven. I order in Chinese fried rice with vegetables and brew a cup of tea.

Neale calls, "Hi Mom, so how much formula has Steven taken in today? And what else is he doing?"

"I fed him one ounce, he fell asleep, and then, interspersed with holding those precious little feet of his, massaging his toes, looking at pages in the animal book, and lots of burping, he managed to consume another three ounces and getting those three ounces into him took about ninety minutes." Another ounce, another half ounce, every drop he swallows is blessed.

"Mom, you really have a lot of patience."

I tell Neale, "Whatever I do I describe to him. So I touch his ears and say, 'These are your ears, Steven, you hear sounds through your ears. See, you have one ear here on this side and another sweet little ear over here on this side!'" Then we laugh.

FEBRUARY 25. The medical staff at the hospital has declared Steven well and healthy enough to make the flight to New York!

Neale called, "Is Annie there yet? Ask her to call me, Mom. I want to talk to her after she has a chance to be with Steven."

So engaged in changing Steven's diaper, listening to his little baby sounds and answering him, I fail to hear any other sound and am happily surprised when Annie walks in, followed by her husband and then Danny. Annie goes directly to Steven, picks him up and immediately falls completely in love with him.

FEBRUARY 27. Tomorrow we fly home to New York with Steven and Tracey and her tons of luggage.

MARCH 30. Every day, around noon, Tracey brings Steven over to Museum Tower. I meet them by the curb with a blanket in my hands to wrap Steven. Tracey takes him out without winter outer clothing. Then I have him to love and care for and enjoy his company. Sometimes Tracey returns in a few hours. Sometimes she doesn't come back for a long time, or until the next day, and I have him overnight. I never know how the day will unfold so I make no plans and allow my days to revolve around precious time with Steven.

Meditation. I feel the presence of my grandma. Waves of kundalini energy pass through my body. I feel Grandma's touch on my shoulders, an extra surge of energy enters through my shoulders and flows through my body; four or five waves of energy. Tears fill my eyes from the sensation. "Sing to Steven," Grandma's message comes through, "You are my sunshine! All is well, Fagala, you are living in beauty and harmony. Sing!"

APRIL 10. Passing by the mirror this morning I see my aura, a vision of beautiful violet light all around me as if I were backlit with violet light. It's a constantly shimmering light. My mind is filled with memories of Mom and Dad, all my cousins, my aunts, my brother and his family.

MAY 22. Tracey's instability is ongoing. Neale called four or five times today. He's looking for a house to bring Steven home to, a house that will accommodate all of us. He's counting on me to bring Steven to Miami and help with Steven's care.

MAY 29. Lunch on Madison Avenue at The Right Bank. I'm seated at a table in the back facing the front entrance of the restaurant. Glancing up, I notice a woman enter the restaurant and this woman looks exactly like Mom! Transfixed, I stare as she advances toward me and as she draws nearer she looks, still, just like Mom. She is shown to a seat at a table adjacent to mine and it's not until she is seated that I realize this woman looks nothing like Mom. But until the very last moment I was sure it was my mother walking toward me. Her hair, her body shape, her hat, even her Asian eyes and nimble walk, altogether created a vision that looked just like my mother. Was Mom's spirit using this woman's body to let me know she's with me?

JUNE 3. Tracey has agreed to move in August to Florida.
Listening to a guided meditation tape by Orin and DaBen, spiritual teachers from a higher finer dimension, who channel through Sanaya Roman and Duane Packer. I find their energies consistently pure. Listener is advised to choose someone and touch them with your awareness. Immediately, I see Neale. I see his heart energy, radiations of golden white light, and we communicate soul to soul. "It's not easy, Mom, I'm working on it but it's not easy." He is referring to resolving his issues with Tracey. I feel our loving connection; it transcends spoken language. The

listener is now advised to take the burden you have been carrying for this person, and give it to the person, whose soul reassures you that this person possesses the necessary strength. (I did not know this meditation is about the transfer of burden) In these highly refined spaces all is truth and wisdom and love. Neale's soul knows this has to be done. I return to conscious awareness with quite a sharp pain in my upper right back, as if surgery had just been performed. So I know the burden has truly been removed. The phone rings, it's Neale.

JUNE 4. Dream. John Kennedy was hanging out in my kitchen, in a house I live in only in dreams. My kids were young and moving about, in and out of the room.

JUNE 7. I'm learning with greater depth what it means to be true to yourself and this leads to an urge to cleanse my life of unnecessary possessions and to tell Danny I want to move.

JUNE 20. Tracey and Neale are having a terrible argument and ask for my help. Silently, I call upon the one who comes to me in dreams and visions, the beautiful god-like being who glows with gorgeous light of turquoise-blue and gold. I have no name for him, always too overwhelmed by his presence to ask, and it almost doesn't matter as his vibration and appearance is outstandingly unique. I feel the familiar waves of energy pass through my body and fill me completely. My Master Guide whispers, "Call them and guide them to do the following: Face each other. Surround yourselves with golden healing light. Recall the endearing qualities you first saw in each other; think about these qualities. Then you are to say to them: I am now going to leave you and you will make a pact between you to act only in ways that lead to your highest good. Whenever you begin to feel negatively toward one another do this exercise."

JUNE 22. Neale is alone with Steven today and can hardly contain his joy. He calls and says to Steven, "It's Grandma! It's Grandma! Want to say hello?"

AUGUST 6. A few short days remain before Steven and Tracey leave New York to live in Florida. How barren the days will be without the light that Steven brings with him wherever he goes. Neale bought a beautiful home in Miami Beach. This phase of my life is now drawing to a close. For the past few years I've been giving away most of my books but it's not enough. I want to travel light through the rest of my life, be free to stand in my own light.

AUGUST 27. Annie gave me a copy of duPont Registry of Fine Homes. A photograph of her new home is in it and also in this same volume, on page 64, is a photograph of Neale's new home!

I go to see Frank Andrews, my psychic friend, and he tells me, "That was you. You, with your high angelic energy, caused it to unfold this way. For both your children. You took the necessary steps here on Earth and bolstered them with your spiritual powers, which are ancient by the way." How could that be? Frank says that someday I will understand.

Tracey called and spoke lovingly. She is happy we have grown close, she loves me and misses me, we did so much for her and Neale when we came down last week, she said. Tonight she left a voicemail of Steven laughing.

SEPTEMBER 2. Listening to a guided meditation. I embark on another past life journey, descending from the grid of light above Earth into ancient Egypt where I am a slender Egyptian priestess worshiping at the statue of Isis, the widely honored great mother goddess. I stand with my arms extended, my body leaning forward gracefully from the waist with right leg extended, my foot set firmly on the ground. Here I live a serene and focused life where my days are devoted to healing and prayer. Life is lived with purity here. My ability as a healer grants me a peaceful, protected life.

The most important task of this life is the bathing of newborns in a basin of holy water drawn from the fountain of the statue of Isis. The water flows from the statue of the revered goddess. Newborns bathed in holy water blessed by Isis are protected from all illnesses, allowing them to grow in strength and good health. Most important work. The selection of infants is implemented by highly trained and gifted seers who utilize various divination methods to determine which infants are destined to contribute to the overall well-being of our society. The most high court also sends before me for healing people of the temple community and government. The seers and the court are held in high esteem and respected by all.

When I emerge from this amazing recollection, back to present time, I experience a powerful rush of kundalini energy. I research Isis in the encyclopedia and learn she was a most powerful goddess, protector of her son, healer, restorer of life, mother goddess. Some months later, browsing a spiritual book store in Miami, I come across an unusual book about Isis. I leaf through the pages and find a drawing of the Fountain of Isis. The fountain is in the center of a small, clear pond. It is the precise image I saw in my past life journey. Prior to the Egyptian life regression I was unaware of Isis, which seems incredible to me now, for now it feels to me that I have always known.

SEPTEMBER 6. Miami. Steven reaches up a little hand. He gently pats and caresses my face. Neale walks over, Steven looks up and says, "Da da da!" his first word.

SEPTEMBER 25. Long awaited visit with psychic, Jim Forgiano. "Usually I see light straight up around the head. With you the light is wide, all around you. It goes up and out. You are very open. You have a spirit guide, male, American Indian. Your guides are bringing in higher guides, Masters, one very high Master will be working with you. Your third eye is open. Your mother just got here, talks a lot. She is saying how much she loves you. Says she was short on these words when you were growing up. But she loves you and is proud of you. Your dad, more so, she says. Can't express how much he loves you. Showing image of you with baby. You and the baby have been together in past lives – mother and son, husband and wife, lovers. When the baby touches your face that's Mom and Dad reaching out to you. Image of Jesus, regarding baby. That's what they're showing me. Loved by many. Known by many. From Mom and Dad: Tracey will not take baby away, can't happen, will not be allowed. Keep doing prayers, your prayers are powerful. Showing your energy out so far. Dad sending image of you looking into the mirror and not seeing true reflection of who you are. You'll see changes in your social structure. Spiritual path. With Annie and her husband, strain between them. There's a powerful struggle. He's latched on to her for a ride, he hitched his wagon to her star. He has to learn. Want Annie to maintain financial independence. Her finances are secure. Your health looks good. Improvement images. See you spending a lot of time in Florida. Annie has powerful work image. One baby. Annie and Neale's houses are synchronicity, complimentary to you. Mom and Dad can be with you and with baby. They are kissing you. Your mom is kissing you and your dad has his arm around you. (I feel a warmth around me and gentle vibrations in my chest.)

OCTOBER 10. Out-of-body experience. Lying flat on my sofa in the study where I like to meditate; sunrise, in all its magnificent glory, pouring in. Suddenly, I feel myself rising above my body to a height higher than where the ceiling is. I look down and see myself lying on the sofa in my long white cotton gown, feminine touches of lace distinctly visible. As I ascend, I watch my body grow smaller. With infinite clarity, images arise in my mind: Annie, Neale, Steven.

I feel spiritual beings around me, on my right side and on my left. I turn my head and see them in human shapes of white light. And each being is an individual part of a unified mind. They communicate telepathically according to pure law, or guidelines. They are sharing their thoughts with me. I feel the exaltation of the unified mind enter my consciousness. "There is that woman in white, she is so serene, she is praying once again for her loved ones. They are all good, they do no harm, they are kind. Her prayers never cease. Let us respond to her prayers."

In this way, their decision to grant my prayers is made, not according to emotional or subjective feelings, but based upon high standards of wisdom and ethics. My mind is linked with theirs! A glorious, Utopian, comforting experience. The sense of oneness, of the universe being a place of harmony pervades my consciousness. In higher dimensions all thought is encompassed by love and harmony. Then, I feel myself descending, the woman on the sofa draws nearer and very gently, I am back in my body, feeling awed and so blessed.

OCTOBER 21. Neale says to me today on his birthday, twice, "You've been a wonderful mother and I love you very much, Mommy."

To comfort him in his constant worry about Tracey running off with Steven, I relay Jim Forgiano's message.

OCTOBER 26. Tracey arrives with Steven for a visit to New York, brings him over to me, and goes off with her friends. After our warm reunion I set him down on my polished wood floor and right away I am dismayed to see that my precious Steven is not crawling properly at all, employing his arms to propel himself forward. So I get down on the floor with him. "See, my love, how Grandma crawls? Now we crawl together, Steven and Grandma. Come, sweetheart, you can crawl just like Grandma." I move his little legs and help him crawl on his knees. In this way the day passes, with nourishment breaks and reading and singing breaks. Steven quickly realizes that this crawling thing is important to learn, and he cooperates happily to achieve success. The next morning he's eager to get down on the floor again. Now we laugh together for Steven is showing me that he is crawling in perfect symmetry!

Tracey tells me Steven drinks his bottle lying on his stomach but I notice immediately that this is a frustrating position and it seems quite unnatural. I turn him over onto his back. "Steven, my little love, try drinking your bottle this way, lying on your back. I think you will feel more comfortable." But still, I am bothered, so I pick up my grandson, hold him securely and sit on the sofa with him resting in my arms. In this way Steven relaxes and empties his bottle.

Annie stops by and while she is holding him on her lap Steven reaches up, places his little hands on her face and snuggles against Annie's face. Annie is delighted.

While Steven naps I stand beside the crib and transmit healing light to him. I do this, also, whenever I am holding him. He looks at me in a most unique way, unusual for a baby, and he holds on tightly to me with both his little hands.

On this visit, assisted by a big dark-brown plush monkey, Steven learns to clap hands. Steven sits facing the friendly monkey, while I sit behind the monkey, holding its floppy arms, singing a silly song, "Abba dabba dabba dabba dabba dabba dab said the monkey to the chimp..."

I clap the monkey's hands in time with the song and to Steven the monkey appears to clap on its own, so we are laughing together. On the last note I sing, "Hey! And I lift the monkey into a little jump. Steven can't stop giggling. Soon my precious Steven reaches forward, grasps the monkey's hands and shows me that he can do it also. Then I set the monkey aside, sing the silly song and Steven claps his own hands. After this, Steven claps for everything!

With great gentleness I encourage Steven to pull himself up in the crib to a standing position. "What a big boy you are, my love, look how you are standing!" Steven, at this stage in his development, requires an abundance of loving encouragement, and with each new accomplishment his face glows with joyful sunshine.

NOVEMBER 23. I notice an unusual freckle in the center of my chest, with a clear overlay and I don't have a good feeling about it. It turns out to be a squamous cell tumor requiring an hour long surgery.

DECEMBER 4. My new agent, Claire Gerus, reads my manuscript, "Sara, Sara," and claims that not only will it be published, it will be made into a film.

Tracey is visiting some friends in New York, leaving Steven at her friend's downtown apartment. Today the tumor was removed. I'm feeling weak, admonished by the doctor as I'm leaving his office, not to strain or lift or bend with fresh stitches. Danny drives down to Tracey's friend and brings Steven back to our apartment. My sweet angel knows something's wrong so with rare sensitivity for a child of his age he sits quietly on my lap and leans his head against me, clearly seeking to comfort me. Neale and Annie call to check in.

December 7. Deep altered state of meditation. I'm at a construction site where Neale is building a house, showing me around. Then he's commiserating with my father. "Grandpa, you don't know how hard it is for me. First, I have my father and he gives me so much heartache. Then I have my beautiful son and just to see him is so much heartache with Tracey." My father's face held deep concern and heartfelt compassion for the grandson he so cherished.

When I emerge from the meditative state I go to the mirror to inspect my wound. The swelling is gone. My skin is flat. And the site of surgery no longer hurts.

A new year, 1999. Our apartment is on the market. The callous, careless way he approaches all interaction with me, the lack which has prevailed for so long of even a single day of kindness, has irretrievably diminished my desire to sustain our marriage. The wheels of destiny are turning and even though it appears from the outside view as if I am the agent of change it feels to me beyond my control.

February 15. Neale called, "Mom, did you have that conversation with Dad? You asked him about selling the Bronx operation and moving down here to help me? Did you make it clear? Does he understand that I need him to help with the used cars down here?"

"We had a very long conversation, Neale. I brought up every advantage, for you, for Steven, for himself, for the future, but all I could get from him is that in two years he'll consider it."

"It's too much for me, Mom, living down here and helping

Dad run the Bronx operation. And now I can't stand leaving Steven."

"Neale, I had terrible arguments with Daddy, when he started piling all those responsibilities on you but he refused to hear me."

"Well, Mom, Daddy is the most selfish guy I know."

FEBRUARY 19. Freezing cold weather. Danny argues against turning on the heat in the bedroom. If I review the forecast of snow and single digit temperatures it's of no account to him and the argument grows unbearably absurd. I wait for him to fall asleep, then as quietly as possible turn the heat on low. He wakes up immediately, turns the heat off and I go to find refuge on the sofa in the study. He follows me, demands I come back to bed. "I came in here to be warm, please leave me alone, go away and let me sleep!" He starts another argument. It's unbearable to live with him. I have another case of hives, this time, the welts are confined to my thighs so I feel fortunate. This man is driving me crazy!

Still, we have our children so we fly down together to Miami every month and stay for ten days. There's a guest house on the property of Neale's new home where at night I lock the door to my own little suite and Danny sleeps in the other room.

MARCH 5. I sign a contract for a corner apartment on the Upper East Side and ought to be feeling very happy. Instead, I'm using all my strength to remain centered as Destiny pulls me toward the unknown.

MARCH 6. Lately, I've been feeling a light touch on my right side. I turn my head and, of course, no one is there.

MARCH 8. Psychic Medium, Suzanne Northrop seminar. Suzanne begins the meditation to call in the spirits and immediately, Mom and Dad are here, peaceful and beautiful, in their youth, and I'm receiving the love they are transmitting. I ask if Tracey will take Steven away from us and they reply very quickly, "No, never, it cannot happen."

Then, to my surprise, a whole crowd of my mother-in-law's family comes in, each one looking directly at me! An uncle who died when I was twenty-two, my mother-in-law and father-in-law, others I never knew but recognize now as family members. Rose, my mother-in-law, is the noisy one, in front and most energetic. "Why are you arguing with my Daniel?" she demands.

"Oh, no, don't do this to me!" I answer. "Why can't you ever say something nice to me? I've been good to him all these years! When will you offer recognition instead of criticism?"

Then my father interjects, "You do receive recognition, Fran. Why do you suppose we are all here? Everyone knows what you do and who you are." So much love is transmitted with my father's quiet words, I'm overwhelmed with emotion. Rose acknowledges my love for Danny, the good I've brought into his life and says, "Yes, you are right."

My father's abiding love and kindness rises above all. And I realize, my father is an alchemist. Even on the other side my father transforms dross into gold.

MARCH 17. Regarding the seven page prologue to my manuscript, "SARA, sara," which I'd sent out to Elie Weisel's office, Mr. Weisel's secretary calls. "Mr. Weisel has read your prologue and he is intrigued. Would you please send the complete manuscript?"

APRIL 10. Neale called, elated to have Steven for three days. He says Steven is walking all over the house now! Tracey still threatens to take Steven to L.A. and I assure Neale that I have it from an excellent source that it will not happen.

APRIL 15. Dad's birthday. I have a session today with Yang, a highly recommended Buddhist shaman. He sees and feels Tracey's energy: drowsy, drug-induced, sleeping a lot, violent, unstable, depressed. Impatient with Steven and spanks him when no one's around, just as I've intuited. Yang foresees Steven eventually full time with Neale.

Yang sees me as sad and isolated. He says my spiritual energy is so dynamic and expanded he's seen similar energy only once before. He sweeps his arms out and indicates swirls, describing my energy as constantly swirling in and out and all around. He sees me as a healer in past lives, especially strong connection with ancient Egypt. I am destined, he says, to become a powerful healer. An extremely powerful energy that few people possess surrounds me. Concentrated, focused, strong, open. First time he has felt this energy with someone. It comes from inside and circulates around me. Very strong connection to past lives. Egyptian life significant.

APRIL 23. Miami. Awaiting our arrival, Neale is holding Steven. His back to me, Steven hears my voice, holds his head completely still. I go to them, Steven turns around and leans immediately into my arms. My love! He leans his head on my chest, holds onto me, and as with every reunion refuses to let go for hours. Tracey won't allow Steven to sleep here. If we go against her will she shows up late at night, grabs Steven from his bed, and creates a huge drama, so we bring Steven back. The look in his eyes when he sees we are leaving breaks my heart and will haunt me forever. I surround him with golden healing light and pray for his protection.

SEPTEMBER 21. Museum Tower apartment is sold. I am renting a studio apartment on East 57th Street until construction is completed on the new building I'm moving into on East 65th Street. Danny is staying in Neale's apartment. I still have hope that he'll decide to go for marriage counseling, that he'll realize he really loves me and doesn't want to lose me. Inside my heart a feeling of deep emptiness prevails. Danny doesn't seem to care about anything concerning us and on some days I'm filled with a terrible dread that my husband might not even love me at all.

OCTOBER 4. On October 4, 1958, I went to a dance and, across a crowded room, fell in love. Today I'm leaving him. When he goes home it will be to a different apartment, I won't be there, and he doesn't recognize the date or the significance of our move away from our marital home. He's carefree at an all-day golf outing. His drawers still hold his belongings and the furniture movers arrive early in the morning. Momentarily, I'm tempted to do what I've always done, pack his stuff for him, but this time I resist.

OCTOBER 7. Annie and Neale are both very sweet and loving to me. Furniture and antiques they like for their own homes are theirs. Some stuff goes to Neale's apartment here in the city for Danny's comfort and a very few articles of furniture for my studio. Everything I own is here in my studio apartment now. Very few possessions. A cleansing I've longed for. A purification.

NOVEMBER 1. Big saga with my spine. Incapacitating pain. Emergency room at Mt. Sinai, CT scan, MRI. Serious disc problems at the top of my neck and at the base of my spine. I can bend a little and sit with utmost care, my thigh is numb.

NOVEMBER 12. Late last night, still suffering terrific debilitating pain, I call on my spiritual companions, "My dear spirit guides, high Masters, Archangel Michael and Raphael, you who have come to my aid in the past, and to the aid of all those who come to me for healing, send me healing, dear Angels and Masters, that I may go forth and fulfill my task of bringing love and healing to Earth." This morning I awaken at sunrise completely pain free.

NOVEMBER 17. I'm at the American Academy of Science, attending Dr. John Mack's seminar. He has asked us to bring to his seminar any messages we may have received from the E.T.s to share at the conclusion of his talk. Nervous, I hesitate while others speak and finally, I summon all my courage, go to the mic and bring forth the message received last night while soaking in the tub.

"This is the message my spirit guide gave me last night to bring here and share with you. We all feel the significance of the coming new millennium and we want to do something meaningful. It's time, dear friends, to bury hatred and all weapons of war with the ashes of the past, all that we have wept over during our collective history on this planet. It's time to begin anew and align ourselves with a pure vibration of love. Each in our own way."

Back in my seat my friends tell me that while I spoke you could've heard a pin drop in the auditorium. A New York Times reporter approached me and asked for permission to print my quote. Afterward, a small crowd came over and surrounded me, offering expressions of kindness.

DECEMBER 1. In my small studio apartment, so as not to disturb my neighbors, I have set the chimes in my tall case clock to 'silent' and the chimes have remained silent since the day I moved in. On this day of my birthday, as I'm lying down to read in bed, adjusting the pillows, the chimes strike a beautiful melody. No hour strikes, only this beautiful melody.

I feel an enormous release of sadness accompanied by the knowledge that the sadness is absolutely unnecessary. I feel renewed, restored to good health. And I receive this message: "Mother of us all, rejoice in your life, rejoice in your inner resource of unquenchable fire! Celebrate your life! Rejoice! Rejoice!"

My depression is over! I'm in my own place, responsible only for my own life. I recall "A Room of One's Own" by Virginia Wolf, smile to myself, and celebrate my life!

DECEMBER 25. Miami. Danny is reading the newspaper in the guest house, in the small sitting room. It's late and quiet, and I decide to join him. We talk together for a few minutes about our children and my husband actually looks into my eyes for longer than a flicker. In that moment of rare harmony between us I tell my husband that I haven't felt loved or emotionally supported in our marriage and that I always feel alone.

Danny looks down, and all around, and then says that I am not wrong, he has not been a hundred percent committed to our marriage! "My commitment," he tells me, "has been to my own personal comfort. I want to live as long as I can."

Thirty-nine years I have lived with him, loved him and cared for him with all my heart, completely devoted and loyal. I arise from the sofa, go into my own little suite and lock the door.

A New Millennium, the Year 2000

APRIL 2. Seminar with Shaman Craig Jungulas who speaks on spirit guides. During his guided meditation I experience the strong fiery heat of kundalini energy at the base of my spine. The energy rises up my spinal column and when it reaches my heart chakra the kundalini energy spreads wide open like a blossoming flower. At lunch break Craig joins me. "Your guides have spoken to my guides," Craig tells me, "And here's the message for you, Why aren't you teaching yet? What are you waiting for?"

APRIL 7. For the opportunity to thank Dr. Bernie Siegel in person for the benefit I derived from his book, "Love, Medicine & Miracles," when I was healing from malignant melanoma, I attend a seminar he is giving.

I am focused on Dr. Siegel's presentation, listening carefully, taking notes. Suddenly I feel a light pressure of being touched on the right side of my face. Very gently, my hair is being stroked.

I feel pressure on my shoulder. I feel a stronger pressure on my head as if I am being completely embraced by an angel.

At the Q & A session I raise my hand, grateful for the opportunity to thank Dr. Siegel in person for the insight and comfort his book provided. Briefly I describe the anxiety of being too nervous to sleep after a malignant melanoma had been removed from my left eyebrow; how I went to my bookshelf in the middle of the night, found his book which I'd bought for no apparent reason almost a year ago, proceeded to read it all the way through until the sun was coming up; how following his suggestion to patients I had drawn a picture of myself as I imagined I would look in the future and in this way discovered that according to Dr. Siegel's guidelines I qualified as an 'exceptional patient.' I told Dr. Siegel, that moment was a powerful turning point in my healing process. I also told him that his revelation about the spirit guide who is always with him was a wonderful gift of sharing which allowed me to then speak more freely about the spirit guide who is always with me. "If Dr. Bernie Siegel, eminent New York oncologist, can speak about his spirit guide, then I can too!"

APRIL 11. Meditation. Feel light electrical currents emanating from my hands, both palms and each fingertip. My face feels as if I am under a heat lamp.

The agent who was interested in "SARA, sara" manuscript has faded into oblivion as every other agent has.

What am I doing on this godforsaken planet?

APRIL 21. Annie says she doesn't know how I do it or what I do, but after we spoke about her stress and did a distant healing for her she felt immensely improved. She thinks merely talking to me is healing.

APRIL 24. Another squamous cell carcinoma, this one on my left arm. A cute freckle I was born with has turned against me.

I have formed a weekly spiritual study group and we meet here in my studio apartment. I have six friends reading "Spiritual Growth" by Sanaya Roman and Duane Packer, meditations and enlightened teachings channeled by Orin and DaBen.

When I invite my friend Robin to join us she becomes emotional and tells me she has just received a diagnosis of breast cancer. She was praying for an angel to come and help her, and just then I called. So I assure Robin that I will help her get through this, not only in the study group but in every way possible.

APRIL 29. Another suspicious growth, this one on my right foot, situated right on the big vein.

MAY 11. Biopsy on the freckle on my forearm, my beloved friendly freckle, indicates level five carcinoma very deep, close to the bone.

MAY 18. I learned from the malignant melanoma on my eyebrow, which was removed by a dermatologist, that there are times when the particular skills of a plastic surgeon are called for to remove skin cancers. So for the procedure on my foot I am going to a plastic surgeon, Dr. Norman Shulman. This is another squamous cell carcinoma. The skin on my foot is extremely thin, due to years of edema, my right leg swelling up every day, caused by a compromised venous system. I view all these skin cancers as a surfacing and cleansing of stress and anxiety. A higher understanding would be to recognize the purification process as it wends its way through my physical body.

MAY 26. Dr. Shulman is wonderful. He opens his office for my procedure on a Saturday when his office is usually closed and he performs the nursing duties himself as well as completing a perfect surgical procedure. Dr. Shulman holds the tumor up for my viewing pleasure; it's the size of a green pea. Humorously, he asks if I want to preserve it. No, thank you, I smile in reply.

During the procedure hundreds of sparks of light surround me. With great love the light informs me, "You needed to endure certain physical trauma as part of the transformation process. The trauma needed to hold validity, yet also be recoverable."

I don't understand why we must suffer so, through the physical body, and I pray to the sparks of light, "Five serious skin cancers ought to be sufficient to satisfy Pluto, planet of transformation, which moved into Sagittarius in August 1995. The arrival of Pluto heralded the malignant melanoma on my eyebrow and hopefully is finding completion on my foot; head to toe. Please," I pray to the Light, "no more trauma to my body!"

The Light responds, "Keep yourself surrounded with loving souls, people who love you. Keep away from souls who choose to learn through the negative path, people who try to bring you down. Negative people, by infusing your life with stress and anxiety, weaken the magnificence of who you are by turning your attention toward survival. Negative forces, concentrated over time, invade the body's cellular structure. Be wise, dearest, and choose your companions wisely."

JUNE 10-17. Spiritual Cruise to Caribbean. My foot is still healing so instead of disembarking at ports I remain on board and read. First day at sea I meet Bernie McGrenahan, my son's childhood friend. Bernie is elated to see me. Hugging me emotionally, he says, "You look just like I remember you!" Later that evening, in my cabin, Mom and Dad come to me carrying a message: "Bernie's long affectionate hugs were from us too! We were there. We are with you, Fran, your foot will heal and you will walk with ease again."

In the morning, Tarot reading with Kim, who is teaching us how to read the cards. "Change the program before he kills you with something. Stay away from him. Your husband has bad, closed up energy. Bad, and he doesn't care at all about your welfare." Whew! I went off by myself to gaze out toward the wide horizon and cast all painful memories into the timeless sea.

A little while before dinner is announced, Bernie finds me in the lounge. "When I was a kid," he says "I saw you as a surrogate mother."

"Bernie, you were such a cute little kid, with those adorable blond curls you had, and you always played so nicely with Neale, I was always happy to have you over!"

"Well, I always enjoyed being in your house, it always felt so serene, and even though I was just a kid I knew it all came from you." Then Bernie says, "By the way, I have to tell you, when I hugged you the other night something strange was going on. It felt as if I was taken over by a force I couldn't control. Really. Actually, and this may sound really strange, but I swear, it felt like a loving force was pushing through me."

"Bernie, do you remember Neale's grandparents, my Mom and Dad? Well, you should know Bernie, of all Neale's friends my parents were particularly fond of you, they really liked you a lot."

"Yeah! I do remember them! Neale's Grandpa was so good-natured, he would jump up and drive us to the pet shop any time we asked! Boy, did we love our fish tanks back then and there was always something we had to go back for! He was a real good guy, Neale's Grandpa, Neale was lucky to have him."

Seance with Suzanne Northrop. Just about everyone in our group is in attendance so the cabin is crowded. Suzanne speaks for each spirit that shows itself. Right away my mother comes in. "Francine! Steven! Our family brought him in. I brought him in! Very much our blood. Very high, good important soul." With a whole crowd of people waiting impatiently to hear from their loved ones, my father now arrives. He talks about his leg and says it would have been contrary to his dignity to have it removed. Suzanne has no way of knowing but the ravages of diabetes on his leg was a conversation my father and I engaged in all the time, so my father, with his customary considerate nature, now sought closure to soothe my lingering doubts. There's more from my father. Suzanne says he's telling us that the loss of his mother affected his entire life, now he's reunited with her.

I'm really getting choked up now. My mother brought Steven in! My father is reunited with his mother, lifelong wounds are being healed! Now Suzanne is speaking for my father again. Your brother has big problems, he's in more pain than you know. Now your father's talking about his photographs and he's happy you have them."

Past life meditation, we each find a partner. Fortunately for me Terra, a channeler, asks to be my partner. When we exchange notes after the exercise Terra says she saw me in the angelic realm, surrounded by angels, an angel myself. Also saw me in lifetimes off planet Earth.

Another past life regression. We are a group of about 20 people gathered in a windowless seminar room, seated on the usual seminar chairs, to experience past life regression. I am expecting to revisit my American Indian lifetime. We are brought to deep state of relaxation and are asked to look down at our shoes.

I look down and see that I am a Roman girl, 17 years old, wearing Roman sandals and a white Roman toga. The toga is draped and fastened on one shoulder with a small medallion depicting my House. My father is a senator in the Roman Senate. I am walking up a slope surrounded by throngs of people who are attired in long brown hooded robes, a Roman girl walking among the Jews. I have been told by a Jewish friend that I must go and see the rabbi who speaks to the people about the 'Word.' The rabbi is Jesus. I am now at the ascent of the hill. I position myself beside an olive tree only several measures from the Master, somewhat apart from the crowd. Jesus is delivering his Sermon on the Mount. "Love thy neighbor as thyself," he exhorts the people. I learn the 'Word' is "Love" and it resonates deeply inside my heart. I am filled with elation to be standing here and listening to the pure wise counsel of the Master. His mission is to bring enlightenment through love, and immediately I feel great love for this man as if he is my brother! The people are enthusiastic, the very air is suffused with love, and they are calling out, "Jesus, King of the Jews! Jesus, King of the Jews!"

I have returned to my father's house, standing in an open-air room with marble columns all around. The floor is composed of blocks of marble arranged in a most pleasing pattern and I notice with pleasure the palm trees planted as sentinels bordering this beautiful room. My brother greets me and welcomes me home. Instantly, I recognize my brother as my son, Neale, in this life. He stands with regal posture and intelligence, and carries himself with strength and dignity as befits the son of a Roman Senator who might himself be called to the Senate one day. My Roman brother's face is the same as Neale's with strong high cheek bones and forehead, straight nose, almond-shaped hazel eyes. My brother and I share a close bond of mutual respect. I am excited to report to him about the man, Jesus.

Father enters our open-air room. My father's silver hair, combed and tied back, shines in the late day sun. Our father has a mighty presence; he holds himself regally and stately. He is well-respected in the Senate.

"Father, father, I have just returned from witnessing a man, he walks among the Jews, his name is Jesus, and he speaks to the people of love! Father, this man's philosophies are great in power! A new form of power to behold! Father, you must come and hear him speak! Hear his message! Bring his message before the Senate! You have the power, Father, to change the course of Roman history!"

My father listens patiently until my fiery enthusiasm grows respectfully still. "Daughter, you are free to follow this man, Jesus, if you wish to do so. However, dear daughter, do not suppose to interfere with the workings of the Great Roman Empire! Now, go in peace dear daughter, and allow your father some respite from a long day of meaningful work."

And so, as a Roman girl in the time when Jesus walked the land, I left my father's house where I enjoyed the most valuable asset of those times, safe passage, and followed Jesus to the end of his life, helping to spread his message of love.

In the evening I attend a show in the ship's plush nightclub. Tonight a comedy show is the featured entertainment and Bernie McGrenahan, now a career comedian, will be performing. Laughter is a wonderful release after a day of deep self-discovery. Now Bernie is onstage, projecting an intelligent, organized presence. He's really funny and I'm laughing wholeheartedly, a portion of his routine anchored in childhood experience. Shifting to a quieter tone Bernie announces, "There's someone here tonight I want to recognize." The audience grows hushed. "When I was a kid, there were times I felt as if my life was falling apart. But there was one place I could go, a place where I always felt safe, a place where I was welcome as part of the family. It was my best friend Neale's mom who gave me refuge in the midst of my personal storm and honestly, I don't know how I would have survived without her. She never asked questions, she just treated me with love. And, ladies and gentlemen, she's here tonight. Francine!" Bernie looked right into my eyes, having already located me in the huge nightclub, "Would you please stand so everyone can see the woman I looked upon as a surrogate mother." The audience of about a thousand people stirs and shifts in their seats. Taking their cue from Bernie, the audience explodes in emotional applause. I'm emotional too, of course, and blow heartfelt kisses to Bernie.

JUNE 22. Difficulty emerging from deeper than usual meditation. My consciousness remains separated from my body! I'm trapped in a dark place of doom where human souls are locked in eternal sorrow. All manner of cries are sounding, near and distant weeping, sobbing. One small child I'm comforting clings to me, crying and clutching my legs, refusing to let go. A crowd of souls who've drawn close to receive comfort are inconsolable. The power of their collective need is holding me back from returning to present reality. I'm fully aware of my body lying across my bed. My consciousness, however, is remaining in that terrible place I can only imagine must be some kind of hell, a place I have visited before, helping trapped souls to understand they needn't remain there. Yet, the trapped souls are unable to accept this understanding. Hell is what they know and where they believe they belong. With simultaneous awareness of my unreachable body, the place I was unwillingly trapped in, and separation of consciousness from physicality, I am not frightened, only determined to regain wholeness. I must call Annie to help me, the sound of her voice will summon me back. The phone lay beside me. I pick it up, feel it's weight in my hand, yet my eyes are unable to see anything. I see a mist of pale gray, nothing else. Suddenly the phone rings, it's Annie, and in a quick snap my consciousness returns to my body.

JULY 7. My daughter's marriage is ending. I'm transmitting healing to her. In a flash I see her sleeping, surrounded by a mist of golden light. An angel, an almost transparent being of radiant white light is leaning gracefully over Annie, ever so gently kissing her cheek. In the space of a second the scene expands with Neale as the focus of healing, quickly followed by the same golden light and angel leaning over Steven. In another second Annie, Neale and Steven are simultaneously all within my consciousness. I glimpse the angel's face and recognize myself!

I call Neale to tell him about Annie's decision. Sympathetic, he calls to comfort her. A few minutes later Annie calls. Her energies are harmonious for now.

JULY 14. Enhancement of a teaching gained from a spiritual experience can occur within minutes or hours or days of the experience. Today I receive deeper insight into the experience of hovering thirty feet above my body; my consciousness open to the thoughts of seven spiritual beings; feeling no attachment to my body, yet aware of owning responsibility for my body.

Above linear time for a moment I belonged to a group of beings who live with full awareness of unity consciousness. The group performs tasks similar to the one I was allowed to be part of, listening to prayers of human beings, assessing merit, intent, purity and light. The group's consciousness is pure in its intention, assessing quotients of love, mercy, wisdom, forgiveness, taking an expansive view of the life of the individual in prayer. It is not the isolated misdeed in our lives which draws focus; it is the accumulation of thousands of deeds and actions, the sum total of our deeds and actions. This information becomes known to the group's unified mind by observation of the light emanating from the body, forming the aura, which in this case appeared pure white with streams of violet, turquoise blue, pink and indigo blue indicating a human being devoted to loving kindness. Apparently, this human being is recognized and known to the group. Scanning the woman's light body enables the group to 'see' the human beings she is praying for and perceive knowledge of them. Just as it helps to know influential people on Earth, it seems it doesn't hurt to have an influential ally in the spiritual realm. We all need someone to pray for us.

While embraced by the group's unity consciousness I perceived my higher self as a more enlightened self than my own limited human self. My higher self, I learned, 'sacrifices' much of its freedom while remaining connected to my body. In actuality my higher self holds an exalted place in the etheric realm, deciding on matters which may enhance or diminish the quality of a person's life. There is no waste of time in these higher spaces. My consciousness did not need to turn and look at my fellow spiritual beings or ask for approval. Harmony of intent leads to swift decisions.

In spirit we carry a force far more apparent than can be perceived in physical form. This force animates us and drives our actions. I now grasp more fully the meaning of what the mystics say about life on Earth being an illusion whereas the endless world, the world of unity consciousness, is the true reality, the source of Earthly events.

JUNE 23. Asleep, I hear very close to my ears, my name being called: f r a n c i i i n e, drawn out and sounding like crystal bells. Two sequences of my name called two times in each sequence. Pure melodious sound.

AUGUST 2. Annie's husband has moved out of Annie's house. It's a difficult passage for my sensitive daughter but she is discovering her own beautiful inner strength.

SEPTEMBER 28. Danny argues about everything. But he is giving serious consideration to seeing a marriage counselor. I awaken with a sickening sense of dread. My right eye is hurting and difficult to open. Another cyst has decided to form under the upper eyelid of my eye. With deep faith and trust in the angelic realm, I lift up my face and call on them, my dear spiritual companions. "With your ring finger delicately touch the afflicted eye," comes the telepathic response. I touch my eyelid, the awful lump of the cyst cannot be denied. And then, what I think at first are tears, turns out to be oil. The lightest oil imaginable has manifested under my fingertip! With slow circular motion I gently massage this magical oil into my eyelid. And miracle of miracles, my eye is healed. The awful cyst dissolves into nothing!

OCTOBER 10. Yom Kippur, anniversary of my father's passing, Danny and I drive up to be with Annie. She has cleansed from her home the energy of her marriage and is moving forward with her life. My heart breaks for the emotional pain my precious daughter, always a help to others and never causing harm to others, has endured in her marriage. I surround Annie with golden light and see angelic beings of light all around her, with one very large angel watching protectively over all. The angels give me confidence that Annie will find her way to happiness.

I lay down at night to sleep, close my eyes and see a dazzling color show. Opening before me, windows and doors of purest color designs aglow with light, beckoning to me to move forward, move into the beyond, into infinity. Each section glorious light-infused color such as we on Earth do not know. When this heavenly display subsides hundreds of sparks of light against a velvet black sky are surrounding me. The clock registers passage of an hour or more. I call on my Guardian Angel who appears immediately, ask for the spirits of my parents to come, who in another minute are here youthful and healthy. Thoughts of love abound for my children. A cloud of pure love energy surrounds me.

OCTOBER 11. Spiritual growth study group continues to meet each week in my little studio apartment. I invite Danny, Just come for a little while and see what we do, but he has no interest.

OCTOBER 31. At lunch with Danny he speaks confidently about moving into my new apartment. Unexpectedly and uncontrollably, I start to shake with fear. I must find some therapeutic guidance. Up in my studio I lie down to breathe, call on Guardian Angel Love and ask for help. My body begins to vibrate with healing energy and within a few minutes I arise refreshed. The phone rings. My new friend Melanie says she's sitting in her office when suddenly she hears a message in her head, "If you're thinking of calling Francine now is a good time." I share my problem with my friend who immediately gives me the name of her therapist, Ezra. I connect with Ezra, feel comfortable with his warmth and sincerity and decide to embark on this new path toward self-discovery, toward finding a new kind of strength. Once again, my angel, available always, helps me overcome life's struggles; my angel hears the cry of my heart!

NOVEMBER 26. Strange dream experience. I'm exiting the lobby of the building I live in on East 57th Street, looking up at an otherworldly metallic ceiling. Outside the building, off to my left, and not very far off or very high, I see a craft and on the whole underside of this craft are blinking rainbow lights. The sight of these beautiful blinking rainbow colored lights is awesome to behold. The craft draws nearer and the display of lights changes to ominous gray. The craft's enormous size blots out the entire night sky above the East Side of New York. I awaken tired with no memory of going through a door, wondering how I got outside or even how I returned to my bed.

DECEMBER 1. My 59th birthday. Closing on my new apartment. Everything goes well. There are messages from Annie and Neale waiting on the answering machine, and a gorgeous floral bouquet from them. I call my loving children. A little later Tracey calls and gives the phone to Steven. I tell him my birthday is today and Steven wants to know, "Where are you, Grammie?" I tell him, I'm in New York and my precious grandson asks, "How can I hug you?" We have a nice long conversation. I'm feeling pretty good today.

THE YEAR 2001. Memorial Day Weekend. Dream. President John Kennedy and Jackie come to greet me. We stroll together on a vast grassy lawn, President Kennedy on my left side and Jackie on my right. Caroline, mounted on a groomed and graceful horse comes riding up to us. Appearing radiantly beautiful and vibrant, Caroline looks at us and smiles. Her horse is dressed in robes of crystal.

In the next scene I am in a pristine, white dormitory room, much to my liking. A large, rectangular window framed in pure white is open wide. I feel that in this room I am younger than my present age. On the other side of the window stands President Kennedy, speaking directly to me, counseling me. President Kennedy is inspirational, telling me I can do anything I choose and be anything I want to be. I listen, paying close attention to his every word. When he's finished delivering his message, the window closes and he is gone. I feel the power of his authority and then, in awe, I offer gratitude.

JUNE 15. I'm living in my new apartment since March 15. I'm assuming more control over my life. I turn the key in the lock, step into my very own place, where I have installed a white limestone floor throughout, close the door behind me, knowing I am safe. Here in my own home my peace and serenity cannot be disturbed.

JULY 18. Past Life Dream. I'm a young woman walking along the Apian Way in Italy, calm, enjoying the graceful canopy of strong trees murmuring in the soft air, the beautiful clear azure blue sky overhead, the road beneath my feet. A car comes into view moving toward me and as the car pulls up closer I recognize the driver is my brother but in this life I am revisiting in my dream he is not my brother. He picks up a revolver from the seat of the car, leans his arm on the rim of the car window, aims the gun directly at me and as he drives by I hear not the gunshot but as I fall down bleeding an almost silent 'Pah.'

JULY 22. Dream vision possible future. Observing from a high position above the water's edge of the East River, off in the distance out at sea, the ship I see appears from my vantage point the size of a toy. Despite this distance I notice the details of portholes and decks. It seems to be a military ship. I see the flash of a missile, an explosion of enormous magnitude occurs, the ship has been hit by a nuclear missile. A tsunami wave hundreds of feet high rolls in toward the city and with this wave the ship, completely demolished, is folded into the sea. The tsunami is fast approaching the shoreline, headed toward us. We better prepare! No time to prepare! The tsunami wave hits the city. Sea water sweeps over everything and in a minute, water has engulfed low buildings and the lower floors of taller structures. Preparation against an overwhelming force such as this is futile. The city is plunged into a fight for survival.

AUGUST 8. Ezra, my kind-hearted therapist who is helping me through the painful phase of marital separation, said to me, "You are an alchemist. You take dross and turn it into gold."

SEPTEMBER 9. Soul travel. In another dimension where all is dark as a moonless night, I go to minister to unhappy souls who have passed on yet cling to the deep sadness of their human life predicaments. A kind of spotlight illuminates the soul I am ministering to. It appears very much like a staged drama in a theater. Tonight I am brought to an older black woman wearing an apron over her flowered cotton dress, weary of standing unendingly beside her push cart of flowers. I reach out my hand to her, "Come with me, dear mother, no longer must you stand here, there is a place in the sunshine where you may rest." She is so sad, afraid to leave this place which is all she remembers of her life. After a while she takes my hand. "You may leave your flower cart here," I tell her. The woman places her trust in me. I guide her to the light where beings of love await her arrival and lead her further toward the brightest horizon.

In my bedroom an aroma of roses surrounds me. Inhaling the rose perfume I am reluctant to open my eyes until the heavenly scent fades away. Consciously awake, eyes remaining closed, I feel a sensation of being rocked in the arms of a large benevolent being as if I were being held in the arms of God. I'm being held and rocked above my bed. I open my eyes, the scent of Roses fades, and I feel the solidity of the mattress supporting my body.

SEPTEMBER 11, 2001. *In Memoriam.*

NOVEMBER 18. During the summer I formed the New York City UFO Community Group in partnership with two friends. It was an idea we discussed whenever we met up at seminars or at a downtown cafe. We three always greeted and parted from each other by joining together in a small circle, arms around each other, heads touching, symbolic of mutual love and deeply felt connection. Our meetings, which synchronistically commenced a week prior to September 11, after which everyone felt a strong need to gather together, are held once a month in the back room of an East Village restaurant. Vibrant and well attended, we provide a warm, safe environment conducive to developing friendships. Some ask to meet more frequently to discuss certain topics in greater depth so I arrange Sunday brunch meetings in my neighborhood. Enduring friendships are formed, everyone asks for healing.

FEBRUARY 19, 2002. My new grandson, Brett, is born, big and healthy, all is well. I fly out to Los Angeles where Brett's mother lives. Neale calls me throughout the day including one moment when Brett was in my arms. "Listen to your Daddy's voice!" and with an intense expression of interest, Brett listened. Later, in my hotel room I held him on my shoulder, he held up his head and looked right into my eyes. And then my beautiful new grandson smiled!

APRIL 19. Tracey is angry; Brett is now here with us, on Earth and she's angry that Neale loves his son and goes to see him. I tell Tracey, Brett's my grandchild and I love him. So Tracey won't speak to me. I'm upset over all of it. How often will I see my new grandson? I speak on the phone to Cheryl, trying to convince her to come back to Miami where Brett can be with his family who loves him.

Golden sparks of light float all around me, mostly around my head. I've noticed that the sparks of light appear on days when my need is greatest. They also appear when something lovely is about to happen. The golden sparks of light are an affirmation of pure love; they uplift my energies, bring me comfort and altogether I am happier and smile more whenever they show themselves.

APRIL 21. All in one day: Tracey called, Steven took the phone and tried to figure out how I could get to where he is and share his french toast with him. Danny called from Annie's house and Annie took the phone. Neale called with a lovely message reporting on the status of Brett and Steven.

JUNE 1. I'm relaxing with a guided meditation tape. The listener is advised to create a sanctuary wherein you will meet your spirit guide. Delighted, I discover I've been transported instantaneously to my sanctuary which I recognize! My sanctuary is a square white room with a large picture window and a most elegant white fireplace. One wall holds bookshelves filled with pristine volumes of enlightening literature handed down from all the mighty sages who have lived on Earth. Elegantly positioned in a corner of my sanctuary, a white desk formed of crystal in the shape of a crescent moon. In a cabinet, a few robes of variously textured cloth are stored. The floor is made of warm natural wood, the beautiful swirls and graining hold stories of trees of Earth. The ceiling is high, peaked and beamed. The fireplace transforms magically into a white screen and on the screen is one word: LOVE.

There are two white chaise lounges in my sanctuary. I recline on one, my spirit guide has assumed a comfortable position on the chaise to my left. My spirit guide wears traditional Native American deer skin clothing and a feathered chief's headdress. In his noble presence I'm awakening to almost forgotten memories. So much more than my spirit guide, he is my soulmate on Earth. We come to Earth together in certain lifetimes for the sake of others, to uplift the existing vibration of the people. A soft golden glow surrounds this magnificent man whose features reflect the beauty of every race of mankind. He smiles a pleasurable and loving greeting. I rise and go to kneel beside him, my right arm leaning across his chest. He strokes my hair comfortingly, reminding me of my courage in assuming this life on Earth without my soulmate. "You, beloved, have passed this way before. Be not afraid as you pass this way again. Always trust in yourself." I am enveloped in abiding peace. I also feel onrushing emotions of relief accompanied by the joy of blissful unity. Together, we gaze at the scene beyond, framed by the picture window: majestic leafy green mountain forest trees. "Notice where we are, my beloved, and when you return to your life on Earth, remember from whence you come. Remember your soulmate! Always beside you!" And then I realize, my sanctuary must be located in a high place because we are gazing at the treetops below! Right outside, framed in the picture window, blue skies, white fluffy clouds.

SEPTEMBER 13. Draw a circle with a zigzag circumference, approximately twelve inches in diameter. Fill the circle with shimmering, dazzling white light, and maintain this vision before your eyes wherever your gaze may fall. You see before you constant rotation and shimmer. This is what I am looking at presently, shimmering on my right hand and arm as I write. My gaze fixed firmly on it the dazzling white light shape expands to almost double size, and even larger! I realize, today is my mother's birthday.

SEPTEMBER 25. In Miami, Danny driving up to Tracey's to pick up Steven, I close my eyes against the sun's glare and go into a private reverie. My consciousness lifts up to ask of God, What am I doing on this planet? A silver cord shoots straight up from my crown chakra. I see the cord with great clarity, but with what eyes I do not know. (Several years later I learned that the crown chakra is capable of opening, allowing the third eye to see above.) The silver cord does not resemble anything of this physical Earth. Strong, tubular in shape, glittering in constant motion, extremely fine and ethereal. It's easy to hold the vision of the silver cord but difficult to adequately describe. The higher part of the silver cord disappears into the upper atmosphere of a glaring hot afternoon in Miami. Yet somehow I know it reached up to the mind of God. Conducted by the silver cord which descended and re-connected with my super-conscious mind I receive an answer from God! "You are here because you are my helper. All that you do you do in my name. All that you do you do with love." Accompanying emotions indescribable. The most gentle, powerful, all-encompassing love going into my consciousness, surrounding me and filling me with a joy so profound as to be unknown within the physical body. The silver cord has strengthened my connection to God. From this moment every thought of mine, every emotion, every word, every action in my life, I will experience on a level of higher awareness previously inaccessible.

SOUL TRAVEL EXPERIENCE. While asleep in my bed, my etheric body, or my soul energy, travels the world. Always guided, always protected, never alone. On this night I find myself in a southern state, possibly Virginia, at twilight on the grounds of a lush estate. Up a gentle slope about fifty feet from where I find myself seated on a garden bench I see a gracious home, built in the year 1880. Grand and stately, a new wing has been added by the owners to accommodate an elegant restaurant. This modern wing is defined by a sweeping corner of floor to ceiling glass panels overlooking manicured lawns and gardens.

Suddenly, a wave of panic courses through the small parties of refined ladies and gentlemen sipping cocktails in the gardens. Everyone is looking skyward and pointing upward. The sky has grown leaden, an enormous tornado is bearing down, its funnel curved askew, moving swiftly toward us yet veering left and right. A small, whimpering child climbs into my lap. I tell him to grasp my neck tightly, hold on and don't let go. With unimaginable speed, not even feeling the grass beneath my feet, I run to the refuge of the house, reach the glass-paneled wall, choose the panel I suppose is the door which slides open in observance of my will, and inside I dash with the child still holding tight. The basement door stands ajar. I carry the child safely down a few steps. Before parting I say to the child, a lovely boy whose fine destiny is bound up in accomplishment of medical cures, "Never forget that an angel came to save you! You have important work to do!"

In the morning, I switch on the TV hoping to learn of a tornado in Virginia. In actuality, a tornado in North Carolina is announced. With inner ears I hear the child describing to unbelieving adults, the angel lady who appeared from nowhere, saved his life and disappeared.

OCTOBER 15. Soul travel experience. I look up into the black night sky and see there three crescent moons shining with magnificent luminosity. Two equally bright, luminous stars are positioned between the crescents. The atmosphere seems like the atmosphere of Earth in a temperate zone but the heavenly bodies appear so much closer than they do from Earth. I am filled with a sense that all of space is near. Four people are present. These four are people who, despite my efforts to create harmony between us, had turned away from having warm relationships with me. I point to the astonishing sight in the sky. They look up at the three crescent moons and the two shining stars and shrug as if this supernal beauty holds no importance for them. I turn my face back to the sky. Numerous bright stars have risen. The three crescent moons are no longer visible. The two shining stars are camouflaged by the other stars.

OCTOBER 25. My friend Phil Imbrogno interprets the experience this way: The two stars are Throne Angels, the highest angelic beings. Because I was comfortable in this place I have been there before, communing with the Throne Angels. The four people had been summoned before them for purposes of healing. The many stars that rose to surround the crescent moons are high spiritual beings who guard the Throne Angels.

NOVEMBER 14. I'm washing my hands and in place of my hands I see a luminous white light. Reflected in the mirror I see where my face is the same luminous light obscuring my face. The light is soft all around. And now I see light beings surrounding me; on my left, on my right, above and behind me. The light beings are golden, tinged with pink, violet, white.

"What does this mean?" I ask the light beings.

"We are with you," was the reply.

The day is filled as always with a stream of clients who arrive at my apartment for healings and I am aware of a profound increase in healing ability.

DECEMBER 12. Two weeks ago a one-half inch brown oval lesion appeared on the upper left side of my nose. It began to change from discoloration to raised skin and in certain light, blue around the edges. I called on my healing angels, stood before the mirror, focused my eyes on the spot, held my left palm open toward it and directed the middle fingertip to the skin lesion. After a few repeated healings the lesion began to appear less 'angry.' Last night I did another healing and tonight, miracle of miracles, only a shadow remains. During last night's healing my fingertip vibrated with concentrated healing energy. It felt as if a high, powerful force was moving through me. Fascinated and completely grateful I watched my own vibrating fingertip blur before my eyes.

DECEMBER 15. The NYC UFO Community Meeting is now renamed the Wisdom Circle and unexpectedly I am now the leader of this group. Through this Wisdom Circle I hope to bring awareness of higher truth and love to people, healing in its highest form.

The lesion on my nose is completely healed and I've gained a wondrous awareness in personal authority which had never occurred to me before: I have the power to heal myself!

Angelic Healing & Light Beings

Brief Summary of Healings

AN ANGEL HEALING, in addition to healing deep wounds of all kinds, is designed to uplift a person's vibration. The person who assumes responsibility for their own process will begin to think and act in higher ways, thus becoming a co-creator in the raising of their own frequency. As the universe desires balance in all things one begins to realize that the universe, in some mystical way, is providing assistance in this process. Opportunities for personal growth arise as well as new people of a higher vibration suddenly entering one's life. Raising one's frequency leads to a life of greater well-being as one leaves behind desire for negative involvement and desires instead to help one's brothers and sisters. One begins to observe the need for help everywhere and experiences desire to respond with an open heart. Raising one's frequency provides a higher understanding of one's life and the pursuit of happiness begins to take on new meaning as love and compassion begin to rule one's actions. Raising one's frequency leads to greater awareness of the multi-dimensional self, an expanded consciousness and inner peace.

NATIONAL BUSINESS CONVENTION in San Francisco. I meet up with Barbara, a long-time friend, suffering with terrible back pain. She is wearing magnets for relief yet the pain persists. We are in a noisy reception hall, loud blaring music, a thousand people milling about. I place my hands on Barbara's spine. She feels a rush of heat, she feels relief, she is amazed. When she goes up to her hotel room Barbara removes the magnets and never needs to wear them again. Her back is fully healed, she and her loved ones are ecstatic. Back in New York she sends me a lovely gift from Tiffany. After a year or so of full relief my friend decides to resume horseback riding. She is thrown by the horse, her back is severely injured, her life is turned upside down and she moves far away.

CLARA, a highly intellectual and spiritually aware woman, seeks help for her ailing mother who resides in a southern state. Since the man she loved has left her Clara suffers a broken heart. There are more broken-hearted people walking on the streets of New York City than anyone can guess. In response to a broken heart a person often creates, for protection, a drawing inward or closing down of the heart chakra. The angels seek to open hearts.

While Clara is relating her story I transmit loving compassion to her heart chakra which helps to open her heart and as the heart opens Clara's story deepens. We seek the seed of sorrow. We seek it on a soul level, to allow the golden healing light to enter into the depths of sorrow and transmute the sorrow into feelings of joy and well-being. When Clara achieves the first flash of deeper insight into the source of her pain we are ready to summon forth deep healing. After working with the 'light' a person may experience extraordinary release and express it through tears. The consciousness is now prepared to accept a powerful healing. The remainder of the healing session is devoted to discussion based on insight gained while immersed in the light. The previously hidden, newly discovered inner self, our life on a soul level, which is always so much more than suspected by any of us, connects easily with the angels. Discovery of one's soul, which is part of God, therefore always Good, ultimately leads to self-love. This may be referred to as true healing. Even if self-love is not completely achieved overnight, receiving permission on a higher consciousness level to love oneself as well as understanding the necessity for self-love, is sufficient to set the process in motion.

As much time as needed in one session is given for healings such as Clara's. We achieve in a relatively short span of time that which might require years of traditional therapy.

Clara received enough relief from the pain of a broken heart to go out on her own and become a practitioner of healing. Turning one's attention outward, in service to others, is a light-filled path toward overcoming depression. With her mother's permission, I transmitted distant healing to her mother which allowed her mother to leave her bed and without using a cane go for a walk in her garden. Mother and daughter discussed the healings and Clara soon began transmitting healing to mother. Self-empowerment.

DIANA IS PREGNANT with triplets. Doctors have detected with ultrasound a sign of possible retardation so she is considering removal of two or possibly three fetuses. While my hands are held above her womb I feel the energies of all three babies, I see the babies and they see me! The babies are calling, "We want life! We want to live!" Physically, the babies are tiny, and their voices are weak, yet the desire to live is powerful and insistent, and more than that, as soon as they became aware of my energy they began to reach out with their combined energies. My hands are tingling ferociously. These babies, if they are allowed to be born, are going to be strong willed.

Diana and I spend hours talking; she has other overwhelming problems in her life. She makes the heartbreaking decision to abort two fetuses and asks me to come over for another healing. Ultrasound has revealed the remaining baby is missing a finger as well as other symptoms which are indications of possible retardation. My hands above her womb I see the baby. He is beautiful and healthy, a really nice baby boy. I listen to Diana's woes, transmit angelic healing vibrations, and tell her what I have seen. She is terribly worried, still unsure, with only a week or so left to decide. A high level of emotion pervades the room, Diana is sobbing, I'm doing my best to remain centered and focused while offering comfort. I call on the angels to help Diana make the choice that will lead to the best and highest good for all concerned. A few days later Diana tells me she's staying with this baby and after he is born I am invited to come over and see him. Mother hands him to me and I'm holding him in my arms. What a beautiful little face he has, rosy and perfect in every way. Altogether he is beautifully formed and strong. His eyes are focused on my eyes and I can see this child is an evolved soul, his attention focused with interest and awareness on my face. The whole of him is lovely and beautiful and the missing finger is as nothing when compared with all the potential held within this baby boy.

EVA HAS RECENTLY been diagnosed with Multiple Sclerosis, needs a cane to walk, seeks relief from symptoms. My hands above her body I feel this woman does not have MS, but in the region of her female organs she is filled with a terrible murky green etheric slime which is expanding and filling up the rest of her insides, creating blockages throughout her entire body. I ask how many children she has and if she had pregnancy problems. Immediately fiercely emotional, she begins to speak about the birth of her son, how his birth affected her, how he messed up her life since the day he was born, nineteen years ago.

"I don't think you have MS, Eva. I see energetic blockages created by whatever the karma is between you and your son. We will do our best to bring you healing by transmutation of unhealthy energy into healthy energy. I feel very positive that we can accomplish this. When you realize that you no longer need to rely on a cane to walk, this will be a sign that the unhealthy energy which has sort of taken on a life of its own is being transformed by the light." Eva returns for a few more healings and I observe that slowly we are making progress in clearing the monumental blockages which were creating a hardening of all her bodily systems. Eva was suffering from a kind of energetic necrosis that was spreading upward from her female organs. But as we work together on the transformation of energy the terrible murky green etheric slime begins to appear less dense and less pervasive. This tells me that the healing process is progressing, the reversal of energetic necrosis is taking place, the angels are responding to our call. When I see her walk in without her cane I will know her healing is being manifested in the physical world. After three very successful sessions I was disappointed to hear from Eva that she decided to stay with her doctor's diagnosis. About a year later I met our mutual friend and the first thing he said was, "Remember the woman who had MS? Guess what? She didn't have MS. And now she's walking without a cane."

FRANK, A WAITER in a nearby cafe where I have lunch, underwent surgery. He's miserable with catheter still in, doctor said it will remain for at least another week. Healing focuses on removing catheter. Frank calls day after healing to report excellent news. Doctor decided to remove catheter, declaring suddenly the catheter unnecessary and Frank is very happy. Nice and easy healing. Wonderful.

Few weeks later Frank is back at work in the cafe. He comes over to my table, smiling and thanking me. "You didn't know this, Frannie, but I've had a drinking problem for a long time and I just couldn't kick it. Since your healing I haven't had a drop and don't even want it anymore!" He brings me a delightful iced cappuccino, "I made this for you myself!" he says, "It's a gift!"

Our angels know our deepest, most pressing needs better than we know. This young man's healing perfectly illustrates the value of having faith and trust in the glorious light beings who, although unseen by us, watch over us awaiting our call to come to our aid and uplift our lives.

GIGI REQUESTS HEALING for her husband who is in a coma. On a cold winter Sunday morning I meet her at the hospital. A few loved ones have gathered to be present for the healing. I observe Sam in his coma and sense a fleeting thought of his which tells me he is not coming back. But ever hopeful, I ask his loved ones to fill their hearts and minds with loving thoughts for Sam. A bit of movement in his toes indicates acknowledgment of the doctor's request to respond this way, but it doesn't feel very heartening to Gigi. Subsequent healings accomplish very little progress. Sam moves his fingers in response to yes and no questions and even lifts a foot but Gigi is despondent. They met late in life, found great happiness together and now this terrible tragedy. She is torn between keeping him on life support or allowing him to pass. Sam was a brilliant man who will never again be as he was.

I suggest a shamanic journey whereby Gigi and Sam will meet soul to soul, bypass physical limitations which will allow Sam to express his desires for himself. During the shamanic journey Gigi and Sam converse in her garden in the higher realm where Sam's mind is fully alert and well. Gigi asks her husband, "Sam, do you want to go on with our life together?" Sam replies, "I will decide in two weeks' time." Nothing is said by him to indicate a future.

Sam is telling his wife that within two weeks he will pass. Gigi's eyes are sad with loss. I'm not sure if she feels as I do but we will allow the future to unfold. She promises to stay in touch. Exactly two weeks later I learn that Sam has passed. Knowing that her husband made his own choice provided immense comfort and consolation for Gigi. Her memory of meeting with Sam in the higher realm where all is truth and love helped her move through the mourning period and enabled her to move on with her life in a healthy way.

THE SHAMANIC JOURNEY is a powerful path to healing. It is a highly organized spiritual journey taken in the presence of spirit guides and under the protective wing of angels. It transpires in a higher realm where all is truth and love. The illusion of life on Earth is comprised of negativity which may be understood to mean that everything negative or restrictive is an illusion, and the shamanic journey bypasses all negativity, all restriction, bringing us above the illusion to ultimate truth where we discover that everything is love. The influence of pure love resonates with the pure light of our soul and in this way our consciousness is forever uplifted. Very few people find the need to undergo a second shamanic journey. Meeting soul to soul with those who play an important role in our lives whether passed over or here with us on Earth; feeling transcendent love which in a flash heals all sorrow; lifelong mystifications unraveled with higher awareness that satisfies for all time; the shamanic journey has proven the most valuable of all healing methods. It reaches deeply into the heart, it soothes and comforts the mind, uplifts the soul.

MOST OF THE HEALINGS I bring through are done spontaneously, when I'm out and about. People I encounter along the way are often moved to disclose their sorrows and pains to me and I offer relief wherever we are. These are usually one time healings which I follow up with supportive distant healings late at night when the electromagnetic frequencies are less active.

An example of this sort of spontaneous healing is the saleswoman who works in Barney's Fine Jewelry Department with whom I chat whenever I stop by; she reminds me of my mother. I recall when my mother worked in Bloomingdale's Fine Jewelry Department and I'd stop by to visit, soon having to leave her standing behind the counter while I walked out into a beautiful sunshiny day. One day my Barney's friend was very distraught. Her daughter was refusing to return her calls. Standing by the counter, holding her hands, I called on our guides and angels and requested healing for the daughter's anger as well as reconciliation with her mother. At home I followed up with distant healings for both mother and daughter. A few days later I stopped by to check on her and the woman greeted me with a big hug. "It's amazing! The very next day after you were here my daughter calls and tells me she loves me and everything is fine since! How did you do that?"

"Honestly, it's not me, it's our angels and spirit guides. Call on them and they will help you!"

Another time, at dinner with friends in a fine Italian restaurant on the Upper West Side, my friend is complaining of a sprained ankle. It's wintertime and she is wearing knee high leather boots. We lift her leg across my knees, transmit healing to her ankle. Later that night my friend calls, greatly relieved. As soon as she arrived home she removed her boots and discovered that her ankle is no longer swollen and no longer hurts.

Occasionally, even ladies' restrooms become settings for spontaneous healings. Once I encountered a woman who was suffering with something quite painful in her eye. I asked her if she'd like my help. She replied, "Whatever you can do to help me, please do!" All I did was wave my hand over her eye once or twice and whatever had been causing the pain dissolved into nothingness.

This is a strange but wonderful phenomenon with cinders or such that are caught in the eye. They just melt away. Similarly with splinters.

Exiting a restaurant one cold winter evening, pausing in the drafty vestibule, my friend suddenly remembers she meant to ask for a healing on her back. I place my hands on her spine for a scant moment. Patrons are coming and going, bar music is blaring, holiday lights are blinking. The next morning my friend calls to report the backache that had plagued her for months simply went away.

These spontaneous healings are wonderful and hold their own kind of joy. Someone is in need, I happen to be with them at that moment, together we enter the realm of angels.

Altogether, on an average day my schedule includes three, four or five clients at my apartment, two or three healings while I'm out and about, distant healings between the hours of midnight and 1:00 A.M., usually a list of ten or so, and long distance telephone healings which are fascinating. People I've never met, living in distant states, find me through recommendation. Everyone who comes to me knows someone who has received healing from me. Everyone who comes to me is being guided by spirit guides and angels.

People call for advice or just to receive comfort. Sometimes people want to learn about healing or metaphysics and ask if I will teach them. I share everything given me for as long as they desire. Some clients go on to become healers themselves.

DECEMBER 31, 2002. Sleeping in the guest room next to Steven's room. Awaken at 3:00 A.M. to a stream of pictures flashing before my inner eye, each one depicting a physical characteristic, accompanied by explanations of differences between myself and my mother's family. Methodically organized close-ups of my physical characteristics including the shape of my hairline, forehead, eyebrows, eyes, down to each individual toe, inspire me to recognize each picture as accurately drawn. This process is repeated for each of my two aunts, four cousins, brother, mother, father. When this slideshow is completed I have an urge to go to the window so I rise from bed, walk the few steps to the windows and draw back the draperies.

I'm gazing out at the eastern night sky above Miami Beach. Far lower than a star I see a circular object lit by a bright central white light ringed by an arc of red lights below and an arc of blue lights above. A consciousness is emanating from the craft. With the aid of Steven's telescope I watch the object shape shift while the blue colored lights pulsate and morph into green and turquoise and the red colored lights into orange and yellow. The colors are not of this world. The colors are radiating a magnificent vibrancy. The colors shine with unbelievable brilliance, the central white light maintaining its own white brilliance while shape shifting. Mesmerized, I stand by the window watching the lights until amazingly the object grows increasingly smaller in size until it blinks out.

Climbing back into bed, one knee on the mattress, I pause and tell myself, This did not just happen. What I have just witnessed must be some kind of dream. But I am awake, here's my knee pressing on the bed. I lie down very much desiring sleep, I have to be awake early for Steven, but another communication ensues.

This time the process consists of video-like displays depicting childhood scenes of family interactions, highlighting differences in consciousness. In each scene my response or behavior comes from consciousness of compassion and love whereas my family member is trapped in drama. I recall each event and remember observing these events as they unfolded in our homes; my awareness of the futility of anger, jealousy, competitiveness; my awareness that all they really had to do was love one another. After a while the process completed and once again I rose from bed, went over to the window and drew back the drapery.

The lighted object, or craft, was again in the eastern sky where it had previously been. Again I am transfixed by a replay of the radiant light show, unable or unwilling to move away from the window, until the lights diminished in size and blinked out.

Climbing back onto the bed I felt this message unfold within my mind, "Trust in yourself. Trust in what you know to be true. You are of us and we are in you." It was 5:00 A.M. Steven came in to sleep the remainder of the night with me. Later, when I awoke, I felt unlike my usual self.

JANUARY 4, 2003. New York. Freezing winter weather. Sun streaming in through the southeastern windows, eyes closed in meditation, I'm warm on my daybed. Coming into gentle focus, manifesting right here in front of me, an ancient man with long white pointed beard, long white hair, attired in white biblical style robes of a homespun appearance. His figure glows, emanating holiness. An ethereal light infuses his pale blue eyes. Quite tall, he holds his outstretched arms palms up as if to encompass the entire room and without moving his lips he communicates with me. It's wondrous to see him, to receive his message.

"Lilacs and Roses," he says, and petals float all around him forming a pedestal beneath his feet which do not touch the floor. "Bluebirds," he says, and enchantingly delicate bluebirds flutter on either side of him mingling with the aromatic floating petals. "Bowers of gardenias," he says and his words are accompanied with imagery. The holy man repeats these phrases three times, radiating comfort, love, playfulness.

"Where are you from?" I ask.

His face and his hands are long and thin, his body is long and thin. In response to my question he points with a single long finger, upward toward the sky. His gentle demeanor is familiar; in the higher realms we know one another well, and I know he will return. He addresses me as 'daughter,' and I call him Divine

Father. "Henceforth, daughter, we shall do healings on Earth as we do healings on the planet we call Home."

I drift into a peaceful sleep awakening an hour later feeling as if I'd slept for ten hours.

JANUARY 20. Steven looks into my eyes with an expression he has that makes him seem all grown up. "I love you, Grammie, I just want to be with you, don't care what I'm doing, even if it's TV, just want to be with you."

FEBRUARY 13. Awake at 6:11 A.M. and see outside my living room window a glowing white light, round and luminous. I'm mesmerized, unable to move. It looks like a full moon has come down to 65th Street to peek into apartment windows. Standing barefoot on the cold limestone floor, I watch as the round light morphs into a tubular shape and back to luminous round with white rays.

"Why are you here?" I ask, immediately aware of vibrations of powerful energy coursing through my body.

"Protection," comes the telepathic response.

I'm tired and my feet are freezing. My eyes remaining focused on the light I step back away from the window where icy air seeps in from outside and return to my warm bed. From my bedroom window the light is still fully visible. Just as dawn is breaking and I'm falling asleep, the light begins to diminish. I watch it separate into two sections. Then I fall asleep.

FEBRUARY 15. Severe back pain, unable to stand up straight. I call on Divine Father, "Divine Father, you have come to me from the higher realms, you call me daughter, declare yourself my healing mentor, please bring healing to my back that I may continue to be of service to others." Left hand on my lower spine I 'feel' a beam of light flash at lightning speed through my left arm and hand and into my spine, a sort of bubble movement, and immediately I am able to straighten up and stand pain free!

FEBRUARY 19. Annie has requested a healing, so late at night I call on Divine Father and focus on Annie's sleeping form. I see his tall figure clothed in beautiful robes of glowing golden light. Standing beside my daughter's bed Divine Father reaches down with both hands and with the most graceful, tender movements uplifts Annie's etheric body high above his head as if she were the most blessed among us. In an instant, radiant healing vibrations from a source higher than himself, immerse Annie's etheric body in a mist of golden healing light. Divine Father, with perfect alignment, lowers Annie's etheric body into her physical body. I draw close to Annie and with loving gentleness smooth her energies, making certain all is well, and kiss her face, feeling her soft sweetness with each kiss.

Annie calls this morning. "Whatever you did, Mom, it worked. I woke up feeling really good, good night's sleep. What did you do?"

I explain to Annie that this one time Divine Father gave me the gift of witnessing. He arranged for me to see and feel the healing, it's transcendent and magical beauty and love, intrinsic to all healings brought through by him.

MARCH 3. 4:30 A.M. Awake to silence except for a small clock ticking. I look outside, no unusual light. A few minutes pass and I look outside again. Facing east I see a huge round white light positioned between a tall building north and a spired building east. The round white light moves imperceptibly in a southerly direction. Transfixed, I watch it progress across the sky low between the two buildings.

"Who are you?" I inquire.

"You are of us," comes the telepathic response.

Protesting, I reply, "My mother gave birth to me, I know this because she described it to me a million times."

"That is of no account," they dismiss my protest casually, "we created you and arranged all the rest. You are of us and we are in you."

The statement comes to me with honest authority and so I accept it as truth.

"Why are you here?" I ask.

"Protection."

The light-ship radiates tremendous energy and within the sphere and in its aura I see constant movement. Approaching the spired building it soon will move out of sight and as I note this, my attention held fast by the light, I am reluctant and sad to watch the light-ship move out of sight. At this moment of parting I feel as if I'm being separated from those who know me as no one here on Earth does. It's 4:50 A.M. I return to bed surprised to feel tears streaming down my face.

MARCH 11. On an afternoon flight to Miami I peer out the window and notice flying not so far away and parallel with our plane a UFO headed north. It appears to be a round white craft trailed by a stream of orange-tinged white. The UFO enters a cloud bank, angles downward for a short distance, suddenly makes a sharp U turn, reversing course, now flying south in slight decline, seeming from my vantage point to slow its speed. Then it moves out of sight.

MARCH 12. MIAMI, 4:55 A.M. Awaken to a soft buzz in my ears, open my eyes and see a pure white enclosure beside my bed, although logically between the bed and the wall there is not enough room for it. I feel as if I've just been inside this vehicle which is rapidly dematerializing. I see now only a curved portion of it which resembles hard white enamel. I see intersecting arcs in motion. Calmly, I watch the structure grow transparent until it disappears.

JUNE 28. MEDITATION. Divine Father is my guide. My apartment is completely filled with golden light. Many glowing angels in attendance, angelic light floods the room. My apartment is transported to a higher realm where melodious angelic singing is heard. Within this environment people are instantly restored to youthful vitality. This happens to me and my children. Bring others with you, I tell my children, everyone you know. I summon all who have trusted in me, then my friends and everyone I've ever known. Everyone is healed!

The angels chorus, "There is more! The blessing has been bestowed upon you, dear Francine."

Out I go, to hospitals. What is your ailment doctor? As I touch the doctor's shoulder with the blessing, "Your ailment is no more. You are blessed for all eternity!" This is repeated. Doctors, nurses. Where are the children? I'm escorted to the children's rooms. Every child is healed, every child returns home to mother! More hospitals, people are lining up to receive healing. I travel the city strong and tireless.

AUGUST 12. In my mind I hear this message: "Take up your pen and write." I stop what I'm doing, pick up my pen and write. "To manifest spiritual healing on Earth one must encompass first and foremost dedication to healing, complete dedication. Dedication includes a process of purification, release of desire to control affairs in the lives of one's brothers and sisters. All who have chosen to incarnate on Earth are brothers and sisters. The energy one commits to control of others, even loved ones, is energy utilized in opposition to the love and light emanating from All That Is, Divine Love, the Heart of God. This flow of love and light is available for all humanity, for every human being, in abundance. The energy of control creates blockages, thereby preventing a brother or sister from receiving their portion of Divine love and light. One who has, in the eternal stream of life, acquired a measure of wisdom, may with a heart of love teach others who seek wisdom.

Another aspect of purification is the response with a loving heart, loving words, loving deeds, to each and every encounter with one's brothers and sisters. A portion of one's encounters may lead to suffering, disillusion, a heavy burden of tears. A loving response lessens one's burdens. Aggression in any form increases one's burdens. An unpleasant encounter met with aggressive response causes darkness to overcome the light. A loving response becomes instantaneous forgiveness releasing the aggrieved and the perpetrator from embattlement. Instant healing.

Another aspect of purification entails honesty and truthfulness beginning with one's own inner dialogue. Pursuit of truth includes a balanced view of whoever may come under scrutiny including oneself. The practice of balancing one's thoughts leads to honesty unattainable otherwise. When emanating from a balanced source the highest ideals of love and compassion grow immeasurably. All truth is contained within the balanced vessel.

The purification process becomes a lonely vigil of one's thoughts and actions. This is intrinsic to manifesting spiritual healing on Earth. An authentic healer will embrace purification with an open heart. To engage in the purification is the highest of all human endeavors for the purification as it proceeds within the heart and mind of one human being gathers great power and increases the flow of love and light from the Heart of God, affecting all others touched by the life of this one. These others affect in turn additional others and so on. In this manner a higher consciousness will become manifest on Earth and all aggression will cease to hold sway over the hearts and minds of Earth's inhabitants.

When an individual soul becomes engaged in the purification process a new and beauteous light begins to emanate from the physical vessel attracting the attendance of God's messengers, the angelic hierarchy, thus stimulating the Heart of God which awaits with infinite patience the purified ingathering of All That Is. When the Heart of God is thus stimulated the flow of love and light increases, providing a greater abundance of love and light on Earth. This in turn allows for awakening to quicken, allows the human heart to more effectively manifest love on Earth. We Are All One."

SEPTEMBER 21. Transmitting golden healing light to Neale's spine. I see streams of strong direct light strike Neale's spine and blend with his spine. The light fills his spinal column so as to turn it into a column of golden light. Streams of light appear as rods held in an unseen hand.

OCTOBER 9. Soul travel. I am in a land of crystal where crystals morph and grow into myriad forms. Encoded within the crystals are the wisdom teachings of all Time. Somehow, messages or teachings are being imprinted on my soul. The crystals are a life form. All around is white.

NOVEMBER 12. Resting on my bed I feel a loving presence enter the room and even hear a subtle movement in the atmosphere of the room. However, I do not see the presence and lie back again. Yet an unmistakable awareness persists. A male presence is standing beside me while I am lying across the foot of my bed, my customary daytime resting place. It's a familiar loving presence who is here to comfort me. It feels like my father.

When I speak to Annie she tells me she, too, felt comforted by an unseen loving male presence in her room. As soon as she realized the presence was her grandpa Annie saw sparks of golden light floating all around her.

NOVEMBER 13. Seeing light in a different way. Awake just before dawn my attention immediately is drawn to a streak of bright red light on the wall below the television which is not on. I look outside and the street lamp on the corner is glowing richly, radiating an enormous profusion of encircling light. The pattern of light encircling the street lamp resembles a greatly enhanced atom, alive with 'speed of light' vibrations. The light of several street lamps visible from my window are appearing to me this way.

NOVEMBER 21. Steven's dream as he told it to me. In his dream Steven saw himself teaching various foreign languages to people. Brett was there learning from him.

Steven asked me, "Grammie, am I kind and wise and good?"

"What do you think, Steven?"

"I think I am."

"And you are, my love, all those and so much more."

NOVEMBER 29. Just before falling asleep at night I feel again, a loving presence beside my bed and open my eyes but the presence remains unseen so I settle down again. Then I feel the presence has drawn very near, leaning over me, whispering in my ear, "Francine, you are going to become a magnificent healer." Twice the presence, familiar and comforting, whispers this message.

DECEMBER 1. Many birthday calls. Three consecutive calls from clients reporting happy successful results and this always gives me great joy. Dinner with Annie and Danny at Oceana. Neale called, very happy that Brett now knows who his Daddy is. Brett showed Neale a photo of them together and pointing to their faces, kissed Neale's face. When Neale picked up Steven at school he reminded Steven to call me, too.

In 1991 when my son, my guide first revealed himself to me and revealed to me what my future held, I asked for a favor in return. "I will do all that Heaven asks of me," I replied, "but in return may I ask for protection for my children every moment of every day of their precious lives. Protect my children from harm and I will do all that Heaven requests of me."

Instantly, my son, my guide agreed and told me that till the end of time our pact shall be regarded as holy and recorded in the Heavenly realms.

DECEMBER 11. Steven called asking for healing for his right arm which is hurting from a flu injection. I saw little white angels, like butterflies, all around his arm. One little angel butterfly alighted on his arm at injection site and kissed it. White light surrounded Steven's arm. Later, Neale called. Steven told me his arm stopped hurting right away.

PARTIAL REVIEW of Healings in 2003. Almost 200 healings by appointment in my apartment. Approximately 1000 to 2000 distant healings, including daytime telephone healings and my list of silent distant nighttime healings. More than 400 spontaneous healings while out and about.

THE YEAR 2005. Stimulated by illustrations I am showing him in Barbara Brennen's "Hands of Light" Steven was full of questions, especially about out-of-body experience. He quickly grasped concepts of the chakra system as well as the spiritual-emotional-physical connection. We talked about auras and Steven was fascinated to learn that I can see my aura in the large bathroom mirror when the light streams in from the window in the next room. He immediately wanted to see his own aura so I showed him how to unfocus his eyes and gaze at a place directly above his head. And Steven saw his aura! His aura is beautiful pink and violet.

MAY 21. Week-long spiritual film cruise with Kathy and Shoshana. Today is the last day of the cruise. 5:19 A.M. Dad's presence is here in my cabin. I feel his love for me. After lunch I feel Mom's presence in my cabin, also strong transmission of love.

After dinner Kathy and Shoshana come to visit on my private deck at the stern of the ship. I lead us into a meditation and after the meditation we discover that each of us received a spiritual message. The message I received was directed at all three of us. The message spoke of the importance of our friendship, urging us not to separate. "Go within. Deep in your heart lies all the knowing you'll ever need. The key to all lies within. Go within your heart. See the self and there recognize God's light."

The three of us standing by the white deck rail, lost in thought, mesmerized by the velvet blackness of a vast starless night. Dark clouds spread high above the ocean interspersed with areas of glowing white light. But, I ask, where is the moon? Can the moon shine in the south while also shining in the east and the west? Bright rays of glowing white light are shining down through the clouds, reflecting on the ocean waves from southern, eastern and western skies. Our cruise ship is sailing north, due to dock at Ft. Lauderdale harbor in the morning. This is our farewell night. We gaze at the sight of mysterious white light brightly lighting up the clouds across the sky until the light fades and the clouds once again hang gray and dark.

It's then I notice a circular opening like a round window in the blackness of space beyond the atmosphere of Earth, contrasted against the dark grey of widespread cloud cover. Within this black circle of space red and white lights dance and loop in dazzling display. Lights zoom across the diameter of the circle, loop around and zoom across to another point on the circumference. They're putting on a light show for us! At first only I can see it. At last Shoshana sees the light show, offered to us as a wondrous gift, a demonstration of Oneness. Just as the circular window begins to close Kathy sees the last of the lights zoom across in a glorious farewell maneuver.

AUGUST 25. Very ill with a terrible flu, lying in bed unable to move, blood pressure dropping, frightened, worried I will pass out lying here alone. I can swallow only a few drops of water. From within my mind the call goes out to Divine Father and in a moment Divine Father is here accompanied by many beings of light all around him, Mom and Dad among them. Somehow they revive me.

"Please tell me," I implore, barely able to move my lips, "does God want to bring me Home?"

Around the room a circle of beautiful spiritual beings of unimaginable radiance, each one focused on transmitting finely-tuned light vibrations. Divine Father, prominent among them, holy and wise, speaks to me of our plan, all the preparation for work yet to be done. The program, it seems, calls for me to become an even more efficient healer in the service of Creator, to help people open their hearts with full awareness of love and kindness. More than thirty years of life on Earth lie ahead for me.

Mom and Dad draw near, and there follows an amazing dialogue whereby my parents explain that they have 'looked into' areas of my life and have gained a deeper understanding of the emotional suffering I endured with Danny of which they had been completely unaware. While they are speaking I am being shown a giant sized glowing crystal ball set in the very center of a dim and silent round space devoid of any other objects and I have the sense that this place is a much revered temple. Souls who seek to learn more deeply the lessons of their lives on Earth may view within this crystal ball full color, holographic imagery of life scenes. My parents, by means of thought transference, show me themselves looking into the crystal ball and seeing Danny and I during one of our terrible arguments when I am begging him to stop running away to play another sport and just stay home with me and the kids, then the aftermath when he has left the house and I am alone. My parents express themselves quite beautifully, free of judgment and negativity, filled with only compassion and love. Feeling so loved and understood, I cry.

Following this I receive a unified, multi-layered transmission from all the light beings in attendance. It seems that Grandma is present as well. "Now is the time to let go of the past and move on into the rest of your blessed life."

Repeatedly the word, NOW, is stressed. Along with a cautionary message, the light beings are communicating to me love, honor and respect. "You must not love, honor and respect yourself one iota less than we do." They call on me to make a vow, now, in their presence, to withdraw my energy from Danny who does not honor nor respect me and to whom I owe nothing. With as much grace as I could summon I vow to withdraw emotionally from him. In these higher realms it is understood that my vow is not even a choice. Sacrifice one's sacred mission on Earth for the sake of pleasing one man? The vow unfolded like a religious ritual, each statement of mine repeated in unison by my beloved spiritual companions. And so it was done.

A great warmth enters my body, my stomach in particular. I feel the heavy energy of illness which has taken hold of my body shift, a subtle movement. I feel the disintegration of sick energy. In its place golden healing light. Then I sleep through the remainder of the day and the entire night to awaken restored to joyful well-being!

SEPTEMBER 19. Walking up Third Avenue feeling lonely and sad. Who am I to imagine myself connected to angels? Where are friends? What am I doing? In my mind I call on my spirit guides to help me rise above the discomfort of this malaise. Just then a woman standing beside me on the sidewalk while we wait for the light to change smiles at me and says, "You look so beautiful! Just look at you!" People waiting at the corner with us turn and smile at me. I return their smiles, and as I resume my walk I smile to my spirit guides.

OCTOBER 25. The sweetest, most melodious music I have ever heard is wafting over me. Melodic chimes of golden bells are sounding all around. Fully immersed in heavenly music suddenly I hear my name being sung as if Heaven is calling to me, healing me, renewing me.

As the light of dawn fills my room I awaken feeling transcendent, risen above the trials and disappointments, the personal loneliness, the human sorrows I don't understand that fill my life. None of it, spirit is always reminding me, is of any consequence in my life. The task of bringing love and healing, transforming disease into golden healing light, has been given me. And when the angels speak, I find myself listening.

NOVEMBER 12. Meditation. Are my thoughts in right alignment with the guidance of angels? Am I holding true to the course set for me and to which I have apparently agreed? Instantly, a vision arises. Four Egyptian males carry on two horizontal poles, a treasure chest. They advance a few steps to emerge from the mists of time, lower the chest to the ground at my feet. The chest opens to reveal its treasure - pure gold bars and golden coins such as I have never seen in this lifetime. I am overwhelmed by the magnificence of this reply. Laughing, I rise up and dance and sing in the company of my spiritual companions.

NOVEMBER 17. Awaken early to the delicate brief aroma of roses. Feel the presence of my mother.

Harold Channer, host of a N.Y. cable TV program, is interviewing me in his downtown studio. At the conclusion of the interview, Mr. Channer turns toward me and inquires, "What would you consider your life accomplishment?"

"So far it hasn't come to pass but I'm always praying for all humanity to rise up and in one voice declare, 'NO MORE WAR! I love my neighbor as I love myself!'"

NEW YEAR'S EVE 2006. The only requirement for acceptance into the path of Light is desire.

JANUARY 22. Aroma of roses surrounds me almost every day.

FEBRUARY 2. Epiphany. The following was given to me in a flash of light:

> The greater portion of our soul resides in exquisitely refined dimensions of light. In the highly refined realms our soul knows individuation within a unified field of consciousness as part of All That Is. The greater

portion of our soul brings us into third dimension reality by utilizing a learned process of creative thought intention which is extended downward into the lower vibrational field of third dimension. Here the soul's highly disciplined and focused consciousness brings into manifestation an energetic living human expression of itself, inbued with a spark of itself - a spark of light - which may be defined as our Life Force.

TO THE GREATER PORTION of our soul we are as a hologram. To us, immersed in the lower vibrational field of third dimensional density, we are solid physicality. We, as an extension of the greater portion of our soul, experiencing physical life on behalf of our soul, endure and eventually master all the trials and tribulations of life on Earth for the exalted purpose of acquiring wisdom. Wisdom acquired through experience as a physical being contributes to the expansion of our soul's awareness which by Divine Law of Service to Others is absorbed into unity consciousness for the highest good of All That Is. We may view this process as humanity's contribution to infinite intelligence. Even getting lost along the way, choosing in opposition to the greatest good, contributes to infinite intelligence, although everything in opposition to the highest good of all prolongs the attainment of ultimate enlightenment on Earth.

THE GREATER PORTION of our soul is our personal "God" who watches over us, loves us as its own creation, provides guidance and awaits with patience our moment of awareness of itself, the greater portion of our soul. For although we are born into an illusion of separation (while within our body which to us is fully physical yet to the greater portion of our soul as seen from the higher realms is a hologram), the spark of our soul that burns within us never ceases yearning for the bliss of unity, truth and pure love. The sacred memory of unity, truth and pure love lies hidden like a rare jewel within the spark of light which suffices as our soul while we are here. This jewel of memory inspires us to seek farther and more deeply for unity, truth and love. And having been born into separation we must become seekers if we are to find our way back to remembering who we truly are and from whence we come. This is occurring now across the entire planet Earth.

OUR ULTIMATE PROTECTION is a strengthening desire to more fully express the highest purpose of every soul on Earth for every soul shares in one mighty sacred purpose above all others. It is to raise the frequency of our beloved planet, to bring about the highest good for all humanity. It is imperative that we awaken, declare our heartfelt desire for peace on Earth, emulate the creativity of the greater portion of our soul, the ability to create by holding a vision here in third dimension as it is done on high, a strong and powerful vision which shall then express in the field of third dimensional reality as a unified desire for peace. We must do this for the highest good of all life everywhere. We must bring about the most phenomenal healing of all time by transforming the blight of conflict into harmony and peace. By joining our consciousness with the higher consciousness of the greater portion of our soul we bring Heaven to Earth and achieve true Oneness, lasting peace on Earth.

FEBRUARY 7. In the aftermath of 9/11 thousands of New Yorkers began to suffer asthmatic symptoms and even more serious illnesses. I am one of these people. My breathing capacity has diminished and this is leading to a diminishment of my well-being. Numerous MRIs, CT scans and all kinds of testing has wearied me and brought me to a moment of choice: undergo surgery or move out from under the toxic cloud that covers the city. Learning the procedural details of the proposed surgery brought me fairly quickly to the decision to move. My apartment sold quickly and I purchased a new apartment in Westchester County hopeful that it will be far enough away to reduce and even eliminate my symptoms, permitting me to avoid surgery and live healthier.

FEBRUARY 19. Moving day. The movers remove from the wall above my bed, my large painting of the San Phillipe Mountains, site of my Hopi medicine woman life. Against the now vacant white wall I see a gathering of my spiritual companions, five gorgeous light beings! Amidst the chaos of dismantling my home an unexpected wondrous gift of joy and love!

OCTOBER 9, 2007. I look into the mirror tonight to see my aura, a bedtime ritual both comforting and calming which I haven't done for a very long time. What I see tonight is astounding. A violet light is glowing all around me. Above my head a horizontal streak of violet light in the shape, I swear, of a halo! I check out the room looking for a violet light shining and reflecting back but with the exception of my usual low light bedside lamp no other light is in the room. Turning back to the mirror I now see an enormous violet aura surrounding my entire body.

NOVEMBER 25. The aroma of roses fills my apartment.

Last night in the midst of an aggravating conversation with Danny the phone suddenly shut off, the TV screen went white and on came a picture of a lavender heart. My spirit guides way of reminding me to let go of the pain.

Message received from my son, my guide:

"The chaos you see around you is momentary and shall pass.

But the loving kindness you bring to each moment is everlasting.

Bring loving kindness to each one.

And your work is perfectly done."

JUNE 10, 2008. Dream. Considering the subject matter the setting for this dream, a store, seems incongruous at first. I'm seated at a counter. A lovely, graceful saleswoman with Asian characteristics has brought out an object for my viewing. With a great ceremony of care and concern for the object's safety, she proceeds to place into my hands a watch of pure solid amethyst. The watch is heart-shaped. With no visible mechanism this heart-shaped amethyst watch is a most unusual artifact. Reverently, I hold it in my hands and marvel at its uniqueness, but the woman gently retrieves it from me. The beautiful amethyst heart-shaped watch had been squashed out of shape and in my hands lay wounded on its side, sadly flattened. Yet the heart's beauty, its unscarred surface, the purity of its inner light remained.

I research the dream elements, meditate on everything I learn, and find some meaning. The amethyst heart is my heart. In a dream a watch often signifies the heart so as often happens with Spirit I'm receiving the message on two levels. The 'saleswoman' was a spirit guide, possibly even the spirit of my mother who worked as a saleswoman selling watches at the Fine Jewelry counter in Bloomingdales and if it was my mother this would explain the setting. As this comes to me now I'm sure the woman was my mother. The tenderness with which she handled the amethyst watch in my dream transmitted a message of understanding sensitivity. Amethyst, an ancient healing stone, signifies peace and serenity. Amethyst power can be accessed to heal body as well as spirit in a gentle, loving way. For psychically sensitive people amethyst can enhance one's third eye vision.

Until the chaos I am currently living with settles down my mother's spirit shall be safeguarding my heart. What chaos can be so powerful as to wound an ancient healing amethyst heart?

White Eagle, the beautiful one who grew up beside me in our past life as Hopi Indians when I was a medicine woman, showed up one day at a conference in New York City. His long dark hair streaked with silver, tied back just as he wore it in Hopiland, he smiled at me and lightning struck. I sat in my seat at the conference while he, a few rows ahead, kept turning around, smiling. The shape of his face, his dark penetrating eyes, transported me back in time and we were riding bareback on White Eagle's palomino pony down to the stream in the forest glade, his long hair blowing in my face. The feel of White Eagle's hair tangling in my face, the scent of his back as I held on, blew softly all around me. In a little while the conference ended, he hurried to reach me and then White Eagle stood before me.

"Danger!" a frantic inner voice whispered. He snapped a photo of me, asked for my address and I wrote it out for him. "What did you just do, Francine?" I asked myself. Intuition warned me, resist him, yet I was hopelessly drawn to him. And in this way White Eagle and Singing Bird reclaimed their lost Hopi passion and brought it into present time.

When I moved up to Westchester, not far from where he lives, White Eagle was waiting for me. We read books together, listened to music, danced in his studio and laughed together, shared our meals, talked about everything, shared longer days together, and gazed up into the night sky together, even communicating telepathically. I understood his art and appreciated his art. Often, when I turned to look at him he was already gazing at me silently.

DECEMBER 15, 2006. Meditating side by side in his studio. His eyes are closed but something urges me to open my eyes so it is with open eyes that I see his etheric body, a great golden light body, emerge from his chest, appearing identical but larger than his physical body. In his light body form he touches my shoulder, all the while remaining connected to his physical body. He imparts a message to me, "We have a beautiful loving relationship. Nothing can come between us."

DECEMBER 20. I'm watching him work on a new mosaic when suddenly he leans more closely over his work, his golden light body emerges once again from the center of his chest and comes once again to stand right in front of me, his left hand reaching out to touch my right shoulder, offering a message, "I love you, Honey." With a feeling of great affection his light body leans over me and then quickly returns to its physical vessel. This astounding experience bound even more thoroughly my heart to White Eagle's heart.

But one day a shattering arrived. Incredibly, a demon also lived inside him. My beautiful man whose hand I loved to hold turned suddenly icy cold, saying cruel things he later said he didn't mean. He behaved uncontrollably rough, our blissful relationship torn apart by sudden outbursts of rage. He begged me not to leave him, earnestly apologizing, promising. Feeling his sincerity I went back, but nothing changed.

And now a dream, perceptively concise, a cautionary, dramatic dream. My heart is torn out! Lying wounded and flat. Flat, flat-lined, death! Alarmed, my guides seek to rescue me, urging me not to allow my love for a man to damage my life force, thereby reducing my effectiveness in the world. "See this heart, feel this heart, hold this heart, know this heart. You are the guardian of this heart, placed on Earth to heal others, and now this jewel of a heart, regarded in the cosmos with utmost reverence, is wounded."

And so the dream of my wounded heart, symbolized by the power and beauty of ancient amethyst, shows me the dangerous outcome of loving with too much attachment, too much of everything and not enough equality. Our spirit guides, highly creative, helpful and wise, do not control us. In all matters we retain free will. And often, we fail to use our free will to bring about the highest good. Instead, bonded to our emotions, our lower body consciousness, we act in opposition to our own well-being.

JUNE 18. Dream. I saw Earth as a dark illusionary world where everyone and everything was one dimensional and compassion non-existent. The world appeared like a giant amusement park yet no one was happy, only going through the motions of one ride after another.

SEPTEMBER 18. I receive a surprise phone call from Brett, my six year old grandson, who has fallen from the jungle gym at school in Los Angeles where he lives with his Mom, and has broken his arm. "Grandma, can you heal my arm?" he asks in his sweet voice. Immediately, I transmit healing to Brett's arm and ask him to call me later, when his homework is done. I tell my sweet grandson, who I don't see enough of and worry about all the time, living so far from his family who loves him, to pay close attention to whatever he feels. Then we say goodbye and I transmit healing light to Brett's arm. What I see is bands of golden light wrapping his arm like an ace bandage with denser light at the site of the break. I also feel as if I am standing by his side; above him are two classic cherubim. I clearly see the break in his bone is uneven, a portion of the bone raised at a slight angle. I visualize the bone properly repositioned.

Much later, when I am sure Brett is in bed, without calling him I transmit another stream of healing light to his arm, again feel my presence beside him and again see an image of golden light wrapped around his arm like an ace bandage. The following day Brett tells me that when he was in bed he felt a big heat sensation in his arm. I follow up with successive healings over the next few nights and then I call Cheryl. She reports that the doctor was pleased to see the swelling quite reduced and the break, which was a troubling uneven break, was now level with the bone.

I'm so glad that by his own initiative he called me for healing. I deeply desire greater closeness with Brett but circumstances beyond my control make it very difficult. I count on our soul connection holding it together until the day when we will be able to spend more time together, and I know we have a soul connection. When he was only two years old I awoke in the night to see my little grandson's light body form standing beside my bed and he spoke to me with a feeling of sadness, "I love you, Grandma." I reached out to touch him and he was gone.

JANUARY 26, 2009. Closing on my new apartment in the Village of Scarsdale, hoping that at last I have found a permanent home.

AUGUST 7. It's becoming impossible to overlook, White Eagle has changed. Friends are calling, "Can't you see he's not honoring you? Why do you stay?" I stay because intermingled with behavior that ought to send me running there are days of beautiful love.

AUGUST 8. In my sleep I receive a phone call from Brett. There's excitement in his voice and he's asking me to come visit at Daddy's house. In the morning Neale calls to tell me Brett arrived at midnight.

JANUARY 2010. Angelic Healing Circle. In Hastings, at a newly opened wellness center housed in an historic Queen Ann style house, approximately fifteen or twenty people are showing up every month since September of last year, for my Angelic Healing Circle. The evening is comprised of guided healing meditations, open discussions centered on Divine Wisdom designed to open hearts and minds to our soul connection with the higher realm. No one wants to leave the warm cohesiveness created in the circle so everyone lingers and friendships are forged.

Excerpt from astrological reading with Doria Gambino: Beautiful new friendships coming, especially females, will become close friends, really close friends. For a reason. Part of soul family. Soul knows them already. All arranged, before you incarnated. You'll be forming whole new social circle. Very spiritual, loving women, men also. Your new circle will support your endeavors, believe in you, are there for you as you embark on your new path. Similar work to each other. All work from love and light. Having this network of people in your life will help you blossom further. This has been pre-arranged. You couldn't have these wonderful friendships and marriage, too. Those two energies incompatible. Now it's time, set before you were born, these soul families reuniting. Soul family reunion. Forming network of loving people, not going to feel alone any more. Not just one person, whole group, come in bizarre ways. Universe will put you in same place when it's time to meet. When you meet one of these people you will just click. Familiarity. Instantly connected. All of this love in your life, these loving true friends. Part of your new reality. Everything in your life is going to change over the next few years, how you spend your time, your social life. Will feel really good and peaceful.

Your abilities as a healer will reach whole new level. You will start channeling in healing type of energies of a very high dimension that were not allowed to be brought to Earth until now. Not that you weren't a good healer before and your intentions always there, it's that the cosmic forces that are guiding this planet would not allow certain higher dimensional energies to come in. The gate was closed. No matter what you did you couldn't have brought those energies through before. You will start bringing those energies through now because now the gate is being opened. The cosmic directors will open the door and allow higher dimensional energies to start coming in. You're tuned into this particular healing vibration to assist larger amounts of people in healing. A lot of people will need intense high level healing. Healing that Jesus is supposed to have done. May not be that instantaneous, but rapidly.

This is wisdom already known in other places in the universe. Will be taught to you so that you can teach it to others. Will allow people to have very rapid healings of very deep rooted problems in their lives.

Once the gate opens you'll start being taught how to do that higher dimensional work. Because healing work is part of who you are, it's innate in you, it's not hard for you to be taught how to do all this. What I'm seeing in my inner vision as I do this reading for you is absolutely amazing. You bringing Heaven to Earth. Exactly. The healing energy you'll be taught is actually tenth dimensional energy, way high energy. And you'll be taught in such a way that makes sense in the Earth realm. Will make sense to you and the people you teach it to.

This is profound. Part of the conditions for this energy, and this is why, the deepest reason why you have to learn to balance relationship dynamics and stop being a caretaker, because when you're given this higher dimensional energy it cannot be used to heal anyone against their free will. You will teach people how to heal themselves and they will have to take responsibility and make the choice to do it, if they do not they will not heal and that is their free will decision. So important that you be balanced. Some people you'll be standing in front of who are really suffering. If they in their free will are not assuming responsibility for their own healing you will have to walk away and accept that. Without sadness.

Here's the ultimate statement about this: the people you play caretaker to don't want to get better. They just want to suck your energy. So you're not helping them. They're just draining you. If someone truly wants healing they will take responsibility for themselves. You will know who to sit with and who to walk away from. This is the dynamic you're reaching. So beautiful. Amazingly wonderful.

THE MAN IN YOUR LIFE is your ultimate karmic teacher before you begin new path. He really is an important person in your life. He's not the right person for you but the issue is, why do you want to be with this man. He always wants to be with you and that's precious to you. This is your weakness, your Achilles' heel. It's in your chart. Until you fix this, another one the same type, will show up. That's the Pluto lesson. Now is the time to learn it. These types of people can't be part of your new reality. Just can't. All the attention he gives you is very strong, but is he treating you with respect? Are your needs being met? You must learn to value yourself to the point where you insist your partner values you and treats you like an equal. As you go through this year's transitions that are coming up for you, new friends, life will change, give you validation. This year's chart is all about you coming into truth in your partnership area. Once you've learned the lesson you are free.

MARCH 1. Water set to boil for tea in a teapot I recently bought, not only for its unusual beauty, but especially because it's made of clear glass. While sitting on my bed, speaking on the phone to my therapist, seeking help with my relationship, the stovetop and teapot are clearly visible through the bedroom door. The teapot had to have been lifted up because suddenly I hear a loud clang, the sound of glass on metal, the sound of the teapot being set back down on the stove. Investigation reveals that the water inside my glass teapot is sloshing back and forth in waves!

At the moment of the teapot movement my therapist, a centered, soft-spoken fellow had been expressing quite strongly frustration with me for not breaking away from my relationship. Describing what had just happened with my teapot I said to my therapist, "I think your outburst rattled my teapot! What powerful energy you have!" He replied, "Not powerful enough to convince you, though! Anyway, I think those spirit guides of yours were adding emphasis to my advice!"

MARCH 10. Directly following a gratifying phone session with a new client who lives in Kentucky I stand before my full-length mirror and offer heartfelt gratitude to my spirit guides. I see in the mirror a shining shimmering golden white light all around my head and shoulders. Light bodies on the left and right of me. The mirror is reflecting right in front of me, a rainbow colored light body. There is a density to the rainbow light body which obscures my physical body and the details of my face. Although it lasts only several fleeting seconds it is so close to me, possibly even blending with me, it's manifestation is gloriously memorable.

The vision of these magnificent light bodies is accompanied by waves of strengthening vibrations in my body as well as an uplifting, comforting message of love. "You are being renewed and rejuvenated such as never seen before, dearest daughter. Your destiny is a great one. You are protected and watched over. No harm shall come to you."

Moments later I am blending honey into a glass of water. I have this deep inner urge to do this and I begin to feel a beautiful sense of lighthearted joy overspreading not only me but my entire home. My spirit guides are sharing their joy with me, urging me to have a 'taste of honey' in celebration of my newly uplifted cellular vibration!

MARCH 16. The mirror is often a portal into other dimensions. Using it with the highest integrity for only good and helpful purposes it can be a window into the heavenly realms where purest love awaits our call. We begin with a desire to see more deeply into ourselves, to know the deepest part of ourselves, our soul. We may approach this exercise as a meditation, quietly and calmly gazing deeply into the mirror, into our eyes, with focused intention, seeking the light of our soul as it reflects back to us. To recognize the light of our soul reflected in our eyes is a moment of pure joy.

By continuing to practice this meditation, growing calmly familiar with our own inner light, one day we may feel inspired to see the greater light of our soul. To see our aura we need the room to be dimly lit by light that streams in from outside the room, a clean white background is most helpful. Stepping back from the mirror to create a measure of distance, continuing to focus on the light of our soul as we see it in our eyes, we may begin to see our aura, the greater light that radiates outward from the spark of light that is our soul, to surround us with our own unique greater light pattern. Each of us walks within an aura of light, our energy field. The human energy field is now being explored by science and will in a short time be accepted as common knowledge.

The aura flows both ways, functioning as a protective net for our physical body. Before it begins to manifest in our physical body illness comes into our aura, our energy field. To see discolored or dim light of illness in our aura is a cautionary gift. Steps we take in our own behalf to reverse the trend of illness are highly effective. Once the energetic force of illness moves from the aura into our physical body the cleansing process, the transformation back to good health, carries greater complexity.

Becoming familiar with our own aura is a most useful tool toward the maintenance of our own well-being. We may then recognize changes in our aura and if we approach this practice in a calm meditative state we will surely be given assistance. We may seek assistance from our higher self or our spirit guides by going inward and asking questions such as, am I lacking sufficient sleep? am I not eating in a healthful way? am I drinking enough pure water? am I overly stressed and if so, what must I do to relieve my stress? Am I expressing anger or hostility toward others? Then we may await a reply which may come immediately into our thoughts or may arrive in a dream, or the answer may come to us through the next article we read or TV program, or person we meet. Most of the time the answer lies inside ourselves. Because stress is the greatest catalyst for illness we must be ruthless in eliminating stress as much as we can and it may be surprising to know that our own attitude is crucial. It is important to remain alert.

And in this vein it is helpful to remember, "To help another is to help oneself; to harm another is to harm oneself."

These are simple, self-directed, self-empowering ways to maintain our own health. As we practice the aura meditation we become familiar not only with our spiritual light but we come to know our own body with greater intimacy as well. Seeking communion with our soul and with our energy field creates a greater personal sensitivity which in turn enhances our humanity. Integration of mind, body and spirit.

MARCH 21. At our "Peace Be on Earth" meeting last night, attended by about twenty-five people, a unanimous request arose for a guided healing meditation. My energy was low last night and I wasn't feeling very confident. Then the noble presence of my spirit guide transmitted to me a knowing that despite my personal reservations we were about to bring through a guided meditation of a higher vibration. I said to my friends, "We're going to go to a place." Everyone remembered that line and after the experience, told me they liked it. This to me was a sign that our higher selves, with higher-self knowing, had joined together for a higher purpose. But entirely focused on the present moment my conscious mind lacked awareness of what that higher purpose was. Helping the people here with me was where my thoughts were focused.

Throughout the guided healing meditation my spirit guide transmitted into my mind a quick flash of descriptive imagery a moment prior to my speaking it. In this way, we brought the people into their light bodies, assisted the people while in their light bodies, to rise above their physical forms. Imagery flashed in my mind showing me a hovering light body above each person. Quickly, a new image arose in my mind depicting a peanut shell shaped cocoon of golden healing light surrounded with pure white light. So I guided the people in their light body forms into their healing cocoons. I watched with open eyes as each one, hovering in their light body forms above their physical forms, moved with ease and grace right into their own personal healing cocoon. Within each one's personal healing cocoon the frequency of light vibrations perfectly matches each one's higher self-vibration, the frequency at which each one vibrates at optimum well-being. Disharmonious frequencies that attach and invade our own higher-self frequencies are brought back into balance by the healing light. After we pass over we are immersed in a similar cocoon for immediate cleansing of lower third dimensional frequencies. The cocoon healing is truly a heavenly experience. And so the room where we were meeting that day, an art gallery, was transformed into a place of heavenly peace and love. Perhaps ninety seconds elapsed when I brought everyone back from their healing cocoons into their physical bodies. The response was wonderful. Everyone experienced a higher frequency of peace and love such as never before. Everyone was smiling and stretching, joyful camaraderie pervaded the entire gallery.

At home that night, quiet and still in my bed, deep spiritual understanding came to me. There is a most loving reason why we have all been blessed this afternoon with a wondrous healing experience the uniqueness of which was exemplified by a harmony of personal healing within a framework of unity consciousness. The reason demonstrates Divine unity consciousness as it exists, however unacknowledged, among human beings and angelic light beings who are here to assist us as we move forward into a new Earth of love and peace.

THE GALLERY OWNER'S beloved husband is suffering terminal illness. She asked me to do whatever I could for her husband who was watching us from his sickbed at home by means of closed circuit TV. The energies of Divine healing co-created by those of us in the gallery was used as a conduit by the angelic light beings for the benefit of our ailing friend. Our higher selves knew this and agreed to join together in service to our friend. This experience, my dear spiritual companions imparted to me as I lay in my bed that night, is a perfect example of how we may bring Heaven to Earth!

MAY 2. In the midst of relationship mayhem. Accompanied by waves of love and a sense of quiet strength I receive this message:

> "You are the still pond
>
> Into which others cast their pebbles
>
> Do not confuse yourself with the ripples."

AUGUST 4. Plagued with back spasms for past few weeks I lie down flat, my usual meditative posture, and call on Starlight, my spiritual soul mate. In desperation I also call on Archangel Raphael, Divine Father and my spirit guide. "My dear spiritual companions, please bring healing to my back. The pain is debilitating."

With absolute faith that a response will be forthcoming I

focus on my breath and grow calm, wondering why I have been so stoic as to endure pain without calling sooner for help. In a few moments I feel soft pressure against my right cheek. Ah, they are here. Allowing my body to relax, silent teardrops escape my closed eyes. I feel the exalted presence of my spiritual companions. I feel, next, a slightly stronger pressure against my hair on the right side of my head. My spinal column is infused with golden healing light. I fall into a calm deep sleep that lasts for ninety minutes. When I awaken the spasms are gone, and the spasms have not returned since that day.

SEPTEMBER 22. Starlight entered my dream state last night and imparted this cosmic vision of Unity Consciousness.

All of the cosmos, every cell in every particle of Creation is One. The minerals and metals of our planet are found throughout the universe, in differing amounts and alloys, but they are the same minerals and metals.

Consciousness of sentient beings affects all matter. Creation manifests in different ways as it comes through individual and group consciousness. Therefore, as all races of sentient beings throughout the universe hold varying frequencies of consciousness matter may be arranged in different forms in various locations throughout the universe.

All beings share in the greater consciousness of Creation and may partake of the greater consciousness of Creation according to their own awareness and development. Scarcity and abundance is ruled by consciousness.

I saw and felt the absolute wonder and grandeur of Unity Consciousness. I felt it deep within my heart. The majesty and glory of it all lies beyond language.

SEPTEMBER 23. Healing with Allison, final stages of liver cancer, at her home, her husband seated by her side. I cannot hold back the destiny or fate of another, especially when faced with advanced disease. For someone suffering in this way the angels bring appropriate comfort.

I take Allison, a gentle woman of an age we consider too young to die, on a shamanic journey where she meets soul to soul with her Mom who is still here on Earth. In the garden of her own creation which exists in the higher realms Allison and her Mom resolve disturbing emotional issues that have troubled Allison for many years. This resolution brings Allison to a place of inner peace for which her soul is longing. In such a circumstance as Allison's the shamanic journey functions also as preparation for the moment of passing. People in their final phase of life almost always call on mother whether mother is here on Earth or has already passed.

I feel the presence of a huge angelic being standing just behind me. The angel enfolds me in its wings and I feel strength flowing into me. After an extremely poignant experience such as this I have a strong urge, before proceeding with the rest of my day, to find a bit of personal comfort. It's a beautiful day and I've parked my car in the shade of beautiful old trees on this quiet street so I open the car windows and breathe fresh air into my lungs. I'm grieving for Allison and for her loving husband. I call on Archangel Michael and watch as Michael surrounds Allison with further blessings and peace of mind and with peaceful sleep in the interim. I remain perfectly still in my car until after an interval of listening to birds and the sounds of passing cars out on the roadway I am ready to resume my day.

I DECIDE to stop in at Traprock for a brief session with Rebecca, a psychic medium. Rebecca says my angels love working with me because to all requests, even those my personality self would prefer to avoid, I always say yes. They have big plans for me, Rebecca says, but I must leave a relationship which is unsupportive of my well-being. She sees two very large angels behind me whose presence I feel. Rebecca goes on to describe a grandfather figure who wears spectacles and smokes a pipe. This strikes a chord with me because I have, over the years, smelled the aroma of pipe tobacco accompanied by a refined presence but having no knowledge of any pipe-smoking ancestors, have not been able to discern who this spirit might be.

AT HOME I lie down across the foot of my bed and call on this grandfather to please come and stand before me and tell me who he is, and within a brief moment he complies! He's wearing an old-fashioned black suit in the style of early nineteenth century. He is of a slender build and a most pleasant countenance. With an energy of educated intelligence he tells me that I was a physician, a student of Hippocrates, renowned, respected, called on from far and wide. In that ancient Greek lifetime grandfather was my student and we were close comrades. In a more recent past lifetime I was a small girl of three when both my parents died of an epidemic. He was my grandfather, my mother's father, and with tender love he cared for me and brought me up. It was in these two most recent past lifetimes that a close and loving bond was established between us.

My body feels warm and I fall into a deep sleep for exactly thirty minutes. When I awake and look into the mirror my eyes and face are glowing. I feel wonderfully regenerated, and with knowledge of my grandfather physician guide staying beside me for assistance in healings, I feel enormously comforted.

I meditate further on this profound experience. I have felt the presence of this grandfather. I remember the aroma of pipe tobacco wafting over me at times when I was alone in Museum Tower. Even though I was perplexed as to who it might be, it was always a most pleasant and comfortable feeling when this happened.*

Also, when I lived in my studio apartment on 57th Street, following a healing session with a woman who suffered from tinnitus I received a message from the great Hippocrates who manifested before me in his spiritual upper body. I saw his face clearly and recognized him immediately. Hippocrates informed me that it was his belief that tinnitus derived from misalignment of the spine, that disharmonious vibrations reverberate inside our eardrums. Excited about this communication, I had left my cozy winter bed right then, in the middle of the night, and opened my encyclopedia to research the great Father of Medicine where I discovered a whole passage dedicated to this particular belief of his.

*Postscript: While reading this over I am struck with sudden awareness: this grandfather figure is the father of my mother! The grandpa I longed to know when as a child I held the accordion his hands had held. And the grandfather whose love I felt instantly when he appeared in spirit form in my dying mother's room. How wondrous, our loving connections that uplift our consciousness into transcendent heart-centered love.

Temple of Light

MY JOURNEY occurred on Sunday night, December 5 but actually on my birthday, Wednesday morning, December 1 I experienced what I believe now was a preparation.

A LITTLE WHILE after awakening on December 1, I felt the presence of my spirit guide urging me to lie down again to receive a message. As soon as I was in position, eyes closed, I 'saw' before me three figures. To my right I saw my guardian angel Love. Directly in front of me and above I saw the one I call Divine Father. To my left I saw Starlight, my spiritual soulmate.

As soon as telepathic greetings were exchanged a force emanated from all three figures which blended just above my heart chakra and entered my body as a single force. This powerful loving force met the spark of light which is my soul directly in the center of my heart chakra and immediately the spark of light expanded to fill my entire body. It settled for an instant and then expanded out beyond my body to encompass me completely in golden light. My mind became illuminated, joyfully infused with awareness of Unity Consciousness. Ancient Egyptian priestess power of 10,000 years ago when I first entered this cycle of incarnation after the fall of Atlantis; Shaman power; Medicine Woman power; blind scholar power of ancient days; all blended within a tiny point of light within my heart and expanded outward with infinite love for all Creation.

ON THE NIGHT of Sunday, December 5 I awoke about 3:00 A.M. feeling fully awake and decided to call on my spirit guides. In a spontaneous burst of emotion perfectly suited for three o'clock in the morning I declared to my guides, and not for the first time, "Oh how I wish I could see where I come from, my true home!"

Instantaneously, I am transported HOME! Standing in the center of a gazebo-like structure created entirely of light, I look down at myself and see that I am formed completely of magnificent deep golden light, shining and radiating, glowing all over. I see density in my arms and legs and also various filaments of light throughout my body. The light has solidity. I am rather tall and in some mysterious way I can see my face as well as if I were also opposite myself. I have large almond shaped eyes and a mouth reminiscent of my human-shaped mouth, sort of smiling but not open. I am completely conscious and aware of my surroundings. To my right but just out of sight I am aware of three spiritual beings, the ones who came to greet me on my birthday, who instruct me to observe all that I could and not be distracted in any way.

I AM AWARE of having no ego presence which is totally liberating. Everything is as it is, there is no judgment whatsoever. I am both calm and joyful to recognize my beautiful light-filled home. I will describe each thing I saw along with accompanying 'knowings' but actually all was taken in at once.

Looking upward I see a golden dome. When healing is

requested a shower of golden-light droplets, like crystal raindrops, shower upon the one standing under the golden dome and this achieves miraculous cleansing of emotional sorrow. Set in an alcove of the spacious room, dominating the space with its incredible beauty, is a pure block of crystal; this is my bed which seems to be the mode by which I receive the greatest emotional healing. The crystal appears to be 10 inches thick and long enough and wide enough to accommodate my light body. Its edges are polished yet also roughhewn. It seems that in addition to the love we have accumulated we bring with us to the higher realms after life on Earth the residue of accumulated emotional pain. Emotional impurities are drawn down by the healing power of the crystal and full restoration of my golden light body transpires. It is extremely beneficial to clear emotional pain prior to taking up our next Earth life. Much attention is given to this task. A graceful, curved pedestal of crystalline light supports my bed. The light extends itself in a long band along the underside of the crystal bed. The white light glows with a slightly different intensity for each purpose. Here on my home planet sleep is very different from sleep on Earth. Ordinarily, life here requires no sleep, one does not tire from one's activities as all action proceeds in harmonious flow with universal frequency, not in opposition to universal frequency. Our individual power and conscious intentions are fully supported on my home planet by each one for the mutual benefit of all. If I should feel depleted while residing in my true home all that is necessary is a restful sleep of approximately one day of Earth time. Restoration following a full Earth lifetime requires for me about a year of sleep on my crystal bed.

THE FLOOR APPEARS SOLID although it too is composed of pure white glowing light that seems to have no source; it feels warm and pleasant beneath my feet. The glow on the floor appears to rise to where our ankles might be if we were to stand on it in physical form. There are glowing white light columns which uphold the golden light domed ceiling. Stirringly beautiful to behold. In between the columns are white light screens. The filaments here are finer and not as dense as the structured parts. Slight spaces can be seen between the filaments. All that is required is a focused thought that you would like to see beyond to the outside landscape and the light screens part or melt away. While in place they provide soothing balanced light. There are no shadows.

There are no kitchen or bathroom fixtures, no dividing walls, only outer walls and those are composed of white light columns which glow softly, subdued yet emanating power and strength. A low perimeter wall rises from the floor to connect the glowing columns. The upper perimeter wall is a screen of white light filaments. These 'windows' light my home and provide privacy. The screen walls of light filaments contribute to the overall atmosphere of serenity and understated elegance.

I AM ALLOWING my gaze to drift over the purity of my beloved home and I see five or six pedestals along the right-side wall formed of white light filaments. These pedestals support beautiful rare healing crystals, majestic in every way. I recall clearly only two of them, retaining only an impression of the others along the wall. The first crystal is completely clear. The one to the right of it is violet in color. My impression remains of other colors but not clear enough to describe. I notice the violet crystal is glowing from within, its healing properties activated by my own focused thought.

Each crystal has been ceremoniously procured and presented to me by our Council of Wise Elders for healing purposes within the Temple of Light. Each crystal, magnificent to behold, represents one long cycle of lifetimes of service, mostly as a human on Earth. I delight as well to rest my gaze upon the glorious jewel stones here in my golden domed gazebo home. Rubies as large as footballs. Jewels, mostly sapphires of varying colors, also very large and polished, are arranged between the white light pedestals holding the crystals. These are also imbued with great healing properties. Also arranged on the glowing white floor are pyramid shaped heaps of marble sized jewels. The jewels remain as arranged, there being no danger of rolling down. They are perfectly interspersed among the pedestals and large jewels. A gorgeous sight, serene and peaceful. There is no excitement in the jewels as we know here as to monetary value. They are what they are and they serve a purpose, each one.

As I stand in the center of my gazebo home I'm given to understand the following: My name, I am reminded, is Harmony. No, I protested, my name is Francine. No matter, they said, here in the endless world you are Harmony. Your name is chosen by the Council of Wise Elders based upon a word that best describes your essence. Each name-word emits a musical note. When your note, your sound vibration, resonates with your light radiance, it is said of you that you have achieved the status of High Master in God's Creation. Here on my home planet, I am told, this status I have achieved.

Additionally, they give me to understand that I was created in the beginning of time. I have completed many long cycles of time on Earth. Life on other planets was not revealed to me. All in this encounter was concerned with Earth. Each time I complete a long cycle and fulfill my mission for that cycle I am presented with one magnificent crystal. This is how the crystals as well as the jewels came to be in my gazebo home. I have returned to Godhead several times they say, only to be sent forth to begin again the Divine labor of bringing enlightenment to humanity. I labor for eons to fulfill this Holy mission. For every lifetime within every cycle, having fulfilled one's mission, an increase in radiance occurs. In this way our very body reveals who we are.

ACTUALLY, the crystals are not 'mine.' I may be considered the guardian of the Temple of Light and work here in the capacity of healer to souls who requisition healing at the Temple of Light. These are souls who have become stuck on one aspect of life and try as they might they cannot overcome. The Council of Wise Elders must first examine the accrued merit of each request. My role is to clear away the layers of emotional pain to prepare them for the guides with whom they will plan their next incarnation. The appropriate jewel or crystal is brought forth for assistance in healing, which here is defined as aiding a higher conscious awareness, building one's ability to hold greater love and light. Needed support is provided to bring each into greater harmony with soul. A cosmic balance is sought. Once healed in the Temple of Light these souls are able to make amazing progress on Earth. I am told they can be recognized on Earth as those who make amazing breakthroughs in any field for the benefit of mankind.

BENEATH THE GOLDEN DOME of my gazebo home I am imbued with understanding of the magnetic pull that Earth has on the consciousness of highly evolved beings. There is something about the dramatic challenges that draw us to return. But even more than that it is the people, the souls we have encountered on Earth who still require assistance on their own individual journeys. In the higher realms we feel a great love for souls who are in human form, we see their struggles and desire with all our hearts to help them move away from suffering into awareness of their true authentic selves where there is no need for suffering. Such an abundance of love is felt for human beings we gladly return to the heaviness of third dimension positive that we will be a true force for good in the world. The possibility of falling into painful situations does not concern us for we clearly see the Grand Play of it all and know it is all a carefully crafted illusion created for the sole purpose of learning. Even those we consider evil or bad are here according to plan to teach others and demonstrate with their lives what must be uplifted and healed.

ON THE LEFT SIDE of my gazebo home there stand on the glowing white floor three crystal volumes, approximately 12 or 15 inches in height. These volumes contain imbedded diamond chips which hold all the teachings of every life lived on Earth. When a lifetime is completed the most significant teachings of that life are transferred from our human memory onto a diamond chip and this chip is imbedded in a crystal book. I open one volume and think, I would like to recall how I learned to ride a bicycle and the dangers as well as the pleasures involved. It is necessary to open only the cover. There in the book is displayed a moving hologram showing my child-self striving to master this one activity. It seems to have been a rather simple accomplishment and joyous memories flood over me. I close the crystal book as one would a scrapbook in grandma's attic; it was enough for this particular visit. When we are in the higher realms we live completely in the moment. There is no past or present. All our learnings are contained within a crystal volume which is available whenever we choose to revisit for any reason.

THE THOUGHT OCCURS to me that it would be very pleasurable to view the outside landscape. The white light screen between one set of white light columns parts or dissolves and there just beyond the gazebo as clear as can be lies the landscape. All is taken in at once. Here is what I see:

Immediately beyond is a crystal clear pond. This pond opens to a narrow connecting stream which flows to another pond and from that pond another stream flows to another pond. I am able to see far distant as the river of ponds curves gently on its way. Beside each pond, I can see as far as three of them, stands a dwelling.

The dwelling directly next to mine is a white house in the style of early 20th century America, perfectly clean and precise. The next dwelling on down the river of ponds is a palace. Broad steps in front, expansive, elegant. Beyond, there's a castle, complete with turrets and pale gray chiseled stones. Very beautiful. The sky is gorgeous cloudless blue. The grass is verdant green, each blade visible about 4 inches high. The grass brings an aroma to the atmosphere, beneficial to experience. The aroma seems to emanate from the ground of this planet and the grass acts as a conduit. So I understand that this planet's purity emanates from its very being and radiates for the benefit of everything. It contributes to the purity of the light, the endeavors that are tried here, the healing which occurs here.

HAVING HEARD of my arrival in the Temple of Light, Starlight my soulmate, enters my gazebo home. We embrace as long separated lovers do everywhere and our light bodies blend in ecstatic joy. We lie upon the crystal bed and in the fullness of our awareness of the eternal power of love we rest briefly until the very moment when I must return to my Earth life where much remains to be completed.

DECEMBER 8. Our spirit guides often speak to us through the books and passages we choose to read. Early in the morning I open, "Bridging Heaven and Earth" by Leonard Jacobson and read, "Through the doorway of the present moment we can call forth our own future which already exists and is fully evolved. We can call forth the highest and most evolved dimension of ourselves." A perfect synchronistic validation of my wondrous visit to the Temple of Light.

DECEMBER 9. While in the Temple of Light I received a wonderful healing. Re-growth of cancerous lesion on my upper lip, site of previous skin cancer removed ten years ago, just flaked off, leaving perfectly smooth skin without a trace of the lesion.

DECEMBER 10. As I stretch my legs in the morning I notice a beautiful light-filled violet orb on my right foot.

JANUARY 3, 2011. My home planet is an administrative planet where important decisions concerning the well-being of the entire universe are weighed and measured by the Council of Wise Elders. The Wise Elders deliberate each issue based on the Law of Wisdom and send their decisions down to other planetary councils. For example, the Wise Elders might have under consideration the following request: "We, the Council of Elders on the planet Venus, have grave concerns regarding planet Earth. Nuclear proliferation as observed on planet Earth poses serious consequences to all of Earth life. We, the Council of Elders on the planet Venus, are at this time greatly alarmed. Our Council seeks permission to intercede, to reverse the dangerous development of nuclear power and weaponry on Earth where the harmony of thought required to create a worthy Council of Wise Elders has not come into being. A nuclear holocaust on Earth is a most serious threat to the life systems of our planet Venus. A nuclear holocaust on Earth is a most serious threat to the harmonious balance of life in our entire solar system."

JANUARY 9. At our Peace Be On Earth meeting I relate to my friends my amazing journey to the Temple of Light and ask if they would like to experience the Temple of Light for themselves. Their reply is a resounding unanimous "Yes!" The room is full with the energy of many spirit guides and angelic beings so I trust this will be a successful transcendent experience for all.

First, I bring everyone through a meditative exercise into their golden light body form which creates a sense of weightlessness. We rise above our physical bodies to arrive instantly in the Temple of Light. My voice is the guide that assists them in seeing the healing crystals, experiencing the cleansing shower of golden light raindrops beneath the golden dome. My voice is the guide that assists them to take in as much as possible the otherworldly beauty and healing powers inherent in the Temple of Light. Together we activate the healing crystals by our thought, each one feels according to their consciousness and inner needs. Together we investigate the crystal volumes that hold the entire history of our soul's journey. Together we absorb the highest frequency available in all the universe to heal our Earthly wounds. And after a while, having accomplished all this as a group, we return to our present time and place.

While in the Temple of Light, even though it was a group visit, each one experienced themselves as solitary. Each one expressed complete amazement at the healing crystal experience. First, we are guided to choose by energetic resonance, one healing crystal in the Temple of Light. As we focus our thought upon the one crystal a light deep within the center of the crystal begins to glow. We feel the energy as it is directed toward our light body form, and people see themselves as various colors in their light body forms; we feel the warmth of healing light permeate our beings. We stand in the glow of majestic healing unimaginable here in third dimension. As an unexpected gift of love we receive from the crystal, a portion of spiritual enlightenment.

At our Healing Circle I offer the journey to the Temple of Light and once again the whole group of about twenty people experience the Temple of Light. Everyone returns with inner peace and eyes aglow with transcendent light.

On the afternoon of our next Healing Circle my spirit guides prepare me with a profound teaching to bring through in the evening. The universe functions like a human body. Just as when one of us suffers any ailment from stubbed toe to serious malady we long for the ailment to heal so we can return to our activities well and whole, so, too, when any part of the Universal Body is out of balance a great longing arises within the universe for re-balance, a return to harmony and well-being. Therefore, my dear friends, know this: whatever steps we take on behalf of our own well-being of mind, body, spirit will receive support from the universe. Helping ourselves is expected to be in alignment with helping others as well. So sharing is key.

As a planet the body of Earth is out of harmony with the flow of universal well-being. This has attracted the attention of other planetary cultures who wish to assist us in healing the wounds of humanity. Also, attention of planetary cultures who wish to take advantage of the disharmony now ruling our beloved Earth. This has caused greater disharmony in the Universal Oneness. Opposing forces now engaged in various forms of disagreement are also joining forces. This must all be reconciled and Universal well-being re-established.

Everything possible is being implemented to assist humanity in personal and worldwide attainment of peace. Large scale worldwide healing not available in the past is now allowed. Healings, peace among neighbors, enlightenment never before available is here now. We must avail ourselves of this amazing opportunity to heal not only ourselves but our brothers and sisters around the globe. If we succeed we will experience a glorious fulfillment within. Our hearts will open. Our third eye will open. Love will prevail. Transparency will prevail. Lies and deception, will belong to the past. And we will, each one of us, find ourselves in a finer higher vibration where all negativity is a thing of the past. Suffering and pain will no longer plague us. So this is our directive: Open our hearts! Let love flow through us!

Driving home afterward, it's eleven o'clock on a cold wintry night. All around me the car is suffused with an aroma of roses. My dear spiritual companions, how you communicate your love for me is truly wondrous!

MAY 18. Unusually deep meditation. In the Temple of Light, in my golden light body form, I am the guardian of the Temple of Light. I am here to receive sorely needed emotional healing so I go directly to my crystal bed and lie upon it. And Jesus is standing by my side! With extended arms the Great One places one hand on my forehead and one hand on my feet. He delivers the ultimate healing. I lose consciousness.

Another deep meditation. Above me, a gorgeous violet light seems to be angelic. The light expands, moves to enfold my shoulders, moving down my body, enveloping me within its violet essence. The light resembles the violet oval light I see every day on my right side, with peripheral vision. Inside the light I see a delicate angel being.

Messages from the Angels

Spring 2011

Warm Loving Greetings to All Our Dear Friends Who Are Holding the Light on Earth

HAVE NO FEAR dearest friends. It may seem as though there is much to fear; we are here to remind you of what you already know deep within your soul. Have no fear dearest friends. To help you remember your true authentic self which lives within you and is a pure, courageous shining light we offer this meditation.

All our messages carry a vibration of love. Allow yourself to feel our love for you while you are reading and experiencing the peace that flows from our hearts to yours. Take a few breaths, feeling the essence of Divine Love coming into your body with each breath. Allow your body to relax.

Imagine right above your head a glowing violet light radiating unconditional love to you. Feel the warmth of the light above you, touching you with great gentleness and tenderness. Now you see within the light a violet angel. See her delicate wings. As you place your attention upon your violet angel she expands, she is standing beside you, enfolding you within her embrace of crystalline purity.

Allow yourself to blend with your violet angel's love. Feel her peacefulness descend upon you, holding you in a place of unconditional love. Her love is soothing you, transforming all stress and anxiety into feelings of joy and well-being. Remain with your violet angel's loving embrace for as long as you desire. When you are feeling peaceful, when you are feeling yourself resonating with all the good in the world you may offer gratitude to your violet angel and say adieu for now.

We will speak again soon.

* * *

Francine Vale

Warm Loving Greetings to All Our Dear Friends Who Are Holding the Light on Earth

WE ARE HERE to remind you of that which is already known to you. With great love we beseech you to remember and to keep this thought before you, before all other thoughts as you go about your daily affairs.

We Are All One.

Events unfolding now are challenging all of humanity to remember the Unity Consciousness, the Oneness of all Creation. The Time is Now for burying all weapons of war in the ashes of the past. The Time is Now for speaking the language of Peace, for keeping uppermost in your minds and hearts, the language of love. Remembering the Unity Consciousness is your shared mission as you approach the end of an Age and prepare to enter into a new Golden Age, that which is waiting for you.

Remember who you are, your greatness and your power. Remember the light of your soul deep within and allow your soul light to expand and fill your entire body. Be your soul light. Shine your light into all the dark corners where light is needed. Share your wisdom with everyone you know.

The Time is Now.

Reach out with your hearts to all your brothers and sisters of sorrow. Reach out with all the love in your heart and live the Unity Consciousness.

We will speak again soon.

* * *

Song of the Heart

Warm Loving Greetings to All Our Dear Friends Who Are Holding the Light on Earth

We are here to remind you of all that is already known to you deep within your heart and soul.

We are here to inspire you to choose always the Path of Light.

We are here to whisper with love in your ear: place your feet upon the Path of Light dear friends, stay on the Path of Light. Immerse yourself in the Light, feel the Love that surrounds you and fills you.

Be aware in your mind of a spiraling upward of consciousness, speedier now than ever before. Be aware of your heartfelt desire and yearning for the health and well-being of Gaia.

Notice the thoughts of your innermost mind, the higher way they are forming. Notice your words, the higher vibration of sound they emit. And notice your actions, the higher expression of your body consciousness.

Look deep into your heart and discover there, love for you. Discover deep within your heart compassion for you. Hold yourself in a place of love and compassion. Feel the love you have for your life, for all the experiences of your life. Feel it fully.

Let the love and compassion within your heart expand outward, let it burst outward from your heart toward the horizon, encircling the world. Feel yourself as one with the Earth. One heartbeat. With every breath share and draw strength from the Oneness. One heartbeat.

We will speak again soon.

* * *

Warm Loving Greetings to All Our Friends Who Are Holding the Light on Earth

THE TIME IS NOW to envision the world you desire for yourself and all those you love.

The Time is Now to choose with conscious intention a world of peace and love, for we see by your light that it is a world of peace and love for which you long. With great love and desire to assist you we invite you now to join together in hearts and minds. Move with us for a moment into Unity Consciousness and envision that loving world of peace for which your souls are yearning.

We envision enlightened humanity expressing loving kindness toward all beings.

We envision a world of days unfolding in ever-expanding goodness and love where all people enjoy the pursuit of their dreams and grow into the fullness of their potential.

Where darkness and imbalance have threatened to overtake humanity with fear and suffering we envision light and balance. We envision light and balance with all our hearts.

We dedicate ourselves to live as our Higher Selves in full alignment with the Universal Laws of Love and Abundance set forth by our Creator who, in the beginning looked upon completed Earth, gazed with satisfaction upon the Garden of Eden and declared that it was good.

This is the sacred goodness we envision in the Time of Now with all our hearts.

* * *

FRANCINE VALE is an author, spiritual leader and visionary. Her past life memories as a Hopi Medicine Woman in the 19th century, a Roman girl who followed Jesus and an Egyptian priestess in the service of Isis continues to inspire and influence her consciousness. Encouraged by the highly evolved spiritual beings who are her teachers, Francine shares all that she has learned. Of prime importance: "Be kind to yourself and love one another."

CPSIA information can be obtained at www.ICGtesting.com
Printed in the USA
BVOW05s2059241114

376589BV00001B/28/P

9 780692 213964